Acclaim for Beth Wiseman

Need You Now

"Wiseman gets to the heart of marriage and family issues in a way that will resonate with readers . . ."

—ROMANTIC TIMES

"With issues ranging from special education and teen cutting to what makes a marriage strong, this is a compelling and worthy read."

—BOOKLIST

"You may think you are familiar with Beth's wonderful storytelling gift but this is something new! This is a story that will stay with you for a long, long time. It's a story of hope when life seems hopeless. It's a story of how God can redeem the seemingly unredeemable. It's a message the Church, the world needs to hear."

—SHEILA WALSH, AUTHOR
OF GOD LOVES BROKEN
PEOPLE

"Beth Wiseman tackles these difficult subjects with courage and grace. She reminds us that true healing can only come by being vulnerable and honest before our God who loves us more than anything."

—DEBORAH BEDFORD, BEST-SELLING AUTHOR
OF HIS OTHER WIFE, A ROSE BY THE DOOR, AND
THE PENNY (COAUTHORED WITH JOYCE MEYER)

The Land of Canaan Novels

"Wiseman's voice is consistently compassionate and her words flow smoothly."

—*PUBLISHERS WEEKLY* REVIEW
OF *SEEK ME WITH ALL YOUR
HEART*

"Wiseman's third Land of Canaan novel overflows with romance, broken promises, a modern knight in shining armor and hope at the end of the rainbow."

—*ROMANTIC TIMES* FOR
HIS LOVE ENDURES FOREVER

"In *Seek Me with All Your Heart*, Beth Wiseman offers readers a heart-warming story filled with complex characters and deep emotion. I instantly loved Emily, and eagerly turned each page, anxious to learn more about her past—and what future the Lord had in store for her."

—SHELLEY SHEPARD
GRAY, BEST-SELLING
AUTHOR OF THE SEASONS
OF SUGARCREEK SERIES

"Wiseman has done it again! Beautifully compelling, *Seek Me with All Your Heart* is a heart-warming story of faith, family, and renewal. Her characters and descriptions are captivating, bringing the story to life with the turn of every page."

—AMY CLIPSTON, BEST-
SELLING AUTHOR OF
A GIFT OF GRACE

The Daughters of the Promise Novels

"Well-defined characters and story make for an enjoyable read."
—ROMANTIC TIMES
REVIEW OF *PLAIN
PURSUIT*

"A touching, heartwarming story. Wiseman does a particularly great job of dealing with shunning, a controversial Amish practice that seems cruel and unnecessary to outsiders . . . If you're a fan of Amish fiction, don't miss *Plain Pursuit*!"
—KATHLEEN FULLER, AUTHOR
OF THE MIDDLEFIELD FAMILY
NOVELS

"*Plain Promise* is Beth Wiseman's masterpiece. It's the story of two unlikely friends' journey toward faith and love. This heart-warming novel brings readers hope and paints a beautiful, authentic portrait of Lancaster County, Pennsylvania. Her characters are so real that they feel like old friends. Once you open the book, you won't put it down until you've reached the last page."
—AMY CLIPSTON, BEST-SELLING
AUTHOR OF *A GIFT OF GRACE*

"I was kind of dreading reading yet another Amish novel as not too many of the more recently published ones measure up to Beverly Lewis or Wanda Brunstetter. However, *Plain Perfect* is the exception rather than the rule. And I couldn't help but keep reading the well-crafted story. The characters could be real, with real-life struggles, and even the Amish had issues to work through."
—LAURA V. HILTON,
LIGHTHOUSE-ACADEMY.BLOGSPOT.COM

THE
DAUGHTERS *of the* PROMISE
COLLECTION

Also by Beth Wiseman

Need You Now
The House That Love Built

The Land of Canaan Series
Seek Me with All Your Heart
The Wonder of Your Love
His Love Endures Forever

The Daughters of the Promise Series
Plain Perfect
Plain Pursuit
Plain Promise
Plain Paradise
Plain Proposal
Plain Peace (Available November 2013)

Novellas included in
An Amish Christmas
An Amish Gathering
An Amish Love
An Amish Wedding
An Amish Kitchen
An Amish Miracle (Available December 2013)

THE
DAUGHTERS *of the* PROMISE
COLLECTION

THREE NOVELS *in* ONE VOLUME

BETH WISEMAN

THOMAS NELSON
Since 1798

NASHVILLE   DALLAS   MEXICO CITY   RIO DE JANEIRO

Plain Promise © 2009 by Beth Wiseman

Plain Paradise © 2010 by Beth Wiseman

Plain Proposal © 2011 by Beth Wiseman

Published in Nashville, Tennessee, by Thomas Nelson. Thomas Nelson is a registered trademark of Thomas Nelson, Inc.

Thomas Nelson, Inc., titles may be purchased in bulk for educational, business, fundraising, or sales promotional use. For information, please email SpecialMarkets@ThomasNelson.com.

Scripture quotations are taken from the King James Version of the Bible.

Publisher's Note: This novel is a work of fiction. Names, characters, places, and incidents are either products of the author's imagination or used fictitiously. All characters are fictional, and any similarity to people living or dead is purely coincidental.

ISBN 978-1-4016-8948-3

Library of Congress Cataloging-in-Publication Data

CIP data is available.

Printed in the United States of America

13 14 15 16 17 18 QG 6 5 4 3 2 1

Contents

Pennsylvania Dutch Glossary

Aamen—Amen

ab im kopp—crazy, off in the head

ach—oh

aenti—aunt

baremlich—terrible

boppli—baby or babies

bruder—brother

Budget, The—a weekly newspaper serving Amish and Mennonite communities everywhere

daadi—grandfather

daed—dad

danki—thank you

Die Botschaft—a weekly newspaper serving Old Order Amish communities everywhere

dippy eggs—eggs cooked over easy

dochder—daughter

dumm—dumb

dummkopf—dummy

Em Gott Sei Friede—God's peace

Englisch or Englischer—a non-Amish person

Es dutt mir leed—I am sorry

fraa—wife

guder mariye—good morning

gut—good

gut-n-owed—good evening

hatt—hard

haus—house

kaffi—coffee

kalt—cold

kapp—prayer covering or cap

kinner—child, children or grandchildren

kumme esse—come eat

lieb—love

maedel or maed—girl or girls

make wet—rain

mami—mom

mammi—grandmother

mei—my

mudder—mother

naerfich—nervous

narrisch—crazy, insane

onkel—uncle

Ordnung, The—the written and unwritten rules of the Amish; the understood behavior by which the Amish are expected to live, passed down from generation to generation. Most Amish know the rules by heart.

Pennsylvania *Deitsch*—Pennsylvania German, the language most commonly used by the Amish

rumschpringe—running-around period when a teenager turns sixteen years old *schee*—pretty

schee beh—nice legs

schtinker—irritable person

scrapple—traditional dish containing leftover pieces of the pig
   mixed with cornmeal and flour

sohn—son

umgwehnlich—unusual

wedder—weather

Wie bischt?—How are you?

wunderbaar—wonderful

ya—yes

Daughters of the Promise Community Tree

Huyards

Abraham (Abe) ⊤ Mary Ellen

Matthew   Luke   Linda (adopted)

Saunders

Kade ⊤ Sadie

Tyler   Marie

Ebersols

Bishop's Grandchildren

Stephen   Hannah   Annie

Millers

Irma Rose (D) ⊤ Jonas — Lizzie

Sarah Jane

Lillian

Dronbergers

Josephine — Robert

Linda

Barbie Beiler

Bed & Breakfast

Stoltzfuses

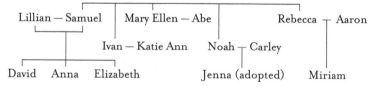

Lillian — Samuel   Mary Ellen — Abe   Rebecca ⊤ Aaron

Ivan — Katie Ann   Noah ⊤ Carley

David   Anna   Elizabeth   Jenna (adopted)   Miriam

Plain Promise

To Rene Simpson, my dear friend who refuses to settle for anything less than true love.

1

THE DEN IN THE OLD FARMHOUSE WAS THE COZIEST room in the house, but a nip still hung in the air. Sadie pulled her sweater from the rack on the wall and tossed another log onto the fire, orange sparks shimmying up the chimney. She walked to the window, raised the green blind, and looked toward the guest cottage about a hundred feet away. She couldn't help but recall the hours she and Ben had spent restoring it five years ago, painting the whitewashed walls, installing carpet, and making it fit for use by the *Englisch*.

Sadie was glad when Bishop Ebersol allowed her to furnish the cottage with electricity last year for use as a rental property. Her current renter had come all the way from Los Angeles, his long, sleek automobile now crowding the inside of her barn. But she was grateful for the income. It had been difficult to make ends meet with Ben gone, though her Old Order Amish community never let her go without.

This time of year, men in the district made sure she had plenty of firewood and kept the snow cleared from her driveway. In the spring and summer, the womenfolk kept her supplied with fresh peas and corn from the family crops, but Sadie, a fit woman at age thirty, kept a small garden on her own. She grew tomatoes, peppers, strawberries, melons, and the like—produce easy to tend. In the fall, her neighbors brought her lots of potatoes. She also had plenty of meat stored in a locker in town, thanks to her best friend, Lillian Stoltzfus, and Lillian's husband, Samuel.

Her shop out front gave her a bit more income. She sold handmade Amish goods that fared well with the tourists. Other women in the district added their crafts to Sadie's, and they took turns tending the store, splitting the profits among them. She turned her head around and checked the clock on the mantel. Nearly seven. She straightened up, tucked loose red ringlets beneath her *kapp*, and bowed her head.

After she thanked the Lord for the blessings of this new day, she grabbed her black cape, bonnet, and gloves. Then she pulled on her calf-high black boots and braced herself for a blast of arctic air. She took a deep breath, swung the door wide, and closed it quickly behind her—gelid wind stinging her cheeks like a thousand tiny needles.

A frosty mix of sleet and snow dusted her cape as she made her trek across the front yard to the shop. How fortunate she was that Ben's old workshop was near the road and visible to tourists. She had cried when she'd given away her husband's tools and turned his favorite place into the shop, but her friends had worked by her side to transform the old building. Then, just two months ago, they opened Treasures of the Heart.

She glanced around at the snow-covered pastures, visions of Ben tending the land still fresh in her mind. Less painful, but still there. It had been four years since the *Englisch* car had sped around a corner of Black Horse Road and into Ben's buggy. She would never forget their crates of fresh vegetables strewn across the road, patches of red, green, and yellow dotting the black asphalt. She envisioned the toppled buggy, their injured horse, who would later have to be put down, and her Ben . . .

When she'd heard the commotion that day, she had run down Black Horse Road faster than she knew her legs could carry her. Jacob King was squatting beside Ben when she arrived, and she knew by the expression on Jacob's face that her Ben was gone.

A glimpse of movement to her right pulled her back to the present. She looked toward the cottage and saw her renter, Kade Saunders, retrieving wood from where she had placed it on the front porch. He was sparsely clothed for such weather, denim pants and a short-sleeved, white T-shirt. Sadie watched him hurriedly scoop two logs into his arms, then drop one before making it to the front door.

She heard him grunt loudly and say something that sounded like cursing. She wasn't sure, but it stopped her in her tracks. She watched him walk backward into the house, cradling the logs in his arms. She couldn't see his expression, but she waved anyway. He didn't wave back. Of course, his arms were full. He kicked the door shut and was out of sight. It was the first time she'd seen the man since he'd arrived three days ago.

She tucked her head to avoid the thickening snowfall and continued toward the shop. It was hard not to wonder what Kade Saunders was doing in Lancaster County for three months, so far from where he lived in California. When he had stopped by to pick up the key, he hadn't looked prepared for the twelve-degree weather—denim breeches, a black overcoat, and white running shoes not fit for two feet of snow. And the man didn't have a head covering. His wavy, dark hair glistened with icy moisture, and his hazel eyes shone with irritation. Shivering as he spoke, he had declined the maid service included in the rental cost but requested that his automobile be protected from the wintry elements. She could see it through the open barn doors.

She rubbed her hands together and recalled the phone call from Mr. Saunders's personal assistant. The woman requested the one-bedroom cottage January through March for Mr. Saunders, but only after insisting that his privacy be respected during his stay. Sadie had hesitated. Her previous renters had been couples and families. How would it look for a single man to be occupying the same property as Sadie for three months, even if they were under separate roofs? Would the bishop be displeased?

As if sensing Sadie's concerns, the assistant said, "Mr. Saunders is quite well-known, and I can provide you with any references you might need."

The woman also asked that the refrigerator be stocked weekly. Sadie's normal rental package didn't include groceries, but Mr. Saunders's employee assured Sadie that cost was of no concern. The fee they'd agreed upon caused Sadie to gasp, but she agreed, grateful for the additional income during the off-season.

Sadie learned that actually finding the products Mr. Saunders desired was a challenge. She'd never heard of Gruyère cheese, for example, so she substituted Gouda cheese instead. His exhausting list of flavored coffees, organic breakfast cereals, and gourmet pastries were also frustrating.

She did the best she could and also threw in some extras. He was, after all, in Paradise, Pennsylvania—the heart of Lancaster County. Wouldn't he want to try Amish favorites, like shoofly pie and chowchow? She provided these for him in an attempt to make up for the items she couldn't find. She'd also prepared him a hearty batch of tapioca pudding, along with a loaf of homemade bread, a meat loaf, and zucchini casserole, and had also included a few jellies and jams she had canned last summer.

But even Mr. Saunders couldn't distract her from thinking about her forthcoming visit from Milo Troyer, her Amish friend from Stephenville, Texas. They had been writing letters for over two years, and he called Sadie every Tuesday night at eight o'clock. They talked for fifteen minutes, a cold fifteen minutes out in the barn this time of year, but she was thankful that the bishop allowed telephones in the barn these days, a luxury that would have been unheard-of in years past. Sadie looked forward to Milo's call all week long, and this spring he would be riding on a bus from Texas all the way to Lancaster County. They decided he would stay with her friends Ivan and Katie Ann for his two-week visit.

With pictures forbidden, she hadn't a clue what he looked like, except what he told her. He was tall and slender, like she was, with dark hair and the customary beard after marriage. His wife died shortly after Ben, and Sadie's cousin had introduced them via mail.

His looks were of no concern though. Milo's heart spoke to her in a way she didn't think possible after Ben died. He understood the grief of losing a spouse, and their hours of consoling each other had grown from friendship into much more. She knew it was God's will for her to move on; it was customary in their community to quickly remarry. But she'd been a widow for four years, and there were no options for remarriage. Perhaps she'd been too picky, but she refused to settle for anything less than something comparable to the love she'd shared with Ben.

She could tell by Milo's letters and phone calls that they would be a good match, and her desire was to begin her life with Milo soon. Milo's correspondence was always upbeat, kind, and filled with hope for the future. He was a hard worker, like Sadie, and family was his top priority. Perhaps they would have the children that she and Ben never did, for reasons the natural doctor in town couldn't seem to explain.

She entered the gift shop, went straight to the gas heaters, and lit them both. Only the cottage had electricity. It'd be cause for a shunning if she connected to the outside world when it wasn't necessary or approved by the bishop. She rolled up the green blinds in each of the four windows. The sun was just starting to rise, giving only a hint of light, just enough for her to attach price tags to some of the quilted pot holders she'd finished the night before. Fridays were usually good sale days, even in the off-season.

If she lived to be a hundred, she'd never understand why the *Englisch* found their way of life so interesting. With less farmland and bigger families, many in her community worked outside the home; it had become a way of life. She felt blessed not to have to travel farther than her own front yard.

The bell on the front door chimed, and Sadie turned to see her friend Lillian walk in. Lillian's mother, Sarah Jane, followed behind her. Lillian and her mother now shared a close relationship. But it hadn't always been that way. Sarah Jane had left the Amish community when she was a young girl of eighteen, and she had protested when Lillian left to come live with her grandparents. But after a few months, Sarah Jane surprised everyone, returning to Lancaster County and being baptized into the faith alongside her daughter. Then when Lillian married Samuel Stoltzfus, a widower in the community with a son named David, Sarah Jane had made her home with her father.

Lillian hung her cape on the stand inside the door. "Whose Mercedes-Benz?"

Sadie ignored the question. She had a hunch the less they all knew about her mysterious guest, the better. "Where's Anna?" she asked instead. Lillian usually brought her daughter, a precious bundle who wasn't much over a year old.

"Anna is with Samuel's sister, Mary Ellen," Lillian answered. She rubbed her expanding belly.

Sadie noticed the gesture. "How are you feeling? Are you still having morning sickness?"

"No more morning sickness." Lillian moved toward the back of the shop and peered out of the window toward the barn. "That's a very expensive car," she said. "Who does it belong to?"

"Kade Saunders." Sadie joined Lillian at the window while Sarah Jane took over pinning price tags on various items. "I don't know much about him. His personal assistant told me he's from Los Angeles. I reckon it's *gut* to have a renter this time of year. These harsh winters tend to keep people away." A tinge of cold air seeped in from outside when her face neared the window. "He's leasing the place for three months."

Lillian pulled her head back and squinted her eyes. "*Ya?* What for?"

"Don't know. But that assistant lady asked me to stock the refrigerator with all kinds of strange foods every week. Some of them I couldn't even find at the market." She paused. "And he doesn't want any cleanup service. I reckon he'll have to wash his own towels and linens in the washing machine and dryer."

"Hmm. That is odd," Lillian mused, still gazing toward the cottage and the fancy car in the barn.

Kade stared at the TV screen and wondered if he could survive without basic cable for the next three months. The antique antenna provided a whopping four channels. No CNN or other national channels, only local news that was fuzzy at best. But this is what he wanted, he reminded himself—away from everything.

He leaned back on the couch and propped his feet on the coffee table, trying to ward off his festering thoughts about Alicia. It wasn't as if she'd broken his heart or anything, but once again he'd let himself be used and fooled by a member of the opposite sex. One shiny new car, a diamond bracelet—and pretty much anything else she'd asked for—and then she was gone. Story of his life. Young, attractive women interested in his money, nothing more.

Kade glanced around at his modest accommodations. This was hardly what he had in mind when his friend Val had suggested he get out of Los Angeles to unwind. Val had brought his ex-wife here and said the peacefulness would help Kade clear his head. Though it must not have worked for Val—he and his wife had divorced shortly after their trip. Val never wanted to talk about what had happened, and he seemed to be mending his soul with travel. Kade could rarely get hold of him these days. But Kade understood. Kade's soul could certainly use some mending as well.

The roaring fire warmed the room, and his refrigerator and pantry were stocked, though he couldn't identify some of his host's offerings. Amish food, he presumed. He wished it wasn't so cold outside, but he didn't feel the need to venture out anyway. That would mean interaction with others, and he wasn't up for that. Besides, he found the simple cottage to be quite cozy. He'd hole up here and try to heal himself of all that ailed him. It was a long list.

For whatever reason, he thought of the Amish woman he was renting from. He couldn't remember her name. But he could recall her ivory skin, incredible blue eyes, and strands of wavy red hair spiraling against her cheek from beneath a cap on her head. She was quite lovely, even without a stitch of makeup on her face and clothed in a baggy dress to her knees. And she was tall and slender. Like Alicia. Kade's brows narrowed as he grumbled in disgust. *Blasted woman.*

Still. It was no reason to be rude to the Amish gal when he'd first arrived—demanding he park his car in the barn and hastily accepting the key before he retreated to his much-needed solitude. Perhaps he could have been a little kinder to the woman. Kade hadn't seen another soul on the property, except for a few women who entered the shop up front each day. He wondered if she took care of this whole place on her own.

He opened the refrigerator and took out the plastic bowl of tapioca pudding. Best pudding he'd ever had in his life. He grabbed a spoon from the drawer and finished the last little bit in the large container, then tossed the empty bowl in the sink, along with the past three days of dirty dishes. He would have been better served to have accepted the Amish woman's house-cleaning services included in the rental. He wondered for a moment if he should reconsider but disregarded the thought. It would require a limited amount of conversation. He began to fill the sink with soapy water.

Thirty minutes later, he was back on the tan couch. He adjusted the volume on the TV, listened to a woman discuss a nearby animal shelter, and then he turned it off. And he sat—thinking.

He crossed his ankles on the coffee table and thought about how successful he'd become by following in his father's footsteps. At thirty-seven, Kade had more money than he'd ever spend in one lifetime. And, he decided, he couldn't be more miserable.

One thing would cheer him up, though—some more of that tapioca pudding from the Amish woman.

In the fading twilight, Sadie braved the below-freezing temperature and pulled two logs from the stack of firewood she kept in the barn, wishing she'd remembered to do it earlier in the day. Her boots heavy in the deep snow, she edged toward the farmhouse, glancing at the cottage lit up by electricity, smoke wafting out of the chimney. Something caught her eye on her renter's front porch. It was the empty plastic bowl that she had sent the tapioca pudding in. Why in the world would he set it on the front porch?

She put the logs down and trudged toward the cottage, the frigid air nipping at her cheeks. She grabbed the bowl, retrieved her wood, and then headed toward the farmhouse. All she wanted to do was climb into bed and reread the letter she received from Milo two weeks ago, to take refuge in his words and combat her dwindling hope.

Following a bath, she lit the lantern by her bed upstairs and pulled out Milo's note.

My Dear Sadie,

I am counting the days until we meet. I will come to see you when the winter weather has passed. I reckon the springtime is when I will come. The sound of your voice helps me to picture you in my head. You are schee, I know. If it is God's will, you will become my fraa and we will be together. The Lord will guide us.

I am reminded of a song from our Sunday singings—"We Have This Moment." The words make me think of you—"Hold tight to the sound of the music of living. Happy songs from the laughter of children at play. Hold my hand as we run through the sweet, fragrant meadows, making memories of what is today. We have this moment to hold in our hands, and to touch as it slips through our fingers like sand. Yesterday's gone and tomorrow may never come, but we have this moment today."

I want to share mei moments with you, Sadie. I will write you again soon.

In His name,
Milo

Sadie folded the letter and pressed it against her chest. She could only pray that Milo would be everything she longed for. While she'd grown accustomed to fending for herself, how wonderful it would be to have a man to help with chores, to hold her, to love her, to grow old with. Maybe God would even see fit to bless them with a child.

"We Have This Moment" was one of Sadie's favorite songs. She recalled another verse from the song—*"Tender words, gentle touch, and a good time sharing, and someone who loves me and wants me to stay. Hold them near while they're here and don't wait for tomorrow to look back and wish for today."*

Please God, she prayed silently, *bless me with companionship as I go forth in life to serve You.*

The ground was solid beneath Sadie's feet as she walked toward the shop, with no new snow since the heavy downfall yesterday afternoon. She wondered if the snow would keep tourists away, but it was Saturday. At least a few customers would rough out the weather. Today's schedule called for Sadie and Katie Ann to work, since Lillian and her mother had worked the shop yesterday. But Katie Ann was down with the flu, and Sadie declined Mary Ellen's help. There wasn't enough going on this time of year to require two women to run the shop. Sadie knew she could handle it on her own. Besides, Mary Ellen had a family to tend to. She, on the other hand, did not.

It was nearing eight o'clock when she lit the heaters and drew the blinds in the shop. Her day had started early that morning. She'd made another large batch of tapioca pudding, thinking her guest might have been requesting more when he left the empty container outside. It was no trouble. She also baked two loaves of bread for an elderly friend down the street, Lizzie Esh. Lizzie suffered with arthritis and had difficulty cooking these days, particularly considering the effort it took to repeatedly knead dough. She planned to run the bread to Lizzie after she closed the shop in the late afternoon.

The container of pudding sat next to her, and she peered out of the back window toward the guesthouse. One light appeared to be on. With her winter cape, bonnet, and boots still on, she decided she'd leave Mr. Saunders's pudding on his porch. Surely he'd come out soon for firewood and see it before it froze.

She was grateful for a pleasantly warmer day, approaching thirty degrees. Nearing the cottage, she saw that Mr. Saunders still had plenty of firewood stacked on the porch, which reminded her that she would need to cart some to the farmhouse for later. Then she heard the music.

Evidently he was awake. She plodded slowly across the yard and stopped at the bottom of the steps. A woman's voice belted loudly above an assortment of instruments. Sadie loved to sing and wondered what it would be like to sing along with actual instruments, something that would never be allowed in her district. Owning an instrument was said to bring forth unnecessary emotions.

This is like spying, she thought, as she held her position, beginning to hum to the rhythm. *Just a little longer.* How could owning an instrument that produced such beautiful sounds be wrong in the eyes of God?

Finally, she placed the plastic container with the tapioca pudding on a small table between two rockers. She turned to leave but hadn't even made it to the steps when the cottage door swung open.

Sadie spun around. Stunned, she faced Kade Saunders standing in the threshold. A flush rose from her neck, accompanied by a knot in her throat as she gulped back her embarrassment. The man was wearing what appeared to be pajama bottoms. He was barefoot, and he didn't have a shirt on. She instinctively threw her hands over her eyes, gasping, but unable to move.

"Wait right here." Kade held his palm toward her and backed into the house.

No problem. She couldn't move. She widened her fingers on one hand to have a peek. He stood in the living area, pulling a white sweatshirt over his head as if sensing her embarrassment at seeing him in such a way. The flush had overtaken her face, she was quite sure. She brought her hands down and began nervously twisting the ties on her black cape. *Pajama bottoms, for goodness' sake.*

When he returned to the door, she stammered, "I . . . I brought you some tapioca pudding."

Kade walked toward her, still barefoot. "Thank you. That was the best tapioca pudding I've ever had."

His shoulder brushed hers as he whisked by her to retrieve it. Her feet were rooted in place when he came back her way; then he stood uncomfortably close to her, facing her. He put one hand on his hip and tucked the pudding container against his side with the other hand. "Do you want to come in?"

"No. I do not." She wished right away that she hadn't sounded so shocked by his offer. He wasn't smiling, but at least he didn't have the irritated look on his face like he did the first day of his arrival. "Okay," he said, then shrugged. "Suit your-self." He turned to head back into the cottage.

Finally, she was able to move her legs and turned to head down the steps, promising herself she would never come back to the cottage until time to deliver more groceries, which she quickly calculated wasn't for another three days.

"Hey," he called out to her.

She had only taken four or five steps into the snow when she was forced to turn around and acknowledge him. "*Ya?*"

"What's your name?"

"Sadie." She offered a brief smile before turning back around.

"Hey, Sadie?"

Again she turned around. "*Ya?*"

"If you like listening to the music so much, why don't you

knock on the door and come in out of the cold next time?" he said. "You don't have to loiter on the front porch."

If only the earth would open up and swallow me, she thought.

"No, no," she mumbled. She gave him a quick wave and began stepping backwards.

She remembered falling. She wasn't sure what she tripped over, but as her legs buckled beneath her, she hit her head on the icy ground.

Sprawled out on her back, she recalled the image of Kade Saunders bolting barefoot across the snow.

2

"GOOD GRIEF!" KADE SPRINTED DOWN THE STEPS, THE frozen ground beneath his feet stinging his soles, a thought that quickly became secondary when he saw splatters of blood around the Amish woman's head. *Oh, man.*

He cradled his hand behind her neck and lifted her head. Not too much blood. But she was out cold. Kade lifted her into his arms in a clumsy, ridiculous way that he was sure would be uncomfortable for her if she had been conscious. His feet were numbing so much that he worried he'd fall with her in his arms. She wasn't fully in his grasp. Her left leg hung loose, her black boot dragging across the snow. Not his most heroic moment.

The icy steps proved challenging. He quickly gave up any hope for gracefulness as Sadie's left calf bounced off of each step. He cringed with each cumbersome movement, his feet practically anesthetized by the slick coldness beneath them.

The central heating from the cottage hit him while he was still on the porch and gave him the extra push to get inside. He wound around the coffee table and laid her on the couch. Kade propped a throw pillow behind her head and wondered if she'd be angry that he let her bleed on her own couch. He'd worry about that later. He wasn't sure Amish people got angry anyway. Kade crouched beside

18

her and gently lifted her head. He fumbled with the string on her white cap, then gently pushed it aside. Strands of red hair escaped, making it difficult for him to see the wound.

Her blue eyes opened wide. "*Ach!*" she screamed, then pushed his hand away. He was startled, but not half as spooked as she was. Then with the power of an army, she thrust her hands against his chest and pushed him to a standing position. When she stood up, a round of dialect unbeknown to Kade followed.

I think she's angry, Kade thought, without a clue about what she was saying.

He stumbled backward. "Hey, hold up, lady. You had a nasty fall, and I rescued you." If you could call it that. She probably had a pretty banged-up shin that she didn't have before.

She was on her feet and scurrying toward the door, trying desperately to tuck her hair beneath the white cap on her head. Kade would've never known her hair was so long, hidden beneath the cap on her head. Now several strands cascaded below her shoulders almost to her waist, wavy and full.

Kade thought he saw tears in her eyes. "Wait," he said. "You banged your head pretty good. Maybe—"

She swung the door open, never looked back, and was gone.

———

Sadie's head throbbed, and she weaved from side to side across the snow. She made her way inside the shop, then reached up and touched a gooey mess on the back of her head. *Blood.*

The recollection of Kade Saunders leaning over her in a most inappropriate way was much worse than the pain she was in. She winced as she recalled the horror and embarrassment of it all.

She should've never agreed to lease to a single man from the city. He'd come to the door in long, flannel pajama breeches—with no shirt on. *Most improper, indeed.*

She was surprised to see Jonas Miller standing outside her shop. What in the world was Lillian's grandfather doing here, especially in his condition? He'd had the cancer for some time now and didn't get out so much as Sadie knew. Plus, it was a frigid day for a ride in the buggy. Sadie's eyes darted to Jessie. Jonas had had that old horse for as long as she'd known him.

Lillian. Was something wrong with Lillian?

"Jonas, what brings you out here on a day like this? Everything is all right, no?" She wiped her bloody hand on her apron.

"Is that blood?" Jonas pushed back the rim of his straw hat, squinted his eyes, and walked over to Sadie. He lifted her hand. "That's blood for sure." He dropped her hand, stroked his beard, and scanned her from head to toe. "Where are you hurt, child?"

"*Mei* head." She pointed to a spot beneath her prayer covering, which was absorbing the slow trickle of blood. "I slipped earlier."

Jonas tilted her head to the side, pulled back her *kapp*, and looked intently at her wound, his touch causing her to flinch. "I reckon you'll live," he said matter-of-factly, then stepped back from her.

That's it? I'll live?

Lillian's grandfather had a way with words—and people— that wasn't reflective of most Amish men she knew. Everyone loved Jonas, but you never knew what might come out of his mouth. And knowing that to be true, her heart skipped a beat when she noticed Kade awkwardly making his way across the snow. At least he was sporting some running shoes, but didn't the man own any boots? And he wore no jacket, only the sweatshirt he'd hastily thrown on.

"Who's the fancy fella comin' across the yard like he ain't got a lick a sense?"

"Kade Saunders. He's renting the cottage for three months." Sadie felt her heart quicken as she saw Jonas eyeing him with suspicion.

"Three months?" Jonas twisted his mouth to one side and narrowed his brows. "He rentin' it all by himself, or he got a *fraa* and *kinner* with him?"

"No. It's just him."

They stood silently as Kade came within listening space. *Please, Jonas . . . be good.*

"I wanted to make sure you were all right," he said to Sadie.

Sadie nodded and opened her mouth to speak. She supposed she should thank him for not letting her lie in the snow and freeze to death, no matter the awkwardness of the situation.

"She's mighty fine," Jonas interjected. "What brings a man like you to Lancaster County for three months in this *kalt wedder*? You runnin' from something?" Jonas stared the man down.

Sadie warmly reflected that if her father was alive, he would have the same question for a man traveling alone, especially a man Kade's age. Sadie figured him to be in his mid to late thirties.

"No . . . I'm not running from anything. I just . . ." Kade looked bewildered by the question.

Jonas stood a little taller. "I come by every day to check on Sadie."

Jonas, that is far from the truth. Sadie arched her brows and shot Jonas an inquisitive look.

"Just so ya know," Jonas added. He didn't take his eyes off of Kade.

Bless his kind heart. Sadie knew Jonas wouldn't be any good to protect her, even if Kade were a threat to her, which she doubted.

Kade folded his arms across his chest, shivered a bit, and smiled. He seemed amused at Jonas's display of chivalry. His dark hair was neatly parted to one side with a hint of gray at the temples. Sadie thought he looked very formal, until he smiled. His teeth were straight and white, but his smile crooked up on one side. It made him look nicer somehow.

But the smile was short-lived. "As long as you're okay." He held up his hand to bid farewell and turned to leave.

"Mr. Saunders?" Sadie realized she'd probably overreacted when she awoke on the couch. But it was so disturbing—his face so close to hers, his hands in her hair.

He turned around. "Yeah?"

"Uh, *danki* for helping me when I fell."

"You're welcome." He didn't smile. Whatever warmth she thought she saw earlier—gone. He was a strange man, that Kade Saunders. Seemed like an unhappy man.

Jonas kept a scowl stretched across his face as he watched Kade walk across the snow. When Kade was out of earshot, Jonas said, "Sadie, I don't know if it's *gut* for you to be out here alone with only him on the property."

"I'm sure he is of no harm, Jonas. The lady who made his arrangements said he has *gut* references." She paused. "I think he might be *somebody*. You know, like famous or rich."

"Well, he ain't nobody 'round here."

"Jonas, what brings you out here on a day like this? It's too *kalt* to be riding in a buggy today, unless you have to."

Jonas pried his eyes from Kade and turned toward her, a blank expression on his face. "What?"

"Did you need something? You didn't really come just to check on me, did you?"

Jonas stood taller, then raised his brows. "I reckon I must have." He paused, as if unsure. "And now that fella knows to mind his manners."

Sadie reached up and touched her head. The ache had lessened, but she was aware of it.

"You better go tend to that cut on your head," Jonas said. He tipped his hat in her direction, as if he was leaving. "You don't need no stitches. A *gut* cleaning oughta do it. And you're probably gonna have a big bump for a while."

Sadie nodded. Before she could say anything else, Jonas was heading back to his buggy. She couldn't help but wonder if Lillian and Sarah Jane knew he was traveling around in the buggy on a day like today. Sadie recalled when Lillian and her mother had frantically showed up looking for Jonas a few weeks ago. Apparently, he'd left without telling anyone, and daughter and granddaughter were worried sick. Sadie hoped this wasn't one of those times.

———

Kade warmed his hands in front of the fireplace and wondered why he kept foolishly walking out into these elements without his jacket. At least he remembered his shoes this time. He couldn't help but smile at the way the old man had tried to intimidate him.

He kicked off his shoes, then pulled off his socks and hung them on a hook on the mantel. Something he'd never done before, but being here seemed to call for it. But then his socks dangling in front of the fireplace reminded him of recent Christmas preparations with Alicia. They had hung stockings at his house for each other. He'd been foolish enough to think Alicia might want to take their relationship to the next level.

His thoughts drifted to the Amish woman, the petrified look on her face when she awoke on the couch. Why didn't she have a husband? She had to be close to thirty and was certainly attractive. Maybe she'd never had a man that close to her before. Kade shrugged. Their simple way of life—buggies, no electricity, the plain clothes—it all seemed so prehistoric in this day and time. Hard to believe people still lived this way.

But the woman had shoved him. Was that allowed by her people?

Kade paced around the small living room, questioning her aggressiveness, and suddenly he realized that for the first time in his life, he had no agenda. Nowhere he had to be. Nothing he had to do. And he could only think of one thing that mildly sparked his interest.

As he dove into the tapioca pudding, not even bothering to serve it up in a bowl, he feared he was a man on the brink of depression—binge eating like some of the women he knew. The thought didn't stop him from shoveling the custard into his mouth. He propped his bare feet on the coffee table and made a mental note: if he had to rescue a damsel in distress again, he would take the time to put some shoes on. He wasn't completely sure that he didn't have frostbite.

He was on the verge of devouring the entire container of pudding when his cell phone rang. He blew out a sigh of exasperation, set the pudding aside, and walked to the kitchen where he'd left his phone on the counter. He glanced at the number.

No, no, no. Not now. Talking to Monica was the last thing he needed. He hit the End button. Her calls were always upsetting—on so many levels.

Sadie opened the medicine cabinet in her bathroom and found something for her head. She parted her hair with her fingers and felt for the cut. The pain led her to it. She gingerly dabbed it with ointment then carefully wound her hair in a bun. After placing a fresh prayer covering on her head, she silently thanked God that it wasn't worse and headed back to the shop.

It was later in the afternoon before she had her first customer, who turned out to be her last customer as well. But the woman from Florida purchased a quilt for seven hundred dollars, two handmade pot holders, and four dolls. *It made for a fair day,* she thought, locking up the shop.

She walked to the road and checked the mailbox. Nothing. She had hoped for another letter from Milo. Disappointed, she headed back down the driveway, taking care with each step. Her eyes drifted toward the cottage. The *Englischer* was staring out the window—at her.

She put her head down and quickened her pace as she made her way to the farmhouse steps. Firewood was stacked neatly on the porch, piled against the house. Lots of firewood—that she hadn't collected. And the empty container of pudding sat on top of the logs. Instinctively, she spun around and squinted to see if he was still there. He wasn't.

She was thankful to have the firewood nearby, and she supposed another batch of pudding was a fair trade. She'd never known a man to eat so much custard. She took the bowl into the house, then remembered the newspaper's prediction of another temperature drop into the teens tonight. Before she kicked off her boots, she went back to the porch for two logs and glanced quickly toward the cabin. No sign of him.

Later that evening, she prepared a fresh batch of pudding, then placed it in her refrigerator. She didn't have anything else to do anyway. Loneliness began to creep in, the way it always did this time of day.

She headed upstairs for bed. It was only Saturday. Three more days until Milo would call. Until then, she'd have to be content rereading his letter. She considered penning him a note, but she'd already put two letters in the mail since the arrival of Milo's last correspondence.

After her bath, Sadie lit the gas heater in her bedroom, climbed into bed, and snuggled underneath a thick quilt, extra blanket, and flannel sheet. She reached for Milo's letter, and her bedside lantern illuminated the page.

When she was done reading, she put the letter back on the bedside table, feeling like it was somehow losing its impact. She tried to stay hopeful, and each letter carried her into another week until she heard the sound of Milo's voice on Tuesdays. But the letters seemed to have slowed down on his end. If she allowed herself to think too much, her heart ached. Two years was a long time to be writing letters back and forth.

She pulled the nightstand drawer open and took out her brush, as she'd done at bedtime ever since Ben died. Then she mechanically smoothed the tangles, careful of her cut. Sometimes, like tonight, her loneliness was beyond tears as she remembered the feel of Ben brushing her hair before bed, something he'd said he enjoyed doing. And, oh, how she'd loved the feel of his hands in her hair, the brush sweeping downward to her waist. She cringed, recalling that Kade Saunders had seen much of her hair when it fell from beneath her *kapp*. *So wrong*. Only a woman's husband should see her hair in length. She drew in a breath, blew it out slowly, and continued to brush, thinking about Ben, about Milo, and strangely enough . . . about Kade.

He was an odd fellow. Void of enough sense to protect himself from the cold too. *But one of God's children*, she reminded herself when judgment cut in. Still she speculated. Why was he here for three months? Why does he seem so angry one minute and then rather heroic the next? But was he? Heroic, that is. It had been unfit for him to be so close to her on the couch. But she was hurt and . . .

She twisted in the bed, pushed the covers aside, and examined her shin. She still wasn't sure how she had acquired the bruise.

Her mind played back and forth about Kade. He embarrassed her when he told her he knew she was listening to the music from the porch. So brazen when he'd said it too. She shook her head, decided not to give him another thought, and closed her eyes to pray.

It was only an hour later when Sadie was startled out of a deep sleep. It took her a few seconds to focus on the battery-operated clock by her bed, illuminated a soft white. Nine o'clock. What could all the ruckus be about? Four o'clock came early in the morning. No one she knew would be visiting at this hour. The noise grew louder, and it was quite clear that someone was pounding on the front door. Loudly.

She pulled her thick robe over her nightgown and headed down the stairs as fast as she could, holding the handrail for support. She couldn't see a thing at first, but the cooler temperature downstairs hit her when she neared the first floor. The fire was still flickering in the fireplace, and the glow from the hearth offered enough light for her to stumble her way across the den. She reached for the doorknob but stopped when she heard *him* yelling—hollering like a madman.

"Sadie!"

Only one thought came to mind, as silly as it seemed. *Serial killer.* She'd read about people like that in the newspaper. He yelled again.

"What is it, Mr. Saunders?" She was shaking all over.

"It's freezing out here! Can you open the door?" His tone was agitated, and she wasn't sure what to do.

"What's the matter?" She fought the tremble in her voice.

"For heaven's sake, woman, please open the door."

Sadie reached for the knob. Then hesitated. "Is anything wrong?"

"Yes. Something is wrong!" he yelled.

She heard him mumbling from the other side of the door. She reached for a scarf hanging on a peg nearby and draped it over her head.

"What is the problem?" She tossed one end of the wrap over her shoulder and assumed she must look a mess.

"I need your help with a problem at the cottage. Can you please open the door?"

Silly, silly woman, Sadie thought. There is something wrong at the cottage, of course. She opened the door. "I'm sorry, I just . . ."

The *Englischer* scooted past her and went directly to the fireplace, stretching his arms near the dwindling fire.

"Don't you own a coat, Mr. Saunders?" Sadie folded her arms across her chest.

He looked down at his jeans and white sweatshirt, then shook his head. "I don't know why I keep running out the door without it on." He shook his head and returned his attention to the fire.

"What is wrong that brings you here at this time of night?" She held her place firmly by the door . . . just in case.

He turned to look at her. "Were you asleep?" He sounded shocked. "It's only nine o'clock."

Sadie prepared to defend her schedule, but he waved his hand as if to say never mind.

"I forget you people go to bed early and get up early."

You people? She pierced her lips together and narrowed her eyes at him.

"Sorry," he said when he saw her expression.

Sadie took two steps forward. "Mr. Saunders, what do you need?"

He sighed. "That phone in the barn is ringing nonstop, followed by the sound of an answering machine picking up. The barn is so close to the cottage, and, well . . . it's irritating me. Why don't you have the phone in the house?"

"The phone is ringing?" Sadie couldn't imagine who it might be. *Milo?* But on a Saturday?

"Yes. It's ringing over and over again. I walked outside to take the darn thing off the hook, but the answering machine had just picked up again. I decided I better come get you when I heard the message."

Sadie's heart flipped in her chest. "What was the message?" Occasionally, Milo left tender messages on the machine. She hoped this wasn't one of those times. A flush was building in her cheeks.

"She said her name was Lillian and that it was an emergency. She said for you to come quickly if you got the message." He paused. "And here's the part that really caught my attention . . ." Kade shook his head, a perplexed look on his face. "She said she needed *my* car."

"What?" Sadie turned and moved toward the door.

"Why would someone named Lillian need my car?" He was hovering right behind her.

Sadie tied the kerchief in a bulky knot under her chin, pulled her boots on, and swung her cape over her robe. Then she bolted out the door.

"Be careful! It's slippery out there!" he yelled as he followed her.

It was snowing again, and the bitterly cold wind blew through her cape as she hurried across the white powder. Lillian would never call this late. And she said it was an emergency. *If she needs a car, something is terribly wrong.*

When Sadie got to the barn, she was numb from head to toe. Her hand was shaking when she reached for the answering machine—another luxury that was unheard-of years ago. She pushed the button.

"Sadie, it's Lillian . . ."

Sadie could hear the *Mr. Saunders* coming up behind her in the barn. "What is it?" He paused, sounding out of breath. "Who is Jonas?"

She gripped her hands together, drew them to her chest, and took a deep breath as she listened to the rest of Lillian's message.

"Oh, no," she said, fighting tears.

3

KADE REMEMBERED HIS COAT AND GLOVES THIS TIME. He carefully backed the car out of the barn and wondered how in the heck he was going to drive in this weather. He was from L.A., for crying out loud.

Sadie waited on the front porch, bundled up like a snow bunny. The last thing he felt like doing was driving around, particularly in these elements, to find a lost old man. Not because he was a cold, heartless kind of guy, but because he'd been this route before. And the end result hadn't been good. Kade thought back to when his mother first told him about his father's Alzheimer's disease. Dad was such a young man at the time too. Not much older than Kade. According to the doctors, early onset of the illness accounts for 5 to 10 percent of those diagnosed, and his father fell into that unlucky percentage. Kade feared losing his mind more than anything else. And it seemed to run in his genes.

Oh man, oh man. The car slid sideways when he tried to turn the Mercedes around. Pulling forward, the tires spun in the snow. He glanced up at the porch and saw Sadie, who appeared irritated at his efforts. Did she want to give it a try? *You don't even know how to drive, and I'm doing the best I can.*

32

Finally the car inched ahead. When he stopped, she was already down the porch steps. She opened the back door and slid into the seat.

"What are you doing? Do you think maybe you should sit in the front seat and help me navigate?" She gave him a strange look, then exited and eased her way into the front seat. All his frustration washed away when he looked into her teary, blue eyes, reflective of the pain in her heart. *This old man must be very dear to her.*

"We'll find him," he said soothingly.

<hr />

"I'm sorry about this." As they pulled onto Black Horse Road, Sadie turned to look at him. He seemed to be concentrating. "But they will need all the help they can get. And Lillian knew there was a car here, so . . ." It seemed strange to be sitting in the front seat with him. Normally, when an *Englisch* driver was called for a ride, she sat in the backseat. Unless, of course, it was a friend of hers. She barely knew her renter.

Kade leaned forward on the steering wheel and struggled to see past the falling snow. "How far down the road is it?"

"Not far." She shook her head. "Poor Jonas."

"Did your friend say how long he's been missing?" Kade turned briefly toward her, then steadied his eyes back on the road.

"Lillian's mother said Jonas left in the buggy after supper, which would mean he went home after he left my shop today. Lillian said her mother tried to talk him out of going for a ride in this *baremlich*—I mean, terrible—weather."

"What's that language you're speaking? It sounds like German."

"Pennsylvania *Deitsch*. It's rather like German, I suppose." She pointed to her left. "Over there."

"Thank goodness," Kade grumbled.

"I'm sorry," she said again. She'd rather not be going anywhere with him either.

"No, it's okay. I just don't know how to drive in these conditions. I'd hate to have an accident."

And mess up this fancy car. Sadie didn't say anything.

"Wow," he said when he pulled into the driveway. "I've never seen this many buggies in one place at one time."

"In our community, everyone helps everyone else, 'specially at a time like this."

"What's everyone going to do? Trudge around in the snow, looking for this guy?"

Sadie knew the look she shot Kade Saunders would have God frowning, and she tried to free herself of the bad thoughts she was having about this man. But even in the darkness, he evidently picked up on her dislike for him.

"I mean, I'll help look, but it's freezing outside, and—"

"We don't need your help, Mr. Saunders. You are welcome to sit in the car, if you see fit." She folded her hands in her lap.

"Of course I'm going to help." She thought he rolled his eyes before continuing. "And you can call me Kade."

Sadie didn't answer. She opened the door and headed toward the crowd of people on the porch.

"Thank you for coming, Sadie. And for bringing the car." Lillian hugged her.

Lillian's mother, Sarah Jane, was talking to the elders gathered at the other end of the porch. Even the bishop had come, and he had to be at least Jonas's age.

"Where do you want us to start looking?" Sadie asked. She scanned the porch. About twenty folks so far.

"Barbie should be here soon in her car. And she's bringing several other *Englisch* friends with cars. Noah and Carley will be here soon, too, in their car. But in this *wedder*, it will take them longer to get here." Lillian looked over Sadie's shoulder. "The *Englisch* man is walking this way. Is he friendly?"

Sadie shrugged. "He has a car."

"Hi." Kade extended his hand to Lillian. "I'm Kade Saunders."

"Thank you for bringing your car, Mr. Saunders." Lillian looked at Kade's running shoes, covered in snow. "Do you have no boots?"

"No . . ." Kade sounded embarrassed. "I wasn't very prepared for this weather. I'm planning to get some in town when the weather clears."

"You won't need them then," Lillian said with a smirk on her face. "*Mei daadi* has an extra pair of boots inside the house. I'll get them for you."

"Thanks," Kade said.

Sadie could hear Sarah Jane instructing the others where to go, areas Jonas might have gone. Her stomach rolled. In this weather, Jonas would freeze . . . She squelched the thought and turned her attention to Kade. He was shivering like a little girl.

"I hate the cold," he snapped as he wrapped his arms around himself.

"I told you, you can sit in the car."

Kade waved his hand in front of her, signaling silence. He'd done that before, and she didn't like it. "I want to help. I'm just not used to this weather. That's all."

Lillian returned with a pair of Jonas's boots and a heavy

coat. Much heavier than the lightweight overcoat Kade was wearing. "Here you go, Mr. Saunders." Lillian offered him the boots and coat.

"Thanks." Kade wasted no time putting on the coat, then pulled the boots over his tennis shoes.

Lillian grabbed Sadie by the arm and began pulling her away from the others. Kade stayed where he was—still shivering.

"The elders will divide up and search the back roads. *Mamm* will stay here, and everyone will be checking back on the hour. When other *Englisch* get here, we'll have several portable telephones to use. Does your friend have one? A cell phone?"

"He's not my friend. He's my renter. But I reckon he has one."

"Sadie, there's somewhere I need you to go, to look for Jonas. Somewhere I don't want the others to know about. I don't even want *mei mamm* to know." Lillian flinched and glanced toward her husband, Samuel, at the other end of the porch. "Actually, there are two places. Samuel will go to one of the spots with Noah and Carley in their car when they get here. Will you and Mr. Saunders go to the other place?"

Sadie knew that Lillian trusted her, and Noah and Carley, to be discreet. Noah was Samuel's shunned brother who had left the Old Order to become a doctor, and who ended up marrying one of Lillian's best friends. They were officially outsiders, but really weren't. The entire community adored them both. Noah's clinic was frequented by the Amish, despite the bishop's initial ruling that their district couldn't patronize Noah's health facility. But ever since Noah had donated one of his kidneys to Samuel's son, David, things had been different. The bishop now seemed to overlook things related to Noah and his shunning.

"Where is it that you want us to go?" Sadie asked.

Lillian frowned and leaned toward Sadie's ear. "There's a little pub down a ways on Lincoln Highway. I fear he might be in there." Lillian stood straight again and waited for a reaction from Sadie.

"Uh, do you mean a *bar* that serves beer and the like?" Sadie had never been in such a place.

"I hate to ask you." Lillian paused. "But once, I was driving the buggy to market, and I saw Grandpa's buggy parked outside the place. I know it was his, because it has that dent on the right side from when Noah backed his car into it one time." She shook her head. "I remember that Grandpa was fit to be tied when that happened. Anyway, I had the baby with me, so I didn't go in."

"What's the other place?" Sadie was wondering if she could choose between the two—if the other spot might not be as bad.

"It's a pub, too, further down Lincoln Highway. It's a little rougher, though. I figured Noah, Samuel, and Carley can take that one."

That answered Sadie's question. "Have you caught him in there before too?"

"*Ya.* I did. And that time I wasn't with the baby, so I went in and coaxed him out. He made me promise not to tell *mei mamm,* which I didn't. It was harmless enough. He was chatting with some *Englisch* men that he knew. But he had no business in such a place, so I kindly told him we needed to be on our way." Lillian's eyes grew glassy. "Sadie, I am *hoping* he's in one of those places on this night. If he's out in this weather . . ."

"We'll leave right now." Sadie turned to see Kade holding his position and making no effort to talk to any of the others. He looked out of place, and she dreaded having to spend more time with him.

"There's Noah and Carley." Lillian pointed to a car coming up the drive. Then she hugged Sadie. "*Danki.*"

Kade was glad to reach the main highway. There was little traffic, and the snow plows were hard at work keeping the streets clear. Driving down Black Horse Road had been an effort. He sure hoped this Jonas fellow was indoors and not out in the weather. It had been just the opposite the day he found his father. Hot. Humid. Kade struggled to push the thought to the back of his mind.

"There it is." She pointed to their right. Looked like a hole-in-the-wall joint. "You don't have to go inside," she added.

"I was just about to tell you the same thing." Kade suspected Sadie wouldn't be comfortable going in such an establishment.

"No, Jonas knows me. I'm not sure he trusts—"

"Me?" Kade grunted. "Yeah, I got that impression earlier today."

"He's very protective of Lillian and all her friends," she said with pride.

Kade put the car in park. "Ready?" He certainly wasn't, but the sooner they got this over with, the better. "Hopefully, we'll find him inside."

She stepped out of the car and pulled the hood of her black coat over her head. Kade found a similar hood on his coat and pulled it on. It was a short walk to the pub, but the snow was coming down in thick blankets. He felt ridiculous in the black galoshes, but his feet were staying dry. He pulled the long, brass handle protruding from the wooden door. Cigarette smoke hit him in the face as he held the door for Sadie. He stayed close behind her.

About fifteen square tables were scattered about the place, each with a red and white-checkered tablecloth and four chairs. Small, glass vases housed worn silk flowers in the middle of the tables, surrounded by salt, pepper, ketchup, and steak sauce. At least it wasn't *just* a beer joint.

Only two of the tables had patrons. A long bar ran the length of the back wall, and it didn't take Kade long to spot an Amish man sitting alone—his straw hat on and a frosty mug in his hand.

"There he is." Sadie pointed. She sounded relieved and wasted no time moving toward him. Kade followed.

"Jonas!" Sadie snapped when she reached his side. "The entire community is looking for you." Relief flooded over her, despite her disciplinarian tone. "We have a car with us. Let's get you home. Thank the good Lord you are safe." She threw her arms around him. He didn't respond, and a chill ran up Sadie's spine. Perhaps he was angry with her for coming.

"Jonas?" She waited for an acknowledgment. He took a drink of what appeared to be beer from a tall, glass mug. Then he turned toward her, stared, and looked past her to Kade.

"Who are you?" He cut his eyes in Kade's direction.

"You saw him this morning, Jonas. His name is Kade Saunders." Sadie stepped back and made room for Kade, who extended his hand to Jonas.

"Nice to meet you, Jonas. A lot of people will be glad you're safe."

Jonas firmly took hold of Kade's hand, stared blankly at him, and then turned to Sadie. "And who are you?"

Sadie's mouth dropped. "Jonas. It's me. Sadie."

Jonas let go of Kade's hand and stared at her. "Sadie who?"

He was playing with her. He had to be. "Why Sadie Fisher, of course." She smiled hesitantly. Jonas didn't.

"Serve these folks a beer, wouldja, Hank?" Jonas said to the short *Englisch* man behind the bar.

"No. *Danki*," Sadie quickly said to the bartender. She knew Jonas's medications caused him to act out of character from time to time, but never anything like this. She glanced at the bartender, who was trying to get her attention with a wave of his hand.

"It's only root beer," the man mouthed in Sadie's direction when Jonas wasn't looking. Sadie nodded.

"Jonas, I don't want a *beer*. We have to go." She gently touched his arm. "Right now. Lillian and Sarah Jane are terribly worried, and—"

"I don't know why they'd be worried. I told Irma Rose where I'd be." Jonas took another drink from the glass.

What?

"Who's Irma Rose?" Kade directed the question to Sadie, but it was Jonas who answered.

"Irma Rose is *mei fraa*. She don't much care for me comin' here, but she don't make too big a stink about it."

"Well, if his wife knows he's here . . ." Kade said to Sadie in a whisper after Jonas turned and focused on the television behind the bar.

"His wife is dead," Sadie mouthed and stared at him.

"Oh, I see . . ."

She faced Jonas. "Jonas, Irma Rose isn't here—"

But Kade interrupted her by waving his hand in front of her again. "Jonas, what's Irma Rose cooking you for supper?"

Huh? Sadie glared at Kade. What was he doing?

Jonas turned to Kade and smiled. "A mighty fine meal it will be. Irma Rose is a *gut* cook. I reckon she'll have me a pot roast when I get home."

"Pot roast, huh?" Kade stepped closer, edging Sadie back a bit. "Nothing like a pot roast. Does she put potatoes and carrots all around it and let it cook all day? That's how my mom used to do it."

Sadie stood quietly.

"Your *mamm* sounds like a *gut* woman. That's exactly the way my Irma Rose does it. Makes for a fine meal indeed."

"Isn't it after the supper hour? I bet Irma Rose has that pot roast ready and is keeping it warm for you." Kade touched Jonas's arm, a gesture Sadie found endearing, considering the way Jonas had treated Kade earlier.

Jonas was focused on the television. A commercial. "Why would anyone cook food from a box?"

Kade kept talking. "I agree. Never as good as a home-cooked meal. I haven't had pot roast in a really long time."

Jonas turned his way. "Irma Rose always makes plenty enough. You wanna have yourself some pot roast tonight?"

"I'd love to." Kade smiled. "And I'm starving. Why don't we head that way?"

It's working. Sadie played along. "I'm hungry, too, Jonas. Can we go now?"

Jonas pushed a five-dollar bill toward the man behind the bar. "Hank, I can't let these two young people starve, so I reckon I'm heading to the *haus.*"

"Okay, Jonas. You take care now." Hank winked at Sadie. "You folks be careful."

Once Sadie had buckled Jonas safely in the front seat of the car, she prepared to close the door. "I will see you at the *haus.*"

"What?" Kade eyed her like she was a crazy woman.

"I have to take the buggy home." Did the *Englischer* think she'd leave Jessie and the buggy here?

"It's freezing out here. You can't drive that buggy home!"

"The boy is right, Lilly. Too cold for you. I'll drive the buggy home." Jonas unbuckled his seat belt, and Sadie ignored the fact he called her Lilly, his nickname for his granddaughter.

"Jonas, you stay put." Sadie slammed the door and began making her way to the buggy. Kade was quickly out of the car and walking her way.

"Just go back to the car and get Jonas home." She shook her head. "I've never seen him like this."

"I can't let you drive the buggy in this weather." Kade put his hand on his hip. "That's insane."

Sadie laughed. "*Ach,* I suppose you will drive it?" She paused, lifted her chin. "And I will drive your fancy car. It can't be that hard."

"Have you ever driven a car?"

"Have you ever driven a buggy?"

The car door opened, and Jonas stepped out.

"Go get him back into the car and take him home!" Sadie stomped her foot. "Please. It's not like I've never driven a buggy in the snow. Now, go!"

<hr />

Kade drove slowly behind the buggy. He kept a safe distance while he watched Sadie maneuvering the buggy like she must have done her entire life. But it seemed wrong for him to be in the warmth of his car while she fought the elements. *She can be a little spitfire when she puts her mind to it.*

"You courtin' her?" Jonas asked after an awkward silence.

"What?"

"That woman. You courtin' her?" Jonas tucked his thumbs beneath his suspenders and turned toward Kade.

Not sure if Jonas knew who *that woman* was, Kade said, "No. We're just friends."

They were hardly friends. He barely knew her.

"Sadie is a special gal. I wasn't sure the poor girl was gonna survive after her husband died."

Kade was glad to see Jonas knew who Sadie was, and the old man had sparked his interest. "When did her husband die?"

"Several years ago." Jonas sighed. "I weren't sure we'd ever get her back to normal again. The girl had a hard time of it. But she's done a fine job tendin' to her farm."

"It's a lot to take care of for one woman."

"She has lots of help from the community. Just until she marries her friend from Texas." He paused and drew his mouth into a frown. "If that ever happens."

"Oh, she's engaged?"

"If you wanna call it that." Jonas shriveled up his nose. "How can you be writing letters to a fella for two years? Seems to me he'd have already made it a point to travel here. But I don't mention that to her."

"They've never met?" *Wow.* Two years was a long time to be corresponding.

"Who's never met?"

Kade assumed he was losing Jonas. "Sadie and the man from Texas."

"Oh. No. They've not met. He better be *gut* to that Sadie if they get a notion to marry. She is special. A *gut* friend to *mei* granddaughter too."

They sat quietly as they neared Jonas's house. Kade couldn't imagine how cold Sadie must be. He felt like a heel. But she was right. He didn't know how to drive a buggy, and she didn't know how to drive a car.

"Bet that pot roast is gonna be mighty *gut.* Hope Irma Rose doesn't fuss because I'm late." Jonas shook his head.

Kade just smiled. He was thankful this night had a happy ending.

His cell phone rang when he pulled into the driveway at Jonas's farm. He picked it up from the console and was surprised to see that it was Val. He glanced at Jonas, who was staring straight ahead, and flipped the phone open.

"Well, hello, stranger."

"Hey, partner," Val said. "I've got some news you're not going to like."

Straight to the point. "That's never a good thing to hear." Kade braced himself. "What?"

"Monica's on her way there."

"What? How does she know where I am?"

"I haven't a clue, Kade. I didn't tell her. I wouldn't do that. I know you need this time to regroup."

"Do you know when she's going to be here?" Kade's chest tightened.

"Any day. That's what I heard via the grapevine from the women at the country club."

"She called recently, but I didn't answer the phone. I didn't want to deal with her. But she didn't leave a message. I cannot believe she is coming here all the way from North Carolina. That's insane."

At least the old man was okay, he thought, putting the car in park. "I'll be there in a minute," he whispered to Jonas, who nodded.

"Kade . . ."

"Yeah?" The way Val said his name indicated there was more. "What else?"

"She's not coming alone."

4

ON THE DRIVE BACK, SADIE SOAKED UP THE JAZZY music filling the inside of Kade's car. She'd already thanked him for what he'd done, but he had waved her off with that bothersome gesture that irritated her more with each shushing movement. Didn't he realize how rude that was?

She breathed in the aroma of leather coming from the black seats in the car, commingled with a hint of Kade's cologne. More gadgets than she'd ever seen lined the console, and he seemed to be controlling the selection and volume of music from his steering wheel. The small confines of Kade's automobile gave her a glimpse into the luxurious way he lived. It all seemed very unnecessary. Did the *Englisch* really need all this to be happy? Kade seemed to need more than most.

She'd be glad to get home. The snow hadn't let up, but Kade seemed to have better control of his automobile as he steered onto Black Horse Road.

"What kind of music do you enjoy?" he asked when the silence grew awkward. "I hope this is okay. It's Dmitri Shostakovich."

Sadie turned toward him. "I mostly listen to country gospel when I have a chance." She paused and looked straight ahead.

"We can't own radios, but we listen to music when we get rides with *Englischers*, and sometimes we attend local festivals when there is a gospel concert—if it's a *free* concert in the park. The bishop doesn't like for us to buy tickets for such events." She glanced back toward him. "But I'm enjoying this music very much."

He smiled. "Do you sing or play any instruments?"

"*Ya*, I love to sing. When I was younger, I attended many Sunday singings. We sing in church, too, but only in High German." She sighed. "We are not allowed to own any instruments, though."

The car seemed to slow down. "What? Really? But why?"

"Owning an instrument would bring forth heightened emotions. It's not necessary to our way of life." She hoped that would end the conversation so she could enjoy the music.

"I don't understand. Singing brings forth emotion too. How can you be allowed to sing but not own an instrument?"

It was a valid point and one she didn't really know how to answer. She'd asked herself the same thing ever since she had first been introduced to instruments during her running-around period. Truth be known, most of the community couldn't remember why instruments weren't allowed. Like much of the *Ordnung*, rules to live by had been handed down from generation to generation, some with little explanation, but followed just the same. She took what she thought would be an easy way out. "We live by the *Ordnung*, which is our order of conduct, and owning instruments is not allowed."

A brief silence followed.

She felt Kade's eyes on her. "I still don't get it." When she didn't respond, he went on. "This arrangement of Shostakovich's is amazing. He is one of my favorite composers." Kade moved his thumb on the steering wheel, and the music grew louder. "Too loud?"

Sadie shook her head. She could feel the vibration from the sounds pulsating against her chest, growing bolder and more intense.

"Well, if anyone is going to bring forth emotion—it's Shostakovich."

Sadie couldn't agree more. She wished he'd be quiet so she could listen.

"Shostakovich ranks right up there, in my opinion, with some of the greatest composers—Bach, Beethoven, Brahms, and Mozart."

Sadie had no clue who he was talking about. But the passion in his voice made her want to hear more. "I think this music is very . . . sweet." She paused, tilted her head to one side. "But sad."

"You have a good ear." He turned to face her, and in the dark she could make out a smile. "Dmitri Shostakovich is known for his ability to invoke extreme emotions, often beautifully sad and sweet at the same time."

"Do you write musical notes or play an instrument?"

"No. I wish. I just enjoy listening to music, all kinds of music." He paused. "Besides, composers are strange people." He chuckled and spoke with an ease Sadie hadn't heard before. "Alexander Robert Schumann lived in the 1800s. He attempted suicide by throwing himself into a river. He was committed to a mental asylum and died not too long afterwards. People speculate that Tchaikovsky committed suicide too."

He seemed to be waiting for a response. *How does one respond to this?* "I expect it's *gut* that you are not one of these strange people, no?"

For the second time, he laughed. "Oh, I never said I wasn't strange. But I'd like to think I wouldn't kill myself." He shrugged. "Guess it depends on what day it is."

Surely he wasn't serious. "Taking your own life is a sin."

"That's what I hear."

They pulled into the driveway. And not soon enough.

Kade prepared a cup of hot tea, shuffled in his socks to the front window of the cottage, and gazed across the snow-covered space that separated the cottage from the main house. For the first time in weeks, he wouldn't mind some company. But the farmhouse was dark. He supposed Sadie wouldn't join him for a cup of late-night tea anyway. As a matter of fact, she'd probably be appalled by the idea.

He couldn't fathom what her life must be like. It looked like all work and no play to him, and without the modern conveniences. But the woman sure enjoyed music. There was a time when a great melody would quiet Kade's loneliness, take him away from all that plagued him, even invoke a sense of spiritual well-being. But not anymore. He still enjoyed a good tune, but any sense of spiritual calm eluded him. God had dealt him a rough blow three years ago. And his life continued to be a mess.

After Monica left, Kade had struggled to move forward without her in his life. Three years of marriage, and she'd split. No divorce. Only separation. Divorce wasn't a concept he'd ever been comfortable with. If two people vowed to love each other forever, then that's what it should be—forever. He'd loved Monica. Despite their problems, Kade would have never considered leaving, especially after the baby came. But three years had passed, and he'd lost hope that they would ever go back to being a family.

Monica, who was ten years Kade's junior, hadn't wanted children. Tyler was a surprise in so many ways. And Kade knew the only reason his wife fought so hard for custody of Tyler was for the money. When Kade thought a relationship might develop with Alicia, he'd called his attorney to draw up divorce papers, knowing that he should be legally divorced before he started dating anyone. But Alicia carted her gifts away before anything serious evolved. He halted the divorce proceedings. He didn't have the energy right now to follow through. There were no other prospects on the horizon, and divorce represented failure in his eyes.

Why hunt him down all the way in Lancaster County?

During the separation, she'd played as mean as any person Kade had ever known. He still loved Monica in his own way, but over time she'd stripped him of the love he once felt for her. During their phone calls, her voice was always laced with anger and resentment, despite the hefty check that she received every month.

Kade could still recall her pulling out of the driveway, Tyler strapped in his car seat, only two years old. It was the only time Kade could remember crying as an adult.

He'd thought about fighting for custody, or at least joint custody. But in the end, he didn't. He convinced himself that his choice to forgo a split arrangement was because a boy needs his mother. That thought was more comforting than the truth.

Kade knew that raising Tyler full-time, or even half of the time, was more than he could handle, and the job took a toll on Monica. Sometimes, she'd call him in the middle of the night, hysterical, complaining about what a bad hand she'd been dealt. But she was the one who left with their son, moved to North Carolina, and often refused to work with his schedule for planned visits. The first year she was gone, Kade traveled to North Carolina several times for his monthly weekend with Tyler, only to show up at an empty house. Monica later said that Kade's refusal to take Tyler overnight didn't provide her with any reprieve, so she didn't feel the need to accommodate him. She was breaking the law by denying Kade access to his son, and he could have pushed the issue. But again, he didn't.

In the rare times he did see Tyler, they spent a few hours at the park before Kade returned him to his mother. He just didn't know what to do with the boy. Tyler was hard to entertain. He wasn't like other kids.

Kade was eaten up with guilt that he hadn't tried harder to spend more time with his son. But there was work. Then there was Alicia, for a while. Somehow, forcing the issue of seeing Tyler kept taking a backseat. Somehow, six months had passed since his last visit. Now Tyler was five years old, and Kade didn't really know his own son. And the part that shredded his insides the most was that he was afraid to know him.

When Tuesday arrived, Sadie had something to look forward to. Today Milo would call, and she couldn't wait to hear the sound of his voice. It had been a long week. She hadn't done more than wave from afar to Kade since the night they went looking for Jonas, but today was the day she'd restock his refrigerator.

At least it wasn't snowing, and the temperature was up into the forties. The sun was shining, and slowly things were thawing out. So far this winter, Lancaster County had gotten more snow than usual. And she just read in the paper that another storm was coming in a week or so.

Sadie pulled on her boots, but decided to forgo her heavy jacket to wear her cape and bonnet instead. It might be a bit chilly with the wind, but she'd been bundled in the coat for days. She welcomed a trip to the market. Just not looking forward to the challenge of finding replacement items for Kade's groceries.

She was grateful that Kade continued to stack firewood on the porch, replenishing as needed. And Sadie continued to make fresh batches of tapioca pudding when the empty container showed up on the woodpile. But he stayed to himself, and that was fine by her.

She'd started this day the way she did every day, beginning with prayer, followed by a bowl of oatmeal. No sense making a big breakfast just for her. After she ate, she'd always do whatever cleaning was on her list for the day. Today, she dusted all the furniture downstairs. Some days it seemed a waste to keep things so tidy when she was usually the only one who ever saw the inside of the farmhouse. But she needed to keep up the practice for when she and Milo started a life together. Plus, she couldn't let Lillian or any of the other women catch her house in a mess.

Next was tending to the few animals she had left—two horses, an old milk cow that no longer produced, and two pigs. It was enough to handle—feeding them all, brushing the horses, and cleaning the stalls. On Mondays, she fired up the gasoline motor for the wringer and washed the clothes, then hung them to dry outside. The clothes would often freeze this time of year, but when that happened, she'd cart them in and drape them across the furniture near the fireplace. There was always something to do, even if it was a simple chore like mending a dress hem. She baked daily for herself, and also for others, like Lizzie. And lately, she'd been baking for her renter as well.

Her schedule varied when it was her day to tend the shop. Lillian's sisters-in-law, Rebecca and Mary Ellen, were taking their turn today, so it worked out that Sadie could go to market. She was getting ready to step into the buggy when she heard Kade call her name.

She turned around to see him walking toward her.

"I'm on my way to market, Mr. Saunders. I'll be back shortly to restock your refrigerator." She pulled her cape tighter around her and wondered if she'd made a mistake by not wearing her heavy coat.

"What happened to calling me Kade?" He didn't wait for a response. Instead, he swooshed his hand the way he does. "Anyway—"

And that was all it took.

"Why do you do that?" She put her hands on her hips and glared at him.

"Do what?"

"That shushing thing you do with your hand. It's most rude." Right away, she wished she hadn't said anything. His face drew a blank. "I'm sorry. I didn't mean to—"

"No. It's okay. I've heard that before, and it's a terrible habit."

He held his hands up as if Sadie had a gun pointed in his direction. "I won't do it again. I promise."

"Is there something you need?"

"Yes. A ride."

"What?" *Impossible.* What was he thinking? She couldn't be seen driving the *Englischer* to town. Besides, he had a car. "I'm sorry. I don't have time today. I have many errands to run. You understand, no?"

He walked around to the other side of the buggy and opened the door. "I must have run over something the other night. I've got two flat tires and only one spare. So, I'm grounded here with no wheels unless you can take me to get a couple of tires. I won't slow you down on your errands."

Rebecca and Mary Ellen would see them leaving, and no telling who might see them at the market. *No, no.* But she was at a loss as to what to say.

Kade sat down on the double seat beside her and closed the door.

She turned to face him. "Mr. Saunders—I mean, Kade—you can't come with me."

"Why?"

"Well, because . . ." She heard her last word squeak out in frustration. "It wouldn't be appropriate." She held her chin high.

"What exactly would be inappropriate about it?" He shifted sideways in the seat and faced her. His leg brushed against her knee. She jumped and scooted away from him.

"Ohhh," he said as he drew out the word. "I think I see." He rubbed his chin and kept his eyes fixed on her. It was most uncomfortable, and she could feel a blush rising from her neck.

"It would be improper for you to be seen with me," he continued, more as a question than a statement.

"*Ya.*" She drew her eyes from his and looked down.

"So, let me get this straight." He paused, but held his position next to her. "It's okay for us to ride together in a car when *you* need something. But now that I need something, it's not all right to be seen together?"

There was humor in his tone, but Sadie found her circumstances anything but amusing. This was serious. And he had a point. How was she supposed to argue? She opened her mouth to speak, but nothing came out.

"Never mind." He opened the door and stepped down. "I'll call someone to come out here and take care of it." He shook his head.

"*Danki*, Kade." She tried to sound chipper and waited for him to respond.

But he just stood there, staring at her. She wanted to look away, but his eyes seemed to lock with hers.

"Well, okay, then," he finally said.

Kade closed the door and turned away without looking back. He began walking toward the cottage.

Sadie felt badly about his predicament, but it didn't outweigh the relief she felt at not having to spend the morning with him or risk being seen. What if Bishop Ebersol or one of the elders saw them together? Sadie knew she was already pushing the limits by housing a single man in the cottage. It had only been allowed because those in charge knew it was difficult to lease the cottage this time of year and that Sadie needed the income. Carting him around town would be looked down upon.

She motioned the horse into action with a gentle flick of the reins.

———

Monica was about two hours from Lancaster County. After three days of driving, potty stops, food breaks, and unfamiliar hotels, she was exhausted. It would have been a ten-hour drive if she had been traveling alone, but with Tyler, that was impossible. Her restless five-year-old was only good for about two hours in the car, and even that was a struggle. She was hoping they could make it to the place she knew Kade was staying without another delay.

In her wildest dreams, she couldn't imagine what would bring Kade all the way to the heart of Amish Dutch country in the winter. Kade hated the cold.

She glanced over her shoulder at Tyler, who had dozed off, and noticed how much he looked like his father.

Monica knew she'd made a mistake by not agreeing to joint custody of Tyler. Turns out, it had backfired on her. She never realized how much work it would be raising Tyler, and it had gotten harder and harder each year. How nice it would have been for Kade to actually keep Tyler for days or weeks at a time in Los Angeles. Instead, Kade barely saw his son and wouldn't even keep him overnight when he did visit. Now, Kade had managed to go six months without seeing him.

But if she hadn't fought hard to keep Tyler, the money wouldn't have been enough to sustain her way of life—a life that Kade had introduced her to. Until now. Her new fiancé had enough money for both of them, and it was Kade's turn to be a parent. She was tired and deserved this opportunity. Her fiancé was kind, handsome, wealthy, and all the things she had thought Kade was when she married him.

Leaving Tyler with Kade would be a high price to pay for her happiness. She loved her son. But she was only twenty-seven years old. She had her whole life to live, and she planned to follow her own dreams—dreams Kade never encouraged. Plus, there would be theater, shopping, nights on the town—all the things she'd missed since Tyler was born.

Monica needed this time to pursue her interest in interior design. Kade had wanted her to stay at home and take care of Tyler, forgoing her own dreams while he pursued his. Well, now it was her turn. Her opportunity. And she was going to take it.

It would be hard on Tyler to leave his school, but Kade would be able to enroll him in another school. Probably even a better school. And Kade would be able to provide Tyler with opportunities Monica couldn't, even with the money Kade gave her.

She twisted her head over her shoulder again. "I love you, Tyler," she whispered, suddenly wondering if she could go through with it.

Kade paid the guy for replacing his tires and huffed out a "Thanks."

The man did a good job and was careful with Kade's car. It wasn't *him* causing Kade's exasperation. Kade was frustrated with the backward ways of the Amish, one redhead in particular. Not that he'd been looking forward to changing his tires in the snow—which would have probably taken him three times as long as the tire guy—he was mostly hoping for a little company following his few days of solitude. He thought the ride in the country might do him good. *Wait till next time* she *needs a ride.*

Who was he kidding? Kade knew he'd help the Amish woman with anything she needed. There was something about her that portrayed both vulnerability and strength. And he wasn't sure which characteristic was more prominent. He smiled, remembering the way she shoved him after she hit her head, deciding strength prevailed. Strange folks, the Amish. You'd have thought Kade was making a pass at her the way she acted.

Kade decided to take advantage of the somewhat warmer weather. Not *that* much warmer, but bearable. He zipped up his jacket and took a seat in one of the rockers on the front porch. Later, he would venture out to keep from getting cabin fever. He knew the towns of Bird-in-Hand and Intercourse were nearby. Maybe he'd do a little sightseeing.

Perhaps Val had been right about coming here. The place had a peacefulness about it that he certainly didn't have in L.A. or any of his other frequented retreats. Almost spiritual.

But Kade resisted the idea. He'd stopped reaching out to God three years ago. He had prayed that all the doctors were wrong about his son, but they weren't. Then Monica had left with Tyler, and Kade slowly shut himself off from communication with God. His parents had raised him in a nondenominational Christian church, and for most of his growing-up years, the Lord was an important part of Kade's life. But it was hard to trust this God he didn't know anymore, or understand.

And Tyler. His only son.

Why? Why would God allow a child to be born into this world who has zero hope for a productive life?

And why was Monica coming here? *If that's even true.*

He'd no sooner had the thought when a car turned into the driveway.

5

THE BLACK CAR DOOR SWUNG OPEN, AND A MATCHING black, spike-heeled boot emerged and landed hard on the packed snow. Kade watched Monica twist toward the backseat, her head topped with short, blonde locks, like he remembered. He watched her lips moving, and his heart raced with long pent-up emotions bubbling to the surface. Anger. Resentment. Regret. Kade knew these sentiments stemmed from his own behavior, as well as Monica's.

Kade saw a crown of light-brown hair bobbing in the backseat. *Tyler.*

He wanted to run to his son, embrace him, and beg the boy to forgive him for his absence. But he was immobilized with fear of the unknown. How much had Tyler changed in the last six months? Kade knew from his past visits with Tyler that his son's ability to reason and understand was one-dimensional at best. Had things gotten worse? *Maybe better.*

He knew he should move. Walk toward the car. Anything.

Monica pulled herself to a standing position and rested her elbows on the car door. "Hello, Kade."

She was as lovely as ever, but his heart didn't skip any beats.

All that they'd had—gone. Too many bitter arguments, too much time gone by. What could she possibly be doing here, so far from home? Kade could think of only one thing. *She's finally come for a divorce.*

"Don't you want to come see your son?" She closed the door and folded her arms across her chest.

Monica was already opening the back door by the time Kade hit the second porch step. He headed across the snow, his heart filled with trepidation, his head swirling with questions. He stared at the back of her black leather jacket while she unbuckled Tyler's seat belt.

Kade swallowed hard. Then inhaled the crisp, cool air, blew it out slowly, and watched it cloud the space in front of him. He recalled the photo of Tyler that he kept in his wallet and wondered again how much his son might have changed. In the picture, it was as if Tyler was looking intently at something, but yet at nothing. A blank stare.

Kade warmed his hands in his pockets. And waited. His heart continued to thump at an unhealthy rate.

Monica lifted Tyler from the seat and placed him on the snow in front of her. He was dressed in blue jeans and a red coat, and he was toting a metal lunch box with Spider-Man etched on the front.

Tyler smiled, and a warmth filled Kade's insides. He remembered the first time Tyler smiled when he was a baby and when his son had taken his first step.

"Hello." Kade leaned down and put his hands on his knees.

Tyler didn't answer. He was taking in his surroundings.

"Can we please go in?" Monica's tone was familiar, laced with attitude. "I've had to go to the bathroom for the last twenty miles, and it's cold out here."

"Monica, what are you doing here?" Kade couldn't take his gaze off of Tyler, whose eyes were all over the place—glancing toward the barn, then the main farmhouse, and back to Kade. Then he'd start all over again.

"Can we talk about it inside?" Monica reached for Tyler's hand. "Tyler, inside."

"Tyler, inside," Tyler repeated.

Kade loved the innocent sound of Tyler's voice, even though Tyler didn't talk much. The testing began six months prior to his second birthday. Six months after Tyler's second birthday, Monica had left. His family gone.

"Sure," Kade said. He motioned them toward the cottage. "I can't imagine what brought you all the way to Lancaster County." He shook his head and followed behind them.

Monica didn't turn around. "Well, I can't imagine what brought you all the way out here either. You hate the cold."

He decided not to bother with an answer. "The bathroom is that way." Kade pointed to his right.

"Tyler, I'll be right back. You sit here and play." Monica eased Tyler to a spot in front of the fireplace. Tyler opened his lunch box and dumped colorful plastic letters all over the tan carpet—the same kind of letters Kade remembered having as a child.

"Whatcha got there?" Kade squatted down on the floor beside Tyler.

Tyler looked at him. Well, not *at* him. At Kade's shirt. Kade glanced down at the word *Nike* printed across the front of his sweatshirt. Tyler was homed in on the word and seemed mesmerized by it. "Nike," Kade said softly.

"Nike," Tyler repeated. Then Tyler turned his attention back to his letters and located an *N*, then an *I*, *K*, and finally an *E*. He placed them in order, and without looking at Kade, said the word again.

Monica entered the room. Kade stood up and turned to face her, excitement in his tone. "He can spell. When did he learn to spell?"

She started to say something on impulse, Kade could tell. But she stopped herself. "During the last six months."

Kade chose to ignore the dig and turned back toward Tyler. "Can he read too?"

"Yes." She sighed. "But Kade, he doesn't know what he's spelling or reading. I mean, he can't comprehend it."

She walked toward the couch, sat down, and crossed her legs. Monica had great legs, but her tight blue jeans didn't have any effect on him.

Kade followed her to the couch, but he didn't sit down. She still hadn't explained the reason for the visit.

"But he *does* read?" Kade knew his tone was filled with hopefulness. Maybe the doctors had been wrong on some level.

Monica rolled her green eyes. "Yes. He reads. He picks up books all the time, and sometimes he reads aloud. But he has no idea what any of it means."

"Are you sure?" Kade felt his hope slipping.

Monica nodded, then said, "Guess you're wondering why we're here?"

Kade arched his brows and waited. It seemed like a rhetorical question.

"Well," she went on, "I'm going to get married, Kade." She paused, as if waiting for a response.

Maybe it should have stung. But Kade didn't feel much of anything.

"But first I need you to sign on the dotted line. I'm sure this doesn't come as a shock to you."

She reached into a big, black bag and pulled out a hefty stack of legal papers bound by a clasp at the top. "Feel free to read through them, but it's a replica of the papers you drew up a while back. A copy had already landed on my attorney's desk when you decided not to follow through with the divorce." She crinkled her forehead. "I never understood why you didn't go through with it. Anyway, the sooner you sign them and get them in the mail, the sooner I can get married, settled, and come back for Tyler."

What? Panic engulfed Kade. *Surely not.*

"I couldn't wait three months for you to get home to Los Angeles, so I packed up as much as I could for Tyler and brought it with me. It's time for you to be a father." Her scalding eyes challenged him to a duel. Well, it was about to be on.

"What?" It was all Kade could muster up.

"Don't look at me like that. I gave up my life to take care of Tyler while you were off building skyscrapers. It's your turn for a while."

Kade narrowed his eyes and inched toward her, towering over her on the couch. "Those skyscrapers provided you with a very nice lifestyle." He glanced over his shoulder at Tyler and lowered his voice to a whisper. "I don't know what you're thinking. You can't leave him here. I mean, I love my son, but—"

"Love him? You don't even know him!" Monica didn't bother

to keep her voice down. The familiarity of her sharp, shrill tone sent a chill up his spine. "I'm going, Kade. And that's all there is to it." She bolted from the couch and headed toward the front door. She turned around as she reached for the knob. "So, you can either help me with his things, or I'll get it all myself."

Kade laughed, despite himself. This couldn't be happening. *Mothers don't do this sort of thing.* "This is ridiculous," he said. He followed her to the door. "If you needed a vacation, or some time to get married, or whatever . . . you could have called me so I could make arrangements."

She stepped outside the door and waited for Kade to join her on the front porch. "Arrangements?" She was yelling now. "I tried plenty of times to make arrangements with you in the past, and it never fit into your schedule, and . . ."

Kade waved his hand in front of her, trying to shush her, and was suddenly reminded of Sadie. He dropped his hand to his side. "That's bull. And you know it. You never wanted to work with my schedule. You intentionally made it difficult for me to spend time with Tyler. You went all the way to North Carolina to ensure it." Kade didn't shut the front door all the way, and he glanced into the den. "Is he okay in there by himself?"

"He's fine."

Kade left the door ajar anyway.

Monica marched to the black Lexus and popped the trunk. Kade followed.

"My family is in North Carolina," she said. "And I wanted to be near them. You had plenty of opportunities to spend more time with Tyler, and you chose not to."

"Don't even bother taking out any of those things." He pointed to the suitcases piled in the back. "I'll get you a hotel room, and we'll figure out what to do in the morning." Kade chuckled in disbelief. "But there is no way you can just show up here and drop off Tyler like this."

One by one, she pulled suitcases out of the trunk and set them on the ground. "I suggest you get these into the house before the snow gets everything all wet."

Monica had that look in her eyes. The look she had the day she took Tyler and left. There was no talking her out of it. But he was darn sure going to try. "Monica, what kind of mother abandons her child like this? Maybe you're just having a rough time right now. And with a little notice, I'd be glad to help out with Tyler."

She practically threw the last suitcase at him, a small, red one. Then slammed the trunk. "Abandoning? Do you want to talk to me about abandoning? You are the one who abandoned your son, and now you can make things right!"

"You left *me*, Monica! I did not leave you. When I said I'd love and cherish you forever, I meant it."

"You are not going to make me feel guilty about this. You are not!" She stormed up to the cottage. Kade was on her heels.

"You've done some crazy things, Monica. But you can't leave Tyler here. I don't know the first thing about taking care of him."

She twisted her head around as she walked up the porch steps. "Well, I guess you're going to learn."

Without missing a beat, she went to the couch and retrieved the big, black bag she had carried in on her shoulder. She reached inside and pulled out a thick, black binder and dropped it on the couch beside the divorce papers.

"That is your Bible, Kade. Read it. It will tell you everything you need to know about Tyler, about his schedule, and every-thing I have learned about having an autistic child. Tyler is considered high-functioning, compared to some of the children in his class who don't speak at all and who can't do simple things, like feed themselves or go to the bathroom on their own."

Kade ran his hands through his hair, exhaled loudly, and said, "I'm sorry, Monica. You can't leave him here. I want to be a part of his life. I always have. But you can't just show up here and do this."

She squatted down beside Tyler, who seemed oblivious to the commotion around him. Cupping his cheeks in her hands, she was crying. "Mommy loves Tyler."

He smiled. "Mommy loves Tyler."

Kade watched in horror. How she could leave a child that she had raised since birth? He knew it was hypocritical, but the thought still surfaced. Second, if she really did walk out that door, what in the world was he going to do?

Monica threw her arms around Tyler. "Mommy loves Tyler soooo much."

"Mommy loves Tyler soooo much."

And with that, she ran out of the cottage. Kade was right behind her and grabbed her arm before she reached her car.

"Let go of me!" There was the hysteria he had heard so many times on the phone. "I have to go! I have to, Kade! Don't make this any harder on me! Do you understand me? I have to go!" She wriggled out of his grasp, and tears streamed down her cheeks. "Read the book. Keep him on schedule."

"Monica," Kade breathed in desperation. He glanced back and forth between her and the cottage. "You can't be serious!"

She slid into the front seat and rolled down the window. "I'll be back for Tyler when we get settled."

"You can't drop him off like this, Monica, with no warning. You have no idea what my schedule is!"

"Oh, I know exactly what your schedule is! You're taking some sort of hiatus from life. You should fire your secretary. All I had to do is get a girlfriend to call your office, and the woman pretty much spilled your entire life story to my friend." Her face twisted with rage. "So you know what, Kade? You can enjoy your little vacation and get to know your son! I need this time for *me!* Do you understand me? So, don't make me feel guilty! Don't you know—"

Kade wasn't hearing her. There was something about her hysterical tone . . .

He began to plead with her again not to do this.

She was still yelling when she rolled up the window.

As she turned the car around and headed toward Black Horse Road, Kade thought about her words. *I'll be back when we get settled.*

Kade wondered if she would come back.

Sadie pulled into her driveway, relieved that she'd be able to get out of the cold. She should have worn her heavy coat. The sunshine and rise in temperature had been misleading. Once on the road to market, her black cape had been no defense against the biting wind.

"Whoa," she instructed Buck, glad the horse no longer lived up to his name.

She made several trips to the kitchen, unloading her bags.

Now she would sort out Kade's groceries and prepare herself for a trip to the cottage. Perhaps he had ventured out to repair his tires now that the weather had improved. But no. His car was in the barn.

She separated Kade's items and began to put her groceries in their proper place, then realized she forgot to check the mail. Without stopping to wrap up, she walked out of the kitchen door and hurried to the mailbox at the end of the driveway.

Nothing. Disappointment tugged at her heart, but she reminded herself that today was Tuesday. Tonight Milo would call, just as he had since they'd set up the weekly phone schedule two years ago, shortly after they began writing letters. The thought lifted her spirit as she headed back into the house.

She redressed in her bonnet, cape, and boots, which not only protected her from the weather, but also from Kade's curious eyes. More than once, she'd caught him staring at her, which made her uncomfortable.

Perhaps Jonas and the elders had been right. How much did she really know about the fancy *Englischer*? Was she really safe out here alone with him? But then she recalled the way he handled Jonas. Sadie didn't think he was dangerous or bad.

Kade's groceries fit in three small plastic bags that she draped over one arm. She pulled the full container of tapioca pudding from the refrigerator and balanced it against her chest. She planned to unpack his things quickly, then scurry back home.

But she'd only taken two or three steps toward the cottage when she heard screams. Continuous shrill hollering, like she'd never heard the likes of before. She stopped walking, stared at the cottage, and listened. Sounded like a child. She turned toward the barn where she could use the phone. In her community, they tried to keep the *Englisch* police out of their lives if possible, but something bad was going on inside that cottage.

She quickly shuffled across the snow with the grocery bags and pudding. Then she stopped and looked toward her shop up near the road. Mary Ellen and Rebecca's buggies were parked outside. Couldn't they hear this child crying for help? She decided they couldn't, and she continued on her trek. But then the shrieks grew louder and louder.

There's no time. She set the food down in the snow and ran toward the cottage instead. With courage she didn't know she possessed, she sprinted up the porch steps and flung the door open. She stood in the entryway, her heart racing. Kade was squatting down beside a small boy in front of the fireplace, begging him to please stop hitting his head on the floor. He looked up at Sadie with fearful, desperate eyes.

"Please help me." He attempted to wrap his arms around the boy, who pulled away and continued bumping his head against the carpeted floor.

Sadie grabbed a throw pillow from the couch and ran to their side. She squatted down beside Kade and placed the pillow underneath the child's forehead. At least the pillow would soften the blows to the boy's head.

"I've tried picking him up, but he bit me," Kade said. He held up his left arm, pushed back his sweatshirt, and revealed a prominent set of teeth marks on his forearm. "I don't know what to do. He's never done anything like this. He's hurting himself, and I don't know how to make him stop, and . . ."

Kade's voice trailed, and his eyes begged her for an answer she didn't have.

"Who is he?" she asked.

"My son." He reached out to touch the boy's head, only to have the child scream even louder.

"Your son?" She narrowed her brows at him. "Have you done something to this child, to make him act this way? Have you hurt him?"

She wished she'd never said it. Kade sat there staring at her in disbelief, his face registering torment, and his eyes glassy and wide.

Sadie didn't wait for him to answer. She had her answer.

"Hello," she said to the boy, in a voice loud enough to rise above his cries. She leaned closer. "My name is Sadie. What's your name?"

No response. She looked up at Kade. "What's his name?"

"Tyler." Kade tried again to reach out to the boy, who began flailing his arms wildly and continued to bang his head on the pillow in front of him.

"Tyler, do you like pudding? I brought your *daed* some pudding." The child stopped screaming, but he continued to bang his head. Sadie looked at Kade, who nodded at her progress, and then she turned her attention back to Tyler. "It is yummy pudding, and I sure would like for you to try some."

Tyler didn't look at her, but his destructive behavior began to subside. "Tyler likes pudding," he mumbled.

She glanced at Kade, who ran his hand through his hair, sighed deeply, and said, "Did you really bring some? Because I'm out of pudding."

The boy didn't seem to hear Kade and repeated, "Tyler likes pudding." He sat straight up, and his eyes began to jet around the room, as if he was searching for something.

"*Ya.* I made you more pudding," she told Kade. "It's outside." Sadie turned back to Tyler. "Why don't I go get you some pudding?" She slowly stood up.

"I'll go get it," Kade said. He jumped to his feet and moved toward the door. "Where is it?"

Sadie kept her eyes on the boy, who had begun playing with plastic letters on the floor next to him, as if nothing had ever happened. "Near the barn, along with your groceries."

Kade was out the door before Sadie could say anything else. *His son?*

She reached over to touch Tyler's arm. He didn't look at her, but jerked away and flinched.

"I'm sorry," she whispered.

Kade returned, dropped the groceries inside the door, and headed toward the small kitchen with the container of pudding. "I'll put some pudding in a bowl for you, Tyler," he said.

Tyler lined his letters up in no particular order. He was calm. Sadie saw Kade searching for a spoon, pulling drawers open. She allowed herself a look around the cottage. It was a mess. Dishes were piled in the sink and clothes strewn across the back of the couch. He really should have opted for the housecleaning service she offered with the rental, although she was glad he hadn't.

"I should go." She stood up and smoothed the wrinkles in her black apron.

"No. Wait." Kade slid a spoon into the bowl of pudding and walked toward her and Tyler. He offered Tyler the bowl of pudding, which the boy accepted. A smile swept across Tyler's face.

"Tyler will be all right, no?" Sadie took a step backward and put some space between her and Kade.

"His mother dropped him off here, so she could run off and get married." Kade put his hand on her elbow and gently coaxed her away from Tyler and toward the far side of the den. "Tyler's autistic."

Sadie didn't know what that meant, but she edged out of Kade's grip and turned to face him. "But you said he was your son. How—"

"His mother and I have been separated for three years, and now she wants me to sign the divorce papers so she can remarry." He pointed to the bound papers on the couch. "She left him here without any warning, and she expects me to keep him until she gets *settled*." Kade shook his head, then looked up at her. "I haven't seen him in six months." Then, as if trying to hide shame, he added, "But I used to see him once a month . . . when his mother would let me."

And this is acceptable parenting in the Englisch *world?* She wanted to ask him why he rarely saw his son, but it was none of her business. "I must go." She turned and headed toward the door.

"Wait." He was following her, so Sadie paused at the door. "Tyler lives a long way from me. That's why I don't see him much."

Sadie nodded.

"Thank you for your help," he said. "Do you want a cup of coffee, or some tea?" His tone was desperate, and Sadie knew he was afraid to be alone with the boy.

"No. *Danki.*" She reached the door and pulled it open. Then she turned to face him again. "Do you need anything? For the boy?"

"I don't know." Kade rubbed his hand against the stubble on his chin. He turned toward Tyler, who was content with his pudding and sighed. "I don't even know my own son."

Sadie couldn't take her eyes from him. Maybe it was the sadness in his voice, but she had a sudden urge to offer him a hug, a thought she quickly squelched, feeling ridiculous. She had no business here. "I'm sorry for the intrusion. I shouldn't have burst through the door like I did, but—"

"No. Thank goodness you did." He smiled. "Turns out the kid likes your tapioca pudding as much as I do."

Sadie looked down at her shoes and hoped he wouldn't notice the flush in her cheeks. "I have to go." She turned around, then walked across the threshold and down the steps, with Kade following her. Thankfully, he stopped at the bottom porch step. Sadie hurried across the snow and didn't look back.

"Thank you again," she heard him say.

But she kept focused on the farmhouse ahead of her, mentally calculating how many days Kade had already been here, and how many days until he'd be gone.

Kade knew he needed to feed Tyler more than just tapioca pudding. He indulged the boy with two more bowls and used the opportunity to begin scanning through the black binder Monica had left him, fighting the wave of panic that overtook him with each page. Kade had never been around Tyler for more than a few hours at a time. How would he ever maintain Tyler's schedule? Up at seven. Breakfast at seven thirty. Brush teeth and get dressed at eight o'clock. Then a gap—go to school at eight thirty and return at three thirty.

He glanced at Tyler when he heard the spoon clink against the empty bowl. But Tyler set the bowl aside and began playing with his plastic letters. Kade kept scanning the pages. Four o'clock, reading time. Four thirty, outside playtime. Five o'clock, sing songs. Six o'clock, more reading. Dinnertime was at seven, followed by brushing teeth and a bath. Bedtime, eight. *Leave the light on* was highlighted in yellow marker.

Kade turned the page to find a list of likes and dislikes. The list of dislikes was far longer than the likes.

Likes to read, sing, play with plastic letters, take his shoes off and on, listen to running water from the tap/tub, carry his Spider-Man lunch box from room to room, and his favorite self-stimulatory behavior is to clap his hands.

Kade took a deep breath and read the column of dislikes.

Does not like to be touched casually—e.g., patted on the head, brushed against, have a haircut, etc. But does like to be hugged tightly and will say the word *hug*.

Does not socialize well with other children, often becoming agitated. Is afraid of the dark. Doesn't like to get off schedule, will scream.

Kade was afraid to move, to breathe, to do anything that might draw attention to himself and distract Tyler's calm mood. He turned the page, still with visions of Tyler's earlier head banging fresh on his mind. During their few visits to the park, Tyler had never behaved in such a way. Tyler had thrown fits before, but nothing like today. More dislikes on the following page.

Doesn't like the television on. *Not much to watch anyway.*

Dislikes any green food—peas, green beans, celery, lettuce . . .

Footsteps moving his way sent a rush of adrenaline through Kade. He closed the binder and looked up to find Tyler facing him. Neither said a word, and Kade feared another explosion. Tyler surely wasn't on his schedule. Kade glanced at his watch. Three o'clock. Tyler would normally be in school. *Please don't scream.*

Kade took in the boy's features, remembering him as a toddler. His blue eyes were still filled with wonder yet seemed to look right through Kade. To Kade's surprise, Tyler smiled, his face lighting up, and Kade returned the smile. "Hi," he said with caution.

"Hi." Tyler kept smiling. Then with his arms at his side, Tyler said simply, "Hug."

"You want a hug?" Kade recalled the bite he received when he'd tried to touch Tyler earlier, but that was before he'd read Monica's notes.

"Hug," Tyler repeated.

Kade pulled the boy to him, slowly at first. But Tyler seemed comfortable, and Kade brought him closer and wrapped his arms tightly around his son's tiny frame. Kade buried his head on Tyler's small shoulder, and for the first time since Monica left with his son, Kade cried.

———

Sadie wrapped her arms around her knees as she sat on the small stool in the barn, shivering and waiting for Milo's phone call. She knew it was well past eight o'clock, and she was tired, cold, and growing irritated. Milo knew she had to sit out in the cold barn, and for him to be late calling was disrespectful.

She couldn't help but wonder how things were going with Kade and Tyler. She assumed Kade's son must be mentally slow. She recalled Martha and Jacob's boy, Amos, who was born a few years back, his mind and behavior different from other children's. A special child of God.

She squeezed her arms around her knees even tighter, the bitter cold a harsh contrast from the more pleasant temperatures earlier in the day. Maybe something had happened to Milo, a situation that prevented him from calling. Worry replaced her irritation as her mind speculated about what could be keeping him from phoning. He never missed a Tuesday call.

Wild dogs howled in the distance, interrupting the eerie quiet that surrounded her. Again, her thoughts turned to her renter and his son. Kade had looked so lost, so unprepared to care for the boy. Divorce. Such a tragedy, a circumstance unheard-of in her community, where marriage was a sacrament, never to be severed. She wondered what could have happened between the two of them. Sadie remembered what a hard time Martha and Jacob had when Amos was born, the difficulties with a special child. All the more reason for young Tyler to have two parents. Perhaps Kade and his wife would not go through with the divorce.

None of her business, Sadie reminded herself. She lifted herself off the stool and picked up the lantern from the small table where the phone rested. She walked toward Kade's sleek, black car and peeked inside, recalling their trip in search of Jonas. Why did anyone need all those gadgets? She shook her head and walked slowly out of the barn, taking careful steps into the snowy yard now icing over as the night temperatures dropped.

The familiar loneliness was her only company. She fought the knot in her throat and picked up her pace, wanting to get inside—secure in her bed, where she could have a proper cry while tucked beneath the thick counterpanes. Milo's Tuesday calls sustained her from week to week.

She heard the cottage door open and briefly spun around to see Kade loading a piece of firewood into his arms, but then quickly turned back toward the farmhouse.

"Hey!"

She wasn't in the mood to make polite conversation, but she stopped and turned around. "*Ya?*"

"Are you all right?" The door to the cottage was wide-open, and Kade had taken a couple of steps further onto the porch, still toting the firewood.

"*Ya.* I'm *gut. Danki.*" She waved, turned around, and quickened her steps. She'd almost made it safely to the farmhouse when she heard him call her name. She sighed, turned around. "*Ya?*"

"Do you want to come have a cup of coffee with me?"

"No. *Danki.*" She turned and walked faster, nearly slipping on the icy snow.

"Please?"

Sadie stopped but didn't turn around. Maybe it was the pleading tone in his voice. Maybe it was her own desperate loneliness, her need to be in the presence of another human being. But suddenly, she found herself considering Kade's offer.

6

SADIE OPENED HER EYES THE NEXT MORNING AT DAY-
break, eyes swollen from crying herself to sleep the night before.
She'd overslept, but who would notice anyway? She rolled onto
her side, tucked the quilt around her chin, and warmed herself
against the chill in the room. Loneliness tore at her heart as she
reached over and draped an arm across Ben's side of the bed. She
closed her eyes and pretended he was lying beside her.

Spending time with the *Englischer* would have been unsuitable
at best, no matter how much she longed for companionship.
Thankfully she'd had the strength to give him a big hearty no
before bolting up the stairs and into the farmhouse. She'd barely
made it into the den when the tears began to spill. *God, please don't
let me be alone the rest of my life*, she prayed.

Today was her day to work at the shop with Lillian, so she
reluctantly pushed back the covers and stepped out of bed. She was
usually a woman of vigor, but now, the hole in her heart seemed to
be dragging her to a place she didn't want to be.

She said her regular morning devotions, praying hard that
God would send Milo to her, that they would fall in love and live
the rest of their lives the way He intended for them, and that they
might be blessed with lots of little ones to fill their hearts with

joy. She knew that to ask for such things was not in line with her upbringing. It would have been better to ask for God's guidance and accept that His will would be done.

Sadie bundled up and headed toward the shop after a few bites of toast with apple butter. She'd already heard Lillian pull up in her buggy twenty minutes earlier. She glanced across the yard at the cottage. All was quiet. She wondered how the boy was doing and how Kade was faring.

When Sadie walked in, the heaters were already lit, and Lillian was opening the blinds. "Sleeping in this morning?" Lillian winked.

"*Ya.* I reckon so." Sadie opened the last blind, flooding the room with sunlight.

"We better enjoy all this sun while we can," Lillian said. She wrapped the cord from the blind around a nail on the wall. "Friday we're in for another hard freeze, and the newspaper said blizzard conditions."

"*Ya,* I heard." Sadie tied off her cord and headed toward the sales counter on the right side of the room.

Lillian marched over to the counter and gazed up at Sadie. "Have you been crying?"

Sadie took a deep breath. "Milo didn't call last night."

"Hmm. Maybe something came up. I'm sure it's nothing to worry about."

"He's never missed a Tuesday call." Sadie began to total up receipts from yesterday's sales.

"Maybe he will call tonight, no?"

Sadie shrugged. "Maybe. But he'll have to leave a message. It's a mite too cold for me to sit in the barn and wait for him to call."

Lillian didn't say anything for a few minutes, but fumbled nervously with papers on the counter. "Mary Ellen said that she and Rebecca saw you go running into the cottage yesterday. She said that you dropped the *Englisher's* groceries on the ground and burst in the front door."

"Were they spying on me?" Sadie didn't look up at Lillian, but kept pushing numbers on the small calculator.

"They said they thought they heard screams coming from the cottage. When they looked out the window, you were running inside. Mary Ellen said they were worried about you, so they watched out the window until they saw you heading back to the farmhouse. They weren't sure how involved they should get."

"As it turns out, Mr. Saunders has a son." She glanced up to see Lillian waiting for more. "He has a wife who he's been apart from for three years. She wants to remarry, so she brought him some divorce papers to sign and dropped the boy off with him. And . . ."

"What?" Lillian's eyes were wide.

"He hasn't seen the boy, Tyler, in six months, and Tyler's mother wouldn't let him see Tyler much before that. Tyler is like Martha and Jacob's boy, I think, screaming and banging his head on the floor when I walked in. I can't help but worry about . . ." She caught herself, looked down, and returned to totaling receipts.

"Worry is a sin," Lillian said. Then she patted Sadie's hand. "God will guide their way. I will pray for them."

Sadie merely nodded. She had included Kade and Tyler in her prayers last night, thinking she'd never seen such a lost man as Kade. *Hopefully*, she thought, *Kade has a good relationship with the Lord.*

Lillian began to sweep the wooden floor, and Sadie silently questioned her own relationship with God. Thoughts had been surfacing that she would never share with anyone, notions that continued to creep into her head, as if put there by the devil himself.

She gave her head a few quick shakes from side to side, as if that would clear the sinful thoughts from her mind. There was no questioning God's will. To do so went against everything Sadie believed in. But she couldn't understand His will for her these days, as her loneliness burrowed deep inside her. Perhaps she just needed to be patient, until the spring, when Milo would be here.

"How's Jonas?" she asked Lillian in an attempt to stem the confusion in her head.

Lillian stopped sweeping. "*Mamm* said it depends on the day. Some days he is perfectly fine. Other days are *baremlich*. He gets confused, wanders off, and tries to take the buggy if it's left hitched up, without letting *Mamm* know where he's going. Things like that. I know it's hard for *Mamm* sometimes, taking care of him on her own. She worries about him a lot."

"Jonas has no business doing such things. Just like the other night—"

"Sadie, I'm sorry I asked you to go into that place to get Grandpa. I should have gone. After all, I've been in those type places before. Before I was Amish."

"You shouldn't be in a place like that while you're pregnant." Sadie recalled the smoke-filled room, the patrons' questioning eyes, and the way Kade had handled Jonas. "You know, it was Kade who convinced Jonas to come with us." She paused. "He seemed to know exactly how to handle him."

"Hmm," Lillian said. "Well, it's a *gut* thing he did." She pointed toward the window. "There's Carley and Jenna."

The bell on the door chimed when Jenna burst into the room. "Hi!" She ran into her Aunt Lillian's arms.

"*Guder mariye, Jenna.*"

"Good morning to you too," the six-year-old answered.

Carley closed the door behind her. "She does pretty well with her Pennsylvania *Deitsch*, huh? With so many relatives speaking the language, Noah has taught her quite a bit. He still remembers much of what he learned before he left."

"*Ya*, she is doing *wunderbaar gut*," Lillian said. She eased out of the hug. "Do you want to go organize the dolls for me, Jenna?"

Jenna nodded and skipped across the store, her blonde ringlets bouncing down the middle of her back.

Carley reached into her purse and pulled out a piece of paper. "Can you look at this and see if I'm missing anything?" She handed the note to Lillian. "Noah and I have a couple coming in from Florida this afternoon. It's a man Noah went to medical school with, and they'll be staying with us for a few days. Of course, they are intrigued by the Amish, so I told them I would cook them an Amish meal."

Lillian scanned the note. "Wow. This is quite an undertaking. Usually turkey roast is reserved for weddings, but they should love it." Lillian ran her finger down the piece of paper. "Barbecued string beans, mashed potatoes, homemade bread, and shoofly pie." She handed the piece of paper back to Carley. "Do you have chowchow, applesauce, and some jams and jellies to serve prior to the main meal?"

Carley grinned. "No. I was hoping maybe my Amish sister-in-law could help me with that."

"Come by the house later, and I'll supply you with everything you need," Lillian said with a smile.

"Or—" Sadie cut in, "I could prepare the meal at my house for your friends."

Carley's eyes lit up. "Really? I know they would love to see the inside of an Amish home." She paused as her face grew serious. "But that's way too much work. I could never ask you to do that."

Sadie glanced at the ground, then sheepishly back at Carley. "I'd truly enjoy the company."

"But what about Noah? I mean, since he's been shunned and all. I wouldn't want to get you in trouble with the bishop."

"I'd be glad to cook for your friends, and I'm not worried about Bishop Ebersol. You know he mostly looks the other way when it comes to Noah." Sadie took the piece of paper from Carley. "What time?"

"Sadie, you're the best!" Carley gave her a quick hug. "You tell me what time is best for you. I'll go to the grocery store right now, buy everything, and bring it here. This is so sweet of you. Noah's friends will be so excited."

"I'm happy to do it." Sadie couldn't tell her how much she needed to have visitors in the house, someone to cook for and serve at her own table. Then she had a thought. "Carley, would you mind if I invited the *Englischer* and his son? The ones who are renting the cottage."

Lillian gave her a strange look, but Carley answered right away. "Of course not! The more the merrier."

Sadie glanced toward Lillian, and then back at Carley. "The young boy is special. I think he might be slow—mentally challenged I believe is the right way to say it." She shook her head. "*Ach*, never mind. I think it might be best not to. I don't know how the child will act, and it might be uncomfortable for your friends. The only reason I thought about it is that the child's mother just dropped him off with Kade, my renter, and the man hasn't been involved much in the child's life. He's clueless what to do with him. And since Noah is a doctor—"

"Say no more," Carley interrupted. "His friend, James, is a doctor too. There will be two doctors, and maybe they can help your friend with his son."

"He's not my *friend*. He's renting the cottage." She let out a long, audible breath. "But he seems rather lost."

"What time do you want to have supper?" Carley asked. "At the usual supper hour, four o'clock?"

"In the past when I've hosted *Englischers* for suppers, I have pushed back supper until seven. How would that be?"

"Perfect." Carley turned toward her daughter. "Jenna, let's go, sweetie."

"Lillian, my table hasn't been full in a long time. Do you, Samuel, David, and Anna want to join us, if it's all right with Carley?" Sadie glanced back and forth between the women.

"That would be great," Carley said as she reached for Jenna's hand.

Lillian rested her hands across her protruding belly. "*Ya*, that would be nice. But Anna has a *baremlich* cold. David is watching her for me today. I didn't want to bring her here like I usually do, for fear she'd get worse being carted outdoors. I think it best to keep her inside. Besides, I promised Lizzie I would bake her some bread. I appreciate the invitation, though."

"Lizzie sure eats a lot," Sadie said. "I told her I'd bake her some bread too. And last week, I took her a meat loaf, and she sent the empty dish back the very next day, by way of Mary Ellen, who'd stopped by to see her."

"She's a dear woman," Lillian said. "Frail little thing. But I agree with you. She eats like a horse. It's a shame she doesn't have children of her own. She does have several nieces and nephews who check on her, but they travel almost an hour to do so, by car from the Beachy Amish community." Lillian frowned. "I don't think they check on her enough."

"She has us to tend to her. Lizzie is easy to love," Sadie said. "I know she gets lonely."

Sometimes Sadie would offer to stay and keep her company, but Lizzie always declined the offer. Maybe Lizzie would accept Sadie's invitation to sit with her if she knew how much Sadie herself wanted the company. One thing Sadie knew about—loneliness. However, she wouldn't be lonely tonight. That is, not until she climbed into bed after her supper guests were gone.

"I'll be back with the groceries." Carley waved, and she and Jenna left.

Sadie began to wonder how she was going to approach Kade about joining them for supper. It seemed a bit forward. *But it's in Tyler's best interest*, she reminded herself.

Kade shifted his position on the couch and blinked his eyes into focus. Tyler was standing beside him, clad in blue-and-white pajamas, a yellow toothbrush dangling from one hand. Kade sat up, placed his feet on the floor, and tried to make eye contact with his son. But Tyler looked past him, although with a hint of happiness on his small face.

"Good morning," Kade said. He glanced at the clock on the fireplace mantel. Seven thirty. Kade reached for the black binder. They were already starting the day late. "Up at seven," he mumbled to himself. "Breakfast at seven thirty. Brush teeth and get dressed at eight o'clock." Then came the huge gap in time from eight thirty to three thirty when Tyler would have been in school.

How could Monica have done this? Kade could have prepared for this, with some warning. And he would have been at his own home in Los Angeles, not in a tiny, one-bedroom cottage in Pennsylvania Dutch country.

He thought about yesterday. There hadn't been any more fits or head banging, and Tyler went to bed right at eight o'clock in the bedroom. Kade left the light on as Monica's instructions suggested. Expecting problems, Kade was up until about one o'clock in the morning, fearful Tyler would get up during the night. But no incidents. And after Kade read every page in the black binder, sleep finally won out.

"Are you hungry?" Kade put the black binder back on the coffee table. Tyler didn't say anything, but he gently touched Kade's knee. Kade wanted to scoop Tyler into his arms, cuddle him, and somehow make up for the kind of man he knew himself to be—the kind of man who would've hired a nanny to do all this if he was home in Los Angeles. For a split second, he considered taking Tyler and going home. Then Tyler smiled. The familiar warmth Kade felt when Tyler arrived yesterday took the fear from his heart, even if only momentarily.

"Let's get some breakfast." Kade stood up and walked toward

the kitchen. He glanced back at Tyler to see him following, still toting the toothbrush.

"Cereal," Tyler said.

"Okay." Kade smiled, glad that Tyler was able to communicate what he wanted. He opened the cabinet where he stored the groceries Sadie brought the day before. Kade's preferred cereal had nuts and raisins, and he wondered if Tyler was going to eat it or not. He pulled a bowl from the shelf and filled it halfway.

Tyler walked over to the small, round table in the corner of the kitchen while Kade poured milk into the bowl. He took a seat at one of the four chairs and kicked his feet back and forth. Kade watched him out of the corner of his eye and allowed himself to fantasize that Tyler was perfect, a normal child.

Kade placed the bowl in front of Tyler and offered him a spoon. "Here's your cereal, Tyler."

"Cereal."

But Tyler didn't take the spoon. Instead, Tyler began tapping his toothbrush on the table, softly at first, then louder.

Kade tried to remember what Monica's notes said concerning ways to handle Tyler's unpredictable behavior, but with all the banging he couldn't think straight. "Tyler, let's don't do that." He reached for the toothbrush and attempted to pull it from Tyler's hand.

Tyler rolled his body from the chair, hit the floor hard, and rocked back and forth on his side, moaning loudly.

"Tyler, are you hurt?" Kade extended his arm downward, remembered the bite, and pulled back. Tyler's groans took on a high-pitched tone, and Kade squatted down beside him, unsure what his next move should be. "Think," he said aloud as he tried to recall the information he'd read the night before. *During a fit, ignore it, and refocus on something else.*

Kade walked to the middle of the floor in the den, scooped the plastic letters into the lunch box, and headed back to Tyler, who hadn't let up. He placed the lunch box beside his son, opened it, and began to randomly line up letters in no particular order. The wailing stopped.

Tyler sat up, as if he was cured of whatever ailed him. He began to sort through the letters, lining them up in what appeared to be a precalculated order, but there were no word formations that Kade could see.

Kade sat down on the floor beside his son and ran his hand through his tousled hair. How was he ever going to do this?

Sadie and Lillian had just finished a cup of chicken noodle soup when Sadie decided she would walk to the cottage to invite Kade and Tyler for supper.

"Go ahead." Lillian reached into a plastic bag beside her chair on the floor. "I need to hem these pants for Samuel anyway."

Sadie pulled her cape and bonnet from the rack. "Maybe it's not a *gut* idea to invite them for supper, but perhaps Noah and his doctor friend can help Kade with the boy."

Lillian glanced up at Sadie, then focused on the needle she was attempting to thread. "He is handsome, the *Englischer*."

"He is odd," Sadie said in a firm tone. "A rich man who needs many gadgets."

"Being rich doesn't necessarily make him odd." Lillian looked up at her and waited for a response.

Sadie moved toward Lillian as she tied the strings on her cape. "It is not normal to be separated from your spouse for three years or to not have a relationship with your child. It's also not *gut* to need so many material possessions, and—"

"But he's *Englisch*," Lillian interrupted. "The *Englisch* collect possessions."

"So many of them? I reckon his home is filled with unnecessary items, like his automobile." Sadie raised her eyebrows. "I've never seen such a car. Lights, knobs, and switches everywhere."

"Sadie . . ." Lillian took a deep breath.

"*Ya?*"

"Only God can pass judgment. Sounds to me like you're judging this man before you really know him."

"Why would I want to know him? I'm just trying to help the boy, maybe get some doctors' advice about how that man should tend to the child. That's all." Sadie tied her bonnet and pondered Lillian's words. "You're right," she mumbled. "It is not my place to judge."

Sadie moved toward the door. "I'll be back."

Once outside, Sadie rigidly held her thoughts in check. She didn't understand why she was picking up unbecoming traits. She'd never been a judgmental person before. It was as wrong as anything she'd been taught. Judging, questioning God's plan for her life—all wrong. She'd need to pray for strength to keep her thoughts pure and righteous. Maybe even speak with Bishop Ebersol about the matters.

She neared the cottage, and a vision of Kade wearing only his pajama bottoms flashed before her. *Surely not.* The man would have all his clothes on this time of day. But she slowed her pace anyway. She leaned an ear inward as she walked. Nothing.

The curtains were closed. She looked toward the barn, and the fancy car was still parked inside.

The porch steps creaked beneath her feet, and she considered turning around. But she knocked, not wanting to get caught loitering on the porch again.

Kade opened the door. Thankfully, he was fully clothed in jeans and a pullover blue sweater. Sadie could see past him to Tyler, who was sitting on the couch, reading a book. *Interesting.*

"The boy can read, no?" Sadie asked. She stretched her neck to peer past Kade.

Kade looked over his shoulder and then turned back to face her. "Yes, but according to my ex, he can't understand anything he reads. In her notes, she says he has hyperlexia. It's a syndrome observed in children who are autistic."

Sadie knew the confusion registered on her face, but she just nodded.

"It's a precocious ability to read words far above what would be expected of a five-year-old." He glanced at Tyler again. "There's a whole bag of books in his suitcase, but he seems fond of the book you had on your coffee table."

"The only book in here is—"

"Come in out of the cold." Kade swung the door wide and waited for her to enter.

"No, I just came to invite you to supper. You and Tyler."

Kade smiled his crooked smile in a way that made Sadie immediately wish she hadn't asked him. "We'd love to," he said in a tone that furthered her regret. She'd need to clarify her invitation.

"*Mei Englisch* friend, Carley, and her husband are bringing guests for supper. They are doctors, and I thought they might be able to help you with your son. I don't know what this 'autistic' is you speak of, but you seem . . ." She paused. His smile had faded, but his eyes were fused with hers, and he was listening intently. "You seem like maybe you need some help with the boy."

"Come in." He gently touched her arm and coaxed her inside. "You're letting in cold air."

She inched inside. The door closed hard behind her, and Tyler looked in her direction.

"Hello, Tyler." She walked to where he was sitting on the couch. "You are reading the Bible, I see."

Tyler didn't say anything, but refocused on the Good Book. Sadie turned around to see Kade standing uncomfortably close to her. She backed up a step. "It will not be a fancy meal, Mr. Saunders. Just a simple—"

"Kade," he interrupted.

"It will not be a fancy meal, *Kade*. Carley and Noah's guests would like to learn more of the Amish ways, and I'm happy to cook for all of them. And you and Tyler, if you wish. Sometimes I host *Englisch* families in my home for supper." She raised her chin and shrugged dismissively. "So this is ordinary, quite common, actually."

Kade folded his arms across his chest. One corner of his mouth pulled into a slight smile. "Sure. Sounds great."

"Am I amusing you, *Kade*?" *This was a bad idea.*

"Yes, Sadie Fisher, you amuse me." His grin broadened. "I get the point—that you're not asking me to supper, not as a date or anything. This is something you do for guests."

In all her years, Sadie was certain she'd never been as embarrassed as she was at this moment. Except perhaps when she awoke on the couch with Kade leaning over her.

"What time?" Kade turned and headed toward the kitchen, but glanced at her over his shoulder. "I was going to make myself a cup of hot tea. Would you like some?"

"No. I must go. Supper is at seven o'clock." She turned to leave.

"Wait," he said as he walked back into the den. He stopped in front of her and put his hands in the pockets of his denim breeches. His forehead creased with worry, and then he sighed. "Maybe it's not such a good idea for us to come."

"Why not?" Sadie's response shone with disappointment, which caught her completely off guard.

Kade leaned toward her and whispered. "Tyler might not be ready for a social environment. I don't know how he'll do." His brows drew downward in a frown. "I don't know how *I* will do."

Sadie looked over at Tyler, who was still reading. Then she smiled at Kade. "Tyler is special. A blessed gift from God. You have to learn his ways. Although he seems happy and *gut* at the moment."

"Right now he is." Kade ran his hand through his wavy, brown hair. "Breakfast was another story."

"Cereal for breakfast," Tyler said.

Kade turned briefly toward Tyler. "Yes, cereal," he said. He shifted his eyes back to Sadie, his expression warm. "He didn't really like the cereal, but we did okay."

"You will be fine, Kade. You will learn Tyler's ways and he will learn yours while he's here."

Sadie continued toward the door and was almost there when someone knocked. *Lillian, perhaps?*

Sadie turned the knob and pulled the door open.

Her eyes grew wide, her jaw dropped, and she fumbled for words that weren't coming. *Definitely not Lillian.*

7

BISHOP EBERSOL TIPPED THE RIM OF HIS STRAW HAT back, drew his brows inward, and stared Sadie down the same way her father had when she misbehaved as a child.

"Bishop Ebersol." Her voice rose in surprise. "How *gut* to see you."

The bishop shifted his eyes and glanced over her shoulder. Sadie could hear footsteps approaching from behind. She stood, waited, and feared what Kade might say.

"Can we help you?" Kade asked. He was so close behind Sadie that she could feel his breath against her neck. *We?* There's no *we*, Sadie thought, hoping he'd hush.

She stepped forward onto the porch, forcing Bishop Ebersol to take a step backward. She twisted slightly to face Kade. "Good-bye, Mr. Saunders. I'm glad to see that your son is doing well." She smiled, then faced the bishop. "What brings you here, Bishop Ebersol?" She headed down the porch steps with hopes that the bishop would follow. He did.

Sadie took two steps into the packed snow and turned to see Kade still standing in the threshold. *Go in the house!*

Bishop Ebersol held firmly to the handrail and made his way down the steps. A man in his seventies, he wore a gray beard that stretched to the end of his chest. But he stood tall in his black overcoat and took each step slow and steady.

"Well, okay . . ." she heard Kade say. "Thanks for coming over. I'll see you at supper tonight."

Sadie cringed and knew she was about to get a good talking-to. She waited for the bishop to catch up with her and wondered if Kade was ever going to go back in the cottage.

"I think it would be *gut* for us to have *kaffi*, Sadie," Bishop Ebersol said in a tone that challenged her to argue. He pulled his coat tight around his neck, blocking a blast of cool air that seemed to come out of nowhere. The sun was shining, but it was a reminder of what was to come. By tomorrow, temperatures would be consistently below freezing. By Friday they predicted terrible conditions.

She'd give thought to the weather later. Right now, she suspected Bishop Ebersol had a few things on his mind pertaining to her renter. She got in step with the bishop and took slow strides toward the farmhouse, and then spun her neck around to see Kade wave. She raised her hand briefly in his direction, turned back around, and prepared herself for the harsh words to come.

They were almost to the house when she saw the mailman pull up to her mailbox, open the flap, and push an envelope inside.

She hoped the bishop wouldn't take too long.

Lillian watched out of the window of the shop as Sadie walked alongside Bishop Ebersol toward the farmhouse, a gloomy expression on her face. Lillian hadn't known what to say when the bishop questioned Sadie's whereabouts, so she had stumbled around saying Sadie was tending to errands around the property. It was the truth, however slightly stretched it might have been. But Lillian saw Sadie walk inside the cottage, and she knew the bishop was already uncomfortable about a single man as her renter.

Lillian shook her head. Sadie should have stayed outside on the porch.

She'd barely sat back down to finish hemming Samuel's pants when she heard the *clip-clop* of hooves. She set the project aside and walked to the front window. *Oh no.*

Lillian walked outside and met her grandfather at the buggy. Before he had time to step down, she said, "Grandpa, does *Mamm* know where you are?"

Jonas Miller scrunched his face in irritation. "Lilly, I am a grown man. I do what I want, when I want." He climbed out of the buggy, opened his black coat, and slipped his thumbs beneath his suspenders. "And *ya*, Sarah Jane knows where I'm at."

"*Gut*, Grandpa." She patted his arm tenderly. "We worry and love you, that's all."

"I know you all think I'm *ab im kopp*, but I reckon I just get confused sometimes." He started walking toward the shop.

Lillian put her arm through his and walked beside him. "No one thinks you are off in the head, Grandpa."

"*Gut, gut.*" He looked her way and smiled. "I was testing your Pennsylvania *Deitsch*, to see if you have kept up with your studies since marrying Samuel."

"*Ya*, I have." She opened the door and motioned her grandpa in. "Are you here just for a visit?" Lillian was still skeptical that her mother knew he was here.

"I reckon I can come just to visit *mei kinskind*, no?"

Lillian closed the door behind them. "You can visit me anytime."

"I see that Bishop Ebersol is here. Sadie get in some trouble for housing that single *Englisch* fella?"

"I don't know. Sadie was a little concerned about that, but Bishop Ebersol said it would be all right for her to rent the cottage. There weren't any specific rules about *who* to rent to, but—"

"Then what's he doing here?" Grandpa placed his hat on the counter.

"I think he's just checking on her, and . . . uh, then she happened to be inside the cottage when he came, and I really don't know what's going on." Lillian shrugged and took a seat on the stool behind the counter.

"I'll tell you what's going on. Trouble. I saw the way the *Englischer* was looking at your friend. You look out for her, Lilly. He don't strike me as the converting type, and he'll steal our Sadie away to the *Englisch* world."

"Grandpa! That is the most ridiculous thing I have ever heard. They barely know each other!" Lillian slapped him playfully on the hand and grinned.

"You didn't know Samuel either."

"That was different."

"I don't know about that, and—"

The bell on the door chimed, hushing Grandpa.

"Is everything all right?" Lillian asked when Sadie walked in.

"*Ya.* Bishop Ebersol asked me a lot of questions, but when I explained about Mr. Saunders's son, he seemed to understand my concern for the boy." Sadie focused on Lillian's grandpa. "Hello, Jonas. What brings you here? Does Sarah Jane know you're here?"

Lillian sighed. She knew what was coming.

"I don't have to tell my daughter my every move. I am a grown man, and I can do what I see fit." Grandpa stood up, put his hat on, and tipped it in their direction. "As a matter of fact, I think I will go for a ride through the country."

"Jonas, I'm sorry if—" Sadie moved toward him.

"No, no. Nothin' to be sorry about." He started toward the door but turned around. "You girls take care of each other."

Kade put Tyler in the bathtub and placed the floating ducks all around him, like Monica had instructed in the black binder. Six little yellow chicks bobbed aimlessly around Tyler, who began to giggle.

Kade smiled. His son was as cute a kid as he'd ever seen. And at times like this, he forgot about Tyler's special needs. But it had been a hard day inclusive of another headbanging incident, and Kade worried how supper with Sadie and her guests would go. He was willing to chance it. He'd been alone and felt sorry for himself long enough. Maybe being around some other adults would do him good. And something about being around Sadie seemed to calm him. Perhaps it was the way she was with Tyler, or maybe because she was pleasant on the eyes. Either way, he found himself looking forward to the meal.

Tyler kept laughing, and Kade was mesmerized by the innocence of it all. He sat down on the tile floor beside the bathtub and watched his son, feeling like he could sit there forever. How had his life spiraled so completely out of control? He had more money than most would ever have, but barely an ounce of happiness. Yet, a bathtub full of yellow chicks was enough for Tyler. Something was amiss in Kade's life, and he'd never felt it more than right now.

He looked up at the ceiling. *What the heck?* he thought. He leaned against the wall and veered his eyes upward. "God, can You hear me?" It had been a long time, and he felt silly. But he pressed on. "Because I'm a mess. I need some help." He shook his head and fought his feelings of unworthiness. He knew from his upbringing that God welcomes those who have strayed, but Kade was struggling to reconnect. Carrying the burdens of his past would only hinder this effort. He knew this. But his regrets pressed down on him like a heavy weight on his chest, testing how much pressure his heart could take.

Tyler was still giggling and pushing the ducks around the tub. Kade was feeling something he hadn't felt before—confusing waves of emotion and an inner voice that seemed to beg him to take a good, hard look at his life, to reevaluate his place in the world.

He'd been crushed when Monica left. Highly perturbed when he lost almost two hundred thousand dollars in a business deal recently. And extremely disappointed when Alicia pulled out of their friendship. He also had a son whom he barely knew, which pained him now more than ever. But worst of all had been finding his father dead near his parents' Malibu home. He recalled his father's lifeless body, his eyes and mouth gaping open. A chill ran up Kade's spine, and he squelched the thought.

Kade's life had had its ups and downs for sure. But these feelings he was having . . . They were different.

Kade pushed one of the yellow ducks back in Tyler's direction.

"My duck," Tyler said as he continued to be entertained by the floating toys.

"Yes, your duck." Kade forced a smile, but he was anything but happy. And he should be—happy. *Shouldn't I?*

Despite the downs in his life, there had certainly been ups. He was wealthy. He'd traveled the world and experienced things most people never would. His doctor had recently told him that he was in perfect health. He had it all, really.

Then why was something pecking away at his insides, like a chisel chipping away at all that he'd ever known, and hinting that there was something else on the horizon?

Contentment? Is this what I'm lacking?

Kade gazed at his son and thought about the life he'd lived thus far. Right now, at this moment, he felt . . . *What do I feel?* He thought about it some more and summarized his emotions.

Fear, regret, hope, and love for my son.

His stomach knotted, and he fought the pangs of shame in his heart. *I want to be a better man.*

Kade looked up again, and this time he didn't feel ridiculous. "Show me the way, Lord. Show me the way."

Kade glanced at Tyler, who for the very first time stared straight into Kade's eyes. Kade didn't even want to blink or move—afraid he'd lose the moment. "Hey buddy," he said softly, wishing, praying Tyler could communicate with him.

The kid got the strangest look on his face. Kade didn't care. He was thrilled that he seemed to be holding his attention. "Tyler?"

Tyler smiled, which instantly invoked a smile from Kade. It was a rare moment, Tyler's eyes fused with Kade's, as if he were looking into Kade's thoughts, his soul.

"Tyler?" His son's eyes were still locked with his.

Tyler opened his mouth to speak, and Kade waited.

Tyler spoke softly, with perfect pronunciation, and with a gleam in his eyes. "The Lord is our King; He will save us."

Then Tyler returned to splashing around in the tub with his ducks, as if something incredibly profound hadn't happened, something that would change the core of who Kade was as a person, a man . . . a father.

———

Sadie pulled the turkey roast from the oven. She placed it on top of the gas range next to a casserole dish filled with barbecued string beans. The potatoes were cooked and cubed, and she had already added butter, milk, salt, pepper, and cream cheese. She'd mash them right before her guests arrived. Her table was filled with homemade bread, applesauce, and an assortment of jams and jellies, and she'd prepared a traditional shoofly pie for dessert. If the supper went as smoothly as the meal preparation, all would be well.

She stepped back to inspect her place settings for seven. Sadie couldn't remember the last time she used the plain white china, a wedding gift from Ben's parents. The long wooden table stretched almost the length of her kitchen, backless benches on either side. She recalled the hours Ben spent making the table, for the large family they would never have.

Sadie closed her eyes for a moment and bit back tears. She refused to allow her shattered dreams to put a damper on this evening. Company was coming, and she felt good about sharing her home and a meal with friends. Carley and Noah were as fine a couple as she'd ever known, and she felt sure their friends would be a pleasure as well.

Kade and the boy. She felt a nervous anticipation about them being at supper. Kade made her incredibly uncomfortable, but she worried for the boy's well-being. Hopefully, Dr. Noah and his *Englisch* friend would be able to guide Kade on how to tend to Tyler.

She adjusted the tall, propane floor lights, one on either side of the roomy kitchen. Then she lit the two white candles in clear glass votives that she'd placed on the table. Everything was ready. She had just enough time to reread Milo's letter that had arrived earlier. But no matter how many times she read it, she couldn't shake her recent doubt that he would ever actually show up. She wanted to believe him. She needed to believe him. Her faith in Milo had been slipping, and along with it, her faith in God's will for her—a sin far greater than her heart could bear. She would need to pray harder that she not be tempted to doubt His plan for her. *God is great, and all things are of Your will*, she silently prayed.

She pulled Milo's letter from the kitchen drawer where she placed it earlier and unfolded the single piece of paper.

My Dear Sadie,

I hope that you are doing gut and that you are staying warm during the kalt wedder. Soon I will be traveling to see you and will finally be able to hold you in my arms. The spring will not arrive fast enough for me. I spend my afternoons working to ready my farm for a visit from you someday, but lately it has made wet on many days in the week.

God continues to bless my new business with more and more customers. Each morning, after tending to the animals, I am able to work in the barn on furniture the Englisch have ordered. It pleases me to work with my hands and be able to make a necessary living. I finished the cedar chest I have been working on for John, the one I wrote to you about. He is most anxious to surprise his wife with it.

Church service will be at my home this Sunday. Mei sisters, Mary and Rachel, will prepare the meal for afterwards, along with mei mamm.

I must go for now, but I will write to you again very soon. You are in my thoughts and prayers.

Em Gott Sei Friede,
Milo

"And God's peace to you as well," Sadie said aloud. She tapped the envelope against her hand a few times, then folded it and put it back in the envelope. *Hmm.* His letters were growing shorter and less enthusiastic, which matched her attitude. Maybe Milo was tiring of their correspondence.

She sighed, and then began to mash the potatoes. Moments later, there was a knock at the door.

Lillian parked her buggy and walked up the dirt driveway to Lizzie's small farmhouse. It was set so far back in the woods you wouldn't know a house was even back there. She'd offered to drop off the bread Sadie had baked for Lizzie this morning because it was on her way home from Sadie's shop.

Surely Lizzie won't need more bread for a few days. As much as she enjoyed the days she worked at Treasures of the Heart, she was always behind on her household chores for that day. Plus she'd stayed late at the shop today to finish reorganizing the quilts by price, a project she shouldn't have started so late in the afternoon. There would be plenty to do when she got home, especially since the baby was sick as well. She'd been up with Anna the past two nights. She was glad Sadie had baked bread for Lizzie and that she didn't have to tackle that chore when she got home.

She knocked on Lizzie's door and heard movement from within the house. Lizzie had to be home. When there was no answer, she knocked again and waited. It was already dark, and the temperature was dipping into the twenties. *Hurry, Lizzie. I'm freezing out here.*

Lizzie hadn't owned a horse and buggy in years and relied on her friends to cart her to town when she was feeling up to it, which wasn't often these days. She mainly stayed to herself. They all felt sorry for Lizzie. Lillian couldn't imagine how lonely she must get.

Definitely movement inside. Lillian pounded hard on the door, and then paced the porch while rubbing her hands together, thankful for her thick, black gloves. From the west end of the porch, she could see a light coming from her grandparents' farmhouse across the pasture. Mom was probably already preparing Grandpa's supper, something fabulous, no doubt. Lillian wished she could head over there, sit down, and eat a hot meal with her mother and grandpa. But too much to do at home.

She'd left a prepared pot of stew in the refrigerator for Samuel and David. She always left something easy for them to heat up on the days she went to the shop. Samuel was a stickler about eating at four thirty.

Her stomach growled. She raised her hand to pound on the

door again, but stopped when she heard footsteps in the kitchen. *Thank goodness.*

"I'm coming, dear," she heard Lizzie call out. "I've been waiting for you!"

Huh?

The wooden door swung open, and Lizzie was grinning from ear to ear. A silly little grin that vanished the moment she saw Lillian.

"What are you doing here, Lillian?" Lizzie didn't open the screen door or invite her in from the cold.

"I brought Sadie's bread for you." Lillian lifted up the plastic bag she had hung across her forearm, with two loaves of bread inside.

Lizzie pushed the screen door open and almost ripped the bag as she pulled it off of Lillian's arm. "*Danki*, Lillian. So kind of you to drop it off." Then she let the screen door slam, smiled briefly, and started to push the wooden door closed.

"Wait!" Lillian said.

"*Ya?* What is it, dear?" Lizzie peeked around the wooden door. Her gray hair was tightly tucked beneath her *kapp*, and she was dressed plain, as she always was. But something was different. Her eyes seemed brighter, her face less wrinkled.

"Is everything all right, Lizzie?"

"*Ya, ya. Wunderbaar gut.*" And she slammed the door closed.

Lillian just stood there. Many times, Lizzie had declined offers of company, but Lillian had just assumed she wasn't feeling well. Quite clearly, Lizzie was feeling mighty fine today. That was the most zest she'd seen in Lizzie's demeanor since she'd known the woman. *Well, that's good*, she thought, as she finally turned to walk down the porch steps. Surprising, but good.

Her feet had just hit the snow when she heard whistling coming from the side of the house. A body rounded the corner, but it was too dark to see. She strained to focus on the approaching mass.

"Lizzie girl, I'm here!" a loud voice bellowed.

Lillian's jaw dropped as the male figure came into view. At about the same time, the man dropped a handful of flowers to the ground.

Lillian closed her mouth, but her eyes were wide.

"Lilly, what in the world are you doin' here?"

Lillian folded her arms across her chest. "I might ask you the same thing, Grandpa!"

8

AFTER INTRODUCTIONS HAD BEEN MADE, SADIE PLACED the turkey roast, mashed potatoes, and green beans on the table while Carley poured everyone a glass of tea.

"This looks wonderful, Sadie," Noah's friend Evan said. The balding man had soft, gray eyes beneath gold-rimmed glasses, and a kind expression.

"*Danki,*" Sadie said. She smiled and took a seat at the head of the table, with Carley and Noah on each side of her.

"And this tea is delicious," Evan added after he took a drink from his glass. "Very sweet, and I like that. The sweeter the better." He smiled.

"We call it meadow tea," Sadie explained. "It grows wild in meadows along the creek."

Evan nodded his approval. Tyler and Kade sat on Carley's bench, and Noah's friends sat beside Noah on the opposite side. Sadie explained that the Amish pray silently before meals and asked if everyone would bow their heads in a prayer of thanksgiving for the food before them.

When they all raised their heads, Evan's wife, Shelly, was the first one to speak. "And it smells fabulous as well," she said.

Noah loaded his plate with mashed potatoes, and everyone

followed by serving themselves whatever was nearby, and then passed each dish to the right.

Kade spooned food onto Tyler's plate, and then his own, each time an item was handed to him. He kept a fearful eye on Tyler.

Amid the small talk, Tyler's hands were all over the place—picking up utensils and then putting them down, sticking a finger in his mashed potatoes, tapping his piece of bread on the table, and then spilling his tea—mostly in Kade's lap.

As the liquid rolled across the table, Tyler began to scream. Kade sat with his mouth open for a moment and stared down at a lap full of tea. Then he shook his head. "I knew this was a bad idea. I apologize to everyone, and . . ." He attempted to calm his son, but Tyler flung himself onto the floor and continued to cry.

Shelly, a tiny little woman with short brown hair, jumped up first and ran around the table to Tyler. Kade had turned around on the bench and was staring hopelessly at his son. Sadie watched Kade's face redden with embarrassment.

Shelly squatted down and reached her hand out toward Tyler, but she pulled back quickly when Kade practically yelled, "Watch out! He bites."

Sadie narrowed her eyes in Kade's direction and fought the urge to tell him that Tyler is not a dog. Then she got up and walked to where Shelly was squatting and joined her. "Tyler likes tapioca pudding. And if Tyler is a *gut* boy, I have some saved just for him."

"Is he . . ." Shelly glanced up at Kade, who was still sitting on the bench, facing them.

"Autistic," Kade answered. "Again, I apologize. We should probably go and . . ."

Tyler stopped crying, and then sat up and looked at Sadie. Sort of. His eyes darted around the room. "Hug, hug, hug."

Instinctively, Sadie started to wrap her arms around him, but she stopped when she recalled how he'd pulled away from her when she was with him at the cottage.

"He actually wants a hug," Kade said. He leaned down toward the boy, but Sadie beat him to it and pulled Tyler into a hug.

Kade dabbed at his soaked blue jeans, and then put the wet napkin on his plate. "I think we'd best go. I apologize for—"

"Nonsense!" Shelly said. "We have three children close to his age at home with my mother-in-law. Rest assured, we've seen bigger messes than this." She smiled in Kade's direction. "You absolutely must stay."

What a lovely person, Sadie thought, as she continued to hug Tyler.

"Heck, I've had a whole plate of food dumped in my lap before," Evan added with a chuckle. "Did she mention that two of our angels are twins? Double trouble on some days." He laughed again.

Kade still looked extremely embarrassed by the whole display, but he managed a smile.

Tyler continued to snuggle against Sadie, and she whispered in his ear. "Tyler, you're a *gut* boy."

He eased out of her arms and smiled. "Pudding."

"*Ya*, pudding for Tyler after he eats his supper. Can you do that?" His big, blue eyes looked through her, but his smile seemed to say yes. He stood up and climbed back into his spot on the bench beside Kade.

"He's adorable," Shelly said. Then she grinned at Kade. "But you're soaked, huh? I've been there."

"I have some clothes in the bedroom that might fit you," Sadie said to Kade. He arched questioning brows. "They were my husband's," she added. Then she couldn't help but grin. "I'll go see about some dry pants for you."

"No, Sadie. Let's all eat," Kade said. "Really, I'm fine for now." He spoke in a way that seemed intimate to Sadie, for some reason, as if they were more than just the acquaintances they were. She knew she was blushing, and she was glad when Noah spoke up.

"Did you say Tyler is autistic?" Noah asked Kade once they were all settled and eating again.

Kade swallowed, and then said, "Yes. He is."

"There's a boy about Tyler's age in the Amish community who is autistic," Noah said before turning to Sadie. "Jacob and Martha, those are the parents' names, right?"

"*Ya.*" Sadie waited for Noah to say more. This is what she'd hoped for.

"The boy's name is Amos," Carley added. "Martha has brought him to the clinic a few times for a recurring cold." She paused. "I've gotten to know a lot of the Amish since I work as a receptionist at the clinic."

Noah finished off a bite of turkey roast. "But unlike Tyler, Amos is nonverbal. He doesn't speak at all. Tyler seems to communicate quite well. Is Tyler enrolled in a school that specializes in behavioral therapy?"

"He has been going to a special school." Kade glanced at his son. "I'm afraid I haven't been around Tyler much. I live in Los Angeles, and Tyler lives with his mother in North Carolina." He paused. "Actually, I haven't seen Tyler in six months. I'm not sure exactly how much he understands at this point."

There was an awkward silence as everyone seemed to be wondering about Kade's statement, but Kade must have decided to make the most of having two doctors present. "In my notes from my soon-to-be ex-wife, she says that Tyler has hyperlexia. Can you explain a little about that?"

"Usually autistic children who present with hyperlexia listen selectively. You'd almost think they were deaf if you didn't know otherwise," Noah said. "I noticed that with Amos in my office. But Tyler seems tuned in to what you're saying."

Kade hung on Noah's words. "What about reading? Tyler reads."

"But does he understand what he reads?" Evan asked. "Although I haven't treated any autistic children, it's my understanding that children with hyperlexia show an intense fascination with numbers or letters, but that doesn't mean they can count or read. Or even if they can, it doesn't mean they can comprehend."

Kade paused, rubbed his chin, and seemed to be weighing Evan's comments. "So, he repeats what he reads with no understanding?" Noah had a mouthful and nodded. Kade went on. "That's what it says in my notes from Monica, my ex, but this afternoon, something . . . something happened, and it was—it was odd."

They all waited. But Kade didn't elaborate.

"Tyler's reading skills can help him to develop language, but it's getting him to understand what he's saying that is the hard part," Noah said.

"He certainly understands tapioca pudding," Sadie said affectionately.

"Tyler likes tapioca pudding," Tyler said. Then he smiled in a way that touched Sadie. *How blessed his mother is,* she thought. And Kade too.

"Maybe he understands more than you think," Evan said.

Kade got the strangest look on his face. "Maybe."

An hour later, everyone was still gathered around the table. Tyler was into his third helping of pudding while the others ate shoofly pie and drank coffee. The conversation had drifted from autism to music, and Kade found someone who shared his passion for the subject—Evan. They talked a lot about things to do with music that Sadie didn't know anything about. But watching Kade have such an animated conversation with Evan, often talking with his hands and laughing, made him seem more *real* to Sadie.

Everyone's mood was light, the conversation good, and they all seemed to be having a good time. A successful supper, despite the rocky beginning. Shelly asked lots of questions about the Amish, all of which Sadie gladly answered. She loved to talk about the beliefs of the Amish, their strong faith and plain ways. However, more than once she felt as though she was ministering to herself about the importance of believing all things to be of God's will.

Twice while she was talking, she had looked at Kade and found him staring at her in a way that she found most inappropriate. She had blushed and felt almost . . . flattered. Tonight, she'd pray to cleanse herself of such thoughts.

"*Ach*," she said to Kade when she was clearing the dishes. "I forgot to round you up some clean breeches. You don't want to walk to the cottage like that. You'll freeze for sure."

He waved his hand to shush her, but then quickly jerked the action to a stop. "Sorry," he said. "It's okay, really. I haven't even noticed it. I should probably take Tyler and be on my way."

"Look." Sadie pointed to the couch in her den, where Tyler had been playing with his plastic letters. "He fell asleep."

"You said earlier that your company builds high-rises," Evan said. "If Sadie's not in too big a hurry to get rid of us, I'd like to hear more about that."

Kade turned to Sadie.

"No rush at all," she said much too quickly. "I'll go get you some pants." She hurriedly left the room and retrieved a lit lantern on a table in the den. She headed down the hall to her bedroom and wondered why she felt elated that everyone—particularly Kade—wanted to extend their visit.

Kade stood up from the table. This had turned out to be the best night he'd had in ages. He was looking forward to spending more time with all of them—especially Sadie. Something about that woman seemed to have a soothing effect on him. He hung on her every word when she talked about her strong beliefs, about God's will, and the ways of the Amish. Several times, he recalled what Tyler had said during bath time. It sent a rush of possibilities through his mind. Could turning his life back over to God quiet the unrest in his soul and lead Kade to the calm existence he longed for? Was God trying to communicate to him through Tyler? *Is God the answer?*

He wasn't sure about any of it, but for the first time in a long time, he felt a sense of hope that seemed to center around the prospect of a relationship with God.

Sadie's wooden table with modest china hardly compared to the tables he'd dined at over the years. Senators, heads of state, religious leaders, and those comparable in power only to others in Kade's elite circle. And yet, it was the best dinner party he could remember attending.

He thought back to dinner in his household when he was growing up. Formality was something that had been handed down from generation to generation. Dressing nicely for the meal was a requirement, and if a child made an outburst at a dinner party, like Tyler's this evening, a nanny would have rushed him away. Kade was twelve before he realized that everyone didn't have live-in housekeepers and nannies.

Tonight the warmth and kindness he felt were real and heartfelt, the conversation was appealing, and the people held no pretenses. He smiled.

"Excuse me, please," he said to everyone.

The hallway was dark as he walked to where he thought the bathroom was. He paused at the first closed door on his right, and then gently pushed it open. Darkness. He remembered Sadie telling Shelly that a lantern was lit in the bathroom. He quietly pulled the door shut and took a few more steps down the hallway to the next door on his right. It was slightly open, and he could see light inside.

He pushed the door wide and walked right into Sadie holding a lantern in one hand, a pair of slacks in the other. They barely bumped, and she stepped back and lifted the lantern to see his face.

Kade could certainly see her face in the dim light—soft shades of ivory skin and blue eyes sparked with indefinable emotion. A strand of wavy red hair had lost its place beneath her prayer covering and draped across her face. She didn't move, didn't breathe, when Kade gently brushed the strand from her cheek. For what seemed like an eternity, they stood in the threshold of what evidently was not the bathroom and gazed into each other's eyes.

"Here," she finally said. She pushed the pants toward him and slowly eased her way around him and was gone.

What just happened?

Sadie rushed down the hall to rejoin her guests.

What was that?

Everyone was laughing and carrying on about their high school years. It was a conversation Sadie couldn't add to, since Amish schooling only ran through the eighth grade.

"Sadie, this is way past your bedtime, I'm sure," Carley said when Sadie took a seat at the head of the table. Only coffee cups and empty pie plates lined the table now, and she fought the urge to yawn.

"It's fine," she said. "I enjoy you all being here."

"Well, it was a wonderful meal," Noah said.

The others all commented about the food, the company, and what a nice night it was. But Sadie barely heard them as her eyes met Kade's when he reentered the room. Then she couldn't help but grin. Ben had been a tall man, almost six foot, five inches. Kade was tall, too, but lacked about three inches of Ben's height, and the black pants dragged the floor.

Kade smiled back at her. "At least they're dry," he said as he glanced down at the floor.

"Tell us a little about your business, Kade, and then we're going to let Sadie get some rest," Evan said. "From what she said earlier, her day starts very early, and I know we're keeping her up too late."

Sadie shook her head and repeated, "It's fine."

Kade glanced at Tyler, who was still sleeping soundly, and then he sat down at the table, but not before giving Sadie a look that seemed to confirm that something had happened in the hallway.

Ridiculous. She pulled her eyes from his.

"Not much to tell," Kade said modestly. "We build high-rise office buildings. We're currently working on two projects, one in Dallas and one in Chicago."

Evan rubbed his chin. "What did you say your last name was?"

"Saunders," Kade said.

Evan's eyes grew wide and assessing. "As in Saunders Real Estate and Development?"

"Yes," Kade answered, as if it was no big matter.

Evan sat up a little taller and looked at Noah. "Do you realize who we're dining with?"

Kade lowered his head, and Sadie could tell he wasn't comfortable with the direction the conversation was going.

Noah smiled. "I do now." He turned to Kade. "I recognize

you now from a recent issue of *Forbes* magazine. You were on the cover."

Kade forced a smile and nodded.

"Uh, no," Evan said. He shook his head. "I didn't see that. I saw Kade on a cover of *Newsweek* a while back."

Shelly's thick lashes opened and closed, her green eyes wide with astonishment. "Good grief," she said softly. "I read an article about you too. And there was a picture of you and the president."

"Of the United States?" Sadie brought her hand to her chest. *Who is this man?*

They all smiled at Sadie's outburst—all but Kade, who shrugged, as if having your picture taken with the president was nothing impressive.

Sadie glanced around her plain kitchen, void of electricity, modern conveniences, and all the things she was sure Kade was used to—things far fancier than Sadie had ever even seen.

Then, as if Carley was reading Sadie's mind, Carley asked, "Kade, what in the world brought you to Lancaster County for three months? This has to be incredibly different from what you are, um . . . used to."

Kade folded his hands on the table and slowly looked around at each of them. He laughed in such a way that it didn't seem genuine, and he shook his head. Then he focused on Sadie and spoke the one word Sadie couldn't have guessed if she had bet all the peas in a summer garden.

"God," Kade said softly. He shifted his gaze to Tyler for a long moment. Then glanced around at each of them again and smiled.

"Seriously?" Shelly asked after a few awkward moments of silence.

Evan twisted his mouth to one side and seemed equally curious about Kade's response. Noah and Carley looked at each other and smiled. They were so in love, the type of love blessed by God. How Sadie's heart ached for such a love as theirs.

Sadie locked eyes with Kade, and as it was in the hallway, she had trouble looking away. So she didn't. Their eyes were still fused when Kade answered Shelly. "Yes, seriously," he said. Then he paused to glance at Tyler again. "And I don't think I realized it until today."

"I think that's as good a reason as any." Noah smiled, dabbed his mouth with his napkin, and then stood up. "I think we need to let Sadie get some sleep."

Carley, Evan, and Shelly all stood up. The two couples hugged Sadie and thanked her repeatedly for a wonderful supper. Kade rose and shook each of their hands, but oddly he made no attempt to arouse Tyler and be on his way home.

"Don't forget Tyler," Sadie teased. She pointed toward the small, tan couch in her den.

"Not likely." Kade stood beside Sadie and waved to everyone as they walked out the door.

She waved good-bye to her guests and attempted to smile, in between darting her eyes at Kade. *He can't stay.*

Then Kade closed the door, as if he owned the place.

Stunned, Sadie turned to face him, but backed up a step when his eyes met hers in a way that was becoming more and more unsettling. She was terribly embarrassed that her guests, especially Carley and Noah, saw that Kade did not leave.

"I'll help you with Tyler." Sadie backed up another step, drew her eyes from his, and headed toward the couch.

"Sadie, wait," Kade whispered.

"*Ya?*"

"I was hoping maybe you and I could talk for a little while." He looked quite silly in Ben's pants. "I promise not to keep you up much longer," he added when she shook her head.

"No. It's not proper for you to be here. You have to go." She edged toward Tyler.

"Wait," he said again. "Who's going to know?"

"I will know," she said in a loud whisper. "And God."

"That's what I want to talk to you about." He moved closer. Much too close.

Sadie folded her arms across her chest. "You want to talk to me about God?"

"Yes. Something happened today, and I need to talk to someone about it, and . . ." Sadie could hear his shirt pocket vibrating, and Kade pulled out the tiniest portable phone she'd ever seen. "Excuse me a minute. It's a friend of mine from L.A."

Kade walked toward the kitchen, and Sadie waited in the den.

"What's up, Val?" Kade asked from around the corner.

Sadie continued to wait. It was quiet for a bit. She squatted down beside the couch and gently touched Tyler's back. So sweet. She wondered how the boy had managed to sleep through all the talking in the next room. The fire was dwindling. She'd need to put another log on before she went to bed. She sighed and wondered how soon that would be. *It is completely inappropriate for him to be here.*

Kade rounded the corner and stopped in the middle of the room. His expression caused Sadie to stand up and take a step toward him. "Kade?"

He put his hand over his mouth and looked down, and then blinked hard.

"Kade, what is it?" She took another step toward him.

His head slowly lifted. "I have to go."

Sadie would have thought, *Thank goodness*, but something was wrong. Terribly wrong. "I'll help you get Tyler," she said, although she didn't move.

"No." He ran a hand through his hair. "I mean, I have to go. I have to leave Lancaster County. I have a flight out Friday morning. Me and Tyler have to go."

He walked to the couch and gently lifted Tyler into his arms, and then buried his face in the sleeping boy's shoulder and stood there holding his son.

Sadie didn't know what to say, what to do. She waited.

Kade lifted his head, and even in the dimly lit room, Sadie could see his eyes glassed over with unspoken pain.

"Kade?" She was now right in front of him, staring into tear-filled eyes that threatened to spill at any moment. She touched his arm, a gesture she wouldn't have considered just five minutes earlier.

"It's Monica," he said softly.

"Monica?"

"Tyler's mother." He stared into Sadie's eyes. "She's dead."

9

SADIE BUNDLED UP FOR THE BELOW-FREEZING TEM-perature and walked onto the porch. Ominous clouds hung low as night gave way to day, and Sadie knew that this morning's weather was the best it would be for several days. The temperature would drop throughout the day and overnight before several feet of snow fell.

Last night, Kade had left immediately after telling her the news about Tyler's mother. He'd clung tightly to Tyler and, with tears in his eyes, mumbled something about a car accident. When the front door closed, Sadie had wept, and then prayed for both of them. They'd be leaving tomorrow morning, and Sadie couldn't help but wonder if she'd ever see them again.

Sadie imagined Kade had scores of people to help him with Tyler when he returned home to Los Angeles. A man of his wealth would surely enroll Tyler in a fine school. But would he ever really get to know that precious child? She was busy speculating about the two of them when she stepped onto the snow and headed toward the shop. The women had decided to meet and devise a plan to check on each other over the next several days. Sadie couldn't remember a storm of such proportion being forecast in Lancaster County. If the weather predictions held true, blizzard conditions were on the way.

She was the first one to arrive at the shop, so she pulled the blinds and started to light the heaters. Lillian and Sarah Jane walked in, and Sadie walked toward them.

"Sadie, have you been crying again?" Lillian asked. "Still no word from Milo?"

"No, I did hear from Milo. It was a short letter, but a letter." She shrugged and then sighed. "But I did shed a few tears last night."

Sadie proceeded to tell Lillian and Sarah Jane the events of the prior evening.

"That's *baremlich*," Lillian said. "That poor child. I guess Mr. Saunders will be getting to know his son on a permanent basis." She shook her head.

"I reckon," Sadie said. She wondered if Tyler would understand the loss or not.

"Well, I have a story that might cheer you up." Lillian smiled at her mother, and then looked back at Sadie. "It's about Grandpa."

Sarah Jane shook her head. "Silly old goose," she said fondly.

Sadie listened with amusement as Lillian told her about finding Jonas at Lizzie's house. "But you think it is *gut*, no?" she asked when Lillian had finished. "Lizzie is a dear woman, and of course, I love Jonas."

"I think it's *wunderbaar gut* that Grandpa has someone to spend time with and play chess," Lillian said. "I was just . . . shocked."

"That must be where Pop sneaks off to sometimes, those times when he is on foot." Sarah Jane hung her black cape on the rack and untied her bonnet. "Because he can walk across the pasture to get to Lizzie's house."

"Does it bother you about—I mean, do you care since . . ."
Sadie tried to reword what she was trying to say. "Your pop was
married to Irma Rose, to your *mamm*, for a long time."

"No, no, no," Sarah Jane said. "I'm happy for him to have
someone to spend time with. The only thing that upsets me is
when he takes the buggy or takes off on foot without telling me
where he's going." She chuckled. "I guess he's mostly at Lizzie's."

Sadie and Lillian locked eyes, both knowing that Lizzie's
house wasn't always the place Jonas went.

Lizzie had been watching the clock for nearly forty minutes.
Jonas said eight o'clock. She reached for the battery-operated
contraption he'd given her yesterday, before he'd been caught
sneaking to her place later that afternoon.

She chuckled. Jonas seemed to enjoy the sneaking around more
than the games of chess they played, always trying to keep his
daughter and granddaughter on their toes. She'd told him repeatedly not to be worrying them in such a way. Lizzie was glad Sarah
Jane and Lillian knew about their friendship now. Maybe she'd get
to see more of Jonas. How she loved that feisty old man. It had been
forty years since she'd loved that way. The good Lord took her
Johnny much too soon. But after all this time, Lizzie had Jonas.

She tried not to pay it too much mind when Jonas called her
Irma Rose every now and then, or when he seemed to think she
was Irma Rose and would recall times they'd spent together.
He'd certainly loved his Irma Rose. She turned up the volume,
twisting the dial on the walkie-talkie just the way Jonas had
showed her. She laughed when she heard his voice.

"Breaker, breaker. You there, Lizzie?"

She laughed harder. "Oh, my!" she said aloud to herself as she fumbled to push her own talk button. "Jonas, is that you?" And, as he'd instructed, she released her hold on the button.

It was quiet for a few moments. "Who else would it be, Lizzie?"

She pictured Jonas at home, with his big, bushy, gray brows edged upward. And she was thrilled that he called her by her name. Lizzie put her hand to her chest and smiled, feeling more alive than she'd felt in a long time. They'd only been spending time together for two months, but during that time, her arthritis had been better, her appetite had improved, and she had a kick in her step that she didn't have before she fell in love with Jonas Miller. Lizzie hadn't shared her feelings, but surely he knew.

"I reckon the weather's gonna be frightful the next few days." Lizzie released the button. She dreaded being cooped up at home with no visitors, no way to leave—and no Jonas to keep her company.

"Gonna miss me, now, aren'tcha?" She heard him chuckle.

Yes, I am. "I'll miss beating you at chess."

"Has that ever happened?" Lizzie heard him snort out a laugh.

"I reckon it's happened several times, Jonas Miller!" She threw her head back and laughed. She felt like a schoolgirl who had a crush on the most wonderful boy.

"You didn't forget our promise we made to each other, did you, now?"

Lizzie pressed her lips together, knowing the serious nature of the promise she and Jonas had made to each other a while back.

They didn't speak of if often, but with each passing day, it seemed more and more important. "No, Jonas, I did not forget."

She could only hope that *he* wouldn't forget either.

Kade watched with fascination as Tyler read the Bible. And he waited with nervous anticipation for Tyler to reveal some sort of message for Kade. But then Kade shook his head and wondered if he'd made too big a deal about the verses Tyler had spoken before. Probably a coincidence, repeating what he'd read.

If that was his line of thinking, why did he continue to encourage Tyler to read the Scriptures? Tyler was content reading, but his son didn't say a word. Kade was jarred from his musings by his cell phone.

"Hey, partner. Monica's parents have made the arrangements," Val said. "Friday at two o'clock in her hometown. You're going to be pushing it to get there from the airport in time. I had Tina at your office arrange for a car to pick you up. Which reminds me, should we go ahead and have someone fly to Pennsylvania to drive your car back? I'm sure you have no intentions of returning there."

Kade still couldn't believe Monica was gone. He had loved her so much at one time, but his heart ached more from those memories than from missing her now. "I haven't really thought about it."

"Is Tyler going to do all right on a plane?"

"I hadn't really thought about that either." Kade knew that was something he'd better think about now. "I didn't see anything in Monica's notes about Tyler *not* flying."

"Listen, I went ahead and took it upon myself to call Penelope and told her to go ahead and start interviewing nannies. And what about a school for Tyler? Do you want him to live at home and attend a special school, or do you want to send him to a school with in-house boarding?"

"What?" This was all happening way too fast. "I mean, I don't know, Val. I haven't had time to think about all these things." His housekeeper, Penelope, had been with him for years, but she wasn't qualified or energetic enough at her age to take care of Tyler. "I don't want him living away at a school, though. I want him with me."

"You still want a nanny, though. Right?"

Kade took a deep breath. "We can talk about all that later." He glanced around the simply furnished cottage, the cozy fire, and Tyler sitting quietly and reading on the floor. And he could see through the window that it was starting to snow. It was like something out of a Thomas Kinkade painting. He wasn't ready to leave.

"Does Tyler seem to understand what happened?" Val asked.

"No. I tried to explain it to him, but he didn't seem to comprehend what I was saying." And that truly saddened Kade. Monica was his mother, and he wished for her sake that Tyler had some sort of feelings about her death, even if only mild ones, to honor the woman Monica had tried to be. On the other hand, he felt relief that Tyler wasn't grieving from the loss.

"So, what do you think about having someone fly there and drive your car back?" Val asked again. "That way you wouldn't have to go back there."

Something about that idea bothered Kade. He couldn't put his finger on it, but Sadie's face flashed before him. He recalled the way they had looked at each other in the hallway, and again in the kitchen. Something about her stirred things inside him. Not manly things, as he would have expected, but more of a spiritual whirlwind. It was confusing, and not something he was sure he was ready to walk away from for good.

He remembered the way Sadie had talked about her relationship with God during dinner. She talked about Him as if He were a close friend of hers, someone she chatted with regularly.

"No, I'll come back to get the car."

"I'm so sorry about all this, Kade."

Kade was sure he heard Val's voice crack, and it touched him that his friend truly felt for his situation.

Val filled him in on a few more details, and they said their good-byes.

Sadie and Lillian closed all the shutters outside the shop in preparation for the storm. Lillian and Sarah Jane said they would check on Lizzie on their way home. Sadie imagined they were curious about Lizzie's friendship with Jonas and wanted to take the opportunity to talk with her. She smiled when she recalled the story about Lillian catching Jonas coming to Lizzie's. How sweet if they were courting at that age, she thought.

Milo's letter was on the kitchen table when she walked into the house through the kitchen door. She didn't have an urge to read it. Instead, she pulled open her kitchen drawer and tossed it inside. It landed on top of some other household papers. It didn't seem to warrant a place upstairs with her other letters, which she had treasured for so long. *Too long.*

Sadie poured herself a glass of meadow tea. She'd just sat down at the table when a loud pounding on the front door caused her to jump up.

She hurried around the corner of the kitchen and flung the door open. Snowflakes dotted a heavy, brown quilt in Kade's arms. "Kade, get that child in here," she said. "What are you doing out in this weather?"

He pulled the quilt back from Tyler's face. The boy was smiling from ear to ear. "Fun!"

Sadie laughed. "Your *daed* bringing you all bundled up out into the snow is fun, no?" She leaned down closer to Tyler.

"The faster I clomped across the snow, the more he bounced, and the louder I could hear him giggling." He set Tyler on the floor, and the boy immediately wrapped his arms around Sadie's legs.

"Hug," he said.

Sadie squatted down and embraced Tyler. "I *lieb* hugging you," she said, nuzzling him closer.

After a few moments, Kade eased onto the couch. Sadie pulled away from Tyler and walked to a rocker on the other side of the room. Tyler followed, and she was surprised when Tyler crawled into her lap.

"Tyler really seems to like you," Kade said, and then frowned. "More than he likes me."

"He's used to having a mother, and . . ." She stopped. "I'm so sorry for your loss, Kade. And for Tyler."

Kade leaned back against the couch. "I loved her very much at one time." He paused and looked hard at Sadie. "But now all I have are memories of that love. I haven't loved her—in that way—for a very long time." He shook his head. "But it's still painful to think of this happening to her." His eyes shifted to Tyler's tiny face, burrowed against Sadie's chest. "I don't think Tyler understands."

Sadie could see the despair etched across his face. "What brings you out in this weather?" she asked when Kade seemed permanently lost in thought. She thought briefly about being alone with him, or at least without the company of other adults, but she suspected these were special circumstances.

"I think Tyler is missing one of his plastic letters," Kade said. He rubbed his stubbly chin.

"I don't know how he knows this, but every time he dumps them from the lunch box, he starts to cry. He keeps holding up the *E* letter, and when I took inventory, it appears that there are four of every letter, but only three *E*s.

Dark circles under Kade's eyes indicated he might not have slept much last night. "Maybe it's in between the cushions on the couch," she said.

Kade began to search the couch, lifting the cushions slightly as he went.

Sadie glanced out the window. Heavy blankets of snow were falling. "Kade, you are going to have a *baremlich* time traveling. It will be much worse by morning. You might not be able to get out."

"I was thinking about that. Maybe I should leave for the airport this afternoon and get a room near there."

Tyler laid his head on Sadie's shoulder, and she gave him a squeeze. "He is such a precious gift from God. You're so very blessed, Kade."

Kade continued to search for the missing letter, running his hand along the part of the couch where the back met with the seat. "Why don't you have any children, Sadie? You're so good with Tyler and all, and I was just wondering. I mean, I know your husband passed, but . . ." He paused and looked up at her. "Sorry. It's none of my business."

"Ben and I wanted children very much. God didn't see fit to bless us with any before Ben died." This was a conversation she didn't want to have, especially with Kade.

"Well, you would have been a great mom." Kade smiled. "Maybe you still will someday. I understand you have a suitor."

"What?" Who had he been talking to?

"Your elderly friend, Jonas. He told me about a man from Texas who is coming to see you soon."

"Ah, yes," Sadie said. She didn't feel the need to elaborate and looked away from his questioning eyes.

"I hope it works out for you."

Maybe it was the way he said it, but somehow Sadie felt the comment was not genuine. "*Danki,*" she answered anyway, and then stood up. She attempted to put Tyler down, but he clung to her neck, so she balanced him on her hip.

Kade stood up, holding the missing *E.* He edged closer to her and gazed into her eyes in a way that he surely shouldn't. Her mouth went dry, and she could feel the flush in her neck traveling upward to her cheeks. When he gently grabbed her forearms, she couldn't have moved if she wanted to. But just when she was sure the unthinkable was about to happen, Kade's eyes drifted from hers. He leaned down and kissed his son on the head.

"Here's your letter, Tyler," he said, still holding one of Sadie's arms. He offered Tyler the letter with his other hand. Then he leaned around his son and kissed her on the cheek. His lips lingered against her skin, and Sadie's heart pounded and pulsed as a wave of panic overtook her. Even with Tyler safely between them, she abruptly pulled away. The feel of a man so close to her, his tenderness, his lips . . .

Oh no. Sadie took an abrupt step backward, and he was forced to drop his hand from her arm. She knew her eyes were reflective of the sinful thoughts racing through her mind. "Please leave," she said softly, refusing to look him in the eye.

"Sadie," he whispered. He took a step closer, but she stepped back further. "I guess, in my world, it's acceptable to make such a gesture of friendship. I'm sorry if I offended you in any way."

Sadie knew that it was not so much his gesture that was inappropriate, as much as her reaction to the feel of his lips on her cheek.

"I won't let it happen again." He stepped back and held his palms up.

She nodded, but wondered if he could keep his word. Or if she wanted him to.

And that thought terrified her.

It was an hour later when Kade loaded the suitcase in his car. He buckled Tyler in the backseat and couldn't stop thinking about Sadie. Evidently, his mild gesture of affection rattled her quite a bit. If she'd only known how badly he'd wanted to kiss her on the lips, she would have appreciated the restraint he used.

He pulled the car out of the barn, edged his way backward in the snow, and then turned the Mercedes around. Maybe he should have left earlier. Much earlier. Large snowflakes froze against the windshield and made it almost impossible to see. He turned up the heat and defrost in the car and headed down the driveway. When he turned onto Black Horse Road, he began to worry that this was a mistake. The snow was much worse today than it was the night they'd looked for Jonas.

He could feel his back tires spinning, and the trees on either side of the road blew wickedly in the wind.

And it's supposed to be worse tomorrow? He couldn't imagine. If he could make it to Lincoln Highway, the snow plows would be in force, and it shouldn't be too terribly bad on the way to the airport. He hoped.

Kade pushed on the gas in an effort to free his spinning tires. But he wasn't moving. "Oh, great!"

"Oh, great!" Tyler echoed from the backseat.

Kade didn't know anything about driving in this slush, but as he revved the engine a final time, one thing was clear. He wasn't going anywhere.

10

SADIE STEPPED ONTO THE PORCH TO RETRIEVE A LOG for the fire.

"*Ach!*" The biting wind nipped at her exposed cheeks and whipped through her cape as she heaved a log into her arms. She was grateful that Kade had replenished the wood stack on the porch before he left. He'd exited so abruptly with Tyler that she didn't have a chance to thank him.

After their encounter, Kade had told her he would be back to get his car and other personal items, but he wasn't sure when. Then he quickly left. But his tender kiss on her cheek replayed again and again in her mind, stirring things inside Sadie that brought on a wave of confusion.

A flurry of snow blew underneath the porch rafters and dusted her dark clothing with sprinkles of white powder. But it was nothing compared to the swirl of activity beyond the porch—whirlpools of wind and snow twirling beneath graying skies, as if churning out one last dance before the lights went out. She flung the door open to go back inside.

"Sadie!"

It was faint, but she heard it—a man's voice. She stopped before crossing the threshold, twisted her head around, and peered into the wintry mix, scanning the snow-covered land. Her eyes tried to focus on . . . *Kade?*

Adrenaline pumped through her and rendered her oblivious to the frigid air as Kade came into view amid the thickening snowfall, carrying Tyler. She dropped the log next to the pile. Inside, she fumbled as she pulled on her boots, gloves, and heavy coat, then bolted out the door and down the porch steps to meet Kade and Tyler.

"What happened?" He was white as the snow and looked like he might keel over any second from exhaustion. She couldn't even see Tyler all bundled up within the same brown blanket as before.

Sadie coaxed them inside, then led them to the fireplace. Kade gently pulled the blanket from around Tyler, who looked around. "Warm yourselves," she said.

Kade's teeth were chattering as he held his hands in front of the fireplace. Tyler began to pace the living room.

"The storm is already too bad. My car got stuck," Kade said. He shook his head. "No one is going anywhere in this. I waited too long to leave."

"I'll go make *kaffi* for us and cocoa for Tyler." Sadie unbuttoned her coat on the way to the kitchen and hung it on the rack. The storm had turned the sky prematurely dark, so she lit a lantern and placed it on the counter.

When she returned with their warm drinks, Kade was putting his gloves back on. "I need to go back to the car and get the suitcase. Tyler won't be happy for long without his letters, plus the black binder is in there, and everything else." He sighed with dread. "Can you keep an eye on Tyler?"

"Of course."

Tyler continued to shuffle aimlessly around the den, clapping his hands.

"It says in my notes clapping his hands is self-stimulatory behavior," Kade said.

Sadie wasn't familiar with Kade's *Englisch* words, but she nodded. The clapping seemed to be entertaining the boy.

"He is going to realize something is missing soon," Kade said. "I'll hurry back."

Sadie peered out the window. "It's almost completely dark outside, and yet still early."

Kade didn't respond, but seemed to be mentally preparing himself to venture back out into the storm. He rubbed his gloved hands together, took a deep breath, and pushed the door from the den open.

Sadie silently prayed that God would keep him safe. Then she brightened the room by placing two more lanterns on opposite sides of the den.

Kade was only gone for a few minutes when she noticed Tyler becoming agitated. The boy's lips curved downward, and he began to run his hands through his hair, causing the light-brown locks to stand straight up.

"Tyler, do you want to read for a bit?" Sadie sat down on the couch and hoped that Tyler would do the same. After a few minutes, he did. Sadie brought the lantern closer and handed him the Bible she kept on the table. She watched him slowly turn the pages, almost as if he was searching for something.

With the boy quiet and occupied, Sadie's thoughts turned to Kade and how different Kade's life would be now, raising his

son full-time. She tried to envision Kade's home, most likely
filled with expensive furniture and trinkets. Such a handsome
man, too, probably with many *Englisch* women pursuing him in
his home city.

She touched her cheek and recalled the gentle way he'd
kissed her, and then forced herself to think about Milo. *I'm tired
of being alone, Lord.* Spring wasn't long to come. Surely Milo would
be here.

But Sadie knew that it was more than just lack of a man in
her life. Questioning God's will was causing her to feel an empti-
ness that went beyond loneliness. Almost as if she were slowly
losing a treasured friend, or not nurturing a relationship that was
vital to her well-being.

Tyler was still flipping pages, and Sadie watched him begin to
turn them slower as he reached the book of Job, and then the
book of Psalms. He ran a finger along each line of tiny print, and
Sadie felt sad that Tyler probably had no understanding of what
he was reading, these words to live by. But she also knew that
God had a special place in His kingdom for children like Tyler,
a reserved seat for His precious little ones who perhaps didn't
have the privilege of understanding His love for them.

Sadie leaned her head back against the couch and sighed. She
felt guilty that she *was* able to understand God's love for her, but
yet she was seeing fit to question His will. Her heart was heavy,
and she feared she'd never find true happiness again. Hope
seemed to be slipping away, little by little. *I want to believe, Lord, that
happiness is coming for me. Please give me the courage and strength to always
know that Your will shall be done.*

Tyler shifted his weight on the couch, and Sadie turned her

head in his direction. He stopped scanning the pages, his small finger parked near the upper-left corner of page 349 of the Old Testament. "Be of good courage," Tyler said slowly. "And he shall strengthen your heart, all ye that hope in the Lord."

Sadie eyed the young boy with wondrous speculation as chill bumps rose on both her arms. "What?" she whispered, unsure if she'd heard him correctly. But Tyler's head was reburied in the pages of the Good Book.

She was still thinking about Tyler's statement when Kade returned. He heaved through the door, slinging snow everywhere, then dropped the suitcase and moved quickly toward the fireplace. "It is unbelievable outside," he said through chattering teeth. He pulled his gloves off and held his palms to the fire.

Sadie couldn't speak as her thoughts spun into a thick mass of bafflement. Speculations about Tyler's words swirled in her head, visions of Kade's kiss lingered in her mind, and she fought to ward off the worry in her heart.

Kade pulled off his coat and sat down on the couch beside Tyler. "Did everything go okay?" He steered his eyes in Sadie's direction.

"*Ya*." Sadie eased into one of the rockers, gave it a gentle push with her foot, and tried to clear her head.

Tyler sat up a little bit taller and glanced toward his father. "Hey, partner," Tyler said boldly.

Sadie giggled, glad for a distraction from her own thoughts. "That's cute, his words."

Kade gazed at his son with eyes longing for more than Tyler was able to give him, but yet tender and kind. Loving. "Yeah, I have a friend who says that all the time too," Kade said. He looked up at Sadie. "My friend Val seems to start every conversation with 'Hey, partner.'"

"Reckon it must be where Tyler heard it."

"No." Kade shook his head. "Val hasn't seen Tyler since Monica took him and left Los Angeles. So, not for about three years."

Tyler began to flip through the pages of the Bible, and Sadie reflected on what Tyler had said before Kade arrived, toying with the idea of mentioning it to Kade.

"Cool beans," Tyler whispered without looking up.

Sadie giggled again at the strange comment, but she thought she saw a troubled expression sweep across Kade's face.

Unease threatened to suffocate Kade as he realized that one of the few things he still held sacred—his friendship with Val— suddenly felt at risk.

"My friend Val says that too." Kade eyed Tyler suspiciously. "Tyler, do you know Val?"

"Val loves Mommy," Tyler said softly. His son didn't look up to see the stunned expression on his dad's face.

But Kade could feel Sadie's eyes on him, and for the moment, he chose not to look at her, fearful she'd see right through him at the rage in his mind—wicked thoughts directed at his dear friend Val. Had the only person he trusted betrayed him?

Kade recalled the conversation when Val told him that Monica was bringing Tyler to him. Val had sounded odd on the phone, but Kade hadn't thought too much about it. Then there was the call from Val about Monica's death. Val seemed shook-up, but

Kade wrote it off as concern about Kade's own situation, not feelings of loss that Val might be having of his own.

It was all clicking—Val's trips, his withdrawal from discussions outside of the business arena, and overall detachment from the friendship. Val wasn't mending his soul. He was planning to marry Kade's wife and raise Kade's son! *When was he going to tell me?*

Val's real estate development company was successful, yet considerably smaller than Kade's corporation. They'd often combined resources to score ahead of the competition, with Kade always pulling most of the load. And he'd never minded. Val was his friend. *Was.*

If Val had come to him, told him that he was in love with Monica—that would be one thing. At least he'd have known that Tyler would be raised by a good man. But to lie and sneak around like this . . .

"Hey, partner," Tyler repeated again with a giggle.

Kade rose abruptly, put his hands on hips, and began to pace. His heart pounded, his stomach churned, and he resisted the urge to verbalize the thoughts in his head.

"Your face is red," Sadie said cautiously.

"That happens when I'm mad, and I am madder than—" He caught himself as Sadie warned him with her eyes to choose his words carefully.

She rose from the rocker, sighed, and said, "'T'will be completely dark soon. Might be best to get Tyler to the cottage before nightfall."

Kade nodded, even though heading back to the cottage was the last thing he wanted to do. The weather was crummy. His mood was worse. Last thing he wanted to do was be alone with Tyler at the cottage. He started the bundling process. First, Tyler's coat and mittens, then his boots. Working slowly, he glanced at Sadie and decided, for once, to say what was really on his mind.

"Sadie." He watched her expression take on a hint of wariness, but Kade pressed on. "I'm having a really bad day." He quit struggling to push Tyler's wriggling foot into the boot, sighed in frustration, and sat on the couch. Tyler stood with one boot on but didn't seem bothered. Sadie waited for him to go on, but she clearly wasn't going to make any offers to console him. He took a deep breath. "Can we stay for a while?"

"I—I don't know if—"

"If it's appropriate," he finished.

"*Ya.*" She pulled her eyes from his—her big, blue eyes that, for an instant, seemed to defy her words. And it was enough to give Kade hope.

"We wouldn't stay long. I thought maybe we could have a cup of coffee and talk. We're both alone out here and could be for days evidently."

Her eyes locked with his in a way that confirmed Kade's initial thoughts. *She wants us to stay.* But Kade also knew that if he didn't work fast, she'd boot them out anyway. He grinned in a playful way. "It's cold outside."

She smiled back. "*Ya,* it is."

"Sadie, no one will ever know that we're unsupervised under the same roof together, I promise. No one is going to be out in this weather, and I won't tell a soul. I would really enjoy talking with you. My life is a mess." He shook his head. "But you seem to have a clearer picture of how to have a more peaceful existence. I'd be interested to hear about that."

"We live in very different worlds, Kade." Something in her tone sealed the deal, and Kade knew they would be staying.

Sadie lit more lanterns than were probably necessary in her kitchen. It was light and bright—nothing like the weather outside, Kade's mood, or the fear she felt at him being here. If Bishop Ebersol knew about this . . . But she knew her fear ran much deeper than getting caught by the bishop.

She tried not to think about it and pulled a container of beef stew from the freezer. As she ran it under the hot water from the sink, she wondered what Lillian would say about this. Of all her friends, Lillian was the most lenient when it came to the Old Order ways, but mostly because she hadn't grown up Amish. Sadie knew that Lillian still struggled with the rules from time to time, but never with her faith—an area Sadie seemed to be having trouble with these days.

Sadie remembered how vibrant she used to feel, how her spirited characteristics had brought her and Lillian together as friends in the first place. Lillian had the same zest for life that Sadie had. Until recently. Sadie's lighthearted spirit had darkened, and it scared her.

She bowed her head but cut her prayer short when she heard Kade returning from the bathroom with Tyler.

"Here is coffee for you, and some milk for Tyler," she said when Tyler and Kade walked into the room. She carried the semithawed stew to a pot on the stove and dumped it in. "Tyler, I think I might have some tapioca pudding in my refrigerator just for you." She turned her head to face him. "Would you like that?"

Tyler didn't respond and seemed more interested in the streams of light shining brightly throughout the kitchen.

"Wow. It's bright in here." Kade walked to the lantern Sadie had placed on her china hutch across the room. "Do you mind if I turn this one off?"

Her eyes grew wide. "*Ya!* I mean, no! Don't turn it off." She turned around in time to see that side of the room grow dark and Kade's brows rise in surprise. "It's all right, I reckon," she added, and then spun quickly around so Kade wouldn't see the pink in her cheeks.

"I can turn it back on, if you'd like," he said cautiously.

Sadie vigorously stirred the stew. "No. It's okay."

She glanced around the room. Darker than she would prefer. A tad too intimate.

Supper was uneventful, except that Tyler burst into laughter for no apparent reason on several occasions, which kept the mood light. And his outbursts had been contagious. Sadie and Kade both laughed along with the boy, and Sadie realized what a long time it had been since she'd had a good, hearty chuckle, the kind of sidesplitting laughter that Tyler's bubbly giggles brought out in her. *Such a sweet sound—a child's merriment,* she thought as she began to clear the dishes.

"Let me help you." Kade stood from the wooden bench.

"No, it's fine," Sadie said. Besides, she doubted Kade had cleared too many tables in his life. For that matter, neither had Ben. In her community, men didn't help with cooking or cleanup. It was work for the womenfolk. But Kade walked toward her with his and Tyler's plates and placed them in the sink.

"I don't remember the last time I've laughed like that," Kade said. He turned around, leaned against the counter, and watched Tyler playing with his lunch box full of letters at the kitchen table.

"Nor do I." Sadie added dishwasher soap to the running warm water. She turned briefly toward Kade, but Kade was still gazing at his son. "He is such a joy, Kade."

"He's so handsome to be so . . ." Kade sighed.

"Special? Is that the word you are searching for?" Sadie placed the first clean dish in the drainer. Kade didn't answer, but instead picked up the plate and began drying it with the dish towel nearby. "No, please. I'll do that," she said. Not only was it not a man's place to take on the chore; it wasn't *Kade's* place to act in such a familiar way.

But Kade finished drying the plate. "Where does it go?"

"Top shelf of the cupboard." Sadie pointed upward to the cabinet on the wall in between them. He edged closer to her, pulled the door open, and put the plate away. He smelled good. Like cologne she smelled on the *Englisch* men in town. Unease settled over her again.

Tyler ate most of his beef stew. Sadie was hoping both Tyler and Kade had forgotten about the tapioca pudding and that they would be on their way soon.

"Thanks for having us for dinner, Sadie. When I asked if we could stay, I didn't necessarily mean you had to cook for us." He smiled his crooked smile, the one that always showed a kinder side of him. "But that stew was fabulous."

"*Danki.*" Sadie glanced at Tyler in hopes that Kade would go join the boy at the kitchen table and not stand so close to her.

"My mom didn't cook a lot when I was growing up. But every

once in a while she'd take over the kitchen from Nelda, and when she did, she'd always cook a roast or stew." Sadie turned to face him as she dried her hands. He was far away, his eyes reflective of times past. "Your stew reminded me of those times when my mother cooked." He paused and looked toward Tyler. "They were good times."

"Was Nelda your servant?" Sadie couldn't imagine such a life.

Kade grinned. "*Servant* might be a strong word. She was our cook, and she also handled parties that my parents hosted, things like that. And she oversaw the other staff—my nanny, the house-keeper, and the yard guy."

Sadie didn't understand. "Then what did your mother do?" Right away, she realized the shock in her voice. "I mean . . . I, uh, didn't mean to be disrespectful. I just—"

Kade chuckled. "It's all right. I know what you meant. And, believe it or not, she stayed really busy. She was involved in a lot of charity events, played tennis twice a week, hosted a literary club once a month, and spent a lot of time traveling with my father."

"Oh," Sadie said.

"It must sound like a shallow way to live to you." Kade cringed a bit.

"*Ach*, no. I would never judge." She recalled Lillian's comments about that very thing, and then added, "I'm sure your *mamm* is a *gut* woman." But how fulfilling could a life like that be? Sadie wondered. Some of her most gratifying moments had been serving Ben his meals, taking care of their home, and growing her own vegetables. And she continued to dream of the day she could mother children of her own.

"Maybe we could have our tapioca pudding in the den

where it's warmer? I noticed you trembling." Kade walked to the kitchen table.

Sadie didn't move for a moment. She knew that her trembling had nothing to do with being cold.

"Tyler, let's put your letters in the lunch box and take them into the den," Kade said. Tyler looked like a fit might be coming, but he allowed Kade to move him into the den.

"I'll be in with the pudding shortly." She pulled the container from the refrigerator and filled three bowls.

"Do you have all these people in your home in the city?" she asked when she handed Kade and Tyler each a bowl of pudding.

"What?"

"These nannies, cooks, and other servants." She didn't wait for an answer, but went to go retrieve her own bowl. Then she took a seat in the rocker across from the couch where Kade and Tyler sat.

"I do have people who live in my home and help with things. I work a lot," Kade said.

"Will these people take care of Tyler when you return home?"

"I suppose so," Kade said after he finished a spoonful of pudding. Then he shook his head, as if something had suddenly angered him. "My so-called friend Val is supposedly checking into someone to care for Tyler."

"This man is no longer your friend, no?"

"No," Kade huffed. "But let's not talk about that. Tell me about you. Parents? Brothers and sisters?"

"*Mei* parents have both passed. *Mei mamm* when I was young, and *mei daed* died a few years back. I have one sister who lives in Ohio."

"My father died when I was nineteen."

Sadie waited for him to mention his mother and whether or not he had brothers and sisters, but he took another bite of pudding. Tyler was starting to get restless, Sadie noticed. He handed Kade his empty bowl and began to bang his head against the back of the couch.

"I guess he's getting tired," Kade said.

Sadie stood from the rocker. "I'll take those." She reached for Kade's bowl as he took the last bite, and then she grabbed Tyler's empty bowl from the coffee table.

They'll be leaving now, she thought as she headed to the kitchen. She washed the bowls and put them in the rack to dry.

She rounded the corner back to the den, prepared to help Kade bundle Tyler up so that they could be on their way, although it didn't appear they were going anywhere. Tyler's head was in his father's lap.

"He must be really tired," Kade said. "Usually he makes it until eight o'clock." He glanced at his watch. "It's only seven."

Sadie slowly backed her way into the rocker.

Tyler's eyes closed, and Kade leaned back against the couch, giving Sadie the strangest look. "You're nervous to be around me, aren't you?"

"What?" She fought the tremble in her voice.

"I mean, I know you're worried that someone will find out that we spent time together, but I also think I make you nervous in general." He paused and tilted his head to one side. "Why is that?"

Sadie sat up straighter. "I assure you, Kade, I am not nervous." He was arrogant, but intuitive as well.

He eased Tyler's head off of his lap, and then he leaned

forward with his elbows on his knees and folded his hands together. "Sadie, I appreciate you letting us stay."

Yes, well . . . now it is time to go.

"And I think I know why you're nervous," he went on.

"I'm not nervous, Kade," she said again with a shrug.

"Sadie, I just want to talk to you. Actually, there is something specific I want to talk to you about." He paused and took a deep breath. "I'm not here to come on to you or anything like that. I'm not going to try to kiss you or—"

She jumped up. "You need to leave, Kade."

"Whoa." He held his palms toward her. "I'm sorry. I just thought you'd like to know that I have no interest in anything but friendship."

"Of course I know that," she snapped in a whisper. "But we don't talk of such things."

He grinned. "Okay, I won't say the word *kiss*." He emphasized the last word.

Sadie put her hands on her hips. "Are you making fun of me?"

His face grew somber. "No. I would never do that. I respect you more than probably any woman I've ever met. Really. You're not like the women I know. And I apologize again. Can we please sit here and talk for a while? I'll put another log on the fire, and maybe we can have a cup of coffee and talk. There really is something I'd like to talk to you about—something Tyler said to me."

Sadie sat back down. She needed to sit down. The conversation had taken a turn that was not fit, but even more bothersome was that Kade said he had no interest in her outside of friendship. Suddenly she wanted to ask him, "Why not?" It was a fleeting thought, but it had popped into her head for reasons she didn't understand. She opened her mouth to tell him that he must leave.

Kade spoke first, though. "Do you believe that God can talk to us through other people? Tyler quoted a Bible verse to me yesterday, and it gave me chills." He shook his head. "It was so perfect for what I was feeling at the time, that I can't stop thinking about what he said, and—"

Sadie had unconsciously put her hand over her mouth.

"Are you okay?" Kade asked.

She dropped her hand to her lap and nodded. "Go on," she said as she thought about whether or not she would tell Kade that Tyler had also quoted a scripture to her earlier, at a most appropriate time.

"The funny thing is," Kade said, "I haven't been on very friendly terms with God lately. I've been distant from any kind of relationship with Him for several years. My faith, or lack thereof, was one of the reasons I came here. Sort of." He shrugged. "Anyway, does that make sense? Have you ever heard of anything like this happening?"

Sadie smiled. "As a matter of fact, I have."

And for the first time since she'd met Kade Saunders, Sadie didn't feel nervous. She stood from the rocker. "Why don't I go make us some coffee?"

11

KADE ADDED ANOTHER LOG TO THE FIRE WHILE SADIE prepared coffee in the kitchen. The fresh-brewed aroma permeated the house, complementing the comfort of Sadie's home. He felt surprisingly at ease here, despite the austere decor and lack of electricity.

Tyler slept soundly on the couch, only his eyes and nose visible under the quilt Sadie had spread over him. Kade was glad he wasn't spending the evening alone at the cottage while Tyler slept. He was anxious to know more about Sadie. Her simplistic life intrigued him, but so did the woman herself. Kade suspected that, despite her nervousness around him, Sadie was more complex than she appeared.

He was tempted to excuse himself, go out on the porch, and make an overdue phone call to Val, but that would only solidify what he already knew to be true. Plus it was too cold to venture outside for anything more than another log for the fire.

"Here you go," Sadie said when she walked into the den, holding two cups of coffee.

"Thanks." Kade accepted the coffee and took a seat in one of the two rockers across from the couch. Sadie sat down in the other chair, and then sipped from her cup. For a few moments, he couldn't pull his gaze from her.

Sadie's blue eyes twinkled in the dim light, but Kade recognized the hints of sadness beneath her radiant glow. He'd seen those eyes in the mirror—the look of loneliness. Her ivory skin, void of any makeup, was flawless, and her lips had retained their youthful color. Loose strands of wavy, red hair wisped against her cheeks from underneath the cap on her head.

The women Kade knew spent a fortune in professional services to render a look that came naturally to Sadie. And she wasn't even trying to be beautiful. He'd never wanted more to tell a woman how lovely she was than at this moment, but she looked up, and her eyes met Kade's. He knew he would alienate her if he voiced his thoughts, probably even win an escort to the door.

"So, about my question," he began instead. "Has anything like what I described, the thing with Tyler, ever happened to you? It left me feeling . . . strange."

Sadie took another sip of her coffee. She seemed more relaxed, he thought. "*Ya*, today."

Then she smiled, broadly. So much so that Kade wanted to smile back at her, but he had questions, so many questions. "What do you mean, *today?*"

She crossed her legs beneath a dark-blue dress and black apron. Only black leather shoes and socks of the same color were visible. "I had the same thing happen to me today." She pushed the rocker into motion with her foot and seemed to be challenging him to question her further.

"Today?" Kade twisted his mouth to one side and narrowed his eyes. "*Today* someone quoted a scripture to you?"

"*Ya.*" She pushed back a strand of hair. "And, like you, it happened at a time when I most needed to be reminded of God's love for us."

"Really? So, this scripture that someone read—"

"It wasn't *someone*, Kade," she interrupted. Her eyes met his in a way that made Kade anxious. Something big was coming. "It was *Tyler.*"

It had been a long time since Kade had felt a jolt like the one Sadie had just given him. "What?"

"I think you heard me." Her tone was strong, but her eyes soft. "I had just said a prayer about . . . about something important to me. Tyler read a scripture that seemed to be speaking directly to me."

Kade could feel the wrinkles on his forehead deepening as he narrowed his eyes in her direction. "Well, these have to be coincidences, right?"

"What do you think?" She raised her brows, challenging him to give this some extra thought.

"I told you, I've rather strayed from my faith for the last few years. It's hard for me to imagine it as anything more than a coincidence." He paused, shrugged. "But if the same thing happened to you, maybe it's plausible." Then he paused again. "No. No, I don't believe that's how God works. Tyler read something and simply repeated it."

"Then why are you so bothered by it?"

He shook his head in defeat. "I don't know."

"Who are we to judge how God works His miracles?" Sadie's glow dimmed. "And who are we to question His will?"

"I guess I question it sometimes."

She took a deep breath. "In my community, we believe that all things are of God's will and are not to be questioned."

"Well, that's impossible." He took a sip of his coffee. "When your husband died at such a young age, was that God's will?"

Crud. Why did he have to go and blurt that out? Her eyes glazed over almost instantly. "Oh, Sadie. I'm sorry. I should have never—"

"It's all right." She rapidly blinked away any sign of tears. "At a time of mourning, I think it's only human to question God's will for a short time. I grieved for my husband, and it was harder for me to see God's goodness during those first few hours."

"*Hours?* What about *months? Years?* I haven't been able to see His goodness for three years, since we found out that Tyler . . . that Tyler was autistic."

"He is a perfect little boy, Kade," she said with such conviction that Kade wanted to believe her.

He kicked his rocker into sync with her rocker and stared at the fire, filled with recollections of Tyler's birth, how proud he'd been, and how he believed Tyler to be the perfect boy. And then, all his hopes and dreams were ripped from him two years later. "He'll never, you know, *be* anything." He turned and looked hard at Sadie. "Please, Sadie, don't get me wrong. I love my son, and I always will. But for me to accept his autism as God's will—well, I can't do that. He'll never play baseball or any other sports. And that's okay. I'm not a huge sports fan anyway. But he'll never do any of the things other kids can do—like ride a bicycle, for example, or climb a tree, or—"

"How do you know these things?"

"He can barely stay focused on anything for more than a few minutes, and he's uncoordinated." He adjusted his sharp tone. "He'll never know what it's like to be in love, or how much I love him, for that matter."

"How do you know?"

Kade shook his head. The woman was beginning to frustrate him. "Because I just know."

Sadie could see the pain in his expression. She thought for a moment about how to help Kade to see things in a different perspective.

"Kade, he'll also never know about murder and crime, or other *baremlich* things that plague the world. And Tyler will always be pleased by the simplest of things in life, like a bowl of tapioca pudding. He'll never suffer grief as we know it, mourn a dear pet's departure, or question a friend's betrayal. Tyler will rejoice in the *gut* moments that he can understand, but not lose himself in the bad moments, like so many of us do."

When Kade continued to stare at her but didn't say anything, she went on. "Kade, if you can believe that all things are of His will, a calm will sweep over you and bring a peacefulness that only comes from God's love."

Sadie felt the sting of her own words, knowing she hadn't been living by what she told Kade. She pulled her eyes from his gaze and sighed.

"Do you really believe that?" He sounded so skeptical. How was she going to make Kade understand when her own ugly doubts were flailing about?

But she sat up taller and confidently said, "*Ya*, I really do believe that." *And I will stop having doubts.*

"I have to admit," Kade began cautiously, "when Tyler quoted that passage from the Bible to me, at that moment I felt the presence of God, and I think I might have had a glimpse of the peacefulness you're talking about." He paused and rubbed his chin. "And for you to have had a similar experience with Tyler—I don't know. It puts a whole new spin on this."

They both sat quietly for a few minutes and stared at the crackling fire as orange embers drifted upward and out of sight. Sadie could hear the thrashing wind beating against the house, and she could feel the cold air sneaking in around the window-pane behind her.

She was glad the conversation had quieted. Kade and she were unequally yoked, and it wasn't her job to minister to him. But no sooner had the thought registered when she realized that by ministering to Kade, she'd been ministering to herself as well.

"It's something to think about," Kade finally said. Then he cocked his head slightly. "How do you do it? Live here?" His voice was tender as he motioned his hand around the room. "Like this?"

"It's the only life I've ever known. I don't need all the material things and conveniences you have in your world."

"But aren't you curious about what you might be missing?" Kade asked. "For example, I know you enjoy listening to music, but yet you don't own a radio. Wouldn't you like to experience the things in our world?"

This was exactly what her parents had warned her about. She could recall her father's words. "To be unequally yoked with nonbelievers will tempt you to stray from our ways and our beliefs," he'd said when she was young.

"I have experienced as much as I need to in your world," she said firmly. "When an Amish teenager turns sixteen, we begin our *rumschpringe*—a running-around period which lasts until we choose to be baptized into the faith or leave the Old Order. During this time, we do many of the things *Englisch* teenagers do. Go to the movies, ride around in cars, visit the shopping malls. Things like that."

"And, obviously, you chose to stay. Have you ever regretted it?"

"Never. Not one day of my life." Her faith might be slipping a tad, but she'd never wanted to live in the *Englisch* world. "We live a simple, mostly uncomplicated life. Can you say the same thing?"

Kade rolled his eyes. "No, I can't. My life has been complicated for as long as I can remember. I wish it was different." He shook his head.

"Then change things."

"I guess in my own way I'm trying, little by little. Coming here was supposed to be a start in that direction, time to get away from everything and everyone, get some perspective. But you see how well that went. My life followed me. First Monica showed up . . ." He looked toward the ground. "Then her death, and then this afternoon I find out that my closest friend has been spending time with Monica, making plans behind my back."

"Do you know this for sure?"

"Yeah, I guess I do. I haven't confirmed it, but some things are starting to make sense now."

Sadie was quiet for a moment, then said cautiously, "If this is true, I bet your friend is hurting."

Kade didn't answer.

"Sometimes when we see past our own pain and into the heart of another, our own self-healing begins."

Kade looked up and turned toward her. "Can you see into my heart, Sadie?"

"I . . . I'm sorry if I offended you. I just—"

"You did not offend me at all, Sadie. I'm serious. Can you see into my heart? What do you see? I'd like to know."

Sadie wasn't comfortable talking to him about such things, but she should have thought about that long before the conversation became so intense. She recalled her own words—and wondered if she could see past her own pain and into Kade's heart. She decided to try.

"I see a man who has been blessed with great wealth, but who is as unhappy a man as I've ever seen." She paused to see him hanging on her every word. "But every now and then, I glimpse a different man, the man you long to be."

Kade stared at her, as if in awe. He let out a heavy sigh. "You are exactly right." Then he surprised her. "What about you, Sadie? I think you, too, have been blessed with great wealth, maybe not monetarily—but a wealth of spirit and faith. But you don't fool me either. I see the sadness in your eyes as well. You do a much better job of masking it than I do, but it's there."

Sadie turned away from him, afraid he'd see her blinking back the tears. "You are exactly right," she echoed. She turned to face him, and they sat staring into each other's eyes.

Then Kade smiled. "If you could do anything in the world, what would it be?"

"What?" She couldn't help but feel lighter suddenly.

"If you could do anything in the world, go anywhere, have anything, Amish or otherwise, what would it be?" Kade rested his elbow on the arm of the rocker and cupped his chin. "Anything."

"You are serious, no?" What a wonderful question, she thought, and an easy one to answer.

Kade nodded. "And if money were of no concern."

She smiled. "I would have a spouse to love and children to care for."

"So, the old adage that money can't buy happiness rings true for you?" His voice was kind, tender. "Of all the things in the world, you'd choose the love of family."

"*Ya.*" She twisted in her chair to face him. "What would you choose?"

And much to her surprise, he said, "The exact same thing."

"You are halfway there." She nodded toward the precious child sleeping on the couch.

Kade rubbed his chin for a moment and stared at Tyler. "Yes," he finally said. "You're right." Then he smiled. "I've never known anyone like you, Sadie."

"Nor have I known anyone like you, Kade." She returned the smile, and they sat silently again, but there was no mistaking the looks passing between them, and it sounded alarms for Sadie. "It's getting late," she said.

"You're right. I'm sorry. I didn't mean for us to stay this long." He stood up and moved toward Tyler.

"Let the boy sleep," Sadie said. "It's too cold to take him outside, and it would be a shame to wake him up. I reckon you can come for him in the morning."

"That would be great." Kade peeked behind the closed blind toward the cottage. Gusty wind continued to mound snow up against the house. "I guess I'm going to miss Monica's funeral."

"I'm sorry. The worst of the weather will be here tomorrow and not start clearing until Saturday or Sunday, and I suspect we might not be able to travel for a day or two after that. My friends and I decided to close my shop until Wednesday."

Kade continued to look out the window. "Wow. I've never seen anything like this. Look at the snow piling against the house." He stepped aside, and Sadie took a brief look but quickly backed away. Kade let the blind go and turned to face her. "What time should I come for Tyler in the morning? I mean, I'll come early. I don't want you to have to feed him breakfast." Kade grimaced. "Breakfast can be an ordeal with Tyler some mornings."

Sadie couldn't remember the last time she'd cooked a big meal for breakfast, with eggs, bacon, homemade biscuits, jams, and jellies. An excitement she hadn't felt in a while rose to the surface. "Breakfast will be at seven o'clock. I will cook for you and Tyler."

"Really?" Kade smiled. "I think that would be great."

But then Sadie began to worry. "Although I . . . I don't cook fancy, Kade. Like those items you have for breakfast. I can make eggs, bacon, biscuits, and—"

"Perfect!"

"Do you like such foods?" She questioned him with her eyes and wondered if he was just saying so.

He chuckled. "I honestly don't remember the last time I had a traditional breakfast. I don't cook, so those breakfast cereals are about all I can handle in the morning. I would absolutely love what you mentioned. It would be a treat."

"All right. *Gut.*" She began to wonder what types of jams and jellies she had, whether she would prepare scrambled eggs and bacon or make omelets. This gave her something to look forward to in the morning. Company for the breakfast meal.

Kade pulled on his coat and gloves. "Then I guess I will see you in the morning," he said.

It was an awkward moment. Even Sadie felt like a hug was in order, but neither moved forward. Instead, Kade turned to open the door. "Bye," he said.

Sadie watched him trudge out into the storm, fighting the wind as his boots sank calf-deep in the snow. She didn't remember ever seeing the weather this bad. Hard to believe that it would be even worse by morning.

Kade couldn't get into the cottage fast enough. He could barely feel his numbed cheeks. Plus, Val had a phone call coming. He flipped the switch on the thermostat in the kitchen, glad to have central heat in the cottage. Sadie's home had been warm enough with the roaring fire and portable gas heaters, but Kade had let the fire die out since he was leaving town—or thought he was—and it was more than a little chilly.

He peeled off the heavy coat he'd borrowed the other night

and hung it on the back of a kitchen chair. What a storm. He'd never seen anything like this, even in all his travels. Kade eased onto the couch and untied his tennis shoes, thankful the black boots had kept them dry. He propped his feet up on the coffee table and looked around the room. It was eerily quiet, but the wind howled with a vengeance outside. In the dark, he could hear icy branches snapping, and it sounded like something flew against the barn. How nice it would have been to curl up on the couch with Tyler in the coziness of the farmhouse. But mention of that would have certainly scared poor Sadie to death.

It was hard to believe that there were women like her around. Honest, decent, and with a goodness he didn't remember seeing in a woman. Sadie was dedicated to living the life she spoke about, driven by her beliefs and a real understanding about a relationship with God. Strong in her faith—and beautiful. He shook his head. Why couldn't he have found a woman like that, instead of the Monicas and Alicias of the world, who were only after his money? But he had to admit, his heart ached over Monica's death. So young. And Tyler's mother. If Kade was honest with himself, he'd have to admit that having Tyler full-time scared him. As much as he wanted to know his son, he also knew it would truly be a labor of love. And what if he failed at it? How would he know if he was a good father?

He pulled out his cell phone, prepared to tear into Val, but Sadie's words kept sounding in his head: "Sometimes when we see past our own pain and into the heart of another, our own self-healing begins."

Kade stared at the phone.

12

LIZZIE AWOKE IN THE WEE HOURS OF FRIDAY MORNING
to the sound of Jonas's voice.

"Lizzie, you all right?"

She rolled over in bed and fumbled for her glasses on the table
next to her. Then she put on gold-rimmed spectacles and blinked
her eyes until the bedside clock came into focus. *Three fifteen. What
in the world?* Her hip popped as she felt around the table for her
flashlight—amid the bottles of pills, tissues, and a glass of water.
When her hand landed around the base of her flashlight, she
turned it on and found the walkie-talkie.

"I'm here, Jonas," she said wearily. "Are you and Sarah Jane all
right?"

It took a few moments before Jonas answered. *"Ya.* But I
woke up worried. You oughta not be there by yourself, Irma
Rose."

Lizzie hung her head and sighed. Then pushed the Talk button. "It's Lizzie, Jonas."

"I know. And it be *baremlich* outside. Don'tcha be goin' out
there."

She grinned. *Why would I be going outside in a blizzard at three in the
morning?* "I won't, Jonas."

162

"*Gut.* Huggy bear don't wanna find you all froze up and buried in the snow."

Lizzie laughed out loud, now wide-awake. She loved when Jonas referred to himself as huggy bear, a pet name he'd chosen for himself. "All right, *huggy bear.* I promise not to go outdoors."

"I'll be seeing ya, Lizzie."

She smiled. *All right, my love.* Her finger was on the Talk button, but Jonas spoke again before she had a chance to push it. "Lizzie?"

"*Ya?*"

She waited for a while, but no response. "Jonas? You all right?" she finally asked.

"I sure am missin' you."

Lizzie touched her palm to her chest and closed her eyes. *Oh my.* "I miss you, too, Jonas."

"Good night, Lizzie."

"Good night."

She set the walkie-talkie back on the table but didn't lie back down. She was fully awake now, and thoughts of Jonas swirled in her head. Lizzie fluffed her pillows behind her and sat up a little straighter. Her hip was aching a bit, and her bedroom was a mite cold, but inside she was warm and fuzzy. She dreamed of Jonas asking her to marry him someday. So many times, Lizzie had fought the urge to tell him how much she loved him, but Jonas was the type of man who needed to do things in his own time. And he'd loved Irma Rose so much. Lizzie knew it was hard for him to give his heart to another.

But tonight he said he misses me. She knew that was a big step for Jonas. He teased her a lot and referred to himself as huggy bear more than she actually called him by the name, but he'd never said he missed her or anything to hint that he might be feeling what Lizzie was feeling.

Sadie flipped the bacon in the skillet, checked on the biscuits in the oven, and then stirred the eggs. Tyler was eating a bowl of tapioca pudding at the kitchen table. She hoped Kade wouldn't mind, but when Tyler woke up on the couch, he had been confused, and the tapioca pudding calmed him down. Sadie was up and cooking before Tyler awoke, but when he stumbled into the kitchen, Sadie could tell by the look on his face that he was not a happy little boy. And one thing Sadie knew to be true—tapioca pudding made Tyler happy.

She glanced over her shoulder at Kade's son. A handsome fellow for sure. Sadie had placed several jars of jam on the table, and Tyler was busy arranging them in a circle between bites of pudding. She smiled. No harm done. She'd been careful to keep knives off the table, or anything else Tyler might be tempted to play with, since Sadie still wasn't sure of his habits.

Sadie prepared some oatmeal, after deciding against scrapple. The mushy mix of cornmeal and flour wasn't for everyone. She recalled when Lillian first arrived in Lancaster County, before she converted. When Lillian found out the traditional dish also contained leftover pieces of pig, she wouldn't touch it—and *still* wouldn't, to this day. "I'm not eating pig guts, toes, and ears," Lillian had said firmly.

Sadie rather liked it. But then, she'd grown up eating it, like most of the people in her community.

"How is your pudding, Tyler? Is *gut*, no?" She wiped her hands on her apron and walked toward him, but he didn't acknowledge the question. He continued to rearrange the jars of jam; then he'd take a bite of pudding, and then start all over again. But all the while, he was smiling. And Sadie was too. The smell of breakfast cooking, a guest for breakfast, a child in the house—it all felt so nice. She even found herself humming.

She walked to the kitchen window and looked outside. The only thing that threatened to put a damper on her spirit was the weather. It was frightful outside, and as the newspaper had predicted, much worse this morning. During the night, she heard branches snapping and loud noises that sounded like small items being tossed around or slammed against the barn or house. She'd tried to secure everything in the barn before the storm, but maybe she'd missed some things.

Blustery winds continued to swirl the heavy snow, burying everything in a blanket of white. Thankfully, no trees grew near her house. In the distance, she could see toppled branches covered in thick ice, the limbs quickly being buried by a mix of ice and snow. Sadie had never seen the weather like this. She began to wonder if Kade would be able to make it the short distance from the cottage to the farmhouse.

She heard a knock, and the kitchen door opened.

"This is unbelievable!" he said when he came in. "I wasn't sure I was going to get here before I froze to death. I can't feel my cheeks."

Sadie put her hands on her hips. "Kade, there is a face covering inside your hood. Why didn't you pull it around your face?" *He really doesn't know anything about cold weather.*

He shrugged, then smiled. "I don't know."

Sadie swiveled toward the oven. "I need to stir the eggs." She could hear his footsteps behind her.

"Hey, Tyler." Kade took a seat on the bench across from Tyler. "What are you doing?"

Sadie pulled the spoon from the skillet and placed it on the counter, then turned to face Kade and Tyler. "He's been having a *gut* time rearranging the jams and jellies," she said. Kade turned toward her and smiled.

Why did her heart have to flutter so when he was near?

After breakfast, Kade helped Sadie clear the table—again—as if it was the most common task in the world. She'd asked him not to, but he'd insisted—again. Kade had carried on all through breakfast about how delicious the meal was, and Sadie knew she'd blushed more than once.

She didn't have much to do this time of year, even more so with the weather this way, but Kade didn't appear in much of a hurry to leave either. Once the kitchen was clean, he sat down on the rug in the den with his son and made words with Tyler's plastic letters. Sadie excused herself for a moment.

She was returning from the bathroom, and as she neared the den, she heard Kade's voice.

"Tyler, I'm going to make a good life for you," he said. "I'm going to be a good father."

His words touched Sadie, and she knew she would continue to pray for both of them, even when they were gone.

Kade glanced up at her when she walked into the den. "We're making words. Do you want to join us?"

This is not the same man who showed up a few weeks ago, Sadie thought, as she sat down on the rug across from Kade.

"My mother loved to play Scrabble when I was a kid," Kade said. "I know this is a far cry from Scrabble, but playing with Tyler like this reminds me of those times. It was one of the few things we did together, usually on a rainy afternoon when I got home from school and couldn't go outside to play, and she couldn't play tennis and didn't have any other commitments."

"Is your *mamm* . . . ?"

"Alive?" Kade pulled his eyes from hers. "No, she died right before Tyler was born. Breast cancer."

"I'm sorry." Sadie could see that it was a tender subject for Kade. "Do you have brothers and sisters?"

"No. I'm an only child." Kade leaned in toward Tyler. "Guess you will be, too, buddy."

They sat quietly for a few moments, and Sadie thought about Kade's comment. *Does he assume he will never remarry and have more children?* It was customary to remarry quickly in her community, after the death of a spouse, but perhaps the *Englisch* did things differently.

After a while, Kade opened up to her in a way that surprised Sadie. He told her how his father had developed Alzheimer's disease as a fairly young man. That it was similar to the confusion that Jonas was having, which explained how Kade had known how to handle Jonas at the pub. He said that, just like Jonas, his father would be lucid some of the time, but then would get disoriented, often while he was at work. When that happened, he would leave and later call Kade's mother from somewhere unfamiliar and tell her he didn't know how he got there.

He went on to tell her that when he came home from college one Friday night, his mother told him that his dad had been missing since the day before. Police, neighbors, employees—everyone was looking for Paul Saunders. Kade ended up being the one to find his father in a field behind a neighbor's estate the next day. He described what his father looked like after being dead almost two days in the hundred-degree heat. The police believed that he'd gotten lost, couldn't find his way back, and ended up having heatstroke. It was a heartbreaking story, and Sadie couldn't imagine what it must have been like for Kade.

"Do you know I never told Monica about that?" He shook his head. "I mean, she knew a little bit about what happened, but I never felt comfortable enough to talk about it."

Sadie was touched by the comment and realized that she felt unusually comfortable talking with Kade as well. An *Englischer* with whom she had nothing in common. She shared her story about her father's death, although thankfully, it wasn't as dramatic—a heart attack. Not long after that, she told him about Ben. Kade listened with compassion and sympathy. By lunchtime, she and Kade were clearly in a new place. It was bewildering, yet wonderful. She hadn't talked to anyone like this since Ben. And, if she was honest with herself, she and Ben seldom had such deep conversations. Their relationship had brought her comfort and reassurance, knowing she was loved unconditionally, but they rarely spoke about emotional matters. Perhaps they'd never needed to.

Kade had suggested that maybe Tyler would like to draw, and Sadie had rounded up a pad of paper and some pens. Circles. Tyler liked drawing circles, and he occupied himself for a bit longer.

"I called my friend Val," he said as they sipped on a cup of hot cocoa. His face scrolled into a frown, and Sadie waited for him to go on. "But I didn't tell him I knew about him and Monica." He paused. "I'm not for sure, and I think I'd like to keep it that way.

Besides . . ." He took a deep breath. "I've known Val for a long time, and I could hear in his voice that he is suffering."

"That must have been very hard to do, no?" Sadie couldn't understand the life Kade led, but she was appreciating her life more and more. Guilt once again rose to the surface as she realized that, despite her own suffering, she'd been blessed in so many ways.

"It wasn't as difficult as I thought it would be. At first, I wanted to lash out at Val. And a few weeks ago, I would have." Kade stood up and grabbed a log from beside the fireplace and tossed it on the fire. "But something about being here, about spending time with Tyler, with you—" He twisted around to face her for a moment, and then returned to the fire, pushing the wood with the poker. "I'm questioning what my entire life has been about. And the kind of person I've been and who I might become." Then he chuckled. "Sounds nuts, huh?"

"No," Sadie said in a somber voice. "I don't think so. It's only natural sometimes to question one's place in this world."

He walked back over to where Sadie and Tyler were sitting on the floor, but he didn't sit down. Tyler toyed with Kade's shoestring, and Kade zoned in on Sadie, a serious expression on his face. "Do you have any idea how much money I have?"

What an odd question. "No, I do not."

Kade grinned. "And you don't care in the least, either, do you?"

Sadie wasn't sure if he was angry or grateful. But he was right. "No," she said simply. In his defense, and to be truthful, she added, "But money is measured in our community, just like in the *Englisch* world. Just not in the same way."

"What do you mean?" Kade sat back down in time for Tyler to hand him a picture of dozens of tiny circles. "This is great, Tyler." He reached out to touch the boy, but Tyler pulled away. Sadie thought about how Tyler had sat in her lap earlier. *Perhaps it's because I am a woman.* But she could see the hurt in Kade's eyes. She took a deep breath and thought out her response.

"There are those in our Old Order district who have more money than others. For example, Elam Lapp has a fine carpentry business. He makes a *gut* living. For Christmas, he gave his seventeen-year-old daughter a solid piece of oak furniture." Sadie paused when Tyler handed her a picture similar to the one he made for Kade. "*Danki,* Tyler." She smiled at Tyler, and then turned back to Kade. "But John King gave his daughter, Ellie, of the same age, an oak box to put on her bedside table, for keeping her personal items in. Not worth nearly as much money, but I bet Ellie found it equally as pleasing, because her *daed* made it for her." Sadie paused. "We do not value money the same way as the *Englisch*. It is necessary for survival, but one man's wealth is not weighed against another's."

"Maybe we're not as different as you think. I'm sure there are similar situations among *Englisch* families."

Sadie couldn't help but wonder what the extent of Kade's wealth was. "Is it rude to ask you how much money you do have?" She raised her brow.

Kade laughed. "I suppose you would think it silly if I said I didn't know?"

"*Ya,* I would." And she meant it. She knew how much money she had, or didn't have, at all times. "We might be plain, Kade, but we know that it takes money to survive. It used to be that our men worked the farms and made a *gut* living, but now only a few are able to do that. Womenfolk help out by working in bakeries and selling jams, jellies, quilts, and crafts. Our way of life is changing a bit, but we still adhere to the *Ordnung* and try to stay as disconnected from the *Englisch* world as we can."

"Why is that, anyway?"

"What?"

"Why do you have to stay disconnected from our world? How does that benefit your community?"

"To be unequally yoked is threatening to our people." This was a conversation he most likely wouldn't understand, but Sadie didn't understand much of what Kade said or believed either.

"How do I threaten you?" He leaned back on his elbows, crossed his ankles. Kade Saunders looked most comfortable in her home.

"I don't question my faith, Kade. Nor do I question the faith of those in my community. We *know* what we believe and practice it in our daily lives." Sadie felt a pang of conscience but pressed on. "That's not to say that someone in the *Englisch* world does not have the same faith that we do. We just don't know for sure. Here in our community, we know, with no doubts. There is no threat that someone will steer us from what we know to be true. It would be unheard-of."

Kade was still resting on his elbows. "So you don't want anyone from the *Englisch* world to tempt you to leave here?"

"No, that's not exactly it. We have an opportunity to leave during our *rumschpringe*. If we choose to leave prior to our baptism, we will not face a shunning. Once we are baptized, we have vowed to God a life dedicated to serving Him by following the *Ordnung*.

We don't feel temptation to leave, but if we are unequally yoked, nonbelievers can cause us to question our faith, and questioning of God's will is not something we believe in." Again, Sadie's guilt came to the forefront, fueled by her own lack of trust in God's will lately.

"So anything that happens, no matter how bad, is God's will?" Kade narrowed his brows and pressed his lips together for a moment. "I admire your ability to believe that."

"There is nothing admirable about it. To question God's will is not something we ever . . ." Sadie turned away from him. How could she continue to preach to him when she was repeatedly failing at this very thing?

She drew in a deep breath, gathered herself, and turned back toward him. "Perhaps I am not the person to tell you of these things."

Kade smiled, his eyes brimming with tenderness and compassion. "I think you are just the right person."

Sadie lifted herself from the floor and walked to the window, confused by how easily she had shared her most intimate feelings with Kade. *He might be* Englisch, Sadie thought, *but he is still a man.* She had been guilty of returning Kade's tender gazes. It had been hard not to, after all they had shared this morning. But she was wrong to encourage any thoughts that might hint at more than friendship.

She stared out the window and wondered if Kade was having any ideas about going back to the cottage. The storm didn't seem any worse, but it didn't seem any better either. Sadie looked over her shoulder at Kade. The man didn't look like he was going anywhere, stretched out across the rug beside his son. She turned back around and couldn't help but grin. If Bishop Ebersol knew about this . . .

But then she reminded herself of the seriousness of her actions. The bishop might not find out about this time spent with Kade, but Sadie knew she was crossing the line. *And God knows.*

She didn't have the heart to force Kade to bundle up Tyler and carry the child out into the storm. With the way the wind was swirling around, it would actually be quite dangerous. Hopefully, conditions would improve soon. She decided to lighten the conversation.

"Maybe when the storm clears, you and Tyler can build a snowman." She walked back over to the middle of the room and took a seat next to Tyler. "Do you think you would like that, Tyler?" Tyler didn't acknowledge the question. By now, he'd drawn mazes of circles on at least twenty different sheets of paper.

"I've never made a snowman," Kade said. He sat up and leaned toward Tyler. "Maybe when the weather gets better, we'll do that together, Tyler."

"You have never made a snowman? Not even as a child?" Sadie raised her brows, thinking how sad that was.

"I grew up in Los Angeles. We don't see much snow. By the time I saw *real* snow, I was too old to build a snowman."

"Nonsense," Sadie exclaimed. "You are never too old to build a snowman. Every year after the first *gut* snowfall, *mei daed* would get up early and surprise me with a snowman outside my bedroom window." She giggled at the recollection. "Each year, he would come up with a different theme for the snowman, or snowwoman, as it sometimes turned out to be." She put her finger to her chin.

"One year, I awoke to find a snowman that was built to look like he was standing on his head. Pop put two sticks up top for his feet, and he made the face upside down on the bottom ball of snow." She laughed. "It was funny. Pop called that snowman 'Sadie's silly friend.' One time, he made two people holding hands. He called them 'the happy couple.' Sometimes, he dressed them in clothes, or had them holding brooms or pots, or some other sort of prop. There was this one time—" She stopped and grinned. "This must be terribly boring for you."

Kade gazed at her with a glint of wonder in his eyes. "Sadie, I don't think there's anything you could say that would bore me."

She pulled her eyes from his and focused on Tyler. "Look at all the circles." She rummaged nervously through the loose papers scattered about. Maybe it was his tone of voice, perhaps the way he'd looked at her, but . . . the alarms were sounding again.

"Sadie?" He leaned back, resting on his palms behind him.

She didn't look up and tried to sound casual. *"Ya?"*

"Look at me," he whispered.

Sadie lifted her eyes to meet his.

"We're not doing anything wrong, Sadie. You do realize that, right?"

"I know that," she said with a shrug. She turned toward the fire. "We need another log, I reckon. I can get it this time." She started to get up.

"I'll get it." But Kade didn't move. "In a minute."

Sadie took a deep breath and waited for him to go on.

"Do you remember what I told you last night?" Kade asked. "I just want to be your friend. I enjoy your company. Everything is fine, Sadie."

"*Ya*, I know." She shrugged again, but Kade was clearly tuned in to her worries.

The last thing Kade wanted to do was rattle his new friend—this amazing, intriguing, beautiful woman. And she had the playfulness of a child at times, like when she talked about the snowmen, her face aglow with memories. *She is something.* But Kade knew he'd need to go easy with any comments or looks that might hint at what a wonderful person he thought she was. He was having trouble, though. This woman was stirring things in him that he didn't quite recognize. In his world, it would only be natural to act on such thoughts, or at least voice them. But this woman's goodness was so *real*, and Kade knew he would never disrespect her in any way.

"Are you hungry?" she asked Kade. "I can hear poor Tyler's tummy growling."

"Tyler's hungry," Tyler said, without looking up from his current project—more circles.

Kade glanced at his watch and couldn't believe it was nearing lunchtime. When he'd sensed that the conversation about the status of their friendship made Sadie uncomfortable, he had changed the subject. Her eyes shone with wonder when Kade told her about some of his travels around the world.

His expression stilled and grew serious. "You know, I'm worried that we might be wearing out our welcome." He sure hoped not, though.

Sadie nodded toward the window. "If you would rather go out into this weather instead of having peanut butter spread on homemade bread, that's fine with me." She grinned.

One minute, she seemed nervous as a cat. The next minute, she was playful and almost . . . flirty. Mixed signals for sure. "I think Tyler and I would much rather stay and have a sandwich with you, as opposed to going out into *that*." He pointed toward the window. "Besides, I don't think I've had a peanut-butter-and-jelly sandwich since I was a kid. And even then, it wasn't very often."

Sadie stood up, smoothed the wrinkles from her apron, and said, "Actually this peanut butter spread is different from the peanut butter in jars that the *Englisch* use. And we like to put cheese spread on our bread and then top it with the peanut spread, but if you'd like—"

"No, no." Kade stood up. "We'll have whatever you're having. Sounds great."

Kade followed her into the kitchen. "Can I help?"

"No, it's fine. You can play with Tyler while I get things ready." She walked toward the cabinet and pulled out a jar of peanut spread, then a jar of cheese spread. Kade plopped himself down on the bench in the kitchen.

"So, it's homemade bread, topped with cheese spread, and then topped with peanut butter spread?" he asked.

"*Ya.* We serve this after Sunday church service, but I eat it sometimes for lunch." She twisted the lid on the peanut spread and placed it on the counter, but the lid on the cheese spread wasn't budging. After banging the edge on the countertop, she tried again.

Kade was on his feet and standing next to her right away. "Here, let me," he offered. The lid unwound with ease, and Kade handed it back to her, but he was in no hurry to leave her side. She smelled so clean and fresh, not bathed in perfume, like most of the women he knew. He breathed in the smell of her one more time before he headed back to the bench.

"Tyler, are you ready to eat?" Sadie walked into the den to find Tyler still occupied with his drawings.

"Tyler hungry."

"You come right this way," she said. "I have a special lunch prepared for you."

Sadie returned with Tyler by her side. "Why don't you sit by your pop—I mean, your *daed*—and I'll get you some milk."

Tyler slid in beside Kade. "You sure have been a good boy, Tyler," Kade said. He was surprised at how self-entertaining his son had been.

"Tyler's a good boy," Tyler said as he reached for the salt in the middle of the table.

"Oh, I don't think we need any salt." Kade reached for the salt shaker in Tyler's hand. Mistake. Tyler began to scream at the top of his lungs.

"What's wrong?" Sadie was quickly by his side.

"He's trying to pour salt all over everything," Kade said, struggling to get the salt shaker from Tyler.

"Maybe you should let him have it," Sadie said.

"In Monica's notes, it said that he'll scream to get what he wants, but that if you give in, he'll always do that." Kade pulled the salt from Tyler's grip. "You can't have this, Tyler," he said in a firm voice. Tyler screamed even more and began to bang his head on the table in front of him.

"Oh, man." Kade ran his hand through his hair. "Tyler, please don't do that." *Think. Think.* "The itsy-bitsy spider walked up the waterspout . . ." Kade began, recalling that Monica had mentioned that he liked that particular song. Tyler stopped crying and wiped his eyes. It was working. "Down came the rain and washed the spider out . . ." Kade was surprised he remembered the song from his childhood. He even remembered the hand motions and began to dribble the rain with his fingers. Tyler started doing the same thing, with a big smile on his face.

Kade was ending the song when Sadie put a plate in front of Tyler. "Here you go, Tyler. My specialty." Then she looked at Kade. "See, you are learning Tyler's ways." Then she giggled.

"What?" He loved the way she laughed.

"It's funny, and nice, the way you sang to him." Her face lit up the playful way it did sometimes. Kade nodded, a little embarrassed.

Tyler dug in almost immediately. "Good," he said, his mouth full.

Sadie placed Kade's plate in front of him. It was the most interesting lunch he'd ever been served. In addition to the sand-wich, there was something on the side that looked like applesauce, and something else he'd seen in his refrigerator at the cottage but hadn't tried.

"That's applesauce and chowchow," Sadie said when she saw him eyeing his plate. She sat down across from them at the table. "It's *gut*. Try it."

The applesauce was fine, but he didn't care too much for the chowchow—mixed vegetables in some sort of pickling sauce. He wasn't much of a pickle eater. "It's great," he lied. The peanut butter and cheese spreads on the bread were delicious, though. *Who would have thought?*

"*Danki*," she said.

After lunch, they resumed their places in the den. Sadie had found several things to entertain Tyler. Two decks of cards, a doll, which oddly didn't have a face, and a bag of building blocks she said she kept on hand for visitors' children. Tyler loved the blocks and stayed entertained for the next four hours, during which time Kade and Sadie swapped stories about their childhoods, their parents, Alicia, Ben, and a host of other topics.

"You are so easy to talk to," Kade said during a break. *I could stay here forever.* He was so detached from the life he knew, and he couldn't remember being happier.

"It's easy to talk to you too." Kade could tell it was hard for her to say, and her eyes avoided his. She glanced out the window. "This is supposed to be the worst of the blizzard," she said. "Tomorrow morning should be much better, but we might be snowed in for a few days."

Excellent, he thought. *Just me, Tyler, and Sadie.* The thought brought him a sense of comfort.

Sadie started to help Tyler build his fortress, and Kade sat watching the two of them. Every once in a while, both Sadie and Tyler would laugh out loud, like when the blocks came tumbling down around them. It was a vision, for sure.

Kade realized that Monica had been put to rest by now, and he'd missed it. His heart ached about missing the funeral and about Monica's death. He was feeling a little guilty that he hadn't thought more about it during the course of the day. To Kade's surprise, he hadn't thought about Alicia in several days either. He wasn't thinking about much of anything—except Sadie and Tyler.

Sadie was at her most beautiful when she laughed. He didn't think he'd ever tire of hearing her laughter. When she looked up unexpectedly and found Kade almost drooling over her, she stopped smiling and looked uncomfortable.

"I'm sorry," he blurted out, shook his head. "It's just . . ." He wanted to tell her that she was a beautiful person, inside and out. But he knew he couldn't. She'd fold up with embarrassment. "Nothing," he said instead. His thoughts were venturing into a forbidden zone, and he kept forcing himself not to look at her lips. Kade knew he needed to leave.

"Tyler, we've outstayed our welcome," he said in a regretful voice. "I should take him and go home. I mean to the cottage."

Sadie's mouth flew open. "The weather is awful outside." She nodded toward the window.

"I know. But at least it's daylight. And it might not get any better. Probably best to go now, before it gets dark." *And before I say or do something I shouldn't.*

"It won't be dark for a bit yet." Kade was more than a little glad that she didn't want them to leave, but just the same, he knew he needed to leave.

He bundled up Tyler, and Sadie retrieved an extra blanket for Kade to wrap around Tyler.

"I wish you didn't have to go out in this, especially with the boy," she said with concern.

"It wouldn't be fair to leave Tyler here with you again," he said. "And actually, I missed the little guy last night." Kade found this thought somewhat surprising, but true.

"I will miss him too." She smiled at Tyler.

"Tyler loves Sadie," Tyler said.

Sadie grabbed her chest, and her eyes lit up. "Tyler, I love you too!"

"Wow. He's never said that to me," Kade said, not hiding his disappointment.

"He will." Sadie smiled.

Before Kade put on his heavy coat, he pulled her into a hug and held her close, begging her with his embrace not to push him away.

And she didn't. Sadie clung to him as tightly as he was clinging to her. Something was happening. They both knew it.

"Thanks for everything," he whispered.

"You are welcome."

But neither of them pulled away. Not until Tyler began to stomp his feet, and Kade forced himself from her arms.

"Bye," he whispered. And Kade picked up Tyler and headed into the storm, protecting his son the best he could.

It wasn't until they were settled in for the night that Kade had a thought. An idea that brought a smile to his face.

Sadie Fisher is in for a big surprise.

13

SADIE SAT ON THE EDGE OF HER BED AND YAWNED. There had been no sleep in between the thrashing winds and her all-consuming replays of the hug she had shared with Kade—the feel of his body next to her, the way he clung to her, as if letting her go would sever whatever it was that was happening between them. And Sadie knew that something was happening, a thought that terrified her. But it had been so long—so long since she'd been held by a man.

She shook her head. A grown woman—an Amish woman, at that—should fend off such temptation, no matter the attraction. But Sadie couldn't deny her attraction to Kade, a man she at first thought to be shallow and arrogant, an *Englischer* she assumed had no regard for anything except his money. In reality, Kade was a lost man struggling to renew his faith and to find his place in this world, not so unlike Sadie in that regard. And now Kade would face those challenges while raising a special child who he didn't know very well. She reached down to tie her shoes and noticed that for the first time in two days, the wind wasn't howling outside.

Maybe the worst of the storm has passed, like the newspapers predicted. She walked to the window and pulled up the blind, and then brought both hands to her mouth and gasped. *I don't believe it.*

Her entire body shook as she laughed out loud at the funniest-looking snowman she'd ever seen in her life. Or snowwoman . . . or snow-*something*.

She peered outside for any sign of Kade. The snow had stopped, and the trees gently swayed against the dying winds. Delicate, orange rays pushed through clouds that seemed hesitant to give in to the sun's full force, revealing a wintry wonderland that glistened with tranquillity for as far as Sadie could see. A welcome sight, indeed. She glanced over her shoulder at her clock. Seven thirty. Granted, she had slept in following her restless night, but Kade must have gotten up early to create the . . . *thing* in front of her window. She bent over laughing, having never felt more flattered in her life.

Visions of her father came to mind. Sadie could almost see him perfecting a masterpiece, applying the finishing touches—a nose, a mouth, a scarf, a hat . . . Although when she looked at the masterpiece Kade had created, she pictured her father with his hands on his hips, head cocked sideways, saying, "What is this silly *Englischer* trying to do?"

It was the worst snowman Sadie had ever seen. Three lopsided balls gave the impression that this snowman had partaken in too much of the bubbly, swaying to one side as if being pushed over by the wind. The middle of the creation was larger and rounder than the top and bottom portion, and Sadie wasn't sure, but it looked like the thing had tiny arms molded out of snow, jetting straight out from each side.

She recognized a green, plastic kitchen glass at the end of one of the limbs. Must be what the snowman drank his bubbly from, she surmised, giggling aloud. Bright-yellow lemons were pushed into hand-molded eye sockets, and Kade had drawn big, black pupils in the middle of each one, giving his snowman a most frightening demeanor. Mr. Scary Snowman had a carrot for a nose—at least Kade had gotten that part right. And there must have been a hundred toothpicks in the shape of a wide grin, making Kade's handiwork the happiest scary snowman she'd ever laid eyes on.

A blue and red tie wound around Mr. Scary Snowman's neck and fell the length of the middle clump of snow, and a blue baseball cap finished off his attire. Sadie shook her head, and then hurried down the stairs two at a time with a childish enthusiasm she recalled having each time her pop surprised her with the first snowman of the season. And the fact that Kade had created this ridiculous structure outside her window touched her in a way she knew wasn't good, a way that made her want to run into his arms and thank him for making her laugh and feel so alive again.

She bundled herself in her heavy coat, gloves, and boots, and she was off. She glided across the icy, slick porch until she reached the steps. Grabbing the rails, she eased down each snow-covered step, and then plowed across the soft snow, periodically sinking to her shins. The wind and snow might have ceased, but it was so cold her teeth were chattering. She didn't care. She was anxious to have a closer look at what she would now call Scary Drunken Snowman.

Cameras were forbidden by the Old Order, but she'd never wished she had one more than at this moment. She stood face-to-face with it and noticed that several of the toothpicks had fallen out of the happy smile, leaving Scary Drunken Snowman with a rather toothless look. She was laughing when she heard the cottage door open. Kade held Tyler's hand as they made their way down the front steps.

"Well, what do you think?" Kade yelled across the snow-covered space between them. He heaved Tyler into his arms and picked up the pace.

Sadie knew she was grinning from ear to ear, and she pinched her lips together to try to stifle the laughter that threatened to erupt. "*Gut*," she said quickly. She pursed her lips together again. Kade was out of breath by the time he and Tyler joined her.

"The baseball cap was Tyler's idea," Kade said with pride, panting a bit. "But I think the tie is what topped him off, don't you?"

"*Ya, ya*," Sadie said. She was still trying not to laugh since Kade seemed so proud of his work. Hard to believe, but she figured she'd better go along. "It's lovely," she said. Then she couldn't hold it anymore. She bent over, put her hands on her knees, and laughed in a way that she couldn't remember ever laughing. It was a gut-wrenching, snorting sort of laugh that she would have been embarrassed about if it didn't feel so good.

"Are you laughing at my snowman?" Kade asked. He lifted his chin and turned toward Tyler. "Do you think Miss Sadie is laughing at our snowman?"

Tyler started laughing so hard that Sadie only laughed harder. "Miss Sadie funny," Tyler said.

"I'm sorry," Sadie managed to say between snorts of laughter. "It's just that—" She started up again.

Then Kade started laughing, and it was as if the world stopped spinning for a few seconds, the three of them lost in a perfect moment. A child's laughter, a glistening snowfall, two grown-ups reveling in silliness. And Sadie planned to enjoy the rarity of such a moment for as long as she could. She gathered herself, leaned down, and rolled the white powder into a perfect round ball.

"I suggest you run!" she said.

Kade looked ridiculous, lifting his legs up to his waist in an effort to step through the snow removing him and Tyler away from her line of fire. "What's Miss Sadie doing?" Kade yelled. His eyes shone with playful tenderness as he looked at his son. And Tyler laughed so hard, Sadie was sure Kade was going to drop the boy.

She heaved the snowball, making sure to hit Kade in the leg, and not Tyler. Then Tyler wanted in on the game, and he squirmed his way out of Kade's arms. Tyler sank into the snow, picked himself up, and started rolling the snow into a ball.

"You're in trouble now!" Kade yelled. "Tyler seems to have easily picked up on this game." Kade leaned down and helped Tyler squeeze the snow into a tight ball. "You better run, pretty lady!"

Pretty lady? Sadie should have been colder than cold, but she felt warm. She hiked her dress up, her big, black boots sinking into the soft snow. It was not her most ladylike behavior, that was for sure, but she bolted across the snow anyway, laughing the entire time.

"Throw, Tyler!" Kade yelled.

And the boy heaved the snowball and smacked her in the middle of her back.

"Are you okay?" Kade seemed serious all of a sudden as he trudged toward her.

She was fine, though, and wasted no time scooping up her own handful of snow. "You better run, the both of you!"

"Run, Tyler!" Kade yelled. He reached for Tyler's hand, and the two of them ambled through the snow.

One thing Sadie knew how to do, and that was to make a fine snowball. She added snow, packed it tighter, and then took aim, thrusting her handmade weapon—right into the back of Kade's head. Over he went.

"Oh no!" she yelled. Kade was facedown in the snow. "Oh no! Oh no!" She fell to her knees and leaned over him. "Kade, are you all right?" Tyler stood at her side, as if he, too, were wondering if his father was going to get up.

Then, without warning, Kade rolled onto his back, grabbed Sadie, and pulled her down beside him, yelling and laughing the whole time. "Gotcha!"

She was completely rattled, yet she couldn't stop laughing as she lay beside Kade in the freezing snow. He reached for her hand, squeezed it, and didn't let go. Then the realization of what was happening hit her hard, and she tried to wriggle her hand from his grasp. He tightened his hold and looked over at her. "I don't remember when I've had this much fun. Please, let's don't analyze it."

But despite the merriment, Sadie pried her hand from his and forced herself to stand up. Kade stood up as well. She reckoned his teeth were knocking together about as much as hers, and Tyler looked frozen as well. "Coffee is what we need, and some hot cocoa for Tyler," she said.

"Yes. Coffee and cocoa," Kade said.

They cumbersomely made their way to the house. Kade carried Tyler. Once inside, Kade added logs to the fire, as if he lived there. And Sadie prepared coffee, cocoa, and breakfast—as if both Kade and Tyler lived there. It should have been awkward. It seemed anything but.

The day was spent much like the previous day, soaking up the heat from the fireplace, playing games with Tyler, and talking—lots of talking. Sadie knew, with every inch of her being, that she was in a dangerous place, but why would God give her a glimpse of something so magical if it were wrong? So she allowed herself to go with it.

In the evening, she said good-bye to both Kade and Tyler, and another hug followed, this one more tender and longer than the time before.

And that's how the threesome spent the next three days—sharing breakfast, lunch, supper, and games and conversation in between. And the now-customary hug ended the day, before darkness settled.

But on this Tuesday night, only a while before Milo was scheduled to call, Kade pulled from the hug and gazed into Sadie's eyes in a way that she knew he was going to kiss her. She'd never wanted anything more in her life, she was quite sure. But she gently nudged him back. He didn't push, and they stared at each other in a way that seemed not to need any words.

"Good night," he said softly.

"Good night." She leaned down. "And good night to you, Tyler."

"Tyler loves Sadie." Sadie pulled Tyler into a hug, and he fell into her arms.

"I love you, too, Tyler."

"He still hasn't said that to me," Kade said. He dipped his head slightly as his eyes darkened with emotion.

"He will." Sadie smiled up at Kade, Tyler still holding tight.

"Come on, Tyler," Kade said. "We better let Sadie get some rest."

Sadie waved to them from the porch as they made their way back to the cottage. She checked the clock on the wall. For the first time, she considered not going to the barn to wait for Milo's call at eight o'clock. He had already failed to call her the week before, and it was dreadfully cold. And if she was honest with herself, she'd admit her head was filled with thoughts of Kade and Tyler these days. She hadn't thought much about Milo, nor had she reread any of his letters. But Sadie watched the clock until time for him to call, and then she headed to the barn.

At ten after eight, she left the barn with a new emotion that Milo didn't call: relief.

The next morning, Sadie heard the snowplows on Black Horse Road. Life would resume to normal. She'd no longer be hidden away with Kade and Tyler. Today, she'd open the shop with Lillian, and yes, things would return to normal.

Then why did she feel that something inside her would never feel normal again? Something had changed. Her spirit had changed, her willingness and ability to feel happiness. She'd been happier than she had been since Ben died.

She recalled her many prayers for God to grant her happiness. And He had. But why this way? It was a reality she couldn't have, a happiness that had no place in her world. She was instantly back where she started, questioning God's will for her.

"I am so glad to be out of the *haus*," Lillian exclaimed when she met Sadie at the shop that morning. "You know how much I love my Samuel, David, and baby Anna, but they were about to make me bonkers." Lillian laughed. "I think we all got a touch of cabin fever." She cut her eyes in Sadie's direction. "Oh, Sadie. I can't imagine how it must have been for you, all these days alone out here. That must have been equally dreadful." Lillian shook her head, frowning.

"*Ya*," Sadie said. "Dreadful." She pulled her eyes from Lillian's, afraid Lillian would pick up on Sadie's variation of the truth.

But her friend went on to ready the shop for business. And without much traffic, since the weather was still uncomfortably cold, Lillian spent most of the morning telling Sadie about her confinement indoors with Samuel and David. "They are so used to being outdoors, it's hard to keep them entertained," she said.

Sadie listened and chose not to share her adventures with Lillian, even though Lillian was her best friend and the one person who would most understand how Sadie had allowed herself to slip into a situation that was unacceptable at best. She'd no sooner had the thought when the bell on the front door of the shop rang. And in walked Kade and Tyler.

"I thought it was time we checked out Treasures of the Heart," he said with a smile.

Sadie jumped up. "Kade, what are you doing here?" She knew her tone revealed the alarm she felt at being around Kade with Lillian in the room.

Kade smiled and seemed to pick up on Sadie's unease. He walked to where Lillian was sitting on a stool by the counter. "Nice to see you again, Lillian." He extended his hand to Lillian.

"Nice to see you as well," she said. "And who is this young fellow?" Lillian leaned down toward Tyler.

"This is Tyler," Sadie interjected. "Isn't he a handsome little man?" Sadie was beaming with the pride of a mother, she knew, but Tyler had stolen her heart, and it was hard to hide.

"Sadie and I were just talking about how miserable we were during the storm. Confined, bored." Lillian shook her head. "We're both glad it's all over."

"I didn't say I was *bored*, though," Sadie rushed to say. She looked back and forth between Kade and Lillian. Kade smiled. Lillian looked confused. But Lillian was quick, and she didn't stay confused for long.

"No, Sadie didn't say she was bored," Lillian said. Then she grinned. "I did all the talking. Sadie didn't say much at all."

"I was by myself, in the house . . . in the night hours. *Ya*, in the house by myself most of the time." Sadie took a deep breath. "Except for playtime. I mean, card time. Or talking time. And we played in the snow once, and . . ." She couldn't seem to stop herself. She took another deep breath, and then glanced back and forth between Lillian and Kade. Lillian was grinning from ear to ear. Kade was a gentleman.

"Well, ladies, we wanted to see your shop and say hello. Lillian, it was a pleasure to see you again." He turned his attention to Sadie. "And Sadie, this is a great place you have here."

"*Danki*," she whispered. Lillian was going to get hold of her the minute Kade and Tyler were out the door. This Sadie knew.

"Oh, and Sadie, I wanted to let you know—Tyler and I are going to venture out this afternoon. I think it's time we see Lancaster County." Kade pointed toward the barn. "My car is back. I arranged for some men to dig it out of the snow and bring it back, but Tyler and I are going to take a cab. Not only do I not drive very well in the snow, but I think that driving, reading a map, and Tyler in the car . . . well, it might be a little much."

"Here, take this." Lillian handed Kade a pamphlet they kept on the counter. "It's an off-the-beaten-path map. It'll take you away from the touristy places to real Amish shops, bakeries, and such. We like to share this with our customers."

Kade accepted it and waved as he headed out the door.

It took every ounce of Sadie's willpower not to say, "Will I see you for supper?" but she reminded herself that things had changed now that the blizzard was over. And she found that thought most depressing.

The bell on the door was still ringing from Kade and Tyler's exit when Lillian said with a grin, "Oh, my. What has my best friend been up to?"

It was early afternoon when Sarah Jane, Katie Ann, Mary Ellen, and Rebecca showed up at the shop, each telling stories about their confinement during the storm. Sadie kept quiet. She had told Lillian about her past few days, but only sparse details. Of course, Lillian filled in the blanks on her own, and there'd been no doubt that Lillian, worldly as she'd once been, was worried about Sadie. "Be careful, Sadie," she'd said. "Kade Saunders is a powerful man who comes from a world you know nothing about."

While that might be true—that she knew nothing of Kade's world—she knew *Kade*, the man. But she realized Lillian had every reason to be concerned.

"Ivan found it to be *wunderbaar gut*, staying in the *haus* for all those days," Katie Ann huffed. "Said it was like a vacation." She shook her head. "A vacation for him maybe. But he was making me *narrisch!*"

Sarah Jane laughed out loud. "I'm sure you girls all had a rough time, but please remember that I was cooped up for six days with Pop."

"*Ach*," Rebecca said. "That's true. I reckon you were more *narrisch* than the rest of us."

They all laughed, picturing six days trapped inside with the lovable, yet mischievous Jonas.

"Do you know that Pop and Lizzie have been communicating with walkie-talkies?" Sarah Jane told them all. "It's the cutest thing in the world, really. But I think if I hear 'breaker, breaker' one more time, I might snap like a twig."

"It's sweet that they are courting," Mary Ellen said.

Sarah Jane took a seat on the stool behind the counter. "I'm happy that Pop seems to have found someone he cares about. He was a wreck after *mei mamm* died."

"Irma Rose was a *gut* woman," Rebecca said.

"But having Pop in the house, in his state of mind, and courting . . . well . . ." Sarah Jane laughed again. "I think you can all imagine; I have my hands full."

"We all love Jonas so much," Sadie said.

"I'm happy to share him with all of you," Sarah Jane said with enthusiasm. "There is enough of Jonas to go around, that's for sure."

"*Wunderbaar gut* to see the sun out," Katie Anne said. She walked to the window that faced Black Horse Road. "And to see the snow-plows out. I've even seen a few cars on the road."

"We had two visitors here in the shop earlier," Lillian said.

"They didn't buy anything, but it's *gut* to see people are getting out and about."

"Is that your *Englisch* renter pulling into the drive in the yellow taxi?" Katie Anne asked. She pointed out the window at a cab turning into the driveway.

"*Ya*, I reckon so," Sadie said. She joined Katie Anne at the window. *And he's in time for supper later.* They hadn't discussed it, but Sadie knew she'd make the offer, bishop or no bishop. Right or wrong. Her time with Kade and Tyler had been some of the best she'd had in years. All the warning bells in the world weren't going to stop her from a night of supper, maybe some conversation, and a goodnight hug. They were simple pleasures, harmless. And maybe if she kept telling herself that, she'd reconcile her guilt.

They all huddled around the window and watched as the cab stopped near the farmhouse instead of the cottage. Then a man stepped out of the car, one tall, lanky leg at a time.

"That isn't the *Englischer*," Rebecca said assuredly. She shot a questioning expression Sadie's way.

She pressed her hand to her chest and pushed the others gently aside. She watched the man turn their way, and she took a deep breath to calm her pounding chest.

"Who is it, Sadie?" Lillian asked.

"Sadie?" she heard Rebecca say. "Are you all right?"

The others chimed in, but their voices were echoes in a tunnel, tuned out by Sadie's own thoughts, fears, anticipation.

There was no way for Sadie to know for sure, yet she did.

It was Milo.

14

Tyler and Kade toured the towns of Bird-in-Hand, Paradise, and Intercourse, stopping at places recommended in the pamphlet from Sadie and her friends. Tyler's highlight of the day had been a buggy ride in Paradise. He clapped his hands throughout the entire ride. Kade knew the clapping was self-stimulatory behavior, as per Monica's notes, but it was the smile on Tyler's face that Kade would remember from this special day with his son. Kade had hoped to take such a ride with Sadie, but when Tyler saw the horse hitched to the buggy on the side of the road, he couldn't resist the massive animal. For fifty bucks, they explored the back roads in Paradise, to Tyler's delight. And the cab driver seemed thankful to be carting Kade and Tyler around for most of the day.

During the taxi ride back to the cottage, Kade admired Amish homesteads cloaked in white along the winding roads, each with a silo and several outbuildings. They passed other buggies along the way, the occupants bundled in thick blankets, the same as Kade and Tyler had been during their ride. Tyler had laughed and pointed at the passersby, sometimes waving. It was their first outing as father and son, and it felt good. Kade was eager to get to know his son better. His fears had subsided, and

Sadie had played a big part in that. She'd been so good with Tyler from the very beginning, so natural. For Kade, it hadn't come easy, but watching her gave him confidence that he could do the job—maybe even do it well.

Kade had been all over the world, but something about Lancaster County provided an elusive sort of peacefulness that Kade hadn't felt anywhere else, as if the Amish held the secret to true contentment, tucked away in their own world detached from modern society—a world Sadie had given him a glimpse of. He thought he'd head back to L.A. once the storm let up. He needed to prepare for Tyler, and he had thirty-six business-related messages on his cell phone that he'd been putting off. And at some point, he knew he needed to talk to Val.

But at the moment, only one thing was on his mind. Actually, two. The bright-eyed boy sitting next to him in the cab, and Sadie. Everything else seemed distant and unimportant.

The driver made his way back toward Sadie's place, and Kade recalled the past few days in vivid detail, zoning in on their goodnight hugs. Never before had a simple gesture of affection moved him in such a way. It wasn't just the feel of her in his arms, her fresh aroma and soft skin—although those things kept him up at night—it was Sadie, the woman. She made Kade want to be a better man.

Kade also felt a new level of responsibility. He was accountable for a lot of people's livelihoods, for billion-dollar business deals, and a host of other things that, at the moment, didn't compare to the job he'd been handed—raising his son.

"Sadie's house," Tyler said when the driver pulled into the driveway.

"Yes, it is. That's Sadie's house." Kade watched his son's face light up and knew that Sadie had the same effect on Tyler as she did on him.

"Tyler loves Sadie," Tyler said.

Me too. The thought hit Kade like a jab in his chest, pushing him to a place he hadn't expected. Did he love her? Was that even possible? The idea had certainly popped into his head as naturally as Tyler had said the words. It was an idea too complicated to explore right now. The end result may not be what Kade wanted, and he was too caught up in the time he had left to worry with what the future might bring. Life was good today, and he planned to live in the present.

"Thank you." He handed the driver a wad of cash, anxious to see Sadie. The driver responded with an enthusiastic "Thank you!" before he drove away.

"Do you want to go say hello to Sadie?" Kade asked Tyler.

Tyler nodded and reached for Kade's hand. It was a first. And Kade knew that at this moment, on this day, he was exactly where he needed to be. Everything else could wait.

They walked toward the farmhouse and eased their way up the icy steps.

Kade heard voices inside. Sadie's voice and . . . a male voice.

"Are you sure?" Lillian had asked Sadie. "How do you know it's Milo? You've never seen him. How could you possibly know?"

But Sadie did know, sure as she'd known anything in her life. Milo's tall stance, his questioning eyes as he scanned his surroundings—yes, it was him. She was sure. And she didn't move.

The ladies turned their attention to her. "He's heading up to the farmhouse, Sadie," Rebecca said. "Aren't you going to go find out for sure?"

"I bet you can hardly contain your excitement!" Mary Ellen squealed.

Lillian's mother nudged the others aside and cupped Sadie's cheek in her hand. "Sadie, dear, it's only natural for you to be *naerfich*," Sarah Jane said. "You've been writing letters to Milo for a long time. And now he's here."

Sadie's feet were rooted to the floor.

"If it's even him," Katie Anne said in a skeptical voice. She poked her head around the others and stared toward the farmhouse. "Sadie, he's knocking on the door. You better go see if it's him." She eased Sadie toward the door, even though Sadie's feet fought to stay where they were.

"It'll be fine," Lillian said as Sadie turned the knob.

The bell on the door clanged as she closed the door and looked toward the farmhouse. She began the long trek to what she had presumed for a long time would be her future. Milo. But her head was abuzz with doubt, fear, worry—and, most of all, Kade.

She was within a few steps of the porch when he turned around. Sadie stood perfectly still, studying him. Handsome. Very handsome. Dark hair and a short beard, and tall, just like he'd described himself. Although he left out that he had stunning, bright-blue eyes, and a smile that stretched wide above a square jawline. Milo, if indeed it was him, had been much too modest about his appearance. Looks were not everything, but there was no denying that Milo's attractiveness caught Sadie's eye.

"Sadie?" His voice was deep.

"Milo?"

His smile widened, and he headed down the porch steps toward her. After stopping for a moment in front of her, taking in her appearance as well, he wrapped his arms around her in what should have been the happiest moment of her life.

She closed her eyes tight. Milo didn't smell like Kade. He was taller than Kade, towering over her by almost a foot. *He isn't Kade.*

"Sadie," he whispered. He held her tighter. "I couldn't wait until spring." He pulled away from the hug, but kept his strong hands on her arms. "I began my travels two weeks ago, but a blizzard kept me away for almost a week. I haven't been able to phone you . . ." He paused and fused his eyes with hers. "Sadie, you are more beautiful than I could have pictured in my mind."

"*Danki.*" She looked away, blushed. "Let's go in out of the cold," she said.

Milo followed her up the porch steps, and Sadie felt as though she were in a dream. She should have been walking on clouds in this dream she'd harbored for two years. But instead, the fantasy of Milo and the reality of him faced off like competing emotions, confusing Sadie so that she wasn't sure what she felt.

Sadie prepared some hot cocoa, then sat down on the wooden bench at the kitchen table across from Milo.

"It's so *gut* to finally be here." Milo's eyes shone. He was everything she imagined him to be. "I reckon that after all this time, you might have been thinkin' I wasn't coming."

Sadie shook her head, though it had been exactly what she'd been thinking. "I knew that someday we would meet." She sipped her cocoa. This man was a stranger, despite all their correspondences. It felt odd for him to be sitting here at her kitchen table.

But now that he was here, Sadie tried to reconcile her thoughts and recall how much she'd longed for this day. *Everything will be fine now.* She planned to continue telling herself that for as long as necessary, until things were as God intended them to be.

"You have a fine homestead," he said. "I'm anxious for you to travel with me to Stephenville. I read much about Lancaster County in the *Budget* and the *Die Botschaft.* And from what little I have seen of your fair county, it has much more population than where I come from. As I wrote in *mei* letters, our Order is small compared to Lancaster County."

How much smaller? She took in a breath and exhaled slowly as she thought about the possibility of living somewhere else.

"I will need to talk with Katie Anne and Ivan to make arrangements for you to stay with them while you're here. They have been expecting for you to be their guest whenever you arrived." Sadie hoped the last-minute notice would be all right with Katie Anne. "Katie Anne is at my shop right now." Sadie pointed out the window, where she could see in the distance all the women still peering through the window toward her farmhouse. She was tempted to close the blind, but instead, she smiled to herself.

"I don't want to be a bother for anyone, and I don't mind getting a room in town or—"

"*Ach*, nonsense. Katie Anne and her husband, Ivan, will love to have you in their home. They haven't been blessed with *kinner* yet, so it's just the two of them."

"Sadie, I feel like I know you so well." He smiled at her, the way a man does when he's smitten. She smiled back, but she wasn't feeling like she knew Milo very well at all. She knew the voice on the other end of the phone, the penmanship in the letters she'd

received. But the man before her seemed like a stranger, familiar
yet unreal.

"*Ya.* It is so *gut* to finally meet you in person," she said. *Very
handsome,* she thought again, as her eyes met his. "How long will
you be staying?"

Milo's forehead wrinkled. "Not as long as I'd hoped. Due to
mei delays with the weather, I will need to leave in a few days. On
Saturday."

"That's only three days from now." After all this time, after
two years, and he could only stay for three days?

He reached over and placed his hand on hers, which rattled
Sadie a bit, but she didn't move her hand. "Come to Texas with
me on Saturday. I have two bus tickets for us to travel together.
You can come before the harvest begins, and we'll have time to
get to know each other."

It was so sudden. Sadie had never been out of Lancaster
County before, much less across the United States to Texas.
"Can't you stay here a bit longer?" she countered.

"I would love to stay in your community, get to know your
family and friends, but I must prepare the fields for harvest. We
only have a small family harvest, and I work at my carpentry. *Mei*
sisters and *mamm* will keep you company when I'm not able to, and
they will introduce you to members of our community, in hopes
that you will want to stay." He paused, then smiled. "In hopes that
you will want to stay with me and become *mei fraa* someday."

They'd talked about it on the phone many times, and corre-
sponded about it in letters as well, but hearing Milo recite their
plans right here at her kitchen table was almost overwhelming.
This was her home. There was her shop, her friends . . .

Milo's expression was kind, sympathetic. He still had his hand atop hers, and Sadie feared her hand was growing clammy at the thought of leaving. "I know how hard it would be to leave your community, the only place you've ever known. Don't think I would take that lightly, Sadie." He gave her hand a gentle squeeze. "But our life will be *wunderbaar gut*, and *mei mamm*, sisters, and the rest of the district will welcome you with their arms and hearts open. Leave with me on Saturday, Sadie? Stay as long as you like." He smiled. "Perhaps, forever."

Sadie couldn't help but smile. He was offering her everything she'd dreamed of. But yet, she felt almost relieved to have an excuse not to go. "I would love that, Milo. But I have a renter in the cottage. He will stay through March, and he has his young child with him."

Milo's face sank, and he took a deep breath. "I understand." Then he forced a smile. "Then we shall enjoy the time we have while I'm here." He gave her hand another squeeze.

"*Ya.* For sure we will have a *gut* time." But all Sadie could think about was whether or not he would be leaving in time for her to prepare supper for Kade and Tyler.

She heard footsteps coming up the steps. And then a knock.

"Excuse me." She pulled her hand from beneath Milo's and walked to the door. When she opened it, she wondered if her face lit up the way her heart did. "Kade, Tyler, come in." Sadie stepped aside and motioned them into the kitchen. "You two come in here out of the cold."

Milo stood up when Kade and Tyler walked into the kitchen. "Milo Troyer," he said, extending his hand to Kade.

"Kade Saunders." Kade returned the handshake, but his eyes cut to Sadie's, his expression reserved.

"Hello there," Milo said to Tyler. As was his way, Tyler's eyes were all over the place, until they landed on Sadie.

"Tyler loves Sadie." He ran to her. "Hug."

Sadie wrapped her arms around Tyler. "Sadie loves Tyler too." She looked up at Milo. "And this is Tyler," she said proudly. "Sit down, everyone." She ushered Tyler to the bench and helped him get situated.

"Uh, no. We can't stay," Kade said. "We came to say thank you for telling us about the off-the-beaten-path tour. We had a great time."

He doesn't look like he's having a great time, Sadie thought, as she tried to catch his eye. But Kade refused to look at her. And his tone hinted that he'd returned to the man who arrived a few weeks ago—cold, aloof.

"I'm getting ready to make supper." Sadie smiled. "Beef stew. Please stay." Her eyes were pleading with Kade, and she couldn't help but wonder if Milo noticed.

"No, I know you've been waiting a long time to meet Milo, so Tyler and I are going to excuse ourselves." Kade walked toward Tyler. "Tyler, let's go to the cottage so Sadie and her friend can spend some time alone."

"No, that's not necessary. I have plenty . . ." Sadie was feeling desperate.

"Sadie's right. Please stay," Milo said. "I was just telling Sadie how I'd hoped she would be able to travel with me to Texas on Saturday, but she explained that she had a renter. It's nice to meet you."

But Kade didn't sit down. He stared hard at Sadie and then looked at Milo. "There's no reason Sadie can't go to Texas with you. Tyler and I will be fine. As a matter of fact, Sadie, maybe you should take this opportunity to go while we're here. I can take care of your animals."

"But you know nothing about taking care of animals," Sadie said. *Why is he doing this?*

"I'm sure Milo can give me a lesson or two before you leave." Kade smiled and arched his brows toward Milo.

"I would be happy to. *Wunderbaar* news!" Milo glanced at Sadie. "Isn't it, Sadie?"

"*Ach*, no. It wouldn't be right." Sadie shook her head with determination. "I provide Mr. Saunders with groceries, and it's not his place to tend to my farm while he is leasing the cottage. I won't hear of it. No. It wouldn't be right." She continued to shake her head.

"No, no. You take this opportunity," Kade said. "Tyler and I will be fine. We are quite capable of getting our own food and taking care of ourselves." He paused. "Unless, you don't trust us here or—"

"Of course I trust you," Sadie snapped.

"Then that settles it." Kade extended his hand to Milo. "Milo, a pleasure to meet you. Enjoy your time with Sadie. She seems like a fine woman. You two go to Texas, and I'll keep an eye on things here."

"You know nothing about a farm." Sadie folded her hands across her chest.

Milo stood up to shake Kade's hand, and as if Sadie wasn't even in the room, he said, "*Danki*, Mr. Saunders. Sadie and I have been waiting for this for a long time."

"As much as I would love to go, I'm afraid Mr. Saunders had a tragedy recently, and he probably has to leave soon. When he leaves, I can come to Texas then."

"No. I'm not leaving. In another six weeks, perhaps I'll be ready to go back to L.A., but for now, Tyler seems to like it here, and I can conduct my business via conference calls." Kade helped Tyler to his feet.

"Milo, will you be staying here with Sadie?" Kade still refused to look at Sadie.

Milo looked as shocked as Sadie. "Uh, no," Milo said. "I will be staying with friends of Sadie's, of course."

"Ah, yes. I suppose anything else would be *inappropriate*." The way Kade said the word *inappropriate* made Sadie want to swat him, a feeling she'd never had before.

Sadie stood dumbfounded as Kade and Tyler walked out the door. "Have a good evening," Kade said.

As he closed the door behind them, Milo said, "What a nice man to offer to tend to the place so you can join me." He sat down across from her. "Sadie?"

"*Ya?*"

"Are you sure you want to come with me to Texas? You seem to be puttin' up quite a fight."

Maybe it was the kind, honest way he directed the question to her, but Sadie said, "Of course I want to come."

He put his hand on hers again. "I know you're nervous. I'm nervous too. But I feel like this is God's plan for us. Everything will be fine."

"*Ya*," she said, forcing a smile. "I should start some supper. Why don't you go rest in the den, warm yourself by the fire."

"I am a mite tired from my travels," Milo said. He stood and walked toward the den, but he turned around before he rounded the corner. "Sadie, you really are a vision. I'm glad I came."

"Me too." She smiled back, although at the moment, Sadie wasn't glad about one single thing. And she'd like to get her hands on that Kade for pushing her into a situation that she didn't have time to think on.

Her eyes were filling with tears, and she was glad Milo was resting on the couch and not insistent on helping her in the kitchen, the way Kade had. No need for him to see her with such worry in her heart. And anger. And hurt. She had thought there might be something between her and Kade. Clearly, she was wrong. He'd practically insisted that she leave with Milo. If he cared one bit, he wouldn't have done that.

The pain in Kade's heart was immeasurable. It was one thing to hear Sadie talk about her past with Ben, but entirely another to envision her with Milo. The thought of her running off to test a potential new life with him was a concept Kade had trouble comprehending, but if he'd learned one thing from Sadie, it was that he wanted to be a better man. Holding her back would be a selfish thing to do. She had an opportunity with this man, a chance at happiness with someone of her own kind. Offering to stay here, alone with Tyler, and pushing her to go with Milo was indeed the most unselfish thing Kade had ever done. She was going to go eventually; might as well be now.

The truth was, he should be going back to L.A., but with or without Sadie here, he wasn't ready to face the real world yet. He planned to use this time to get to know his son. As he watched Tyler rolling across the floor in the den, giggling, Kade thought about how much things had changed between him and his son since Monica had dropped him off. They still had difficult moments, but he was learning about Tyler, finding out the things that made the boy laugh, things that made him sad. Tyler had his own personality, despite his challenges.

His thoughts returned to Sadie. The immediate connection she'd made with Tyler, the conversations she and Kade had shared, the way she felt in his arms, the smell of her. Yes, it was best that she go. If she didn't go now, Kade might say something to try and convince her to stay, or worse, tempt her away from a faith and place that she belonged. And even Kade didn't have the heart to do that.

After Tyler's bath, Kade tucked him into bed and said prayers with him, something they had started doing a few days ago. Tyler repeated each prayer along with Kade. This was a special time for Kade, but he had to admit, he was still waiting for another message. He wasn't willing to write it off as a coincidence, nor was he willing to accept it as divine intervention from God. Either way, he always waited anxiously, just in case.

Tyler had been tucked into bed for about an hour when Kade heard a pounding on the front door. He closed the book he was reading and edged off the couch in his socks and sweat pants. He pulled the door open to find Sadie standing on the porch, her cheeks red and her teeth chattering.

"What are you doing here? It's freezing! Get in here." Kade grabbed her by the arm to drag her inside.

"Not until you dress properly," she said, freeing herself of his grip. Sadie lifted her chin and looked away from him.

"This is ridiculous." But Kade walked into the bedroom and threw on a sweatshirt. He'd barely gotten it pulled over his head when he returned to the door. "Better?" he asked. He motioned her inside.

"What do you think you're doing?" she asked once he'd closed the door behind her.

"Would you like to take your coat off and stay awhile?" It was sarcastic, and she didn't find it amusing.

Sadie walked up to him with a fire in her that Kade hadn't seen before. "You cannot boss me about my life, Kade Saunders."

"I didn't realize I was *bossing you*, Sadie Fisher." He smirked, amused at her angry display and choice of words, then crossed his arms. "You'll have to be more specific."

"Don't play with me, Kade." Sadie actually stomped her foot. "Couldn't you tell that I didn't want to go to Texas right now? I was trying not to hurt Milo's feelings. Now I have to go, because you made it so very convenient for me to do so."

"I thought I was doing you a favor. You said you've been corresponding with Milo for over two years. I thought my staying here to watch the place would give you an opportunity to get to know this man. I thought you'd be happy."

"No, you didn't." There was a lethal calmness in her blue eyes. "You were just trying to be powerful, because that's the way you do things in your world."

"Sadie, who am I to tell you what to do? If you don't want to go, don't go." Kade shrugged. "I don't know what the big deal is."

"Evidently, you do not." She turned to walk away, but Kade gently grabbed her arm.

"Hey, hey. Come back here. Talk to me, Sadie."

She shook free of his hold. Kade watched her backing away, tears in her eyes. It was breaking his heart. Now was his chance.

She was feeling something for him too. If he was ever going to tell her how much he cared for her, now was the time—and he would probably screw up her life in the process. Kade took a deep breath.

"What do you want me to say?" she asked.

Kade walked toward her, but she backed up a safe distance. "Come here, Sadie." He held his arms out to her. He couldn't help it. God forgive him, he couldn't stand to see her like this. So torn. She looked shattered, as shattered as he felt. "Come here," he repeated, stretching his arms out further.

"I can't," she said.

"Then why did you come here?" Kade took a step forward. She didn't back up.

"To see . . . to know if . . ." A tear spilled over, and Sadie let it run the length of her cheek without taking her eyes from Kade's.

I love you, Sadie. He wanted to tell her so much that it physically hurt. But he said nothing. *It's the right thing to do.* But couldn't he at least hold her, comfort her, one last time? Soon she would grow close to Milo, as it should be, and Kade would lose her forever. He moved toward her again.

"To know if what?" he asked. "Why are you crying?"

She looked embarrassed all of a sudden and turned her eyes away from him. He grasped both of her arms and pulled her toward him, and then he lifted her chin and forced her to look into his eyes, eyes longing for the same thing hers did. Then Kade did the hardest thing he'd ever done in his life.

He readied himself, stood tall, and firmly said, "Go be with Milo. Go to Texas, Sadie."

She jerked free of his hold, turned, and ran for the door. And she never looked back. If she had, she would have seen the tears filling Kade's eyes.

What have I done?

15

LIZZIE WAS AS NERVOUS AS ANY A PERSON COULD BE. She fumbled with her *kapp* as if she hadn't been wearing the prayer covering for the past sixty-plus years, poking at loose strands of gray hair that kept falling forward. She had known Samuel Stoltzfus since he was a baby, and she'd taken a liking to his wife, Lillian, right away. And Jonas's daughter, Sarah Jane, had always been mighty good to Lizzie. There was no need for all this fuss just because she was going to supper at Jonas's house.

She was honored when Jonas invited her on behalf of them all. It was a big step for Jonas, and Lizzie suspected it might mean that Jonas was ready to take their friendship to the next level. She wanted to make a good impression. *So silly,* she thought. These were all fine people whom she'd known for years.

The sound of a buggy approaching gave her the push she needed to tame her unruly tresses. A final poke beneath her prayer covering, and she was ready. She bundled up in her heaviest coat and pulled on her boots, glad she'd worn two pairs of thick, black tights beneath her best blue dress. She molded her black gloves around her tired old hands and pretended for a moment that she was a young woman. Lizzie closed her eyes and imagined what it would be like to live the next fifty years with Jonas—that she was a woman in her youth, vital and strong.

She sighed, smiled, and realized she would be happy to take what she could get where Jonas was concerned. A week, a month, a year, or twenty years, she wanted to live out her days with Jonas by her side, caring for him, doting on him, playing chess with him, and loving him. She waited on the front porch for him to halt the buggy and come help her down the porch steps, which he insisted on. Her kind, chivalrous huggy bear.

"Sarah Jane's got a mighty fine meal planned for you," Jonas said, his shoulders squared and his chin held high. He met Lizzie at the top of the porch and offered her his arm, which she gladly latched onto. "She's lookin' forward to having the *kinner* and you all over for supper. Lillian said to apologize to you that we're eatin' so late. She had a doctor's appointment this afternoon in the city, and it ran a bit late."

"Is everything all right?" They took the porch steps slow and steady, each holding a handrail, and each other.

"*Ya, ya.* One of those regular checkups 'bout the baby. Everything is *gut.*"

Jonas helped Lizzie into the buggy and handed her a thick, brown blanket.

"*Danki*, Jonas," she said.

A short ride later, they rounded the corner at Jonas and Sarah Jane's house.

"I reckon the whole bunch is already here," Jonas said. He parked the buggy and helped Lizzie down. "Now, don't you be nervous, Lizzie. They all love you." He winked.

But do you love me, Jonas? She nodded.

Samuel and his son, David, were already sitting at the table when Lizzie and Jonas entered the kitchen from the porch. Anna was snacking on crackers in a high chair while Sarah Jane and Lillian scurried around the kitchen.

After the greetings, Lizzie asked, "Can I help with anything?"

"No, Lizzie, *danki*. You sit down and visit while we finish up here," Sarah Jane said. She stirred a pot on top of the stove.

"David, how are you feeling?" Lizzie asked. Samuel's son had undergone a kidney transplant this past year, and the boy looked like he was doing well, a healthy color in his cheeks.

"I feel *gut*." The fifteen-year-old smiled.

"And I see little Anna is growing like a weed." Lizzie reached over and tenderly touched the child's cheek. "So precious." What a lovely family. Lizzie wanted to be a part of it.

Jonas sat at the head of the table and instructed Lizzie to sit at the other end. It felt strange to sit in Irma Rose's spot, but she was honored to do so. Samuel and his wife sat on one side, and Sarah Jane took a seat beside David after she placed the stew in the middle of the table.

"Let us pray," Sarah Jane said. They all bowed their heads. Lizzie had so much to be thankful for.

"Now, let's eat," Jonas said when he felt they'd prayed for long enough. He smiled at Lizzie and winked, and she knew everything was going to be fine.

"This stew is *wunderbaar*, Sarah Jane," Lizzie told Jonas's daughter. "I'd be honored to have this recipe."

"Remind me after supper, and I'll be happy to jot it down for you," Sarah Jane said. "There's a secret ingredient in it."

Lillian laughed. "There's no secret about it, *Mamm*. I know what's in it, it's—"

"*Ach!* Don't say," Sarah Jane interrupted. "These boys will tell everyone."

"Sarah Jane, you think you be havin' a secret, but I know your special ingredient," Jonas said with a wink. "Pickle juice." He paused to chew a piece of meat in the stew. "You put a squirt of pickle juice in everything. Irma Rose, you taught her that, didn't ya, now?"

The room went silent, and Lizzie could feel all eyes on her. Just for this one day, in front of his family, Lizzie had hoped Jonas could remember that she was Lizzie. She could feel her face reddening, and her hands began to tremble, making it difficult for her to hold on to her spoon. Then she dropped the utensil, full of stew, and made a mess on the floor, like a small child.

"I'm so sorry, I—" She choked back tears.

"Don't you give it a second thought." Lillian was on her feet right away and retrieved the spoon. She had a fresh one in Lizzie's hand in no time. "Anna makes a mess all the time. We're used to it."

Lizzie forced a smile. She knew Lillian's intentions were good and her words said in the spirit to make Lizzie feel better. But Lizzie wasn't a baby, and she should be able to hold her own spoon and carry herself at supper, for goodness' sakes.

"Lilly, how did Sadie fare out there during the storm with the *Englischer* renting that cottage of hers?" Jonas asked. "I don't trust that fella."

"Now, Grandpa, that *fella* helped us the night you were— the night we couldn't find you," Lillian said. "He seems nice enough."

"A man like that might try to steal our Sadie away from here." Jonas sat up a little taller. "You want your best friend to be leavin' us?"

"Didn't you hear?" Lillian's eyes grew wide, and then she turned toward her mother. "Didn't you tell Grandpa, *Mamm?*"

"Tell me what?" Jonas stopped chewing and eyed his daughter. Lizzie was glad the focus was not on her.

"*Ach.* I guess I forgot. Milo showed up."

Even Lizzie had heard of Milo, and she thought Jonas might drop *his* spoon at the mention of this news. "The pen pal from Texas?" he asked.

"*Ya.* And if you're going to worry about anyone stealing Sadie away, you better worry about him."

Jonas grunted. "At least he's Old Order. Sadie wouldn't be veering from her faith and facing a shunning."

"I don't think you have anything to worry about," Lillian said.

But something in Lillian's tone made Lizzie suspect that maybe there was something to fear.

"Irma Rose, pass those rolls over here, can ya, please?"

Lizzie took a deep breath. Sarah Jane reached over and clutched Lizzie's free hand as she looked at her father. "Pop, this is Lizzie," she said in a firm voice.

Jonas looked up and seemed to realize what he'd done. "I'm sorry, Lizzie," he said, regret in his voice. And then he kept staring at her.

Lizzie grasped her spoon extra tight and said, "It's all right, Jonas."

But Jonas didn't look all right. His gaze lowered, as did his voice. "No, it's not all right," he said.

Everyone was quiet again for a few moments, and Lizzie knew she was trembling. It happened when her nerves got the best of her.

But then Lillian began to talk about her visit at the doctor's office, the mood lightened, and they all finished supper without incident. When it was time for Jonas to take Lizzie home, each one of his family hugged her neck and thanked her for coming. Given the circumstances, she figured things had gone rather well.

Jonas was quiet on the drive home.

"*Danki* for having me to supper with your family, Jonas," Lizzie said.

He nodded as he turned onto Lizzie's driveway, but he said nothing. Something was terribly wrong. Maybe it was a bad idea to have supper where he'd dined with Irma Rose for most of his life. Or perhaps she was being her normal worrisome self. She sat up a little taller. "Will I be seeing you for chess tomorrow? I think we have a rematch to play." She offered him a hopeful smile.

Jonas didn't answer and pulled the buggy to a stop. "Whoa, Jessie."

Lizzie fought the tears building in the corners of her eyes, and her heart was thumping madly. *Please, Jonas. No.*

Jonas hung his head. "Lizzie . . ." He gazed in her direction, and even in the darkness, his eyes told the tale. "Let's get you in out of this cold, and we'll talk inside."

He walked around to her side of the buggy and helped her down. And as she'd done before, she locked her arm in his and they headed up the porch steps. Lizzie held on extra tight.

"A game of chess before you go?" She tried to sound as cheerful as possible, even though her heart was breaking.

Jonas's eyes narrowed as he walked Lizzie to the bench at her kitchen table and motioned for her to sit down. He took a seat beside her.

"You don't have to say anything, Jonas." Lizzie lowered her eyes.

Jonas reached over and held her hand. With his other hand, he lifted her chin and gently turned her face toward him. "Lizzie, you are a special woman. A *gut* woman." She began to cry, and Jonas brushed away a tear with his thumb. "But I can't do this."

Lizzie pulled her hand from his and wept into her palms, not wanting him to see her like this, but unable to control the grief of not having him in her life.

Jonas stood up. "I'm sorry, Lizzie. I've only loved one woman. And it might be my silly way of thinking, but I feel like I'm betraying Irma Rose. I'm sorry. I think it'd be best if I not be comin' around anymore like this, and—"

"No, Jonas." She cried harder. "Please don't do this. We've enjoyed each other's company so. Surely, we can continue on in a friendly manner. We can still play chess, and you can still be my huggy bear, and—"

"Good-bye, Lizzie."

Lizzie followed him onto the front porch. "Jonas?"

He stopped, and then slowly turned around. "*Ya?*"

Lizzie wiped her eyes and caught her breath. "You can always come back, huggy bear."

He gave a sympathetic smile, and then he was gone.

Lizzie clutched her sides and wept, watching until he was out of sight.

Kade dressed Tyler the next morning and indulged his son by letting him lick the bowl clean of the tapioca pudding. "That might be all the pudding we have for a while," he said to Tyler. But then added, "Until I get things fixed with Sadie."

He'd had a sleepless night. Sadie's tearful face, her pleading eyes. He couldn't let her leave for Texas, not like this, anyway, with so much unsaid. It was a mess, and he wasn't sure how he was going to fix things, but her leaving because he forced her to go didn't seem to be the answer.

"Let's go, buddy." He helped Tyler get his warm clothes on, although it was a sunny day outside. Maybe they would be able to shed some of this winter gear later this morning.

First stop, a flower boutique. It had been a long time since he'd given a woman flowers, but it was the thing to do when you'd made one cry. "Let's go get Miss Sadie some flowers. What do you think about that?"

"Love Sadie." Tyler smiled.

"Me too, buddy. Me too."

Kade pulled his car out of the barn for the first time since the blizzard, and he found a flower shop on Lincoln Highway.

He knew that extravagant would not impress Sadie. Quality of the bloom itself would. He had heard her talk more than once about how the Amish prided themselves for toiling the land and producing quality products. Roses. Elegant and traditional. He chose two dozen, realizing when he left that a dozen might have been more appropriate. "We'll just say a dozen of them are from you," he told Tyler.

His son had behaved so well in the flower shop, Kade decided to stop at the bakery and reward the boy with a whoopie pie.

"Tyler, you do realize that you won't always be able to eat tapioca pudding and whoopie pies, right?" Kade smiled. Tyler shoved the last bite in his mouth, and then grinned back at his father.

"Let's head to Sadie's and see if we can fix things somehow."

It was close to lunchtime when Kade pulled into Sadie's driveway. He wasn't sure if she'd be at her shop again today. Even when it wasn't a scheduled day to work, the ladies seemed to gather there. Kade would stop there on the way to the farmhouse.

"Hello, Kade," Lillian said when he and Tyler walked in. "Is everything all right?"

"Yeah. I was looking for Sadie. I figured I'd stop here on the way to the house."

"Actually, she told me to help you with anything you might need while she's away."

Kade took a step forward. "What do you mean, *away?*"

Lillian set aside some sort of knitting project she was working on. Her eyes grew serious. "Kade, she left for Texas this morning with Milo."

Despair gnawed at Kade's heart. "For how long?"

"I don't know. Possibly a few weeks. Maybe longer." Lillian didn't seem surprised by Kade's reaction to the news.

"I thought she wasn't leaving until Saturday. Why'd she leave today?"

Lillian's questioning eyes met with Kade's. "You tell me."

Kade realized that Sadie must have confided in Lillian, but he was unsure how much she knew, and he didn't want to get Sadie in any trouble with her friend. "I'm guessing maybe she was upset with me?" Kade posed the question as if he might already know the answer.

"This is an opportunity for her to find happiness, Kade," Lillian said. "I don't want Sadie to leave here. She's my best friend. But I want her to be happy."

He shoved his hands in his pockets and sighed heavily. "That's exactly why I told her to go."

"I am sensing that was hard for you to do."

"How much did she tell you?"

"Enough."

Kade needed a spark of hope. "Can you maybe throw me a bone, here? I mean, does she care about me in the least?"

Lillian smiled. "I think you know the answer to that."

Tyler walked up to Lillian and touched her on the leg.

"Well, hello there, Tyler," she said.

"Kade loves Sadie." He smiled broadly.

"Wait! No. I mean, I never said that," Kade said. He turned to Tyler. "Tyler, why did you say that?" Then Kade remembered—Tyler had told him earlier that he loved Sadie, and Kade had said, "Me too, buddy." He couldn't make his child out to be a liar. "Okay, I might have sort of said it."

Lillian cocked her head to one side. "And how does one *sort of* say it?"

Kade put his hands on his hips, paced around the room. "I thought I was doing the right thing."

"You did do the right thing," Lillian said.

"Then why do I feel so crummy?"

"Kade, what did you think would happen if feelings continued to develop between the two of you? That Sadie would leave everything she loves, her friends, her family, and travel to a life that is foreign to her?"

"Didn't she just do that?" He was sure his hurt shone through in his sarcastic tone.

"You know what I mean. Or, even a further stretch, were you willing to give up all you know to be a part of Sadie's life here? If the answer to both those questions is no, then you did the right thing by letting go of Sadie, no matter your feelings for her."

Lillian was right. It was the reason Kade told Sadie to go to Texas in the first place. He just didn't realize it was going to hurt so much. "You're right." He had no one to blame for his defeat but himself. A knot churned his stomach.

"But if there is anything you need, one of us is here at the shop during the day. I'm filling in for Mary Ellen today, as she has a sick child. We mix things up a bit, but one of us will be here— short of a blizzard." Lillian smiled.

The only thing Kade needed was Sadie.

"Thanks," he said. He motioned Tyler toward the door.

———————

"What do you mean you won't be seeing Lizzie anymore?" Sarah Jane asked her father over lunch a few days later. "I thought the two of you enjoyed each other's company, enjoyed playing chess together."

"*Ya,* we did." Jonas opened the *Budget* and scanned the pages. It didn't appear that he felt the subject warranted further conversation, but Sarah Jane suspected it did.

"What happened, Pop?" She folded the kitchen towel over her arm and stood beside her father, who was seated at the kitchen table.

He peered above the paper and cut his eyes in her direction. "I reckon this is not conversation for a father to be havin' with his daughter."

Sarah Jane chuckled. "Pop, I'm a middle-aged woman, not a child. And you sure did seem happy when you were spending time with Lizzie." She paused and recalled the way Lizzie gazed at Jonas during supper the other night. "And Lizzie sure is crazy about you."

Jonas folded the newspaper, blew out a breath of frustration, and looked up at Sarah Jane. "Lizzie is a *gut* woman. But it seems rather silly to be courtin' at my age." He took a sip of the sweet tea Sarah Jane had prepared for him.

"Why? Why is that silly, Pop? I think you should do whatever makes you happy." She walked to the counter and finished preparing a turkey sandwich for him. When he didn't answer, she took him the sandwich, then took a seat across from him. "Why is it silly, Pop?" she asked again.

Jonas took a big bite, chewed it, and thought over his response. "She's not my Irma Rose. Sometimes I might think she is." His face twisted into a scowl. "I know I get a bit confused sometimes, and I reckon it ain't fair to Lizzie." Her pop held his head high. "I've only loved one woman, Sarah Jane. My Irma Rose. Your *mamm.*"

"Pop, I know how much you loved *Mamm*. But that doesn't mean you can't be happy with someone else too. I think *Mamm* would want that, and she thought the world of Lizzie. It just makes me sad, because the two of you seem to get along so well."

He took another bite of his sandwich, mulled it over some more. Then he swallowed and shook his head. "Something 'bout seeing Lizzie sitting there in Irma Rose's chair just—"

Sarah Jane reached over and touched her father's hand. "Go on," she said.

"It didn't seem right, I reckon. And it can't be *gut* that sometimes I think Lizzie is Irma Rose." Jonas pushed back his plate, half a sandwich still left. "I choose not to talk about this anymore, Sarah Jane."

She was clear on the rules. When the man of the house said a topic was not up for discussion, it was not to be debated. But Sarah Jane had spent a large part of her life living with the *Englisch*, and she tended to push when she shouldn't. "All I'm saying, Pop, is that—"

Jonas spun around. "Sarah Jane, did you not hear me?"

"*Ya*, Pop." His face was fire red, and Sarah Jane didn't want his blood pressure to get any higher. Between her father's cancer and the onset of Alzheimer's, they had enough to deal with. Maybe there would be a better time to talk about this, when her father wasn't feeling so sensitive. He'd been sulking for the past several days.

"I'm gonna go over to Sadie's place, check on that *Englisch* fella. He oughta not even be left alone out there. Might steal everything Sadie's got." Jonas put on his straw hat and grabbed his long, black coat from the rack.

Sarah Jane grinned. "Pop. Surely you're not serious. That man is filthy rich. He's not going to steal anything from Sadie. That's ridiculous." She cleared the plates from the table.

Jonas grumbled, and Sarah Jane couldn't make out what he said. "What?" she asked.

"I said I think I heard the word *filthy* in there somewhere." He pulled his coat tight. "I'll be back later, Lilly."

Sarah Jane watched him walk out the door and hoped he would be safe in the buggy, realizing he had just called her *Lilly*.

Jonas headed down Black Horse Road toward Sadie's place. He slowed down and hesitated at Lizzie's driveway. She'd been pretty torn up when he last saw her, and the vision haunted him. But he sped up again and passed her house. No good could come of his spending time with Lizzie. Jonas was sure she wanted to marry him, and that was something he wasn't about to consider. Irma Rose would be throwing stones at him from heaven.

But he couldn't help but wonder how Lizzie was and what she might be up to right now.

Jonas pushed the thoughts about Lizzie aside and turned into Sadie's driveway. He stepped out of the buggy onto the packed snow, glad the sun was out and warming things up a bit. Jonas knocked on the door of the cottage.

To his surprise, a small person answered. A cute youngster. Must be the slow child he'd heard the others talking about. "Hello. Where is your pop?" Jonas asked.

"Pop, pop, pop!" the boy yelled, but he didn't move from the door. "Pop, pop, pop!"

Jonas couldn't help but grin. The young lad was beaming and cute as he could be.

He heard footsteps approaching and saw the *Englischer* coming up behind his son.

"Jonas." The fella looked surprised, ran his hand nervously through his hair. "What brings you here?" Then he looked down at the boy. "Did you meet Tyler? Tyler, this is Mr. Jonas."

"Just *Jonas* will be fine," he said. "Hello, Tyler." He tipped his hat in the child's direction. "I'm just checkin' on you." Jonas lifted his chin, eyed the *Englischer*. "Why are you still here? I understand the boy's mother passed. Don't you need to be gettin' back to the city?"

"I probably do." Kade shrugged. "But I'm not ready to face my life back there, plus I told Sadie I'd take care of things around here while she's gone, which reminds me . . ." He put his hands on his hips. "Her *friend* forgot to show me how to take care of these animals."

"*Ach*, you mean Milo, her future husband?" Jonas asked. Then he laughed. "I reckon to venture that you don't know a thing 'bout tending to Sadie's animals."

"I don't believe I've heard anyone say that Milo is her future husband."

Jonas was enjoying the *Englischer's* irritation, which he knew was wrong in God's eyes. But he couldn't help himself. "They'll be wed soon enough, I reckon."

"Whatever." Kade rolled his eyes. Jonas grinned. "Is there

something you need, Jonas? Tyler, why don't you go play with your letters." Kade motioned for Tyler to step into the house, and the boy did so.

Jonas pushed back the rim of his hat. "Just checkin' on things." He paused, then sighed. "But I reckon since I'm here, I'd best show you how to tend to Sadie's animals since you said you'd take care of that, which was probably a silly thing to do."

"It can't be that hard. Let me throw on my shoes and coat, and get Tyler dressed. We'll be right back." He paused at the door. "Do you want to come in, out of the cold?"

Jonas shook his head. "I'm plenty fine right here."

"Okay." Kade closed the door.

It just didn't make no sense to him why the *Englischer* didn't go back to where he came from, unless he had some pretty strong feelings for Sadie. After a couple of minutes, Kade and the boy were back.

"Come on, Tyler." Kade escorted Tyler through the doorway and closed the door behind him. "We're ready."

When they got to the barn, the boy's eyes lit up at the sight of Sadie's two horses. He ran to the stall and climbed up on the first notch of the gate.

"You like the horses?" Jonas asked. He patted the boy on the head. The child jerked away from him like Jonas had hurt him.

"He doesn't like to be touched," Kade said. "Well, I mean, he does. He likes to be hugged, but he sort of lets us know. He doesn't like to be touched otherwise."

Jonas nodded, although he wasn't sure he understood what Kade meant by that. "This here is Sugar, and that one is Spice. Silliest names I've ever heard for horses." Jonas shook his head.

"Sugar!" the boy echoed enthusiastically. Jonas couldn't get over what a handsome youngster he was. He had to admit, if he was fair, the boy did get his looks from his father.

"They like to have their noses scratched. See here." Jonas showed the boy how to scratch Sugar's nose, then Spice's. Then he walked around the barn and showed Kade where everything was kept. Feed, supplies to clean the stalls, horse grooming brushes. "You'll be needin' to tend to the pigs as well." Jonas stopped and studied Kade's fancy clothes. "You gonna be able to handle all this?"

"It doesn't look like all that much. Feed the horses, clean the stalls, brush them. Check their water. Feed the pigs. Did I miss anything?"

Jonas narrowed his brows. "I reckon not." He had to admit, it warmed his heart to see Tyler having such a good time. "He seems to have taken a special liking to the horses." Jonas pointed to Tyler, who was still scratching the horses on their noses.

"Yes, he does. I'm still trying to learn the things he likes and doesn't like. He's autistic. Do you know what that means?"

"I reckon I don't much." But Tyler looked to Jonas like he was just being a normal little boy at the moment.

"Well, for example, he can read. But he doesn't understand what he reads. I guess you could say he has a limited understanding about some things."

Jonas could see the worry in the *Englisher*'s heart for his boy. "He looks like he's having a mighty *gut* time right now."

Kade smiled, donning the proud look of a father. "Yes, he does look like he's having a *gut* time."

"*Ach*, you speaka *da Deitch?*" Jonas grinned at Kade's attempt.

"No, not much. Only what I've picked up from Sadie." Jonas watched Kade staring at the boy, as if worrying about the fact that he was different.

"Children like Tyler are a special gift from God. There's a special place in heaven for them," Jonas said.

"That's what Sadie said." Kade didn't look up though. He kept staring at the boy.

"Sadie is a smart woman."

"Yes, she is."

Jonas wasn't sure about this *Englischer*, but one thing was for certain—he appeared to be hurting about several things. Mostly his son. And Sadie being gone. Jonas knew what it was like to be detached from a child. Sarah Jane had left them when she was eighteen to live in the *Englisch* world. They'd only been blessed by her return a few years ago. And Jonas also knew what it was like to love someone you couldn't have. He'd been in love with Lizzie for a while now, even though it was a dishonor to Irma Rose. Jonas could tell that Kade was in love with Sadie—something about the way he spoke her name. And Kade certainly had worry in his heart about the boy.

"How would you boys like to take a ride in my buggy into town? I wonder if Tyler would like that."

Kade looked confused. Rightly so. Jonas had given the man a rather hard time since he'd arrived in Lancaster County. "Seriously?"

"*Ya, ya.* We best enjoy the sunshine. We can have coffee in town." Jonas figured it might keep his mind off Lizzie. He didn't have anything else to do anyway.

"That would be great. Tyler, you ready to go for a ride in the buggy?" He turned toward Jonas. "Thanks, Jonas. This will be fun for Tyler, and there is something important I want to ask you."

Jonas couldn't imagine what Kade wanted to talk about, so he shrugged. "Let's be on our way, then."

16

IT WAS TWO WEEKS BEFORE LILLIAN RECEIVED A LETTER from Sadie. She'd reprimand her friend later for not checking in sooner, but for the moment she was thrilled to pull a letter from her mailbox.

"Look, Anna, a letter from Sadie," she said to her little one. Anna was cutting another tooth and a bit fussy, so Lillian set the letter aside and gave Pete a flick of the reins. "We'll read the letter when we get to *Mammi* Sarah Jane and *Daddi* Jonas's *haus*. How's that?" Lillian pushed back Anna's soft hair from her face and checked the buckle on Anna's car seat. Many of the Amish carry their babies on their lap, but Lillian wasn't comfortable with that. Maybe it was the time she'd spent in the *Englisch* world, where car seats were a necessity, but she wanted Anna safely strapped in, even in the buggy.

Lillian reached down and rubbed her expanding belly. *Less than two months to go*, she thought, as she pulled onto Black Horse Road. The weather had warmed to a cool thirty-eight, and the sun was making a regular appearance. Still cold, but a welcome relief following the nasty blizzard they'd recently gone through. Lillian was looking forward to spending the day baking and chatting with her mother. And she was looking forward to reading Sadie's letter. She couldn't imagine what adventures Sadie must be having, since she'd never been far from Lancaster County. Since Lillian had lived in Texas prior to converting to the Old Order Amish in Pennsylvania, she was anxious to hear what her friend thought about the Lone Star State, and more important, how things were going with Milo Troyer.

But as Lillian headed down the road, she felt compelled to make a stop along the way. She knew her grandpa wasn't spending time with Lizzie any longer, and Lillian thought she'd check on her. The first few days after their initial breakup, her mother said Grandpa had been a bear to live with, moping around the house, complaining that Sarah Jane didn't play chess with him enough, and even complaining about the food her mother was cooking. But then, her mother had told her that an unlikely friendship had developed. Grandpa had been spending his free time with *Englischer* Kade Saunders, who as it turned out, proved to be a challenging chess partner.

It didn't make any sense to Lillian, though. What could those two possibly have in common outside of chess? Grandpa had bordered on being mean to Kade since the moment they met, citing his distrust for the man on more than one occasion. Lillian guided Pete down the drive to Lizzie's house. She unstrapped Anna and grabbed a loaf of banana nut bread she'd made, along with a container of chicken soup. Balancing Anna on her hip, she struggled up Lizzie's porch steps.

"Lillian, how *gut* to see you," Lizzie said. "Come in, child. Come in."

"Hello, Lizzie. I brought you some banana nut bread and some chicken soup." She set Anna down on the wooden floor once they were inside.

Lizzie squatted down to Anna's level. "You are getting so big."

Lillian set the soup and bread on Lizzie's table. "I hope you don't mind us stopping by. I was worried about you."

Lizzie stood up. "*Ach,* I be fine," she said. "And you stop by for any reason, anytime. And, oh, how I'll enjoy this bread and soup."

"No, Anna," Lillian said when Anna reached for an apron Lizzie had hung on a nearby rack. Lillian turned toward Lizzie. "She's a handful these days."

Lizzie walked to her cabinet and pulled a box of crackers down. "Can she have some of these?"

"Sure." Lillian set Anna in the wooden armchair at the end of Lizzie's table. Once Anna was settled, both women sat on either side of the table. Lillian glanced around the kitchen and saw a frightful mess—dishes in the sink, open containers of food left unattended on the counter, and the floor didn't look like it had seen a broom in weeks. "Lizzie, are you doing okay these days?"

"*Ya, ya.* I do just fine." Lizzie smiled.

Lillian was wondering how long it had been since Lizzie's nieces, or anyone, had visited.

"How about a glass of sweet tea?" Lizzie stood up and walked toward the counter. She pulled two glasses from the cabinet.

"That would be *wunderbaar,*" Lillian said. She continued to study Lizzie's kitchen. There were several pill bottles to one side of the sink. Two of the bottles were knocked over and empty. Lillian stood up and walked to the sink. She picked up one of the bottles. "Lizzie, do you need me to get these filled for you?'"

"No, no. Those are old bottles. I have *mei* refills upstairs by the bed." Lizzie placed two glasses of tea on the table, along with a glass of milk for Anna. "Can she drink from a glass?"

"*Ya*, she does, with some help. Sometimes she still takes a bottle, but we're trying to wean her from that." Lillian took a sip of tea and struggled to gulp it down. Sweetest tea she'd ever had, and she wondered how long that pitcher had been in Lizzie's refrigerator. She grabbed Anna's plastic glass filled with milk before Anna had a chance to get it to her lips. "Actually, Anna had a bottle before we left. Maybe just some water for her?"

"*Ya, ya.*" Lizzie smiled and went to retrieve a fresh glass. As Lizzie pumped water from the sink, Lillian sniffed the milk. Then grimaced and set the glass aside, confirming what she'd feared.

Lizzie returned to the table and handed Anna the glass. "Oops," she said when water trickled down Anna's chin.

"She's still a messy drinker when it comes to cups," Lillian said. She wiped the water from Anna's chin with her thumb. "Lizzie, is there anything you need?"

"No, I have all that I need. But *danki*, Mary Ellen, for bringing me the bread and soup. Is for sure I will enjoy it."

Lillian decided not to correct her on the name. Instead she smiled. "You're welcome, Lizzie." Lillian stood up. "I best be off. *Mamm* is expecting me. But Lizzie, I'd be glad to pick you up anything you might need from town."

"No, dear. I'm fine." Lizzie stood up and patted Anna on the head. "You take care of this little one and tell your *mamm* and Jonas I send my best."

Lillian nodded, unsure whether to tell Lizzie how much she knew her grandfather missed her. But Lizzie was smiling and seemed glad she'd stopped by. She didn't want to cause any upset for Lizzie.

"Whoa, Pete," Lillian instructed the horse. She pulled off on the side of Black Horse Road to read Sadie's letter before she arrived at her *mamm's*. Anna had dozed off in her carrier, and Lillian wanted to enjoy a quiet moment reading what Sadie had been up to. She pried the envelope open and pulled out the letter. Lillian took a deep breath and unfolded the white paper. She wanted Sadie to be happy, just not so far away in Texas.

Dear Lillian,

I am sorry it took so long for me to pen this note. It was a long travel on the bus from our home to Texas. But there was much to talk about with Milo during our trip. He is a kind man and everything I had hoped he would be. Milo's family has made me feel welcome. He has three sisters—Ellen, Hannah, and Lavina. Between them, they have twelve children. Milo's mamm, Martha, is a gut woman, and I like her very much. His daed, John, I don't see much. He is a hard worker, always busy making furniture or tending to chores around the farm. I am staying with Martha and John while I am here.

Milo is a hard worker too. He stays busy at his farm and with his wood-working projects, and he comes to his folks' haus in the evenings to pick me up, just like if we were young and courting. We even attended a Sunday singing, although I felt a mite silly at my age.

I'm not sure if this is an Old Order District, or just a gathering of Old Order families. There are only a few families left, and almost everyone works in the city. Milo is one of the few who farms his land, but he also must hold a construction job in town to make ends meet. Their ways are different than our ways. Shunning is almost unheard-of, and the supper hour is at 6:00 instead of four. They sleep later too, until 6:30. I like that part.

I miss you, Lillian. And Rachel, Mary Ellen, Katie Ann, and Sarah Jane. And I miss Jonas, his protective ways of me. I must tell you, in confidence, I miss the Englischer and his boy very much. Can you please write to me and tell me how they are doing?

Lillian, I will need to sell my farm to have a life here with Milo. We discussed him moving to Lancaster County, but it seems to make more sense for us to live amongst his large family. I will continue to live with his folks until a time when we see fit to marry, which most likely will be after the fall harvest in November. As our Order has done in the past, please offer my land to someone in the Amish community first. I'm sure Bishop Ebersol can handle the arrangements.

I will be back on April 1 to gather my things. Kade and Tyler will be gone by then. I hope that my renters have not been too much trouble. The boy loves tapioca pudding, and Kade eats just about anything, but I don't think he knows how to cook much. And Lillian, Tyler likes to read books. He doesn't really understand them, but I have a big box of books suitable for him in my bedroom. I collected them over the years for a child of my own, but please give them to Tyler. Milo's family has many books here, if God should ever bless me and Milo with a child.

If it's not too much trouble, can you please show Kade how to make tapioca pudding so he can make it for the boy when he returns to his home in Los Angeles? Or maybe he can give the recipe to whoever might be tending to Tyler.

I must go, Lillian. Please write to me very soon.

Em Gott Sei Friede,
Sadie

"God's peace to you, too, my friend," Lillian whispered. She folded the note and put it back in the envelope, most disturbed by the tone of Sadie's letter. It seemed to Lillian that Sadie was masking sadness, not once mentioning that she loved Milo, and focusing instead on the needs of the *Englischers*.

Lillian whistled Pete into action and continued down Black Horse Road to her *mamm's* house. She headed down the long driveway and fought the worry in her heart about Sadie. But what a surprise she had when she pulled near the house.

Grandpa, Kade, and the boy were busy making a snowman in the front yard. It seemed strange to Lillian on several levels. One, she'd never seen her grandfather frolicking about in such a playful way. Two, Kade Saunders was laughing and playful as well, a far cry from the stuffy *Englischer* who had shown up several weeks ago. And most of all, she couldn't get past what good friends Kade and her grandpa had become.

She headed toward the house with Anna on her hip. "Hello," she hollered to the trio as she made her way up the porch steps.

"Hello, Lilly." Grandpa packed another mound of snow on their structure, and then held Tyler in his arms so the boy could place a carrot nose on the snowman. Kade waved, but quickly refocused his attention on his project.

"What have I told you about carrying that baby when you are this pregnant?" *Mamm* met Lillian at the steps and pulled Anna from her arms. "It's still slippery out here, and last thing we need is for you to fall with this baby in your arms."

"I'm fine, *Mamm*," Lillian mumbled. She turned to have a final look at her grandpa, Kade, and Tyler. "What are Kade and his son doing here?"

Sarah Jane put Anna in a high chair and offered her some crackers. "I told you, your grandpa and Kade have developed quite a friendship. Pop is either there, or Kade and the boy are here." Her *mamm* paused, raised her brows. "Want to hear something even more shocking?"

Lillian sat down on the bench in the kitchen. "I don't know," she said hesitantly.

"Your grandfather is teaching Kade the *Ordnung*. Kade asked him to."

"What? Why?" Lillian paused for a moment. "Kade Saunders can't possibly be thinking of staying here. That's ridiculous, a man of his stature and wealth. I mean, why would he do such a thing?"

Her mother shrugged. "You tell me." Her mother walked to the refrigerator and pulled out a tub of chicken salad. She began to spread the mixture on slices of bread she had laid out.

"*Mamm*, if he's staying because of Sadie, that is the wrong reason to join the community." Lillian shook her head.

Sarah Jane placed her hands on her hips and faced Lillian. "Are you sure you are one to speak against this?"

Lillian's jaw dropped. "I didn't convert to Amish to be with Samuel, *Mamm*, and you know that."

Her mother didn't say anything, but continued to spread chicken salad on the bread. She topped each mound with another piece of bread. Then she turned around and winked at her daughter. "I never said you did."

Lillian always believed that she would have converted to the Amish faith, with or without Samuel by her side. But was she being honest with herself?

"A man like Kade doesn't leave the *Englisch* world, *Mamm*. He's been on the cover of *Forbes*, for goodness' sakes. He's a millionaire. A person like that doesn't give it all up to become Amish, for a woman or otherwise."

"I approached this very subject with your grandfather. He said Kade is a miserable, unhappy man in search of the same peacefulness that you came here looking for."

"It's not the same!" Lillian insisted. "He has a life. Millions of dollars, people counting on him, probably lives in a mansion. People like him don't do things like this." Lillian folded her arms across her chest.

"Lillian, you know it's not our place to judge Kade's heart in this matter." Her mother reprimanded her with her eyes, and Lillian recalled being on the other side of this conversation with Sadie recently. Lillian had accused Sadie of this very thing where Kade was concerned.

"I know, *Mamm*," she said, then sighed. "But how in the world did Kade and Grandpa become friends in the first place?"

"I think your grandpa took a liking to the boy first and then got to know Kade." She twisted around and smiled. "And it didn't hurt that Kade turned out to be quite the chess player. To tell you the truth, Lillian, I'm relieved your grandpa has someone else besides me to play chess with. I don't have time to always be indulging him. Kade seemed to take over where Lizzie left off."

Lillian sighed. "We need to talk about Lizzie, *Mamm*. I think—"

"You think what?" Her grandpa burst through the kitchen door, followed by Kade and Tyler. "Is lunch ready?" he asked next. "We done worked up an appetite." He hung his straw hat on the rack and sat down at the head of the long, wooden table, and then turned toward Lillian, his face as serious as she'd ever seen it. "What about Lizzie?"

"Hello," Lillian said to Kade; then she turned to Tyler. "Hello, Tyler. Did you have fun making a snowman?" The boy's eyes jetted around the room, but he smiled for an instant in Lillian's direction.

Grandpa grunted. "Tell me about Lizzie," he demanded.

Lillian pursed her lips together for a moment, then said, "She doesn't seem like she's doing very *gut.*"

Grandpa sat up a little taller and narrowed his eyes in Lillian's direction. "What do you mean?"

"She's just—just out of sorts a little." Lillian paused. "I mean, Lizzie's house has always been so tidy, but today when I stopped by there, dishes were piled in the sink, the milk she offered Anna was sour and smelled as if it had been in there for weeks, and . . ."

"And what?" Grandpa asked.

"She called me Mary Ellen when I left." Lillian turned toward her mother. "*Mamm*, I think we need to go over there later and help Lizzie clean up. I would have done it while I was there, but I had Anna, and I'm limited by what I can do with my big belly and all. Maybe we can—"

Grandpa was on his feet. "Sarah Jane, I'm taking the buggy out for while."

"Don't you want lunch?" she asked. "I have your sandwich ready." Her mother held a plate toward him but was left standing there as Grandpa scrambled out the door.

There was no doubt in Lillian's mind where Grandpa was

headed. And since she'd already stirred things up in one couple's tattered love life, why stop there? "I received a letter from Sadie today," she said, trying to sound casual.

"What?" Kade asked, his eyes wide. Then he tried to readjust his excitement. "I mean, how is she doing?"

Kade didn't fool her for a minute. "Fine," Lillian said. Selfish thoughts plagued her mind—*if Kade were to convert to the Amish faith, Sadie might come home.* "Well, I *guess* she's fine," she added.

"What do you mean, you *guess*?" Kade accepted a plate from Sarah Jane. "*Danki,*" he said smoothly.

Lillian laughed.

"What's so funny?" he asked.

"I'm sorry." She laughed again. "It sounds funny to hear you speaking Pennsylvania *Deitsch.*"

"Lillian," Sarah Jane began in a tone that Lillian was familiar with. "I don't think anyone laughed at you when you were learning the *Deitsch.*"

But Lillian didn't apologize. She tapped her finger to her chin, eyeballing Kade.

"What do you mean you guess Sadie is fine?" Kade asked again.

"She wants us to have Bishop Ebersol take care of selling her farm."

"What? Why?" Kade's voice rose in surprise. "Why would she sell her farm? To move to Texas? She doesn't even *know* that Milo person. I thought she was just going for a visit?"

Sarah Jane sat down at the table with her own plate. "It does seem a little fast," she said.

"Evidently she is going to stay in Texas. She and Milo are

talking of marriage, maybe in November," Lillian said. She looked at Kade. "So, I guess you won't need to be continuing your studies of the *Ordnung.*"

Kade reached over to wipe chicken salad from Tyler's chin. "Why is that?"

"I guess I figure, what's the point?" Lillian shrugged, then took a bite of her sandwich.

Her mother glared in her direction. "It's probably none of your business," Sarah Jane said.

"No, it's all right." Kade took a deep breath and stared hard at Lillian. "I guess you think I have alternative motives for learning about the Amish ways?"

"It crossed my mind." Lillian smiled.

Kade took a bite of his sandwich. "Hmm," he mumbled.

"I can't imagine, in my wildest of dreams, why a man of your stature would be so interested in our ways. I can't help but wonder if it's because—" Lillian could feel her mother's glare blazing into her skin, but she went on. "Because of Sadie."

"It is exactly because of Sadie." Kade's expression challenged her to argue.

"Well, that's the wrong reason to—"

But Kade interrupted her. "Sadie represents the kind of person I want to be, a Christ-centered person, a person of faith. I want to be a good father, a good man . . ." He paused, his eyes filled with hope. "Sadie makes me want to be a better person. So, yes, my decision to study the *Ordnung* is because of Sadie."

"She's not coming back," Lillian stated emphatically.

"Does that mean I can't stay, in search of my own peace? It

seemed to have worked for you. Or did you convert to be with Samuel?"

"I did not convert just to—" Lillian's voice rose, bristling with indignation. "You don't know what you're talking about anyway, and—"

"You don't know what you're talking about either." His angry gaze swept over her.

"Both of you, stop it!" Sarah Jane interjected. "You sound like two bickering children." She shook her finger at Lillian. "You are in no position to judge what Kade is doing." Then she pointed the same crooked finger in Kade's direction. "And you are in no position to judge Lillian's actions. That is for God, and God only. So both of you settle down."

Tyler began to slam his hands on the table, as if sensing the upset in the room, which caused his tea to spill. Then Anna began to wail.

"See what you both have done," Sarah Jane said. She picked up Anna and paced the kitchen, while Kade attempted to comfort Tyler.

"Hey, buddy," Kade said. "Everything is okay. Let's don't do that." He looked up at Sarah Jane. "Sorry about the mess."

"It's no problem," Sarah Jane said. "I'm going to go take Anna upstairs and see if she needs a diaper change.

Kade began to sing "Itsy Bitsy Spider" to Tyler, and Lillian bit her bottom lip to stifle the giggle she felt. Kade seemed so incredibly out of character.

There she went—judging again.

Tyler stopped slamming his hands against the table and refocused on his sandwich. Kade smiled. "Go ahead. Laugh. I know you're dying to, but it's the only thing that seems to calm Tyler down." He reached for a nearby towel and began wiping up the spilled tea.

Lillian grinned. "I'm not making fun. Really. I think it's sweet the way you sing to him."

Kade's face turned red, and he shrugged. "It's a far cry from a high-profile life in Los Angeles, huh?"

He sounded almost embarrassed as he said it, and there was something touching in his voice, combined with the way he tenderly smiled at his son. "*Ya*, it is," she said softly, wondering if perhaps he was telling the truth. Maybe even a wealthy, influential man like Kade Saunders was simply seeking contentment, the way she was when she came to Lancaster County.

"I came here to get away from life. It was never my intention to stay here, far from it." He smiled. "Then I got to know Sadie, particularly during the blizzard, and—and something about her, the calm, the goodness." He shrugged. "I'd like to see what it's all about, that's all."

"Fair enough," Lillian said. She knew what it was like to feel lost, detached from God. She also knew what a miraculous thing it was to reconnect with God and to trust in His will. "Grandpa is a *gut* teacher, I'm sure."

Kade smiled. "I don't think he cared for me too much at first, but Tyler seems to have stolen his heart, and we're sort of a package deal."

"Grandpa seems to like you just fine," Lillian said.

"He's quite the chess player." Kade paused. "Quite the *man*, actually. I'm honored to know him."

Lillian smiled. "We all are."

Jonas removed his straw hat and stared at the simple tombstone in front of him, no different from the other plain markers in remembrance of those who'd passed—except this stone marked the spot where his beloved Irma Rose was laid to rest. He bent to one knee, his tired old bones cracking in opposition, and he bowed his head to thank the Lord for the life he'd lived, for the blessing of living so much of it with Irma Rose.

He folded his arms atop his knee, his hat dangling from one hand. His heart was heavy, not so much for Irma Rose as for another in need.

"Irma Rose," he began, "I don't want a lashing from you when I get to heaven, so I reckon I'll run somethin' by you." He paused, scratched his forehead. "It's Lizzie, Irma Rose. I think she's in trouble, and I reckon I'm 'bout all she's got, and—"

Jonas shook his head. That wasn't the truth. Not all of it anyway.

He glanced around the small cemetery, sprigs of brown poking through the melting clumps of snow. Sunshine beamed across the meadow in delicate rays, as if God were slowly cleaning up after one season, in preparation for the next. Soon it would be spring, Irma Rose's favorite time of year, when new foliage mirrored hope for plentiful harvests, when colorful blooms represented life, filled with colorful variations of our wonderment as humans.

"I love you, Irma Rose. I've loved you since the first day I saw you, sittin' under that old oak tree at your folks' house, readin' a book. You musta been only thirteen at the time, but I knew I'd marry you someday." Jonas smiled at the recollection of that young girl, so long ago. "And we had a *gut* life. I miss you every single day." He swallowed back emotion. "But I've grown to love another woman, Irma Rose. Lizzie. She's a fine woman, and I'd like to do right by her and love her openly the way she loves me. But I've been holdin' back, out of my loyalty to you, my wife."

Wet snow was soaking through the knee of his pants, numbing the joint to a point he feared he wouldn't be able to hoist himself up. But it didn't seem right to speak about such things towering over her, so he endured, and went on. "I'm gonna ask Lizzie to marry me, Irma Rose. And I reckon I've come here for your blessing."

17

SADIE HELPED MILO'S MOTHER, MARTHA, CLEAN THE breakfast dishes. Daylight shone through the kitchen window as the clock on the wall chimed seven times. It still seemed odd to Sadie that breakfast was served so late in the morning. At home, she would have already had breakfast, done her baking, given the house a once-over, and tended to the animals.

She glanced around Martha and John's kitchen, not unlike her own, except dark-blue blinds covered the windows instead of green. And Martha had a few decorative trinkets placed about the room, items Bishop Ebersol wouldn't have taken a liking to—a colorful fruit print propped up against the counter backdrop, a stained-glass picture hanging in the window, and three ceramic dogs grouped together on the hutch. All items that served no purpose, but gave the room a certain luster. Even though this house was simple in nature, Sadie knew she was a long way from home.

In the den, Martha and John's furniture had decorative carvings etched into the wooden rocking chairs, and multicolored throw pillows lined a long, tan couch. A colorful rug was the focal point in the room. Milo's community abstained from electricity, owning cars, having a telephone in the house—most of the other rules that Sadie's district adhered to—but things seemed more

casual, lacking the discipline Sadie was used to. Even church service was only an hour and a half, as compared to the three-hour
worship she was accustomed to. Although, truth be told, that was
okay by her.

She placed a plate in the cabinet and stared out the window
toward flat, brown land that stretched as far as she could see. No
dips or meadows, just barren land waiting for spring to arrive.
And it was warm in Texas. It was the first week in March, but the
thermometer on the tree outside the window read seventy-two
degrees. She wondered if snow still covered the ground at home.

Homesickness set in right away, but Sadie did her best to push
through it, basking in her time with Milo and getting to know
what would potentially be her new family come fall. It was all
lovely. Milo's family was wonderful, and Milo was a gentleman
in every way. He was perfect for her, just as she'd hoped.

Milo lived on the adjoining property. Sadie could see his
house from the window. She'd had supper there several times,
always with Martha and John present, or with other members of
Milo's family, as it should be. But she and Milo still found plenty
of time to be alone and get to know each other.

He was quieter than Kade and didn't seem to possess the same
playfulness. Somehow, she couldn't picture Milo rolling around in
the snow or making a snowman. Come to think of it, she'd never
thought Kade could be capable of such behavior. The memory
always brought a smile to her face.

Milo didn't seem to enjoy deep conversation the way Kade did
either. Twice, she'd tried to talk to Milo about Ben, how she felt
after his death, and the struggle to move forward. He'd seemed
very uncomfortable and changed the subject both times. Once,

Sadie had tried to spark up a conversation about faith. She hinted at her own need to understand God's will sometimes, but she was careful not to say too much. Rightly so. Milo didn't want to hear of such questionings when it came to the Lord. And she knew he was right to feel that way, which added another layer to her guilt. She had no reason to doubt, after all. God had sent her the perfect man to spend the rest of her life with and blessed her with an opportunity for a new beginning. She knew there was nothing to gain by comparing Milo to Kade.

Her *Englisch* friend had aroused feelings in Sadie she thought were long gone and had awakened her to the fact that she was still a woman—a woman who longed to be held, touched, and loved. But he was not the right man for her. Her place was here, with Milo. To consider anything else would only cause heartache. She should have never allowed herself to get close to Kade or Tyler.

It wasn't only Kade and Tyler that Sadie missed—it was also Lillian, Mary Ellen, Rebecca, Katie Ann, Sarah Jane, and Carley. Hopefully, one of the women would be able to continue to run Treasures of the Heart, even after the farm was sold, a thought she chose to push aside, knowing Lillian most likely had begun that process. She had worked so hard to get the shop up and running. How Ben had loved that farm.

Surely, over time, she wouldn't feel so homesick.

"What is it, dear?" Martha touched Sadie lightly on the arm. "You look a million miles away."

"I guess I was just thinking—" Sadie wasn't sure how much to say. Martha and her entire family had been more than hospitable; they'd welcomed her as part of their own family.

"Let's sit a bit." Martha motioned toward the den. "It's normal for you to be feelin' homesick, ya know?" Martha said when they sat down in the rockers.

Sadie nodded, but there was a catch in her throat as she opened her mouth to speak.

"This is all very new to you. A new place. New folks to get to know."

"*Ach*, I'm fine. Really." Sadie smiled.

Martha pursed her lips, folded her hands in her lap, and then took a deep breath. "Sadie, I know that your parents have passed. And I'll not try to assume the role of your *mamm* . . ." Martha paused, her hazel eyes radiating with kindness. "But if ever there is a time when you need to talk, for certain you can come to me. Milo is my son, and you seem to make him very happy. But you must feel right in your own heart too."

"Milo is wonderful," Sadie said, surprised Martha would doubt her intentions. "I care for him very much. It's just that—" She couldn't tell Martha that her own heart belonged to another, someone she could never be with. "I am a bit homesick. I mostly miss *mei* friend, Lillian, and several other ladies in my district." She smiled. "And Lillian's grandfather, Jonas, is also very special to me." Sadie lowered her head. She was telling the truth, just not the entire truth.

"*Mei* daughters all care for you very much, and with time, you'll make lots of new friends here." Martha reached over and patted Sadie's hand. "Will just take some time."

Time. Yes, time, Sadie thought. She was exactly where she needed to be.

Kade tucked the quilt up around Tyler's neck, thankful his son was taking a nap. Kade needed time to think. In nine short weeks, he'd had a life overhaul. Monica's death. Full custody of Tyler. His friendship with Sadie. And now, he was learning the ways of the Plain people of Lancaster County from a kooky old man he'd grown to love. Jonas was completely opposite from his own father, yet they were each independent keepers of great knowledge. Kade's father was wise in ways of the world—an innate ability to turn a buck into a million, a way with people that had earned him trust by unlikely parties, and Kade respected him more than any man he'd ever known. Yet Kade couldn't deny that his relationship with his father consisted of a detached type of love that ran both ways.

Jonas's distrust for the *Englisch*, as he called them, had shone through from the beginning—particularly a wealthy *Englisch* man with a past far more complex than Jonas could imagine. But once the elderly man saw past the image of Kade and his wealthy lifestyle, Jonas dove deep into Kade's spirit, got him to think about deeper questions. For reasons Kade didn't understand, Jonas had allowed himself to become both mentor and friend to Kade.

Repeatedly, Jonas had told Kade that a life among the Amish would never work for Kade. And it sure seemed that way. Every reason Jonas cited made perfect sense, yet Jonas continued to teach Kade, almost as if he was testing his will. And Kade continued to soak up Jonas's teachings with an insatiable thirst that he couldn't quench, although logistically it made no sense.

Kade's search for real contentment had been unattainable for his entire life, and Jonas seemed to hold the key that was opening up possibilities for Kade, possibilities for happiness that had nothing to do with money or material possessions—things Kade already knew could not bring the type of fulfillment he was looking for. Jonas spoke about God so passionately and with such ease, Kade felt compelled to learn more. Eventually, Kade opened up to Jonas in a profound way; Jonas had nudged him to feel things he'd never felt before. Once he even cried in front of Jonas, who merely said, "Welcome the Lord, Kade."

Some days, Jonas checked out for a while. Sarah Jane said the doctors were not completely sure whether it was his cancer medications or the progression of Alzheimer's that made him mentally lapse. Kade believed it to be the latter. He recognized the symptoms. He'd been through it with his own father, and as distressing as it was to relive, Kade guided Jonas back to reality as best he could. He needed Jonas. And in some way, Kade felt like Jonas needed him too.

Sadie. He thought about her constantly, wondered how her new life in Texas was working out. He constantly fought to keep his heart from turning bitter. Why would God introduce him to such a woman if she was destined to love another man? He often fantasized about having a life with Sadie in this wonderful Amish community, but it seemed so far-fetched that his mind wound in circles and always came back to the most prevalent question, *what am I doing here?*

Kade picked up his cell phone from the coffee table, the flashing red light indicating a message. He'd been avoiding the link to his previous life for days—but he knew that to move forward, he had to take care of what was behind him. He dialed his voice mail. Forty-two new messages. His heart raced, not from anticipation

but from dread. To go back to his house, his money, his friends—
a term he now used loosely—seemed like a prison sentence. He
couldn't go on living the way he had been. Something had been so
amiss in his life, and that something was God.

The heart of the people in Lancaster County was unlike anything Kade had known, and he clung to their beliefs like a drowning
man to a life preserver, clutching the one thing that could carry him
to safety—a relationship with God and His Son, Jesus Christ. And
yet the logical side of his brain continued to reprimand his choices,
begging him to rethink this absurd behavior.

Seventeen voice mails were from Monica's mother, checking
on Tyler. He owed Andrea a call and regretted not calling her
before now. Plus, he'd never returned Val's first batch of messages,
and now there were eight more from him, all pleading with Kade
to call him—once stating that he had something important to
talk with Kade about. The rest of the messages were from board
members, business contacts, and people representing Kade's interests on various fronts. He knew he'd shown the irresponsibility of
a young teenager, off on a *rumpschpringe*, as Jonas would call it. And
yet, he listened to all the messages, placed the phone back on the
table, and chose to talk to no one.

No one on that phone list anyway. He wanted to talk with
someone else. "Dear heavenly Father . . ." he began.

Jonas knocked at Lizzie's door for the third time—resolved that if
she didn't answer, he was going in anyway. To worry was a sin, but
it pulled at Jonas like a weight, dragging his spirit down. He
needed to know if Lizzie's current state was his fault. He'd thought

he was doing right by Irma Rose not to act on his feelings for Lizzie, but when Lillian said Lizzie wasn't doing so good, he knew he'd been wrong to abandon her the way he had.

Finally, the door opened, and Jonas was shocked at what he saw. Lizzie's long gray hair cascaded down around her shoulders. So silky and smooth, Jonas resisted the urge to stroke it with his hand. She looked like she'd been in her blue dress for more than a day or two, and as Lillian had said—the place was a mess. As improper as it was to behold Lizzie's hair, unbound and flowing freely without the confines of her prayer covering, Jonas suspected there might be bigger issues at hand.

"Lizzie, you all right?" he asked hesitantly from the front porch.

Lizzie stepped back and motioned for Jonas to come in. "*Ya*, I'm *gut*, Jonas. Just a bit tired, that's all." She sat down on the bench at the kitchen table. "Please, sit down, Jonas."

Jonas removed his straw hat and hung it on the rack inside the door and studied her for a moment. Didn't she realize she was missing something? He tugged on the full length of his beard, clamped his lips tight. Then he asked, "Lizzie, do you know that you don't have your *kapp* on?" Right away, he wished he hadn't mentioned it.

She jumped up, bumped her knee on the table, and brought both hands frantically to her head. "*Ach*, no." Tears welled in the corner of her eyes. "I'm so embarrassed. I'm so—How could I not know that?"

Jonas wasted no time moving around the table. He placed his hands firmly on each arm and gazed into her eyes. "We won't tell a livin' soul 'bout this, Lizzie. I reckon it is just fine."

"It's not fine." She cradled her face in her hands, and Jonas could feel her trembling.

He wrapped his arms around her and pulled her close. "Lizzie, don't cry." She felt so tiny pressed against his lanky, thin build. What a pair they made. "I've missed you, Lizzie. I'm sorry that—"

She eased him away, turned, and walked out of the room. When she returned, her hair was tucked beneath her prayer covering, her head held high. Jonas wanted to take her in his arms again, but her expression was solemn, and Lizzie didn't seem excited to see him, the way he'd hoped. But Jonas knew something that would cheer her up. He cumbersomely dropped to one knee and balanced his weight by holding on to the kitchen table.

"Jonas, I think I've had a stroke," she said matter-of-factly, with no regard for Jonas's obvious intentions. "Maybe you ought not be thinking what you're thinking, and stand up," she said in a bossy tone he hadn't heard from her before. Jonas wasn't sure he could stand up. His old joints had had one too many trips to the bended-knee position today. "Get up, now," she demanded.

He eyed her with amusement. Lizzie was trying her best to look tough, but she looked downright silly to him. "Lizzie, what do you think you're doing?" he said, still on bended knee, one hand resting on the kitchen table.

"What do you mean?" She cupped her small hips with her hands.

"Why are you trying to be all tough and mean when you ain't got a mean bone in that tiny body of yours?" He grinned.

"Did you hear what I said, Jonas? I think I've had a stroke. I'm not sure, but somethin' ain't right in my mind." She took a deep breath, then lifted her head a little higher. "I reckon that's what happens when a person has a stroke. I remember when it happened to Anna Mae last year. She got all crazy in the head."

"What's all that got to do with me being down here on this floor like this, and you trying to be all . . . whatever it is you're trying to be?" He groaned a bit, but kept himself in proposal position.

She shook her head. "I never want to be a burden on anyone."

Jonas bellowed out a hearty laugh.

"Do you find this funny?" She pressed her thin lips together.

"Lizzie," he began, "I don't know what's goin' on half the time, so I reckon it'd be a fair shake as to who'd be a burden to who. Don'tcha think?" He groaned.

"Jonas, maybe you should get up from there."

"I'll get up when I'm *gut* and ready, when I've tended to my business," he grumbled.

Jonas straightened his back as best he could and gazed into her eyes. "Lizzie, I want you to marry me, move in over with me and Sarah Jane, where we can tend to ya."

Her big, brown eyes went wild with fury—almost rabid, like his old hound dog years ago. She was as frightful a woman as he'd ever seen. "Is that a yes?" He cowered backward a smidgen.

"I don't need no one tending to me!" she hollered. "Why would I want to marry a man just so he could *tend* to me? That's as wrong a reason as I can think of, and—"

"Lizzie!" he snapped.

She closed her mouth and waited for him to speak.

Jonas drew in a deep breath. "Woman, don't you know how much I love you? After Irma Rose died, I never expected to love another, Lizzie." He paused, seeing her eyes soften. "But I do, Lizzie. I love you. I love the time we spend together. I'm at my best when I'm with you. And you'd do this old man an honor by becoming *mei fraa* and growing old with me."

"We're already old," she said smugly. "And what if I've had a stroke? What if my mind is going? What if it's something else?"

Jonas snickered. "Lizzie, I'm not even sure I can get up off this floor of yours, and who knows if I'll drop dead tomorrow. I got the cancer, ya know. And we already know I don't be remembering things so *gut* these days. But I say we go nuts together and make the best of it."

It warmed his heart to hear Lizzie laugh. "You're a silly old man, huggy bear."

"That's what they tell me, that daughter and granddaughter of mine. So what do you say? Wanta get married to this silly old man?"

"Oh, Jonas. Yes." Her voice bubbled with joy.

He was tickled by her reaction, but there was another issue at hand. "Lizzie."

"*Ya?*"

"I can't get up." Jonas tried to push his weight upward, but the pain in his legs was unbearable.

"Here, let me." Lizzie wrapped her arms underneath his and pulled with all her tiny might.

Slowly, Jonas rose to his feet, amid all the crackling in his joints and bones. "And I don't see no reason to wait until November to get married either."

"Folks will expect us to wait till after the fall harvest," she said.

Jonas grinned. "I don't know 'bout you, but I ain't got a fall harvest."

"Oh, Jonas," she said again, her eyes twinkling.

"Now, that's my Lizzie," he said, and then wrapped his arms around her.

"And you're my huggy bear."

She pulled back a little and looked up at him. "Who will you have to stand with you?"

Jonas thought for only a moment. "I reckon it should be Samuel."

"That's lovely, because I am going to ask Lillian to stand with me. How sweet to have husband and wife!"

He couldn't help but smile at Lizzie's girlish enthusiasm. He was feeling a tad giddy himself. "Not one of your kin?" he asked after a moment.

"They are *gut* girls, my nieces, but I hardly ever see them. Your granddaughter has always checked on me regularly, her and Sadie both." She paused. "I hope Sadie finds happiness in Texas, but I'll sure miss having her here in Lancaster County. Such a *gut* girl."

"Sadie is special," Jonas said fondly.

"Jonas?" Lizzie's enthusiasm floundered a bit. "Do you reckon I'm losing my mind? I've never forgotten to wear *mei kapp*." She lowered her head.

Jonas lifted her chin gently with his hand. "Lizzie, there ain't no shame in gettin' old, and I don't think you're losin' your mind." He chuckled. "No more than I am. But I do think we need to have Noah take a look at you. If you be forgettin' things, might be easy to fix."

Lizzie glanced around at her house, and Jonas felt sorry for her, knowing she was embarrassed, but not wanting to say anything.

"I've been so tired, Jonas," she said softly as she eyed the dishes in the sink.

He pressed his palm to her cheek. "We'll help each other grow old. We'll do it together."

Lizzie smiled and molded herself into his arms.

Kade looked at the calendar hanging on the kitchen wall. One more week. That's all he'd signed on for—three months. Jonas told him that Bishop Ebersol sold Sadie's farm right away to Lester Lapp, who'd agreed not to take possession until Sadie returned to collect her things, which wouldn't be until he and Tyler were gone.

Sadie loves this place, Kade thought, as he stood staring at the calendar. *But she must love Milo more.* He fought the bitterness that continued to creep into his soul when he thought of Sadie playing house with Milo in Texas.

Tyler was on the floor, playing with his letters, so Kade allowed his mind to drift into a world where his thoughts were clean and pure, a place with no worry, no deadlines, no distrust, fear of failure, fear of death, fear in general—a world where God sat beside him as a good friend and mentor. A world like he'd found here in Lancaster County.

But he had a home, and soon he'd be leaving to go there. Somehow, he needed to bottle up everything he felt here and take it with him. He and Tyler were certain to have great challenges when they returned. Tyler seemed to have settled into the routine of life here. His tantrums were still a daily occurrence, but Kade was learning, and together they would make it through the transition. Guilt at his own absence from the boy's life still stabbed at his heart, but that was slowly being replaced by a love that Kade had never known.

His thoughts were interrupted by a pounding on the door. Tyler beat him to the door and wrapped his arms around Jonas's legs.

"Here's *mei* boy," Jonas exclaimed like a proud grandfather. Kade knew Jonas was going to miss Tyler.

Jonas walked in the door, the way any good friend does, and helped himself to a seat on the tan chair next to the couch. A light jazzy mix resounded from the small radio. "Sounds like craziness, that music." He removed his hat and looped his thumbs through his suspenders.

Tyler resumed his position on the floor, and Kade sat down on the couch and propped his white socks on the coffee table. "It's jazz," Kade said. Then he shook his head. "That's one thing that would be difficult to give up if I stayed here."

"We both know that ain't possible," Jonas said with conviction.

"Why do you do that, Jonas?"

Jonas innocently raised his brows. "What's that?"

"You act as if I could never make the necessary sacrifices to conform to your life. How do you know that? After all the conversations we've had, you know me pretty well, and you know what a mess my life has been. Why do you assume I could never be happy here?"

"Could you be? Happy here, that is."

Kade was suddenly stumped. Usually, Jonas held firm to the

conviction that Kade's staying was not an option. "I'm happy here now."

"Because you're on vacation," Jonas said. "But a man like you doesn't exchange the things you have for our way of life."

Kade thought long and hard before he spoke. "Jonas, I've been a wealthy man my entire life. Money, possessions, great business success—I've had it all. And yet, I don't have an ounce of the peace of mind you have. And those material gains are no longer alluring to me, and to tell you the truth, I'm not sure they ever were. It's all I ever knew. Had I not come here for a reprieve from my life, I'd have never known this way of life even existed. So, I really don't think it's fair for you to judge my intentions."

"Is that what you think I'm doing? Judging you?"

Kade eyed Jonas curiously. This was the wise man he'd grown to love, pressing him in ways that often confused him. "Yes, I think you're judging me."

"Then stay," Jonas said, his face somber.

"What?"

"You heard me, my *Englisch* friend." Jonas remained serious, his eyes fused with Kade's. "Just stay."

It became apparent: Jonas was going to miss Kade as much as Kade was going to miss the old man. "But I—" It was a fantasy to think about living here, and the reality didn't align with the dream. Although he feared leaving Paradise might kill him, he knew he didn't have a choice. "I have responsibilities that I've ignored for too long," he finally said.

Jonas was quiet for a moment. "Kade, I reckon you're gonna find that you're not the same man you were when you arrived here." He paused, stroking his beard. "But the things you have learned here, along with your renewed relationship with our Lord—this feeling of wholeness—you can have it anywhere. There is no reason you can't live your life among the *Englisch* with a new sense of freedom. You'll take it all with you, Kade. God is not geographically prejudiced, presenting Himself more to us than those out in the rest of the world. You can seek Him out from anywhere. His Holy Spirit dwells within you."

Why was it, when Jonas spoke to him like this, that Kade had a hard time controlling his emotions? "You don't know how much I'd like to just never go back, Jonas." He paused and fought the unwelcome tremor in his voice. "I'm afraid, Jonas—I'm afraid that the world out there"—Kade swung his hand toward the door—"will suck the life out of me again—will steal my will and all that I've gained here."

"You still have much to learn," Jonas said. "Fear hinders a man. Once you stop being afraid, your life will change in ways you've never imagined. Fear keeps your heart closed and prevents the Lord from reaching you."

"Are you scared, Jonas? I mean, the cancer and all."

"I'm human, Kade. I'd be lying if I said that leaving my loved ones didn't cause me pain. Chances are, I'll never see the child that Lillian carries grow much past a toddler, if that much. I worry about leavin' Lizzie, how she'll be when somethin' happens to me. It worries me to leave Sarah Jane, Lillian, and the rest of the people I care about, even though worry is a sin." He paused. "I am human. But am I afraid of death? The answer is no."

They sat quietly for a few moments. Then Jonas said, "I came here to tell you some news." He grinned. "Me and Lizzie are getting married."

Kade shot Jonas an instant look of approval. "Jonas, I think that's great."

"We ain't farmers with harvests to tend, so I reckon we'll be gettin' married next month. The twentieth of April is the day we picked. Sure would mean a lot to us—to me—if you could be here."

Kade was deeply touched. "I wouldn't miss it," he said.

"I know it's a long way to travel, but sure would be *gut* if you could bring Tyler."

"We'll do our very best to be here."

Kade's cell phone began to ring. "The closer it gets for me to leave, the more this thing rings." He reached for the phone, pushed the End button, and tossed it back on the table. "That cell phone is one thing I wouldn't miss if I lived here."

Jonas stood up. "See you for supper? Sarah Jane is makin' meat loaf."

"That sounds great." Kade walked Jonas to the door.

———

Sadie hung up the phone in Martha and John's barn. She didn't leave a message. She wasn't even sure what she would have said if Kade had answered. But she felt compelled to make the call, hoping that Kade would say something, anything, to cause her to return to her home, to a place in his arms, to the fantasy world she created of them sharing a life together.

In reality, if he had answered, she would have probably told him that she was happy in Texas, and that she was merely calling to check on Tyler.

But happiness was not the emotion that overflowed from

Sadie's heart, particularly after what Milo had told her, "Bishop Ebersol left a message, Sadie. Good news. Your farm has been sold."

She fought back the tears building in the corner of her eyes, looked up to heaven, and begged God to give her the strength to stay on the path He has chosen for her.

Sadie knew she should be counting her blessings, but Milo's words kept ringing in her head like gongs of forthcoming doom.

18

KADE'S RETURN TO HIS OLD LIFE LOOMED OVER HIM like a dark cloud, and in a mere two hours, he'd be home, back to a world filled with shrewd business deals, high-powered luncheons, and enough vanity to choke on. And beautiful women—lots of beautiful ladies interested in a place on Kade's arm—all with the same selfish pursuits of furthering their own social status. Then, of course, there was Val.

The captain's voice sounded through the plane, something about arriving in Los Angeles early, but Kade's mind was elsewhere. He thought about Monica and how her life was cut tragically short. He reached over and stroked Tyler's head while he slept, knowing that change was not easy for his son. *I wonder if Penelope knows how to make tapioca pudding.*

The flight attendant stopped her cart in the aisle. "Cocktail, sir?"

Kade shook his head.

He constantly thought about Sadie and how much he missed her—the sound of her laughter, her loving ways with Tyler, and, of course, their hugs at the end of the evenings. And even the firm way that she kept Kade in line. He recalled the way he'd almost lost his cool about Val, but Sadie warned him with her eyes when unsuitable language threatened to spew from his mouth. And she'd always kept a safe distance from Kade, even though Kade often saw the longing in her expression to do otherwise. He smiled as he thought about the way she'd scolded him about his dismissive hand gestures, a habit Kade had just about kicked. Memories of her calmed him, but also tormented him. Sadie could never be his, and that badgered his heart unmercifully, testing his resolve to quiet his troubled spirit.

Kade rested his head against the back of his seat, closed his eyes, and pretended he was back with Sadie in the middle of the blizzard, back in the warmth of her company. There was no sex. No false promises. No pretending. No lies. Just Sadie being herself—honest and pure, loving and kind.

Now he was homeward bound and feeling more destitute than he'd ever felt, with each passing mile putting more distance between the place and the people he'd grown to love.

But knowing he'd go back for Jonas and Lizzie's wedding gave him a tiny bit of comfort, and he wondered if Sadie would be back for the wedding, and if she'd have Milo with her.

Sadie kept hearing the words pounding in her head. "Your farm has been sold. We can travel to Lancaster County and collect your things soon."

Milo hadn't formally asked her to marry him. It was an assumption, and Sadie hadn't done anything to dispel or confirm it. They spent time together, and Sadie had laughed and carried on as a young girl during courtship. But Kade and Tyler were always in the back of her mind. She knew it would be a sin to marry Milo when her heart belonged to another man. But now her farm was gone.

Sadie waited until Martha and John traveled to a neighbor's house for supper, declining the invitation because of a terrible headache. She made her way to the barn and prayed silently that someone at Lillian's house would hear the phone ringing in the barn. She'd never needed a friendly voice more than now. But when there was no answer, she dialed the number to Jonas and Sarah Jane's house.

The phone rang six times, and Sadie was about to hang up when the ringing stopped. She heard a raspy voice say hello.

"Jonas, is that you?" she said. "Jonas?"

"Who be callin', please?"

"Jonas, it's Sadie!"

"Sadie, it's *wunderbaar gut* to hear your voice. How are you, my child?"

And that was all it took. She yielded to compulsive sobs.

"Sadie?" His voice was comforting, compassionate. "Tell me your troubles, dear Sadie."

"My farm is sold," she babbled while wiping her eyes.

"*Ya*, it is. Isn't that what you wanted?"

"Yes," she lied softly. "I'll be coming to collect my things soon."

She heard a sigh on the other end of the line. "So, you will be staying to make a life with Milo in Texas?"

"*Ya*." She bit her lip.

"And this makes Sadie cry?"

"*Ach*, I'm being silly." She sniffled, dabbed at her eyes. "Milo is a wonderful man, and he'll make a fine home for me here in Texas.

I'll be traveling back by bus in two days. I reckon I'm homesick, and it will be *gut* to see everyone, especially Lillian and you."

"We all miss ya, Sadie. But we want you to be happy. A *gut* girl like you deserves to be happy." He paused. "Are you happy, Sadie?"

"*Ya*," she said as convincingly as she could. "Milo is wonderful. He'll make a fine home for me here in Texas."

"*Ya, ya.* You just said that." Jonas paused again. "Are you *in lieb* with him, Sadie?"

She couldn't lie to Jonas, but she couldn't quite tell him the truth either. "He's a fine man. It's all happening so fast, I reckon."

"Sadie . . ." She could hear Jonas inhale deeply on the end of the line. He took his time releasing the breath. "We can't force God's will or try to guess what His plan is for us. It is important that you not let your own wants and needs block out His voice. Listen to Him, Sadie."

Sadie sighed. "I know you're right, Jonas." What a wonderful bishop Jonas would have been. So wise and kind. But Sadie knew Jonas lacked the harsh discipline to enforce the rules, as was expected by the bishop. His heart, though, was always in the right place. She was glad he answered the phone today.

Silence stretched the distance between them, and she waited for Jonas to speak. "I have news, Sadie."

"About Kade and Tyler?" she asked.

"Uh, no. 'Tis 'bout me and Lizzie."

"Oh."

"Ain't no need to sound so disappointed. My news might shed some light on Kade and Tyler as well. I've asked Lizzie to marry me."

"*Ach,* Jonas! That's so *gut,* so very *gut.* Lizzie is a fine woman, but . . ." How did this shed any light on Kade and Tyler?

"I know you're coming home in a couple of days, but I'm sure hoping you'll somehow be able to be at my wedding. It'll be a few weeks from now. The twentieth of April is when I'll take Lizzie as *mei fraa,* and we'd be mighty glad if you could be here. But I understand if that's too much traveling too close together."

"That is a lot of traveling. Texas is a long way from Lancaster County." Her heart was breaking. "But I want so very much to be there, Jonas."

"Kade and the boy will be here to see me and Lizzie wed." Jonas tempted her with his tone.

"I'm surprised," she said. "I mean, I received a letter from Lillian telling me that the two of you had become friends, but—"

"He's a fine man."

"*Ya,*" she said softly. "How is Lillian and everyone else?" She clamped her mouth tight and fought the tremor in her voice as she wiped another tear from her cheek.

"My Lilly is doin' fine." He paused for several long moments. "Come home, Sadie," Jonas finally said. "Just come home."

Penelope was standing in the front yard when the cab rounded the circular drive in front of Kade's house. And so was Val.

Kade sighed from the backseat. Tyler had been restless, fussy, and downright mean during the taxi ride from the airport to Kade's home in Los Angeles, trying twice to bite Kade. But Kade knew Tyler was rattled by the plane flight, change in schedule, and new surroundings. His son needed stability, and the day had been void of a normal routine.

Kade was exhausted, stressed, and not in the mood to face Val.

"Welcome home," Val said when Kade stepped out of the cab with Tyler.

Ignoring Val's extended hand, Kade reached in his pocket for his wallet and handed the driver a hundred-dollar bill. "I'm really sorry about the ride."

"No problem." The driver accepted the generous tip, but Kade saw him roll his eyes.

"How big he is!" Penelope rushed to Tyler. "Hello, Tyler."

Tyler's eyes grew wide and fearful. "Hug," he said to Kade. Tyler wrapped his arms around Kade's legs, and that one small gesture made up for the entire day. Kade scooped Tyler into his arms. "He's had a hard day. Hello, Penelope." He hugged his longtime house-keeper as he balanced Tyler on one hip.

"So good to have you both home," she said.

Kade took a deep breath and extended his hand to Val. "Hello, Val." He set Tyler down beside him and grabbed their suitcase. "I need to get Tyler something to eat and introduce him to his new surroundings."

Val followed a few steps behind. "Penelope found a school for Tyler, but he would have to live there most of the time. It's the best school for autistic children in the area, and—"

"Tyler will be living here with me." The thought of anything else caused Kade's stomach to churn.

"I've prepared your favorite meal, Mr. Saunders. I've made ratatouille."

Kade recalled the eggplant casserole with tomatoes, zucchini, and onions. It was one of Penelope's specialties. As they all continued up the walkway to the front double doors, he said, "That sounds fine, Penelope." Then he turned toward her as she walked alongside him. "But feel free to tone things down in the future. Even meat loaf and stew would be fine with me." He thought about the fabulously simple meals Sadie prepared for him.

"Oh, and Penelope—" Kade walked ahead of her and through the front door with Tyler. "Call me Kade from now on."

He glanced over his shoulder in time to see Penelope give Val a confused look. Kade didn't comment. He motioned Tyler ahead of him on the spacious, tiled entryway—an entryway as big as Sadie's entire den. It felt unusually cold and distant here now.

"Tyler, this is your new home." Kade watched his son eye the massive room ahead of them. And then Kade began to examine the room himself, making a mental note of all the things that had to go, things that could hurt Tyler—like the abstract sculpture atop a marble stand to the side of the fireplace. Spiked, fluted spurs extended from a solid bronze base and shimmied aimlessly into the air about three feet. Once considered his most prized possession, he now regarded his first piece of fine art as a danger for his son. If Tyler pulled on the marble base, and the sculpture were to fall with all those spikes . . .

Kade surveyed the rest of his house. More sculptures, exotic finds, rare collections, priceless vases, glass tabletops with sharp edges, and the list went on.

"Penelope, we are going to make some major changes around here. There are many things in this house that can hurt Tyler. I want to start selling some of these items, tone things down a bit, provide a simpler atmosphere, one safer for my son. No sharp edges, dangerous sculptures . . ." Kade pointed to the sculpture a few feet ahead of them. "Objects like that."

"Yes, Mr.—I mean, Kade."

Mr. Saunders may have been the man who left three months ago, but Kade was the man who came back. He didn't want to remember the person he used to be. "Penelope, I have some issues to discuss with Val. Would you take Tyler into the kitchen and get him something to eat? If you have any problems, call for me." He paused. "Do we have any pudding?"

"No, Mr. Saunders." Penelope blinked her eyes closed, then opened them. "No, Kade."

"Tyler loves tapioca pudding. Maybe you could make him some soon. But for now, he seems to like bread with peanut butter, and maybe some cheese spread on it. Do we have anything like that?" Without waiting for an answer, Kade said, "Nothing that requires a fork, only a spoon. He likes mashed potatoes also."

"Yes, Kade." Penelope held her hand out to Tyler. "Come with me, Tyler."

"Oh, he doesn't like to be touched," Kade said. "I mean, not unless he asks for a hug. And that lunch box he's carrying, he takes that everywhere. I have a list of his likes and dislikes, Penelope, that I can go over with you later. But no worries. Tyler will be spending most of his time with me."

"What?" Val asked.

"Tyler, go with Ms. Penelope, and I'll see you in a minute."

"Tyler go with Ms. Penelope," Tyler repeated.

"He knows my name." Penelope sounded proud as she guided Tyler toward the kitchen.

Kade waited until they were out of the room before he turned to Val and wasted no time getting to the point. "I'm sorry for your loss, Val. About Monica. She was a fine woman, and of course, she's Tyler's mother. So my grief and sympathy span several levels." He paused to see Val's jaw drop. Clearly, his friend was expecting a verbal lashing. And a couple of months ago, that's what Kade would have done. "My preference would have been for you to trust our friendship enough to tell me that you were seeing her, but what's done is done. Moving on, though, I know you have stock in Saunders Real Estate and Development, and a vested interest since your company has done several deals with us. So, I want you to know that I am addressing the board tomorrow, resigning as CEO, and putting my shares up for sale." Kade fused his eyes intently with Val's. "I'll trust you to keep this information confidential until I speak with the board tomorrow."

Val nodded, and his jaw dropped even further.

"I'm stepping out of the rat race, Val. I want to spend time with Tyler." Kade began sorting through the pile of mail on the counter at the bar.

"May I?" Val asked. He rounded the corner of the wet bar and helped himself to a glass. "I think I need a drink." He paused, narrowed his eyes at Kade. "Don't *you* need a drink? Scotch?"

Kade realized he hadn't had a cocktail since he'd been gone. "No, thanks. But help yourself."

"What happened to you in Lancaster County?" Val filled the small glass and took a giant swig.

"My priorities have changed, that's all."

"I'll say." Val chugged the drink. "Kade, about Monica . . . I was going to tell you."

"It doesn't matter at this point, does it?"

"I suppose not." Val walked around the bar to where Kade was standing. "Your father started Saunders Real Estate and Development, Kade. How can you give it all up?"

Kade looked up at him. "Just doesn't seem important anymore." He motioned around the room. "None of this seems important."

Val shook his head. "Kade, I can understand you wanting to be a good father to Tyler, but I hate to see you start making rash decisions because you've spent a few months with the Amish. What? They brainwash you or something?" Val grinned.

"Yes. That's it, Val. They brainwashed me." Kade rolled his eyes. "If you don't mind, Val, I want to check on Tyler, and I have mounds of mail to go through. I have a lot of lifestyle adjustments to make." He extended his hand to Val. "No hard feelings."

Val was slow to grasp Kade's hand. "I'm glad about that, Kade."

When Val was out the door, Kade headed to the kitchen to spend some time with his son. He wanted to show Tyler around the place and start making the changes he knew were necessary to accommodate Tyler's needs.

Sadie and Milo sat quietly at the train station, tickets in hand. As planned, they would travel to Lancaster County, where a moving van would meet them at Sadie's farm, or the farm that used to be hers. Her things would be loaded and hauled to Texas. She sat thinking out how this had gone from a visit to a full-blown move so fast, and with a wedding planned for November. She hadn't argued against any of it, going along with each of Milo's suggestions. It was, after all, her chance at happiness.

However, waves of panic surged through her, threatening to suffocate her. She tugged on the neckline of her dress and endured stares from the *Englischers*. She'd never felt more on edge. She was overcome by an urge to run, and she knew if she didn't speak up now, it would be too late.

"Milo," she said softly.

He reached over and grabbed her hand. "*Ya?*" His profile was strong and rigid, his blue eyes kind, but questioning. A muscle flicked in his jaw, as if the expression on her face brought forth worry.

What a wonderful man, she thought. *What a wonderful father he would make.* Indeed, he was everything she asked God to provide for her.

She inhaled a deep breath and blew it out slowly.

"There's something I need to tell you," she finally said.

19

SADIE WALKED ACROSS HER YARD, NO LONGER COVERED in snow like when she left. She stumbled up the porch steps, toting the cumbersome suitcase, and walked into her den. Actually, Lester Lapp's den. She set the luggage down and looked around. Her first order of business would be to visit with Lester and see about buying the farm back. Lester was a kind man, and Sadie felt sure he wouldn't hesitate to sell back the property that had been in Sadie's family for generations. She tried to shake the forlorn expression on Milo's face when she explained that she wouldn't be moving to Stephenville.

She'd been home about fifteen minutes when she heard a buggy coming up the driveway.

"Lillian!" Sadie yelled as she ran down the porch steps. "I missed you so much," she said when Lillian got out of the buggy.

"We all missed you too."

Sadie could barely get her arms around Lillian. She pulled back from the hug and said, "You are huge."

Lillian groaned. She took hold of Sadie's arm and motioned toward the porch. Then her friend lowered herself onto one of the rockers. "I know. The doctor said it should be any day. And I'm miserable." Then she smiled. "But I sure am glad you're home. I have to admit, I wasn't all that surprised when you left word that you were coming back—alone—to stay."

"Why do you say that?" Sadie wondered if Lillian knew her secret.

Lillian shrugged. "I don't know. Maybe because this is your home. Or maybe because I wasn't sure Milo was the right one."

"But you only met him briefly before I left for Texas. How could you possibly suspect that he wasn't the one for me?"

Again, Lillian shrugged. "You didn't have that look. You know. The look a person has when she is *in lieb*."

"I wasn't in love with Milo, but I guess I thought I could be. His family was so wonderful, Lillian, and you should have seen the look on his face when I told him I would be traveling alone and not returning to Texas." She shook her head. "In so many ways, he was perfect. I hope I haven't made a *baremlich* mistake."

"What are you going to do now?" Lillian twisted uncomfortably in her seat.

"I'm going to go right over to Lester Lapp's house and buy back my farm. I'm sure he'll sell it back to me, and—" Sadie stopped when Lillian's face went white. "What's wrong?"

"Didn't anyone tell you?"

"Tell me what?"

"Lester Lapp closed on the farm, and the very next day, he sold it to someone else—an *Englischer*."

"What?" Sadie grabbed her chest with both hands. "Who?"

Lillian shrugged. "I don't know. I heard the news from Mary Ellen, who found out from Rachel. And evidently, Rachel got word of it while she was at the farmer's market."

"*Ach!* It's Dale Spalek—that *Englisch* fella in town. He's been try-ing to purchase property along our road for years. Remember when he tried to purchase the Lantz place? But Amos Lantz wouldn't sell to him." She gasped. "Probably for tourists. They will want to use my shop out front to sell overpriced things to tourists! Mr. Spalek has two stores in town already. He doesn't need my family farm." Sadie looked at her friend. "Lillian, what am I going to do now?" She covered her face with her hands. "I've made such a mess of everything."

After several moments of silence, Sadie uncovered her face and stared at Lillian. Something was wrong.

"Uh-oh. It appears I've made a mess too." Lillian's eyes were wide as she slowly focused on the water seeping over the edge of the chair.

Sadie tucked her chin to her neck. "Did you wet yourself, Lillian?"

Lillian scrunched her face up. "No, silly. My water just broke!"

"Pop!" Sarah Jane yelled throughout the house. "Pop! Sadie left a message on the barn phone! Lillian is in labor, and Carley is taking them to the hospital. Pop, where are you?" She ran upstairs and checked every room, then checked each room downstairs again. "Where is that man?" she grumbled. "Pop!" she yelled again. "Barbie is on her way to get us."

Twenty minutes later, Barbie was in the driveway. Sarah Jane made one last scan of the house and then hurried down the porch steps.

"Where's Jonas?" their *Englisch* friend asked when Sarah Jane climbed into the front seat.

Sarah Jane pulled on her seat belt. "I don't know. I reckon he must have gone to Lizzie's without telling me. He still does that, sneaks off." She blew out a sigh of exasperation. "Sometimes I think he enjoys the thrill of sneaking around, when there is no need to. All he does is worry me when he does that."

"Do you want to swing by Lizzie's house and see if he's there?"

"No. I don't have time to be chasing him around today. Lillian is in labor, and I want to be there. I'm sure he's all right. He always is. Pop is so mischievous, like a child sometimes. He frustrates me. But I'm hoping once he and Lizzie get married, he will stay close to home where I can keep an eye on him."

"How's his cancer?" Barbie asked. She turned off of Black Horse Road onto Lincoln Highway.

"Most days he does fairly well, although he gets confused sometimes." She paused and thought for a minute. "The doctors say he might have a touch of Alzheimer's, but honestly, I think sometimes it's his medications. I think they make him a tad loopy."

"Jonas is such a dear. You know, everyone who meets him loves him."

Sarah Jane laughed. "I think Pop scares some people when they first meet him. It isn't until people get to know him that they realize what a big teddy bear he is. You know, he'd do anything for anyone. Pop has a huge heart."

"I guess you're right. Years ago, I suppose it did take Jonas a while to warm up to me. That seems like such a long time ago."

"You've been a *gut* friend, Barbie. Pop loves you. So do I." She smiled at her friend as they made their way toward Lancaster General. "I can't wait to see if Lillian has another girl or a boy!"

The plan was simple, Jonas thought, lying out in the field halfway between his house and Lizzie's farm. Strap on his walkie-talkie, sneak across the field between their farms now that the snow had cleared, then call her on the walkie-talkie and tell her he was sitting on her front porch. She would have been tickled pink at his playfulness.

Instead, he had tripped and stumbled, then landed flat on his back. Now he couldn't seem to move. It had been downright frustrating to hear Sarah Jane hollering for him, and even more so, to watch his daughter ride off with Barbie. *And where are they going anyway? It's almost my lunchtime.*

He unclasped the walkie-talkie from the clip on his suspenders and groaned from the pain in his back. "Breaker, breaker," he rasped. "Lizzie, you there?"

"Is this my huggy bear?"

"Lizzie, I got myself in a bit of a predicament." Jonas tried again to shift his weight.

"You all right, Jonas?"

He noticed his straw hat about a foot over, reached to grab it, but the pain was too much. "Lizzie, I took a fall, and I'm laid out here in the field between your *haus* and mine. Ain't a thing you can do either."

"I'm comin', huggy bear."

"You ain't comin' out here, Lizzie. It's too far for you to walk.

Nearly half a mile, I reckon." *She'd never make it,* Jonas thought, hoping she would have the good sense not to try. Lizzie could barely get up and down her own porch steps and around her house. "Lizzie," he said again when there was no response. "Don't you leave your house. Someone will be by to check on you. Just tell whoever it is to come fetch me out in this field."

"That could be hours from now. Or days, Jonas. I'm on my way," she said.

Hardheaded woman! "Lizzie, don't you dare. I'm ordering you to stay there. Do you hear me?"

"I'm not your *fraa* yet, Jonas Miller. I don't reckon you can be ordering me to do anything."

Jonas sighed, and even that small gesture sent a ripple of pain throughout his body. His pain from the cancer had gotten worse lately. His doctor wanted to put him on medication to manage his discomfort, but had also said it would make him out of sorts. He figured he'd live with the pain, as he was out of sorts enough as it was. Plus, he needed his mind in the right place if he was going to take care of Lizzie.

"*Ach.* No, Lizzie," he whispered to himself. He saw her tiny frame, a dot in the field, moving his way. He pushed the button on the walkie-talkie. "Lizzie, you go on back to the house. You'll catch a chill, and it's too far for you to come out here."

Silence for a few moments. Then Jonas heard her on the walkie-talkie as he watched her taking baby steps across the field. "I'm comin', Jonas."

He didn't have the strength to argue.

"It's a girl," Samuel told the crowd in the waiting room of Lancaster General. "We will be calling her Elizabeth."

"Wonderful news," Sarah Jane said. "How's Lillian?" It had been a short labor and delivery, barely four hours.

"She's *gut*. You can go see her." Samuel couldn't wipe the grin from his face, and Sarah Jane was a proud grandma yet again.

She stood up, hugged Samuel, and headed toward her daughter's room.

"*Mamm*," Lillian whispered when Sarah Jane walked in. She was holding little Elizabeth in her arms. "Isn't she beautiful?"

Sarah Jane held back tears of joy. "Oh, Lillian. She certainly is. Just beautiful." She gently touched the baby's cheek, and then cupped Lillian's face. "She will be a fine baby sister for Anna and David. I think David will want to come in. Is it all right if I go get him?"

Lillian nodded, but her eyes were fused with the new bundle in her arms.

Sarah Jane thought for a moment. "As a matter of fact, sweetie, I think I better go. I couldn't find your grandpa before I left. He probably snuck off to Lizzie's, but he'll be hungry and sorry that he missed all this."

"It's fine, *Mamm*. Send David in. You go find Grandpa."

Sarah Jane kissed her daughter on the forehead. "Do you need anything? I will be back first thing in the morning."

After Lillian assured her that she and the baby were fine, Sarah Jane excused herself, wishing she could stay, and trying not to be irritated with her father.

Lizzie fell for the second time, and she heard her hip pop. As she lay in the field, new spring growth poked her legs and back.

"I'll be there soon, Jonas," she said into the wind. With every ounce of strength she possessed, Lizzie pulled herself to a standing position. She stifled a cry of pain as she edged forward, almost dragging her right leg behind her. Her heart was racing much too fast, and it was difficult to breathe. But her huggy bear was in trouble. She could see him up ahead, sprawled out and not moving.

"Please, Lord," she prayed, "let me make it that far."

She pressed forward, not knowing what she would do when she reached him. But something inside her drove her onward, to Jonas, to her love. "I'm coming," she whispered. And with each painful step, she held her chin high and fought the urge to quit, to lie down, to rest.

But she fell again, and this time the pain in her hip caused her to cry out. It felt dislocated, completely out of joint. She closed her eyes, grimaced, allowed herself to feel the pain, and then she struggled to stand up again. "Please, Lord," she said. "Just let me lie beside him, hold his hand."

Her legs wouldn't lift her, and Lizzie feared she had gone as far as she could. She'd lie here in the field, within only a few yards of him, until someone found them. "Jonas!" she cried with all her might. And then she laid her head back, tears flowing down her wrinkled face. "I can't do it," she cried. "I'm sorry, my love." And she closed her eyes.

It was a few moments later when the breeze carried the sound of his voice. "Lizzie?"

"Jonas?" She struggled to lift her head. "Jonas?" she asked louder.

"I'm here, Lizzie. But I can't move."

Lizzie pushed herself up onto her elbows and realized something. Her upper body was working far better than her lower body. She inched along on her elbows, dragging her legs behind her. "I'm coming, Jonas."

"Stay there, Lizzie. I'll come to you," Jonas said.

She fell onto her back and waited. But nothing.

Lizzie lifted her head. "Jonas?"

But there was silence. "Jonas!" she yelled. "Jonas! Answer me, you silly old man!"

She propped herself back up on her elbows and dragged herself forward through the tall weeds, a few inches at a time, not sure she'd ever felt such pain or determination. Then she saw him—inching toward her, his face filled with pain, but with the same determination she had. "Jonas," she whispered. She continued to pull herself toward him.

"Lizzie." His voice was low and hoarse. "Wait. I'm almost there."

But Lizzie pressed forward, her heart pounding through her chest, both hips preventing her legs from assisting with her efforts. And finally . . . she was within two feet of him. She lay on her stomach and reached her hands as far as they would stretch. Jonas did the same.

"You silly woman," he breathed as his fingers met with hers.

"You silly old man." She intertwined her hand with his and stared into his tired eyes. "I'm so tired, Jonas."

"I know. I'm tired, too, Lizzie."

"Maybe we should rest for a bit."

As they both closed their eyes, Lizzie felt the crisp winds

swirling, heard the rustling weeds swooshing to and fro around them. A tiny insect buzzed in her ear, but she was too exhausted to wave it away. Jonas clutched tightly to her hand, and Lizzie could hear his labored breathing. She would figure out what to do after a little rest.

"I think little Elizabeth looks like Anna," Sarah Jane told Barbie on the drive back to the farm. "They both have those incredible blue eyes like Samuel."

"I can see Lillian in both the girls too, though." Barbie turned toward her and smiled. "Beautiful children."

"I'm so thankful this was a short, easy delivery for Lillian. You know, she had quite a time when Anna was born. Twenty hours of difficult labor."

Barbie nodded as she turned onto Black Horse Road. "I remember. We thought Lillian would never have that child."

"*Danki* for taking me to the hospital, Barbie. I have a fresh batch of cookies I'd like to send home with you for Thomas and the boys."

"That's not necessary, Sarah Jane. I wanted to go." She snickered. "But I'll still be glad to take those cookies off your hands. Do I dare ask if they are my favorite?"

"Raisin puffs. Your favorite." Sarah Jane unclasped her seat belt. "Come in. Let's have a cookie. Hopefully, Pop is home and found himself something to eat."

"Well, the buggy is here," Barbie said. "Your dad didn't get far. If you'd like, I can swing by Lizzie's on my way home."

"I might have you do that, if he's not inside. He could be

napping by now, though. He usually lies down about this time of—"

Barbie grabbed her forearm hard. "Sarah Jane!" She pointed toward the wide-open meadow spanning the space between their farm and Lizzie's house.

Sarah Jane's heart pounded violently. "Oh no," she said. "Pop!" she yelled. "Pop!"

Her legs were already moving toward the field when she realized there were two people lying amid the tall weeds. She broke out in a run, praying aloud. "Please, God, please, God, please, God . . ."

"I'll call 911!" Barbie yelled.

Sarah Jane ran as fast as she could across the meadow. "Pop!"

20

Sadie left the hospital, elated for Lillian and the birth of Elizabeth. But she also felt a profound sense of panic at her own situation. Her farm was gone. And somehow, she was going to have to buy it back.

She thanked Carley for bringing her home, although she'd never felt more homeless or unhappy in her life. God presented her with an opportunity at happiness, with Milo and his wonderful family in Texas, and she had ungraciously walked away from all He offered. She hung her cape on the rack and sat down on the bench at the kitchen table. Maybe she'd made a terrible mistake by not giving things more time between her and Milo.

But every time she'd start to get close to Milo, Kade's face would pop into her mind. She wished she had never met Kade Saunders. Then she would have fallen happily in love with Milo and lived the life she was meant to live. Now, the familiar bitterness she tried so hard to steer away from crept back in. Why would God show her a glimpse of true love with a man she could never be with? Questioning Him was driving her right back to a place she didn't want to be.

Her thoughts were interrupted by the sound of horse hooves coming up the drive. She pulled herself up and went to the door, although she was not in the mood for visitors. After a few moments, she recognized her guest, and this was the one person she was glad to see on this gloomy afternoon.

"Hello, Lester," she said to Lester Lapp. The elderly man hobbled up the porch steps and tipped his straw hat in her direction.

"Sadie, it's *gut* to see you home."

"From what I understand, I don't have a home. I was hoping to buy back my farm from you, but I heard it's already been sold again."

Lester pulled off his hat, scratched his head. "Ya know the only reason I bought this place so quickly, Sadie, was so the property wouldn't go to an *Englischer*. Bishop Ebersol had your power of attorney, so I snapped it up." He paused. "And I'd have sold it right back to you if I'd known you were comin' back."

"Then why did you sell it?" She knew her tone was accusing, but he just said he didn't want the property to go to an outsider.

He took a deep breath and walked to the rocker on the porch. He eased onto the seat, but Sadie kept standing. She folded her arms across her chest and waited for an answer.

"Mary has the cancer," he said. "I'm sure you know that."

Sadie softened her look and voice. "*Ya*, I do. I'm so sorry, Lester. How is she?" She genuinely cared for Mary and Lester, but Mary had been diagnosed with breast cancer months ago. What did this have to do with her farm?

"The city doctors are trying an experimental medication on Mary, and the cost is two thousand dollars a month. I know the community would draw from our fund to cover it, Sadie, but it puts a huge burden on our district. When someone offered me double what I paid for your farm, I reckon I didn't see past the fact that the fella was *Englisch*. That money will go a long way toward Mary's care." He shook his head. "I'm real sorry, Sadie. I figured you to be stayin' in Texas, making a life there."

"So did I," she mumbled.

"Maybe you can buy it back from the *Englischer*? I'll give you the profit I made to do just that."

Sadie knew the sacrifice Lester was making by extending such an offer, but she also knew that the community would cover Mary's medical expenses, one way or the other. If she didn't get her farm back, she was homeless.

"Why would anyone offer twice what the property is worth?" she finally asked. "I don't understand. Mr. Spalek is very greedy to snatch up my property from you, offering to pay such a ridiculous—"

"Whoa, there," Lester interrupted. "It ain't Dale Spalek who bought the property. It was your friend . . ." Lester ran a hand through his long beard. "What was that fella's name?"

"What? Who?" No one Sadie knew had that kind of money or intentions.

"Why, it was that Saunders fella. Kade."

"What?" she asked again. Her blood was starting to boil as she realized that Kade was indeed the only person she knew with the means to purchase her farm at double the value. "Evidently, he is not my *friend*. Why would he want my farm?" she demanded.

Lester shook his head. "I don't know, Sadie. But yours wasn't the only place he bought. He bought the old King place too. Isaac had that place priced way too high, and that's why it's been sittin' there for almost two years. But Mr. Saunders paid top dollar for all ninety-eight acres."

"I don't understand." Sadie folded herself into the rocker. "Why would Kade Saunders be buying up property in the middle of our community?" Then a thought hit her. Maybe he was coming here to live. Seemed a far-fetched idea, though.

"That ain't all," Lester said. He lifted his chin, challenging her to question him.

"What do you mean?"

"That twenty-acre tract right next to Noah's clinic. It's been for sale nearly six months. Saunders bought that too."

Sadie's eyes grew wild. Kade wasn't moving here. He was just buying up all their property for some commercial use, because he had the money to do it. She'd never been more furious. How wrong she'd been about him. *Greedy, greedy.* He'd gotten a taste of their quiet community and decided to profit from it.

"Is there any more? Did he buy anything else?"

Lester stood up. "Not that I know of, Sadie. I'm real sorry. But you take the money I made on your place so that you can purchase you somethin' else."

Sadie wanted to tell him that this was her family property and that she didn't want anything else, but Lester looked tormented, and she knew he had plenty to worry about with Mary.

"I'm going to talk to Mr. Saunders," she said. "And when I get done with him, he's going to sell me back my farm for what I sold it to you for, and you're going to keep that extra money to tend to Mary's medical needs."

"Why would he sell it back to you for such a loss?"

"Because he can afford to."

And with that, Sadie bid Lester good-bye and stomped toward the phone in her barn. Kade Saunders was about to get a piece of her mind.

It amused Kade to see the stunned looks on the board members' faces when he announced his resignation from Saunders Real Estate and Development. As he stared at the twenty dropped jaws, he decided to give them a moment to let the news sink in. He supposed that three months ago, if anyone had predicted such a maneuver, he'd have laughed. But he wasn't the same man he had been three months ago.

"What happened to you during your hiatus?" Larry Paulson bravely asked when no one else spoke up.

"Nothing happened to me, Larry. My situation has changed, that's all. As I'm sure you are all aware, I have full custody of my son, Tyler, following the death of his mother. Tyler has special needs, and I choose to be a hands-on father."

Mouths were still agape, and Kade's colleagues couldn't seem to grasp the concept. All except for one, Sheila Burns. A mother of four, her eyes were sympathetic, and she had a slight smile on her face. "I think it's a wonderful thing you're doing, Kade," she said.

Sheila wasn't the only female, or mother, in the room. However, the other four women present didn't seem to share Sheila's understanding.

"Kade, we all have children," Carol Watkins said. "And some of our children have special needs as well. But we don't give all this up, everything we've worked hard to achieve. Are you sure you've thought this through?"

Kade looked at Carol, then at Larry, Sheila, and continued around the room until he'd made eye contact with each and every one of them. Then he said, very simply, "Money will not buy any of us happiness. Everyone in this room has more money than they will ever spend in a lifetime. And how many of you can say, in all honesty, that you are truly happy and at peace with yourself and your life?"

While Kade might not have made such a comment several months ago, strangely enough, his colleagues seemed to consider his statement. No one said anything.

A knock at the conference room door pulled them all from their musings.

"I'm sorry to interrupt, Mr. Saunders," Mindy, the receptionist, said. "But there is a woman on the phone who insists she must talk to you. I told her repeatedly that you are not available, but she said it's urgent."

"Who is it?" Kade asked.

"She said her name is Sadie. She said you rented a cottage from her?"

Kade's heart thumped anxiously. "Put her through to my office." Then he turned to the board members. "Please excuse the interruption. I need to take this call." He left the room and walked a few paces to his office down the hall.

He answered on the first ring. "Sadie, is everything all right? How are you? Where are you? It's so good to hear—"

"How dare you!" she yelled into the phone, startling Kade.

"How dare I what?"

"You bought my farm from Lester Lapp for a ridiculous amount of money. And now, I need you to sell it back to me for what Lester originally paid for it. That is my family farm, Kade!"

Kade couldn't help but smile. "So, you are in Lancaster County, not Texas?"

Silence for a moment. "*Ya.* Now, will you sell me my farm back?"

"Of course. Why aren't you in Texas?"

He heard her sigh on the other end of the phone. "*Danki, danki.* I was feeling homeless."

"Sadie," he said soothingly. "I'll draw up the papers and get them to you. And, of course, for the same price you sold it to Lester Lapp. Now, why aren't you in Texas?"

"Why did you buy so much property in Lancaster County, Kade?"

"Why do you keep answering a question with another question?" It was wonderful to hear her voice. He could visualize her face, the way she bit her lip and twisted her face into a scowl when she was angry.

"Are you planning something? Something bad? Are you trying to bring your *Englisch* business into our community, Kade? Because we won't hear of such a thing, and—"

Kade smiled. "I sure have missed you, Sadie Fisher. I have missed you a lot. Now again I'll ask, why aren't you in Texas?"

A moment of silence, and then she said, "It wasn't right for me."

"*It* wasn't right for you, or Milo wasn't right for you?"

"Both," she conceded.

Kade wasn't sorry in the least to hear that news. It was a huge bonus to his already developed plan he'd put into action.

A huge perk, indeed. "I'll be coming to Lancaster County for Jonas and Lizzie's wedding in a couple weeks. It will be wonderful to see you."

He waited for her to reciprocate, but he only heard silence. "You still there?" he finally asked.

"*Ya*, I'm here." Her tone seemed laced with skepticism, and Kade felt the need to make her understand how much he missed her.

"I meant what I said," he began. "I've really missed you. I've wanted to contact you, but I didn't want to interfere with the new life you were pursuing." He waited again. Then he grinned. "You missed me, just a little, didn't you?"

He waited, then was elated to hear her say, "Just a little."

And that would be enough for now.

"How is Tyler?" she asked.

"He is adjusting, but he misses your tapioca pudding. Penelope, my housekeeper, made him some, but he doesn't eat it by the bowlful the way he does yours."

She chuckled, music to Kade's ears. "Are you bringing Tyler to Jonas's wedding?" she asked.

"Jonas would kill me if I didn't bring Tyler. I think he likes Tyler more than me."

"*Ya*, I understand that you and Jonas formed quite a friendship while I was away."

"Shocking, huh? We got off to a rocky start." Kade paused. "He's a fine man, Jonas."

"The best," she said.

Mindy's voice came across the intercom. "I apologize again, Mr. Saunders. It seems there is another call from Lancaster

County coming in. And the woman also says it's urgent. Do you want to take a call from Sarah Jane Miller?"

"Yes. Put her on hold. I'll pick it up," Kade said.

"I heard what that woman said," Sadie said, sounding alarmed. "Why is Sarah Jane calling you?"

"I don't know. Do you want to hold on while I find out?"

"*Ya.*"

"Okay, sit tight." Kade pushed the hold button and clicked over. "Sarah Jane? What is it? Is everything all right?"

Kade listened intently, and a minute later, hung up the phone.

He clicked back over to Sadie. "Sadie, it appears I will be traveling to Lancaster County sooner than I thought."

21

As the cab pulled up in front of Jonas and Sarah Jane's house, Kade counted the buggies. Twelve. A small crowd, but that's the way he understood they wanted it. He helped Tyler out of the taxi and paid the driver.

This trip to Lancaster County had consumed Kade's thoughts for the past three days, since Sarah Jane's phone call. Tyler didn't do very well on the plane last night, and an unfamiliar hotel room only added to the mix, rendering them both without much sleep. Then more problems this morning when Kade realized he forgot Tyler's favorite breakfast cereal. You would think a hotel could round up some Honey Nut Cheerios.

He hated to be late to anything, particularly an occasion such as this. He glanced at his watch. Eight thirty. They were a half hour late.

Sarah Jane warned him on the phone that the service would last from three to four hours, and Kade had considered just showing up for the last hour. But somehow, that seemed disrespectful. It would be a long morning with Tyler, but Kade figured he could slip outside with Tyler from time to time, if necessary.

"Tyler, we need to be very quiet inside," Kade told his son.

They headed up the porch steps, and Kade decided it would

be best to enter through the kitchen. He quietly pulled the screen door open and tiptoed in with Tyler by his side. Kade handed Tyler a candy sucker, saved for this very moment. It wasn't the recommended parenting tip, but Tyler smiled and began licking the lollipop. They walked around the corner and into the den.

Everyone was seated on wooden benches that had been lined up and angled toward the front of the room. Women were on one side and men on the other side, except for a few who were huddled around Jonas and Lizzie. Kade swallowed hard. The small congregation was singing a song in German, slow and without any musical accompaniment. Kade and Tyler slipped into the back row on the men's side of the room, the song filling the room with enough sound to cover their movements.

Tyler seemed mesmerized by his surroundings, and his eyes darted about in every direction. But the minute the music stopped and the bishop began to speak, Tyler made their presence known.

"Good!" he yelled.

Kade wasn't sure if Tyler meant the candy, the singing, or something else, but every person in the room turned around to look at Kade and his son. Sheepishly, Kade smiled and waved to his friends. Some returned the gesture, and Bishop Ebersol continued on with the service. Kade took a deep breath and hoped that Tyler would be able to refrain from any more outbursts. Then he saw Sadie in the front row.

She stared at him and smiled faintly. It was torture for him to be only a few yards away from her and not be able to talk to her. He desperately wanted to tell her how much he missed her. But there would be time for that later. Kade was glad to be back in

Paradise for a few days. He planned to have Sadie's property transferred back into her name and get his other plans rolling. But mostly, he was looking forward to spending time with Sadie.

Bishop Ebersol began to speak in German or Pennsylvania *Deitsch*. Kade couldn't tell the difference. The German language and the Pennsylvania *Deitsch* dialect sounded a lot alike to Kade. Twice, the bishop translated, seemingly for Kade's benefit, the stories of the Old Testament. Tyler yelled, "Good" two more times, but the bishop merely went on, and the attendees smiled.

Anywhere else, Tyler's interruptions might not have been so well received, but here—in Lancaster County—things were different. Kade's eyes shifted to Tyler, who was now reading the Bible he'd brought with him, his finger running along each line of fine print. Right away, Kade recalled Tyler's past Scripture quotes to both him and Sadie. Each time Kade saw his son pick up the Bible, he still felt a level of anticipation at the possibility of another revelation.

About an hour later, Kade and Tyler slid from their places on the back bench and went outside. Kade was shocked that Tyler had made it that long, and Kade had to admit it felt good to stretch his legs. As much as he respected, admired, and often longed to be a part of the Amish community, he couldn't quite get used to the lengthy worship services. Twice, he'd attended with Jonas before he returned to Los Angeles. Jonas had said, "Ya get used to it." Kade knew it was an honor to be invited to an Old Order church service, not something most of the outside world would ever have the privilege to experience.

He smiled as he recalled times spent with Jonas. And with Sadie.

Fifteen minutes later, Kade told Tyler it was time that they headed back in. Kade was worried he'd miss the main event, but they came back just in time. He helped Tyler to his seat and scooted in beside him. Kade smiled when Bishop Ebersol began the part of the service he was looking forward to the most.

"It is a blessed day," Bishop Ebersol began. "We are gathered together for this joyous occasion, to unite Jonas Ivan Miller and Elizabeth Mae Esh in holy matrimony . . ."

Jonas glanced Kade's way and smiled, then focused on his bride-to-be. What a scare those two had given everyone. Sarah Jane had told Kade on the phone about the adventure that had landed both Jonas and Lizzie in Lancaster General a week earlier. Luckily, neither was injured seriously. Following their one-night stay at the hospital, both Jonas and Lizzie wanted to push the wedding up. Sarah Jane had laughed, saying they'd both be safer if they were together.

Kade gazed at the couple. Jonas stood tall and proud, and Lizzie was a glowing bride, clothed in a blue dress, white apron, and white prayer covering, her face radiant as she smiled at her husband-to-be. He remembered Sarah Jane saying that when Lizzie and Jonas had split up for a short while, Lizzie'd had a bout with forgetfulness. They worried that she might have had a stroke, but Lizzie had been so depressed, she'd forgotten to take some of her medications. There was no evidence of a stroke.

Kade could hear sniffles throughout the room, and he struggled with his own building emotions. It was a glorious day, and Kade was honored to be included.

Everyone seemed to breathe a sigh of relief once Jonas and Lizzie had repeated their vows to each other. *What a blessing this day is,* Kade thought with a smile.

When Bishop Ebersol closed the service, Jonas and Lizzie made their way through the small crowd. It was heartwarming to see Jonas practically pushing past everyone to get to Kade, extending his hand two feet before he arrived. "I was worried you might not make it."

Kade latched onto his friend's hand, but then pulled him into an embrace. "I wouldn't have missed it, Jonas."

Lizzie joined her husband. "It's so *gut* you and the boy are here, Kade." She leaned in to hug Kade.

Kade's eyes scanned the room. "Where's Tyler?"

Jonas pointed to the far corner. "With Sadie. We see who's number one on his list." Jonas chuckled. "And I thought it was me."

Sadie hugged Tyler and caught Kade watching her. Kade took a deep breath. Being here—with Jonas, seeing Sadie, the feel of the place, the fellowship, the spirituality in the room—Kade felt almost overwhelmed. And to think that these people have this every single day.

He couldn't take his eyes from Sadie, who was now holding Tyler, laughing, and whispering something in his ear. There were so many things Kade wanted to say to her. But just then, Jonas spoke to him.

"Kade, me and Lizzie have something to give you, later, when things calm down a bit. Just don't run off until we're able to talk with ya for a few minutes."

"I'm not going anywhere, Jonas. I can't think of anywhere

I'd rather be. And I'll be staying for several days. There are some things—"

"Kade! Wonderful to see you," Noah Stoltzfus said. The doctor extended his hand to Kade.

"Great to be here," Kade responded. "It was a beautiful ceremony."

Jonas and Lizzie excused themselves to mingle with the other guests. "Just remember what I said, Kade," Jonas reminded him. He tipped his black hat as he walked away. Kade nodded in acknowledgment.

"I'm very excited about our project, Kade," Noah said when Jonas and Lizzie were out of earshot. "What you're doing is a wonderful thing, a great thing for the community. I think it will be wonderful for Tyler too."

Kade turned back toward Noah. "This place, and everyone here, will be good for Tyler."

"I agree," Noah said. He rubbed his chin for a moment. "Listen, I don't want to be overstepping my bounds—"

"What is it?"

"Well, as we discussed, I haven't mentioned your plans to anyone. But I was wondering if Sadie knows?" He paused. "I mean, people talk, even here, and word around the community is that perhaps something is going on with you and Sadie, and—"

"What?" Kade frowned. "I'll do whatever I have to do to protect Sadie's reputation. We're just friends, and Sadie has been very good to Tyler and me. If people are talking—"

"Wait, wait. Hold on, there, buddy," Noah said. "That's how we in the *Englisch* world think, but that's not what I meant. Sadie's reputation isn't being questioned. That would never occur to anyone here. What I meant was—in the words of the Amish—there is talk that a courtship is going on, even perhaps long-distance. I think that got started when Sadie returned from Texas, with no plans to marry Milo. I'm mostly wondering if you are considering converting?"

"I know people will probably think that, especially when we move here to stay. But God led me here, and this is where Tyler and I will stay." He paused for a moment. "Do I fantasize about what it would be like to convert, to be with Sadie as a family? Yes, I do. We became very close while I was here, and I care about her a great deal. But Noah, I'm wise enough to realize that a decision like that must be carefully weighed, and a change in faith of that magnitude would require more time, and a better understanding of the *Ordnung*."

"I'm glad to hear you say that. Because an Amish woman would never allow a man to convert to the Plain ways just so he could be with her." Noah smiled. "Listen, I grew up Amish. If I can help you with anything, let me know. But I am thrilled that you and Tyler will be moving here, and I'm very happy about our project."

"So am I."

Kade looked across the room at Sadie walking toward him, holding Tyler's hand, and he wondered if he was being honest with himself. A large part of his intent in coming to Lancaster County was to be with Sadie, in some capacity. Could he really be happy being just her friend? Could he overhaul his life to that extent that he could claim a place in this fine community, a place with Sadie?

He looked around the room and smiled. *Maybe so.*

Sadie had tried to stay focused on Jonas and Lizzie during the ceremony, but she couldn't stop thinking about Kade and Tyler in the back row, so close. Sarah Jane told her they would be staying for a few days. Kade's words—*I've missed you*—resounded in her head.

Now she was anxious to get to Kade, when Lillian grabbed her arm.

"Thank the good Lord this all went well today," Lillian said. "Grandpa and Lizzie are so happy, and both of them know *who* they are and *where* they are today." She smiled, then spoke to Tyler. "Hello, Tyler."

"Hello, Tyler," the boy repeated to Lillian.

"It's a *gut* day for everyone," Sadie said. She fought to keep her eyes from drifting in Kade's direction.

"You know," Lillian said with a twinkle in her eye, "there is a rumor circulating around the community."

"Gossip and rumor are sins," Sadie said as she winked at Lillian. "But tell me."

Lillian leaned in close. "Rumor has it that Kade is staying here."

"I know that," Sadie said. She was somewhat disappointed Lillian didn't have anything juicier than that. "He'll be staying for three days."

Lillian grinned. "Uh, no, my friend. That is not what I meant." She folded her arms across her chest. "Rumor is that he will be *staying*. Moving here."

Sadie twisted her mouth from side to side, thought for a minute. "I wondered why he was buying so much property here."

She paused. "But I can't imagine what kind of business he would conduct in our Amish community."

"Maybe it's not business," Lillian said. "Maybe he's moving here to be with you!"

Sadie narrowed her eyes. "Lillian, that is ridiculous! He's not Amish." *But oh, how I wish he was.*

"People convert. Look at me. I did." She smiled.

"I know, Lillian. But people like Kade don't do that. Besides, we don't have that kind of relationship, nor would I ever hear of a man converting to our faith for the wrong reasons. I'm sure Kade's motives are—"

"Did I hear my name?"

Sadie had gotten so caught up in the conversation that she didn't realize Kade was standing beside them. "Kade," she said, her cheeks flushing. She felt like she might cry all of a sudden.

"I missed you," he whispered in her ear, and Sadie allowed herself to bask in the feel of his closeness.

But she pulled back, unsure what Lillian would think, and wondering if Lillian had heard what Kade said. "It's so *gut* of you to come to Jonas and Lizzie's wedding," she said.

"I wanted to be here. For a lot of reasons." He smiled.

"I better go find my family," Lillian said. "*Mamm* is proudly toting little Elizabeth around. And David has Anna. As much as I'm enjoying this break, I'll let you two talk." She grinned at Sadie, which caused Sadie to blush again.

"It's good to see you, Sadie," Kade said when Lillian was gone.

He seemed so familiar, as if no time had passed. Sadie gazed into his eyes, wondering, speculating. Then the words flew from her lips. "Are you moving here?"

Kade didn't seem at all surprised by the question. "Yes," he said smoothly.

People were bustling past them, particularly the womenfolk, and Sadie knew she needed to head to the kitchen and help prepare the meal. But she had so many questions. "Why? Why are you moving here?"

Kade's eyes darkened a bit. "I thought you might be glad I was moving here." He touched her arm. "Can we go outside for a minute to talk?"

"I need to help with the food, and—"

He tugged at her arm and guided her to the door in the den, which led outside. "Just for a minute." Tyler had taken a seat on the bench with Jonas, and Kade called Jonas's name. "Will Tyler be all right with you for a few minutes?"

Jonas looked up and nodded.

Sadie glanced over her shoulder, but everyone was busying themselves.

Once outside, Kade practically dragged her around the corner of the house, out of sight.

"Kade, stop it." She wiggled free of his hold on her arm. "What if someone sees us? Why are we hiding back here? I need to be inside helping with—"

"I missed you, Sadie," he said again. Kade pulled her close, and she gasped unexpectedly, afraid to stay in his arms, and yet not wanting to push him away either. His lips were so close to hers, she could feel his breath. He was going to kiss her, and what a mess that would make of things. Sadie knew she didn't have the strength or desire to stop him. *God, forgive me.*

But he didn't kiss her. Instead, he spoke softly, but intently, gazing steadily into her eyes—eyes Sadie knew reflected the fear in her heart. Fear he'd stay, fear he'd go.

"I'm not the same man I was before I came here, Sadie. Call it a spiritual awakening, or a spiritual cleansing of sort, but I'm not the same. I want a different life for both Tyler and me. I want that life to be in Lancaster County. I think the world of Jonas . . ." He paused. "And you. I don't have any expectations past knowing that I need to leave the city, my life as it was, and to start fresh. Basically, I'm taking the steps I feel comfortable with, based on what I believe is God's will for me. I plan to take things one step at a time. I hope I can count on your friendship."

It should have been what Sadie wanted to hear. But she was disappointed and wondered why. She already knew that men like Kade didn't give up their lives to become Amish. But that thought only brought up more questions. Her mind was buzzing, and she was having trouble thinking straight.

"I know you need to go inside to help with the meal," he said. "Could Tyler and I come by this evening?"

Sadie nodded mechanically. Saying no was not an option, this much she knew. "I'll cook supper," she said.

"Wonderful," he whispered. And then he was gone.

It was later in the afternoon when Kade asked Sadie if she could keep an eye on Tyler while he joined Jonas out by the barn, away from the others. Inside the barn, Jonas retrieved a metal box from the corner of his workbench, although Kade could tell there hadn't been any actual projects going on for quite a while. Cobwebs covered the vise grip bolted to one corner of the long, wooden table, and sandy dirt covered most of the surface. Jonas pulled an envelope from the metal box and motioned for Kade to sit down on a nearby bench. Jonas sat down on a wooden chair across from him.

"Kade, between my medications for the cancer and this Alzheimer's disease, my mind is a mess," Jonas began. "Some days I reckon I do real *gut*, but some days, I'm not sure who's who or where I'm at. Before things got too bad, I decided I wanted *mei* kin to know how I felt about them, how they added to this *wunderbaar* life the Lord blessed me with. So, I scribbled some letters to *mei* family, telling each one of them my most private feelings, things I might not be able to say in person." Jonas pressed his lips together. "We feel things just like other folks, Kade. But as Amish men and women, we know it's not always proper to say what's on our minds."

Kade listened intently, not sure where Jonas was going with this.

"These are the letters." Jonas held up the envelope. "Lizzie made a promise to me that she'd make sure to give each letter to each person if I die, or if I just go nuts." He lightly tugged at his long, gray beard. "And Lizzie has letters, too, to her kin. I'd promised to give them to each person." Jonas shook his head. "But we recently combined all our letters in this envelope. We fear that we could both not have our right minds at the same time, and no one would find the letters, or at least not for a while. And we reckon it might help our loved ones know what they meant to us, to help them durin' a time of grief, or even worse— if we were still on God's earth but not in our right minds."

"I think that's a nice idea, Jonas."

Jonas handed Kade the envelope. "I'd like for you to make sure everyone gets these letters at the right time. I reckon if somethin' happened to Lizzie, my mind would be like slosh, and I'm worried I'd forget where I put them."

"I'd be honored, Jonas." Kade accepted the envelope. "I will take care of this, if ever there becomes a need."

"*Ach*, there will come a need." Jonas chuckled. "Just ain't sure when."

"Can I ask you . . ." Kade hesitated. "Why me?"

"Why not you?"

Kade smiled. That was Jonas's way, and as Jonas had stated before, he wasn't comfortable being open with his feelings. But Kade knew it was an honor to be asked to do this on behalf of both Jonas and Lizzie.

"I feel better we've handled this, Kade. I trust you to take care of it." Jonas took a deep breath. "But now I reckon I need to talk to you about something else."

"What's that?" Something in Jonas's tone worried Kade.

"You ain't gonna like it, but I'm gonna speak the truth."

"Okay," Kade said.

Jonas took another deep breath. "I know you're planning to move here, Kade, and I'm pleased by this. I also know that you gave Noah a large amount of money to open a school next to his clinic, a school for special children, like Tyler and some of the others in our community. This pleases me also."

Kade opened his mouth to ask how Jonas knew this, but Jonas flashed his palm forward.

"And I know you plan to live on the other farm you bought, the King place." He paused. "'Tis *gut* as well."

Kade heard the *but* coming, loud and clear.

"But until you know if you plan to convert yourself to the Amish faith, renounce your worldly ways, and live as one of us by putting your faith in all that is God's will—then you need not be courtin' Sadie in any manner."

Kade wasn't sure he understood what Jonas was telling him. "But we can be friends, right?"

Jonas took off his hat and placed it on his knee. His eyes shone with implacable determination as he spoke. "If you have any thoughts of comin' here to test the waters, spend time with Sadie, and then make a decision one way or the other, it ain't right. You kids spent a lot of time together durin' the blizzard, and I looked the other way. But with you comin' here to live, it's only right that I tell you how I feel."

"I'm not sure I understand." Kade tipped his head to one side.

"I believe the *Englisch* say, 'You can't have your cake and eat it too.' And what I mean 'bout that is, you find your way *first*, Kade. Don't be courtin' Sadie without having made a commitment to the faith. Ain't fair to her."

Kade sat quietly for a moment.

"Can you say with certainty that you are going to leave all your worldly ways behind you and become a true member of our community through baptism?"

"Well, no, not yet. But I'm selling most of my personal possessions, donating them to charities, downsizing my life, all in an effort to see—" He stopped. Jonas was right. He was reducing his material baggage, and he was trying to turn his life over to God. But he hadn't made a final decision to commit to the Amish ways.

"When you can look me in the eye and tell me that you are

ready to live as an Amish man, then, and only then, would it be appropriate to court our Sadie. You may think that you might want to be Amish, but more time is needed. I reckon I will continue to teach you the ways of the *Ordnung* as long as my mind allows me to, if you'd like."

Kade considered Jonas's comments. "I want to learn everything I can. I guess I thought that I could still spend time with Sadie while I was doing that, and—"

Jonas was shaking his head. "It's not right, Kade."

"But Bishop Ebersol wouldn't have to know," Kade said.

Jonas's expression was solemn and reprimanding. "But you will know. God will know." Jonas stood up. "I will leave you to think on this."

Kade sat in the barn for about twenty minutes, thinking about everything Jonas said. With much regret, he knew what he had to do.

He found Sadie in the house with Tyler. They were smiling and laughing. It was a picture-perfect moment, and he was about to ruin it.

22

SADIE UNLOCKED THE DOOR AT HER SHOP. THEN SHE sprung open the windows and allowed the crisp April winds to blow in, bringing with it the sweet smell of wildflowers. She inhaled, hoping the aromas would fill her senses with the tranquility of the season. Spring was her favorite time of year, but on this day, it was taking all her effort to enjoy the beautiful weather.

She'd heard that Kade and Tyler were settled in at the King farm, even though she hadn't heard from him since the day of Jonas and Lizzie's wedding. Following his abrupt departure from the wedding, he'd returned a few weeks later to take up residence less than a mile away from her.

Her last conversation with Kade replayed again and again in her mind, and each time her thought process concluded, she was right back where she started, wondering what her future held.

Kade had canceled supper that evening with only a vague explanation. "I want to be a better man, Sadie," he'd said. "And I think I'm going to need some time to myself, just Tyler and me, for a while. Do you understand?"

Sadie didn't understand, but she'd nodded just the same, unsure what had changed since earlier in the day. She had wanted to ask him, how much time? And why did he have to distance himself from her in such a way? But then he added, "Only God can see past this moment, so I promise to walk with Him and see where His road leads me."

And that was something Sadie couldn't argue with, no matter how much she wanted to.

Yet, after all this time, she hadn't laid eyes on him, and Sadie had decided that Kade's promise to walk with God was not leading him toward her. Otherwise, surely he would have been by for a brief visit or something. She'd also heard rumor that Kade was involved in a business deal with Noah. *It's okay for him to socialize and do business with other members of the community and not me?*

Bitterness tugged at her heart—a heart filled with holes that she was tired of plugging. First Ben. Then Milo. And now Kade. Each bringing his own heartache. Sadie was done opening her heart or praying for a happy ending. Instead, she busied herself with other things and constantly prayed that God would help her understand His plan for her—a plan that seemed destined for her to be alone. But she knew that marrying a man she didn't love would have never brought her true happiness. Better to be alone.

"It's a gorgeous day," Mary Ellen said as she walked into the shop.

Rebecca followed behind her. "*Ya.* I love this time of year."

Both women walked over to Sadie, who stood near a rack of quilts on the far wall.

"I'm just adding this quilt to the others," Sadie said. It wasn't her scheduled day to work, and she had lots to do at her house. She heaved the quilt onto a large wire hanger for such a purpose. "I've already put a price tag on it. Sarah Jane dropped it off yesterday."

"I reckon you'll be readying your *haus* for church service this Sunday?" Mary Ellen asked. She helped Sadie straighten the quilt on the hanger.

"*Ya*. I'm getting ready to head to the house now."

Sadie hadn't hosted worship service at her house in almost nine months, which was about the amount of time it took to circle back to her after other members of the community took their turns. There was much to do in order to ready the house for such a gathering, a group of almost one hundred. And she only had today and tomorrow to do so. Samuel and several other men would be by tomorrow to help line up the wooden benches she kept in the barn and to remove the panel in her den for the occasion. The wooden room divider, a common addition to most Amish homes, separated Sadie's large den into two rooms. But on worship day, the two cozy areas became one large space big enough to host everyone.

Ben had loved having church service in their home. She missed him now, more than ever. And despite her bitterness, she also missed Kade and Tyler.

How naive she had been. She'd thought that Kade was moving here to be close to her, when he was really only here for business opportunities, opportunities he only knew about because of acquaintances that Sadie had introduced him to. He didn't even bring Tyler by to see her. Nothing. Her anger at him kept dragging her down. Eventually she'd have to pick herself back up, determined not to let Kade Saunders get the best of her.

Even all these weeks later, she could still see his face, feel his arms around her, and hear the sound of his laughter. She missed Tyler, too, his gentle ways, his innocent giggle. She recalled the way he'd clung tightly to her at the wedding. If she allowed herself to think too much about the two of them, it always brought forth tears. And there was way too much to do today to allow herself the luxury of feeling sorry for herself. So, with that thought, she bid good-bye to Mary Ellen and Rebecca and trudged toward home, to begin a thorough cleaning of the farmhouse.

―――

Kade and Tyler spent most of their time with Jonas, at his place, when they were not in their new home. Not a day went by when Kade didn't long to see Sadie. Tyler was adjusting to his schedule, and Mary Ellen's daughter, Linda, babysat him when it was necessary for Kade to be without him. Today was one of those days.

"Thank you, Linda," Kade said when the girl arrived to keep an eye on Tyler for a while. "I shouldn't be gone more than an hour or so." Tyler liked the teenager, and Linda seemed to enjoy taking care of Tyler as well. However, today, Linda had a strange look on her face.

"Is something wrong?" Kade asked.

Linda walked to the window and pointed outside. "Is that yours?"

"Yes. What do you think?"

Linda raised her brows, and her eyes were as large as golf balls. "Do you know how to drive a horse and buggy? And where did you get *that* horse?"

Kade smiled. "Jonas has been teaching me. He's been letting me drive his for about two weeks."

"Where'd ya get that horse?" Linda's eyes were still wildly curious.

"From Big Jake, down past the Gordonville Bookstore." And what a deal he'd gotten. He couldn't wait until Sadie saw him pull up in his own buggy for church service this Sunday. It would be Kade's first time to attend worship since he'd been back, and a bonus that it would be at Sadie's house, a place filled with grand memories for him. He knew enough about the *Ordnung* at this point to know that pride was an unacceptable trait, but he suspected the emotion might surface just the same.

"That's what I thought," Linda said smugly. Then she abruptly spun around and faced Kade with warning eyes. "You bought Loco."

"What?"

"We call 'im that cuz he's a crazy horse. That's why Big Jake ain't been able to sell him." She paused and tapped her finger to her chin. "But I reckon you got him all the way here, so you must know what you're doin'." Linda shrugged.

"Well, actually—" Kade scratched his forehead. "Big Jake brought Loco, as you call him, early this morning. He hitched the horse up to the buggy for me. I purchased the buggy yesterday from Lester Lapp. He delivered it."

Linda giggled. "So, you ain't ever been behind the reins with Loco then, huh?"

"Loco, loco, loco!" Tyler exclaimed from his spot on the floor where he was playing with his letters.

"That's right," Linda said. "Your Pop is loco if he gets in the buggy with that horse a-pullin' 'im." She shook her head.

Kade felt a hint of nervousness, but if he was going to give the Amish life a try, he needed to live as they did. He had been doing a pretty good job so far. No electricity, for starters. It wasn't in the King house when he purchased it. Plus, he'd come a long way with his studies of the *Ordnung*. It was all strange and new—wonderfully strange and new. He and Tyler were settling into this peaceful community, and Kade had never been so relaxed in his previous life in California. Only one thing was missing, and he was working on that.

He was probably the richest Amish wannabe in history, but he was living proof that money didn't buy happiness, and he'd spent the last few weeks spreading his wealth around to those who needed it the most. He did miss one thing—his music. He missed listening to the radio. Most of what made up his past life—the business meetings, unscrupulous deals and people, the rat race—he was glad to be rid of.

He would miss a few people at his office, along with neighbors down the street. And he'd miss Penelope. He'd even miss the doorman at his favorite restaurant. The elderly man had opened the door for Kade at the eatery for seven years and then parked Kade's car, always with a smile on his face and, Kade believed, with the Lord in his heart. In many ways, the man had shone a wealth of spirit that Kade had never possessed with all his money. Until recently, Kade only knew the man as Jerry. But Kade made sure that Jerry wouldn't need to park another car for the rest of his life, unless he chose to do so.

Since he'd been gone, several high-profile publications had offered a pretty penny for an interview about Kade's transformation, and he'd declined. He knew they would print their own version of what they would call an early midlife crisis.

"And another thing." Linda's voice interrupted his thoughts. "I don't reckon it's right for you to be driving the buggy around like that." She pointed to Kade, dressed in his blue jeans, white T-shirt, and tennis shoes. "You don't look Amish."

"I'm not Amish. Not yet."

"Then why are you wantin' to drive the buggy?"

This girl was frustrating him. "Because I need to be able to get around, and I'm trying to live—"

"I seen a car in the barn." Her hands landed on her hips.

Kade sighed. "I'm trying to live the Amish way. But I guess I'll just take my car," he conceded, deciding Linda was probably right. "I'll be back in an hour or so then."

"Take your time. Me and Tyler will be just fine."

Kade pulled into Noah's clinic about ten minutes later.

"Hello, there," Noah said when he walked in. "Perfect timing. I don't have another patient for about a half hour. That will give us time to talk." He motioned Kade down the hall and toward an office on the right. Kade took a seat in front of Noah's desk in one of the two high-back tan leather chairs.

"These are the plans I had in mind." Kade handed him a rolled sheet of paper. "I'll leave this with you to take a look at. See what you think, and we can talk next week."

Noah tapped his pencil on the desk. "Lillian told Carley that you haven't seen Sadie since you've been back. I thought . . . Well, let's just say I'm surprised."

"It hasn't been easy," Kade said. "I want to spend every waking minute with her, but Jonas made a good point when he said I need to decide if I truly want to convert to the Amish ways before I pursue Sadie. So I guess I've been trying to do that."

"Sadie's pretty upset," Noah said. "According to Carley, Sadie thinks you only moved here for business reasons, and the other girls aren't saying otherwise. They're afraid you won't make the commitment, and they don't want to see Sadie get hurt."

"Makes sense. Sounds like all those women really watch out for each other."

"They're all daughters of the promise," Noah said.

"What?"

"Each one of them has been on a journey toward faith, hope, and love—a spiritual journey. These women all have a very strong faith, even my wife, Carley, who isn't Amish."

"Noah, you walked away from being Amish. How can I be certain converting is the right thing? I mean, I want to be with Sadie, but I honestly don't even know if she'll have me. Plus, I really do want to make a decision of my own volition."

Noah shifted uncomfortably in his chair. "I'd be lying if I said I wasn't surprised that you're considering such a radical change. But I will tell you this—these people live the life they believe in. They don't just talk about it or admire what it stands for. They live it. Each and every day. And as someone who has lived it before, I can vouch for the tranquillity that such a life has to offer."

"But you left." Kade needed more.

"Yes, I did. But I have Amish roots that will never be completely severed. Part of me will always be Amish, even though I don't mention that to most folks. I'm a blessed man, Kade. I get to live among them, take care of them, and yet still follow my own calling. At one point, I turned it over to God, and He showed me my place in this grand community."

Kade didn't say anything. How was he to know if he was truly following God's plan or if he was just running away from a life that caused him heartache?

"One thing I should mention, Kade," Noah went on. "You don't have to be Amish to have a relationship with God. The kind of peace you're looking for can be found anywhere." He paused, then smiled. "I think it's just easier to recognize that peace here in Lancaster County."

"I feel better than I've felt in my entire life, Noah," Kade said. "I have hope. Does that make sense?"

"Yes. It does." Noah smiled. "But once this school is built, what are you going to do with yourself? Somehow, I don't see you as a farmer. No offense intended."

Kade chuckled. "None taken. I don't know the first thing about farming. But I guess if it's meant to be, God will open doors for me."

"Yes. I believe that to be true. When things come very easily to us, it is usually because we are taking the path God wants us to take. Too much opposition means we are straying from His plan."

Kade smiled. "This has all happened easily for me—disbursement of funds, rearranging my life, finding the King farm, all of it. Tyler has adjusted well, and he seems to like it here too."

"I will continue to pray for you, my friend. You'll make the right decision."

Kade stood up and shook Noah's hand. "Thank you, Noah."

As Kade got into his car, he knew he needed to talk to Sadie on Sunday.

"Are you sure he's coming?" Sadie asked Lillian Sunday morning.

"Grandpa said he is." Lillian set a large bag on Sadie's counter.

"There are seven loaves of homemade bread in here. But we might want to warm them a bit later."

Sadie nodded, then moved to the far corner of the room to make way for Samuel and his brother Ivan to carry another bench through the kitchen and into the den.

"I don't know why they're not carrying those things through the den," Lillian complained.

Sadie shrugged. "What did Jonas say about Kade?"

"Just that he's comin'. That's all."

Sadie's hands landed on her hips. "Why do you never want to talk about Kade? He has been here for weeks, and I know he spends a lot of time with Jonas. And yet, I reckon no one tells me anything, and—" Sadie choked back tears.

"Sadie, don't cry." Lillian hugged her friend. "I've been worried to voice my opinions just yet."

"But why? You are my best friend. You know how much I care for Kade and Tyler, and still you won't open up to me about why he's here or what Jonas is saying. Nothing. I don't understand."

Lillian kissed Sadie on the cheek, then brushed a tear from her face. "I think you will understand soon enough."

Sadie was having one of those days where she couldn't stop feeling sorry for herself, yet those emotions were mixed with extreme levels of excitement at the prospect of seeing Kade and Tyler. But if he really cared for her, why hadn't he been around?

"Well, I don't understand. That's for sure." She shook her head and began hastily unpacking the loaves of bread from the bag. "I don't understand at all."

Jonas arrived at Kade's farm at seven thirty Sunday morning, with Lizzie by his side. Kade had forgotten that he'd asked Jonas for a ride to the worship service this morning. He didn't want to drive up in a car. But that was before he'd gotten a buggy and horse.

"Good grief," Jonas said. He stepped out of the buggy and walked toward Kade, who was standing in the front yard with Tyler. "What have you done?"

"It's our clothes, huh?" Kade felt ridiculous. He'd picked up clothes for him and Tyler at an Amish-owned shop in town.

Jonas stroked his beard. "No, you look mighty fine. Yes, you do. You both make fine-looking Amish gentlemen." Jonas pointed across the yard. "But, *what* have you done?"

"Oh, I was going to surprise you. I bought a buggy and—"

"Loco. You bought Loco! Boy, what were you thinkin'?"

"Big Jake said he's a great horse, and he gave me a really good deal on him. I'm taking the buggy to church."

Lizzie walked up beside her husband. "Is that Loco over there?"

Jonas began laughing so hard that he had to lean down and put his hands on his knees. Then he snorted, and said, "*Ya*, that's Loco, all right. And Kade thinks he's gonna have Loco pull that buggy all the way to Sadie's place."

Lizzie grabbed her chest and gasped.

Kade frowned. This was humiliating. "Don't let the name fool you," he said casually.

"*Ach*, we're not!" Jonas exclaimed. "Ain't foolin' us one bit. That horse is crazy as can be. And so are you if you think he's gonna get you to Sadie's in one piece."

"I'm counting on it." Kade held his chin a little higher. "Tyler and I were getting ready to leave."

"You do what ya want, but the boy rides with Lizzie and me."
Jonas shook his head. "It's your funeral."

Kade's stomach twisted. How bad could this horse possibly be?

"Kade, I think maybe you best be ridin' with Jonas and me,"
Lizzie said softly.

"No, I'm taking Loco, and I'm driving this buggy to Sadie's
house!" It was becoming a matter of principle at this point.

"Fine. But the boy comes with us."

"Fine."

Jonas turned to leave with Lizzie and Tyler, but turned back.
"*Ach*, wait. I almost forgot. I brought you something." He pulled
the seat of the buggy forward and reached into the backseat. He
pulled out . . . *What? A radio?*

He handed it to Kade. "I know it's not fancy, like what you
must be used to, just a battery-operated device, but it'll serve its
purpose."

Kade accepted the radio but eyed Jonas with skepticism. "But,
Jonas, it's not allowed. If I'm going to really be Amish, then I
shouldn't have it." He pushed the radio back toward Jonas.

"Hogwash. Lots of folks have radios." He grinned. "Be best
to listen to it in the barn, though."

Kade folded his arms across his chest, atop his new suspenders. "If I recall, I suggested not telling Bishop Ebersol something
not too long ago, with regard to Sadie, and you said, 'But you will
know and God will know.'"

Jonas twisted his mouth to one side. Then he leaned in toward
Kade, a twinkle in his eye. "I reckon you need this to check the
weatherman's forecast, no?"

Kade grinned back at his friend. "I suppose so."

"As you grow in faith, you'll know which rules are meant to

be bent, and which ones ain't." He winked at Kade. "And there's a little something for Sadie inside that trapdoor on the radio." Kade pushed the button marked Eject, and a CD popped out. *Favorite Country Gospel Tunes*, he read aloud.

"The girl loves music."

"I know." Kade smiled, remembering how Sadie had loitered on the cottage porch, listening to his music playing, and how much she enjoyed listening to the jazz melodies in his car. So much had happened since then.

"I figured there's a chance the two of you might be seeing each other in the near future." Jonas paused and stared warmly into Kade's eyes. "You're ready, Kade. And it's truly been an honor to travel on this journey with you."

"The honor has been mine, Jonas." It was a special moment, and Kade could feel God working in his life in so many ways.

"Hope you live long enough to enjoy the radio." Jonas snorted, tipped his hat back, and headed to his buggy.

Kade shook his head, a smile on his face. Then he headed to his own buggy. And Loco.

⸻

It was ten minutes until eight when Jonas pulled up with Lizzie. Most of the people Sadie expected to attend were already there. She was surprised to see Tyler with Jonas and Lizzie. Obviously, Kade wasn't coming after all.

She hugged Jonas, then Lizzie, when they stepped out of the buggy.

"Hello, Tyler," she said, squatting down.

Tyler wrapped his arms around her neck. "Sadie, Sadie," he said, almost bouncing up and down.

"I'm so glad you came, Tyler." She looked up at Jonas and tried to sound casual. "I suppose Kade isn't coming?"

Jonas let out the silly snort he was known for. "*Ach, ya.* He's comin' all right. Just ain't sure if he'll arrive in one piece."

Sadie stood up. "What do you mean?"

Before Jonas had time to answer, all their attention was drawn to the noise coming from down the road. Sounded like a man yelling.

"I reckon that's him coming now," Jonas said.

"What's all the racket?" Sarah Jane stepped onto the porch, then eased her way to the yard where Sadie, Jonas, Lizzie, and Tyler were standing. The rest of the people who had gathered in the den made their way outside.

"Oh no!" Mary Ellen screamed. "Someone is in that buggy, and the horse is out of control!"

Dirt flew from beneath the wild animal. And the group could hear a man yelling, "Whoa! I said whoa!"

"That ain't just any horse," Jonas said. "That's *Loco*. And the crazy person in the buggy is Kade Saunders."

"What?" Sadie couldn't believe it. "How do you know? What is he doing with Loco?" She shook her head. "Surely not." Sadie grew concerned. *Please, God, don't let anything happen to Kade.*

"I told Jonas when we left Kade's *haus* that we shouldn't be lettin' that boy behind the reins with that crazy horse leading the way," Lizzie said.

"What? Jonas, how could you?" Sadie started down the driveway toward the road. The large crowd began to follow.

"Pop!" Sarah Jane said. "Why didn't you stop him? We all know that horse is crazy! And shame on Big Jake for selling it to Kade!"

Sadie's heart was thumping hard against her chest. They all continued down the driveway and were almost to the road when Kade came barreling by. The buggy wheels were lifting off the ground, and Kade was yelling at the top of his lungs. A memory surfaced in Sadie's mind—one of Ben lying on the road among the scattered fruit, the buggy toppled. It sent a chill up her arms.

Jonas shook his head. "I warned the boy."

"You should have stopped him!" Sadie yelled.

Lillian then faced off with her grandpa. "Shame on you, Grandpa!"

"You girls need to quit blaming an old man for a young man's stupidity." He shook his head. "It ain't right."

No sooner had Kade passed them by than he came barreling back by in the other direction.

Jonas snickered. "I reckon he's gettin' control of that animal after all. He got him turned around."

Lillian gave her grandpa an incredulous look. "But he passed us up again. And at warp speed, I might add!"

"This is *baremlich*! What do we do?" Sadie looked to Sarah Jane for guidance.

Samuel was already in his buggy, and preparing to go after Kade, when they heard the buggy coming back down the road in their direction. Kade was no longer yelling, and he eased the buggy onto the driveway. Everyone cleared out of the way.

Once Kade was able to stop the buggy next to the house, the crowd headed back up the driveway and watched Kade step down.

"Sorry I'm late," he said after taking a very deep breath. Then he walked toward the house, turning back once to address the group. "That's quite an animal." He arched his brows and smiled.

"That is one brave human being," Jonas said. "Brave indeed."

Sarah Jane poked her father on the arm. "Shame on you, just the same," she said.

"*Ya*, you should have stopped him, Grandpa!" Lillian brushed past Jonas.

Similar sentiments were spewed in Jonas's direction by most of the other women, including Sadie.

She heard Jonas whisper innocently to his wife, "Why they blaming me?"

Sadie was just thankful that Kade was all right.

Kade barely gave Sadie the time of day after the three-hour worship service, though, in his defense, she'd been busy in the kitchen. Kade sat with the men for the noon meal, and as customary, the women served them first, so there hadn't been much of an opportunity to talk to him. By the time Sadie sat down to eat, most of the men, including Kade, had congregated out by the barn to tell jokes. Afterward, the younger men stored the wooden benches back in the barn.

When the afternoon wrapped up around two o'clock and everyone began to say their good-byes, Sadie noticed that Kade seemed in no hurry to leave. Quite the opposite. When the den cleared, he parked himself on the floor with Tyler—in the same spot that they'd sat together so many nights during the blizzard. It was unsettling, and Sadie wasn't sure what she would say or do if he stayed. He'd been absent from her home for so long, but never from her heart.

"'Twas a *gut* day," Jonas said to Sadie on his way out the door. Everyone had left except for Jonas, Lizzie, Sarah Jane, Lillian, and Lillian's family. But as the others made their way toward the door, Jonas turned and took a few steps back into the den. "Need a ride there, little fella?" He looked at Kade and said, "I don't reckon you need to be carryin' the boy in that runaway ride you got." He chuckled.

But before Kade had a chance to answer, Lizzie spoke up. "Kade, do you think Tyler would spend the night with us tonight? We'd be glad to carry him to our house." Then Sadie saw her wink at Kade.

"What's going on?" Sadie whispered in Lillian's ear.

Lillian had little Elizabeth Mae in her arms, while Samuel stood nearby, toting Anna. David was walking out with Sarah Jane. "I don't know." She shrugged.

Kade and Jonas exchanged grins. Then Kade smiled at Lillian.

"You are not telling me the truth," Sadie whispered to Lillian. "Something is going on, and everyone seems to know but me."

Lillian kissed Sadie on the cheek. "You'll know soon enough."

Sadie looked back toward Kade. "I think Tyler would love to spend the night," Kade said. "How does that sound, Tyler? Do you want to go stay with Jonas?" Kade squatted down on the floor and started to help Tyler put his letters in the lunch box. "No promises, Jonas. I don't know how Tyler will do."

"Tyler loves Jonas," his son said.

Jonas's face lit up. "I think we'll be mighty fine."

Kade waited until everyone was out in the yard before he approached Sadie. "I thought maybe we could talk?"

"Can't imagine 'bout what," she said, shrugging as she refused to make eye contact.

"Just give me a minute to tell them a few things about Tyler." Kade whisked past her and out the door.

Sadie began to rinse the last few dishes in the sink. When she heard footsteps, she looked over her shoulder. "Hello, Tyler."

The boy had his arms outstretched. "Hug," he said.

"Oh, sweetheart. Of course." Sadie dropped the towel on the counter and walked toward him. She wrapped her arms around him, and Tyler did the same. With his head on her shoulder, he spoke softly. "Be strong in the Lord, and in the power of His might."

Tyler pulled away, then smiled.

"I see you've been reading your Bible," she said. "Ephesians 6:10. You are such a sweet boy." Once again, Tyler's quoting of the Scripture seemed to come at an opportune time. Sadie was trying hard to be strong in the Lord and in the power of His might, trusting that His will would be done.

"Tyler loves Sadie."

Sadie blinked back tears. "Oh, Tyler. Sadie loves you too."

Then he ran outside.

After a few minutes, when Kade didn't come back into the house, she walked out onto the porch to find him sitting in one of the rockers. "What do you want to talk to me about?" she asked. Everyone was gone, and he was just sitting there.

He stood up. "Let's take a walk. It's a beautiful afternoon." He reached out his hand to her.

She ignored his gesture and asked, "What do you want, Kade?" She didn't need to take a walk. She needed to understand why everyone was winking and snickering earlier. She needed to know why Kade had avoided her for weeks, as if she had imagined what they'd shared.

Kade walked toward her, and she stepped back, feeling vulnerable all of a sudden.

"Come here, Sadie," he whispered. He drew even closer to her.

"What do you want, Kade?" She was almost yelling. "I haven't seen you in weeks. You just left, and you said you needed time by yourself with Tyler, and I thought—" She hung her head.

"You thought what? That I didn't care about you?"

She glared at him. "*Ya.* You left. And you've been back all this time, without so much as a visit." She turned away from him. "I think you best go."

When his arms wrapped around her waist, Sadie was paralyzed. She could feel his breath against her neck. "Sadie," he whispered. Then he gently turned her around to face him, holding her out at arm's length. "Have you taken a *gut* look at me today?"

She couldn't help but grin at his use of the *Deitsch.* Then she scanned him from head to toe. "*Ya.* I took notice earlier, and you make a fine-looking Amish man."

"That's why I've been staying away, Sadie."

He pulled her into his arms, and his lips drew close to hers. She began to tremble. "Why?"

"Because I needed to make a decision about my faith, my life, and not do it based on my feelings for you. I needed to know if this—being Amish—was right for me. And you, my dear friend Sadie, would have only clouded my judgment." He gazed into her eyes. "Do you remember what I promised? To walk with Him and see where His road leads me. It brought me right here, to you."

His lips met hers tenderly, and Sadie fell into the moment, as if she'd waited her entire life for him. "I love you, Sadie," he said. "And if you'd allow me, I'd like to court you properly. I spoke with Bishop Ebersol yesterday about my intentions to be baptized into the faith, and also sought his permission to court you. So, it's with his blessing that I am here."

Her knees began to fold underneath her weight, and tears threatened to spill over. Could this be happening? At last? It was as if the heavens had opened up and shined light down on the two of them. "Kade—"

He brushed the tear from her cheek. "Do you think you could love me, Sadie? Because I have this dream I've been harboring for weeks, that you, Tyler, and I could someday be a family. I needed to know in my heart that I was following God's plan for me, and—"

"I love you," she said, putting a gentle finger against his lip. "I've loved you for a long time."

Kade kissed her again. Sadie closed her eyes and gave thanks and praise to God. She wasn't going to be alone after all. She would be with the ones she loved most. "You know," she said softly as Kade gazed into her eyes, the back of his hand stroking her cheek. "I can tell Tyler has been reading his Bible, because once again he quoted a Bible scripture to me. Today, in the kitchen, before he left."

"What did he say?" Kade asked. He leaned back from her slightly, his eyes still fused with hers.

"He said, 'Be strong in the Lord and in the power of His might.'"

Kade looked down, then lifted his eyes to hers. "He told me the same thing out in the yard when I told him good-bye." Then Kade pulled her close, and she could feel him trembling. "He . . . he also told me he loves me," Kade added in a shaky voice. "It was the first time."

"Oh, Kade."

Sadie knew that she and Kade were both on the path that God had planned for them.

She glanced upward and there were just two words on her mind.

Thank You.

Reading Group Guide

1. In the beginning of the story, Sadie is convinced that Milo is perfect for her even though she has never met him in person. If Sadie had never met Kade, do you think she would have ended up marrying Milo?

2. Kade travels to Lancaster County to escape his life, but ends up finding more than he ever anticipated. What are some things that he discovered in Lancaster County? Have you ever traveled somewhere and expected one thing, only to find another? What do you think would have happened to Kade if he had never visited Lancaster County?

3. Twice, Tyler quotes readings from the Bible to both Sadie and Kade. Do you think these are coincidences, or was God trying to reach Sadie and Kade through Tyler? Has there ever been a time when you felt God was trying to reach you through another person?

4. Jonas breaks off his courtship with Lizzie because he feels guilty about Irma Rose. What factors influenced his decision to reconsider and ask Lizzie to marry him?

5. Why do you think Tyler is able to tell Sadie that he loves her early on, but he doesn't tell Kade until the end of the story?

6. Kade lost his faith in God when Tyler was diagnosed with autism. Have you ever turned your back on God when you felt He let you down? What made Kade seek to reestablish a relationship with God?

7. The Amish adhere to the rules of the *Ordnung*, the written and unwritten rules of the Amish, the order by which the Amish are expected to live. Do we, as Christians, have an *Ordnung*? What are some of the unwritten rules that Christians are expected to live by?

8. Jonas is outspoken, but wise. He tells Kade, "Until you know if you plan to convert yourself to the Amish faith, renounce your worldly ways, and live as one of us by putting your faith in all that is God's will—then you need not be courtin' Sadie in any manner." What if Kade hadn't taken Jonas's advice? Would things have turned out differently for Sadie and Kade?

9. The Amish struggle to live a good life and be the best they can be, but they are human. There are several instances in the story when Amish characters judge others. Can you name some of the scenes where judgment is carried through?

10. When Monica drops Tyler off with Kade, did you sympathize with her situation, or did you feel like she was only being selfish with little regard for Tyler's well-being? Do you think Monica would have come back for Tyler if she hadn't been killed?

11. Kade's friend Val betrayed him, yet Kade chooses to forgive him. Have you ever felt betrayed by someone but chose to forgive that person?

12. Kade and Jonas develop an unlikely friendship, which begins when Jonas takes a liking to Tyler. Is this another possibility that God is working through Tyler to unite two people who have something to offer each other? If so, how do Kade and Jonas help each other?

Acknowledgments

I THANK GOD EVERY DAY FOR THIS BLESSING HE HAS bestowed upon me. I'm incredibly grateful for the opportunity to share my stories through words that glorify Him.

This journey would be impossible without the support of my husband, Patrick, who is willing to forego dinners, live with a messy house, and put up with me when the deadlines close in. I love you so much. And thank you for reading everything I write, as you promised in our wedding vows. (What a guy!)

I also couldn't do this without the love and support of a very special friend. Barbie Beiler reads each of my books before they go to print, and her Amish background helps me to keep the books authentic. Barbie, I not only appreciate all that you do, but I value our friendship more and more each day.

Another special person gets tons of credit when it comes to my books. To my editor, Natalie Hanemann, you are amazing. I hope we are on this incredible journey together for a very long time. I can't imagine anyone else by my side, teaching and encouraging me the way you do, my friend.

My fiction family at Thomas Nelson—you are all so special. I keep a picture of you all above my computer to keep you close in my heart all the time. Thank you for everything you do.

A special thanks to my agent, Mary Sue Seymour, for being a friend as well as a great agent.

Rene Simpson, it's an honor to dedicate this book to you. Your work with autistic children is inspiring on many levels, and your hands-on experience helped me immensely during the writing of this book. Your young students are very fortunate to have you in their lives. And I am blessed to have you as one of my best friends.

Renee Bissmeyer, thank you for reading behind me as I wrote *Plain Promise.* You keep me going when the going gets tough! I will always value our life-long friendship.

Special thanks to my sister-in-law, Valarie Spalek, for testing the tapioca pudding recipe, and to my mother-in-law, Pat Mackey, for testing the zucchini recipe. You gals are the best!

To friends and family not mentioned here, please know how much I appreciate all you do to encourage and support my writing. Blessings to you all.

Plain Paradise

To Barbie Beilor

1

JOSEPHINE DRONBERGER ADJUSTED HER DARK SUN-GLASSES as she stared at the faceless dolls on display. She lifted one to eye level then eased her way closer to Linda. Turning the figure about, she pretended to study it even though her eyes were on the seventeen-year-old Amish girl standing with two friends at the neighboring booth.

She inched closer, as if somehow just being near Linda would comfort her. Then she heard one of the girls talking in Pennsylvania *Deitsch*, the dialect most Amish speak and one she regularly heard at the farmer's market. Josie pushed her glasses down on her nose and slowly turned to her left, feeling like the stalker she had become over the past few weeks. She drew in a deep breath and blew it out slowly.

Two of the girls were wearing dark green dresses with black aprons. Linda was clothed in a dress of the same style, but it was deep blue, and Josie instantly wondered if Linda's eyes were still a sapphire color. All of them wore prayer coverings on their heads, as was expected. Not much had changed since the last time Josie had been in Lancaster County.

She watched one of the girls fondling a silver chain hanging on a rack filled with jewelry. Linda reached forward and removed a necklace, then held it up for the other girls to see. Again they spoke to each other in a language Josie didn't understand.

Josie knew she was staring, so she forced herself to swivel forward, and once more she pretended to be interested in the doll with no face, staring hard into the plain white fabric. Until recently, that's how Linda had looked in Josie's mind.

She placed the doll back on the counter alongside the others and then wiped sweaty palms on her blue jeans before taking two steps closer to the girls who were still ogling the necklaces. Jewelry wasn't allowed in the Old Order Amish communities, but Josie knew enough about the Amish to know that girls of their age were in their *rumschpringe*, a running around period that begins at sixteen—a time when certain privileges are allowed up until baptism. Josie watched Linda hand the woman behind the counter the necklace. Then she reached into the pocket of her apron and pulled out her money.

Josie moved over to the rack of necklaces and glanced at the girls. Linda completed her purchase, then turned in Josie's direction so one of her friends could clasp the necklace behind her neck. Josie stared at the small silver cross that hung from a silver chain, then she let her eyes veer upward and gazed at the pretty girl who stood before her now, with blue eyes, light-brown hair tucked beneath her cap, and a gentle smile.

"That's lovely." Josie's words caught in her throat as she pointed to the necklace. Linda looked down at the silver cross and held it out with one hand so she could see it, then looked back up at Josie.

"*Danki.*" She quickly turned back toward her friends.

No, wait. Let me look at you a while longer.

But she walked away, and Josie stared at the girls until they rounded the corner. She spun the rack full of necklaces until she found the cross on a silver chain like Linda's.

"I'll take that one," she told the clerk as she pointed to the piece of jewelry. "And no need to put it in a bag."

Josie handed the woman a twenty-dollar bill and waited for her change. She glanced at the Rolex on her left wrist. Then she unhooked the clasp of the necklace she was wearing, an anniversary present from Robert—an exquisite turquoise drop that he'd picked up while traveling in Europe for business. She dropped the necklace into her purse while the woman waited for Josie to accept her purchase.

"Thank you." Josie lifted her shoulder-length hair, dyed a honey-blonde, and she hooked the tiny clasp behind her neck. The silver cross rested lightly against her chest, but it felt as heavy as the regret she'd carried for seventeen years.

Josie straightened the collar on her white blouse. She cradled the small cross in her hand and stared at it. There was a time when such a trinket would have symbolized the strong Catholic upbringing she'd had and her faith in God. But those days were behind her. Now the silver cross symbolized a bond with Linda.

Mary Ellen scurried around the kitchen in a rush to finish supper by five o'clock and wondered why her daughter wasn't home to help prepare the meal. She knew Linda went to market with two friends, but she should have been back well before now. Abe and the boys would be hungry when they finished work for the day. Mary Ellen suspected they were done in the fields and milking the cows about now.

She glanced at the clock. Four thirty. A nice cross-breeze swept through the kitchen as she pulled a ham loaf from the oven, enough to gently blow loose strands of dark-brown-and-gray hair that had fallen from beneath her *kapp*. It was a tad warm for mid-May, but Mary Ellen couldn't complain; she knew the sweltering summer heat would be on them soon enough. She placed the loaf on the table already set for five. Her potatoes were ready for mashing, and the barbequed string beans were keeping warm in the oven.

The clippety-clop of hooves let her know that Linda was home. Her daughter had been driving the buggy for nearly two years on her own, but Mary Ellen still felt a sense of relief each time Linda pulled into the driveway, especially when she was traveling to Bird-In-Hand, a high-traffic town frequented by the tourists.

"Hi, *Mamm*. Sorry I'm late." The screen door slammed behind Linda as she entered the kitchen. Her daughter kicked off her shoes, walked to the refrigerator, and pulled out two jars of jam. "We lost track of the time." Linda placed the glass containers on the table.

"The applesauce is in the bowl on the left." Mary Ellen pointed toward the refrigerator, then began mashing her potatoes.

Linda walked back to the refrigerator to retrieve the applesauce, and Mary Ellen noticed a silver chain around her daughter's neck, tucked beneath the front of her dress. She remembered buying a necklace when she was Linda's age, during her own *rumschpringe*. No harm done.

"I see you purchased a necklace." She stepped in front of Linda and gently pulled a silver cross from its hiding place. "This is very pretty." Mary Ellen smiled before returning to her potatoes. "But I reckon it'd be best if you took it off before supper, no? Your *daed* knows there will be these kinds of purchases during *rumschpringe*, but I see no need to show it off in front of him."

"But it's only a necklace. That's not so bad." Linda reached around to the back of her neck, and within a few moments, she was holding the chain in her hand. "Do you know that Amos Dienner bought a car during his *rumschpringe*?" Linda's brows raised in disbelief. "His folks know he has it, but they make him park it in the woods back behind their house." She giggled. "I wonder what *Daed* would do if I came home with a car and parked it back behind our house?"

"I think you best not push your father that far. He has been real tolerant of the time you've spent with *Englisch* friends, riding in their cars, going to movies, and . . ." Mary Ellen sighed. "I shudder to think what else."

"Want me to tell you what all we do in town?" Linda's voice was mysterious, as if she held many secrets.

Mary Ellen pulled the string beans from the oven. "No. I don't want to know." She shook her head all the way to the table, then placed the casserole dish beside the ham loaf. "Be best I not know what you do with your friends during this time."

"*Ach, Mamm.* We don't do anything bad." Linda walked to her mother and kissed her on the cheek. "I don't even like the taste of beer."

Mary Ellen turned to her daughter and slammed her hands to her hips. "Linda!"

Linda laughed. "*Mamm!* I'm jokin' with you. I've never even *tried* beer." She twisted her face into a momentary scowl, then headed toward the stairs. "I guess I'll go put my new necklace away."

Mary Ellen believed Linda. She trusted her eldest child, and she was thankful for the close relationship they shared. Linda's adventurous spirit bubbled in her laugh and shone in her eyes, but she was respectful of her parents and the rules. If going to the movies and buying a necklace were the worst things her daughter did during this running-around period, she'd thank God for that.

"Something smells mighty *gut* in here." Abe came through the kitchen entrance, kicking his shoes off near Linda's. Mary Ellen could hear her sons padding up the porch steps.

Eyeing the growing pile of shoes, she said, "I don't know why everyone insists on comin' through the kitchen when there is a perfectly *gut* door that goes from the porch to the den." She pointed to the shoes. "I reckon I'd like to have those dirty shoes in my den and not in my kitchen."

Abe closed the space between them, kissed Mary Ellen on the cheek, then whispered in her ear. "But you are always in the kitchen, and it's your face I long to see after a hard day's work." He pulled her close to him.

"Abe . . ." She nodded toward her two sons, who were now adding their shoes to the others, and she gently pushed her husband away. "The children." She tried to hide her reddening cheeks, but she was thankful that her husband of nineteen years could still cause her to blush. He winked at her as he took his seat at the head of the table.

She heard Matthew make a small grunting sound before sitting at one of the wooden benches lining the sides of the oblong table. Mary Ellen glanced at her oldest son, noticing his slight smile. He looked exactly like his father, minus the beard. Dark brown hair, broad shoulders, and a distinctive square jawline that ran in the Huyard family.

She shivered when she thought about how Matthew only had one more year until his running-around phase, and Luke was only a year behind him. Three children all in their *rumschpringe* at the same time. Unless, of course, Stephen Ebersol proposed to Linda soon, as they all suspected would happen any day. Linda would be eighteen in August, and they'd been dating for over a year. Mary Ellen knew there would be enough time to plan a wedding by this November or December—the time designated for weddings, after the fall harvest—but she hoped they would wait until the following year to wed. Another year of dating would be good for them.

"Someone's here," Linda said as she walked back into the kitchen. "I saw a buggy comin' up the drive from my upstairs window."

"It's the supper hour," Abe grumbled.

Mary Ellen wiped her hands on her apron and joined Linda by the screen door. They waited until a face came into view.

"It's Lillian!" Linda darted down the porch steps.

Mary Ellen knew how much Linda loved her aunt. When her brother Samuel had married Lillian several years ago, Lillian became a wonderful stepmother to David, Samuel's son. Then they added two lovely daughters, Anna and Elizabeth, to their family. But Mary Ellen couldn't help but worry why Lillian would show up at suppertime. *I hope Jonas is all right.*

Lillian's grandfather, Jonas Miller, had been battling cancer and Alzheimer's disease for years, but he'd taken a turn for the worse recently. Everyone adored Jonas. He was a pillar of faith in their community and had an unforgettable—if not contrary—charm that drew people to him.

"Is everything okay?" Mary Ellen opened the door and motioned Lillian inside. Linda followed.

"Hello to everyone," Lillian said with a wave of her hand, but it wasn't in her usual chipper manner. "I'm sorry to come callin' at this time of day. I can see you are about to eat. But I was on my way home from work, and this was on my way, so I told Samuel I was going to stop in."

Mary Ellen took a step closer to her sister-in-law. "Is it Jonas?"

"*Ya.*" Lillian hung her head for a moment, then looked back up at Mary Ellen. "*Mamm* had to put him in the hospital this morning. She can't get him to eat, and his blood pressure has been really high."

"Oh, no, Lillian. I'm so sorry to hear that." Mary Ellen shook her head. "I could see this comin'. He looked awful poor last time I saw him." Jonas lived with his daughter, Sarah Jane, and his wife Lizzie, but Mary Ellen knew most of the caregiving fell on his daughter. Lizzie was up in years, and even though she was in much better shape than her husband, she still had medical needs of her own.

Lillian sighed. "As you can imagine, Grandpa was not happy about it." Then she smiled. "He said the *Englisch* will kill him before his time."

Mary Ellen smiled in return. "The *Englisch* will have their hands full with Jonas, I'm sure."

Jonas's offbeat personality wasn't typical of someone in their district. But poor Lizzie. Jonas married Lizzie almost four years ago, after his first wife had passed. Lizzie was going to be lost without Jonas.

Abe stood up. "I'm sorry to hear that Jonas is down, Lillian. Is there anything we can do for your family?"

"No, Abe. But *danki*. Samuel and David take care of things at

Mamm and Grandpa's. I just wanted to let you know. Grandpa is in Lancaster General."

"Can we visit him?" Linda asked.

"*Ya.* He can have visitors." Lillian paused. "I best be gettin' home. I have to stop by Rebecca's and pick up Anna and Elizabeth. And Samuel and David will be hungry."

Matthew stood up from the table, then Luke rose alongside him. "Lillian," Matthew said, "we'll help any way we can."

Luke straightened as if to reach the same height as Matthew, but he was still an inch or so shorter. "Me too, Lillian. I'll help."

Her youngest son sported the Huyard jaw too, but Mary Ellen always thought he looked more like her own father, from what she could remember; he'd died when she was a young girl. Her mother still lived nearby, and they saw her from time to time. But Abe's parents lived in a neighboring district, and they didn't get to see them as often.

Abe shook Lillian's hand, as did both his sons. It warmed Mary Ellen's heart to see the fine young men her boys were turning into. She followed Lillian out the door, Linda by her side.

She hugged her sister-in-law, and Linda did the same.

"We're here for you, Lillian," Linda said. "Tell Sarah Jane and Lizzie, okay?"

Mary Ellen echoed her daughter's sentiments, and they both waved as Lillian drove away. Abe and the boys were waiting patiently when they returned to the kitchen. Mary Ellen took her seat at the opposite end from Abe, and Linda slid onto the wooden bench across from the boys.

"Let us pray," Abe said. They all bowed their heads in silent prayer.

When they were done, Luke picked up the bowl of mashed potatoes and asked, "Is Jonas gonna die?"

"Don't say that!" Linda blasted. "He's just sick, and he's in the hospital until he feels better." She snatched the potatoes from her brother's outstretched hand and cut her eyes at him, mumbling something under her breath.

"Watch your tone, Linda," Abe warned.

Mary Ellen knew Abe didn't like much conversation during the supper hour, and he certainly didn't like any upset. Or visitors for that matter. But he loved Lillian, and Mary Ellen knew that he was glad she stopped by.

Mary Ellen also knew that she would need to prepare her children about Jonas at some point. Jonas was like everyone's grandpa, and Lillian shared him with the community, but it was evident to Mary Ellen that Jonas was on a steady decline.

Luke had taken his first ride on a scooter as a young boy, with Jonas coaching from the sidelines, and Jonas had given Matthew lessons driving the buggy when Abe was busy in the fields. But it was Linda who had spent the most time with Jonas, particularly over the past couple of years. Jonas had taught her to play chess, and Linda took every opportunity to sneak off to challenge him to a game. It was only a matter of time for Jonas, and all the adults knew it. The cancer had been getting worse and worse.

"Jonas could get better." Linda swirled her fork amidst the string beans. "They have chemo—chemo something—that cures cancer."

"It isn't a cure, Linda," Abe said. "It's a treatment. I reckon sometimes it works, but . . ." Her husband's voice trailed off when he saw his daughter's eyes tear up. "We will say extra prayers for Jonas during our devotions each day."

Mary Ellen spooned potatoes onto her plate. She wasn't sure

what to pray for. To pray for an extension of Jonas's life could cause much pain and suffering for him.

"Tomorrow, I have some sewing to do, *Mamm*, but not too much else. I was planning to spend the day with Stephen after that." She paused with her fork full of beans. "Maybe Barbie will take Stephen and me to see Jonas."

Barbie was their *Englisch* friend who ran Beiler's Bed and Breakfast off of Lincoln Highway. She was wonderful about providing rides for people in their district. Barbie's husband grew up Amish, and even though he was no longer Amish, they had strong ties to the community.

"That would be nice," Mary Ellen said. "But doesn't Stephen have to work at the furniture store tomorrow?"

"No, Abner gave him the day off because he worked all last week and then on Saturday too."

"I reckon it would be all right, if you finish your chores around here in the morning."

After they finished supper, Abe retired to the den, and the boys headed outside to tend to the two horses. Linda was helping Mary Ellen clear the table when they heard a car coming up the driveway.

"Are you expecting someone?" Mary Ellen tried to keep the edge from her voice. Linda's *Englisch* friends showed up too often these days. Mary Ellen knew this was normal for someone Linda's age, but it bothered her just the same. When she faced up to the reason why, it was because she had less time with Linda, and she was forced to accept the fact that Linda wasn't the same little girl who had glued herself to Mary Ellen's side since she was young. They'd always been close, and Mary Ellen wanted to selfishly savor the time she had left with Linda before her daughter would go and make a home with Stephen.

"No. I'm not expecting anyone." Linda put two dirty dishes in the sink, then strained to see out the window, past the begonias blooming on the windowsill. "It's a blue car, the kind that's like a truck and a car all in one."

Mary Ellen walked to the kitchen door and watched the blue SUV pull to a stop. Linda walked to her side.

"She's pretty," Linda said as the woman exited her automobile and stepped gingerly onto cobblestone steps that led to the porch, wearing high-heeled silver shoes.

Mary Ellen agreed. The tall *Englisch* woman was thin, yet shapely, dressed in denim pants and a white blouse. Her hair was the color of honey and rested slightly above her shoulders. Her dark sunglasses covered a large portion of her face, but her painted features were most attractive. Mary Ellen didn't recognize her to be any of their non-Amish friends.

Linda let out a small gasp as the woman neared the door, then whispered, "I saw her at market today."

The woman came up the porch steps. "Hello," Mary Ellen said. "Can we help you?" She pushed the screen door open.

"Mary Ellen?"

"*Ya.*"

The woman pulled the dark shades from her face, and Mary Ellen tried to recall where she'd seen the woman before. She was now most familiar looking, but Mary Ellen couldn't place her.

"I—I was hoping to talk to you." The stranger's bottom lip trembled, and she sucked in a deep breath. She glanced at Linda, then back at Mary Ellen. "Alone, if that's okay."

"Is something wrong?" Mary Ellen pushed the screen door wide. "Would you like to come in?"

The woman didn't move but bit her trembling lip for a moment and pushed back her wavy locks with her hand. "You probably don't recognize me. It's been a long time since I've seen you, and—" She took another deep breath, and Mary Ellen struggled to recall where she knew the woman from. "My name is Josie. Josephine Dronberger. I mean—well, it's Dronberger now. It used to be Josephine Wallace."

Mary Ellen's chest grew tight as she remembered where she'd seen the woman before—no longer a scared seventeen-year-old girl but a mature woman, beautiful and fancy. Mary Ellen fought a wave of apprehension that coursed through her. Instinctively, she pushed Linda backward and stepped in front of her.

"*Mamm*," Linda whispered with irritation, stumbling slightly. "What are you doing?"

Mary Ellen ignored her daughter as her heart thumped at an unhealthy rate. She gazed intently into the woman's eyes, which were now filling with tears.

"I'm sorry to just show up like this, but I—"

"Now is not a good time," Mary Ellen interrupted. She held her head high, fighting her own tears as well. She stepped backward, pushing Linda along with her, until the screen door closed between her and Josephine. "Perhaps another time." She managed a tremulous smile, but she knew Linda would question her about who the woman was the minute Josephine was gone.

Josephine's lip began to tremble even more, and a tear spilled over thick lashes, which she quickly wiped away. "Please. I'll just leave you my number. Maybe you can call me when it's a better time. Please . . ." She reached into the back pocket of her blue jeans and pulled out a card.

Mary Ellen watched with fearful fascination at how Josephine's brows cinched inward, how she slowly closed her eyes, and the way her trembling mouth thinned as she pressed her lips together. The same expression Linda had always had when she was hurting a great deal about something.

"*Mamm?*" Linda edged around her mother, gave Mary Ellen a questioning look, and then stared at the woman. The resemblance was eerie, and Mary Ellen wondered what might be going through Linda's mind.

"*Ya,*" she said to Josephine. "I—I will call you when it's a better time."

Josephine pushed the card in Mary Ellen's direction. "Call me any time. My home phone number and my cell number are both on the card." She sniffed. "I'm sorry."

Mary Ellen took the card, and Josephine smiled slightly, then fixed her eyes on Linda.

"I will call you." Mary Ellen hastily pulled Linda into the kitchen enough where she could push the wooden door between them and Josephine. It closed with a thud, and Mary Ellen's stomach churned with anxiety. Linda was going to have questions, but she needed to talk to Abe first. She needed Abe to tell her that everything would be all right.

Linda ran to the window and watched Josephine get in her car. "*Mamm,* who is that woman? And why was she crying? Why were you acting so strange? Do you know her, or . . ."

Mary Ellen pressed her hands against her chest, still standing and staring at the door, only half hearing Linda's queries, and wondering how the years had gotten away from her without them ever telling Linda that she was adopted.

2

JOSIE SAT ACROSS FROM HER HUSBAND, PICKING AT HER stuffed pork chop and pushing her peas around her plate. Mary Ellen's fearful expression kept flashing through her mind. The last thing she wanted to do was cause Linda and her family any pain, but there just had to be some way for her to share in at least a small part of Linda's life.

"Honey, you're barely touching your food." Robert gazed at her speculatively from his chair on the other side of the dining room table. "Are you feeling all right?"

She scooped some peas onto her fork and forced the bite into her mouth. "I'm eating," she said and began to chew. Maybe her response would convince Robert that her condition hadn't worsened—at least not today. She swallowed, then glanced around the kitchen in their new house, at all the boxes still left to unpack.

"I'm going to hire someone to come unpack these boxes. I don't want you to have to do that." He paused. "Or I can unpack some of them tonight."

"No. I want to do it." She smiled at her husband of twelve years. "But tonight, I just want to cuddle with you on the couch, watch television, and relax. I have all day to unpack these boxes, and I know you're tired from work."

Josie recalled her first trip to Paradise nearly six months earlier, just to verify that Linda still lived with her parents in the Amish community. A woman at the Bird-In-Hand market confirmed that she did. Then, when Robert agreed to relocate to Paradise, Pennsylvania, so that Josie could be near Linda, he'd attained husband-of-the-year status in Josie's eyes. Robert uprooted his law practice, after ten years of working to establish a healthy clientele at the firm he founded. They didn't know anyone in the small town of Paradise, and while geography wasn't an issue for some of his clients, he still lost more than half. Robert had insisted that he was ready to downsize and not work as much, but Josie also knew that he wanted to spend more time with her. Especially now.

"I'm not that tired. Amanda and I finished setting up a filing system today." Robert ate the last of his pork chop, then placed his fork across his plate. "She's a sweet kid. I think she'll work out just fine."

Amanda had answered an ad Robert ran in the local paper for a secretary. He had hired her on the spot, and he was paying her big city wages as opposed to what would be the norm here in Paradise. And Josie knew why. She suspected that Amanda probably had a hard time finding a job, and Robert was always out to help those in need. He took more pro bono cases than he did paying ones.

Robert's new secretary was a petite nineteen-year-old girl who lived nearby in the city of Lancaster, about twenty miles from Paradise. Josie met her on her first day of work over a month ago. Robert had prepared Josie in advance, so she wouldn't be shocked when she saw the girl. Amanda's lips were unnaturally enlarged, almost exuding a duck-like appearance. She'd been born with a cleft palate, which she'd had surgically corrected when she was a young child. However, according to Amanda, it left her lips unusually thin with a scar in the middle of her top lip and impaired her speech. When she turned eighteen, she used the money she'd saved working summer jobs to have her lips enlarged with injections, a new procedure the plastic surgeon promised would enhance her physical appearance and possibly improve her speech.

It didn't work, perhaps because Amanda also had scar tissue on her lip from a childhood bicycle accident. The swelling in Amanda's lips hadn't gone down for the past year, and she didn't have the money to sue the plastic surgeon or get any help for herself. Robert filed suit against the plastic surgeon almost immediately, in an effort to compensate Amanda for her past year of suffering, and offered his services to her for free. There was no guarantee that the plastic surgeon would be held accountable, but Robert met with a local doctor, Dr. Noah Stoltzfus, who was helping him arrange for Amanda to have corrective surgery, regardless of the legal outcome.

When Robert met Noah, who ran a clinic in the heart of Amish Country, he liked the doctor right away. The two had been developing a friendship ever since. Josie wasn't surprised. Everyone loved Robert. No one more so than his wife though.

"Well, I'm a little tired." Josie settled back against her chair and yawned. "But I'm thankful not to have a headache today. That last one I had stayed with me for almost four days."

Josie watched him clear their plates from the table. He was eight years older than her, having just celebrated his forty-second birthday. Josie thought he'd only gotten more handsome with each passing year. He was thirty when they'd married and had a full head of dark hair. Now, his thick mane was a salt-and-pepper mixture that lent him an air of sophistication. His eyes were shades of amber and green that changed in different lighting, but they always brimmed with tenderness and passion. Robert wasn't nearly as polished as his two partners had been in Chicago, but it was her husband's ruggedness mixed with a sense of humble power that attracted her to him in the first place.

She stood up, followed him into the kitchen, then joined him at the sink. He rinsed, and she loaded the dishwasher.

"Do you think she'll call you?" Robert handed her two spoons.

"I hope so." Josie sighed. "Mary Ellen was having a routine night with her family until I showed up." She tucked her chin as her eyes filled with water. "I should have sent a letter first, giving them all some sort of warning that I was coming. I just thought that if I spoke to Mary Ellen and Abe in person, it would be harder for them to say no about me seeing Linda."

Robert turned off the faucet, wiped his hands on a towel, and turned to her. He clutched her forearms in his strong but gentle hands. "Josie, I know you don't want to hurt anyone. But I also know how much you've been looking forward to meeting your daughter. And I'm afraid you can't have it both ways. I mean, this will be hard for everyone concerned." He sighed, then gently lifted her chin. "It's going to take some time for this to soak in for Mary Ellen and Abe. They'll need time to talk to Linda, and I'm not sure I'd be expecting a call from them right away. Josie, you're a good person. I've never known you to intentionally hurt anyone. Over the years, when we've talked about your daughter, you always said that someday you wanted to meet her." He shrugged. "Maybe *someday* came before you were ready."

"I gave birth to her, Robert. Does that really make her my

daughter? She has a family. A family that I am about to disrupt."
She rested her head on his shoulder. "I feel obsessed with knowing
her, but I worry about the price of my happiness. Is it really fair to
Linda that just because my circumstances have changed, now it's
okay to seek her out? Plus, Mary Ellen's expression is etched in my
mind, Robert." She looked up at him. "She's so scared. I'm sure she's
afraid of losing her daughter and thinks I will try to be a mother
to Linda. You and I know that won't happen, but I just need . . ."
Robert wiped a tear from her cheek. "I need to know her."

Robert tilted his head slightly and gazed lovingly into her eyes.
"Honey, we talked about all this before we made this move. I love
you with all my heart, and I know how important this is to you,
but you can change your mind at any time."

She ran her finger under her eyes and cleared runny mascara. "I
love you so much. And I'm so sorry, Robert. I'm sorry I couldn't give
you children. I'm sorry that I'm so obsessed about meeting Linda.
You moved your practice for me to be near her. I'm just so—"

Robert gently put a finger to her lip. "Josie, you're my world. I
want you to have a peaceful feeling in your heart, and I've loved you
since the day I met you. But there's always been something amiss
for you. Maybe meeting Linda will fill that void." He smiled. "You
certainly can't go on following her around town."

"I know." She shook her head, twisted her mouth to one side.
"I've been a stalker."

Robert handed her a bowl. "Okay, my little stalker, let's finish
these dishes, and then you can go take a hot bath."

Josie turned toward him again. "What did I ever do to deserve
you?"

"Yeah, you're a lucky gal," he teased.

She poked him in the ribs, and he chuckled.

But he was right. She was incredibly lucky to have him in her life. Especially now.

———————

Mary Ellen clutched the sides of her white nightgown and paced the wooden floors in her bedroom, dimly lit by one lantern on her nightstand. *Help me, Dear Lord in heaven, to handle this situation the right way. I need your guidance. Please help me to do Your will without letting my own fears hinder me.*

Abe walked barefoot into their bedroom, his dark hair still wet from his shower and wearing only his black pants. He stroked his beard, which reached the top of a muscular chest covered with wavy brown hair.

"We've made a terrible mistake." His eyes drew together in an agonized expression as he faced Mary Ellen. "We should have known this might happen someday, that the girl's mother—"

"Abe, *I'm* her mother! She's *my* daughter." She walked over to him and fell into his arms. "What does she want after all this time? Why is she doing this to our family?"

"Now, Mary Ellen . . ." He ran his hand the length of her hair. "We must be faithful and trust God to see us through this. Linda is a strong girl, and she—"

"What if she doesn't forgive us for not telling her?" She leaned her head upward and searched his eyes. "Abe, what if she leaves us?"

Abe pushed her gently away and kissed her on the cheek. "She *is* going to leave us soon, Mary Ellen. She's almost eighteen. I reckon she'll marry Stephen and start her own life within the next year or two."

"You know what I mean. What if that Josephine woman has come to claim her, after all these years?"

"*Mei lieb*, it will be up to Linda to decide if she wants to know this woman. You are her *mudder*. You will always be her *mudder*." He sighed, pulled away, and then walked to the other side of the room. In the moonlight, his profile was somber. "But this will be hard for our *maedel*." He shook his head again. "We should have told her."

"Why didn't we?" Mary Ellen walked to the small mirror hung from a silver chain on the wall next to her chest of drawers. She reached up and touched her cheek. "She looks like me. Everyone says so." But then she recalled how much more Linda looked like Josephine, and her heart landed in the pit of her stomach.

"After we asked the community members not to tell her until we felt she was old enough to understand, I reckon the years just got away from us." Abe sat down on the bed. "And now she is a young woman."

Mary Ellen spun around and faced her husband. "I could just not call her back. Maybe she will go away, leave here."

"Mary Ellen, you can't do that." Abe raked a hand through his hair.

"Why not? I don't have to call her." She responded in a tone she'd often scolded her children for using.

Abe patted the side of the bed.

"I can't call her, Abe. I'm afraid," she said while sinking down next to him. She swiped at her eyes and laid her head on his chest. He wrapped an arm around her shoulder.

"I will call her first thing tomorrow morning," he said with authority. "All this guessing about her intentions will do us no *gut*."

Linda sat down on her bed, reached over and flipped on the switch of her battery-operated fan, then leaned her head in front of it to dry her hair a bit. In the evenings, she tried to be the first one in the upstairs bathroom, but tonight both Matt and Luke managed to get their baths before her. Now she'd end up going to sleep with wet hair.

She pulled the comb through tangled strands that ran to her waist and thought about her mother's reaction to the *Englisch* woman who'd shown up earlier. She'd never seen her mother react in such a manner, and Linda couldn't stop speculating about who the woman might be. Although, she had a hunch.

Her parents had celebrated their nineteenth wedding anniversary recently, and Linda knew they were happy, but she'd heard her mother jokingly refer to *Daed's* first girlfriend on occasion—a woman he'd dated before he'd started to date *Mamm*. But Linda thought her name was Naomi, not Josie. And Josie clearly wasn't Amish. *Maybe she was Amish at one time.*

She sat up taller and almost gasped as she recalled what happened to Lena Ann Zook. Lena Ann's husband ran off and left her for another woman, a woman he was seeing behind Lena's back.

No, no, no. Her father would never do that.

Bet that's what Lena Ann's children thought too. She held her head upside down to dry the back of her hair in front of the fan.

She thought about what had happened today, the woman's tearful expression as she pleaded for a return call, and how *Mamm* didn't seem to recognize the woman until she identified herself. When Linda questioned her mother afterward, she had been sharp and told

Linda they would discuss it later. Whoever the woman was, Linda hoped she wouldn't be back. She'd never seen *Mamm* behave in such a way, and one thing was for sure: that woman seemed like trouble.

Abe fastened his suspenders and headed down the stairs, breathing in the aroma of frying bacon and fighting fears about what the day might bring. He'd prayed long and hard last night about this situation that was sure to bring upset to his family, and he'd asked God to guide his words and his actions. He'd prayed for all of them. Josephine too.

He dreaded making the phone call to Josephine, but he knew Mary Ellen didn't have the strength. His wife had tossed and turned most of the night, and there was a sense of desperation surrounding her that Abe could relate to. He hoped his precious daughter could forgive her parents for not sharing the truth with her before the truth came calling unexpectedly.

Mary Ellen was standing at the stove when he entered the kitchen. She flipped the bacon, then turned toward him. Her eyelids were swollen, and Abe wished he could ease her pain. He offered her the best smile he could muster and tried to hide his own fears as he sat down at the kitchen table.

Mathew and Luke waited patiently as Mary Ellen and Linda finished preparing breakfast. Abe didn't have much of an appetite this morning. He gazed at his beautiful daughter who was scurrying around the kitchen, and he wondered how different Linda's life would have been if Josephine had raised her. He thought back seventeen years ago and realized that Josephine was the same age as Linda now, when she showed up on their doorstep.

At the time, Abe and Mary Ellen didn't think it was in the Lord's plan for them to conceive a child since Mary Ellen had been unable to get pregnant. But after they'd adopted Linda, Matthew came two years later, then Luke a year after that. Abe's eyes drifted to Linda's bare feet as she moved toward the refrigerator and pulled out two jars of jam. She had the chubbiest little feet for someone so thin. Adorable feet that she'd loved for Abe to tickle when she was a little girl. Abe swallowed hard as Linda's entire childhood flashed through his mind, and he couldn't seem to take his eyes from his daughter.

"*Daed*, do you need something?" Linda stopped in front of him, holding the jars of jam, her brows raised.

Abe shook his head and fought the unsteadiness in his voice. "No."

Linda shrugged as she walked to the other side of the table.

Matthew and Luke were rambling on about an *Englisch* girl they saw in town who had purple hair, but Abe didn't hear anything else after that. His head was filled with what ifs as he watched Linda place the jars on the table. Mary Ellen would fall to pieces if Linda chose to leave the community to be with her birth mother. Abe filled his lungs with air, then blew out slowly, knowing Mary Ellen would not be the only one to despair if Linda chose a life outside of the community.

But there was one factor largely on their side. Stephen Ebersol. Linda claimed to be madly in love with him, and suddenly Abe found comfort in that thought. For the past few months, he hadn't wanted to hear talk about his daughter and Stephen. He wasn't ready to let her go just yet and hoped that Linda and Stephen would date for another year before mentioning wedding plans.

Now, though, he found himself hoping Stephen would take that next step soon.

"Abe, do you need anything else before I sit down?" Mary Ellen's eyes were heavy with worry, and Abe wished he was able to mask his own emotions better.

"No. *Danki*, though." He forced a smile in Mary Ellen's direction.

Once Mary Ellen and Linda were seated, they bowed their heads in prayer. Luke, Matthew, and Linda filled their plates and, between bites, discussed their plans for the day. Linda was planning to ask Barbie to take her and Stephen to see Jonas after she finished her morning chores, and Luke and Matthew were going to give the barn a fresh coat of white paint, a job that would take them most of the week.

Abe watched his wife trying to keep face in front of her children, smiling when called for, and commenting when appropriate. But he'd been married to Mary Ellen for a long time, and Abe knew it was taking all her effort to keep herself together.

After breakfast, Mary Ellen waited until the children were out of earshot before she spoke of the situation.

"Are you going to call her first thing this morning?" She clutched her apron with both hands. A moment later, she shook her head and paced the wooden floor. "No, no. Maybe I should do it. Maybe I should call her." She stopped walking, then spun to face him. "Abe, let's just don't call her."

Abe got up from the table and walked to his wife. "You know we must call her." He reached for his hat on the rack, placed it on his head, then embraced Mary Ellen. "But I reckon she wouldn't be up this time of morning." Abe eased Mary Ellen out of his arms and nodded toward the window. Only a hint of daylight was visible as the sun began to creep over the horizon. "I have some things to tend to in the barn, and when the daylight is full, I will call her."

Abe was thankful the bishop had started allowing phones in the barns a few years back. Otherwise, he would have to trek over to the Lapp's shanty, and he didn't feel like bumping into anyone right now. He needed time to think.

Mary Ellen folded her hands in front of her and stood a little taller. "I will meet you in the barn after I finish a few things indoors. I should be there when you call her."

Abe nodded. Offering to make the call was the manly thing to do as head of the household, but he'd be glad to have his wife with him when he confronted this woman who threatened to cause much upheaval in their world.

Josie threw her arm across Robert's side of the bed. Empty. She wiped sleep from her eyes, blinked the alarm clock into focus, and forced herself to sit up when she saw that it was almost nine o'clock. She rarely slept that late unless it was a weekend and Robert was by her side. Normally, she got up when Robert left for work during the week, around seven o'clock. Then she recalled the sleeping pill she took the night before, an old prescription that she held on to for nights when she couldn't sleep. She knew sleep wouldn't come, and her doctor had already told her that the pills were compatible with her other medications, if she needed them.

She couldn't help but wonder if Mary Ellen would call today, even though Robert warned her that it might be a couple of days.

She eased her way out of bed and into her robe. It took her

a few moments to recognize the faint beep she was hearing from downstairs. When she realized it was her answering machine, she was suddenly alert and bolted down the stairs. She maneuvered around the maze of boxes in the living room and headed toward the kitchen, her favorite room in the house. She needed its light and cheery atmosphere, with white cabinets and powder blue countertops, lightly-dusted yellow paint on the walls, and a large window that looked out onto freshly tilled soil where Robert had recently planted a garden. Josie had tried to discourage him from the large undertaking, but Robert had always lived in the city, and he wanted to have homegrown vegetables. There was certainly enough room on the five acres that surrounded their new home.

Josie grew up picking peas in her grandparents' garden when she was young. By the time she was ten, she'd made up her mind never to have a garden. Nana and Papa's farm had been right in the middle of Amish Dutch Country in the town of Paradise, where they'd raised their daughters, Josie's mother and her older sister Laura. Every summer, Mom and Dad would drag Josie and her brother, Kenny, to help with Nana and Papa's garden. It was about an hour's drive from where Josie and her family lived in Harrisburg.

Josie loved visiting her grandparents and especially enjoyed playing with the neighboring Amish children. She just didn't care for gardening and always seemed to be the one to stumble into something poisonous or somehow annoy a stinging insect.

Her grandparents had died within a year of each other during Josie's first year of college. Kenny accepted a job in Florida after graduating from college, and he married Stephanie about two years later. When the first grandchild came a few years ago,

Mom and Dad sold the family home in Harrisburg and moved to Florida. Josie hadn't seen her parents in three years.

She recalled her phone conversation with her mother on the night she'd called to tell her that she and Robert would be moving to Lancaster County, to Paradise, to be near Linda.

"You are making a mistake. Why do you want to travel back in time, Josephine?" her mother had asked. "You will only open old wounds. Let the past be the past. Besides, you have far more to worry about than establishing a relationship with that girl."

But for Josie, it was hard to find any peace without facing her past, and she was running out of time. Now, back in Paradise, the past was everywhere.

Josie recalled her trip to the doctor, when he confirmed that she was indeed pregnant at seventeen-years-old.

"Your grandparents are not to know about this," her mother had said on the way home from the appointment, echoed by her father later that evening. "You will go and stay with your Aunt Laura in Chicago until we figure out the best way to handle this."

Mom and Dad told Nana and Papa that Josie was going to Aunt Laura's to finish her last year of high school and then attend college there. But she never saw another day of high school and got her GED instead. College in Chicago did follow but only after Josie was summoned to Paradise to hand her newborn to Mary Ellen and Abraham Huyard just two weeks after she'd given birth. Two glorious weeks during which Josie had called the baby Helen, the name she'd chosen for her daughter.

Josie had begged her aunt and uncle to let her stay with them. She could raise the baby and work. Aunt Laura had said she couldn't go against Mom and Dad's wishes, which were for

Josie to return to Lancaster County and sign adoption papers that had already been drawn up. She remembered the pain of handing over her baby to Mary Ellen on the front porch steps of the farm, where she'd just visited yesterday. Her parents had stood tall behind her. Josie felt like they were forcing a punishment on her by making her give away her baby. Her little Helen.

But it wasn't my fault. I trusted Mr. Kenton.

Larry Kenton was a math teacher at the high school in Harrisburg, and all the girls had a crush on him. But it was Josie he befriended and invited to his house on a cold, December evening, enticing Josie with an offer to help her study for her final exam in trigonometry. She was flattered when he kissed her and told her she was the prettiest girl in the school, but when his hands began to roam, Josie realized that she was in way over her head. She'd kissed boys but never anything beyond that.

Chills ran up her spine as she struggled to push the event from her mind. But at the forefront of her thoughts stayed the hurt and disappointment that her parents wouldn't stand up for her. *He was an adult. A teacher.*

"You were alone with that man in his home, Josephine," her father had said when Josie told her parents what happened three months later, when she was fairly certain she was pregnant. "I'm not sure what you want us to do about this. Larry just doesn't seem like the kind of man who would force himself on someone."

Although her mother was more sympathetic, Josie knew that her parents, pillars of the community, didn't want such a scandal. Their Catholic upbringing prevented them from considering anything but adoption. Mom had met Mary Ellen and Abraham through mutual friends, and Mom knew they'd been trying to have a baby but couldn't conceive. Large families were important to the Amish, and Mom told Josie she was doing God's work by giving her baby to Mary Ellen and Abraham.

She'd hated her parents for a long time after that. Even though she returned to Chicago, her relationship with her aunt was also strained. She went to college during the day and worked nights for three months until she was able to get a small apartment near the campus. Two years later, she had an associate's degree in business management and not much of a relationship with her family. And that was okay.

Over the years, Josie was sure Mom and Dad had run into Linda from time to time before they'd moved to Florida, but Mom swore that she broke contact with Mary Ellen and Abe after the adoption, feeling it was best for everyone. In the beginning, Josie phoned her mother often from Chicago, and with each phone call, Mom had done her best to convince Josie that she would be ruining Linda's life if she caused a ruckus by returning to Lancaster County and seeking claim to her daughter.

Mom and Dad had visited her in Chicago a few times and attended her marriage to Robert, but nothing was ever the same between them. She'd never forgiven them for making a decision that should have been hers to make.

But Linda was seventeen now. And Josie was back in Lancaster County. She didn't care what her parents or anyone else thought about her moving here.

She stared at the number one blinking red on the answering machine, took a deep breath, and then pushed the Play button. At the last second, she wondered if someone other than the Huyards had left a message. Her heart thumped as she waited and hoped to hear Mary Ellen's voice, but instead, a deep, raspy voice came through.

"Hello. This is Abraham Huyard calling for Josephine Dronberger."

3

LINDA TOOK SHALLOW BREATHS AS SHE WALKED DOWN the hallway at Lancaster General. She tried to avoid the odor, which smelled like something *Mamm* used when she cleaned the basement. With each tiny inhalation the stench found its way to her nostrils, igniting memories of the last time she had been in this hospital five years ago. Her Uncle Noah had given her cousin, David, one of his kidneys, but before David was transferred to Philadelphia for the transplant, the family had spent a lot of time here. Both Noah and David were healthy now, but it was a scary time for everyone then. And it made Linda even more fearful about seeing Jonas. She wished Stephen hadn't been called into work at the last minute.

She gently pushed open the door to Jonas's room. Lizzie, Jonas's wife, sat on one side of his bed, and his daughter, Sarah Jane, on the other. Jonas was lying flat on his back with lots of tubes and wires running everywhere, and Linda's chest grew tight for a moment, until Jonas tilted his head toward her and smiled. His cheeks were sunken in and his complexion a grayish-white color—like his hair and beard—but when he smiled in her direction, he was still the same old Jonas she loved.

"Linda, so *gut* to see you." Jonas quickly turned to his daughter who occupied the chair on his right. "Sarah Jane, get up." He raised his brows and lifted his chin.

"No, no," Linda said when she saw Sarah Jane cut her eyes sharply at her father. "I don't need to sit down. I'm just fine standing."

Sarah Jane stood up, shaking her head at Jonas, then turned to Linda and smiled. "You sit and visit with Pop. I need some *kaffi* anyway." She scooted around Linda and coaxed her toward the chair, then faced off with her father. "Pop, I'm not sure it's necessary to speak to me in such a tone. I would have gladly gotten up for Linda, and I could certainly use a break from you."

"*Gut.* Take Lizzie with you and the two of you go do something. All this hovering makes a man nervous. I ain't gonna die in this hospital; I already told you that. And I ain't gonna eat any more of that mush they call food in here either." Jonas swooshed a hand toward Sarah Jane. "Go, now." He turned toward his wife. "The both of ya's."

Lizzie placed her knitting needle in her lap beside a blue roll of yarn. She leaned closer to her husband. "I love you, Huggy Bear. But you are a cranky old man when you are feeling down."

Jonas grunted. "I've told you a hundred times since you locked me up in this place that I don't feel all that bad."

Lizzie stood up, leaned over, and kissed Jonas on the forehead. "We'll be back soon." She pushed a fallen strand of gray hair underneath her *kapp* and walked toward Linda. She smiled and patted Linda on the back. "Enjoy your visit, dear. If we're not back by tomorrow, you'll know we've left him in your hands."

Over the years, Lizzie's sense of humor had begun to mirror Jonas's. Linda suspected that to live with Jonas, a person needed to stay light on their toes and find humor in every circumstance.

"We wouldn't do that to you, Linda. Not to worry," Sarah Jane said to her before turning to Jonas. "Be *gut*, Pop." She playfully pointed a finger in his direction, then she and Lizzie headed out the door.

Jonas rolled his eyes and grumbled. Linda walked toward him and sat down where Sarah Jane had been. "Are you in pain?" It was the one thing that scared her. Pain. She didn't tolerate it well, and she didn't like to see others suffering.

Jonas propped himself up taller in the bed. "Why didn't you bring the chess set? I haven't played chess since the last time you and me played."

"I—I didn't know if you would be well enough to play. But I can bring it next—"

"No, no." He waved his hand in frustration. "There won't be a next time." He leaned closer to Linda. "I reckon they won't be back for a spell, so you got plenty of time to get me out of here."

Linda arched her brows in surprise and stifled a grin. "What?"

He edged upward in the bed even more. "I think they hid my breeches in that closet." Jonas pointed to a cabinet on the far wall. "If you can fetch me those, I'll worry about all these contraptions they have me hooked up to." He paused and twisted his mouth to one side. "Might try to round up my shoes too. And a shirt."

Linda realized that he might be serious. "Jonas, you can't just leave. I reckon that's not how it's done."

He worked his legs to one side of the bed, swung them over, and kicked Linda in the shin. "*Es dutt mir leed,*" he said, apologizing, but planted his feet firmly on the tile floor.

Linda jumped from the chair and put her hands on her hips.

"Jonas, for sure you can't seriously think I'm going to help you to—"

Jonas latched onto her arm. "The *Englisch* will kill me in here. I got a *gut* month or two left, and there ain't no need for them to rush me on to heaven." He released her arm and pointed to his own. "They got me hooked up to all kinds of mind drugs." His brows cinched together in a frown as he shook his head. "There ain't a need for all this. Yesterday, colorful flowers started blooming in the corner over there." Jonas pointed to his right. "They were growing right out of the tile floor." He sighed. "Now, Linda, I'm not a well man, but I reckon there ain't no flower garden growing in that corner."

"Jonas, have you told Sarah Jane and Lizzie all this?" She dropped her arms to her side in frustration. "You can't just pull those tubes out and leave." She shook her head.

Jonas reached for his straw hat on the nightstand and placed it atop his matted hair, then he stroked his beard. "They're keeping me hostage, that daughter and wife of mine."

Linda fought a grin. "Jonas, no one is keeping you hostage. Everyone just wants you to feel better. Don't you want us to be able to play chess when you're feeling up to it?"

Jonas scanned the room with glassy eyes. "Where ya reckon they'd put my suspenders? I've lost so much weight, *mei* breeches will fall plumb down to *mei* ankles."

Linda hoped Sarah Jane and Lizzie would be back soon. "I think you better wait until Sarah Jane and Lizzie get back."

Jonas grunted again. "Those two are the guards in this prison. They ain't gonna help me one bit." He looked up at Linda, his eyes serious. "I'm doing this with or without you. I thought I could count on you."

She sat down and reached for Jonas's hand. It had to be the medications that were making him act like this, a stretch even for him. "Jonas, you know you can count on me, but I'm sure we can't just pull those tubes from your arm. That wouldn't be safe at all. I know you don't like it in here, and I—"

"Hello." Linda immediately recognized the voice and spun around to face Stephen. Relief washed over her.

"I thought you had to work." She released Jonas's hand, stood up, and walked to Stephen, wishing she could fold herself into his arms the way she had last Sunday after the singing. Every time she thought about the kiss they'd shared behind the barn after he brought her home in his courting buggy, she went weak in the knees.

"The *Englisch* worker showed up after all, so Abner told me I could leave if I wanted. I got a ride from Mr. Lauder at the bank next door." Stephen slid past her, but not before winking in her direction, which did cause one knee to buckle. His brown eyes were flecked with gold, like sun-kissed wheat in the field. Stephen's hair changed colors with the seasons, and already his tawny locks were turning a golden shade of blond, which framed his bronzed face in the bobbed haircut Amish men wore. After working long days in the fields, his skin was already tanned, his hard work evident by the way his shoulders filled out his blue shirt. Linda loved everything about him. Stephen Ebersol was as wonderful on the inside, kind and unselfish, and always the first one to volunteer when the community needed someone to take on an extra project. Maybe that was because Stephen was the bishop's grandson, but Linda suspected it could be something else.

Linda felt like Stephen worked harder than most, as if it

might make up for the one thing he was particularly self-conscious about. He was born with one leg almost two inches shorter than the other one, and even though he had special shoes to even out his tall stance, he walked with a slight limp and couldn't run very fast, something she knew had bothered him when they were younger.

Over the past year, they'd shared picnics, Sunday singings, and spent all their free time together, but when Linda suggested they go for a swim at the creek, Stephen made up an excuse not to go. She knew it was because he didn't want her to see him without his shoes on, which would make him off-balance. The only thing off-balance was Stephen's way of thinking. She loved him, and to her, he was perfect.

"Hello, Jonas." Stephen extended his hand to Jonas.

"Stephen, you're just in time." Jonas latched onto Stephen's hand. "Linda was just about to break me out of this jail."

Linda tried not to giggle. Jonas was a mess sitting there on the side of the bed wearing nothing but his straw hat and a white hospital gown. She shrugged in Stephen's direction, glad that Jonas was feeling good enough to behave in such a manner.

"Break you out of here?" Stephen smiled benignly. "Jonas, you know we can't break you out of here."

"Well, then—" Jonas reached for the tube running into his arm and Linda gasped. Thankfully, a voice erupted throughout the room.

"Jonas Miller, what in the world do you think you're doin'?" Lizzie marched to his side, slapped her hands to her tiny hips, and leaned her face to his. "This is why we can't leave you for a minute."

Sarah Jane was quickly at her father's bedside. "Pop, you'll be glad to know that we ran into the doctor on the way to get *kaffi*, and they are going to release you, if that's really what you want. But they won't be able to monitor your pain as closely if you aren't in the hospital."

"I'm not in any pain." What little color Jonas had in his face when Linda arrived was quickly draining as he sat on the edge of the bed, and she noticed his hand trembling. Just sitting on the bed seemed to have zapped his energy.

"Pop, you will have to wait until the nurse comes in and unhooks you from everything. Now lie back down." Sarah Jane helped her father back into bed. He grumbled but seemed to be relieved after he was on his back again. "Are you sure this is what you want to do?"

Jonas took a labored breath, then reached for his daughter's hand. He spoke softly. "Take me home, Daughter. I want to watch the sun rise in the mornings and set in the evenings." With glassy eyes, he turned to his wife. "Like I've done my entire life. It's where I want to be."

It was a side of Jonas that Linda had never seen, and she suddenly felt as though she were intruding on a very private moment. Worse, the realization of what Jonas meant punched her in the gut. Stephen's hand brushed against hers, and he discretely looped his pinky finger with hers.

"All right, Huggy Bear," Lizzie said tenderly. "You rest now."

Sarah Jane was still holding her father's hand, and Linda could see her eyes clouding with tears. "I'll go check to see how much longer it will be before you can get released." She blinked back tears, then turned to Linda. "Here, Linda. Come sit. Visit with

Jonas while I go find the nurse." Sarah Jane eased her hand from Jonas's and motioned for Stephen to come closer. "Come over here. I'll be back shortly."

Linda sat down and Stephen stood by her side. "Maybe when you get home, you'll feel like playing chess." She tried to sound hopeful.

"A game of chess will be *gut*." Jonas smiled, but Linda could tell it was forced, and she didn't want him to have to make an effort like that for her sake. His eyes began to close, and after only a few moments, Jonas was snoring lightly.

"It doesn't take much to tucker him out." Lizzie gazed at Jonas, rubbing his forearm with her hand. She looked up at Linda and Stephen. "But I know it means a lot to him that you both stopped by."

"We—we love . . ." Linda swallowed hard and fought to steady her emotions. Stephen put a hand on her shoulder.

"When you get Jonas home, if there is anything you need, anything at all, please get word to me, Lizzie." Stephen's warm smile matched his tone of voice.

Lizzie nodded. "We will have lots of help from everyone, I'm sure. *Danki*, Stephen." Lizzie stared at her husband in a way that caused Linda's heart to ache. *Jonas is going to die.*

"You children should go and enjoy this beautiful weather."

It seemed clear that Lizzie wanted to be alone with her husband, and Linda felt like tears were going to spill over at any minute, so she and Stephen excused themselves. Linda just wanted to get in the hallway before she completely broke down in front of Lizzie.

Once outside the hospital doors, that's exactly what happened. She folded onto one of the benches in the courtyard on the east side of the hospital and buried her face in her hands. Stephen sat down beside her and draped an arm around her shoulder.

"Did you not realize how sick Jonas is?" His voice was comforting, but his words stung.

She pulled her hands away, swiped at tears, and then turned to face him. "I guess not. Jonas has been sick for years, and somehow he always seems to get better." She paused, sniffled. "Remember three years ago, when the doctors told him that he couldn't attend Kade and Sadie's wedding? They said he was too sick and made out like he was going to die any minute." She shook her head and grinned. "But Jonas said he wouldn't miss the wedding for anything, and he insisted Sarah Jane and Lizzie take him. Remember?"

"*Ya*, I remember." Stephen took a deep breath, and with his free hand, he reached for hers and held it tightly. "Jonas is a fighter, but Linda—"

"Don't say it. Just don't say it. Jonas is so special. To everyone."

Stephen nodded, gave her hand a squeeze, and they sat quietly for a few moments.

"How'd you get here? Barbie?"

"*Ya*. She'll probably be here any minute to pick me up. She was going to run some errands."

"I guess I'll catch a ride too. Anything special you want to do the rest of the afternoon?" Linda snuggled closer, but Stephen pulled his arm from around her shoulder and put a tiny bit of space between them when two doctors walked into the courtyard, though he kept hold of her hand. Most men in their community weren't comfortable with much public affection, and Stephen was no exception.

Linda twisted slightly to face him and wished they could just go somewhere, anywhere, so Stephen could take her away from her worries about Jonas. She knew that to worry about such matters was a sin and that Jonas would have a special place in heaven when he arrived, but the thought of not seeing him anymore, playing chess, listening to his wise advice—she just couldn't imagine. Poor Lillian. And Sarah Jane and Lizzie. There would be a huge void in so many lives when Jonas passed.

"Anything with you is fine," Stephen said after the doctors passed by them. Linda could feel her cheeks blush and wondered if Stephen could read her mind, if he knew how much she longed for him to propose. She'd be eighteen in August, on the seventeenth. That wouldn't leave much time to plan a wedding for November or December of this year. Weddings were always scheduled after the fall harvest. Besides, her parents would argue that she was too young to get married, even though *Mamm* and *Daed* were married at seventeen.

"There's Barbie." Stephen pointed to the white minivan, then turned back to Linda, arched one brow, and eased into a smile. "Wanna go to the old oak tree?"

Linda knew what that meant. The old oak tree was a place where couples went to be alone, a huge oak in the middle of a field off of Leaman Road, with arched branches that formed a globe around those who ventured beneath the protective limbs. She felt her face reddening even more, and she nodded.

"We'll get Barbie to just take us to her bed and breakfast, and we can walk to the old oak from there." Stephen stood up, offered Linda a hand, and she rose from the bench along with him, relieved their *Englisch* friend wouldn't know their destination.

Mary Ellen paced the kitchen. She'd sent Matthew and Luke over to Samuel and Lillian's house with two shoofly pies she'd baked that morning, along with a big container of high fiber balls. She knew how much her brother liked the fiber balls filled with peanut butter, honey, raisins, chocolate chips, and coconut. Truth was, she needed to keep busy to keep her mind occupied.

Abe's conversation that morning with Josephine was brief, but they agreed that Linda's birth mother would visit tomorrow morning at ten o'clock. That meant that Mary Ellen and Abe would have to tell Linda the truth this evening, and Mary Ellen's stomach was rolling with anxiety. It was only fair to discuss the matter with Linda first, and privately, so sending Matthew and Luke to Samuel's house worked out perfectly since Linda was due home any minute to help with supper preparation. Mary Ellen dreaded the conversation they would be having with Linda, but waiting could worsen the situation if Linda found out the news some other way. What if Josephine decided not to wait and went to Linda directly? She jumped when the screen door slammed.

"It's just me, Mary Ellen." Abe hung his hat on the rack near the door, then ran a hand through his hair. "It's gonna be all right." He walked to the refrigerator and poured himself a glass of meadow tea, took a few gulps, and then took a seat at the kitchen table.

Mary Ellen brushed flour from her black apron and resumed her pacing.

"Sit down, Mary Ellen. Rest. I know you're nervous, but we will have to trust the Lord to guide us to say the right things."

"There is no *right* way to tell our daughter that we've lied to her for her entire life." Mary Ellen bit down on her lower lip, then eased onto the bench across from Abe. "I've always been close to Linda, and I'm afraid that when she finds out this news, that— that we will lose that."

"We didn't lie, Mary Ellen." Abe raised his shoulders, then dropped them in frustration. "It just didn't come up."

Mary Ellen slammed a hand on the table, something she would normally never do. "Abe! We didn't tell our daughter that she is adopted. Don't you think that should have *come up* at some point?" She regretted the tone she took with her husband, and she could see the anxiety in his expression, the fear in his eyes. But her own worries were overwhelming her as she wiped sweat from her brow. A knot was building in her throat, and the last thing she wanted to do was cry in front of Linda when she arrived. Mary Ellen wanted to calmly tell Linda that it didn't matter one tiny bit who gave birth to her, that she loved Linda as if she'd carried her in her own womb, that she was her daughter, no matter what. And she'd prayed all night that Linda would somehow understand.

"Mary Ellen, where is your faith? It's God's will that things are working out this way. You know that, no?"

To question God's will is a sin, but Mary Ellen had never questioned His will more than at this moment. "Things better work out, Abe." She sat up a little straighter, raised her chin. "We will just explain this to her, and then things will resume the way they were."

"I hope you're right." Abe's tone was doubtful, and doubt was not what she needed from her husband right now. She always relied on Abe's strength, and she needed him to stay strong for her, for them.

Mary Ellen stood from the table, twisted her apron strings, and paced some more, apprehension rippling through her body like a tidal wave that threatened to destroy her. Instead of focusing on her own failure to tell Linda the truth, she wanted to lash out at someone, and she knew Abe wasn't any more at fault than she was.

"I just don't know why she would want to ruin all these lives like this, that Josephine woman." She shook her head, then stopped pacing and turned to Abe. "I reckon she's not a *gut* Christian woman, or she wouldn't be doing this."

"Mary Ellen, you don't know that. I'm sure this is hard on her too."

She clenched her lips tight and bit back words that the Lord would surely not approve of.

Abe turned toward the door when he heard the clippety-clop of hooves, then stood up and walked to the threshold. Mary Ellen followed him and together they peered through the screen. They watched Linda walk up the driveway, then hop barefoot across the cobblestone steps that crossed the yard. When she reached the porch steps, she closed the distance between her and her parents and smiled. A smile that quickly faded. She stopped on the other side of the screen, facing them. No one moved or said anything for a few seconds.

"What's wrong?" Linda's brows narrowed, and she glanced back and forth between Mary Ellen and Abe.

Mary Ellen pushed the screen door open and motioned Linda inside. "Linda, we need to talk to you."

4

LINDA SCOOTED PAST HER PARENTS AND INTO THE kitchen and wondered if she'd done something wrong. She was a little late to help prepare supper, but it didn't even look like *Mamm* had started yet. Her time with Stephen at the old oak tree had helped to ease her worry about Jonas. It wasn't just the few kisses they shared, although those would keep her up at night, but the deep conversation. Stephen's faith seemed stronger than Linda's, and he had a way of making her understand about God's will, something that the *Ordnung* taught was not to be questioned. But when something bad happened, Linda tended to question the event just the same. She suspected that Stephen would follow in his grandfather's footsteps someday and become the bishop. And hopefully, she'd be by his side as the bishop's wife.

"What's wrong?" she asked again when both her parents just stood off to one side of the kitchen, her mother's face drawn into an expression of dread. Her father's brows furrowed as he stroked his beard.

"Let's go into the den." *Daed* led the way, and Linda glanced at her mother as they followed him into the den, but *Mamm* just took a deep breath and kept her head down.

Linda sat down on the couch, and each of her parents took a

seat in the rocking chairs across the coffee table from her. That
was usually where they sat when they were reprimanding her or
one of her brothers. Again, she tried to recall something she might
have done to upset them.

"We have something to tell you, *mei maedel*, but first I want you
to know how much your *mamm* and I love you. You are our daughter always." *Daed* swallowed hard, and Linda's chest tightened.
Could something have happened to Jonas since she and Stephen
left the hospital? She sat quietly and waited, but she noticed that
her mother wouldn't look at her.

"Your *mamm* and I tried to have *kinner* for almost two years
before we—before you were born," her father began. "We went to
the natural doctor who sent us to an *Englisch* doctor in Lancaster.
But I reckon no one could figure out why we couldn't have a child."

This seemed an inappropriate conversation, and Linda's anxiety heightened as she wondered where her father was going with
this. She sat up straight on the edge of the couch and folded her
hands in her lap. Her mother had never talked with her about
where babies came from; it just wasn't a conversation that a mother
would have with her daughter. These things were learned when a
girl got married. But Linda's *Englisch* girlfriends had educated her
about the matter early on in her *rumschpringe*.

"We wanted a child so badly," her mother chimed in. "A little
one to love." *Mamm's* eyes filled with tears, and Linda tilted her
head to one side and gazed at her forlorn expression. Then it hit
her, and her embarrassment reddened her cheeks as she gasped.

"Do you think Stephen and I are—" She didn't even know how
to speak the words. "We would never. I kissed him, but that's all."
Linda tucked her chin. "Maybe I shouldn't have, but I know that

won't make a baby." She looked up to see both her parents' jaws simultaneously dropping.

"No, no," her mother said as her cheeks took on their own rosy shade of red. "That's not what we were thinking."

"Then what is it? You're scaring me."

Her mother left the rocker and joined Linda on the couch. She grasped Linda's hand tightly within hers, then looked intensely into Linda's eyes as her own eyes clouded even more with tears. *Mamm* opened her mouth to speak but sighed heavily instead and turned to *Daed*.

Her father leaned forward, put his elbows on his knees, and rested his chin on his hands. Linda's heart was thumping so hard it was making her chest hurt. "When we couldn't have a baby of our own, we were given another woman's baby to raise. We signed papers that a lawyer wrote up."

She didn't understand. "What woman gave you a baby?" She glanced around the room. "And where is this baby?"

Mamm cupped Linda's face with both hands. "*You* are that baby, *mei maedel*. I did not carry you in my womb. Another woman did. You're adopted. The pretty woman that came to the house. She is your—your mother."

Linda eased out of her mother's grasp. "This can't be so." She turned to her father. "*Daed*, tell me this isn't true."

Her father left the rocker and bent on one knee in front of Linda. "You are our daughter. You will always be our daughter. Just because you do not carry our genes, it makes you no less our child. We love you, and that will never change. Do you understand?"

"No. I don't." She edged further away from both of them as her chest rose and fell with labored breaths. Tears threatened to spill, but she blinked them back. Too many unanswered questions. "Are you saying that the *Englisch* woman didn't want me, so she gave me to you?"

"Linda, she was only seventeen years old at the time. Your age. She didn't know how to care for a baby. And there was no father around or in the picture to help her." Her mother reached out to her, but she jerked away.

A father. The sting continued to worsen. "Where is my father then?" She glanced up at the person she'd believed to be her father her entire life, and indeed her tears did spill over.

"I—I am your father, Linda. I will always be your father." *Daed* swiped at his eyes, something Linda had never seen him do before. "As for the man whose genes you share, we do not know about him."

Linda jumped from the couch and put her hands over her face. "Why are you telling me this now?" Her voice was elevated and cracked as she spoke. "Isn't this something I should have known before now?"

"*Ya.*" Her mother stood up and walked to her. "Linda, please, try to understand. We made a mistake. We should have told you when you were younger, but it just didn't matter to us. You have always been our daughter, and nothing was going to change that."

Luke and Matthew. "Do Luke and Matthew know about this? I reckon they should be told too."

Her father was now beside her mother on the couch, both of them with teary eyes. "We thought you should know first." *Daed* sighed, his voice filled with anguish.

Linda swallowed hard and knew this would be difficult for Luke and Matthew. She looked at her parents. *Parents?* She'd never felt more lost than at this moment. Her thoughts momentarily trailed to the *Englisch* woman. No wonder *Mamm* was so upset. But she would need to be strong for her brothers, despite this complete lack of responsibility by her parents.

"I reckon Matt and Luke might not understand this either. When you tell them that they were adopted, they are going to take it even harder. How could you do this? How could you not tell us—"

Her father grabbed her arm gently. "No, no, Linda." He shook his head. "*Mei maedel,* your brothers were not adopted."

She wanted to run into her mother's arms and beg her to say this wasn't true, but *Mamm* only nodded in agreement, muttering how sorry they were.

Sobs of grief began to rack Linda, and she was having trouble breathing. "You mean, I don't have any brothers either?" *Dear Lord in heaven, do something. Please. This can't be true.* "But you said you couldn't have any *kinner* of your own."

"We didn't think we could, Linda, but we were able to have Luke and Matthew. We don't know why, but the Lord graced us with the boys, and—"

"I'm not your daughter! I have no parents. I have no brothers." Her sense of loss was suddenly beyond tears, quickly being replaced by anger. She backed away from her parents. "I have no one."

"Linda, my beloved daughter. I am your mother. We are your parents. It will always be that way. We love you, Linda. Please forgive us for not telling you this sooner. Please, Linda . . ." *Mamm* reached for Linda again, and this time Linda stepped even further away from them.

"We know this is hard, Linda, but over time you will realize that we are still your parents, no matter what." Her father continued to fight a buildup of tears in his eyes, and there was a part of her that wanted to run to him, to them both, to comfort them, ease their pain. But she felt suffocated by her own grief.

"Why are you telling me this now?"

Her parents looked at each other, and then her father spoke. "The *Englisch* woman, she wants to see you. She wants to meet you tomorrow morning and spend some time with you."

"But you don't have to go." *Mamm* stepped forward. "We will just tell her that you are not interested in meeting her, and—"

"I want to meet her. *She* is my *mother*." Linda kept her voice steady and cut her eyes at Mary Ellen. *Mary Ellen*—the person who raised her. She should have felt remorse at the way her cutting words sent tears streaming down Mary Ellen's face. But instead, she twisted the dagger. "What am I supposed to call you both now? *Mary Ellen* and *Abe*?"

"Watch your tone, Linda," her father said as he wrapped a protective arm around his wife.

Linda grunted, stood taller. *They can't tell me what to do. They aren't even related to me.*

"We know that you're hurt, dear, but nothing has to change, and—"

"Stop it! Everything has changed." Linda wrapped her arms around herself, never needing a hug from her mother more than at this moment. The woman she thought was her mother. From someone. Someone who loved her.

"Please, Linda . . ." her mother cried as she reached out to her. "Please, my darling baby . . ."

"I'm going to Stephen's. He'll be my family someday! Then I'll have a family!"

She ran out the door, down the porch steps, and didn't stop running until she got to Black Horse Road, where she collapsed onto the gravel shoulder and sobbed. It took a few moments for her to realize her toe was bleeding and only another minute or so before a buggy came along. She wiped her eyes, then blocked the sun's glare with her hand until the buggy came into view.

Her cousin David. She waited while he pulled to a stop beside her.

"You okay?"

David was two years older than Linda, and he'd been through a kidney transplant, so she wasn't sure he'd have much sympathy for her throbbing toe, but her bloody foot was the least of her worries. David jumped from his topless courting buggy and ran to her side. He knelt beside her and put a hand on her shoulder.

"Here, let me see." He lifted up her dirty bare foot covered in blood. "Ouch," he said as he crinkled his nose. "That's a nasty cut, but I reckon it doesn't look like you need any stitches. I'm on my way to *Onkel* Noah's clinic. You wanna go and have him clean it up?"

Linda stood up, wiped her eyes, and shook her head. "No. Can you just take me to Stephen's *haus*? Please, if you don't mind."

"Sure." David helped her into the buggy, then went around and got in beside her. He'd barely settled into a steady trot when the tears started again. She just couldn't seem to stop. "Does it hurt that bad?"

She heard the concern in David's voice, much like that of a protective brother. "It's not my toe. It's—it's . . ." Linda covered her face with her hands. "David, I'm adopted. My parents aren't my parents."

"What?" He twisted in the seat to face her, a confused expression on his face.

"I just found out. *Mamm* and *Daed*..." she paused as she sniffled. "I mean *Mary Ellen* and *Abe* told me that I have a birth mother, someone who gave me to them when I was a baby. And I'm so upset, and ..." She lowered her head, then looked David's way. He was staring straight ahead, keeping the horse at slow pace. After a few moments, he turned her way.

"Linda, I'm sure that news was a shock." He glanced back and forth between her and the road, then steadied his gaze on her. "But ..." He gave her a small smile. "I think I'd like to thank your folks for raising such a wonderful cousin for me."

Linda tried to manage a smile through her tears, but the news was too raw for her to pretend for more than a moment that she was anything but destroyed.

David slowed the buggy before he reached Stephen's house and eventually came to a stop. He turned to face her in the seat again, then wrapped his arms around her, which only caused her to cry more.

"Linda," he finally said in a soothing tone. "Mary Ellen and Abe are your parents, no matter what." David gently eased her away. "You know how much they love you."

In her heart, Linda knew it to be true, but the reality of the situation was overwhelming her. "Why didn't they tell me? Why would they keep something like this from me?" Then she had a horrible thought. She took a deep breath. "David, did you know about this? Since *mei mudder*, I mean Mary Ellen, is your *daed's* sister."

"She's still your mother, Linda, and no, I didn't have any idea about this." David pulled his straw hat off and ran his forearm over a sweaty forehead. "I think of Lillian just like *mei mamm*, and I know Lillian loves me just like her own son. I reckon you don't have to be born into a family to be a part of it."

Linda knew that when Lillian married Samuel, she'd raised David as her own son, but somehow her situation seemed much different. "It's the betrayal. The fact that no one told me."

They sat quietly for a few minutes. "So, what now? What are you going to do?"

Linda recalled the looks on her parents' faces. *On Mary Ellen's and Abe's faces.* Every time she mentally corrected herself, the pain she felt was even worse. She shrugged. "I don't know. I'm supposed to meet *her* tomorrow."

"Still want to go to Stephen's? I reckon you look a mess." David grinned, poked her in the arm. They'd grown up together, and David had always been like the older brother she didn't have. Again, she thought about Matt and Luke.

Linda sniffled. "*Ya.* I need to see Stephen."

David nodded, then flicked the horse into motion. "Linda, everything's gonna be all right. Mary Ellen and Abe love you, and that's what matters. It was just God's will that the other woman helped them out."

Linda shrugged. "I guess. I'm just not sure how I feel about all this." However, the look on her parents' faces was enough for her to know that, despite her own hurt, they were suffering too.

Stephen pushed back his hat, looped his thumbs beneath his suspenders, and walked across his front yard toward David's buggy, wondering what would bring Linda to his house so near the supper hour. He watched Linda hug her cousin before she stepped out of the buggy and shut the door. David waved, and Stephen returned the gesture, but he couldn't take his eyes from Linda as she ran barefoot across the yard.

"What's wrong?" She was a few feet from him when he noticed blood on the top of her bare foot and tears rolling down her cheeks. "What happened?"

She threw her arms around his neck. "My life is ruined."

"What?" He held her for a few moments, then gently eased her away and looked down at the blood on her foot. "Do you need a doctor?"

She swiped at swollen eyes and shook her head. "No. My foot is fine."

Stephen raised his brows and gazed into her eyes. "Then what is it?"

"I'm adopted!" She took a step backward and clinched her fists at her sides. "Abe and Mary Ellen aren't my parents, Stephen! A woman named Josephine is my mother. I don't even think I really have a father. Luke and Matthew aren't my brothers." She squeezed her eyes shut as tears rolled down her cheeks. "I'm adopted! And no one bothered to tell me until my *mother* showed up at our house yesterday."

Stephen swallowed hard and searched for something to say. He stepped toward her and touched her arm. "Are you sure?"

Her eyes flew open in a rage. "*Ya*, I'm sure. They—Mary Ellen and Abe—just told me." She covered her face with her hands and mumbled something Stephen couldn't understand, then she moved forward and buried her face in his chest. "Tell me it isn't true."

He wrapped one arm around her back and cradled the back

of her neck with his other hand. "I'm sorry, Linda. What can I do?"

"Just hold me." She pressed her body closer to his, and Stephen struggled to stay focused on the issue at hand.

After a while, she pulled from the embrace and gazed into his eyes. "It hurts, Stephen. Make it stop."

"I—I . . ." He raised his shoulders and dropped them. "I don't know what to say, Linda." How could he ease her pain if this was really true?

She tried to blink back more tears, but they spilled down her cheeks as she continued to wait for him to say something. He knew he was failing miserably, so he stepped forward and cupped her cheeks in his hands, then kissed her softly on the lips. He couldn't stand to see her hurting like this, but he wasn't sure what he could say to make her feel better. She returned the kiss, then eased away, and her eyes begged him to say something more to comfort her.

He took a deep breath. *Please, God. Let me say the right thing.*

"Linda, I don't think Mary Ellen and Abe could love you any more than they already do, and I reckon they are your parents no matter what." He paused as she sniffled and wiped her eyes, seeming to wait for more from him. "I've seen you and your *mamm* together, and I don't think anything is going to change between the two of you."

"Everything has changed." She tucked her head and sniffled again.

Stephen gently lifted her chin. "Linda, Mary Ellen is your *mudder*. Talk to her." He kissed her on the forehead. "Let me take you home."

She nodded as she bit her bottom lip.

"It'll just take me a minute to ready the horse and buggy. Wait here. We can talk more on the way to your house."

Stephen ran toward the barn, moving as quickly as he could. His grandfather was due for supper any minute, and the last thing Linda needed was for Bishop Ebersol to question her tears right now. Stephen knew his grandfather would find out soon enough. *Daadi* always found out everything.

Linda listened to Stephen do most of the talking on the way home. He was sweet for trying to make her feel better, insisting that not much would change for her. But he was wrong. Everything was going to change.

When a crisis had presented itself in the past, she always went to her mother. *This is a crisis . . .* Right now, she wanted to go inside, and have her parents reassure her that she was, indeed, loved. She told Stephen good-bye, and they shared a brief kiss in the driveway.

"It's going to be fine, Linda," he said one last time as she exited the buggy.

She crossed the yard, then stepped on the cobblestones that led to the porch steps. She thought about how Matt and Luke were not her true brothers, and she began to cry again.

Linda looked up when she heard the porch screen slam and saw her mother standing on the porch with her arms stretched wide. Her mother, not Mary Ellen. *This woman is my mother, no matter what.*

Linda ran to her as fast as she could, and *Mamm* wrapped her arms around her tightly.

"I'm sorry, *Mamm*," Linda cried.

"No, my precious daughter. I'm sorry."

At breakfast the next morning, no one said much. Mary Ellen served scrapple and some dippy eggs, along with some flapjacks, because they were Linda's favorite. They decided the night before that Abe would talk to Matt and Luke when they went to market later in the morning while Linda was spending some time with Josephine.

Mary Ellen recalled her conversation with Linda late last night. When she'd heard her daughter crying, she went to her room, and they'd spent the next two hours talking. She prayed that she had convinced Linda that everything was truly going to be all right and how very much she loved her. That nothing had to change.

Mary Ellen glanced at the clock. Straight up ten o'clock. Abe and the boys had left nearly two hours ago, and Linda had busied herself cleaning the upstairs. Mary Ellen hadn't seen her or heard any movement from upstairs in about an hour. She finished running a damp mop across the wood floor in the den and headed toward the stairs. When she got to Linda's room, she knocked.

"Come in."

Mary Ellen slowly pushed the door open, and Linda was sitting on her bed in her newest dress, a purple one the color of a ripe plum, the one Mary Ellen had made for her just last week. Her black apron was a newer one, bold in color and not faded by multiple trips through the wringer. Linda was twisting one of the ties on her *kapp*, but not one brown hair was out of place, each strand tucked neatly beneath the prayer covering. Her black leather shoes shone as if Linda had run a wet cloth across the top, and her ankle-high black socks were neatly folded to the rim of her shoes.

When Mary Ellen sat down on the bed beside Linda, her

daughter stopped twisting the tie of her *kapp*, folded her hands in her lap, and took a deep breath. Mary Ellen patted her leg. "She will be here any minute. It's ten o'clock." She paused and waited for Linda to say something, but Linda merely bit her bottom lip and stared at the floor. "You can change your mind," she said softly, wondering if the hopefulness in her comment had shown through.

Linda shook her head but didn't look up. "No. I'm going."

Mary Ellen had prayed last night, and again this morning, for the Lord to lift the worry from her heavy heart. But that was only the beginning of a long list of prayers that weren't normally included during her devotions. At Abe's insistence, she'd prayed for Josephine, although she wasn't sure what to pray for. If things went well between Josephine and Linda, would she lose her daughter? She tried to banish the selfish thoughts, since apparently Linda hadn't changed her mind about the visit. Mary Ellen couldn't stop thinking about what Linda and Josephine might do together, what places they might visit, conversations they might have.

"*Mamm?*" Linda twisted her neck and looked into Mary Ellen's eyes.

"*Ya?*"

"What do you think she wants?" Linda paused and chewed on her lip again for a moment. "I mean, will she want to be my mother? Because I already have a mother."

Mary Ellen felt better than she'd felt since Josephine came calling. She smiled at Linda, reached for her hand, and squeezed. "I'm glad to hear that." She thought for a moment. "I reckon she wants to know you. That's all. Maybe have a place in your life."

"What kind of place?" Linda's confused expression, paired with her questioning eyes and fidgety feet, took Mary Ellen back to a time when Linda was five-years-old and being reprimanded for picking all the strawberries in the garden before they were ripe and giving them to their dog Buddy.

Tires churning up loose gravel on the driveway diverted both their attention, and Linda suddenly turned pale. Mary Ellen knew that she must be strong for her daughter.

"Linda, you go and have a *gut* time." Mary Ellen cupped Linda's cheek and smiled. "You are very pretty, like her."

"I'm nervous, *Mamm*."

"I know. Me too."

Linda threw her arms around Mary Ellen. "I'm sorry for how I behaved yesterday." Mary Ellen gently nudged her away and pointed a finger in her direction.

"Do not apologize to me, Linda. I should be apologizing to you. I hope that you can forgive your father and I for not—"

"*Mamm*, I already have forgiven you." Linda sighed. "I thought a lot about this last night, and I know you and *Daed* are hurting and worried. But you will always be my parents."

"*Danki* for saying so. We love you very much."

Then they heard a knock at the door.

5

JOSIE CHECKED HER LIPSTICK IN THE REARVIEW MIRROR, ran a hand through her hair, and wondered if she should have worn something different. After several outfit changes, she'd chosen a pair of capri jeans, a tan T-shirt with no imprint, and flat brown sandals. She'd toned down her jewelry also—only her wedding ring and small silver hoop earrings. It was a far cry from what she knew Linda would be wearing, but she didn't want to come across as flashy, so she'd ditched spiked heels for sandals, left the Rolex at home, and even gone light on her makeup today.

She took a deep breath before she stepped out of the car and wondered if she should have taken Robert up on his offer to come with her. She took in her surroundings and saw that she'd parked near two buggies. One was the familiar box-shaped buggy Lancaster County was known for, and the other one Josie recognized to be a spring buggy, without a top, room for four, with a storage area in the back. In this warm weather, she'd seen lots of spring buggies on the roads.

Josie glanced around the property as she made her way across cobblestone steps that led to a long wooden porch with two entryways. It seemed to Josie that the Amish must get on hands and knees to trim their grass so perfectly around every flower bed, cobblestone, and planter that occupied the space between the gravel driveway and the front porch. Every tree in the spacious yard was encased by a pristine flower bed sporting red, pink, and white blooms. The white clapboard house appeared to have a fresh coat of paint, and in grand contrast, the home had a green tin roof that matched the roofs of two barns nearby.

A horse whinnied from the barn to Josie's left, and she turned to see the animal poke his head out opened shutters, as if voicing a hello in her direction. It was picturesque, and under different circumstances, Josie knew it would be a calming, peaceful place. But as she headed up the porch steps, Josie's heart was pounding against her chest and beads of sweat were accumulating on her forehead.

Two doors led into the house, and Josie headed to the one directly in front of the porch steps, which appeared to be the main entrance. As she drew near, she could see through the screen door and into a den, then she heard footsteps, and the door swung open.

"Hello," Mary Ellen said softly. She motioned for Josie to come in. "Linda will be down in a few minutes. Please, have a seat. Can I get you some tea or *kaffi*?"

Josie hesitantly sat down on the tan couch, folded her hands in her lap. "No, thank you. I'm fine."

Mary Ellen's home was tastefully decorated with more décor than other Amish homes Josie had been in when she was younger. She'd heard that the bishop was more lenient about allowing a few ornamental trinkets here and there, as well as conservative wall hangings. As she glanced around, Josie thought this could have been any number of non-Amish homes in the area. Two oak rockers faced the couch with a matching coffee table in between, and a colorful rug rested beneath the setup. A large leafy ivy was in a planter in the far corner next to a bookshelf that went almost to the ceiling, filled with books, cards, and various games. A large framed picture of a cottage nestled among colorful foliage resembling a Thomas Kinkade painting hung above the fireplace, and on each side of the mantel were large glass lanterns filled with a yellowish liquid.

Spying the lanterns was a reminder that this was indeed an Amish household, and Josie glanced around to see no electrical outlets, overhead light fixtures, and of course, no television or radio. But it was still much more ornate than what she remembered. One thing still stood true; the Amish didn't believe in photographs, taking them or posing for them, so there were no pictures of family scattered about the home. Josie instantly realized that there would be no pictures for her to see of Linda growing up. What did she look like when she was two-years-old? Five? Thirteen?

Mary Ellen sat down in the rocker facing Josie on the couch, but it was only a few moments later when they both heard footsteps coming down the stairs. Both women stood up. Josie watched as Linda descended the last few steps, then paused before she slowly entered the den.

"Hello," Josie said tenderly to the girl in the deep purple dress who stood before her. *My daughter.* She held her position and waited for Linda to come a little closer.

"Hi." Linda's eyes locked with Josie's, but only for a moment. "What time would you like me to be home, *Mamm?*"

Mary Ellen smiled, but Josie could still see fear etched into her expression. "Take as long as you like," she said bravely. Then she walked to Linda, whispered something in her ear, and pulled her into a gentle hug. After a moment, she eased away and turned to Josie.

"Katie's Kitchen is a nice place for lunch. They haven't been open long, and we try to support them, since they are Amish-owned and operated." She paused, then shrugged. "Linda likes it there, but I'm sure anywhere will be fine."

"I think Katie's Kitchen sounds nice for lunch." Josie glanced at her wrist and remembered she hadn't worn her watch. "Probably a little early for lunch." She turned to Linda. "I thought I would take you to my home, if you'd like. We could talk there, maybe have some tea or coffee. Then we can head to Katie's Kitchen later. If that's okay? I'm open to anything really. It doesn't matter. Is there something else you'd like to do? Or maybe . . ." Josie stopped when she realized she was rambling. Then she had a thought, an idea that perhaps would make the entire day easier on everyone. She turned to Mary Ellen.

"Mary Ellen, would you like to come with us?"

Mary Ellen's eyes widened, and she glanced at Linda, but ultimately shook her head. "No, I think it'd be best if you two spent some time alone."

"But *Mamm*, she said you can come, and—" Linda's pleading voice made Josie realize just how nervous Linda was. *I'm nervous, too, sweetheart.*

"No, Linda. I have much to do around here." Mary Ellen took a step backward, waved, and said, "Now, go and have a *gut* time." Mary Ellen continued to ease backward until she had almost rounded the corner into the other room. "Have fun," she hoarsely whispered, and Josie could see Mary Ellen's eyes clouding with tears.

"Are you sure you don't want to join us?" Josie's heart ached for Mary Ellen.

"It's okay. Let's go," Linda said to Josie when her mother shook her head again. "*Mamm*, I'll be home this afternoon." Then Linda said something in Pennsylvania *Deitsch* to Mary Ellen—something Josie didn't understand—but Mary Ellen smiled, then she left the room. Linda followed Josie out to the car.

"Does this car have air-conditioning?" Linda climbed into the passenger seat up front and strapped on her seatbelt.

"Yes, it does." Josie turned on the air-conditioner as soon as she started the engine.

"Some of the *Englisch* don't use their air-conditioning, or they don't have it in their cars. I don't know which." Linda looked out of the window as they drove down the driveway.

"I can't imagine not having air-conditioning. Even though it's only May, it's already really warm." Josie glanced at Linda, who was staring at her. "I mean, I know you're used to not having air, but I guess it's just hard for me to imagine."

Linda finally pulled her gaze from Josie and looked straight ahead. "It's not so bad."

A few awkward moments of silence ensued. "So, would you like to see my home?"

Linda shrugged. "Sure."

"It has air-conditioning too," Josie said with a grin, trying to lighten the mood. Linda didn't say anything and kept her eyes on the open road ahead of them. Josie turned off of Black Horse Road and turned left onto Lincoln Highway.

"That's Barbie Beiler's place." Linda pointed to a bed and breakfast on the right. "Do you know her?"

"Uh, no. I haven't met very many people since I've—since I've been back." The questions were sure to come, and Josie hoped she could explain things in a way that Linda could understand. And forgive her.

"She's a *gut* friend. She gives us rides and helps us with things." She turned toward Josie, twisted her mouth to one side, and then asked, "Are you married?"

Wow. That came without much warning. "Uh, yes, I am." Josie pushed a strand of hair from her face. "His name is Robert."

"Is he . . . ?"

Josie turned her head to face Linda.

"Is he . . . my father?"

"No, oh no. He's a wonderful man, but he isn't your father. We've been married for twelve years."

"Do you have other . . ." Linda drew in a deep breath. "Do you have children?"

"No, we weren't able to have any. I mean, I wasn't able to have any more children after you were born."

"I have a lot of questions." Linda's voice was soft as she spoke, void of much emotion, and Josie worried what must be going through her head.

"And I will answer them all, as best I can." She pulled into her driveway.

Josephine's house was a big brick mansion and looked a lot like Barbie's bed and breakfast. "Just you and your husband live here?"

"Yes." Josephine turned off the car and opened her car door. Linda did the same, then walked alongside Josephine on the way up the sidewalk. She smelled good, sweet like honeysuckle. "Are you wearing perfume?"

"Yes, I am. Do you like it?" Josie turned the key in the front door. Linda nodded and tried to see through the fancy glass, but Josephine pushed the door open before Linda could preview what she was walking into. A whoosh of cool air hit her in the face, and she could hear soft music playing. Josephine pushed the door wide and motioned for Linda to walk in ahead of her.

Linda was barely inside the door, but she knew for sure that this was the fanciest house she'd ever been in. Her eyes drifted upward to a light that hung high in the entryway with lots of twinkling bulbs and dangling crystals that shone onto a white tiled floor. Farther in front of her, she could see wooden floors spreading throughout a large den area, but these floors were glossy and bright, unlike those at home. Josephine's furniture was rich-looking, and her blue couch spread in a half-circle around the room.

"Come on into the kitchen, and I'll pour us some tea." Josephine walked ahead of her, and Linda followed, walking slow, taking it all in.

When she entered the kitchen, she immediately felt more comfortable and was glad Josephine had suggested talking in here. The yellow walls and blue countertops made this room seem warmer, not so fancy. She saw familiar electric gadgets on the counter. Nothing out of the ordinary. She'd been in plenty of *Englisch* homes. Then her eyes rested on something new.

"What's that?" She pointed to a silver-shaped box with some sort of metal pipe coming out of it.

Josephine was pouring two glasses of tea but looked up. "Oh, that's an espresso machine. Robert and I often have a cup of cappuccino at night."

Linda stepped closer to the appliance to have a better look. "Is it like *kaffi*?"

Josephine placed two glasses of tea on a kitchen table that didn't look like any table Linda had seen before. It was all glass and had six high-back chairs with thick blue cushions. In the center, a pretty glass vase held a mixture of flowers and greenery, although the flowers weren't like anything Linda had seen in Amish gardens either.

"It's coffee, Italian coffee. It has milk foam on top." Josephine raised her brows. "Want me to make us each a cup?"

Linda stepped back from the elaborate coffeemaker. "Oh, no. That's all right. You've already prepared us tea." She nodded toward the two tall glasses of iced tea on the table but glanced back at the coffee machine on the counter.

Josephine ran her hand through hair that was the color of wheat, not brown like Linda's, and then she smiled. "You know, I think a cappuccino is just what we need. It sure sounds good to me. Why don't I make us some?"

"Okay." She liked coffee, although *Mamm* didn't encourage drinking too much of it. But she was anxious to see the machine work and to see coffee with foam on top.

Josephine began a process that captured Linda's attention, especially when Josephine poured milk into a small pitcher, then placed it under the pipe that made all sorts of odd sounds.

"We're steaming the milk now." She smiled at Linda. "I like to sprinkle nutmeg and cinnamon on mine. Do you want me to do that to yours too?"

"Sure." Linda watched her add white foam on top of two cups

of steaming coffee, then sprinkle the spices on top. "Josephine . . ."
She stopped and realized she had yet to call this woman by name.
"What do I call you? I mean, I have a mother and all."

Josephine carted the two cups of coffee to the table, pushed
the two glasses of tea to the side, and pulled out a chair for Linda.
"Here, sit down," she said.

Linda sat down and waited for her answer.

"My name is Josephine, but my friends and family call me Josie."
Her face shone with kindness, and Linda took a deep breath and
tried to settle her nerves. "Linda . . ." She paused, placed an elbow
on the table, then rested her chin atop it. "I would never expect
you to call me mother. Of course, you have a mother. I am just
hoping to be your friend, in whatever capacity you will allow me. I
just want to get to know you." She smiled. "Taste the cappuccino."

Linda brought the porcelain cup to her mouth and blew.
"Hot," she whispered, then took a sip. "It's *gut*." She took another
swig. "It's very *gut*." It was the best coffee she'd ever had.

"I'm glad you like it. Robert and I became fans of cappuccino
about six years ago. Now it's our thing to curl up on the couch
and have a cup in the evenings. Some people can't do that because
the caffeine will keep them up at night, but it doesn't bother us."

Linda took another sip and thought about how she'd like to
drink this kind of coffee every day.

"Josie? It's okay if I call you that?" Linda set the cup down and
Josie nodded.

"Of course. Josie is just fine."

Linda's stomach churned with anxiety, but she had to know.
"Why did you give me away? What would make a mother not
want her baby?"

Josie's eyes instantly clouded with tears, but Linda knew she needed this question answered first, before she and Josie could even move forward as friends. Josie stirred uneasily in her chair and tried to blink back tears.

"I wanted you very much," she said as a tear rolled down her cheek. She quickly wiped it away. "But my parents didn't want me to raise a baby. I was only seventeen at the time. Your age." She smiled at Linda, even though another tear trickled down her cheek. "But I wanted you very much. Handing you over to your parents two weeks after you were born was the hardest thing I have ever done. I prayed each day that you would be cared for and grow up to live a good life. My parents said that I was doing what God would want me to do, since Mary Ellen and Abe couldn't have children. Or, they didn't think they could at the time."

Linda was relieved to know that Josie had wanted to keep her, but equally as relieved to hear her speak of God. "I only found out about all this yesterday. My parents never told me that I was given to them."

"I know. Your father told me that on the phone when we arranged this meeting. I'm sorry, Linda. I know this must have been a shock to you." Josie took a sip of her coffee, then leaned back against the blue cushion. "But not a day has gone by that I haven't thought about you. I wanted you to be old enough to understand why I did what I did and to know that I loved you from the moment I laid eyes on you." Long black lashes blinked feverishly to keep more tears from falling. "I have a whole box full of pictures that I took that first two weeks after you were born."

"You do?" Since photos were not allowed, Linda had no idea what she looked like as a baby.

"Do you want to see them? Do you think your parents would mind?"

"They won't mind. *Ya*, I'd like to see them." Linda thought for a moment. "Do you have other pictures? Of you?"

Josie's eyes lit up. "I have lots of photo albums of me as well, but do you really want to see those?"

Of course I do! "*Ya*, I do, but . . ." Something was still looming over them.

"What is it, sweetie?"

Maybe it was the way Josie called her "sweetie," but Linda felt warm inside and comfortable enough to ask, "What about my father? What happened to him? Why did the two of you not get married?"

Josie rubbed her forehead with her hand, the one with the big ring on her finger. "We didn't love each other. He was older than me . . . and I didn't want to do what he wanted to do, but he forced me to, and . . ." She paused. "Linda, are you following what I'm saying?"

Linda shook her head. "No."

"Linda, he forced me to have sex with him, and that's how I got pregnant. He was not a very good man. He died a long time ago. I'm sorry to tell you this."

Linda could feel the flush in her cheeks. "Oh," she said softly, unsure how she felt about this news. They were quiet for a few moments. "Did he hurt you? This man who is my father."

Josie reached over and placed her hand on top of Linda's, and it felt strange, but nice. "My biggest hurt was losing you. And all that matters at this point is that we are becoming friends, and that you know that I always loved you, and never wanted to be away from you. Each year on your birthday, I'd have a cake, and I'd light candles for however many years old you were, and I'd sing to you."

"Really?"

Josie nodded. "Do you want to look at pictures now, while we have time before we go to lunch?"

"*Ya*, I would."

Linda had helped Josie lug several photo albums from her bedroom to the kitchen. Josie looked at them, scattered all over the kitchen table, most of them she hadn't opened in years. She'd tried not to bring the albums with pictures she wouldn't want Linda to see, like the one of her with her girlfriends at a bachelorette party when she was in her twenties, the time when a male dancer showed up. It was innocent, but Linda might not understand. Then there was the one when she and Robert were in Mexico, and Josie remembered the skimpy bikini she'd bought for that trip. Her mind was racing when Linda reached for one of the photo albums and opened it.

"Is that me?" She pointed to a baby in a pink T-shirt that said, *Mommy loves me.* Linda's eyes were glowing and hopeful.

"No, sweetheart. I'm afraid that's me." Josie remembered putting her two weeks' worth of photos in a little blue album, only big enough to hold single shots of Linda. She picked it up and handed it to Linda. "These are pictures of you."

"But the name on the front says Helen." Linda looked up at Josie with big blue, questioning eyes.

"That's what I called you. For two weeks anyway. I named you Helen."

Linda smiled. "Can I look at them?"

"Of course." Josie scooted her chair close to Linda. She wanted to put her arm around her, to hold her close. But just sitting next to her daughter, in her home, would be enough for now.

Linda giggled, and Josie's insides warmed like that of a proud mother. "That's me?" her daughter asked. "I look like a frog!" She laughed again.

Josie playfully poked her in the arm, smiling ear to ear. "Don't you dare say that about my beautiful baby! You did not look like a frog. You were beautiful, still are." She took a chance and put her arm around Linda, and instantly she felt Linda stiffen up and edge forward in the chair. Josie eased her arm back down to her side and refused to let that small thing derail the wonderful time they were having.

"Look at you there." Josie pointed to a picture of herself holding Linda on her aunt's couch, with her arm stretched wide. "I held the camera out and took that picture of us, that's why it looks kinda odd."

"You're so young." Linda turned toward Josie, frowning.

Josie stared at the picture. She remembered buying the disposable camera and hiding it from her aunt. Aunt Laura had thought it best for Josie not to keep any pictures of the baby, but Josie took pictures of Linda every chance she could. "I was your age. Seventeen. Almost eighteen."

"I'll be eighteen in August."

Josie smiled. "I know." She choked back tears as she thought that perhaps this year she would light candles and sing to her baby in person. To Helen. To Linda.

"I like the name Helen."

"I like the name Linda too." Josie watched her flip through the photos, slowly, as if memorizing each and every one.

When she looked at the last picture, she turned to Josie, her expression serious. "Did it hurt? To have a baby?"

"They say you forget about the pain, and I guess that's true, but I do remember it being rather painful." Josie handed Linda another photo album. "This one is pictures of me, before you were born. It was my sixteenth birthday."

Josie watched in awe as Linda smiled and studied the photos. "I look like you, no?"

"Yes, you do." She covered her mouth with her hand and fought the knot building in her throat.

Josie watched Linda scan each and every photo album and answered all her questions about those in the pictures. It took over an hour for her to go through them all.

"*Danki*," she said when she closed the last album.

"You're very welcome. Do you want to go to Katie's Kitchen now?"

"*Ya.*"

Josie left the albums on the table, found her purse, and they headed out the door. "Do you have a boyfriend?"

"*Ya.*" Linda smiled as her cheeks turned a rosy shade of pink. "His name is Stephen Ebersol."

"Oh, I'd like to hear all about him at lunch, if you'd like to tell me."

"*Ya*, I would."

Linda was glowing, and Josie knew that this was the happiest day of her life. And since the doctors had told her to enjoy each and every day she still had, that is exactly what she planned to do.

6

MARY ELLEN PACKED A BASKET WITH A LOAF OF ZUCCHINI
bread, two loaves of regular homemade bread, and a generous
supply of raisin puffs. Her nephew, David, loved the fluffy cookies rolled in cinnamon and sugar. She knew Lillian was racing back
and forth between her own home and her *maam's* so she could help
take care of Jonas and Lizzie. It was a small offering, but if Mary
Ellen were honest with herself, she also needed the distraction to
keep her thoughts from venturing to Linda and Josephine.

She hitched up the spring buggy, loaded the basket in the
back, and headed to Lillian and Samuel's. On the way, though, she
barely noticed the gentle breeze and colorful foliage. Every time
she thought about Linda and Josephine spending the day together,
her stomach twisted in knots. And she wondered how Abe's conversation was going with Matt and Luke. Would their boys be just
as upset by the news of Linda's adoption as Linda? *I should have gone
with Abe to tell them.*

"Whoa." She pulled the buggy to a stop next to the family
buggy parked at Lillian and Samuel's, picked up her basket, and
headed to the house. Lillian met her on the porch.

"How are you holding up?"

"What?" Mary Ellen offered her the basket. "What do you mean?"

Lillian pushed back a strand of loose hair, tucked it beneath her *kapp*, then stepped closer and accepted the basket. She put her free hand on Mary Ellen's forearm. "David told us. About Linda. About her being adopted. I honestly didn't know."

Mary Ellen wasn't surprised that Linda had confided in her cousin; they'd always been close. "It happened so long ago, way before you married Samuel. We just don't speak of it, so I'm not surprised that Samuel didn't tell you."

"When I asked Samuel about it, he said he just never thought to tell me, that Linda is just as much a part of this family as anyone." Lillian opened the screen door and motioned Mary Ellen into the kitchen. "Here, sit down. Samuel and David are working in the barn, and Anna and Elizabeth are down for their naps. This is a perfect time for us to talk."

Mary Ellen took a seat on one of the wooden benches in Lillian's kitchen. "They're together now. Linda and her mother."

"*You're* her mother, Mary Ellen. Nothing is going to change that."

"And Abe is telling Matt and Luke this morning." Mary Ellen covered her face with both hands and shook her head. "We made such a mistake, Lillian." She pulled her hands away and rubbed tired eyes. "We should have told Linda and the boys about this a long time ago, way before Josephine came callin'."

"Maybe so. But, Mary Ellen, love runs much deeper than a bloodline. You know that. No one is ever going to replace you as Linda's mother."

Mary Ellen was quiet for a few moments. "I know nothing about this woman Josephine. Is she a good Christian woman? Will she be a *gut* influence on our Linda?"

"Linda might not even want to have a relationship with this woman. They might just spend the day together and that will be it. Linda might just be curious now that she's been told, and she might not want to see this woman again."

Mary Ellen sighed. "Lillian, I know it's wrong of me to want that, but that's exactly what I want. God help me, but I don't want that woman in our lives. I'm praying about it constantly, and I know my thoughts aren't Christian, but I can't help it."

"Did she seem nice?"

"*Ya*, she did. She even invited me to go with her and Linda."

Lillian sat up taller. "Why didn't you?"

Mary Ellen shrugged. "I reckon we've made a mess of things up to this point, and I felt like Linda should have this time with Josephine by herself." She paused. "She's very pretty, the *Englisch* woman."

Lillian smiled. "So are you."

Mary Ellen forced a smile. "*Danki*, Lillian." But these days when Mary Ellen looked in the mirror, she no longer saw the person she remembered herself to be. Instead, the face that stared back at her had tiny lines feathering from the corners of each eye, and depending on the hours of sleep she'd had, often dark circles underneath eyes that seemed smaller somehow, less vibrant. And her hair, once a silky dark brown, was now speckled with gray. She thought about Josephine's honey-blonde hair, her perfectly made-up face, and the way her clothes complemented her shapely figure. Mary Ellen knew that vanity is a sin, but as her thirty-eighth birthday approached, it was hard not to see the physical changes taking place. She glanced at hands worn by years of hard work, and she suspected Josephine used fancy lotions to keep her hands smooth and young-looking.

"How is Jonas?" Mary Ellen was ready to talk about something else.

Lillian blew out an exasperated breath and rolled her eyes. "Demanding." She smiled. "It's a *gut* thing we all love Grandpa so much, because some days he is just a *schtinker*." Lillian shook her head. "*Mei mamm* and Lizzie have their hands full. I go by there every day and try to help, but it's hard because I have *mei* own family to take care of too."

"Is there anything I can do?"

Lillian pointed to the basket. "I don't have to bake any bread tomorrow morning since you brought us that basket. *Danki*, Mary Ellen. That's a big help."

"I'll do whatever I can." Mary Ellen reached over and placed her hand on Lillian's.

"*Danki*. We're all getting by just fine, but when Grandpa gets in one of his nasty moods, it's just terrible. I know he feels badly and all, but yesterday he demanded that someone shave his beard off. We didn't know what to do."

Mary Ellen let out a slight gasp. "Why? That would be unheard of."

"*Mamm* tried to calmly remind him that when a man gets married, he never shaves his beard." Lillian stifled a grin. "Do you know what he told her?"

Mary Ellen arched her brows. "No tellin'."

"He told *Mamm* that there are tiny little people living in his beard and that they talk all the time, keeping him up at night. Then he talked ugly to *Mamm* and told her he'd shave it himself."

Mary Ellen chuckled, but quickly bit her bottom lip. "I'm sorry, Lillian. I know it's not funny."

"It's okay. It's hard not to laugh at something so out of character for Grandpa."

"What did Sarah Jane do?"

Lillian smiled. "*Mamm* told the little people in his beard to be quiet, then pretended to give them one of Grandpa's sleeping pills."

"Did that work?"

Lillian shrugged. "Seemed to."

Mary Ellen thought for a moment. "Does Jonas understand what's happening?"

"*Ya.* He does. When his mind is *gut*, he says he is ready to go be with the Lord."

They sat quietly for a minute.

"How is Lizzie handlin' things?"

"Pretty *gut* on most days, but I heard her crying in the bathroom the other day. She won't show much emotion in front of anyone, especially Grandpa, but I know she's hurting."

"Of course she is." Mary Ellen paused. "The world won't be the same without your grandpa in it."

"No. It won't." Lillian's eyes filled with water. "But how blessed we all are to know him and have him in our lives."

Mary Ellen nodded as she blinked back her own tears.

Abe loaded the last of the tools he'd purchased at the farmer's market, while Matt and Luke stowed several bags of groceries in the buggy, items from Mary Ellen's list. His wife had offered to be with Abe when he told Matt and Luke about Linda's adoption, but Abe feared his wife's current state of mind might only make things worse. Matt and Luke were young men, and Abe reckoned he should be the one to talk to them. He waited until they were clear of the city and moving down Black Horse Road toward home.

Matthew was in the front seat with Abe, and Luke sat beside the groceries and tools in the backseat. Abe slowed the horse to a trot and took a deep breath.

"Boys, there is something I need to talk with you about." He held the reins with one hand as he tipped his hat back with the other, wiping sweat from his brow.

Neither boy said anything. Matt seemed preoccupied with a flyer he was reading, something about an upcoming Mud Sale in nearby Strasburg.

"It's about Linda," Abe continued.

"What's she done?" Matt didn't look up, but snickered.

Abe sighed as he stifled his irritation at Matt's comment. "She didn't do anything."

Matt closed the brochure. "Then what is it?"

Abe stared straight ahead and wondered why he hadn't planned out this conversation. He'd prayed that it would just come to him. "Your sister is adopted. Your *mamm* and I adopted her when she was two-weeks-old. We should have told you before now, but as we speak, Linda is spending time with the woman who gave birth to her." Abe glanced to his right. Matt's eyes were wide, his jaw dropped. "I'm sorry we didn't tell you before now."

"Are you serious?" Matt raised his brows at his father.

"*Ya.* I'm serious."

Matt looped his thumbs beneath his suspenders and sat taller. "I knew there was something different about her. That explains it." Then he chuckled.

"Shut up, Matt! Just shut up! You're just stupid, and . . ." Luke slammed both hands on the top of the seat in front of him.

"No, you're stupid!" Matt twisted in his seat, his eyes blazing with anger.

"Whoa!" Abe quickly pulled the horse and buggy to the side of the road. "Both of you, stop it this minute!"

"*Daed*, is it true?" Luke leaned forward into the front seat. "Is Linda really not our sister?"

Abe twisted in the seat to face his youngest son, whose eyes were filled with tears. "Linda will always be your sister. No matter what."

"I don't understand then." Luke's bottom lip trembled.

Abe looked at Matt, who was staring straight ahead, his lips pressed firmly together. Matt always hid his feelings with anger, so Abe wasn't surprised at his reaction. He focused on Luke as he spoke.

"Your *mamm* and I tried to have children for quite a while. When the Lord didn't bless us with any, we began to think that perhaps we just weren't able to have any *kinner*. Linda's birth mother was seventeen and pregnant at the time, and a lawyer made an arrangement for us to raise Linda as our own."

Matt kept staring straight ahead, but grunted. "*Ya*, I reckon someone should have mentioned this before now."

"Does Linda know yet?" Luke's voice trembled as he spoke.

Matt spun around. "Aren't you listening? *Daed* said she's with that woman now."

"Matthew, that is enough. You watch that tone of voice. Do you hear me?" Abe leaned forward toward his son.

Matt turned back around and stared straight ahead. "Yes, sir."

"Linda's my sister." Luke held his head up high. "No matter what."

Abe smiled. "That's right. Nothing is going to change."

"Everything has changed." Matthew shook his head, and Abe knew that his oldest son was taking this harder than he let on. When Abe saw Matt's bottom lip quiver, he reached over and laid a hand on Matt's shoulder.

"I know you boys are hurting right now. Your *mamm* and I are hurting too. But this will take a toll on Linda more than anyone, and I need you boys to be strong for her. She is still your sister."

Abe faced forward, grabbed the reins, and flicked the horse into motion. He looked forward, but he saw Matt swipe at his eyes.

He knew his boys were strong young men. It was just going to take them a little time. That's all. Time.

We should have told them all sooner.

But for now, there was nothing else to say. Abe raised his chin and kept his eyes straight ahead.

Josie pulled the car to a stop in front of Linda's home, sad that their time together was coming to an end.

"*Danki* for showing me all the pictures and for buying *mei* lunch at Katie's Kitchen." Linda reached for the handle on the passenger door, but first turned to Josie and smiled. "And for letting me put on some of your perfume."

"You're welcome." Josie's mind was spinning. There hadn't been enough time. Linda pushed the car door open. "Linda?"

"*Ya?*"

Josie couldn't say anything for a moment; it was like looking into a mirror seventeen years ago, except that Josie would have been wearing blue jeans, a T-shirt, and her hair in a ponytail, but Josie recognized herself in Linda's face for sure. "Would you like to do something on Saturday? I don't really know what's allowed, and I wouldn't want to do anything to upset your parents. I guess movies aren't something you can do, or—"

"I can." Linda's face brightened. "I'm in *mei rumschpringe*, so I can go to movies and do things in the *Englisch* world."

"Want me to pick you up around noon?"

Linda tapped her finger to her chin. "Would you mind if we made it around three, so I'll have time to finish my Saturday chores?"

"Sure."

Linda smiled, then pushed the door open and stepped out of the car. Josie watched her walk up to the house, unfamiliar feelings rising to the surface and filling her with a love she didn't think she'd ever known.

As Linda tiptoed into the house, an overwhelming feeling of guilt overtook her. She'd had a good time with Josie and found her to be kind, generous, and fun to be around. Linda liked the way she smiled, too, the way she looked. She was pretty, and Linda couldn't help but wonder if people thought she was pretty too, like Josie. She sniffed her wrist, the spot where Josie had sprayed the sweet-smelling perfume.

"Hello."

Linda jumped when she heard her mother speak to her from the bottom step of the stairs. She was holding a broom, and more guilt consumed Linda as she realized that her chores fell on her mother today. Linda crossed the den and reached for the broom.

"I'll finish up. I'm sorry I was gone so long. I didn't know—"

Mamm pulled the broom back. "No, no. I'm done, and no harm done. Let's sit. I want to hear all about your day with . . ." She paused. "What is that sweet smell?"

Linda could feel her cheeks reddening. "Josie let me try a little of her perfume." She held her wrist up, just in case her mother wanted to get a better whiff. She didn't. Linda followed her to the couch and took a seat beside her.

"Did you go to Katie's Kitchen?"

"*Ya*, we did. Anna Marie was our waitress." Anna Marie was Ben and Martha King's daughter, and Linda had grown up with her.

"Did you tell Anna Marie who—who you were dining with?"

Linda shook her head. "No, *Mamm*."

Her mother let out air she'd seemed to be holding. "What else did you do?" *Mamm* clenched her lips tight, and Linda wasn't sure how much to say.

"Not much." She shrugged.

Mamm twisted on the couch to face Linda. "Linda, you don't have to be afraid to share with me." She looked down. "Or, if you're not comfortable, I understand."

Linda didn't say anything for a moment as she tucked her chin. Then she looked up to see her mother waiting for some sort of response. "She's nice."

"*Gut.*"

This was the first time Linda had ever felt awkward talking to her mother, yet it was the one time when she felt like she needed her the most. "She has the fanciest house I've ever seen, *Mamm*.

And it's big." She paused and checked her mother's expression. *Mamm* smiled, but not a full smile. "She's married too. But they don't have any other—I mean any children."

Her mother nodded, then her eyes warmed, and Linda's stomach settled a little bit. "You're very pretty, like she is." *Mamm* pushed back a strand of hair that had fallen from beneath Linda's *kapp*.

"I always thought I looked like you," Linda said sheepishly. "That's what everyone always said."

"*Ya*, people have always said that. They say you have my cute little pug nose." She playfully poked Linda's nose. Linda smiled.

"*Mamm*." Linda reached for her mother's hand. "You should have told me a long time ago about Josie."

Her mother twisted her head and stared at the wall to their left. "I know."

"But nothing is going to change. I love you. You are my mother and will always be my mother."

Mamm kept her head turned toward the wall but reached up and swiped at her eye. When she turned to face Linda, all Linda wanted to do was crawl in her lap like she'd done when she was a little girl and have her mother stroke her head, the loving way only a mother can. When *Mamm* opened her arms, Linda folded into them, and they both held each other for several minutes.

"She wants to see me again on Saturday afternoon," Linda said after a while. She felt her mother instantly stiffen, and she wondered if perhaps she'd forbid her to go.

"I suspected that she would want to spend more time with you." *Mamm* eased out of the hug, cupped her hand under Linda's chin, and said, "And that is all right."

Linda felt relief, but there was something about the way her mother spoke that made Linda suspect that it wasn't as all right as *Mamm* let on.

Josie had a spring in her step that she didn't remember having for years, and it had been a long time since she'd used her fine china and set the table in the formal dining room, complete with candles and fresh flowers. She stepped back to inspect her work. *Perfect.* She heard the front door open, glad that Robert was on time. She had so much to tell him. The timer on the oven dinged, and she headed back to the kitchen. She pulled the pan from the oven just as Robert entered the kitchen. She looked up in time to see him glance into the formal dining room.

"I take it things must have gone well today." He placed his briefcase on the kitchen counter, waited for her to put the pan down, then wrapped his arms around her.

"Oh, Robert. It was a perfect day." She buried her head in his chest and squeezed him tightly.

He gently eased her away. "Josie, I'm so glad, and I want to hear all about it, but I have some news for you."

She arched her brows. What could possibly be more important than her news?

"Remember Dr. Noah Stoltzfus, the doctor who put me in touch with some people at Lancaster General regarding Amanda?"

She nodded.

"Well, Noah also knows someone whose specialization is the type of inoperable tumor that you have."

No, no. Don't ruin this day. She pulled away, turned her back toward him, and combed a hand through her hair. "Robert, I don't want to see any more doctors. I've seen plenty, and they all say the same thing."

Robert gently spun her around, cupped her cheek, and gazed lovingly into her eyes. "Just one more, Josie. Please. Do it for me."

Josie twisted her mouth to one side, then the other. "I thought Dr. Stoltzfus ran a small clinic and catered mostly to the Amish community."

"He does. But he used to work at Lancaster General, and he has friends there. You know how hard it can be to get an appointment with a really good specialist. It can take months." They both looked at each other, and there was no need to verbalize what was on both their minds—how many months? "Please," he said again, his eyes begging her. He kissed her on the cheek. "I invited him and his wife for dinner. Can we set two more place settings?"

Josie pushed away from him. "Robert, why didn't you give me any warning?" She thrust her hands on her hips. "And I have so much to tell you about my day with Linda, and . . ."

"I know, baby. I tried to call all the way home and kept getting 'call failed' . . . And I want to hear every little detail about your day with Linda. I'm so happy for you. But I think it's important for you to meet Noah. I've met his wife several times when I've been at his clinic. I think you'll like her."

Josie let out a heavy sigh. "I guess I don't have much choice. Let me go get two more place settings."

Robert gently grabbed her arm. "Hey, come here, you." He pulled her close again, cupped the nape of her neck, and whispered, "I'm not giving up. Do you hear me?"

Josie eased away and looked him in the eyes. "This was such a good day for me, Robert. I just want to share it all with you, and I'm so tired of talking about medical stuff."

"Tonight, over a glass of wine, after our guests are gone, I want to hear every little detail of your day with Linda." He paused with pleading eyes. "But let's hear about Noah's specialist. Please."

Josie forced a smile for Robert's sake. She'd accepted her fate years ago. It terrified her, but she'd accepted it. Robert hadn't. "I hope they like beef parmesan and fettuccini," she said in a pouty voice.

"They will love whatever you made. They will love you." He kissed her on the lips, then pulled away when they heard a knock at the door.

"They're here."

7

JOSIE HAD BARELY ADDED THE EXTRA PLACE SETTINGS when Robert opened the door.

"Carley, Noah, so nice to see you." Robert stepped aside so the couple could enter. Josie joined them in the foyer, and she tried to mask her disappointment by forcing a smile. Good thing she'd chosen her good china.

"This is my wife, Josie."

Josie extended her hand to Carley, then to Noah. "So nice to meet you both."

Robert motioned everyone toward the living room, and he wound his way around the wet bar in the corner. "Can I get anyone a drink before dinner?"

"No, we're fine," Noah said as his eyes scanned the room. "This is a beautiful home you have."

"It really is." Carley smiled at Josie.

"I'm still unpacking boxes. I should already be done." Josie waved her arm around the room where a few boxes were still pushed up against the walls.

"It takes time." Carley smiled warmly. "But you've done an amazing job so far. It's really pretty."

I want our home to be perfect for Robert after I'm gone. "Thank you."

She paused. "Robert said you have a daughter?" Josie walked toward the couch, sat down, and motioned for Carley to do the same. Robert and Noah sat down in high-back chairs facing the couch. "I thought he said her name is Jenna? How old is she?"

Carley's face lit up at the mention of her daughter, and Josie could certainly understand that. "Jenna is nine, and we've had her for four glorious years. We adopted her when she was five."

"Really?" Josie crossed her legs and leaned forward. "From an agency?"

"No. Actually, Jenna's parents died and her older sister, Dana, had been raising her, but when Dana went off to college, she asked Noah and me if we would like to adopt Jenna. Noah was a good friend of their family before he and I got married." Carley paused. "I couldn't have any children, so we felt very blessed to be able to adopt Jenna."

"Josie recently reconnected with her daughter that she gave up for adoption," Robert said, much to her horror. How could he possibly bring up something so personal to these people she didn't even know? She cut her eyes at him in a way that told Robert he'd messed up. "She was very young," he added, as if that would make up for his blunder.

"Well, we are big advocates of adoption," Noah said. "I think it's a wonderful thing you did. You said you recently reconnected?"

Even though Noah directed the question to Josie, Robert stepped in once more. "The main reason we moved here is so that Josie could find her daughter. She's seventeen now. This is where Josie used to live, in Lancaster County."

"It was an open adoption," Josie added. This was not how she had envisioned her night at all, sharing something so personal with total strangers. She'd looked forward to a quiet dinner with Robert and an opportunity to share everything with him about her day with Linda. To make things even worse, a knot was building in her throat, and she choked back tears. She could feel Carley's eyes on her.

"Josie, I'd love to see your house." Carley stood up, and Josie stood up beside her.

"Sure."

"You girls go ahead," Robert said. "Okay with you, Noah? I'll show you around later."

Noah nodded, and Carley followed Josie around the corner and down a hallway lined with four bedrooms. "This is our bedroom," Josie said as her emotions about everything continued to build.

Carley didn't seem too interested in the bedroom, but instead stood staring at Josie, and then did the most unexpected thing. She walked toward her, grabbed her hand, and said, "You looked like you were about to lose it in there. Are you all right?"

Josie clutched this stranger's hand. Shallow gasps escaped, she bit her lip, and shook her head. As a tear fell, she let go of Carley's hand and wiped it away. "I'm so sorry. I've just had a very emotional day, and I just didn't expect Robert to bring up the subject of Linda."

Carley's eyes were kind and sympathetic. "Yes, I could tell that it bothered you. You don't even know us. Is that your daughter's name? Linda?"

"Yes. I spent the day with her today for the first time since I gave her up for adoption seventeen years ago."

"Oh my gosh. We shouldn't even be here." Carley shook her

head. "I'm sure you want to spend time with your husband and tell him all about it." She smiled. "Instead, Robert drags in dinner guests."

"No, no. It's fine, really." Josie was starting to feel somewhat comfortable around this woman. "It's just very—very personal."

"Of course it is. We don't have to talk about it at all. I just thought you might want to get away from the men for a few minutes. Men. They're so insensitive sometimes."

"Yes, they can be." Josie appreciated Carley's attempt at lighthearted humor.

"When we adopted Jenna, I worried about so many things. I know that I was on the other end of the spectrum, but if you ever want to talk, please call me. I know that tonight, Noah wants to talk with Robert and you about a specialist at Lancaster General who deals with the kind of tumor you have." Carley took a deep breath. "Wow. You have a lot going on, huh?"

Josie smiled. "You could say that. But I know everything is going to work out fine."

"I will pray for you, Josie. For you. For Linda. And for good news from this new doctor."

Josie smiled and thanked her, even though she knew prayers would go unanswered. Why would God possibly help someone who'd turned away from Him a long time ago? Josie could recall a time when she had a closer relationship with God, before she married Robert. But Robert didn't believe in God, and slowly over time, Josie's own beliefs had veered to questioning whether or not such an entity existed.

But with little time on her side, she couldn't help but speculate about God. And the possibility of heaven. Or hell.

After dinner, Josie served everyone coffee in the living room. Noah said Dr. Phillips had agreed to meet with Josie on the following Thursday at Lancaster General to evaluate the tumor growing inside her brain stem.

"Thank you for setting up this appointment." Robert took a sip of his coffee. "We really appreciate it."

"Yes, we do," Josie echoed to be polite. She'd enjoyed meeting Noah and Carley. Dinner conversation had been light and engaging, but she was ready to spend some quiet time with Robert, fill him in about her day with Linda.

"We'd like to put you on our prayer list at church," Noah said. "There's nothing like the power of prayer."

"That would be great." Josie glanced at Robert, who merely smiled. "We'd appreciate that."

"I don't know if it's ever come up, but I grew up Amish." Noah pushed back dark wavy locks, and Josie tried to envision the doctor with a bobbed haircut and sporting suspenders and a straw hat.

"Really?" Josie's eyes grew wide. "What happened?"

Noah set his coffee cup down on a coaster on the coffee table. "I had a strong calling to become a doctor." He paused. "If I'd made that decision before I was baptized, things would have been a lot easier. Instead, I was baptized into the faith, then chose to leave, and I was shunned by my family."

"Oh, no." Josie said. "I remember when I was growing up here, I heard of a man getting shunned. I didn't know him very well, but I just remember that he couldn't have anything to do with his family, not even sit down and have a meal with them."

"I had a terrible time understanding the whole shunning process," Carley chimed in. "But, luckily for Noah, his family eventually came around, and the bishop has pretty much looked the other way and allowed members of the community to visit his clinic."

"So, you have a good relationship with your family now?" Josie took a sip from her own cup of coffee.

"Yes, I do. But it took a while. My brother, Samuel, had a really hard time accepting me back into the family. It's a long story. I ended up giving my nephew one of my kidneys, and I think everyone had to take a good long look at the whole issue of shunning."

"Wow. That's amazing," Josie said. "How is your nephew now?"

"David is great. He's had no trouble since the transplant." Noah paused, glancing at his wife. "We've all been very blessed. My other brother, Ivan, and both my sisters eventually came around, and we don't flaunt it in front of the bishop, but we all spend time together. My sister, Mary Ellen, was sort of the cheerleader, pushing everyone to play nice." He chuckled. "And my niece, Linda, even worked for me for a couple of weeks a year or two ago, doing some filing for us. So, we've all come a long way."

Josie's heart began to thud against her chest. She glanced at Robert who had begun to squirm in his chair, then Robert stood up, and offered to pick up everyone's coffee cup, almost a rude gesture that the night should come to an end. Josie knew he didn't mean it that way, and she could tell by her husband's worrisome expression that he was fearful Josie had heard Noah loud and clear.

"Linda is your niece, and Mary Ellen is your sister?" Josie stood up when Carley and Noah did.

Robert set all the dishes haphazardly down on the coffee table, spilling coffee out of one. "We'll have to do this another time," he said smiling. "This has been great getting together like this."

Carley and Noah began to move toward the door. "It really has been fun." Then Carley turned to Josie. "Oh, and yes, Linda is the name of Noah's niece and Mary Ellen is his sister."

The two women locked eyes, and Josie knew her own eyes were big as golf balls. As if connecting to Josie's thoughts, Carley's bulged too. "Linda . . ." she whispered. "*Your* Linda?"

Josie nodded to Carley.

Friday morning, Mary Ellen was busy deep cleaning the down-stairs in preparation for worship service at their home on Sunday. Abe and the boys were at her brother Ivan's house, helping him paint his fence, and Linda had gone along to visit with Katie Ann. Mary Ellen knew that Katie Ann was lonely, no children to take care of. No one was quite sure why they hadn't been able to have children. Once, Mary Ellen mentioned the possibility of adoption to Katie Ann, but Katie Ann wouldn't hear of it. "The Lord will bless us when He's ready," she'd said. Ivan and Katie Ann certainly knew that Linda was adopted, so she didn't understand why they wouldn't mull over the possibility, but it was not her business.

Her thoughts drifted back to Linda and Josephine as she fin-ished up dusting, giving the mantel a final swipe, when she heard a knock at the door.

She saw Noah at the screen door. "I needed a break." She pushed open the door to the den. "Come in, *mei bruder*." She nar-rowed her brows. "What are you doing here? Shouldn't you be at the clinic?"

Noah blew out a heavy sigh and scratched his forehead. "Yeah, but I need to talk to you about something."

Mary Ellen stuffed her cleaning rag in the pocket of her black apron. "You look so serious. Everything is all right, no? Jenna, she is okay? Carley?"

"Yes. Everyone is okay." Noah sat down on the couch. "Do you remember when I told you that I'd recently met an attorney that I was helping find a doctor for his receptionist?"

Mary Ellen sat down on the couch beside Noah and thought for a moment. "No, I don't think so . . . *Ach*, wait, the girl with the disfigured lip?" Mary Ellen recalled a conversation she'd had with Noah a few weeks ago at his office. She'd taken Matt to see his uncle for a deep cut he'd gotten while working out in the barn. As Noah stitched up Matt's arm, he'd told her about the lawyer he'd met who offered to help his receptionist. "I remember, you said you thought a lot of this man."

"Yes, I do. He seems to go out of his way to help others, often without taking any money for his services. I admire his work ethics." Noah sighed. "Carley and I dined with him and his wife last night."

"That's nice," she said hesitantly. She knew Noah well enough to know that he was trying to get to a point, and it must be an important point to cause him to leave the clinic on a Friday morning to come talk to her.

Noah blew out a long breath. "Samuel told me about Linda, about her being adopted. He didn't want me to find out from someone else, since her birth mother has come looking for her."

I should have known what he was coming to talk about. "It has been a *hatt* situation." Mary Ellen rubbed her forehead. "We just never spoke of it, and of course, we took Linda in when you were away."

Noah stood up from the couch. He didn't look like a doctor in his blue jeans, loafers, and a bright yellow shirt—a "golf shirt" is what he'd called it in the past, which didn't make much sense since Noah didn't play golf. Noah always dressed that way when he worked at the clinic. Seemed to make people in the community more at ease when they saw him wearing it, as opposed to what doctors usually wore, either starched white shirts or those blue pants and shirts that looked like pajamas.

He tucked his hands deep into the pockets of his pants and paced for a moment. "Robert is the name of my friend." He glanced at Mary Ellen. "His wife gave up a baby for adoption."

Mary Ellen rose from the couch and walked toward him. "Why would they, Robert and his wife, do such a thing if they are married?"

"No, no. *They* didn't give up a baby; *she* did. A long time ago."

Mary Ellen tilted her head to one side and waited for Noah to go on.

"His—his wife's name is Josephine."

Mary Ellen put her hand to her chest and hoped that Noah wouldn't confirm what she knew to be true.

"Yes, Linda's mo—I mean the person who gave birth to her."

"And you are friends with these people?" Mary Ellen's brows leaned into a frown, and she knew that she had no right to feel betrayed, yet she did.

"I've been friends with Robert for weeks, but I only met Josephine last night when Carley and I ate dinner with them. I've been trying to help them—"

"I don't want to hear." Mary Ellen held one hand in the air, then turned her back to Noah. "I have to hear about Josephine from Linda, and it's hard for me." She covered her mouth with her hand, as if that would prevent her from spewing the vicious thoughts in her mind where Josephine was concerned. She'd given her baby away, and she should have respected that decision. Mary Ellen turned slowly around to face her brother. "Do you understand, Noah? Do you understand that her being here is a complete upset to our household? Not only was Linda upset, but Matt and Luke began to question whether or not I'd actually given birth to them, even after Abe talked with them. It's just all been terrible, and I'm afraid . . ." She choked back tears.

"Afraid that Linda will leave to go be with Josephine and live in the *Englisch* world?" Noah put a hand on her shoulder. "That's not going to happen."

"How can you be so sure?"

Noah stared long and hard into Mary Ellen's eyes. "Josie is sick."

"What do you mean, sick?" Mary Ellen folded her hands in front of her.

"That's what I was trying to tell you. I'm helping them get in to see a specialist at Lancaster General. It usually takes months to get an appointment to see Dr. Phillips, but I knew him well when I worked with him at the hospital, and he is doing this as a special favor. When Robert told me about Josie, I wanted to help, to make sure they'd utilized all their options."

"What do you mean, this utilizing of options? What does that mean?" *And what is wrong with her?*

"Mary Ellen . . ." He paused as his eyes saddened in such a way that Mary Ellen feared what he would say. "Josie is going to die within six months because she has an inoperable tumor on her brain. I want Dr. Phillips to have a look at her. He could be their last hope, and Dr. Phillips is a brilliant surgeon."

Mary Ellen folded at the waist and grasped her knees. "Oh, no." Her insides twisted in agony as a stab of guilt bore into her heart.

Noah wrapped his arm around her shoulder. "Mary Ellen, are you all right? I didn't realize that you knew Josie that well, or at all. I mean, I know Linda will be upset." He paused. "She just wants to know Linda while she has a chance. They moved here just for that reason."

"Oh, no," Mary Ellen said again. "Dear Lord, forgive me. Oh, Heavenly Father, forgive me."

Noah latched onto her shoulders and forced her to a standing position. He faced her and said, "Mary Ellen, what is it? Tell me what's wrong."

"Oh, Noah," she cried. "I've done a horrible thing. I've sinned a far greater sin than I could have imagined myself to do. Oh, Noah." She leaned into his arms. "This is my fault. It's my fault she's dying."

Noah pushed her away. "What? What are you talking about?"

"I prayed, Noah. I prayed to God to make her go away, to leave here, and—"

"Mary Ellen, listen to me. This is not your fault. Josie has been sick for a long time. Do you hear me? You didn't have anything to do with her brain tumor."

Mary Ellen sniffled and felt her guilt subsiding a little, but then she thought about the beautiful *Englisch* woman only a few years younger than her and how her life might be tragically cut short. Only moments earlier, she was wishing and praying for Josephine to go away, but never like this. Then she remembered the specialist and hoped her guilt would be even more relieved. "Will your friend, this Dr. Phillips, be able to save her?"

Noah sighed. "I don't think so. But I want him to review her test results, just to be sure."

They were quiet for a minute. Mary Ellen sat down on the couch, propped her elbows on her knees, and put her chin in her hands. "Linda finds out that she has a mother, only to have her taken away."

"You're her mother, Mary Ellen." Noah sat down beside her.

Mary Ellen rubbed her tired eyes and sat quietly, thinking. Then she turned to Noah. "You will let me know about this meeting with Dr. Phillips, if he can help her or not?"

"Yes. I will."

"Maybe we shouldn't say anything to Linda until we know for sure."

"I agree." Noah paused. "Mary Ellen, do you think maybe it's Josie's place to tell Linda?"

Mary Ellen swallowed hard. "*Ya*, I reckon so."

"I need to get back to the clinic." Noah stood up and walked toward the door. Mary Ellen got up and followed him. "I just wanted you to know what's going on. Linda might need you more than ever in the near future, especially if she gets close to Josie."

Mary Ellen nodded, then thanked Noah for stopping by. After the door closed between them, she stood where she was and bowed her head.

Forgive me, Lord.

8

STEPHEN HELPED LINDA'S FATHER AND TWO BROTHERS set up benches in the family's den in preparation for worship service the following day. When Stephen's family hosted worship, they removed a wall partition that separated a small den from a larger living area, but the Huyard's den was exceptionally large and all the benches fit nicely after moving the couch and two rockers into another room.

As was tradition, they lined several rows of benches for the men facing one way and more benches for the women facing toward them, leaving room in the middle for Stephen's grandfather, the ministers, and deacons.

Stephen poked his head into the kitchen and saw Linda pulling a loaf of bread from the oven. Someday, she'd be baking bread in a home they would share together, just as soon as Stephen could build up enough courage to ask Linda to marry him. He loved her plenty, that was for sure, and they were both planning to be baptized in the fall, but being married to Linda would mean that she'd see him without his elevated shoe on, hobbling around the house off-balance. She'd told him over and over that it didn't matter to her one bit.

He smiled when he recalled Linda pulling her dress up slightly above her knee to reveal a birthmark she'd had since birth, an oblong circle of red that ran a good four inches up her leg. "See, I'm not perfect either," she'd said.

But she was perfect. Warm, loving, beautiful, and a great cook. He'd eaten plenty of meals with the Huyards since he and Linda had started dating a year ago, and many of those meals Linda had prepared. She was going to make a wonderful wife, and Stephen knew he needed to just go ahead and do it, ask her to be his *fraa*. They would publish their announcement in the paper and most likely wait until the following November or December to get married, when they were both almost nineteen and after they'd both been baptized into the faith.

Stephen helped Luke shift the last bench into place just as Linda rounded the corner into the den.

"Looks *gut*." She folded her arms across her chest. "And I finished all my chores."

Good. Stephen was ready to have some alone time with Linda. He playfully raised one brow in her direction and waited until Luke was out of earshot. "Let's get out of here." His eyes met with hers, and he couldn't wait to hold her in his arms, kiss her again.

"I can't. Josie is picking me up at three. Didn't I tell you?"

Linda had filled him in about her time with Josie, but he couldn't recall her saying that she was spending Saturday afternoon with her. He was pretty sure she hadn't or he would have remembered, but he tried to mask his disappointment since he knew all this was hard on Linda.

"I'm sorry." She reached up and touched his arm. "But we'll see each other here at worship tomorrow."

"*Ya.* It's all right. I know it's important for you to get to know this woman."

She kicked at the wood floor with her toe and tucked her chin. "I guess. It's just all strange." Linda lifted her face to his, gazed into his eyes, and pressed her lips firmly together for a moment. "I just don't know what she wants from me. I mean, she's nice enough and all, but I have a mother."

"Maybe she just wants to be your friend."

"That's what she says." Linda tilted her head slightly to one side. "Do you think it's okay to be friends with her?"

"*Ya,* I reckon so."

"I think we're gonna go eat and go to a movie." She shrugged. "Which I guess is all right since I'm at the age to do these things."

Stephen nodded, disappointed he wouldn't be spending the afternoon with Linda, but glad that she seemed to be handling this news about her mother much better than she had in the beginning. He thought back to her uncontrollable sobs when she'd first told him.

"Want to walk me to my buggy?"

She smiled, and he hoped there would be a good-bye kiss in store for him, but when they got out to the buggy, Linda's aunt and uncle, Katie Ann and Ivan, were just pulling in.

"It wonders me what brings them out here." Linda brought a hand to her forehead and blocked the descending sun as they pulled in. "We see *Onkel* Samuel and *Aenti* Rebecca, and even *Onkel* Noah and their families all the time, but we only see *Onkel* Ivan and *Aenti* Katie Ann at worship usually."

"Why do you think that is?" Stephen whispered as Katie Ann was climbing out of the buggy.

Linda shrugged. "I don't know." She waved her hand. "Hi *Aenti* Katie Ann and *Onkel* Ivan."

Katie Ann lifted a brief hand in Linda's direction, but kept her head down as she walked toward the house. Ivan trailed behind her and smiled briefly.

"*Mamm* said she thinks they're sad because they don't have no *kinner*," Linda said after her mother let them into the house. "They're old not to have a family."

"Hmm." Stephen zoomed in on Linda's lips again. Then he gently pulled her toward him. "I guess I'll see you tomorrow." He quickly brushed his lips against hers, and the feeling sent the pit of his stomach into a wild swirl. He couldn't wait to make Linda Huyard his wife.

Josie was anxious to see Linda, and she'd spent way more time than probably necessary planning out their afternoon. She reached up and fondled the cross necklace and wondered if Linda would be wearing hers too.

Linda was waiting in the yard when she pulled in, and Josie was glad to see a smile on her face as she crawled into the front seat.

"I have that same necklace." Linda pulled her necklace from beneath the collar of her dark blue dress.

Josie smiled and waited for her to buckle her seat belt before she pulled out. "I know. I bought mine that day at the market in Bird-In-Hand when I saw you purchase one just like it." She glanced briefly in Linda's direction. "I hope that's okay." She shrugged. "I guess I just wanted us to have something—something the same."

Linda smiled. "It's fine. I'm glad we both have one."

Josie was happy to see Linda relaxed, and she had high hopes for the afternoon. "I thought we could go see a movie, and then, if it's all right with you, I'd like for you to meet Robert." Josie couldn't wait to introduce Linda to her husband. After Carley and Noah had left the other night, Josie and Robert stayed up late talking about Linda and what a wonderful day Josie had with her daughter. And Robert had apologized for bringing up the subject of adoption in front of Noah and Carley, although they both agreed that it was best to know that Noah was related to Mary Ellen and Linda, especially in light of the friendships that were forming.

While Josie thought Carley was nice enough, she had no plans to get close to anyone. Only Linda. What was the point anyway?

"I'd like to meet your husband." She raised her eyebrows. "What movie?"

"There're several playing." Josie reached into the backseat and handed Linda the newspaper. "Here. You pick."

"Hmm." Linda scanned the movie section. "How about this one?"

Josie slowed the car down as she approached a buggy in front of her, then carefully sped up and made her way around it. She leaned over to see which movie Linda was pointing to. "It's rated R. How will your parents feel about that?"

"*Ach*, it'll be fine."

Linda spoke with such confidence that Josie immediately suspected it would not be fine. "Have you ever seen an R-rated movie?"

Linda sighed. "No."

"I just don't want your parents upset with me. I know that at your age you're given some freedoms, but that movie is going to be . . . *steamy*, I guess is the word."

Linda grinned. "It's a love story." She paused. "Please."

Josie couldn't say no. Under different circumstances, she might have told her they'd do it another time, but time wasn't on Josie's side. "Okay." She hoped the movie was a mild R.

Only twenty minutes into the movie, Linda whispered to Josie that she had to go to the ladies' room. Josie suspected that her hurried departure had something to do with the content on the screen. The movie was anything but mild, and more than once, Josie saw Linda's eyes widen with disbelief. No violence or language to speak of, but there was enough bare skin to make up for it, and Josie felt terrible for taking Linda to see the movie. Even though she was of age, it was quite clear that she was shocked by what she saw. Josie was glad that Linda was in the bathroom when things began to really heat up on the screen.

"We probably should have seen something else," Josie said when she found Linda standing outside the bathroom, her hands folded in front of her, her eyes cast down. Josie wondered if she was praying.

"I'm sorry, Josie." Linda looked up at Josie. "I reckon that movie is not for me. I kept thinking what *Mamm* would think, and . . ."

"No, don't apologize." Josie touched her arm and motioned her to walk alongside her and toward the exit of the theater. "I should have known you wouldn't like the movie." Josie silently blasted herself for agreeing to that particular movie. A good mother would have insisted they see something different.

They walked quietly for a few moments, and Linda waited until they were in the parking lot before she commented again.

"It wasn't that I didn't like it." Linda tucked her chin as Josie unlocked the passenger door. "It just—it embarrassed me."

Josie nodded, opened Linda's door, then walked to her side of the car and climbed in. "I shouldn't have agreed to that movie." *Mary Ellen wouldn't have.* Josie started the engine and backed out of the parking space.

"Josie?" Linda twisted beneath her seatbelt until she was facing Josie.

"Yeah?"

"Is that really how a man and woman are together when they're in *lieb?*" Her cheeks reddened, but her eyes pleaded with Josie for an answer.

Josie thought about Robert, their relationship, and how very much she loved him. "Yes, it is." She turned toward Linda, whose expression was drawn into a frown. "Linda, what is it?"

"I don't understand."

Josie drew in a breath, quite sure it was not her place to explain about sex to Linda. "Which part do you not understand?" *Oh dear.*

Linda avoided looking at Josie. "*Mei Englisch* friends told me how—how babies are made." She paused, glanced briefly at Josie, then looked away. "*Mamm* said I would learn when I get married, but I'm curious about one thing."

"Okay." Josie fearfully waited for Linda to get to the part that she didn't understand.

Linda shifted her weight, folded her hands in her lap, and stared straight ahead. Josie wondered if she was just going to drop it.

"It's just that—" Linda turned to face Josie, but then turned quickly forward again and shook her head. "I reckon I don't know how to ask . . ."

Josie pulled onto the main highway then briefly glanced at Linda. "I know we don't know each other well at all, Linda, but if you want to ask me something, anything at all, you can."

Linda shook her head. "Such matters should not be talked about."

"Okay." Josie waited since Linda's mouth was open, as if she was going to keep talking anyway.

Linda arched one brow. "They didn't show everything in the movie, did they?"

"No, they didn't. Most of what they showed leads up to intercourse."

Linda's face drew a blank. "Leads up to what?"

Surely in this day and time, Amish or otherwise, a seventeen-year-old girl would know what intercourse is. "Intercourse. You know what that is, right?"

"Of course." She sounded a bit irritated that Josie even had to ask. "It's a neighboring town," Linda finished confidently.

Josie stifled a grin. Lancaster County was known for the odd names of towns. Towns like Bird-In-Hand and Intercourse. She remembered questioning the unusual names when she'd lived here as a kid. Surely Linda knew that Intercourse referred to more than just the name of a town?

"Linda, you do know that intercourse means something else, besides just the name of a town, you know that, right?"

Linda faced her, widened her eyes. "What does it mean?"

It seemed too soon for Josie to be having this talk with Linda and way too late for Linda to just now be discovering this word or learning about the act itself. Josie sighed and feared she was stepping on Mary Ellen's toes in a big way. But as delicately as she could, she explained lovemaking to Linda. She watched Linda's eyes grow big as golf balls.

"But the couple in the movie weren't married." Linda sat up taller as she twisted to face Josie.

"No, they weren't."

"But that's wrong, then, no?"

Josie let out an uncomfortable sigh. "I suppose it is."

Linda tapped her finger to her chin. "I have one question," she said in a determined voice.

"What's that?" Josie pulled into her driveway.

"Does it hurt?"

Josie thought for a moment. "Well, I suppose the first time it can . . ."

Josie barely had the car in Park when Linda reached for the car door and jumped out. Josie grabbed her purse and also exited the car. She saw Linda standing on the other side. Josie stared at her across the hood. "Linda, it's just—"

But Linda waved her hand as if she didn't want to hear. "It doesn't matter. I'm not doing it. Ever!"

Josie hid her smile with her hand. "Linda, I'm sure that you will change your mind about that." She walked to the other side of the car, and together they began to walk up the sidewalk.

"Please, don't speak of this in front of your husband." Linda's eyes grew fearful and her expression serious.

"I won't," Josie assured her as she put the key in the door, but she hadn't even twisted the knob when the door flew open.

"Hello. This must be Linda." Robert extended his hand to Linda, and Josie felt an unfamiliar sense of pride. *Yes, this is my daughter.*

Linda tucked her chin, something Josie noticed she did when she was feeling uncomfortable. She wanted Linda to feel comfortable around Robert. Her husband promised to look after Linda, financially or otherwise, after Josie was gone, and Josie hoped the two of them would be close. Then a pain surged through her head, and she reached for her temple. *No. Not now.*

Her head began to throb the way it did before she had an episode, and she could feel her mouth going dry. Robert's eyes met with hers as she and Linda walked through the doorway. He knew right away what was happening; he'd seen it plenty of times.

"I'll get your pills," he whispered. He put a hand on her shoulder. "Is it a bad one?"

Linda walked into the living room while Josie and Robert lingered by the door. "I don't know yet," Josie said. She squeezed her eyes closed.

"Are you all right?" Linda was walking back toward them.

"I just have a headache. I'll be right back." Josie moved past Linda and headed toward her bedroom, her legs shaky, her balance off, and vivid colors flashing around the room. Her doctor said the symptoms were similar to a migraine, but Josie knew what it was, and just knowing that a tumor was pushing on her brain stem often caused her to have a panic attack, wondering if this was it. Her doctor said he thought she had several months left, but he also told her he wasn't God, so there were no guarantees.

Josie sat down on the bed, reached for the pill bottle on her nightstand, and popped two of the pills, knowing they would make her sleepy. She'd fight to stay awake and spend time with Linda. She took a deep breath, closed her eyes, and hoped the pills would take effect soon without completely knocking her out.

God. She thought about Him a lot lately. It was hard not to.

She'd grown up in a religious household, and even though her parents stopped going to church when she was in junior high, Josie had continued on for a couple more years. Then Robert came along. Such a good man, but he had lots of valid arguments against the entire concept of God, life after death, and the teachings of the Bible. But now, more than ever, she found herself recollecting her time at church, the fellowship, the prayer, and the relationship she thought she'd had with God. *Illusions. Not real.* Must have been, if she was so easily swayed away. *Is there a heaven? Did Jesus really die on the cross to save us? Is there a hell?*

As the pain began to subside, Josie did something she hadn't done in many years. "If You are there, please take care of my daughter when I'm gone," she whispered, then thought for a moment. "Maybe you could even give me a little sign that you're there."

She knew the headache wouldn't completely go away for a while, and she wanted to spend time with Linda, so she picked herself up off the bed and made her way downstairs. Linda was sitting on the couch watching television. She didn't see Robert anywhere.

"Did Robert abandon you?" Josie sat down beside Linda, who smiled.

"He's getting us all a piece of pie."

Josie kicked off her brown flip-flops, crossed her legs, and brushed a piece of fuzz from her blue jeans. "First a steamy movie and now TV. Your mom would kill me."

Linda pointed to the television. "Look, Josie! It's the man in the movie we just saw."

Yes, with clothes on. "It sure is." She turned her head from the television and gazed at Linda. She'll marry her boyfriend next year and go on to have babies. She has her whole life in front of her, a life that she will share with Mary Ellen and the rest of her family. As it should be. What Josie wouldn't do to stand on the sidelines and watch her grow and become a wife and mother. She swallowed hard.

"I watch television with my *Englisch* friends at their homes. *Mamm* knows. But once I'm baptized into the faith, I won't do those things."

"You're close to your mom, I can tell."

"*Ya*, I am." Linda turned back to the television, but then Robert entered the room balancing three pieces of key lime pie.

"Here you go, ladies." He handed the first piece to Linda, then passed a plate to Josie.

Linda took a bite of pie and swallowed. "This pie is very *gut*, did you make it?"

"No. Robert brought it home the other night. Honey, didn't you pick it up at that bakery on Lincoln Highway?"

Robert had a mouthful, but nodded.

Josie wasn't hungry, and she was afraid the pie wouldn't stay down, but she took a small bite just the same.

"Linda, did Josie tell you that I have to go out of town for two weeks?"

"No, I haven't had a chance to," Josie cut in.

"I have a trial that's been going on for years, and it looks like it is finally going to wrap up, but I have to go to China." Robert took another bite of pie, then went on. "Anyway, maybe you could stay here with Josie while I'm gone."

"Robert, no." Josie's tone was sharp. She couldn't believe he would ask Linda this. "I'll be fine."

"I just thought that it might be a nice way for you two to have some girl time together, that's all." Robert's expression grew solemn.

Robert had done everything humanly possible to get out of the business trip, but Josie kept urging him to go. She knew it was important to him, but he didn't want to leave her alone. Much to her horror, he'd even called and asked her mother to come stay with her, starting next week when he had to leave. Josie had quickly called her mother and squelched that plan. One day with her mother would be too much for Josie, even though Mom was ready and willing to come be with her. Josie had two friends back home that she stayed in touch with, and she was sure that Kathy or Paula would come and stay with her, but she refused to disrupt their lives for this. She'd look forward to a visit from her friends when it was convenient for them. Robert's parents, sweet as they were, could barely take care of each other.

"No, Robert. Linda can't just give up her life to come stay with me for two weeks, I'm sure." Although, there was nothing Josie would like more.

Linda glanced back and forth between the two of them. "No, I couldn't," she said sheepishly. "I have many chores to tend to at the farm." She paused and smiled. "But maybe I can come visit some."

"Anytime." Josie set her pie on the coffee table after taking only one bite. "I guess I ate too much popcorn at the movies," she lied. Her head was splitting, and she needed to lie down.

Robert sat up taller in his chair. "Baby, are you okay?"

Don't alarm Linda. They'd discussed this. Josie didn't want Linda to know about the tumor. Not yet. She didn't want Linda to feel sorry for her.

"I'm fine, Robert."

Linda placed her clean plate on the coffee table. "*Danki*, Mr. Robert. This was so *gut*."

"You're very welcome, Linda. And just call me Robert."

———————

Linda nodded. Robert looked older than Josie, but he sure seemed to love her very much. He looked at her the way Stephen often looked at Linda and also like the man in the movie looked at that woman. Linda cringed and wondered how she'd ever have a baby if making one would hurt. She knew that actually having the baby hurt; Aunt Lillian had said it hurt bad. But Linda always figured that once she was in a family way, the baby was coming out no matter what. It never occurred to her that the making part would be painful.

She glanced around the room at all the paintings on the walls as she enjoyed the cool air-conditioning. She thought about what it would be like to stay here for two weeks. Linda had seen Josie's bathroom on her first visit, and she couldn't imagine what it would be like to take a bath in a tub twice as big as the one at home. She envisioned herself taking a long soak in bubbles up to her neck.

"Maybe I could spend one night?" She smiled at Josie.

"That would be great!" Josie reached over and squeezed her hand. This was all very confusing, but Linda couldn't help but like her birth mother. She and her husband both seemed very kind. "Any night you want," Josie added.

"Josie, I'm going to try one more time to get out of this trip. I'm just not comfortable leaving you alone, and—"

"No, Robert. I already told you that I'll be fine. Really." Josie glared at her husband, and Linda didn't understand why he didn't want to leave her. *Daed* had left *Mamm* several times for a few days to go purchase farm equipment in another town. Of course, *Mamm* had her *kinner* around, and Josie didn't have anyone.

Linda faced Robert. "What day do you leave, Mr. Robert? I mean—Robert." Linda couldn't help but wonder if Josie had fancy lotions and bubble baths in her bathroom too.

"I leave on Tuesday morning."

"Monday is wash day, but Tuesday is a slower day. Maybe I can spend the night with you on Tuesday night, if it's all right with you. And with *mei* parents."

"I would love that." Josie slapped her hands to her knees. "I'll cook us something. Anything you'd like. Do you have a favorite?"

"I like meatloaf and potatoes." *Mamm* made the best meatloaf, but for some reason, she hadn't made it in a while.

Linda watched Josie and Robert glance at each other and smile, even though Linda wasn't sure why.

"Then meatloaf and potatoes it is." Josie was smiling, and Linda wanted her to be happy. But she wanted *Mamm* to be happy, too, and she wasn't sure if this news would make her mother very happy, or if *Mamm* would even allow her to stay overnight with Josie. But the thought of bathing in that warm bathtub, with the air-conditioning running, and maybe even the television on, told Linda she was going to ask for permission.

But she couldn't help but be leery as to exactly what Josie wanted from her and how much she had to give in return.

9

Mary Ellen always enjoyed having worship service at their home, and her family hosted about every nine months. Much preparation went into readying the house. On this Sunday morning, she was pleased at how well things had come together. Her house was clean, benches were in place, food was prepared and ready to serve, and Linda had stayed unusually close to her throughout the morning.

Her daughter didn't say too much about her visit with Josephine, just that she'd had a good time and that they'd gone to the movies. And she mentioned meeting Josephine's husband, commenting that he seemed like a good fellow. Mary Ellen still wasn't comfortable with the situation or pleased that Josephine had disrupted their lives in such a way, but Noah's information certainly shed new light on the circumstances. It stood to reason that Josephine would want to know her daughter. Mary Ellen's heart ached when she thought about Josephine's short future, but she also wanted to make sure that Linda was grounded in her faith and would stay on course with her studies of the *Ordnung* in preparation for baptism. Mary Ellen and Abe had worked with all the children from the time they were young to make sure they had a good understanding of the code of conduct by which they lived, so that each one would know the *Ordnung* well and be able to choose baptism into the community.

Mary Ellen glanced at the clock as time for worship service drew near, then looked out the window to see a line of buggies coming up the driveway. Her yard was green and plush, her flowers in full bloom, and Abe had even cleaned up the inside of the barn, knowing the men would gather there in the afternoon to tell jokes and possibly sneak a few cigars, or even a glass of homemade wine. Everything was ready.

"Stephen's here." Linda bounced across the living room and out the front door. Mary Ellen watched through the window as the two met in the front yard, showing no affection, but Mary Ellen could see the looks in both their eyes. She was quite content knowing that Stephen would someday be her son-in-law. They were both still young, but Mary Ellen hoped he would ask her to wed soon. Somehow, in her mind, that would solidify Linda's staying in the community and dissolve the threat that Josephine brought into their world. Even though Linda was of age to experience her running-around period, Mary Ellen knew that her exposure was heightened when she was in Josephine's fancy house and doing things Mary Ellen certainly wouldn't approve of.

At eight o'clock everyone was seated, and the service began with thirty minutes of song in High German, followed by the opening sermon which always lasted about twenty minutes. After the sermon, there was a short silent prayer before the deacon read a Scripture verse. Mary Ellen caught Linda and Stephen winking at each other from across the room. However inappropriate, Mary Ellen couldn't help but smile.

Two hours into the service, they listened to the minister give the main sermon, and today he seemed to be speaking directly to Mary Ellen. "We don't always understand the circumstances that we find ourselves in, but we must remember that to question His will is a sin and often leads us down a path that is not of His choosing."

Mary Ellen knew she'd been guilty of questioning God's will from the moment Josephine showed up on the doorstep. However, she tried to recall that day Josephine arrived at Mary Ellen and Abe's house seventeen years ago. She suspected it was just as hard on Josephine then, if not more so. Mary Ellen cringed when she thought about the way Josephine's mother spoke to Josephine all those years ago, and it had been clear at the time that Josephine was being forced to give away her child. Perhaps Mary Ellen and Abe should have backed out of the adoption because of that.

Her thoughts were interrupted when the congregation began to sing, and she regretted allowing her mind to drift and missing the end of the sermon. She sang with conviction her praises to the Lord for the next fifteen minutes of the service, and then worship came to a close. She hurried to the kitchen to start getting things ready for the meal.

She bumped into her friend, Sadie Saunders, who was with her husband, Kade, and their two children. They chatted for a moment, then Mary Ellen excused herself.

"I'm going to put the meal out so everyone can get started."

Sadie handed Kade their daughter, Marie. "I'm coming to help."

By the time Mary Ellen and Sadie worked their way through the crowd to the kitchen, several of the ladies were already putting the food on the counter. Every two weeks after worship service, the noon meal consisted of the same thing. Mary Ellen had wondered for years if that would ever change, but it didn't appear so. Ten loaves of homemade bread sat next to large containers of peanut butter and cheese spreads. Sandwiches were made by swiping both spreads onto the bread. The tastes complemented each other, and they'd all been raised on it. Occasionally, an *Englisch* person was invited to worship service, and they were always interested in the consistency of the peanut butter spread, which was made using traditional peanut butter, but with added ingredients that made it sweeter and thinner.

Pickled beets, seasoned pretzels, pickles, and snitz pie were always served as well. On this late morning Mary Ellen's stomach was growling, and she was wishing for more than the usual offerings.

"I notice that none of Lillian's family is here. Not her, Samuel, or the children. And neither are Jonas, Lizzie, and Sarah Jane." Sadie twisted the lid from a jar of pickles and placed them on the table. "It wonders me if everything is all right."

"I haven't heard anything." Mary Ellen poured the homemade pretzels from a plastic bag into a large bowl as speculations about the family's absence began to stir worry. "I reckon maybe Linda can pay them a visit this afternoon, see if everyone is all right. She enjoys visiting with Jonas."

"Did I hear my name?"

Mary Ellen turned to see Linda snatching a pickle from the jar on the table. "We're just concerned that Samuel, Lillian, and the children aren't here, and neither is Jonas, Lizzie, or Sarah Jane. I was wondering if maybe you'd like to go check on them in a while."

Linda nodded with a mouthful, then swallowed. "*Ya.* I noticed they weren't here. I hope Jonas is all right, but don't you think Barbie or someone would have gotten word if—if something bad happened?" Linda paused, bit her bottom lip, and waited.

"I think so." Mary Ellen comforted herself with that thought.

"*Mamm* . . ."

"*Ya?*"

"Do you think I could drop off a piece of snitz pie for Josie and her husband on the way? I mean, if there's any left." Linda tucked her chin, then raised her eyes to Mary Ellen. "They seem to like pie," she said sheepishly.

"I reckon that would be all right." Mary Ellen recalled her conversation with Noah and she offered another silent prayer for Josephine.

Linda shared a kiss with Stephen back behind the far barn after almost everyone had gone home later that afternoon. His touch sent a tingle up her spine and caused her body to react in ways she didn't exactly understand. She immediately thought about the movie she'd watched with Josie, and she edged away a bit.

"Have you told your *mamm* that you want to spend the night at Josie's house on Tuesday?" Stephen pulled his arms from around her waist and sat down on a nearby stump.

"Not yet. I'll talk to her tonight." Linda was dreading having to ask permission. She could see the tension in her mother's expression anytime Josie was mentioned.

"Linda . . ." Stephen pulled his straw hat off and swiped his forearm against beads of sweat building on his forehead. "I reckon you gotta be careful 'bout what you're doing."

She sat down on a stump facing him, rested her elbows on her knees, and cupped her cheeks. "What do you mean?"

"Gotta be careful 'bout getting unequally yoked with outsiders. We hear about it at worship and in our studies of the *Ordnung*." He twisted his mouth to one side. "That's all I'm saying."

Linda sat up straight. "I know that."

"*Daadi* says that lots of them are *gut* Christians, but we don't know for sure, so it's best to stick with our own, not be tempted by their ways."

Just because your grandfather is the bishop . . . "I'm just enjoying my freedom during my *rumschpringe*, that's all." She paused, feeling defensive. "It wouldn't hurt you to do a few things in the *Englisch* world, while you can. We'll be baptized soon enough, and you'll never be able to experience some of those things."

Stephen shrugged. "I reckon I don't care to experience that stuff. I'm happy here. With you." He reached over and latched onto her hand.

"I'm happy here, too, with you." Linda blew air upward to clear a strand of hair that had fallen from beneath her *kapp*. Stephen pulled his hand from hers and was gently brushing the hair from her face when they heard footsteps coming around the corner of the barn.

"*Daadi.*" Stephen rose from the stump as his grandfather approached. Linda stood up also.

"Hello, Bishop Ebersol. Lovely worship service today." Linda forced a smile. Bishop Ebersol made her nervous, always had. His gray beard stretched the length of his chest, and his bushy brows jetted inward, giving him the appearance that he was always angry. He was tall, slightly bent over, but with an air of authority and the appearance of someone who demanded instant obedience. Stephen said he just looked scary but really wasn't.

"Linda, I came to speak with you about this woman, Josephine." Bishop Ebersol looked briefly in Stephen's direction, as if he wasn't sure whether to continue talking to her in front of his grandson.

"*Ya.*" Linda waited as she twisted the strings on her apron.

"This is an *umgwehnlich* situation." The bishop paused, then narrowed his eyes, which only made him look even scarier. "My door is always open if you would like to talk about this."

Linda nodded, but knew she'd never approach the bishop about anything if she didn't have to. She recalled a time when she was about ten years old, when the bishop came to her house to speak with her parents. She could still recall the scared look on both her parents' faces when Bishop Ebersol pulled into the driveway that Saturday afternoon. Linda never did find out what happened, but just his presence still sent her knees to shaking.

"*Danki*, Bishop Ebersol," she finally said. Although if she needed to talk to anyone, she knew exactly who it would be, and she'd be seeing him later. Jonas.

The bishop glanced back and forth between her and Stephen, and Linda could feel her cheeks reddening. Bishop Ebersol just seemed to know things, and Linda wondered if he knew she and Stephen had been kissing behind the barn.

"Stephen, I think your parents are preparing to leave." The bishop raised his brows, as if waiting for Stephen to walk back to the house with him.

"*Ya, Daadi.*" Stephen gave Linda a quick wave good-bye, followed by a wink when his grandfather wasn't looking, and Linda watched them both walk back to the house.

About fifteen minutes later everyone was gone, and Linda loaded up two pieces of snitz pie in a basket, prepared to stop by Josie's house before going to see Jonas to make sure everything was all right. It made sense that Jonas, Lizzie, and Sarah Jane couldn't make it to worship, but it seemed odd that *Onkel* Samuel's family wasn't there either, unless Jonas was in a real bad way. She decided to go by and see Jonas first.

When she pulled in, she saw several buggies out front, and her heart began to pound against her chest. She parked alongside a buggy she thought she recognized to be Lillian's, and when she took a peek inside the buggy, she saw the car seat her aunt and uncle used to cart baby Elizabeth around in. She hurried to the front door and knocked.

Linda could tell her aunt had been crying when she looked at Lillian's face. A knot rose in her throat as she fought the tremble in her bottom lip.

"Hello, Linda." Lillian pushed the screen door open and motioned for her to come in.

"*Mamm* wanted me to come and check on everyone, since no one was at worship today." She wanted to just go home. David's eyes met with hers when she walked into the den, and she could tell her cousin had been crying as well. Her knees began to tremble.

"Jonas has had a hard day." Sarah Jane placed a hand on Linda's shoulder. "But I know he would want to see you."

"Is he in pain?" Linda cringed and drew in a deep breath and held it.

"He is feeling better than he was earlier today." Sarah Jane motioned her toward the stairs. "Go on up, dear. Lizzie is upstairs with him."

Linda didn't move. "I can come back another time."

Sarah Jane smiled, but her eyes welled with water. "I think you should go see him now."

Oh, no. Dear God, don't take Jonas. Not yet.

Linda's feet were rooted to the floor, and she glanced at David. He nodded toward the stairs. "He'll want to see you," her cousin said.

Linda left them all, and the sound of sniffling echoed behind her as she made her way up the stairs. She didn't turn around and silently prayed that Jonas was not in any pain. When she pushed open the door to Jonas's bedroom, she wanted to pinch her nostrils as the smell of sickness hit her in the face, but even worse was the way Jonas was propped up in the bed, his hands folded across his stomach. Like he was dead.

"Hello, Linda." Lizzie cupped her hand to her husband's cheek. "*Mei lieb*, Linda is here."

Linda stood in the doorway not moving as she watched Jonas's eyes slowly open. He licked parched lips as white as the rest of his face, and Linda closed her eyes for a moment.

"Linda," he whispered. "I'm glad you came. I've been . . ." Jonas took a deep, labored breath. "I've been wanting to talk to you."

Lizzie stood up from the chair beside Jonas's bed. *Don't leave me in here with him, Lizzie.*

"I'll be back in a bit." Lizzie clutched the footboard on the bed as she eased toward Linda. "Go sit. Talk with Jonas, dear."

Linda nodded, but didn't move. Then Jonas's lips parted into a slight smile.

"Don't look so scared." Jonas licked his lips again. "Could you pour me a glass of water?" He pointed to his nightstand where a pink plastic pitcher was surrounded by pill bottles, a box of tissues, several small white cups, and a pair of reading glasses.

"*Ya, ya.*" Linda moved quickly to the pitcher, filled the glass, and hurriedly handed it to Jonas. She waited for him to finish sipping the water. "Are you in pain?"

Jonas raised his brows. "I'm dying. I reckon so."

"*Ach,* no. How bad? How much pain?" She sat down in the chair, reached over, and touched his arm. "What can I do?"

"Tell me about meeting your birth mother."

Linda wiped clammy hands on her black apron. "Right now?"

"Unless I die while you're talking. Then be best to stop and go get Lizzie."

"Jonas!" Linda wished he was teasing, but his expression was pained and it seemed to take effort to keep his eyes open. Then he smiled.

"I ain't gonna die this very minute. Tell me about meeting Josephine."

Jonas's voice took on the tender tone Linda loved, and she watched his eyes widen with concern.

"I reckon it's all right. Meeting her, I mean." She paused, pulled her eyes from Jonas's, and tucked her chin. "I wish someone would have told me." She looked back up at him. "You knew, didn't you?"

"We all knew. And then we didn't know." He slowly raised his hand to his beard and stroked it slowly. "We forgot, Linda."

"What?"

"We forgot," he repeated as he gave a slight shrug. "You were as much a part of this family as if our blood ran in your veins. We simply forgot."

Linda pulled her eyes away again, not sure how to respond, but feeling like she wanted to crawl in the bed beside Jonas and have him wrap his arms around her. She blinked back tears.

"Dear Linda, from the time your mother held you in her arms, you were Mary Ellen and Abe's child. There is no love like that which a parent has for a child. It's a different kind of love. I reckon I'd lay myself out on a train track for Sarah Jane." He chuckled. "Don't know if I'd do that for Lizzie or not."

Linda smiled.

"You won't understand what I'm tellin' ya until you have *kinner* of your own."

"*Mamm* and *Daed* will always be *mei* parents. That will never change."

"Of course not. And I reckon they'd lay themselves on the train track for you and both your brothers." Jonas raked his hand through his beard again. "But here's where it gets tricky." He squinted in her direction and then pointed a finger at her. "I reckon Josephine would lie down on a train track for ya too, give her life willingly for you. That puts you in a unique position. All these people that love you. Do you have room in your heart for all of them?"

She thought about what Jonas was saying for a few moments.

"I don't really know Josie, though. I don't know how I feel." It was true. Linda liked Josephine, but . . . "I can't love her just because—because she is the one who gave birth to me."

"True." Jonas smiled slightly. "But I reckon she already loves you an awful lot."

Linda sat quietly for a moment. "I don't think *Mamm* likes this, me spending time with Josie. And I don't want to hurt her."

"Every wise woman buildeth her house: but the foolish plucketh it down with her hands."

Linda recognized the verse from Proverbs.

"Your *mamm* is a wise woman. This might be *hatt* for her, but she will make *gut* choices. Which you must do also." Jonas smiled, and his eyes clung to hers. "Keep your love for one another at full strength, because love covers a multitude of sins."

"The Book of Peter," she whispered, then smiled.

"*Ya.*" Jonas reached for her hand. "I will miss you, *mei* dear sweet Linda. And I will miss our games of chess."

Linda squeezed his hand as a tear rolled down her cheek. "Are you scared, Jonas?"

"No." He answered quickly. "I feel the presence of Jesus around me, Linda. I'm not afraid. Be strong in faith, Linda. Always."

"But—but, are you afraid it will hurt, that there will be pain?"

"When I go to be with my Father, there will be no pain. Only love."

Linda felt another tear run down her cheek. "Oh, Jonas . . ."

Jonas squeezed her hand as his own eyes clouded with tears, then the door creaked open.

Linda saw her uncle's face peer into the room. "Hi, *Onkel* Noah." She brushed away tears, sniffed, and sat up taller in the chair.

Noah walked to the other side of Jonas's bed and touched his arm. "I have some news."

"Just tell me." Jonas shook his head. "How long do I have? Weeks, days, or hours?"

Linda choked back tears and pressed her eyes tightly closed, not wanting to know.

"Actually . . ." Noah said slowly. "I think you're going to be around a lot longer than that."

Jonas's eyes opened wide. "I know you're the doctor and all,

Noah, but with all due respect, I feel like I could go at any minute. Downright awful is how I feel."

"I know. I just got back from the lab. You're having a reaction to one of your medications. Once we take you off that medication, you are going to feel better." Noah patted Jonas's arm.

Linda brought her hands to her mouth and stifled a gasp.

"You hear that, Linda?" Jonas's lips parted into a smile.

"*Ya*, I did!"

"I reckon you better go get my Lizzie and tell her I won't be heading to heaven just yet." He chuckled, and Linda realized by his reaction to the news that Jonas could say whatever he wanted—that he was ready and not afraid to die—but Linda could see that he was relieved to have more time. Maybe God knew that he just wasn't ready yet. "And next time you come, you bring the chess board."

"I will, Jonas. I will." She kissed him on the cheek, said her good-byes to Noah and those downstairs, and then headed to Josie's to deliver the slices of pie.

10

JOSIE WISHED ROBERT WAS HOME TO GET HER PILLS from upstairs. Clearly, one pain reliever hadn't been enough when her headache had started up again. She lay back against two blue throw cushions on her couch. Robert had left over an hour ago to visit an Amish man named Kade Saunders, someone he'd met through Noah. Mr. Saunders needed an attorney to handle some routine business for him, and although he refused to talk business on a Sunday, he'd invited Robert to his home for tea this afternoon.

Josie picked up the *Forbes* magazine Robert had left on the coffee table with Mr. Saunders's picture on the front. The magazine was dated ten years ago, and Josie couldn't understand how a man of Kade Saunders's wealth and power could give all that up to be Amish. She shook her head, which only made the pain worse. She tossed the magazine back on the table, then closed her eyes, and draped her forearm across her forehead. She fought the tears building. Crying would only make her head hurt more.

As the pain beat against her temple like a steel drum, the pain in her heart was equally fierce. She had the most wonderful husband on the planet. She had a daughter she was just getting to know. A beautiful home. And a tumor that would eventually kill her. When? Her stomach was constantly churning with fear and apprehension. Void of hope, Josie wondered why she was even bothering with any of this—getting to know Linda, unpacking the boxes in their home, or even getting dressed in the morning. She'd be gone soon, and with each passing day, routine things were beginning to seem pointless.

Her lids rose slowly when she heard a knock at the door. She let out a heavy sigh, and pulled herself to a sitting position, her head throbbing to the point she felt like she might vomit. *Please, make it stop. Please.* She wasn't sure who the thought was intended for, but if there was anyone out there—God, a supreme being, or anyone to offer aid—she was willing to try.

Josie stumbled to the door as strobe lights flashed in her head and caused her vision to blur. She glanced at herself in the mirror by the front door, and she knew that she should care how she looked. No makeup, slept-on hair, and a raggedy T-shirt and blue jeans. But the pain in her head was overriding everything else. Robert had offered to stay home, and she should have let him. She wasn't up to seeing anyone. Josie pulled the door open and attempted a smile when she saw Linda.

"Hi." She tried to sound as chipper as she could.

"I brought you and Robert a piece of snitz pie. I made it." Linda pushed a small basket, almost like a miniature picnic basket, toward Josie, and a smile lit her daughter's face in a way that made Josie just want to drop to her knees and beg to live.

When the doctor first diagnosed her, Josie went through all the emotions, even had counseling. She thought she'd been handling her fate with a sense of bravery, mostly for Robert's sake, but as Linda stood there in the doorway, smiling and offering her pie, every valiant bone in Josie's body crumbled, and her loneliness and hopelessness welded together in an upsurge of fear. Her lip began to quiver. She latched onto the basket.

"Thank you." Josie bit her bottom lip and tried to calm the rest of her body, although the pounding in her head was causing her to feel faint.

Linda's eyes narrowed with concern. "Josie? Are you all right?"

"Oh. Yeah." Josie drew in a deep breath and blew it out slowly. "I just have a really bad headache, that's all." *I want to invite you in, but I feel so awful.*

Linda stood there, her bright blue eyes confused as she tilted her head slightly to one side. "Is there anything I can do?"

Josie's thoughts churned inside a splitting head that couldn't seem to decipher much of anything, but one worry bounced ahead of all the others. *What if this is it? What if I never see Linda again?* She stepped aside and motioned for Linda to come in. "Visit with me for a while."

"Sure." Linda hesitated as she stepped through the door, and Josie caught another glance of herself in the mirror.

"Sorry, I know I look a mess. My head is just really hurting." She sat down on the couch, and Linda took a seat right beside her, then surprised Josie by reaching for her hand.

"Let's pray." Linda squeezed Josie's hand, closed her eyes, and bowed her head. Josie waited for her to say something, but Linda just kept her chin tucked and her eyes closed tightly. She knew how devout the Amish were in their faith. Maybe Linda had some sort of inside track to God, if He existed.

"Okay," Josie said, hoping Linda would open her eyes and say a prayer on Josie's behalf. At this point, she was willing to try anything.

Linda opened her eyes and looked at Josie. "Oh, we usually pray silently. Do you want me to offer a prayer aloud?"

Josie was so touched by her offer, along with the fact that she was even here, that she nodded. "Please."

Linda bowed her head again and closed her eyes as she kept a tight hold on Josie's hand. "Dear Blessed Father, please cure Josie's headache if it is Your will. Help her to not feel pain. Be with her on this day, and . . ."

Josie pulled her hand from Linda's, brought both hands to her face, and began to sob. Even for Linda's sake, she couldn't hold it together when something so powerful seemed to be latching on inside of her and threatening to deny her the resolve to be strong, to accept what was happening to her. She didn't want to be strong.

"I'm so incredibly unworthy." Josie cried harder, knowing that if a God existed, He'd never help her. She had been gone far too long, and to come to Him in a time of need when she'd never graciously thanked Him for all He'd given her . . . it seemed a futile attempt at the eleventh hour to reach out to someone she wasn't even sure she believed in.

Josie felt Linda's hand on her shoulder, a gesture which caused her to cry even harder, only elevating the pain in her head.

"We are all unworthy." Linda's voice was calm, nurturing, like a mother. Josie pulled her hands from her face and gazed into her daughter's eyes. "But God is good. He knows we are all unworthy, and He loves us just the same, and He wants to help us. Please, Josie. Don't cry."

Josie swiped at her eyes, sniffed, and smiled at Linda. "Thank you." *But the prayers won't do any good; my fate is sealed.* Josie stared at

Linda and wondered how she'd given birth to someone who possessed such goodness.

"Would you feel better if you lie down? I'll go so that you can rest." Linda stood up, and Josie wanted to hug her more than anything in the world. Josie stood up alongside her.

"I want you to stay, but I'm so sorry that my head hurts so much." She brushed a strand of hair out of her face.

"No worries." Linda smiled. "We have Tuesday night."

Josie walked with Linda to the door. "Yes, we do. And I'm looking forward to that." When they got to the door, Linda pulled it open, scooted over the threshold, and turned to face Josie.

"I hope you feel better." She smiled, and Josie wanted to cry again.

"Thank you so much for stopping by and bringing us the pie. Do you want your basket back?" Josie twisted around, ready to go get the basket.

"I'll get it Tuesday." Linda stared at Josie with concern in her expression. "Where is Robert?"

"He is visiting a friend, but he'll be back soon."

"All right." Linda gave a little wave. "See you Tuesday."

Josie smiled, closed the door, and leaned her head against it. She felt the tears building again, and she fought the urge to cry, to feel sorry for herself. Instead, she raised her head, ran a hand through her tangled hair, and headed back to the couch to lie down. Then the strangest feeling came over her. All her thoughts quieted, and a sense of peace flowed over her. She reached up and touched her forehead.

Then she realized she felt no pain at all. Her headache had vanished. Gone.

Linda gave her horse a flick of the reins and pulled out of Josie's driveway. She'd never seen anyone in such pain from a headache, and that kind of pain scared her more than anything else. Hopefully, Josie would be feeling better by Tuesday. And maybe she'd offer up that big bathroom. Linda smiled as she pictured herself lathered up in sweet-smelling bubble bath, soaking in the big tub while watching television. Maybe she'd even call her *Englisch* friend, Danielle, while she was bathing. She wondered what such luxury would feel like. Then she recalled Stephen's warning, to watch out for those unequally yoked. They'd been taught that their entire lives, and she didn't need him to remind her of it. She knew what she was doing. But she didn't understand Josie getting so upset during prayer. It must have been the pain that caused her to act in such a way.

She glanced to her left as she came over a hill and passed a buggy coming from the other way, no one she recognized, but she nodded in the woman's direction. No other buggies or automobiles shared the street with her for as far as she could see beneath a cloudless blue sky, just the open road winding between fields of freshly planted soil that filled her senses with hope for a plentiful harvest. She leaned her head back as the warm breeze blew against her face, and she thanked God for the beautiful land, the cows mooing in the distance, and the sense of calm that she felt at this moment. Then she prayed for Josie again.

As she neared the bridge at Ronks, she recalled her first kiss with Stephen. Late at night, they'd traveled on foot scooters and secretly met underneath the bridge after everyone was sleeping. She could still remember the feel of his lips meeting with hers for the first time. They'd met several more times since then, always late at night after their families were asleep. Linda knew her father would tan her hide if he knew she snuck out that late and scooted all the way to the bridge at Ronks, but it had become their special place.

She guided her buggy underneath the crimson structure with openings at both ends and smiled when she thought about how much the tourists loved the covered bridges. Sometimes they would gather off the side of the road and take pictures. But not today; all was quiet. She glanced to her left as she made her way under the bridge to the spot where Stephen had first kissed her. A white piece of paper was stuffed between two pieces of wood with a pink ribbon tied around it. She passed by it, but then pulled her horse to a stop and eased him slowly backward. Pink was her favorite color, and even though she wasn't allowed to dress in it, she'd told Stephen repeatedly it was her favorite. She squinted at the rolled up piece of paper bound by a thin strip of pink. *Surely not.*

Smiling, she stepped down from the buggy and walked toward it. She pulled it from its resting place and unrolled it. Her heart began to flutter as she read:

> Sunshine is smiling upon you, like a wave of happiness; never to diminish or fade, like the love in my heart.

She brought the letter to her chest and closed her eyes. *Stephen.* More than once, he'd said, "The sunshine is smiling on you." It was just something he said, and it always made her smile. She crawled back into the buggy, checked to make sure no one was coming in either direction, then she reached for a pen in the buggy's storage compartment.

You are my sunshine, that wave of happiness that I carry with me
when we are apart; like the love also in my heart.

They'd never told each other that they loved each other face-to-
face. This was the closest Stephen had come to doing so, and she
wanted to make sure he knew how she felt as well. She rolled the
note back up, tied the pink ribbon around it, and walked over to a
slightly different spot from where it was before.

As hooves echoed beneath the tunneled bridge, Linda visualized
her marriage to Stephen, the exchanging of vows in front of their
family and friends. She'd envisioned the event so many times that
she could even see her mother and father smiling to her right, her
brothers standing to her left, and her cousin, Rachel, as her maid
of honor. Bishop Ebersol always seemed less scary in the daydream,
almost smiling as he said, "We are gathered here today to bless the
marriage of Linda and Stephen . . ." It would be a perfect day.

Josie. Her vision clouded. Where would Josie be? She would
have to be there. Where would she be sitting or standing? Would
Mamm still be smiling? Would Josie bring her husband, Robert?
The daydream vanished completely as she thought about Josie's
place at her wedding—and in her life.

Mary Ellen handed Abe a piece of rhubarb pie, then joined him
at the kitchen table with her own piece.

"Where's Linda? I haven't seen her since right after worship service." Abe glanced at the clock on the wall. "Be time to start supper
soon, no?"

"*Ya.* Probably shouldn't be having this pie; it's going to spoil our appetites." Mary Ellen tapped her fork gently on the plate. "She went to go check on Jonas." She took a deep breath. "And to drop off two pieces of pie for Josephine and her husband."

"You say that like it irritates you." Abe took a bite of pie and swallowed. "Now that we know that she's . . . ill, I hope you won't prevent Linda from seeing her."

Mary Ellen plunked her fork down on the plate, louder than she'd intended. "Of course I'm not going to keep Linda from seeing her. I'm not some kind of monster, Abe."

"I never said you were, Mary Ellen. You're a *gut* woman. I also know that you feel real threatened by Josephine, but Linda is our daughter. That ain't gonna change." He shook his head. "We better just count ourselves blessed that Linda forgave us for not telling her that she was adopted. This whole thing could have gone another way, and we were in the wrong about not telling her a long time ago."

"I know all that, Abe."

"Maybe we oughta have Josephine and her husband to supper sometime. Might be *gut* for Linda if we are friendly with them, and—"

"I will not." Mary Ellen sat taller. "It's fine for Linda to get to know her birth mother, I suppose, but I just can't do that."

"Why?" Abe raised his brows, and she didn't like his tone.

"Because—because I just don't think . . ." She picked up her plate and got up from the table. After she placed the uneaten piece of pie on the counter, she spun around to face him. "It would just be too awkward, Abe."

"Doesn't have to be." Abe scooped up the last of his pie and closed his mouth around the fork.

Mary Ellen folded her arms across her chest. "Why are you pushing me on this? Linda can visit Josephine, but I don't have to entertain her in my home, Abe." She shook her head. "I just don't want to do that."

Abe shrugged. "All right."

"This is dangerous, Abe. But you just don't see it."

Abe chuckled, and Mary Ellen took two steps toward him. "You think this is funny? It's dangerous enough that Linda spends all that time with her *Englisch* girlfriends, but it's her *rumschpringe*, so not much we can do about that. But, not only is Josephine unequally yoked, she is the girl's kin. Linda could choose a life with her, and . . ."

"Are you listening to yourself? Josephine doesn't have much *life* left, Mary Ellen."

"What if she exposes Linda to her fancy life so much that Linda decides to leave?"

"She ain't goin' anywhere. She's gonna marry Stephen, and our *maedel* is grounded in her faith. You are worrying about something that ain't ever going to happen."

Mary Ellen picked up Abe's empty plate and placed it in the sink. "I hope you're right."

"There's our girl now." Abe pointed to the window, and Mary Ellen saw Linda turning the buggy into the driveway. "I hope everything is all right with Jonas. That poor fella has been fighting this cancer for years, and every time I think it's come his time, that old coot pulls through again." Abe followed Mary Ellen to the window and wrapped his arms around her waist. "Everything is going to be fine, Mary Ellen."

They watched Linda move the horse toward the barn, then they sat down on the couch in the den for their usual reading time.

Mary Ellen looked up from her Bible when Linda walked in a few minutes later. Abe had his head in a book that had a man on a motorcycle on the cover.

"How is Jonas?" Mary Ellen marked her place with her finger.

Linda fell into one of the rockers and crossed her legs. "He looked bad when I got there, *Mamm*. I thought he was going to heaven any second. The worst I've ever seen him." Linda shook her head, and then her face brightened. "But then *Onkel* Noah showed up and said that Jonas's medications were making him sick, and he said he'll start feeling better now that they know to take him off some of his pills."

"What did I tell you?" Abe looked above his gold-rimmed reading glasses at Mary Ellen.

"*Ya*, Jonas always seems to overcome and surprise everyone, but Linda . . ." Mary Ellen paused. "You do know that Jonas is still on a downward spiral. He's eaten up with the cancer. It is just a matter of time."

Linda smiled. "Miracles happen sometimes."

Mary Ellen was proud of her daughter's faith, and she silently reprimanded herself for questioning the choices she'd feared Linda might make. "*Ya*, they do." She smiled back at her beautiful girl, even though Mary Ellen didn't think God granted the type of miracle Linda was searching for. Jonas had beaten the odds for a long time, and Mary Ellen feared his time was near.

"*Mamm? Daed?*"

Mary Ellen waited for Linda to speak, but she tucked her chin the way she did so often. "*Ya?*" she finally asked when Linda looked up at her. "What is it?"

Linda avoided eye contact. "Josie wants me to spend the night at her house Tuesday night. Tomorrow is wash day, and I think if I work late tomorrow, I can get some of Tuesday's chores done. Do you think that would be all right? Her husband is going out of town for two weeks." Linda pulled her eyes away from Mary Ellen's. "Actually, he asked me to stay with her for two weeks, but—"

"Two weeks!" Mary Ellen slammed the Bible shut. "That's impossible. How could she even ask you such a thing?"

"She didn't ask me, her husband did. But *Mamm*, I told her I couldn't, of course."

Linda's eyes started to fill with tears, and Mary Ellen instantly regretted her reaction. Once again, she hadn't trusted her daughter's judgment.

"I think one overnight visit would be fine." Abe said and glanced at Mary Ellen before turning to Linda. "As long as you can get your chores done." He looked back at Mary Ellen. "Don't you think, Mary Ellen?"

"*Ya*, I reckon so." She took a deep breath and blew it out slowly. "I'm sorry I snapped at you, Linda. It's just that the *Englisch* often don't have an understanding about how busy our day is, and I just wasn't expecting you to say two weeks." The nerve of her husband to even ask Linda such a thing. Then Mary Ellen felt her heart sink into the pit of her stomach. The woman is sick. Of course he doesn't want to leave her alone. *I am a mean, selfish woman. Forgive me, dear Lord.* "Does Josephine have any kin here in town?"

"No, she doesn't." Linda scowled, a confused expression on her face. "And her husband doesn't seem to want to leave her alone." She glanced at her father. "But you've left *Mamm* for days when you've had to go out of town. Maybe it's different since *Mamm* has us with her." She shrugged. "I don't know."

Mary Ellen silently prayed. Somehow she needed to try to make up for doubting Linda, questioning the Lord's will, for not telling Linda she was adopted, and mostly for the ugly thoughts she'd had about Josephine since she'd come into their lives—a woman with little time to live and who'd given birth to their beloved Linda.

Mary Ellen raised her chin and folded her hands in her lap. "It is your *rumschpringe*, and Josephine is your birth mother. Maybe you should go and spend the two weeks with her."

Abe's mouth dropped open, and Mary Ellen held her breath as she waited for Linda to answer. And, again, she prayed—that this wouldn't backfire on her.

11

STEPHEN BROUGHT HIS FOOT SCOOTER TO A HALT AND pulled the note from the bridge, his pulse racing as he wondered whether or not Linda had found the note and responded. He uncoiled the paper and exhaled a long sigh of contentment as he read.

You are my sunshine, that wave of happiness that I carry with me when we are apart; like the love also in my heart.

He pulled his pen from within his front shirt pocket.

My dearest Linda, There is much to be discovered in an ocean. It can be shallow. It can be deep. Life it can give. Life it can take. Never to be taken for granted. Found all around us, making the world smaller. My love for you is like an ocean.

Stephen shook his head. *If my buddies knew I wrote this stuff* . . . But Linda loved his poems, and that's all that mattered. He continued.

I love you. Will you marry me?

Always, Stephen

Every time he'd tried to ask Linda to marry him, he froze up with worry about things he needn't be worrying about. *Hopefully, she will think this is romantic and not dumb.* He quickly stuffed the note back in between the wood slats, then scooted off as the clouds became shaded with orange and the sun settled on the horizon in front of him.

Linda could hardly believe she was going to go stay with Josie for two weeks. She'd never had a vacation, and even though Josie's house was only a few minutes from home, this would certainly seem like a holiday. She pinned the last towel on the line, after getting up early to start the wash this sunny Monday morning.

She still didn't understand why *Mamm* was allowing this. A tiny part of her was hurt that her mother suggested she go stay with Josie for two weeks. Had something changed for *Mamm*? Did she no longer feel like Linda's mother? Linda didn't ever want *Mamm* to feel that way, but she wouldn't turn down the offer. Again, she thought about the luxuries in Josie's house. Air-conditioning, for starters. And that bathtub. She smiled to herself.

"Almost done?"

Linda twisted her neck to see her mother approaching. "*Ya.* Last load." She picked up the laundry basket to head back inside, but *Mamm* inched closer to her, then put her arms around Linda's neck and pulled her close.

"Do you know how very much I love you?"

Linda eased away from her. "*Mamm*, I won't go tomorrow if you don't want me to."

Her mother kept hold of Linda's arms and gently ran her hands up and down. "No. I think you should go."

Linda tucked her chin, but *Mamm* gently eased her face back up, then locked eyes with her. "I'm so sorry, *mei maedel*, for not telling you about your adoption." She smiled, gazed into Linda's eyes, and then spoke softly, with such tenderness that Linda considered not going. "Everyone always says how much you look like me, and I think we just really started to forget."

"That's what Jonas said." Linda smiled back. "Are you sure that it's okay with you if I go, *Mamm*? I don't want this to hurt you." She shrugged. "I probably won't like it there." Linda cringed inside as she told the tiny lie.

"Josephine gave you life. She gave you to us to love and raise. I think she is deserving of a chance to know what a lovely young woman you have grown into. But Linda . . ."

Linda waited. *Mamm* frowned a bit and just stared at her for a moment.

"There will be much temptation in Josie's world. All the things that are forbidden to us. Televisions, radios, electricity, and everything modern that we don't agree with. I know this will be like a vacation for you, away from all the hard work, but I will pray constantly that you remember the *Ordnung* and stay steady in your faith. I know it's your *rumspchpringe*, and to worry is a sin. I'm going to work hard to keep worry and fear from my heart." She paused. "Your *daed* and I love you very much."

Linda threw her arms around her mother's neck. "I love you too, *Mamm*. And you will always be my mother. Always." She eased away. "And no worries. My life is here, with all of you, and with Stephen. Please don't worry."

"Things are *gut* with Stephen?" Her mother's eyes brightened.

"*Ya*. I love him very much."

"I think he is much in *lieb* with you as well." *Mamm* playfully arched her brows a couple of times. "Perhaps a proposal will be in order soon, no?"

Linda giggled. "I hope so!"

They started toward the house with Linda carrying the empty laundry basket. She wanted to assure her mother what she knew in her heart to be true. "I won't be tempted, *Mamm*. I know things will be different at Josie's house, but it's only for a couple of weeks so I can get to know her better—as a new friend."

"I know, dear. I trust you to make wise decisions."

It was after dark when Stephen came calling Monday evening. They were just finishing up family devotion time when Linda heard a buggy pulling up.

Daed scowled from his seat on the couch. "A little late for that boy to be showing up here."

"Linda will be busy the next couple of weeks, Abe. I'm sure they want to spend a little time together." Mary Ellen winked in Linda's direction.

"Don't seem fair that Linda gets to go stay with that woman for two weeks." Matthew shook his head. "I reckon we are supposed to take care of her chores while she's gone on her little vacation?"

Daed closed the Bible and peered over his reading glasses. "Watch yourself, Matt."

"I tried to do as much as I could before I leave tomorrow." Linda stood up from the rocker so she could let Stephen in.

"Well, it ain't enough to make up for two weeks," Matthew grumbled as he walked out of the den.

Luke didn't say anything, but Linda suspected by the scowl on his face that his thoughts matched Matthew's. Maybe this whole thing was a bad idea.

"It's late, Linda. Keep your visit short." *Daed* set the Bible on the coffee table next to one of two lanterns that illuminated the den, then stood up. "I'm heading to bed. Outten all the lights when you come in."

"*Ya, Daed*. Good night." Linda picked up the flashlight by the door, opened the screen door to the den before Stephen had a chance to knock, and met him coming up the porch steps.

"I'm glad you came. I have something to tell you." She latched onto his hand and pulled him down the steps toward the garden.

"I'm happy to see you too." He chuckled as Linda pulled him toward the entrance to the garden surrounded by a white picket fence. She shined the light on the latch, flipped it open, and wound her way to a white bench on the far side of the garden and sat down. Stephen took a seat beside her.

"You are never gonna believe this." She turned off the flashlight and blinked her eyes into focus in the dark until Stephen's handsome face was illuminated by the full moon above them, a spark of mischief in his eyes. "I'm leaving tomorrow to go stay with Josie for two weeks."

Stephen's expression soured instantly. "What?"

"Josie's husband is going out of town for two weeks. At first, I was only going to spend one night, but *Mamm* and *Daed* said I can go stay with her for two weeks, to get to know her."

"Why?"

"What do you mean, why?"

Stephen shrugged, and even in the darkness, she could see his mouth take on an unpleasant twist. "I don't know. Seems odd."

"It's not odd." Linda pulled her hand from his. "Why do you say that?"

"Why would you even want to stay with her for two weeks, in the *Englisch* world?"

"I told you. To get to know her."

Stephen eyed her with a critical squint. "And your parents are allowing this?"

"*Ya.* They are."

Linda didn't want to squabble with Stephen about this or put a damper on his visit. "Did you get my note?" She broke into a wide open smile, hoping to lift his mood.

"*Ya,* I did. And I left you another one."

"*Ach, gut!* I'll go by and get it on the way to Josie's tomorrow." She reached for his hand again. "I really do love your poems, Stephen."

"I think you'll really like this one." He leaned in and kissed her gently on the lips. "I'll be anxious to hear what you think." Then he pulled away hastily. "Am I going to see you during these two weeks?"

"Of course. Josie isn't going to keep me under lock and key. She'll probably even drive me places, if need be."

"Okay. Thursday, I get off work early. We could go to the creek and swim?"

Linda couldn't believe it. Stephen never wanted to go swim at the river. "Sure. That'd be great. What time?"

"I'll pick you up at four o'clock." He leaned in and kissed her again, longer this time, as he cupped the nape of her neck. "I want to know what you think about the poem I left you."

"I will love it, I'm sure."

"I really hope so."

Stephen kissed her again, and Linda was certain that everything in her life was going to turn out perfectly. *Mamm* was coming around about Josie, she and Stephen were growing closer, and Linda was about to embark on a two-week adventure filled with fancy bubble baths and air-conditioning.

Tuesday afternoon, Josie was anxious for Linda to arrive, and thankful to be having a headache-free day. She had meatloaf in the oven and potatoes were peeled and ready for boiling. Robert had called her from the airport before his plane left for China, and she'd assured him that she would be fine while he was away.

"I shouldn't be going," he'd told her again. "I don't want to leave you alone."

Josie promised to call if there was a problem and told him he could catch the first plane back home, though there usually was nothing to do except take the Vicodin and steroids. Each episode just had to take its course. Josie reached down and rubbed the top of her right hand with her other hand. Still no feeling. It had been that way since yesterday morning, but she knew if she told Robert, he would cancel this important business trip.

She lit two candles in the living room and put on some soft music and hoped Linda would enjoy her overnight stay. Josie had her room all ready. She couldn't remember a night this important in a very long time. She wanted everything to go perfectly and for

Linda to like her, to know her, to have a tiny bit of Josie's heritage to carry with her in life.

No tears today. Only happy thoughts. She recalled how her headache had gone away on Sunday after Linda prayed with her and how she'd followed up with her own prayer. It didn't mean there was a God, but perhaps she could allow the possibility to give her a tiny bit of hope. She'd told Robert what had happened, but he'd firmly said that the medicine had just kicked in. He was adamant that God had nothing to do with anything. "I wish there were such a being, Josie," he'd said. "I wish that more than anything on this earth, but you know I just don't believe that. But, Josie, you need to believe what's right for you. Don't let my beliefs interfere."

Josie found that interesting, since Robert had always given up a hundred arguments to any point she'd made about God early in their relationship. Eventually, she'd had to admit that Robert's point of view made much more sense than hers. But with her own mortality hanging in the balance, she wished there was something to believe in. She needed hope. As she felt the knot forming in her throat, she shook her head. "No, not today," she said aloud.

A loud knock interrupted her thoughts, and she hurried to the door and pulled it open.

"Wow. That's a lot of luggage for one night." She smiled at Linda who was standing on the doorstep with two fairly large suit-cases. Mary Ellen was turning the buggy around, and Josie waved, but Mary Ellen didn't see her.

Linda awkwardly cleared her throat. "Actually, *Mamm* and *Daed* said I can stay for the whole two weeks." Linda tucked her chin. "I probably should have asked you first."

"Oh my gosh! No! Are you kidding? Get in here, you!" Josie

grabbed one of the suitcases and motioned Linda in. "I'm so excited. This is going to be great."

Linda's face lit up, and she scooted in the door. "I smell meatloaf."

"Yep! Just for you." Josie thought she might burst. *Two whole weeks with my daughter. Thank you, God!* The thought came out of nowhere, but it seemed fitting to thank someone, anyone, for this wonderful luck. "I can't wait to tell Robert when he calls that you are staying for the entire two weeks. We are going to have so much fun." Linda followed her through the den and to the stairs. "Follow me upstairs, and I'll show you your room."

Linda followed Josie up the stairs and down a long hallway, until they got to a door at the end on the right.

"This is your room. It's right across from my room, in case you need anything." Josie walked inside and set the suitcase she was carrying down before motioning for Linda to come in.

"This is the room I'll be staying in?" Linda gasped as she set her other suitcase down. She brought both hands to her chest as she took in her living quarters for the next two weeks. "I've never seen such a bed." She walked to the large bed in front of her, topped with a floral bedspread in shades of ivory and rose, and there were four large satin throw pillows resting against two pillows in rose-colored shams. It was too fancy to touch, and Linda couldn't believe she would be sleeping here. She glanced up at the ivory sheer draped over four large posts on each corner of the bed. It peaked in the middle, forming an arch above the bed, like something a princess would sleep in.

Linda moved toward a piece of furniture in the corner. A

hairbrush and hand mirror rested atop the off-white finish, along with a crystal vase filled with bright red roses, the kind Mr. Buckley sold at the flower shop in town, ones that were especially big. Ivory-colored walls were topped with a border consisting of three different shades of roses, and lacy curtains covered two windows. Next to the bed was a small end table with a white lamp. A pink alarm clock and a Bible were on the table next to a telephone.

Josie moved toward a six-drawer dresser along one of the walls, also painted an off-white shade, and pulled open the first drawer. "These are all empty. You can put some of your clothes in here." She pointed to the closet. "The closet is empty as well."

Linda glanced around the room and noticed the television suspended from the wall in the corner of the room. A white rocking chair occupied the other corner of the room. She was afraid to touch anything.

"I hope you like roses." Josie smiled. "I love roses, and I was hoping you did, too, when I started decorating this room for you."

"You decorated this room for *me?*"

Josie nodded, then walked to the closet and swung the door wide. Linda was pretty sure the closet was as big as her entire bedroom at home. "This is probably more room than you need, but every woman should have a big closet."

Linda stared at the couch against the wall across from the dresser. It was an odd-shaped couch, with only half a back that swayed downward, covered in a velvety-looking light pink fabric.

"That's a chaise longue." Josie walked toward the piece of furniture, then sat down. "If you lean back like this, you can see the television really well from here." She twisted her neck back toward the bed. "But you can see it just as well from the bed."

Linda eyed the flat, square television in the corner and wondered if it had a controller to change the channels, like at her *Englisch* friends' houses. Her eyes veered back to the table by the nightstand, and sure enough, there was a television controller beside the alarm clock.

"Do you like the room?" Josie bit her bottom lip.

"Like it? I love it, Josie. I've never seen anything like this." She ran her hand along the delicate bedspread and wondered what it was going to feel like to be wrapped up in the covers with the princess dome overhead. With the television on. She turned around and faced Josie. "*Danki*, Josie, for making this such a beautiful room and for inviting me to come stay with you."

Josie moved toward her and smiled. "You are very welcome." She turned toward the door. "I'll tell you what. Why don't I go finish dinner, and if you'd like, you can take a bath, and then we'll eat, curl up on the couch, and just make it like a slumber party and talk. There's a bathroom down the hall." Josie pointed to her left. "Or, even better, if you'd like to take a bath in our room, there is a big Jacuzzi tub you can soak in."

"*Ya, ya.* I'd like that." Linda didn't even try to contain her excitement. She'd been fantasizing about taking a bath down the hallway, with the big tub, phone, and television set. *But Josie's bathroom is probably even grander.*

"Great. Come on. Follow me. I'll show you where everything is."

Linda crossed the hallway behind Josie, and suddenly her own quarters seemed modest in comparison to Josie's bedroom, if that was possible. Josie's bed angled from a corner of the room and reminded Linda of a sled, the way the base of the bed curved at the bottom. It was much larger than the bed in Linda's room and was covered with a dark blue bedspread and topped with lots of white lacy pillows. Everything in this room was made of dark wood, which made it all seem so formal. There was an entire sitting area off to one side with high-back chairs and a full-sized couch. Why did anyone need all this den furniture in a bedroom?

She wanted to keep looking around Josie's room, study the big framed pictures of landscapes on the wall and the smaller ones of people on her dresser, but she followed Josie into the bathroom.

This is no bathroom. She didn't even see a commode. This room was surely larger than her bedroom at home.

"There are towels in the cabinet." Josie pointed to her left, but Linda could hardly take her eyes from the tub, which she reckoned would hold four people if need be.

"That's some bathtub." Linda eyed the massive, bronzed faucets and water spigots all inside the white enclosure.

Josie walked to the tub, turned the faucet on, then pointed to some buttons on the side of the tub. "You can adjust the jets however you like. Just push these buttons when the tub gets full." She walked to the marble counter and pulled a pretty blue basket full of bottles and tubes toward her. "And there are bubble baths, lotions, and all kinds of goodies in here. Just help yourself to anything."

Linda recalled the baths at her house, lit by lantern if she didn't beat Matt and Luke to bathe in the evenings. Soaps and shampoo that she and *Mamm* made on a regular basis. The small battery-operated fan to keep the sweat from building the minute you stepped from the claw-foot bathtub onto the brown rug. Creaky wooden floor, gas heater in the wintertime, and always, no matter the season, the same towel all week long.

"Here's the remote for the television." Josie handed the

channel changer to Linda. "You should have plenty of time to take a nice soak before I finish dinner." Josie smiled. "Linda, I'm so glad you're here."

Linda glanced around the room, anxious to enjoy a bath in this super fancy tub, but she couldn't shake the feeling that she had forgotten something.

"I'm glad I'm here too."

"Okay. Yell if you need anything."

Linda nodded, then Josie left the bathroom and closed the door behind her. A sweet aroma filled her senses and drew her to the basket of goodies on the counter. She fumbled through the items and chose more than was probably necessary, then set the bubble baths, gels, and shampoo on the platform beside the tub, alongside the channel changer.

She giggled as she pushed the button on the tub. Water started to bubble up like the brook behind her house after a hard rain. She hastily got out of her clothes, tossed them on the tile floor, and removed her *kapp*. Her brown hair fell to her waist, and she dipped her toe into the warm water, then climbed in. As she got comfortable in the tub, she reached for the channel changer and pushed the On button. She wondered what it would be like to take a bath in this tub every day. Hopefully, she'd be doing it for the next two weeks.

She twisted her mouth to one side. Despite the perfect moment, there was something bogging her down, that feeling like you've forgotten something. *What is it? What is it?*

Then she remembered.

12

STEPHEN PASSED THROUGH THE COVERED BRIDGE ON his way to the furniture store on Tuesday evening, anxious to see what Linda's response was to his written proposal. She'd said she would get the note on the way to Josephine's, which would have been way before now since he'd worked late. His stomach swirled and his palms went damp as he pulled the buggy to a stop and reached for the coiled paper. But the swirling turned into a heavy knot in the pit of his belly when he unrolled it.

He sighed, then rolled the note back up and retied the ribbon around it. As he placed it back in between the supports on the bridge, he figured she must have forgotten to pick it up on her way, which irritated him probably more than it should have. She didn't know it was a proposal.

Stephen motioned the horse into action and continued toward the store. He'd check again tomorrow on his way home from work.

He couldn't seem to shake the worry he was feeling about Linda staying with her birth mother for two weeks. It was only natural that she'd want to get to know the woman, but that thought didn't lessen his fear. Stephen saw the way Linda eyed fancy items when they were in town sometimes, and he wasn't sure how strong her attraction to material things was. He shook his head, resolved to trust her. Linda was strong in her beliefs, and he'd keep the faith that she would stay in line with the *Ordnung*.

Still, it irritated him that she didn't swing by the bridge earlier, when she knew there was a note waiting for her.

Linda dried herself off with a towel so plush it felt like silk against her skin. She glanced at the phone in the bathroom and thought about calling Stephen's house and leaving a message on their phone in the barn, but she didn't want someone other than Stephen to get the message, which was most likely what would happen. She'd have to go by the bridge tomorrow to get his note. She was glad she'd remembered what she'd forgotten.

Her suitcases were still across the hall in her room, so she bundled up in the towel, tiptoed out of the bathroom, and walked through Josie's room toward the door. She paused and gazed at the beautiful pictures hanging on the wall, floral landscapes with cottages.

She passed by a large cherry wood dresser with a tall etched mirror. Pictures lined the top of the dresser, and her eyes were drawn to a photo that appeared older than the others and showed a sleeping baby dressed in pink. *Me.* She held the towel in place with one hand and picked up the framed photo with the other and wondered if the picture had always been on Josie's dresser. She set it down and walked to her own room and breathed in the fresh scent from the roses. *This is paradise.*

She pulled a brown dress over her head, brushed out her wet hair, and started to go down the stairs, then she remembered something. Linda went back into Josie's bathroom and reached for the blow-dryer and fumbled to turn it on. She'd never used one before, but she quickly found the On switch and aimed the warm air at her scalp as she raked a hand through her hair. When she was done, her hair was still damp, but it had a smoothness she didn't get from air drying it at home, or when she dried it in front of the battery-operated fan in her room.

She hung the blow-dryer back on the hook beside the sink, then reached for a tube of perfumed lotion she must have missed earlier. She smeared it on her hands until they were soft and felt elegant. If Stephen could see—and smell—her now . . . Linda smiled and then headed down the stairs.

Josie struggled to mash the potatoes. Her entire right hand was numb now and part of her arm. She knew all too well that she was supposed to call the doctor if she began to experience numbness on the right side of her body. *Not tonight.*

She bowed her head as visions of her youth came flooding back, a time when prayer was something she practiced daily. Now, it just felt awkward. But it had worked before, when she had her headache, and she was willing to try anything. *God, please help me to stay well enough to enjoy this time with my daughter. Don't let me get sick—or die—while she's here. Please.*

She raised her head in time to hear Linda coming through the den. Josie took a deep breath, forced a smile, and put the potatoes on the table in the dining room with her left hand.

"Josie, that bathroom is wonderful. That was the best bath I've ever had in my life!" Linda was glowing, and her daughter's youthful zest sucked the fear and worry right out of Josie's mind.

"Good, I'm so glad. I thought you might like taking a bath in my room, in that big tub." Josie felt a bit guilty, knowing that Mary Ellen and Abe couldn't—and wouldn't—offer Linda the kind of luxuries that Josie had enjoyed for most of her life.

"Can I help you do something?" Linda folded her hands in front of her, and Josie didn't think she'd ever seen a more beautiful image. *My daughter. In my home.*

"No." Josie forced herself to look away from Linda. She felt like she could stare at her forever. She'd waited so long for this. "Everything is ready." Josie motioned for Linda to take a seat across from her at the table where she'd arranged two place settings.

Linda hesitated but slowly sat down. She stared at the china, stemware, and serving dishes on the table. Josie had wanted to set the perfect table, but this might be too much for Linda.

"Hey, I said this was going to be like a slumber party, right?" Josie cupped her hips with her hands. "Why don't we take our plates into the den, curl up on the couch, and eat in our laps while we watch TV?"

"Really?" Linda smiled as Josie picked up her own plate with her left hand. "Let's just fill them and take them to the living room."

Josie set her plate on the table beside the meatloaf and then picked up a spatula with her left hand to scoop out a small portion. "Help yourself."

Linda didn't move, though, and her brow creased with worry. "What's wrong with your hand?"

Josie looked down at her arm, swallowed hard, and tried to control the panic she felt when she saw her right arm jerking like it had a mind of its own. "Oh, it's just—oh, it's nothing. It just happens sometimes."

Linda stood up and rounded the table, then stared down at Josie's twitching arm. "It's not nothing. Does it hurt?"

"No. It doesn't hurt at all. I'm just having some motor function issues. It'll go away in a minute." Josie piled some potatoes on her plate, more than she'd ever eat. "Here, sweetie. Fill your plate, and we'll go pick out a movie." She nodded toward the potatoes.

Linda didn't move. "Does the doctor know?"

"Yes, it's really no big deal." Josie shrugged. "I take medicine for it. Sometimes it's worse than others."

"But it doesn't hurt?"

Linda seemed unusually preoccupied with pain, and Josie wasn't sure whether or not to question her about it. "No, it doesn't hurt. I promise."

Hesitantly, Linda went back to the other side of the table, picked up her plate, and began filling it.

"How do you stay so thin, eating like that?" Josie grinned, but she could feel her right hand starting to twitch even more.

Linda was focused on the salad Josie had prepared and helping herself to a nice-size portion. "I reckon it's because we work a lot. There's lots to do on a farm."

"Oh my gosh!" Josie clamped her eyes closed for a moment. When she opened them, Linda had stopped serving herself salad and was staring at Josie. "I almost forgot. The doctor's office left a message and changed an appointment I have from Thursday to tomorrow, so I have a doctor's appointment at ten o'clock in the morning at Lancaster General." She paused and offered Linda what she hoped was a comforting smile. "Just routine." One more doctor confirming what she already knew to be true. *Mrs. Dronberger, the lesion in your brain stem is inoperable, and since all other treatments have failed, we are sorry to tell you . . .* She'd heard it enough to recite it for them.

"Is it for that jerkiness in your hand?" Linda gazed up at her with such concern in her eyes that Josie swallowed a knot in her throat.

"Yes, but it's not a big deal." Josie lifted her plate with her left hand. "Let's go sit on the couch and eat."

"*Mei onkel* is a doctor. Do you want me to have him look at your hand, maybe you won't have to go all the way to Lancaster General? *Mei onkel* has a clinic right here in Paradise."

Josie knew Linda was referring to her husband's friend, Noah Stoltzfus, but she didn't mention it. "Actually, I'm going to see a specialist." Josie nodded for Linda to follow her into the living room. She sat down and tucked her legs beneath her. Robert hated to eat anywhere but the dining room table, so this was a treat for Josie as well, watching television while eating. It angered her that her hand had picked this night to act up, but she'd ask Dr. Phillips about it in the morning.

"Is it serious?" Linda sat down on the opposite end of the couch, keeping her feet together on the floor while balancing her plate in her lap. She stared hard into Josie's eyes.

Josie hated herself for lying, but she was not going to mess up these two weeks. "No, it's not."

"*Gut.*" Linda sighed with relief, then bowed her head.

Josie did the same, but she didn't want to talk to God right now. She opened one eye and watched her right hand twitching. Maybe it wasn't so much that she didn't believe in God; maybe she was just madder than heck at Him. The issue was becoming more and more confusing for her.

Mary Ellen tried to focus on the book she was reading in bed, but she couldn't get her mind off of Linda.

"Mary Ellen, you're tapping your feet together." Abe gently nudged her foot with his. "You always do that when you're upset or worried about something." Her husband pulled off his reading glasses and set the book he was reading aside, the one with a motorcycle on the front. "Linda is fine."

"You don't know that, Abe." Mary Ellen glanced at the book on his nightstand and arched one brow. "There's much temptation in the *Englisch* world."

Abe followed her eyes to the bedside table. "*Ya*, I reckon there is. But Linda will make *gut* choices." He paused, then grinned. "Now quit eyeballing my book like I've turned to the other side." Abe settled back against his pillow and stretched his legs.

"I just don't see why you read such nonsense." She pointed to Abe's reading material. "What could a book like that possibly have to offer you?"

Abe shrugged. "It just interests me, those bikes. How fast they can go, what size motors they have, and how much the *Englisch* will pay for one." He chuckled. "I reckon it's just something to do, Mary Ellen. You worry too much. About everything."

Mary Ellen sat up taller and narrowed her eyes at him. "I do not." She folded her arms across her chest. "I worry about what needs to be worried about."

"Well, my motorcycle book shouldn't be one of those things." He pulled her close. "And I feel like we are past the worst part with Linda. My biggest fear was that she wouldn't forgive us, and she did. Now, let our *maedel* spend some time with Josephine, while she can. And try not to worry."

Mary Ellen sat quietly for a while as shimmering rays of light from the lanterns danced on the clapboard walls. She wondered what Linda and Josephine were doing right now. What did Josephine cook, or had they gone out to eat? Would they stay up late talking or go to bed early? What plans were they making for tomorrow?

She gave her head a quick shake and tried to clear the worry from her heart. Abe was right. She was worrying too much. But one thing scared her more than Linda leaving the community— picking up the pieces of Linda's broken heart if she got too close to Josephine. Did Josephine even think about that before she plowed into their lives?

Linda threw her head back on the couch and couldn't remember the last time she'd laughed so hard or had so much fun.

"That is a funny story. What did your mother do?" Linda tucked her white nightgown underneath her legs on the couch and twisted to face Josie. "I bet you got punished, no?"

"Oh, yeah." Josie smoothed wrinkles from her peach-colored robe with her left hand. Linda could still see Josie's right hand and arm twitching, but she tried not to stare. "I was grounded for a month after that."

"Grounded? Like being punished?"

"Yep. I was punished. I couldn't go anywhere with any of my friends." Josie shook her head, but she was grinning.

"Was it worth it, though? I mean, do you wish you hadn't done it?" Linda tried to picture Josie and her friends filling up a fountain in a nearby town with bubbles, so much so that the bubbles spilled across two blocks into the streets.

"It didn't seem like it at the time because we were in so much trouble." Josie rolled her eyes. "It ended up on television because the bubbles were slowing traffic, then one of the girls bragged to someone, and we all eventually got caught." She giggled, and for a moment, she seemed like she was Linda's age. "But no. No regrets. It's just one of those things we did as kids. No one got hurt, and . . ." She smiled. "And now I can share it with you, something to remember someday when . . ." Josie drew in a long breath, shook her head a bit. "Anyway, it's just a fun story to remember."

Linda had done her share of talking throughout the night too. She'd told Josie all about Stephen, including how she'd forgotten to check for a note by the bridge. "That's so romantic," Josie had said. And she'd shared about her own school years. Josie had already known that Amish children only went to school through the eighth grade, and Linda certainly didn't have any fun stories to share like the ones Josie had. But Josie hung on Linda's every word, in a way that no one had done in a long time. Like she was someone truly special.

"I bet you are not used to staying up this late." Josie glanced at the clock on her mantel. "It's almost midnight."

"It's all right." Linda couldn't take her eyes from the clock. "That's so pretty."

"That clock? Yes, it is. I brought that back from Germany about six years ago when I went with Robert. That mahogany finish is gorgeous."

"I love the way it chimes too. Little chimes every fifteen minutes, longer on the half hour, and then even longer on the hour. I just love that."

They sat quietly for a moment. "You can have it," Josie said sheepishly after a while. "I'd be glad for you to have it."

Linda's eyes widened. "No, I could never." She shook her head, but still couldn't take her eyes off the clock. Sitting about a foot high on the mantel, the timepiece wasn't really fancy, just beautiful. Simple and lovely.

"Linda, I'd really like for you to have it. I don't want to do anything to upset your parents, but I know clocks are allowed. Please take it as a gift from me."

Josie's voice was begging her to reconsider, and Linda could picture how beautiful the clock would look on the mantel at home. *In Mamm's home.* "No, I really can't." She turned to Josie. "But it's nice of you to offer." She tucked her chin.

"You know, Robert says I do that a lot too."

Linda looked up. "What's that?"

"We both lower our heads and look down when we feel uncomfortable and shy about something."

Linda made a conscious effort not to do it again, even though she wanted to do it at this uncomfortable moment.

"When you were born, you had a birthmark above your right knee. Do you still have it?"

Linda untucked her legs from beneath her on the couch and stretched her right leg. She raised her nightgown to reveal the mark. "*Ya,* I still have it all right. It's big too." She shrugged and put her gown down. "But it's all right. It's always covered by my dress."

They were quiet for a few moments again.

"Linda. It's a dream come true for me, you being here. I've dreamed about this since you were born. Thank you for staying with me." Josie's eyes filled with water as she reached over and clasped

Linda's hand, and Linda wished she could feel what Josie was feeling, but it was all just too new. She was still getting used to the idea that Josie was her birth mother, but she didn't remember Josie giving her to her parents, or understand how hard that must have been. She wanted to return the affection Josie had been showing her all evening, but she wasn't sure how. She eased her hand free.

"It is late, no? Maybe we should go to bed." She stood up and cupped a hand over her hair, which she'd pulled into a bun on top of her head.

"Sure. I know it's late." Josie stood up too, but her expression reflected her disappointment. Josie's hand and arm were still shaking.

"Can I come with you to your doctor's appointment in the morning?"

"Oh, I don't know. Don't you want to sleep in, and when I get back we can go do something? You don't want to hang out with me at the hospital. Sometimes, you have to wait, and—"

"I don't mind. I'm sure I'll get up in plenty of time to go."

"Okay." Josie frowned a bit. "If you want to."

"Oh, and Josie?"

"Yes?" Josie blew out a candle on the coffee table.

"Stephen asked me to go swimming at the creek on Thursday. Is that all right with you?"

Josie touched Linda's arm with her left hand. Linda could see her right arm twitching out of the corner of her eye, but she kept her eyes on Josie's.

"I want you to do anything you want to do while you're here. Anything. And by all means, I refuse to interfere with your love life. Definitely go swimming with Stephen."

Linda smiled. "*Danki*, Josie. For everything."

Josie wrapped her arms around Linda and held on for what seemed like forever, and Linda returned the hug. It had been such a wonderful night, hearing about Josie's life, sharing her own life with—with her friend. In Linda's mind, she knew that's all Josie would ever be, and she hoped that Josie would be all right with that too.

Once upstairs, Josie threw herself on the bed. No headache, and she was eternally grateful for that, but the sporadic jerking of her right hand and arm both bothered her and worried her. But tonight, she just wanted to bask in the feel of having Linda under her roof for the first time in twelve years. No, fourteen—fourteen years. No, she's . . .

How old is—is?

Linda. That's her name. Linda. Linda is . . .

Josie grabbed her head with her only good hand. No headache, but something wasn't right. She bolted straight up on the bed, as if sitting up would send a rush of blood to her head and clear the fog that seemed to be wrapping around her brain like a cocoon.

What's happening? Why can't I remember how old she is? I should know this . . .

13

GROGGY FROM SLEEP, JOSIE SAT UP IN BED AND LOOKED down at her hand and arm. She brushed her hand, then her arm, against her leg and smiled at the returned sensation. Closing her eyes, she took a deep breath. "Linda is seventeen years old. Her birthday is the seventeenth of August," she said in a whisper. Everything was back to normal.

She glanced at the clock on her nightstand about the time the phone started ringing, and she answered it on the first ring. A fuzzy voice spoke on the other end of the line.

"Robert, is that you? I can barely hear you."

"Josie, are you okay? Is everything all right?"

"Everything is great. Fabulous. I'm having the best time with Linda." No way she was going to mention the numbness in her hand and arm last night or the slight loss of memory. This trip was important to Robert. "As a matter of fact, I smell bacon. Linda must have gotten up early and made breakfast." *Wow.* She swung her legs over the side of the bed and ran a hand through tousled hair. "How was your trip? Are you at your hotel yet?"

"Josie, can you hear me?"

"Yes, honey. I'm here. Where are you?"

"I'm still on the plane. I've been sitting on the plane for two hours. Something's going on, and they won't let us get off the plane."

Josie's heart thudded hard in her chest. "What do you mean something is going on?"

"I don't know, hon. I can't understand the people speaking in Chinese around me. I'm sure everything is fine, but we aren't being allowed to get off the plane. That's all I know. But . . ."

"Robert, you're breaking up."

"Josie, it looks like they're letting us off. I'll call you tonight, okay? I can barely hear you."

"I love you. Can you hear me?"

"Yes, babe. I love you too. Call you tonight."

Josie sighed a breath of relief as she hung up the phone, though a thread of worry still lingered. She'd feel better when Robert called tonight.

She heard a noise from downstairs and quickly pulled on her robe and headed down the steps.

"Smells like coffee in here." She shuffled across the tile floor in her socks.

"I wasn't sure how to make the cappa cappa—"

"Cappuccino." Josie reached for two cups in the cabinet. "I think regular coffee sounds great this morning. And I smell bacon."

"I already made breakfast, I hope that's okay. It's keeping warm in the oven."

Josie's eyes widened. "Linda, you're my guest. You didn't have to do that."

"*Ach*, I know. But I wanted to. I didn't know if your hand and arm would be . . ."

Josie held up her arm, then wiggled her hand. "Look. Good

as new. And no, I don't mind that you made breakfast. What a treat!"

"I made bacon and eggs with onion, bell pepper, tomatoes, and some bacon bits I found in your refrigerator." She pointed to the other side of the counter. "And some toast." Linda smiled as she stared at the toaster. "Much better than broiling it in the oven."

"Thank you. You must have gotten up early. I'm sorry I didn't get up in time to help you."

"No. I like to cook. *Mamm* says it's important to be able to cook *gut* for a husband."

"She's right. Although . . . I'm afraid that if I had counted on that for Robert to marry me, I'd still be waiting." She tipped her head to one side and twisted her mouth. "I'm not a great cook. If the truth be told, I was worried about the meatloaf."

"No, it was *gut*."

"Are you s-u-r-e?"

Linda giggled. "*Ya*, I reckon I'm sure." She pulled a skillet of eggs from the oven and placed it on the kitchen counter. Then retrieved a plate of bacon.

"Do you want to eat on the patio?" Josie pointed to the large window in the kitchen. "It's lovely out there this time of day. The birds are just starting to wake up, and it's not too hot."

"Sure."

"We probably need to leave for Lancaster about nine fifteen." She paused. "Are you sure you want to go?"

"*Ya*. I'll just wait for you. It's no problem."

Josie wanted Linda by her side constantly; she just didn't want to take a chance that Linda would find out about her illness. Not yet. "Okay. We'll do something fun afterward."

They filled their plates and moved to the patio. The glass table was surrounded by flowering potted plants, and it offered a nice view of Robert's garden.

"What do you have planted?" Linda pointed to the garden as she took a seat in one of the chairs.

"Oh, that's Robert's garden. I think he has tomatoes, cucumbers, and some peppers. I'm not sure exactly."

"We musn't forget to water it while he's gone." Linda smiled, then bowed her head.

Josie lowered her chin. *I'm dying. If you're there, stop me from dying.* Her silent plea was laced with bitterness, and an instant pang of guilt stabbed at her heart, which caused uncertainty. *If I don't believe, why do I feel guilty?* She didn't need this type of confusion this morning. She raised her head and waited for Linda to do the same, then they both began to eat.

Josie and her daughter. On her patio. She was determined to live in each special moment without dreading the future.

Josie sat in an oak chair with a worn leather seat, facing a desk covered with papers and file folders, and she wondered how Dr. Phillips kept anything straight in this mess.

"Mrs. Dronberger." Dr. Phillips walked in and extended his hand. "It's nice to meet you."

"Nice to meet you too." Josie stood up to shake his hand, then sat back down when Dr. Phillips took a seat behind the desk.

"I've reviewed all your files and test results. Has anything changed since Dr. Stoltzfus had your records forwarded to me? Any new symptoms or problems?"

Josie knew if she told Dr. Phillips about the numbness in her hand and arm, he most likely would subject her to further testing, or worse—admit her to the hospital. She'd waited too long to spend time with Linda. "No. Still just a lot of headaches."

"Well, I'm going to recommend that you stay on your current meds for now, and I really don't see the need for another MRI just yet, since you just had one a couple of weeks ago. But I would like to schedule you for one thirty days from now, so we can see what that tumor is doing." He pulled off a pair of dark-rimmed reading glasses and placed them on the desk. Dr. Phillips was a well-built man of around fifty, Josie assumed, with a full head of gray hair and eyes that seemed careful not to reveal too much information. Josie assumed they trained for that in medical school.

Josie nodded and waited for the doctor to go on. He rubbed his eyes, then replaced his glasses with a sigh. Josie knew what was coming.

Dr. Phillips opened a file and read for a moment. "I see where you had radiation therapy two years ago." He glanced up at Josie.

"Yes. I did. And I was hopeful for a while. The tumor regressed, and my symptoms subsided. For a while." She paused, crossed her legs. "But then I had a seizure."

He read some more, then removed his glasses again. "Mrs. Dronberger, I see where you've also had chemo, and that failed as well. The only option left would be for me to try to remove that tumor, and . . ." He shook his head. "I don't think I could give you more than a five percent chance of surviving the surgery." He paused, as if waiting for a reaction that wasn't coming. "Is this even an option for you?"

"No. I want to live out however long I have, not die on an

operating table." She folded her hands in her lap. "This is what I've been told repeatedly. Five percent."

"That lesion is located in an . . ." He stopped and pulled a large envelope from underneath the file. "Here, let me show you." Dr. Phillips pulled her MRI out and faced it toward her. "Do you see this?" He pointed to the lesion that Josie had seen a hundred times before.

She smiled politely. "Yes."

"Where it's located in the brain stem makes it almost impossible to get to. I imagine most doctors wouldn't even consider it. And I'll be honest with you, I've never successfully taken out a lesion of this size in this location, but there is a small window of hope should you ever feel that you want me to try."

"Five percent isn't much of a window, Dr. Phillips." She folded her arms across her chest. She knew this would be a waste of time, but she'd endure for Robert, who couldn't pass up any opportunity to get another opinion, even though they were all the same.

"No. It's not." He gazed at her, in the familiar, sympathetic way she'd gotten used to. "But, Mrs. Dron—"

"Just Josie."

"All right. Josie, if your quality of life should come to a point where you are willing to take the risk, you should have that documented." He paused. "For example. If you should lose the ability to remember, to think clearly, and it's evident to your husband that your quality of life is suffering greatly, you might want to make sure that he has power of attorney to make decisions for you. It might be that at that point, the surgery would be an option. Do you understand?"

"Yes, I understand. My husband already has my power of

attorney for such things." She glanced out the window and wished she'd never come here, never allowed herself to have the tiniest glimmer of hope. She just wanted to pretend for two weeks that everything was normal.

They sat quietly for a few moments.

"Josie, have you had any type of counseling? Perhaps a support group of others who are going through what you are?"

"I've been in counseling, Dr. Phillips. I understand what's happening."

"Understanding it and dealing with it are two separate things."

Josie stared out the window of the eight-story building. "I'm dealing with it the best anyone can, I suppose."

They were quiet again.

"Do you have any questions?"

"Nope." She turned toward Dr. Phillips. "I appreciate you seeing me on such short notice, but honestly, Dr. Phillips, you aren't telling me anything that I haven't already heard."

"Then you do realize how your body will begin to shut down? Numbness, particularly on the right side. Motor functions will be affected, and even memory disturbances." He wiped his forehead with his hand, then continued. "There will be increased brain pressure as the lesion expands, Josie. The headaches will become debilitating and could even cause some changes to your personality. I'm assuming all of this has been covered by your doctors before me?"

"Yes. It has." She forced a smile. "I understand."

Dr. Phillips tilted his brow and looked at her uncertainly, waiting for more. Finally, he said, "Well, all right. Then I suppose we'll have another look in a month."

Josie nodded, stood up, and extended her hand. "Again, thank you for seeing me on such short notice."

What Dr. Phillips didn't understand was her ability to program herself for the situation. She'd learned that a long time ago. When she didn't want Robert to worry, there was a program for that. When she didn't want a doctor to see her cry, there was a program for that. When she needed to pretend that this was all a false reality, a program for that. She'd been doing it for so long, sometimes she actually believed she'd never have to face the grim reality before her.

She rubbed her hands together as she walked down the hallway. *Good.* Complete feeling. It had been like that all morning. She was glad she didn't mention anything about the numbness to Dr. Phillips.

After she made her appointment for an MRI in a month, she walked into the waiting room to find Linda surrounded by four women. They all had their heads bowed and were holding hands. Linda looked up when she entered the room.

"I'm sorry. I have to go." Linda stood up. "I will pray for each of your loved ones."

One woman hugged her. "Thank you."

Josie waited until Linda walked to where she was standing a few feet away.

"Normally, it's not our place to minister to others, but all these women are sad about a very sick loved one, so we all prayed together. I told them of the Lord's peace and how he never abandons us in our time of need." She smiled, then her expression grew serious. "What did the doctor say about your hand and arm?"

"Oh, it's fine. Just a neurological problem from the headache.

No biggie." *If there is a hell, I'm going there for lying.* "Let's forget all this and go do something fun."

Linda didn't move. "Are you sure that's all he said?"

Josie nodded. "I told you, no biggie. How about a trip to the mall? Does that sound good? And maybe get some lunch after that? By then, we'll be hungry after that fabulous breakfast you made." She headed toward the exit. Linda followed, waving at her new friends on the way out.

"Sure. That all sounds fine."

Linda had been to the mall plenty of times with her *Englisch* friends since she'd begun her *rumschpringe* almost two years ago, but her friends clearly didn't have the wealth that Josie had.

Linda thumbed through the blue jeans on the rack while Josie was in the dressing room.

"No one has to know if you want to try them on."

Linda turned to see Josie standing beside her with several pairs of pants and a couple of shirts draped over her arms.

"*Ach*, I couldn't." Linda wondered if she would look like the women in the fashion magazines, or even like Josie. She smiled. "Or could I?"

"It's only clothes. And you're just giving them a try. It's your running-around period, right?"

Linda thought for a moment, tried to visualize herself wearing the stylish blue jeans. "Okay." She picked out a size she thought might fit and also grabbed a pink, lacy blouse, then walked to the dressing room.

After she slipped out of her dress, she pulled the tight blue jeans on, then slipped the blouse over her head. She had a slender figure like Josie's, but enough curves to fill out the *Englisch* clothes. Vanity and pride were forbidden, and guilt rose to the surface as Linda studied herself in the mirror, but she pushed it aside, and just for this moment, she pretended she was one of the fashion models in the magazines. She put her hand on her hip and turned slightly to one side, the way the girls in the magazines did. She pushed her chest out a bit, puckered her lips, and wished she could pull her hair from the prayer covering to make the look complete.

"Can I come in?"

Linda's heart jumped in her chest when she heard Josie's voice, and she could feel the red taking over her cheeks. "Uh, wait. Um. Just a minute." She gathered herself, then opened the curtain.

"You look adorable." Josie smiled. "Do you want me to get them for you?"

"*Ach*, no. I'm not allowed."

"Okay. I understand. Like I've told you, I don't want to do anything to upset your parents. I just wasn't sure if you were allowed since it's your *rumschpringe*."

Linda recalled the time Marian Kauffman wore blue jeans into town while she was in her running-around period. Her parents had found out, and even though they weren't happy, they didn't do anything because certain behavior is allowed during that time. Josie closed the curtain.

"Wait." Linda pulled it open again. "I reckon, maybe it might be all right." She lowered her head, but quickly raised it, now that she was aware she tended to do that.

"Great. I'll meet you at the register."

Linda stood looking at herself in the *Englisch* clothes, and suddenly she thought of her mother. Her *real* mother.

"Where are the clothes?" Josie asked when Linda met her by the register.

"I changed my mind."

Josie's brow crinkled as she spoke. "Are you sure?"

"*Ya*, I'm sure."

"Okay." Josie looked at her own pile on the counter, then glanced at Linda. "You know, I think I have plenty of clothes." She turned to the clerk. "I've changed my mind too."

As they exited the mall, the sun felt good against Linda's cheeks, a welcome contrast to the cold in the mall. Josie draped an arm around Linda's shoulder, and for whatever reason, Linda thought of *Mamm* again.

Late that afternoon, Linda helped Josie fold clothes she'd pulled from the electric tumble dryer. How much easier wash day would be with such modern conveniences, but she noticed right away that Josie's dried clothes didn't smell the same as her clothes at home, a certain freshness that could only come from line drying.

She handed Josie a folded pair of blue jeans.

"Those used to be my favorite jeans, but I've lost about ten pounds, and they don't fit very well any more."

"I like the beads along the waist." Linda studied the sleek design, then glanced around the room, making double sure they were alone. "Can I try them on?"

Josie handed her the jeans. "Of course you can. You can have them, if they fit, but only if you're comfortable with that."

"No. I just want to try them on."

"Here try on this blouse with them. That's one of my favorites." She handed Linda a bright red blouse with lace on the collar. "It'll be our secret."

Linda darted up the stairs with the clothes and returned feeling as pretty as Josie. She'd left her hair in a bun atop her head but shed her *kapp*. "What do you think?"

"I think you look beautiful! But Linda . . ." Josie's expression softened into a nurturing look she'd seen on her mother's face. "I think you look beautiful in your Plain dresses too. Simply gorgeous."

Linda knew that looks were of no concern. They shouldn't be anyway. It's how she'd been raised and what she truly believed. But it felt good to bend the rules just a bit. She'd never been in any real trouble, and if this was the worse thing she ever did during her *rumschpringe*, her conscience could handle it.

Josie had turned on some music. Another thing they didn't have at home. Songs of worship during church service were only sung in High German. There was some harmonizing at Sunday singings, but nothing like this. Instruments were forbidden in their community, said to invoke too much unnecessary emotion. But when Josie's hips started swaying to the music, Linda found her hips moving to the tune as well.

"Oops. I forgot to turn on the dryer after I pulled this load out. Be right back." Josie headed past the kitchen to the large laundry room. Linda kept swaying her hips to the music until she heard a knock at the door.

"Can you get that?" Josie yelled from the back part of the house.

Linda walked to the front door, pulled on the knob, and swung the door wide.

Without even thinking about how she was dressed.

14

"STEPHEN!" LINDA STOOD FROZEN IN THE DOORWAY. "What are you doing here?"

Stephen eyed Linda up and down in the blue jeans and bright red shirt. He was speechless, but he could feel his mouth curving upward into a smile. This is exactly what he'd feared, his Linda succumbing to temptation. But seeing her in the tight jeans and lacy red shirt showed off curves he didn't know she had, a figure she'd kept hidden beneath her Plain dresses. It wasn't anger bubbling to the surface, something entirely different. Stephen swallowed hard.

"I just wanted to make sure you were all right. You told me Monday that you'd go by the bridge, and my note was still there tonight on my way home from work." He frowned. "I reckon you weren't that interested in what I had to say."

She stepped onto the front porch and closed the door behind her. "Of course I'm interested in what you have to say. You know how much I love your poems."

"You don't even have your *kapp* on." He looped his thumbs beneath his suspenders and scowled.

She mumbled something under her breath, shook her head, then folded her arms across her chest. "I know what you must be thinkin', but I'm not straying from our ways. I was just trying some of Josie's clothes on. For fun." Her expression challenged him to quiz her further, so he just shrugged.

"If you say so." He tipped his straw hat in her direction. "I'll let you get back to what you were doin'."

She grabbed his arm. "No, wait." Then she threw him a smile, the kind that always made him melt. "Where's my note? Is it still there?"

Stephen recalled the proposal he'd written. "No. I threw it away."

"Why?" Her lip folded into a pout.

"Because it just didn't seem important anymore." Stephen wondered how much of the *Englisch* life Linda was going to get involved in. Maybe he should just walk away from her for good. What if his grandfather saw the way she was dressed? Another part of him wanted to drop to his knee right then, to assure that she would marry him and remain a part of the community. But he shifted his weight and stared back at her with the same challenging look.

Her expression softened. "Anything you write to me is important. I'm sorry that you're mad."

"I'm not mad, Linda. I just figured you would have been by our spot under the bridge before now, and . . ." He paused with a sigh. "I'm just surprised to see you in Josie's *Englisch* clothes. You sure you ain't gonna jump to the other side?"

She stepped forward, her arms still crossed. "Stephen, I cannot believe you would even ask me that."

He shrugged again. "Well, it just wonders me to see ya dressed like this."

"It ain't . . ."

Linda stopped when the front door swung open. "Hello."

If Stephen wanted to know what Linda would look like when she got older, now he knew. Linda looked exactly like her birth mother, but with darker hair instead of blonde, and minus the lines around the older woman's eyes.

"You must be Stephen," the woman said with a smile. "I recognize you from Linda's description. I'm Josie." She shook Stephen's hand, then turned to Linda. "You're right. He is very handsome."

Linda's cheeks reddened, but it warmed Stephen's heart to know Linda had said that, even though vanity was to be avoided. He forced a half-smile.

"Come in." Josie stepped backward and pushed the door wide.

Stephen raised one brow at Linda, who nodded.

Once inside, Linda excused herself. "I'm going to go change clothes." She scurried up the stairs, and Josie motioned for him to sit down on the couch. Josie sat down in a chair on the other side of the coffee table. He glanced around the fancy home, not comfortable in it and not comfortable being alone with Josie. He resented the time Linda was spending with her, and he was afraid it would show. Too much temptation for Linda. Then he recalled his reaction to Linda in the *Englisch* clothes and decided maybe he'd best just work on his own temptations.

"It's so nice to meet you . . . um . . . oh gosh. Um . . ." Josie rubbed her temples with both hands. "I'm sorry. It's nice to meet you . . ."

"Stephen."

Josie closed her eyes, slowly reopened them, and dropped her hands in her lap. "I'm sorry. I knew that." She attempted a smile.

"So, I understand that tomorrow you and Linda are going swimming at the creek?"

"*Ya.*"

"That should be fun. I know Linda is looking forward to it." She appeared as if she was trying to smile again, but instead cringed so badly that Stephen felt himself cringing just watching her.

"You all right?"

"Actually, I have a really bad headache." She stood up. "I need to go take something for this. I apologize for leaving you downstairs by yourself."

Before Stephen could answer, she was hurrying up the stairs with one hand holding her head. It was only a moment later when Linda came down the stairs.

"Josie said to apologize again for leaving you." Linda sat down beside Stephen on the couch. "She gets really bad headaches sometimes."

Stephen was glad to see Linda back in a dark blue dress and black apron. "You look beautiful." He reached for her hand and squeezed. "You don't need all that fancy stuff."

"I know that. I was just, you know . . . playing dress up." She smiled.

Stephen decided to take advantage of them being alone, in the nice air-conditioned house. He leaned over and kissed Linda softly on the lips, then said, "I just don't want you to get too used to all this."

"I'm not. I'm just trying to get to know Josie, and all this comes along with Josie. That's all."

"You plannin' to see your folks during the two weeks?"

"*Ya.* I thought I'd go spend the day Sunday with them. There's no worship service, but I'd like to just be there." She scowled, then leaned closer and whispered. "We don't have any kind of devotions here, and I miss that. I really do."

Stephen was glad to hear that she missed it. "Maybe you should bring it up, see if she'll share devotion time with you."

Linda tipped her head to one side. "I think I will. I'd enjoy that."

Josie popped two Vicodin in her mouth and downed the pills with some water she had on her bedside table. This was a bad one, and when the phone started to ring beside her, she thought her head might explode. She grabbed it on the first ring.

"Josie?"

"Robert? I can barely hear you." It hurt to talk, and as much as she wanted to talk to Robert, she was hoping he'd keep it short.

"Honey, listen. Something's happened. Have you been watching TV?"

Josie took a deep, cleansing breath and tried to fight the pain enough to understand what Robert was saying. "No. What do you mean something's happened? Are you all right?"

"Yes. I'm okay. But they are having their own version of 9-11 over here, and over eleven hundred people are dead from an explosion at last count. Turn on CNN."

"What? Oh, my gosh! But you're okay? Robert, you're in a safe place, right? Should you come home?" Josie stood up, kept one hand to her head, and wandered restlessly around the room.

"Josie, listen to me. I am in a very safe place, far from where the explosion occurred, so don't worry. Things will settle down again soon, but I just didn't want you to see all that on television and worry. I am perfectly safe where I'm at."

"Thank God," she whispered.

"What?"

"Thank goodness." She spoke loud and clear. "Thank goodness you're safe."

"I love you, babe. I'll try to call you later, but if not, we'll talk tomorrow."

"I love you too, Robert. Be safe."

Josie hung up the phone and decided to head downstairs to check on Linda and Stephen and to turn on the television. Her head was still killing her, but she knew the meds would take effect soon, and she wanted to see what was going on in China.

"Where's Stephen?" Josie glanced around the living room.

"He went on home. Said to tell you it was nice to meet you."

"I feel badly that I had to leave him like that, but I had a really bad headache come on." She reached for her temple and could feel the sharp pulse against her fingertip.

"Is it better?"

"No. But it will be. I just took some pills." She reached for the remote. "Robert just called, and there's been a big explosion in China. He's far away from the action, but he said it's just like 9-11 was here." Josie pushed the On button.

"Oh, no. Really?"

"Well, I don't think planes crashed into buildings, but there was an explosion, and Robert compared it to 9-11."

Josie began flipping channels until she reached CNN. She focused on the television, thankful that the Vicodin was kicking in. "That's horrible."

Live coverage from Beijing showed bodies covered with dark sheets among the wreckage of the explosion. It had occurred at a twenty-six-story high-rise not far from Peking University. The newscaster said that a well-known terrorist group had already taken credit for the despicable act.

Josie watched the details unfolding. "I'm glad Robert called to tell me he was okay. I'd have been worried to death if I'd turned on the TV and saw this." She shook her head. "So many dead. So tragic." Josie continued to view the devastation. Her heart hurt for all of them. "As bad as this is, at least it wasn't a direct hit on the university where all those young people go to school."

Josie heard a sniffle and turned to Linda. Tears were streaming down her daughter's cheeks, then she began to sob loudly. Josie ran to her side and threw her arms around her.

"Linda?" Josie held her tightly; she was trembling. "Sweetheart, are you all right?"

"Those people, they are dead, no?" Linda pulled away from her, swiped at her eyes, and pointed to the television. "The ones covered up."

Josie gazed into Linda's eyes as her daughter stared in horror at the disturbing images on the television, right about the time the newscaster said, "The death toll has now reached twelve hundred and twenty-two."

"Yes. I believe those people are dead."

Linda shook her head and covered her face with her hands. "I can't watch any more. I'm sorry, Josie."

"No, it's all right. We don't have to watch it." Josie clicked the remote and the screen went black. "I'm sorry. I didn't realize you would get so upset or I would have never turned it on, Linda. I'm sorry."

"We read about 9-11 in the newspaper when it happened here, but it's so much worse to see it on television. We need to pray." Linda reached for Josie's hand. "We need to pray for all those people in that place and for all those families who lost loved ones." Linda sniffled and bowed her head.

As Josie lowered her head, she squeezed Linda's hand tightly. Maybe some of Linda's faith would rub off on her.

Stephen scrubbed his courting buggy with soap and water so it would be nice and clean tomorrow when he picked up Linda to go swimming at the creek. Every time he envisioned the two of them in their swim clothes, and him without his elevated shoe, his stomach twisted with anxiety. But if he was going to marry Linda, this was something he knew he was going to have to get past.

He glanced over his shoulder when he heard a buggy pulling onto the driveway, then dried his hands and waited until his grandfather came to a stop.

"*Gut-n-owed.*" The elderly bishop stepped with care from the buggy, his gray beard spanning the length of his chest.

"Good evening to you, *Daadi.*"

"Where is the rest of the family?" His grandfather tipped his straw hat back as he approached Stephen, his back curved forward as he walked.

"Hannah and Annie are helping *Mamm* make supper," Stephen responded about his only two siblings, "and I reckon *Daed* is bathing already."

"*Gut.* We can talk before your supper."

Stephen removed his hat, wiped sweat from his brow, then placed it back on his head. "Is something wrong?" Stephen recognized the expression on his grandfather's face. Usually, it was directed at a member of the district who had displeased him. Stephen couldn't think of anything he'd done to warrant it.

"No, nothing is wrong, but I have concerns, Stephen."

Stephen's brows shot upward. "About me?"

His grandfather stroked his beard. "I understand Linda is staying in the *Englisch* woman's house for two weeks, no?"

"*Ya,* she is." Stephen was wondering who told him but surmised it could have been anyone. Nothing stayed a secret around here for long.

"Does this concern you? Her being there?"

"No. Not at all." Stephen's stomach flipped a bit when he realized he'd just lied to his grandfather. "I mean, maybe a little. But Linda's faith is strong, and she'll only be there for two weeks."

"Don't underestimate the bonds of blood. That woman is Linda's kin." Bishop Ebersol stood taller as he spoke and lifted his chin. "Linda is at a time in her life when she can choose the life she wants to live." His eyes narrowed in speculation. "Do you think she is continuing to practice the ways of the *Ordnung?*"

"*Ya, Daadi.* I reckon Linda just wants to get to know her mother. That's all. Then she'll come home."

"Very *gut* then. I was just on my way home from the Miller farm."

"How is Jonas?" Stephen knew that when Jonas passed, lots of people would be devastated. He was such a fixture in the community, such a wise soul, and everyone loved him. Linda would be very upset.

"Jonas is doing poorly. The doctor told the family that he is rapidly declining." His grandfather shook his head. "He will be greatly missed."

Stephen hung his head, not wanting to think about Jonas passing.

"I know it is almost suppertime. Tell the rest of the family I will be by with your *mammi* on Sunday for a visit." He turned to leave, but turned briefly around. "Keep Linda on course, Stephen. This is a delicate situation, her being with the *Englisch* woman."

"I will, *Daadi*."

Stephen recalled seeing Linda in Josie's *Englisch* clothes. He sure hoped he could keep Linda on track.

———————

Linda couldn't sleep that night. All tucked in under the covers of the princess bed, her mind raced with thoughts of what she'd seen on television. There was much in the *Englisch* world she didn't understand. She'd enjoyed her bath for the second night in Josie's big bathroom, but if all this sadness came with Josie's world, Linda was sure she didn't want any part of it for long.

She was disappointed that she'd been so caught up in her new surroundings that she'd forgotten to check the bridge for Stephen's note. But at least they would have tomorrow, an afternoon swimming in the creek. Linda didn't really care what they did, as long as they were together. Tomorrow, she'd reassure Stephen that the only things she wanted were to be in his arms and to be a member of the community. Maybe soon, he would think about asking her to marry him.

Linda closed her eyes and tried to sleep, but her mind was as restless as her body. She missed *Mamm* and *Daed*, even Luke and Matthew. She'd only been there since Tuesday, but it seemed longer.

Josie looked at the clock on her nightstand. Eleven thirty, and each minute seemed to be ticking by a hundred times faster than the last one. She'd never been more frantic to get her affairs in order than she was right now. She scanned the pile of personal mementos and keepsakes in front of her on the floor as her right hand began to shake again, something it had done several times during the course of the evening.

Linda had gone to bed early, and Josie sensed something was wrong. She wasn't sure how much of it had to do with the tragedy on television or if it was something else. Either way, Josie wanted Linda to know everything about her, and her entire life was poured out on the floor of her bedroom. With her left hand, she picked up a picture of her and her mother at the beach. Josie remembered her father taking the picture when she was about ten. She and her mom had made a sand castle together and were proudly displaying it for the camera.

Josie tossed the picture into the pile she didn't plan to leave for Linda, but then picked it up again and wondered if her mother would speak to Linda at Josie's funeral. Would they establish any kind of relationship after Josie was gone? Mom was not the kind of influence Josie wanted for Linda. All Mom cared about was status and what people thought, nothing like sweet Linda. Josie supposed she'd die without seeing her mother again, and sadly, that was all right with her.

Robert didn't call again tonight, but he'd said it might be tomorrow, so she tried not to worry. She had the television volume in her bedroom on low, and at last count, fatalities were at fifteen hundred. She recalled Linda's reaction to the news again and wondered if bringing her here was a mistake. Such innocence. And Josie was exposing her to life in a world she'd been sheltered from.

She slammed her right hand down hard on the carpeted floor, hoping the blow would jar some feeling into the numb limb. Nothing. She picked up a picture of her and Robert on vacation in Italy. It was one of her favorite pictures of Robert, handsomely dressed in cargo shorts and a white T-shirt, and she was wearing a yellow sundress and looked so happy. Robert was going to be a lost soul when she was gone. She recalled the first time she met Robert, through mutual friends, and the only blind date she'd ever been on. He'd stolen her heart on that first encounter at the Italian restaurant on Mason Boulevard.

Josie lay down in the middle of the floor, surrounded by tokens of her life lived thus far, a life soon to end, and she allowed herself to feel the pain in her heart, the fear of the unknown, and the absolute sense of loss she felt about not growing old with Robert and not being able to spend more time with her daughter. It was her most pitiful moment, she was sure, as she pulled her knees to her chest and sobbed.

"I don't want to die." She tucked her blue satin pajamas tight around her knees and hugged her legs. "Please, God. I don't want to die. I don't want to die. I'm afraid. I'm so scared." She sobbed hard, stifling her cries so as not to wake Linda.

And then she felt it.

His presence.

And then she heard it.

His voice.

I am here My child. The fool hath said in his heart, There is no God.

15

JOSIE AND LINDA SPENT THE MORNING WATCHING television, mostly sweet loves stories. Josie didn't turn on the news, and while she tried to focus on the movies she and Linda had picked out, her mind wandered. Linda had asked her if she was worried about Robert, and she said a little bit, which was true.

Josie could tell that Linda was anxious to see Stephen, mentioning their planned swimming trip several times. Linda seemed nervous as well and explained that girls in her district wore either shorts and a shirt to swim in or a one-piece bathing suit. She also said some of the girls wore a two-piece swimsuit, but she didn't own that kind and didn't think she'd wear it if she did.

Linda had left to try on her suit for Josie, and when she entered the room wearing her swimsuit, Josie rose from the couch. "That looks really good on you." Linda had chosen a dark blue, one-piece bathing suit.

"*Danki. Mamm* approved of this one when we went shopping in the city."

"Are you going to Pequea Creek?"

"*Ya.*" Linda tugged on her swimsuit in an effort to cover more of herself. Josie remembered her own breasts being larger than most girls' too.

"Sweetie, you're all in there. I promise." Josie smiled warmly. "Stephen will think you look great."

Linda blushed slightly. "It feels strange not to have my *kapp* on." She reached up and touched the clip that held her hair in a tight bun on top of her head. "What are you gonna do this afternoon, Josie?"

"Well, I thought I might take a little nap and then make us some dinner for later. Do you like lasagna?"

"*Ya!* I have that when we go to Paradiso. *Mamm* and *Daed* take us there about once a month. Do you know how to make lasagna?"

Josie smiled. "Actually, I make pretty good lasagna. So, I'll make that, a salad, and some garlic bread for us to eat when you get home from your swim with Stephen. How's that?"

"Sounds *gut*."

Josie heard the clippety-clop of horse hooves.

"There's Stephen." Linda headed toward the door. "I'll see you later."

"Have fun."

Josie watched out the window as Stephen pulled away with Linda beside him in the buggy. It was a bright, sunny afternoon, and the cool water in the creek would be a welcome relief from the heat. Josie remembered those days from her own youth. But twenty years ago, Amish girls wouldn't have been caught dead in a swimsuit like Linda was wearing, no matter how conservative. Times were changing. Even for the Amish.

Though she didn't have a headache this afternoon, Josie lay down on the couch anyway. She hadn't slept much last night. She couldn't shake that voice she'd heard. Her religious background had certainly taught her everything she needed to know about God, about Jesus. She'd studied the Bible. She'd gone to Bible study. And for a time, it seemed to make sense, even though she never felt any real connection to God, even back then.

Robert had so many valid arguments against the concept of God. "Josie, some humans need something to believe in, or there would be even more chaos than there already is," he'd said. "I'm not one of those people. My mind just can't grasp the concept of this higher power." He'd talk about evolution, how an all-powerful God wouldn't let people suffer this way, and on more than one occasion, he'd mentioned the possibility of otherworldly entities being in control. "There are too many pieces of the puzzle missing, parts of the Bible missing, cover-ups by religious rulers. It's just not an idea I can buy into."

But what if Robert was wrong? He was the most giving, loving, generous, and sincere person she'd ever known. Robert wasn't capable of telling a lie, and he lived each day to serve others. If what she'd been taught in Sunday school was correct, Robert was going straight to hell for not believing in God and His son, Jesus. And if there is a God, how could such an entity send such a good man to the depths of hell for all eternity?

What about me? What do I really believe? Am I changing my tune at the eleventh hour on the off chance that there might be a God, so that I'm not damned to hell? Is it too late for me? Again, she recalled the feeling she'd had the night before, the voice she thought she'd heard, and the calm that had spread over her. She'd felt like a child, wrapped in the comforting arms of a parent, unconditional love that could be felt to the core of her being.

She closed her eyes and tried to reconcile her thoughts, her feelings. But nothing made sense anymore.

Linda dipped her toe into the cool water at Pequea Creek and wondered when Stephen was going to shed his trousers, shirt, and shoes. She knew this was uncomfortable for him, but if they were going to be married someday, he was going to need to get past this. *If I can wear this bathing suit . . .*

Reflections of everything around them bounced off the clear blue water as sunshine streamed down through the trees, leaving patches of glassy stillness on the creek's surface. Linda poked the water with her foot until it made ripples across the reflection of her face.

"It's chilly." She turned to Stephen. "You coming in?" Linda eased down the creek bed until she was knee-deep in water.

"*Ya.*" Stephen sat down on the ground and fumbled with his shoes. Linda made it a point not to watch. She heard him toss his boots to the side and then the sound of him pulling off his trousers. She was sure Stephen had a bathing suit on underneath his brown pants, but the sound of him pulling them off, then tossing them on the ground, sent a ripple of anticipation through her. She turned around in time to see him toss his blue shirt and suspenders onto the pile and shivered at the sight of his beautifully proportioned body in nothing but a pair of gray and white swim trunks. He held his head high above a confident set of shoulders and broad chest, even though his square jaw tensed visibly. A gentle breeze blew his tawny-gold, bobbed hair as he stepped toward the water's edge with precise footing—as if he'd practiced it a thousand times.

Linda eased backward in the water until she was chest deep,

and it only took Stephen a few moments before he was facing her. Their eyes met in a new and unexplored way, and Linda wondered what was going through Stephen's mind. He leaned forward and kissed her tenderly on the lips, and the feel of his naked chest against her invoked both excitement and fear. She backed away, bit her bottom lip, and eased herself into deeper water.

Then without warning, she cupped her hands in the water and splashed Stephen in the face. Things were getting too intense, too serious.

"Hey!" He splashed her back, and in no time, they were carrying on like playful kids, instead of the young adults they were. And this felt better. There'd been enough serious moments in her life lately, and today she just wanted to play and have fun, put her worries aside.

And that's exactly what they did for the next two hours.

Abe wished he could do something to ease the worry in Mary Ellen's heart. His wife wasn't sleeping well, tossing and turning all night long, and during the day, she worked so hard he thought she might keel over.

"Mary Ellen, if everything isn't perfect while Linda is away, the boys and I will survive. You don't need to work so hard." He watched her scrubbing the floor after they'd finished supper Thursday evening.

"I reckon I can't have the *haus* a mess, Abe." She scrubbed the wood floor even harder with the sponge in her hand, although Abe hadn't a clue what she was scrubbing. It looked clean to him.

He squatted down beside her and eyed the floor. "What ya scrubbing, Mary Ellen? It ain't dirty."

She stopped abruptly and fired him a look. "Luke spilled orange juice here earlier, if you must know." Mary Ellen resumed the scrubbing as if she was mad at that floor.

He grabbed both her shoulders and pulled her to her feet even as she resisted. "Abe, what are you doing?"

Then he wrapped his arms around her. "I'm giving you a hug and hoping to pull some of the worry from your heart." He eased away and cupped her cheek. "I know you are working so hard to keep your mind off of Linda, but I worry *mei fraa* is going to just fall over with exhaustion." He kissed her on the cheek. "*Mei lieb*, everything is going to be all right."

Mary Ellen shrugged. "I know that, Abe. There's just lots to be done, that's all. I am still expected to have a clean home, and that is just what I plan to do." She dropped to her knees and began to scrub again.

Abe blew out a breath of exasperation. "All right, Mary Ellen. I'm going to go secure things outside. Paper says we're in for a nasty storm later. Luke and Matt are already out there tending to the animals."

"Fine."

Abe shook his head as he headed out the kitchen door. Poor woman was going to be exhausted if she kept on like this. But, truth be told, he was missing his Linda more than he cared to let on, and it had only been two days.

Mary Ellen rubbed the sponge across the floor with a vengeance God wouldn't approve of, anger and bitterness with every swipe. Sending Linda for two weeks was her idea, and Mary Ellen didn't think she'd regretted anything more in her life. She'd never been away from her daughter, for starters, but every time she envisioned Linda with Josie and all her fancy things, she went into some sort of jealous tailspin that was not in her normal character. Jealousy is a sin, and she'd prayed that God take away these feelings ever since she'd dropped Linda off on Tuesday.

The woman is dying. How can I be harboring such nasty thoughts toward her? She'd been praying constantly to rid herself of such notions. Mary Ellen knew she'd been selfish and mean-spirited, but Josephine Dronberger hadn't thought things through either. Linda would be devastated when Josephine passed. Didn't Josephine ever stop to think that maybe it would have been best for Linda if she'd never shown up here?

Linda was terrified of pain and saw pain as the gateway to death. Mary Ellen reckoned all that started when Linda was a young girl and witnessed their cow having a troubled birth, which killed both the momma and the calf. Mary Ellen had reprimanded Abe repeatedly for allowing Linda to see that. Mary Ellen had been at market when it happened, and six-year-old Linda cried for days afterward. Once Luke sliced his finger on a saw blade in the barn, not even enough for a stitch, and Linda passed smooth out and busted her chin. Linda couldn't stand to see someone in pain.

Mary Ellen stopped scouring the spot, took a deep breath, and bowed her head.

Dear Lord, release me of the bitterness I feel for Josephine, this woman who so graciously gave us Linda to raise. Now, in her time of need, please guide me to do right by her, to shed all jealousy where she is concerned, and to help her any way I can as her time to join You draws near. In Jesus' name I pray, God. Give me strength.

Mary Ellen stood up, dropped the sponge in the sink, and headed out to see if she could help Abe and the boys get things ready for the storm.

Stephen hobbled out of the water, anxious to get his shoes back on. He towel dried as best he could before pulling on his pants and shirt over his swim shorts, then quickly pulled his work boots back on. He'd felt confident in the water where Linda couldn't see his awkwardness, but back on land, he needed his shoes on to feel normal.

"You worry too much about that." Linda waded her way out of the water, thrust her hands on her hips and stared at him. "About your foot."

Aw, don't bring it up. "I ain't worrying." He pulled his suspenders up over his blue short-sleeved shirt.

"I reckon you seem like you're worried about it." She pointed to her leg. "What about my birthmark? Should I be trying to cover that up around you?"

"It ain't the same, Linda." That birthmark was the last thing he'd been looking at.

She reached for a towel she'd left on the bank and wrapped it around herself. "I just want you to know that I love you just the way you are."

He turned quickly toward her. She was white as snow, her eyes wide, and biting her lip. "What did you say?"

"I, uh . . . you know what I mean. I just like you for being you." She turned away from him, and Stephen walked to her, wrapped his arms around her waist.

"No, that's not what you said." He kissed the back of her neck. "You said—"

"No I didn't!" She spun around. "Because I would never say something like that first, Stephen. It just—it just slipped out, and—"

"Linda." He cupped her beautiful, soft, pale cheeks in his hands. "I love you."

She didn't smile. "Are you just saying that because I did? On accident?" She twisted her mouth sideways, lifted her chin.

"Don't you even read my poems? I've done everything but scream it to you. I love you, Linda. With all my heart. I've loved you for a long time."

She giggled. "Since when?"

Stephen smiled. "I reckon since you stubbed your toe on the playground in first grade. You cried so hard, I wanted to hug you, even back then. And don't you remember, I gave you the pie in my lunch that day?" Stephen chuckled. "I loved you then, 'cause I reckon rhubarb pie is my favorite, and I gave it to you."

"I do remember that." She lowered her head for a moment. When she looked up, her eyes were teary, but in a good way. "I love you, Stephen Ebersol."

Now is the time to ask her. Stephen opened his mouth to ask her to be his wife, the way he'd so romantically—or cowardly—done in the letter, but the words just weren't coming. "Linda . . ."

She waited.

"Linda . . ."

Just then, thunder boomed overhead amidst clouds that had darkened within the last few minutes.

"I love you, Linda." He kissed her gently. "But we better get home."

"*Ya*, look at the clouds coming from the west." She pointed to a large mass of blackness moving in their direction.

They hurried to Stephen's topless courting buggy. "It's gonna make wet before I get you back to Josie's, I reckon."

Linda shrugged. "We're already wet anyway." There was a loud clap of thunder. "But thunder and lightning scare me." She squeezed her shoulders together and closed her eyes.

Stephen flicked the horse into action. "Don't worry. I'll get you home safely."

They'd barely pulled out onto the road when the sky opened up.

When they got to Josie's, Linda gave Stephen a quick kiss in the driveway. "Don't come in. Get home before the storm gets worse. And be careful." She turned to leave, but spun back around, as if waiting for something.

"I love you, Linda."

Her face brightened beneath the droplets of rain. "I love you too, Stephen!"

He watched her run up the walkway, turn the doorknob, and get safely inside before he turned to leave. Blackness engulfed the skies above him, and the thunder was so loud he jolted every time it echoed overhead. He considered asking Linda if he could stay for a while, but his house was less than fifteen minutes by buggy. Surely, it'd be all right. Stephen backed the buggy out of the driveway.

Mary Ellen closed the window above the kitchen sink when rain began to spray through the screen.

"Luke and Matt, go close the windows upstairs. I know it

might be hot for a spell with all the windows shut, but otherwise we're going to be sleeping on wet linens later."

Both boys headed toward the stairs as Abe came in from outside. He pushed the wooden door closed behind him.

"What a storm. We sure need the rain but maybe not so much of it at once." Abe pulled off his soaked straw hat and hung it on the rack by the door, then raked a hand through his hair. "Everything is secure outside."

A loud clap of thunder rocked the house and rattled the china in her cabinet. "That was close." Mary Ellen walked to the window and peered outside. "And it's raining so hard, can't see a thing." She paused, turned to Abe. "You think Linda is all right? She gets scared during storms like this, even at her age."

"She's fine, I'm sure, Mary Ellen." Abe headed toward the back of the house, presumably to check the other windows.

"I hope Josephine doesn't leave her alone during the storm for anything. Linda would be terrified." She shook her head. "She might pretend otherwise, but I know my daughter, and every time it storms, I coddle her like a baby. She puts her hands over her ears, Abe, and she gets very scared."

"Mary Ellen, Linda is fine."

"I know she thinks she's grown up, but in so many ways she is still so young."

"She's a big baby. She always gets scared when there's a storm." Matt rolled his eyes as he walked into the kitchen. He opened the refrigerator and pulled out a pitcher of tea, then pulled a glass from the cabinet.

Luke followed his older brother. "She ain't no baby. She just don't like thunder."

Mary Ellen narrowed her eyes in Matt's direction. Then she turned to Luke. "That's right, Luke. She just doesn't like thunder."

"Hope she's havin' fun on her little vacation." Matt walked to the window by the kitchen door and looked outside. "Sure ain't fun around here, having to help with girl chores." He sat down on a bench at the table and drank his meadow tea.

"*Ach*, Matt. I've asked you to do very little since your sister has been gone. Now stop your complaining."

Her oldest son rolled his eyes again.

"You will find your *daed* taking you out to the woodshed if he catches you rollin' your eyes at me like that." Mary Ellen knew Matt was much too old for that type of discipline, but as of late, he'd developed a disrespectful attitude.

Luke pulled the wooden door in the kitchen open and watched the lightning flash for a moment before holding his hand up in everyone's direction. "Listen. Do you hear that? I think it's the phone ringing in the barn."

Linda. "I'll go." Mary Ellen closed the door, reached for the umbrella behind it, then swung it wide again.

"You will do no such thing, Mary Ellen." Abe latched onto her arm. "Do you hear how close that lightning is? You'll get soaked, and by the time you get there, that phone will have stopped ringing."

Mary Ellen jerked from his grasp and stepped into Abe's galoshes that were by the door. "I told you. Linda gets scared when there is a storm, and the sound of my voice will comfort her. I'll just call her right back and talk to her for a minute."

Abe was shaking his head as she brushed past him. She stood on the porch staring at the torrential rain and cringed as another burst of lightning lit up the sky, followed by a deafening eruption of thunder. Her heart thudded hard as she made her way across the yard to the barn. Like her daughter, she was not a fan of raucous storms.

As Abe predicted, the phone had stopped ringing by the time she got to the barn. The answering machine light flashed one. Mary Ellen set the umbrella down and pushed the button.

"*Mamm*, I'm so scared. *Mamm*, I'm really scared!"

I knew it. Mary Ellen reached for the phone to call and comfort her daughter, but she stopped when she heard Linda go on.

"*Mamm*, call me back. It's about Josie. I'm scared. She's not breathing."

16

LINDA WATCHED TWO MEN IN WHITE UNIFORMS HUDDLE over Josie, and lights from the ambulance flashed through the window of the house. The rain continued to pound outside, and one of the men had placed a plastic mask over Josie's face and said it would help her to breathe.

"*Onkel* Noah, is she going to be all right?" Linda had known to dial 9-1-1 when she walked into the house and found Josie lying on the kitchen floor in the middle of red sauce and a broken casserole dish. Lasagna noodles and meat were strewn across the tile floor. After she called the emergency number for help, she'd called her uncle, and then her mother.

"Josie had a seizure." Noah put his hand on her shoulder. "But she is going to be all right."

Linda didn't have any idea what that was, but she knew she'd never been so scared in her entire life. "What is that? What caused it? Did her bad headaches cause her to have a seizure? What now? Is she going to the hospital?"

"I'm not going to the hospital. I'm fine."

Linda turned to see that Josie had pulled the mask from her face. Linda pushed her uncle out of the way and squatted down beside Josie on the floor. "Josie, oh Josie. Are you okay?" She latched onto her hand. "Are you hurting? Are you in pain?"

"No, sweetheart. I'm not in any pain. This has happened before, but it hasn't happened in a long time. I'm sorry you had to see this."

"Mrs. Dronberger, we're going to have to take you to the hospital for evaluation."

"No. I'm not going."

Her uncle moved toward them and knelt down. "Linda, Josie was breathing, but she was unconscious when you found her." Her uncle leaned down closer to Josie. "How long has it been since you've had a seizure, Josie?"

Josie reached up with her left hand and rubbed her eyes. Linda noticed Josie's right hand was jerking like before. "I don't know, Noah. I guess maybe about a year. They were pretty regular back when—" Josie stopped and looked at Linda for a moment, then back at her uncle. She didn't go on.

"When is Robert due back in town?"

"Not for another week and a half." Josie sighed. "He was far enough away from the attacks in China, and he was going to try to finish his business since he made the long trip."

Linda glanced back and forth between her uncle and Josie. *Do they know each other?*

Linda had called her uncle because he was a doctor, but he and Josie sure seemed familiar with each other.

"I think we need him to come home sooner, Josie. You shouldn't be alone." Her uncle's forehead wrinkled with worry.

"She's not alone. She has me. I'm staying here for the whole two weeks, while Robert is in China."

"Honey, I think Josie is going to need more care than you can probably give her." Uncle Noah was talking to her like she was a child.

"I can take care of you, Josie." Linda folded her hands in her lap as she began to wonder what was wrong with Josie. She turned toward her uncle. "Did this happen 'cause of her headaches?"

Linda watched Uncle Noah and Josie lock eyes briefly.

"Yes, it happened because of my headaches." Josie smiled at Linda. "You know how bad they get sometimes."

The men in the uniforms were packed up and looked like they were ready to leave. The taller man handed Uncle Noah a piece of paper. "Dr. Stoltzfus, she really should go to the hospital, but we'll leave her in your care if she'll sign this release form saying she refused to go."

"Josie . . ." Uncle Noah sighed. "How about it?"

"I'm not going, Noah. And you know why. This is going to happen again, and . . ." Josie looked at Linda again, then back at Uncle Noah. "And there's nothing that can be done."

"I can take care of you Josie," Linda repeated, although the thought terrified her. "Just tell me what to do."

"Linda!"

Linda turned and saw her mother's comforting face. She jumped up and ran into her mother's arms as Mary Ellen walked into Josie's kitchen. "Are you all right?" *Mamm* held her tight.

"I was so scared," Linda whispered in her mother's ear. "I didn't know what to do. I called 9-1-1 like you always told us."

"You did the right thing." *Mamm* eased out of the hug and made her way toward Josie and Noah.

"Is she all right?" *Mamm* directed the question to Noah.

"I'm fine." Josie sat up, then looked at the mess in her kitchen and at her clothes. "I sure made a mess, though."

"We're going." The two uniformed men waved and headed

out the front door. "Take care, Mrs. Dronberger," the taller man said before he closed the door behind them.

"Josie, you can't stay here by yourself. What about your mother? Do you want me to call your mother?" Noah stood up.

Linda watched Josie's face turn a bright shade of red. "No. Do not call my mother. I don't want her around me."

Noah let out another sigh. "Then let's get Robert on the phone and have him come home early."

"I don't want to do that." Josie's eyes filled with tears. "This case is so important to him." She paused and looked at Linda. "But I know it's not fair for Linda to stay."

"I have told everyone that I can take care of Josie." Linda glared at Noah, then looked at her mother with pleading eyes. "Besides, maybe it won't happen again. Josie's had some headaches but nothing like this."

"It will happen again." Josie turned her head away from everyone, and Linda was sure they were not telling her something.

"Does Robert have his cell phone over there? I'll go give him a call." Uncle Noah stood up and pulled his cell phone from the pocket of his white doctor's coat.

"Yes, he does."

"He wasn't near any of the trouble, was he?" Noah took a few steps toward the other side of the room.

Josie was still facing away from everyone, and Linda saw her wipe away a tear. "No. He wasn't near there."

Linda wasn't sure what to do. *What is happening?* Her uncle walked into the next room. Linda could hear him talking but couldn't understand what he was saying.

"Here, let's get you cleaned up." *Mamm* squatted down beside

Josie on the floor. Josie wiped her hands, covered with sauce, on her blue jeans, then covered her face with both hands. "I'm sorry, Mary Ellen. I'm sorry for everything. I should have never . . ."

Normally, if someone was crying, *Mamm* was the first one to offer comfort, but *Mamm* just sat there and seemed unsure of what to do. Linda knelt down beside her mother.

"Josie, it's all right." Linda grabbed her hand and squeezed at about the same time her mother wrapped an arm around Josie. Together, *Mamm* and Linda pulled Josie to her feet.

"Linda, why don't you clean up this mess, and I'll help Josie upstairs to get some fresh clothes on." *Mamm* said it in a tone that meant there'd be no argument. Linda nodded.

Mary Ellen kept an arm around Josephine's waist as they headed up the stairs. Josephine grasped the handrail with one hand and draped her other arm across Mary Ellen's shoulder. Mary Ellen could feel her struggling to pull herself up the steps with each heavy step they took. Josephine kept mumbling how sorry she was. For everything.

"Are you sure you didn't get cut by all that glass in the kitchen?" Mary Ellen paused on the step when she felt Josephine leaning on her even more. Josephine took a few moments to catch her breath, then shook her head.

"No. I didn't get cut." She sighed. "I'm just really tired."

"Can you keep going?"

Josephine nodded. "I think so."

Mary Ellen tightened her hold around her and edged them upward.

When they walked into Josephine's room, Mary Ellen couldn't believe her eyes. She hadn't really noticed the downstairs too much with all the ruckus going on, but now that things had settled down a bit, she took in her surroundings. She'd been in plenty of *Englisch* homes over the years, but nothing like this. Why in the world would anyone need all this?

Mary Ellen cringed when Josephine sat down on the bed and smeared what appeared to be spaghetti sauce all over her blue bedspread, even getting a little on one of the white throw pillows. But she didn't seem to care. Josephine wasn't crying anymore. Her expression was blank as she stared into the far corner of the room.

"I never should have come here." She turned to Mary Ellen. "This is all going to be too hard on Linda, and it was selfish of me to want to get to know her. Selfish of me to put her through all this."

Mary Ellen didn't say anything.

"But now I don't know how to undo it." She shrugged. "I guess Robert and I could just leave, and—"

"And leave Linda hanging, thinking her mother abandoned her?" Mary Ellen stared hard into Josie's eyes. "I don't think that's an option at this point."

"Then what should I do, Mary Ellen?" Josephine threw her hands in the air, then slammed them down beside her. "I've already said how sorry I am about everything." Then Josephine started to cry again. Mary Ellen sat down on the bed beside her. Her own dress was covered in sauce anyway.

"I just want to protect my daughter. That's all I've ever wanted to do." Mary Ellen felt her own eyes watering, but she was not about to let herself cry. "We are going to have to tell Linda about your—your condition at some point. But today is not that day. She has been through enough for one day."

Josephine sniffled. "I agree." She stood up. "I'm going to go get cleaned up. You can go downstairs if you want. I'll be down in a minute."

"I'll wait for you." Mary Ellen met Josephine's eyes. "In case—in case you need help or feel ill."

"Thank you."

Mary Ellen glanced around the room after Josephine went to the bathroom to change. So many things. So many things she has exposed young Linda to. Mary Ellen shook her head. Then she just waited. Wondering. Worrying.

"Okay." Josephine came out of the bathroom wearing a fresh pair of blue jeans and a pink pullover shirt. She stopped in the middle of the room. "I guess I better go see when my husband will be home." But she didn't move and instead started to tear up again. "I hate this. I just hate it. I hate all of it. If there is a God, He wouldn't let all this happen!" Then she dropped to her knees right there in her bedroom, as if she could no longer carry the weight of her situation. Mary Ellen put her hands on her chest and wondered if she'd heard correctly.

She walked to Josephine, who was sitting on her heels, covering her face with her hands. "I have no hope, Mary Ellen. Do you know what it's like to face death with no hope?"

Mary Ellen dropped down beside her. "Josephine, what are you saying?"

Josephine uncovered her face and brushed away tears with only her left hand. Mary Ellen could see her right hand twitching in her lap. "You heard me, Mary Ellen. You can add that to your list of reasons to hate me."

"That's not fair, Josephine. I never said I hated you." Mary Ellen took a deep breath. "These are hard times for all of us, but I never said—"

"It doesn't matter." She lifted her head, then stood up, sniffling, struggling to gain control of her emotions. "I miss my husband very much. Let's go downstairs. I want to know when he'll be home."

Mary Ellen followed Josephine downstairs. How could anyone face death and make such comments? It was the saddest thing she'd ever heard.

When they got downstairs, Linda was scooping up the last of the broken glass and Mary Ellen heard Noah telling Linda how he knew Josie, that he was friends with Josie's husband.

Noah walked toward Josephine. "Josie, there're more problems in China. Robert is fine, though."

"What? Did something else happen? More attacks? Robert said he was far away from everything."

Mary Ellen was thinking that this woman really couldn't take any more today.

"No, nothing else happened, but the airports are closed indefinitely for those who aren't citizens, those traveling with a passport."

"What?" Josephine looked like she might collapse again. Mary Ellen stepped toward her but stopped when Linda rushed to Josephine's side.

She watched her daughter—*their* daughter—put her arm around Josephine. "It's all right. We'll figure something out. I'll stay here with you."

Mary Ellen's eyes welled with emotion at the nurturing kindness in Linda's voice. And she knew right away what she needed to do.

She raised her chin, folded her hands in front of her, and spoke directly to Noah. "Josephine will come and stay with us. In our home." She swallowed hard, then glanced at Linda. A smile spread across her daughter's face. Josephine, however, was staring at Mary Ellen as if she'd lost her mind.

"Mary Ellen, I don't know if . . ." Noah's brows furrowed as he spoke. "Are you sure that's a good idea?"

"Absolutely not," Josephine interjected.

"Why?" Linda was quick to ask. Mary Ellen watched her daughter gaze at Josephine with eyes that begged her to reconsider. "You can stay in my room. I have two beds. It would still be like a sleepover, but at my house."

"She's right." Mary Ellen moved toward them. "It makes the most sense. Until Josephine's husband gets home, she should stay with us. She can still . . ." Mary Ellen looked down for a brief moment, then faced Josephine. "You can still get to know Linda, and there will be several of us around so that you are not alone, just in case this should happen again."

"Mary Ellen, can I talk to you outside?" Noah's voice was firm, but Mary Ellen didn't care. She knew that this was the right thing to do for all concerned.

"Of course. We can talk outside while Linda helps Josephine pack a few things."

Josephine moved away from Linda, walked toward Mary Ellen, and faced her. Mary Ellen couldn't tell if she was angry, relieved, or a combination of some other emotions that Mary Ellen wasn't familiar with.

"Mary Ellen, I appreciate the offer, but I—"

"Do you have a better one? Offer, that is," Mary Ellen asked in a challenging tone.

Josephine just stared at her. Speechless.

"Scoot. Both of you. Go pack while I go talk to Noah." She turned around. "Noah, let's talk." She marched out of the kitchen and into the living room. Or den. Or family room. Or whatever this oversized room filled with unnecessary items was.

"What is it, Noah?" Mary Ellen folded her hands across her chest.

"You have no idea what you are getting into." Noah shook his head. "It's noble what you're trying to do, Mary Ellen, but if Josie is starting to have seizures, she is going to start going down quickly. Are you really prepared to take care of her? What if it's weeks before her husband can get back?" Noah leaned closer and whispered. "Not to mention, that no one in this charade has told Linda that Josie is going to die."

"The Lord will guide us, Noah. And I believe this to be His will."

Noah put his hand on his hip, then ran a hand through his wavy dark hair.

"You need a haircut." Mary Ellen smiled at her brother.

"Seriously, Mary Ellen. This could be a huge undertaking if her husband doesn't come back soon. I will give you some literature that explains all about seizures and what to do if she has another one, but the best thing to do would be to call 9-1-1 if Josie begins to exhibit any symptoms that another seizure is forthcoming." Noah shook his head and sighed. "This is too much for you, Mary Ellen. Maybe after a day or two with you, you can convince her to call her mother. I understand from her husband that they don't have a relationship. He told me once that her parents forced her to give up Linda for adoption, and she never forgave them. But who knows . . . there might be more to it than that. At this time in her life, I would think that she needs her family."

"Linda is her family, and in that respect, I reckon I will have to be her stand-in family."

Noah leaned over and hugged her. "You're a *gut* woman, Mary Ellen."

"*Ach*, I see you still speaka the *Deitsch* sometimes," she teased.

"*Ya*. I do."

She stayed in Noah's arms, his words lingering in her head . . . *You're a gut woman*. She hadn't felt like a very good woman lately. And maybe inviting Josephine to stay at their home was a mistake. But one thing bothered Mary Ellen far more than her own troubles.

If there is a God, He wouldn't let all this happen. I have no hope, Mary Ellen. Do you know what it's like to face death with no hope?

Josie loaded clothes into a red suitcase while Linda sat on the bed and waited.

"What do you think your father will say about me coming to stay?"

Linda stretched her arms behind her and leaned back. "I reckon it'll be just fine with him." She nodded her head with confidence and smiled.

Josie smiled back at her, even though she wasn't convinced. "I'm surprised that your mother asked me to come stay. But it's very kind of her."

"*Mamm* is wonderful. You'll love her cooking too."

Josie looked down at her suitcase. "I think that's probably all I'll need." She zipped it closed, then sat down on the bed beside Linda, away from the splattered sauce. She put her hand on Linda's knee. "I'm sorry about today. We didn't get to eat lasagna, and I didn't get to hear about your day with Stephen at the creek."

Linda smiled again. "We'll have lots of time to talk since you'll be staying in my room."

"Sure that's okay with you?"

"I'm sure. It'll be fun." She giggled. "You don't snore or anything, do you?"

Josie chuckled lightly. "Robert says I do sometimes." Then she thought about Robert being so far away, near all the chaos. "I hope he's all right."

"We will say special prayers for him. I'm sure he'll be fine." Linda paused. "Josie, there's something I want to ask you."

Josie pulled her hand from Linda's knee, smoothed wrinkles from her pink shirt, and twisted to face her. "What's that?"

Linda locked eyes with Josie. "Tell me what's really wrong with you. I want to know the truth."

17

JOSIE PULLED HERSELF TO A STANDING POSITION BUT kept her back to Linda. She squeezed her eyes closed for a moment and pondered how to avoid a lie and still stay true to Mary Ellen's wishes.

"I have really bad headaches that cause me to lose control of my motor functions, and sometimes I have seizures." Josie turned to face Linda and shrugged. "And that's the truth. Sometimes I feel really bad. Other days are good."

Linda's accusing gaze burned through Josie, and she wondered just how mad Linda was going to be when she became privy to the entire truth, not just bits and pieces of the truth. She didn't want Linda to look at her the way Robert did sometimes, with pity in his eyes.

"What causes these headaches?" Linda stood up and folded her arms across her chest. Then she slammed them to her side and stomped one foot. "Please, Josie. I know you're all not telling me something, and I'm not a child!"

Josie jumped, caught off guard by Linda's display. "I know you're not a child. I never said—"

"Then tell me!" Linda took a step toward her. "Just tell me what's wrong with you."

Josie turned her head toward the bedroom door as it swung open.

"What's all this yelling in here?" Mary Ellen's lips thinned with irritation as she shifted her gaze back and forth between Josie and Linda, finally centering on Linda. "What are you yelling about?"

Linda lowered her head, then looked back up at Mary Ellen. "I know there is something else wrong with Josie. Something she's not telling me. Do you know too, *Mamm*? Is there something you're all not telling me?"

Mary Ellen's face clouded with unease. She glanced at Josie, then back at Linda. "Why do you ask such a thing, Linda?"

"I can just tell, *Mamm*. By the way you are all behaving. Even *Onkel* Noah. And I am old enough to know what's going on."

Mary Ellen moved across the room until she was right in front of Linda. "Everything will be fine." She reached out to touch Linda's arm, but Linda backed away as she gritted her teeth and released a heavy breath through her nose.

"Linda." Mary Ellen's voice was disciplinary. Josie got the impression that this was not Linda's normal behavior. "Why are you acting in such a manner?"

"Because you are not telling me the truth!"

"Hey, hey." Noah walked into the room. "What's going on?"

Linda ran to her uncle and threw her arms around him. "*Onkel* Noah, please tell me the truth. Everyone is treating me like a child. There's something wrong with Josie, and you all aren't telling me."

Noah eased her away, cupped her cheek in his hand, and stared lovingly into her eyes. Then his eyes locked with Josie's. "Tell her."

Mary Ellen took a step toward him. "But Noah, I don't think this is—"

Noah silenced her with narrowed eyes. "There is never going to be a good time, Mary Ellen."

"Tell me what?" Linda ripped out the words as she faced her mother, then shifted her angry gaze to Josie. "Tell me what, Josie?"

Josie was frozen in limbo, in a place where no good would come from whatever response she offered. A war of emotions raged within her, but she knew the time of reckoning was upon them, so she tried to mask her inner turmoil with a deceptive calmness. "Linda, what we've told you is true. We just didn't tell you everything, because I wanted time for you to get to know me. Time for me to get to know you." She searched Mary Ellen's eyes for guidance, but Mary Ellen was biting her lip, holding her breath. "Linda, I have a brain tumor. A tumor that they can't operate on or take out, and . . ." She searched for the words as her bottom lip began to tremble. "I'm sorry."

"What do you mean, *sorry?*" Linda choked out the words in a small voice.

Josie knew that a good mother would keep her raw emotions in check, keep in tempo with what needed to be said, but the words caught in her throat. "I'm—I'm dying, Linda."

A black silence surrounded them as they waited for Linda to react, and then Josie saw Linda's mouth begin to move, but she couldn't grasp what she was saying. Josie could feel the color draining from her face as tiny bolts of light shimmied in front her, purple rods of warning, a sign that another seizure was forthcoming. *I've never had two in one day.*

She could see Linda moving toward her through eyes she was

struggling to keep open, and the tip of her tongue edged toward the roof of her mouth as if magnetized by something out of her control.

"She's having another seizure," Noah said.

It was the last thing Josie heard.

When Josie opened her eyes, it took her a few minutes to figure out where she was, then she hazily remembered Noah carrying her to his car. She blinked her eyes into focus to find a room full of people hovering around her, and she scanned the rustic room until she saw Linda. Josie could tell Linda had been crying, and she longed to ease her suffering.

"How are you feeling?" Mary Ellen was standing at the foot of the bed. To her left were Noah and Linda. A man she didn't know and two teenage boys were standing to her right.

"Tired." She reached up and touched the side of her head, then pulled back when pain speared through her temple.

"You fell before we could get to you." Noah sighed. "You've got a pretty good knot on your head, but luckily the floor was carpeted."

"Josephine, I'd like you to meet my family." Mary Ellen walked to the older man's side. "This is my husband, Abe. And these are our two boys, Matthew and Luke."

They each moved forward and shook her hand, then she studied them for a moment. The taller boy, Matthew, was wearing a dark brown shirt, and his brother was wearing a dark blue shirt like their father. They all had on black pants and suspenders and made for a handsome trio.

"Your family is lovely." Josie forced a smile for each of them, even though her head was splitting. Then she homed in on Linda, and tried to fight the tears building in her eyes as she whispered, "I'm sorry."

Linda shuffled closer to the bed and reached for Josie's hand. "*Danki* for telling me." She smiled. "We are all going to be praying for you constantly."

"Prayers are being offered across a broad network of prayer groups as we speak." Noah smiled. "I've already called Carley, and she's put the wheels in motion. Before we even hit the driveway, thousands of people had started praying for you, Josie."

Josie glanced at Mary Ellen, and for a moment, the women just stared at each other. No words were necessary. Mary Ellen knew her secret. Thankfully, it didn't appear that Mary Ellen had shared Josie's lack of faith with the other members of her family. Josie wasn't sure how Mary Ellen's husband would feel about having a nonbeliever under their roof. Josie knew how devout the Amish were. If Mary Ellen didn't want her here, she certainly could have used that as an excuse.

Josie finally pulled her gaze from Mary Ellen's when the oldest boy turned to his father and spoke. "*Daed*, I'm gonna go get the horses put up."

"You boys go ahead." Abe nodded at the boys, who seemed anxious to be on their way.

"Josie, I'm going to go," Noah said. "If you have any problems at all, call me on my cell phone." Then he eased closer, touched her arm. "These seizures are going to come with more frequency, but I'm going to talk to a neurologist I know and see if we can get you something stronger to help with that. And I'm going to give

Mary Ellen some information about what she needs to do if it looks like you might have another one. It's important that you get lots of rest too." He paused, his brows wrinkling. "I'm sure plenty of doctors have told you what to expect?"

She nodded and wondered if she should be in the hospital, although she knew that realistically this could drag on for months. This was such an imposition on Linda's family until Robert returned. She tugged at her pink blouse with her left hand and pulled it away from her body, shaking it. *So hot.* A tiny fan on the nightstand blew full force in her direction, but it did little to help with the still heat inside the room. Green shades were drawn high above two open windows on the wall to Josie's right, but no breeze blew through the screens. *How can they sleep in this heat?*

Josie scanned her surroundings. As Linda had told her, there were two beds in the room. In between the beds was a wooden nightstand with one drawer—a simple but lovely piece of furniture, with a pitcher of water, two glasses, a Bible, and a box of tissue on top. And a lantern. Josie eyed the relic and wondered if she was making a mistake. No electricity. The heat. No television. Sometimes, television was the only thing that kept her mind on something other than her own fate.

An oak dresser was against the wall opposite the beds, another well-crafted piece of furniture. One rocking chair was in the corner, and there were no wall hangings except for a calendar and a small mirror.

Then she glanced up at Linda and realized that none of that mattered if she could spend time with her daughter.

After Noah left, Mary Ellen asked Linda to go start supper

while she spoke with Josie. Linda pouted a bit, but left, promising to return shortly.

"How is she?" Josie propped herself up higher in the bed. "I don't really remember anything."

Mary Ellen walked to the window and lowered the blind a few inches to block out the sun as it began to set. Then she turned to Josie. "You were in such bad shape at the time, she said very little. I will try to talk with her more later." She paused. "Or . . . she'll be in here with you. Perhaps you would like to talk with her about it."

Josie nodded. "Thank you for having me in your home, Mary Ellen. I know this must seem awkward—"

"The bathroom is down the hall to your left. You'll find everything you need in there if you'd like to bathe later."

"Okay." Besides the obvious, Josie could feel the other elephant in the room. "Thank you for not saying anything about my—my lack of faith."

Mary Ellen stared blankly at her for a few moments. "Is it something you're ashamed of?"

"No." Josie didn't mean to sound so defensive, but Mary Ellen didn't seem affected by her tone.

"Do you not know of the Lord? Were you not educated as a child?"

"Oh, I was educated. I just don't think I ever really *got* it." Josie pushed back the light sheet that was covering her legs. "And then I married Robert, and he doesn't believe in God. At all. And his arguments against a higher power seemed valid." She leaned her head backward against the wall. "I guess it's been so long now since I've thought about God, I just—I just figure it's too late for me. Although, the other day . . ."

Mary Ellen sat down on the edge of the bed, waited for Josie to go on.

"I felt something." Josie recalled the voice in her head. *I am here My child. The fool hath said in his heart, There is no God.* "I was praying, and I heard something, and it seemed so real."

"I thought you didn't believe." Mary Ellen arched her brows.

"I don't, but . . ."

"Then why would you pray?"

She shrugged. "I'm dying, Mary Ellen. I guess I was willing to try anything."

They sat quietly for a moment.

"My husband is a good man." Josie reached for the cup on the nightstand, poured herself some water, and took a big gulp. "He really is. He does for everyone but himself. He is the most kind-hearted, loving, generous person I've ever known. Robert is full of goodness."

Mary Ellen's expression was somber. "Why do you feel the need to defend him?"

"I know how strong your faith is, Mary Ellen. All the Amish. I just don't want you to think he's a bad man. Or . . . that I'm a bad person for not believing."

"It's not my place to judge. Only God can do that."

It grew quiet again, and Mary Ellen stood up. "I'll let you rest." She turned to leave.

"Mary Ellen?"

She turned to face her. "*Ya?*"

"What if I'm wrong? About God?" She pulled her knees to her chest.

Mary Ellen locked eyes with her, a kindness in her expression that Josie hadn't seen from her before. Softly, she said, "Exactly. What if you are wrong?"

Then she turned and left.

———⟨⊛⟩———

Mary Ellen met Linda coming up the stairs.

"I put the chicken in the oven and peeled the potatoes. Can I go visit with Josie for a little while?"

"*Ya.* But first . . ." Mary Ellen pushed back a loose strand of hair that had fallen from beneath her daughter's *kapp.* "Are you all right?"

"*Ya.*" She sighed. "I reckon it just doesn't make any sense. For me to get to know her, only to have the Lord call her home. And she's so young."

"You know we don't question His will."

"I know, *Mamm.* I just wish things could be different, and I'm going to pray that God will heal Josie."

Mary Ellen kissed her on the cheek. "You're *mei gut maedel.*" Then she brushed past her down the stairs and crossed the den to the kitchen. Abe was sitting at the kitchen table.

Mary Ellen picked up a fork and poked the potatoes that were simmering in a pot on the stove. "It won't be ready for at least thirty minutes."

Abe picked up the *Die Botschaft* and began to flip through the pages. "Sure smells *gut.*"

After only a few moments, he closed the newspaper. "Mary Ellen, I reckon I gotta tell ya . . ." He peered into the den to see if anyone was there, then lowered his voice. "I'm surprised 'bout you asking her to stay here."

Mary Ellen set the fork on the counter and took a seat across from her husband. Keeping her voice low, she said, "She doesn't have anyone to tend to her until her husband can get home from China. Might only be for a day or two."

Abe looped his thumbs under his suspenders. "It's a *gut* thing you are doing, especially for Linda." He paused and rubbed his tired eyes. "I suspect Linda knows by now what's happening with Josephine?"

"*Ya.* She does. And Abe . . . she seems to be handling the news better than I would have expected." She reached over and put her hand on his. "And, of course, she is praying for the Lord not to call Josephine home just yet."

"We should all pray that the Lord's will be done, whatever that might be. But it's only human to pray for extra time for those we care about."

"Like Jonas. You know I've been praying extra hard for that old man since he was first diagnosed with the cancer years ago. I reckon all the prayers from everyone in the community have kept him alive, do you think?"

"We must be careful what we pray for. Jonas is hurting these days, and to pray for him to stay on this earth doesn't seem right."

"That's true."

They sat quietly, and Mary Ellen considered telling her husband about Josephine's lack of faith but decided against it. It wasn't their way to minister to others, to teach them about God.

But Josephine had said she didn't have any hope. Everyone should have hope.

Linda walked into her bedroom, and Josie was standing by the window looking out. She turned around when Linda entered.

"It's beautiful here."

"What are you doing out of bed?" Linda lifted the pitcher to see if Josie still had water, then joined her by the window. "*Onkel* Noah said you need to rest."

"My headache is better, and I can't just stay in bed."

Linda's stomach twisted with anxiety. First Jonas. Now her own—mother. So much loss. She worried how much her heart could take. Why would God introduce her to this woman, only to take her away?

"Josie, how long—how long do you—how much time . . ."

"A few months. Maybe six."

Linda sat down on Josie's bed; her knees felt like they might give beneath her. Josie sat next to her.

"But I plan to sing loudly at your birthday and watch you blow out your candles this year."

Linda covered her face with her hands and started to cry. "This seems so unfair."

Josie put her arm around Linda's shoulder and squeezed as her own eyes welled with tears. "You know what they say, life isn't fair."

Linda wiped her eyes and turned to face Josie. "Are you scared?"

"Yes."

They sat quietly for a few moments. Linda could see Josie's right hand twitching. *Please God, don't let her have another seizure. Please keep the pain away and help her not to be scared.*

"Maybe you will get better, no?"

Josie shook her head, then cupped Linda's cheek and gazed into her beautiful sapphire eyes. "No, Linda. I'm not going to get better. I have an inoperable brain tumor in my brain stem. Eventually, it's going to disrupt my motor skills much more"—she glanced down at her trembling hand—"much more than just my hand and arm. I'll forget things, won't be able to keep my mind clear, and the seizures will come more often. I'll most likely slip into a coma at some point." She paused when a tear rolled down Linda's cheek. "The highlight of my life is this time I have with you."

"Oh, Josie." Linda threw her arms around her neck.

"My sweet baby girl."

Then Josie cried in a way Linda had never heard a grown-up cry. Deep sobs that caused her whole body to shake. Linda fought her own emotions and held Josie as tight as she'd ever held anyone.

"Don't be scared," Linda whispered. But Josie just cried harder.

Linda thought about what might make things easier for Josie. Then she had a thought.

Josie joined the family for breakfast the next morning, even though Mary Ellen offered to bring her breakfast in bed. Josie remembered eating the morning meal with her Amish friends on occasion when she was younger. There was always a bountiful layout of food, just like Mary Ellen's table now. Eggs, bacon, homemade biscuits, lots of jams and jellies, and a traditional dish called scrapple, a mushy cornmeal mix made with leftover parts of a pig, something Josie didn't like as a child and didn't plan to eat this morning. She didn't have much appetite, but would try to eat some eggs and maybe a biscuit just to keep her strength up.

After Mary Ellen filled the last glass with orange juice, she sat down at the head of the table across from her husband. Josie was sitting beside Linda on one of the wooden benches across from Matthew and Luke. They bowed their heads in silent prayer. Josie clamped her eyes closed.

I don't want to die. I'm scared. Please, help me. It was wrong to ask for help from an entity she wasn't sure was even real. But the "what if" of the situation was gnawing at her, and again, she recalled the voice she'd thought she heard. She drew in a deep breath. *Thank you for this time with my daughter.*

She opened her eyes when she heard the clanking of silverware across the table. Both boys were diving into the scrapple as if afraid they wouldn't get enough, then scooped generous amounts of scrambled eggs onto their plates. Josie helped herself to a small spoonful of eggs and reached for a biscuit after the boys were done.

"That's rhubarb jam." Mary Ellen pointed to a small jar in the middle of the table.

Josie smiled, then reached for the jar and spread some of the bright red mixture onto her biscuit.

Matthew grabbed two biscuits and began loading them up with jam. "We got a rooster that's *ab im kopp, Daed.*" He reached across his brother and pulled back a handful of bacon. "He's crazy as I've ever seen."

"I noticed that bird didn't seem to be acting right the other day," Abe said as he eyed his son's helping of bacon. "I'm sure everyone would like some bacon, Matt." Abe arched his brows and a slight grin formed.

"Oh." Matt put two pieces back.

"*Ya*, that rooster done slammed into the barn the other day," Luke added with a chuckle. "I know it ain't funny, but after it did that, it got up and ran all around the yard, chasing them hens."

"Like a drunkard," Matt said.

Linda giggled, which was music to Josie's ears. "You've never even seen a drunkard, Matt."

"Have so. At the Mud Sale in Gordonville last year. He was wobbling and ran into a wall. Just like that rooster."

Everyone laughed in between bites, and Josie recalled family breakfasts at her house when she was growing up. They'd certainly lacked the warmth of this family's. Her family's meals had been about appearance and formality, and even though Josie and Robert were fortunate to have nice things, Josie had always tried to make their home seem warm and inviting. She looked around at everyone at the table—this perfect family—and smiled. *Linda's had a good life.*

Josie did the best she could, picking at her food enough to not hurt Mary Ellen's feelings, although she avoided the scrapple.

"I can't eat another bite." Josie waved her hand in front of her when Mary Ellen placed some apple turnovers on the table next to Josie. "It was all wonderful, Mary Ellen."

Mary Ellen smiled, then pushed the plate toward her boys. "These are Matt's favorite."

Josie watched Mary Ellen serving her family, and she didn't think she'd ever seen anyone more cut out for mothering than Mary Ellen. Josie looked down at all the food left on her plate, then folded her arm across her stomach which was upset to the point that she fought the urge to leave the table.

When Abe and the boys finished their apple turnovers, they

excused themselves, and Josie picked up a few dishes to help Mary Ellen and Linda clear the table.

"You don't have to do that," Mary Ellen said to Josie. "You're our guest. And you should rest."

"Please don't treat me like a guest. I want to help. It's the least I can do, Mary Ellen. Really."

"How are you feeling?" Linda narrowed her brows at Josie, like a little mother hen.

"Pretty good." Except for her stomach, that was the truth. Josie's head wasn't hurting, and she could certainly handle a tummy ache in comparison to the headaches.

Linda turned to her mother and whispered something Josie couldn't hear. Mary Ellen nodded, turned to Josie, then back to Linda. "I think that's a *gut* idea," Mary Ellen said.

"Josie, there's someone I'd like for you to meet." Linda stashed a jar of jam in the refrigerator. "Do you feel up to a ride in the buggy to go visit a friend of mine?"

"Sure." Josie wasn't sure about any sort of travel, but Linda looked so anxious and excited for them to go that Josie would just hope her stomach didn't get any worse.

"I'm gonna go ask the boys to get the buggy ready." Linda scurried across the kitchen and bolted out the door.

Josie picked up a kitchen towel and started drying the plates that Mary Ellen was putting in the rack to drain. "Who does she want me to meet?"

Mary Ellen handed Josie a clean plate and smiled. "A very special man. His name is Jonas."

18

JONAS SHIFTED HIS BODY IN THE BED AND RECONCILED that there was no comfortable position anymore. Not a part of his body that wasn't hurting these days. He had one thing left to do, and then he hoped that the Lord would call him home. Clenching as another wave of pain overtook him, Jonas tried to focus on the life he'd led. He wondered if there was a man alive who'd been as blessed as he had. He'd shared the majority of his life with a wonderful woman, his beloved Irma Rose. And when God saw fit to call her home, he'd been blessed with his Lizzie.

So many people he'd loved, and he'd been loved by so many. His daughter, Sarah Jane; his granddaughter, Lillian, and her family; and a community full of family and friends whom he'd watched grow up, marry, and have families of their own. Yes, he'd been a blessed man. *But I'm ready, Lord.* Just this one last thing to do.

"They're here." Lizzie pushed the bedroom door open.

Jonas could see his friends standing behind Lizzie, and he forced a smile, determined to hide the constant ache in his bones while he visited with Sadie and Kade.

"Come in, you two." He wearily motioned with his hand for them to come closer. "*Danki* for coming."

Lizzie smiled at her husband, then eased out of the room.

Kade moved ahead of his wife and latched onto Jonas's hand. As Kade stood before him in traditional Amish clothing, Jonas recalled the first time he met Kade. He was a fancy, rich, *Englisch* man without a clue about real life. More money than any man could spend in a lifetime but as miserable as any a person could be. Jonas recalled mentoring Kade, teaching him about the *Ordnung*, and helping him to grow his faith. An Amish man teaching an *Englischer* about the *Ordnung* was out of the ordinary, but Jonas had seen something in Kade worth the effort. And he was right. Kade donated his wealth wisely within the district and to those outside the community in need. He'd set up a fine school for children with special needs, like his own son, Tyler, who was autistic. And he'd married the lovely Sadie, a woman most deserving of a good man. Like Jonas, Sadie had been widowed. Her first love passed on at a young age, so Jonas was glad that she was able to start anew with Kade, and Jonas had recently heard that Sadie was pregnant again.

"I brought the letters." Kade handed a large envelope to Jonas, and Sadie joined her husband at Jonas's bedside. Sadie leaned down and kissed Jonas on the forehead.

"Hello, Jonas."

"Dear Sadie. You look lovely."

She rubbed her slightly expanded belly. "*Danki*, Jonas."

Jonas reached into the envelope and pulled out the letter addressed to Linda. "Kade, reach into that drawer." He pointed to the bedside table. "Pull out that letter addressed to Linda. I'd like to replace Linda's letter with a new one."

Kade pulled out the letter Jonas had written to Linda when he heard her birth mother was in town.

"Jonas, these letters are a beautiful idea," Sadie said as her eyes filled with tears.

"No tears, my sweet Sadie. This old man has lived a blessed, full life. I'm ready." Jonas paused and looked back and forth between his friends, knowing this could be the last time he saw them. He could feel his body shutting down. And he'd seen Irma Rose twice this week just sitting across the room smiling.

Jonas had written the letters four years ago, figuring he'd be gone way before now. The letters told each person what they'd meant in his life. He'd never been good at expressing his feelings, and he wanted all of them to know that his life was blessed and he was a better man for knowing them all. He'd updated the letters over the years—most recently Linda's. The arrival of Linda's birth mother was surely an upset to his young friend, and he wasn't going to be around to see her through this.

There was a letter for Lizzie and one for his daughter, Sarah Jane. There were letters for Kade and Sadie, Carley and Noah, his beloved granddaughter, Lillian, and her husband, Samuel. Plus there were letters for all the children, young and old, whom he'd loved and watched grow, many of whom he'd never see marry and have children of their own. He was going to particularly miss seeing his great-grandson, David, marry and have *kinner*. The boy had survived a kidney transplant and was now a grown man of nineteen. But this is how it was supposed to be. A man can't live forever.

"I hear we have another young one on the way," Jonas said when he saw Kade's eyes filling with water. His good friend tried hard to blink back the tear, but it spilled onto his cheek anyway. Jonas reached for Kade's hand and held it tightly.

"*Ya*, we do." Sadie swiped at her eyes. "Jonas . . ." Her voiced cracked a bit, but then she smiled. "If it's a boy, we would like to name him Jonas."

Jonas wasn't sure he could keep his own emotions in check. He took a deep, labored breath. "Nothing would please me more."

They all shifted their eyes to the bedroom door when it creaked open.

"Jonas, you have two more visitors." Lizzie smiled. "I just wanted to let you know. Linda is here. And she's brought—she's brought a friend. But you take your time, Sadie and Kade. Sarah Jane and I will visit with them downstairs." Lizzie closed the door.

Kade said he would like for them all to pray, and Jonas was pleased that it was Kade who made the suggestion.

Jonas realized this was going to be harder than he'd suspected, saying good-bye to his loved ones.

Josie wasn't sure about Linda's reasoning for bringing her to a dying man's house. Nor could she understand Mary Ellen's way of thinking, agreeing that it was a good idea. Didn't Linda or Mary Ellen consider that Josie wouldn't want to see this in particular? Sadness filled the air around them and threatened to suffocate Josie. She'd have enough of this when her own time came.

"More coffee, dear?" Jonas's wife, Lizzie, offered to refill Josie's cup, but Josie shook her head.

"No, I'm fine."

For nearly fifteen minutes, Josie and Linda made small talk with Lizzie and Jonas's daughter, Sarah Jane. Josie's stomach was better, but she really just wanted to go home. She was starting to get tired already, and she missed Robert.

A few minutes later, a couple descended the stairs. Sarah Jane made introductions, and while Josie suspected Sadie and Kade knew she was Linda's birth mother, no mention was made. Sarah Jane had simply introduced Josie as a friend of Linda's, and once Kade and Sadie were gone, Lizzie escorted them up the stairs.

"I know this man is a friend of yours, Linda," Josie whispered to Linda, "but maybe I should just stay downstairs."

"Everyone should meet Jonas." Linda smiled. "Jonas has something for everyone, whether it's words of wisdom, or just a simple prayer to offer on their behalf. He's a special person."

"But he's so sick and I don't want to intrude." *Mostly, I don't want to stare death in the face.* If it had been anyone else dragging her up the stairs, Josie would have refused to go, but it seemed important to Linda that Josie meet this man.

Lizzie turned her head around. "You're not intruding, dear." Then she chuckled. "My Huggy Bear can be a bit gruff sometimes, so if he acts like that, you just ignore him."

Josie nodded. *Great. An old, dying man, who is also gruff.* She was getting more and more upset that Linda brought her here. But when they reached the top of the stairs, Linda grabbed Josie's hand and smiled, and any anxiety Josie felt melted away.

"You are a popular old man this morning," Lizzie said when she pushed the door open. "Linda and a friend of hers, Josie, have come for a visit." She turned to Linda and grinned. "You make him behave, Linda."

"I will, Lizzie."

The older woman left the room—a room that smelled of disinfectant and sickness. Josie hoped they wouldn't stay long, and she lagged behind near the door as Linda walked to the bedside and kissed the old man on the cheek. Josie suspected he must have been a handsome man at one time with his square jaw and big blue eyes, but now shades of gray beneath his lower lids were accentuated by his pale color, and his features were sunken in beneath a tangled mass of gray beard.

"Sweet Linda," he whispered. He attempted a smile, but Josie saw him cringing with pain.

"Jonas, are you in pain?" Linda clasped his hand within hers. "I thought Noah was changing your medications and that you would feel better."

The old man sighed. "He lied." Then he grunted but with the corner of his mouth tipped up on one side. "They did change my medicines, but turns out this old body just has too much going on inside to hold up much longer."

"We will pray right now, Jonas." Linda's voice was desperate as she bowed her head.

Jonas gently lifted her chin and gazed into her eyes. "Don't pray for me to stay on this earth, dear Linda. I'm ready to go home." He tenderly brushed a tear from her cheek with his thumb. "You are a special one." Jonas glanced at Josie, then back at Linda. "Introduce me to your birth mother."

Josie straightened, shocked that he would verbalize her true relationship to Linda.

"Jonas, this is Josie." Linda waved Josie to move closer, and she inched forward. She extended her hand to Jonas.

"Nice to meet you, Jonas."

His touch was frail, but he locked onto her hand and stared into her eyes. "Nice to meet you too."

"Oh, no!" Linda slapped her hands to her sides. "I forgot

something in the buggy. Stay here, Josie. I'll be right back." Linda scurried across the floor, opened the door, slammed it closed, and left Josie with her mouth hanging open, prepared to oppose being left alone with Jonas.

She pulled her gaze from the closed door and slowly turned to face Jonas. She smiled and glanced at the water pitcher on his nightstand, just like the one in Linda's room. "Can I get you a cup of water?" She moved toward the nightstand.

Jonas shook his head and scowled. "Now, why do you reckon that girl left you here with me? You do realize we've been set up?"

Josie couldn't help but smile at his honesty. "Yes, it appears that way."

Jonas arched one brow high. "Why is that?"

Josie shrugged. "I—I don't know." But she had a pretty good idea. "Probably because I have cancer too."

He cringed, but raised his chin as he spoke. "Ah, yes."

"You say that like you already know."

"*Ya*, I do. Noah was worried about Linda, and he told me you were ill."

"Did Noah tell you that I am staying with Linda and her family until my husband returns from overseas?"

His eyes widened. "No. I didn't know that."

Josie looked toward the floor. "I had a seizure while Linda was staying with me. I guess everyone got worried, because I don't really have any family here, and I passed out and spilled spaghetti sauce everywhere, and—and I'm sorry. I know I'm rambling." She looked up and locked eyes with this man, and the strangest feeling came over her. "Why am I here?"

"I don't know."

Josie shook her head and sat down in a chair by Jonas's bed. "I'm sorry I asked that. What a strange thing for me to say."

"Why do you think you're here?" His face twisted in pain.

"Oh, no. What can I do?" Josie leaned forward, but he waved his hand and seemed to let the pain take its course, then took a deep breath and refocused on Josie.

"So? Why do you think you're here?"

Josie leaned back against the chair and sighed. "I think Linda is hoping that by talking to you, that I won't be afraid of dying." She locked eyes with his. "Are you afraid?"

"No."

"Just like that? Just no? You don't have the least bit of apprehension about dying? Because, I have to tell you . . . it terrifies me."

Jonas smiled. "Now we know why you are here and why we've been set up to have this little chat."

"Why?"

He grimaced. "Because you are afraid of dying, and I'm not."

"Sir, with all due respect . . ." Josie paused and thought about whether or not she should speak her mind. "You are much older than me. I'm only thirty-four-years-old, and I've recently met my biological daughter. I'll never see her marry, have children, or any of that. I feel cheated."

"By who?"

"By God!" It just slipped out, and Josie regretted immediately that she'd said it. "I'm sorry, I just . . ." She fought the knot building in her throat. "If there is a God, I don't understand why He'd cut my life short after I get the only thing I've ever wanted, a relationship with my daughter. I have six months, at the most!

That's not long enough. I want more time. I'm afraid." Josie didn't understand what was happening to her, why she'd opened up to this complete stranger who had enough problems of his own. She cupped her face in her hands, embarrassed at her display, but too upset to have any dignity.

Jonas twisted his mouth to one side and stared at the woman before him, a woman with no hope. *I guess there are two things I have left to do, instead of just one.*

Jonas reached his hand straight out. "Take my hand." She was hesitant, pulling her hands away from her tear-streaked face, but she eventually latched onto his hand. "You are afraid because you don't believe, is that it?"

"What if there is nothing after this?"

"What if there is?" Jonas tilted his head slightly.

"But there's no way to know, one way or the other."

"Of course there is." *Oh, Lord, I need more time with this one.*

You don't have much time, My son.

Jonas sighed. "Does Linda know this? Is that why she brought you here?"

"No. Linda just knows that I'm afraid. Mary Ellen knows, though."

Jonas lay quietly for a moment. "Listen to me, Josie. Listen very carefully. I don't have much time. Mary Ellen is a *gut* woman. Listen to her. Trust her. She will show you the way. Oh, dear child. Learn of our Lord and His son, Jesus. While you can."

"I want to believe. I need to believe. I need hope, Jonas. I need something . . . I need . . . I don't know . . . I just need . . ."

"God." He squeezed her hand as best he could. "Open your heart, not your mind. Forge out falsities, and make way for His words to reach you. Once that happens, you will be filled with hope, and your fears will be no more."

She shook her head. "You seem like a very kind man, and I very much regret that I won't get to know you better. But I don't know how to do that."

"Then I will show you."

Lord, give me the strength, the knowledge, and the words to perform this last task for You, to help this soul find her way to You through Jesus.

"Close your eyes and picture the most perfect place imaginable, and then add the happiest moment in your life to that picture."

Josie closed her eyes and whispered, "When Linda was born."

"How do you feel?"

Her eyes were still closed, and Jonas gave her a reassuring squeeze with his hand, glad she couldn't see the look of agony on his face as another shot of pain seared down his spine.

Josie smiled. "I feel like I want to love unconditionally, this beautiful child, for the rest of my life."

"That is how God thinks of you. He loves you now, the same way He loved you when you felt His love through the gift of a child."

Her eyes opened, and her face filled with anger. "But He took that child away from me."

"Did He?"

"Yes, God took my baby away from me to be raised by someone I didn't even know. My own flesh and blood. And now I am dying, and I won't even get to see her grow into a mature woman."

"This angers you that God would do this?"

"Yes!" She stared at him with tears pouring down his face. "I am angry with God!"

Jonas breathed a sigh of relief. "Then tell Him that."

"What?" Her face twisted into confusion.

"Tell God that you're mad at Him. If you don't believe in Him, what harm can it do?"

"I don't know. It doesn't seem right to blame . . ." She let go of Jonas's hand and brought both hands to her head. He could see her right hand trembling, and Jonas worried he might be pushing her too hard.

"And yet, you do. Blame Him."

"I'm confused. I'm scared. I need something, and I don't know what it is. I feel lost."

"We all feel lost before we are found, dear Josie." Jonas sighed. "Look at me."

She sniffled, then pulled her hands away from her face.

"I'm leaving soon. I can feel it. And I regret that you and I won't have more time together. So, I'm going to offer you these parting words." He took a deep breath, hoping, praying that Josie would understand what he was saying. "*The fool hath said in his heart, There is no God.*"

Josie felt like she might faint when she heard Jonas speak the words she'd heard before—words not harsh, threatening, or fearful, but a declaration that brought on emotions Josie couldn't quite identify.

She stared at Jonas, wishing she would have more time with this man. Linda and Mary Ellen were right. There was something special about him.

"Jonas, is it too late for me? Too late for me to reconcile with God?"

His eyes were barely open, and his lips moved slowly. "It's never too late."

"But won't God think I'm just trying to get in His good graces because I am—I am not going to be here long?"

Jonas fought to keep his eyes open. "Josie, you don't sound like a woman who doesn't believe, but a woman who has lost her faith somewhere along the line. God doesn't care what brings you to Him, just that you go to Him. Pray, Josie. And talk to Mary Ellen. She is a wise woman."

Josie couldn't picture chatting with Mary Ellen about God. Then Robert flashed into her mind. *I miss you so much, Robert.* What would Robert think about her attempt to have a relationship with God? Would he think she was silly? She stood up from the chair and walked back and forth across the room, eventually zoning in on a calendar on the far wall with bright yellow flowers for the month of June. She stared at the colorful blooms as her mind raced.

"How will I know I've connected with God?"

"You will know."

Her back was still to Jonas as she folded her arms across her chest. She noticed her right hand trembling. "I don't think I could ever believe in miracles, but I want to go with an inner peace in my heart, hope for something after this life. My husband doesn't believe, but I should make my own choice. I haven't really allowed myself to explore the possibilities." She sighed. "I'm confused, I admit, but Jonas, I feel something I haven't felt throughout all of this." She relaxed her arms and reached up and touched the yellow flowers on the calendar. "I feel a glimmer of hope. Thank you for talking with me." She turned and faced him.

"Jonas?"

He smiled as he stared off in space at the rocker in the corner of the room. "Irma Rose is here. God's peace to you, Josie."

And he closed his eyes.

19

JOSIE'S VISIT WITH JONAS WORE HER OUT MORE THAN she'd expected it would, and she'd spent the remainder of the day napping on and off. It was eleven that night when Josie's cell phone buzzed on the nightstand between her and Linda, and she quickly reached for it.

"Robert, I miss you. Hold on." She jumped from the bed, tiptoed across the wooden floor, and stumbled down the stairs in the dark. "I'm going outside so I don't wake Linda up," she whispered. "Are you all right?" She groped her way through the den and onto the front porch.

"I'm fine, sweetie, but I am so frustrated. Still trying to get out of here. Are you all right? How are you feeling? Any more seizures?"

"I'm okay. I had another seizure after Noah called you, but I haven't had one since then. No headache either. I miss you so much, Robert. But don't worry about coming home. I'm with Linda, sleeping in the same room with her. If anything happens, she's right there, plus I'll really get to know her this way. So you should plan to finish your business there. Really. Even if the airports open in the next few days."

"No, Josie. I should have never come. I should have never, ever left you. I just want to come home and be with you. Maybe Linda

581

could stay with us some of the time, but I don't want to be away from you. This whole trip was a bad idea. I love you so much, baby. I'm going to hope the airports reopen soon, and I'll be on the first flight."

"I love you too, Robert." She paused. "You're never going to believe what happened this morning."

"What's that?"

"Linda took me to meet a friend of the family. Well, actually, I think he's a relative by marriage, but anyway . . . he was a wonderful old man, and Robert—he died right in front of me in his bed at home."

"What? Oh my gosh! Are you all right? That must have been horrible."

Josie thought for a moment. "You know, I'd just met the man, but I cried when he passed. Strange, huh?"

"Why would Linda take you there, to a dying man's home?"

She sighed as she recalled Jonas taking his last breath, unsure how much to share with Robert. "She said he was special and that she wanted me to meet him."

"Hmm . . . Seems odd."

"I wish I would have had more time to spend with him." She paused with a smile. "His name is Jonas. This entire community seems rocked by the loss. Poor Linda cried really hard earlier tonight. And, Robert, she climbed in the bed with me, and I just held her. It was the first time I felt like—like a mother."

"Oh, baby. I'm so glad you're getting to spend time with her. I know how much you wanted that."

"And you made it possible. You are the best husband in the entire world, and I don't deserve you."

"I'll do anything for you, Josie. You know that. You're my wife, and I love you."

Josie had thought a lot about her life all day, on and off between naps, about the possibilities of something to look forward to. She'd prayed tonight, really prayed. Prayed for strength and courage, for Linda, for Jonas's family, and for the knowledge to understand what having a relationship with God really means. Maybe she'd imagined it, or was just relieved not to have a headache, but a calm had settled over her.

"Jonas talked with me about God, Robert."

"He's Amish. They have a very strong faith. I'm not surprised."

Silence dredged a gap between them, and Josie felt oddly detached from Robert for a moment. "Linda and I prayed together tonight too. For quite a while." More silence. "Maybe we're wrong, Robert. About God. I mean, who's to say that just because we don't have something tangible, that a higher being doesn't exist?"

"Sweetheart, I have told you from the day we met that it's important for you to form your own opinion about this. I don't think I ever forced my beliefs on you, did I?"

Josie knew he hadn't. She'd just listened to his arguments against God and decided for herself that no God of hers would strip her of her child and deny her the ability to have another one. She recalled when Jonas said she was angry with God. Josie wondered if she'd always been angry, which made it easier to pull away from Him. Maybe she'd always believed.

"No, you didn't force anything on me," she finally said. "But I think I want to investigate the possibility of something after this, Robert."

Another silence, then Robert said, "Then you should." He paused. "But Josie, I won't change what I believe."

"I know."

She'd been married to Robert for twelve years, and at this moment, his last comment bothered her more than any harsh words they'd ever exchanged. How would this affect their relationship?

"I'm hoping the airports will reopen in a day or so, and I'll keep you posted. Josie, I am keeping my phone with me at all times. Please, baby, call me if you need to anytime, and make sure Linda and her family have my phone number to call if anything—happens. I mean, if you have a seizure or something."

"I will." She took a deep breath. *Please God, keep Robert safe.* Josie realized that prayer came easier with each passing moment, and she wondered why.

"Well, I guess I better go, but I'll call you tomorrow. I love you."

"I love you too, Robert."

The next day, the community celebrated the life of a man they'd all loved. There was much admonition for the living as well as respect offered for Jonas. A hymn was spoken, not sung, and following the service, Jonas was laid to rest in a hand-dug grave next to his beloved Irma Rose, his wooden coffin plain and simple with no ornate carvings. As customary, friends and family gathered for a meal at Jonas's home following the service.

Linda didn't think she'd ever stop crying, plus the thought of going through this again with Josie was overwhelming.

She glanced around the kitchen as the womenfolk worked to set out the meal and fill tea glasses. Jonas's wife, poor Lizzie, had only shared a few years of marriage with Jonas, but Linda didn't doubt for a minute that her love for Jonas was immeasurable. Linda watched the frail, gray-haired woman pouring tea with shaky hands and swollen eyes. Linda scanned the room to see where she might be needed, but everything to do with the meal was being handled. She slowly walked from the kitchen to the den and scanned those mourning.

Her *Onkel* Noah and *Aenti* Carley were sitting on the couch, entertaining their daughter, Jenna. Kade, Sadie, and their two children sat on the far side of the den, with Kade's arm wrapped around Sadie who was crying softly. Jonas's daughter, Sarah Jane, brushed past Linda and offered tea to several of the men. Linda heard her sniffling as she passed back by her. Uncle Samuel was sitting in a rocking chair with his two young girls in his lap, and her cousin, David, stood nearby. Linda had already seen Lillian in the kitchen, not much good to anyone. Her poor aunt could barely function.

Jonas was going to be missed, and Linda's heart hurt for all the friends and family who'd gathered at his home today. She passed back through the den and into the kitchen. Josie was helping her mother line up loaves of homemade bread on the counter, assisted by two other *Englisch* women, Barbie Beiler and Lucy Turner. Linda didn't think Josie and her mother were exactly friends, but they were respectful of one another, and Linda was just glad that Josie felt well enough to come today. Yesterday had been a bad day, and Josie hardly got out of bed after they'd visited Jonas. Another headache.

Linda wasn't sure how Josie would feel about coming to a funeral, but she'd insisted that she wanted to pay her respects to this very special man.

"Linda, can you open that door?" Her *Aenti* Rebecca nodded toward the door in the kitchen as she carried a tray with full glasses of tea. "I want to get these to those outside in this heat."

"*Ya.*" Linda pushed the screen door open and let it slam behind her. She walked down the porch steps and into the yard. When she stepped around to the side of the house to have a moment to herself, she heard voices coming from the back.

"I don't care, Ivan."

Linda recognized the voice to be her *Aenti* Katie Ann.

"Please, Katie Ann . . ." her *Onkel* Ivan said. "I've said I'm sorry a hundred times."

"And it wonders me if you mean it one bit. The fact that Lucy Turner is even here turns my stomach."

"It's a funeral, Katie Ann. I reckon it's not like I invited her or nothin'."

"She's not even friends with Jonas. Barbie Beiler has been a wonderful friend to Jonas, and of course, she should be here. But that Lucy woman is only here for one reason, and you know what it is!"

Her aunt rounded the corner, and her eyes widened when she saw Linda. "Linda!"

"Uh, sorry. I was just trying to get away from the crowd for a few minutes." Linda could feel the heat building in her cheeks, unsure if it was from being caught listening or from the conversation she'd just overheard.

Katie Ann folded her arms across her chest and marched past Linda mumbling something under her breath. Linda quickly followed before Ivan came around the corner.

Stephen drank a glass of tea out in the front yard following the meal. He watched Linda and Josephine walk to her car and get inside. It appeared they were enjoying some air-conditioning for a few minutes. Stephen sighed as he recalled seeing Linda in the fancy blue jeans and red blouse at Josie's house.

Two more times, his grandfather had spoken with him about Linda and shared his concerns about her relationship with her birth mother and about stretching privileges during *rumschpringe*. Plenty of times, Stephen had watched his grandfather warn parents when their children were stepping outside the boundaries set forth by the *Ordnung*, but lately Stephen found himself worrying about Linda and her role within the community. Stephen had never felt the need to explore the *Englisch* world. His place was here. With Linda. Or so he'd thought.

He took another sip of tea. "Avoid getting too close to those who are unequally yoked," his grandfather had told him.

His thoughts were interrupted when he saw Kade Saunders gathering the immediate family on the front porch. Most everyone else had gone home, but a few people were still cleaning up for Lizzie and Sarah Jane, including Stephen's mother and sisters.

Stephen sipped his tea and held his position, not wanting to intrude. But he could hear from where he was standing. He could also see Linda included in the group.

"Jonas left some special instructions for me to share with those he was particularly close to." Kade reached into a large envelope and began distributing smaller envelopes. When he was done, he addressed the entire group. "Before you open your letter, I have this note to read to you from Jonas."

> *My dear friends and family,*
>
> *I am a blessed man to have shared in all of your lives. I've watched many of you grow up and have families of your own. We've celebrated the gut times and struggled through the bad times together through prayer and fellowship. I reckon each letter is my way of letting you know what you mean to me.*
>
> *Take care of each other through love and prayer.*
>
> > *In His Name,*
> >
> > *Jonas*

Stephen regretted the fact that he wasn't getting a letter and that he hadn't been closer to Jonas, since Jonas was often called upon like he were the bishop himself. Everyone spoke of Jonas's wisdom and fun-loving personality. Perhaps, that was why his grandfather had never encouraged his family to be close to Jonas. *Jealousy?* But that's a sin. Surely *Daadi* wouldn't think like that. Stephen watched each person walk away with their letter to a quiet spot. Linda went to the far side of the yard and sat down in the grass underneath a shade tree.

Linda peeled open her envelope and eased out the letter, knowing she would treasure Jonas's final words for the rest of her life. She took a deep breath and read.

> *My Sweet Linda,*
>
> *If you're reading this, I'm dead and buried, six feet under. Everyone is probably moping around, crying and the like. Now, no need for all that, mei*

maedel. *I'm with our Lord, and I reckon by the time you get this, me and Irma Rose will be sipping cider on the front porch of our heavenly home, looking down on our loved ones, and hoping you folks can behave yourselves.*

Although, it ain't likely that you'll disappoint me. What a fine young woman you are. Always polite and eager to help others, much like your mother. You will be a fine fraa *and* mamm *some day, and I regret that I won't be around to see you in this role, but I will be smiling from above. I'm not sure if there is a greater love than that of a mother, and as of recently, I reckon you have two. How blessed you are, even though I know it is a confusing time. Somehow in all of this, I see you as the strong one, the binding glue so to speak, in this threesome.*

And be not conformed to this world: but be ye transformed by the renewing of your mind, that ye may prove what is that good, and acceptable, and perfect will of God.

May the will of God be done, and may you grow and prosper in His name.

Now, I have some final thoughts for you. I reckon you'll end up marrying Stephen Ebersol. Don't let that scary grandfather of his get you worked up. You young folks don't see Bishop Ebersol as the man he truly is, with three times the wisdom as your old friend Jonas here. Bishop Ebersol just ain't all warm and fuzzy like I am.

Linda grinned. She could picture Jonas roaring with laughter as he wrote the comment about his warm and fuzzy self.

Go to him, Linda, if you need to. For anything. He is a wise man who has much to offer.

I have always thought of you as one of my grandchildren, Sweet Linda. You've always been precious to me.

Loving thoughts from above,

Jonas

Linda pulled her knees to her chest, then buried her head and wept.

She jumped and lifted her head when she felt a hand on her shoulder. Stephen brushed away a tear on her cheek.

"I wish I had received a letter from Jonas. I know he was a *gut* man."

Linda swallowed back tears. "*Ya*, he was. The best."

"Let's go to the creek when we leave here and get away from all this sadness and just be together for a while."

"*Ach*, I don't know. Josie is staying with us. I don't know." Although there was nothing she wanted more. She could tell Stephen wanted to kiss her, but there were too many people around, and public affection of that type was frowned upon.

"I understand. How's it going with Josie at your house?"

"So far, so *gut*." Linda felt tears building again. "I just can't believe that we'll be having a funeral for Josie. I don't know how I'm going to get through that."

He reached for her hand and squeezed. "I will be by your side, you won't be alone. Let's pray for Josie." Stephen bowed his head and closed his eyes. Linda did the same.

Dear Lord, please don't let Josie be in pain, and please let her stay with me for as long as it is Your will. If You could see fit to let her stay with me for a long time, that would be so gut. *Say hi to Jonas for me.* Aamen.

They both lifted their heads when they heard footsteps.

"Hello you two." Carley squatted down beside them. "Jonas will certainly be missed."

"*Ya*, he will," Linda said as Stephen nodded.

"Linda, I've already spoken with Josie, and there is something I want you to know. There are so many people praying for Josie.

I know you don't have a computer, but prayers for her are flying across the Internet and people of every denomination are praying for her. She is on our prayer list at church. Barbie Beiler has also added her to their church list, and tons of people you've never even met are praying for Josie. I just wanted you to know that."

Linda let a tear spill over, then hugged her aunt. "*Danki,* Carley."

"You're welcome."

Josie sat down at the bench in the kitchen when the strobes of light began to flash. *Please, not now.* A few women were finishing the cleanup, including Mary Ellen. Josie thought about what Noah's wife, Carley, had said. About all the people praying for her. What a sweet gesture from so many people whom she'd never meet.

It had been a long day, and Josie could feel the weight of her emotions turning into a bad headache. But she had no regrets at coming. She didn't know Jonas, but something about their one encounter propelled her to be present at his funeral.

"Josie, look at me." Josie tried to blink her eyes into focus. Mary Ellen had a hand on her shoulder. "Are you all right?"

"I—I think so. It's just my head. I'm sorry. I don't want to cut your time short. I'll be fine."

"Nonsense. We're done. I'll find Abe and gather Linda and the boys."

Josie watched Mary Ellen quickly walk away, and she pondered the oddity of this situation—Mary Ellen taking care of her. And, to her surprise, Josie welcomed Mary Ellen's nurturing ways, something she'd never had from her own mother. Even though Mary Ellen was only a few years older than Josie, she felt safe in her presence. *This must be how Linda has always felt. I wonder if I could have been as motherly and nurturing as Mary Ellen.*

"Hi, Josie. *Danki* for coming. I'm Lillian." The woman Josie already knew to be Jonas's granddaughter sat down beside her.

"I hope I'm not intruding, but I met Jonas one time, and I just felt something . . . and I—I don't know. I just wanted to be here. And also for Linda."

Lillian's eyes were swollen from crying. "Grandpa had that effect on people." She smiled. "He would be glad to know you're here."

They sat quietly for a moment.

"Linda thinks the world of you," Josie finally said.

"Linda is very special. When I first came to the community, after being in the *Englisch* world for most of my life, Linda was so welcoming. I liked her right away."

Josie fought the pressure in her head. The strobe lights had stopped, but the pain in her temples was making her stomach churn. "Was it hard for you to leave, I mean, leave the *Englisch* world and become Amish?"

"Hmm. I wouldn't say it was hard." Lillian twisted her mouth to one side. "Challenging, perhaps. But once I realized that the only way to true inner peace was through a relationship with God, then it was easy."

"So, you didn't always believe?" This piqued Josie's interest.

"No, I didn't. I didn't understand." Lillian paused and twisted on the bench to face Josie. "My grandparents taught me about the *Ordnung*, about trusting in God's will, and ultimately I became a Daughter of the Promise."

"What is that?"

"It's when a woman takes a spiritual journey to find the meanings of faith, hope, and love."

Hope. I need that more than anything. "It sounds wonderful."

"It is an amazing journey, especially when you are first establishing a true relationship with God and you see the immense changes in your life." Lillian stared off in space for a moment. "My grandpa was a huge part of that process for me, and of course my grandma, Irma Rose, who died several years ago. Without them, I'm not sure where I'd be." Then she smiled. "And, my husband, Samuel, was right by my side while I learned about the Lord."

"I understand from Linda that you and your husband went through a lot with his—I mean *your* son, David. Linda thinks the world of David too."

"It was tough times four years ago. David needed a kidney, and Noah was the only one who was a match in our family. Noah had been shunned, and it was a rather big mess for a while. But David is healthy now, and over time the community has welcomed Noah into their hearts and homes."

"I can't help but notice how everyone in this community joins together, in good times and in bad. I remember that from when I was growing up here. I had a few Amish friends."

"How is it going, staying with Linda and her family in their home? Miss that air-conditioning?" Lillian smiled. "It was the hardest thing for me to give up."

Josie liked Lillian. Even during this difficult time, she was making an effort to get to know Josie, and Josie was touched. "It was a little warm last night. Although I suspect my husband will be home from overseas soon, and I'll be returning home."

"I'd like to pray with you, if that's all right," Lillian said.

"I'd like that."

"Normally, we pray silently, but I'd like to offer a prayer aloud for you."

Josie nodded, welcoming this thoughtful gesture.

"Please Heavenly Father, be with my new friend, Josie, and stay close to her during difficult times, both now and in the future. Bless her with Your healing touch, and wrap Your loving arms around her. In Your name we pray."

Josie tried to stifle her sobs, which would only make her head hurt worse. "Thank you. I don't know why that's making me cry." She faced Lillian. "I just appreciate it so much. And it's such a sweet thing to do."

Lillian gazed long and hard into Josie's eyes, and Josie had the strangest feeling that Lillian knew her secret, although she was sure Mary Ellen would never share something so private. "When I first came to know the Lord, I cried a lot. It's a spiritual cleansing of sorts. Maybe that's the case with you." Lillian smiled.

Josie didn't respond. She swiped her eyes and wondered what was taking Mary Ellen so long, even though she was enjoying this time with Lillian.

"Lillian, I've been looking for you. I thought you were outside." Sarah Jane hurried into the kitchen. "Hello, Josie. I'm sorry to interrupt."

Josie remembered Jonas's daughter from her visit to see Jonas. "No, that's fine," Josie said as she stood up.

"*Mamm*, what is it? You look frantic." Lillian rose from the bench also.

"This!" Sarah Jane held up an envelope, much like the ones several family members and friends had received earlier.

"Your letter? What about it? I got one too."

"Not like this, you didn't." Sarah Jane's eyes widened as she grinned. "I already opened my personal letter from Pop. But this is a second letter addressed to you, me, and Lizzie. You're never going to believe this." She pushed the letter toward Lillian. "Read it. See for yourself!"

20

LILLIAN OPENED THE ENVELOPE HER MOTHER HANDED to her just as Lizzie walked into the kitchen and after Josie excused herself to go look for Mary Ellen.

"My Huggy Bear is just full of surprises." Lizzie sat down in a chair at the far end of the table. "I couldn't believe my eyes when Sarah Jane showed me the letter."

"Leave it to Pop to do something like this without telling us." Sarah Jane sat down on the wooden bench, propped her elbows on the table, and rested her chin on her hands. "What was he thinking?"

Lillian unfolded the white piece of paper and read.

Lizzie, Sarah Jane, and Lillian,

You three girls have probably given me more grief over the past few years than all the folks I've ever known—always hovering over me, trying to take care of me, and bossing me around.

Lillian covered her growing smile with her hand. She couldn't help but laugh at her grandfather's ways, even at the end.

But I love you girls with all my heart, and I hate that I won't be around to take care of you all—especially you, Lizzie. Lillian, you have Samuel; and

Sarah Jane, I reckon you do all right on your own, but you two take care of my Lizzie.

Now, for the matter at hand. Lancaster County is growing more and more populated, with less farmland for future generations, which makes the land prices mighty high. I reckon by the time Lillian's young girls are grown and married, their husbands will be forced to work only in the Englisch *world, unable to tend to the land we love and make a* gut *living at it. We are getting further and further away from our Amish roots with each passing year, and it wonders me if generations to come will hold steadfast to our deep satisfaction to work the land in hopes of a plentiful harvest.*

In the valley beneath Colorado's Sangre de Cristo mountains, small Amish communities are gathering. I've purchased one thousand acres there, in a place called Canaan, Colorado. There are two farmhouses on the property, over two hundred years old and in need of much repair. I believe that more and more of our people will move west due to overcrowding and high land prices here. So, my girls . . . this is my way of safeguarding future generations.

Beautiful country there, and it's available to you if you should want or need it. Kade Saunders has all the details.

Calm down, Sarah Jane. I can see your face as you read, wondering how I did this. There's this thing called the Internet down at the local library. Puts you in touch with anyone, anywhere. I had to bend a rule on my way out.

In His Name, and loving you all,
Pop—Grandpa—Huggy Bear

"Close your mouth, Lillian," her mother teased in reference to Lillian's jaw, which hung to the floor. "I had the same reaction."

"*Ya*, I was shocked as well." Lizzie shook her head.

"Why would Grandpa think that any of us would split the

family up and leave? We all love it here." Lillian cringed. "Does this mean Grandpa hasn't even seen the property he bought?"

"Hello, ladies." Kade walked into the room. He chuckled. "Leave it to Jonas to do something like this. I didn't know about this until an attorney knocked on my door yesterday with this letter and deed to the property, with instructions from Jonas for me to deliver it all to you. And to answer your question— apparently Jonas has not seen his purchase. Amazing that he would buy property over the Internet, sight unseen, and not tell anyone."

"Well, we'll just sell it," Lillian said. "We don't need a thousand acres in Colorado. That's the craziest thing I've ever heard of."

"I agree." Lizzie shook her head again. "Silly old Huggy Bear knows I could never make a trip like that."

"Kade, would you be able to handle the details of selling the property for us?" Sarah Jane folded her hands in front of her. "We'd pay you, of course."

"I would be glad to." Kade rubbed his chin. "Although . . . I did some research last night and never underestimate Jonas. He got a great deal on this property, in a beautiful location. Land in Lancaster County is almost six times as much as in Colorado. It's not as crowded there, and the acreage Jonas purchased is in a very rural area. I know exactly where Canaan is, I've been there. It's near Monte Vista. You might not want to make this decision so hastily."

"What decision?" Samuel walked into the kitchen carting Elizabeth in his arms and with Anna by his side.

Lillian covered her face with her hands for a moment, then blew out a breath of frustration. "Can you believe that Grandpa bought a thousand acres in Colorado without telling anyone? Property with two farmhouses in a rural area. He left a letter for *Mamm*, Lizzie, and me. We just were just telling Kade to make the arrangements to sell the property."

Samuel stroked his beard and didn't say anything, and Lillian watched his brows narrow speculatively.

"Samuel? Doesn't it shock you that Grandpa would do something like this?"

"*Ya.*" Samuel glanced back and forth between Lillian and her mother. "But I think we should go. Move to Colorado."

Lillian thought she might fall off the bench. "What?" She sat up taller. "We're not going anywhere."

"Samuel, why would you say that?" Sarah Jane edged closer to him and extended her arms to take Elizabeth. "Come here, sweetie. Come see your *mammi.*" Then she narrowed her eyes at Samuel. "I love you, Samuel, but the thought of you taking my grandbabies makes me want to smack you."

"I reckon we can talk about it later." Samuel looped his thumbs under his suspenders. "Are you ready to go, Lillian?"

Lillian stood from the table. "I guess so, but I'll tell you right now, Samuel Stoltzfus, we aren't going anywhere, so there is nothing to talk about later." Lillian eased Elizabeth out of her mother's arms, kissed her *mamm* on the cheek, and said, "Let me know if you or Lizzie need anything."

She said her good-byes to the others, then she and Samuel loaded the girls into the buggy. David would be leaving in his own courting buggy. She waited until they were heading home on Black Horse Road before she broached the subject of Colorado.

"Samuel, why would you say that about moving to Colorado?"

She curled her mouth into a frown. "Our families are here. We could never do that."

Her husband was quiet for a moment. "I guess you're right."

Lillian could see their farm up ahead, and she thought about all the work Samuel had done to the property and everything she'd done to make it a home for all of them. "There must have been some reason you said that, Samuel." She cut her eyes in his direction.

Samuel shrugged. "*Ach*, I don't know. It was just a thought."

Lillian sat taller as they pulled onto the driveway. "I could never leave here."

Samuel didn't say anything.

Josie felt drained by the time they returned from the funeral, and after helping Mary Ellen carry in casserole dishes she'd taken to the funeral, Josie sat down in one of the rockers in the den and pushed herself into motion.

Mary Ellen walked into the den and put her hands on her hips. "You look terrible."

Josie lifted her brows. "Thanks."

"You've done too much today. Why don't you go lie down before supper?"

"No. I'm fine. A little tired, but I'm just thankful that my headache went away." She pointed to her hand. "And look. No bothersome jerking either."

Mary Ellen pushed back a strand of hair that had fallen from beneath her prayer covering, then she wiped her hands on her apron. "I'm making a very simple supper, so I don't need any help, if you'd like to rest. Besides, Linda should be home from her walk with Stephen soon."

Josie kept rocking. "Your bishop didn't have much to say to me today. I tried to talk to him."

"Bishop Ebersol? *Ya*, that's Stephen's grandfather. He's been the strictest bishop we've ever had." Mary Ellen shook her head. "Too strict, if ya ask me."

Josie thought for a moment. "He probably wouldn't like me staying here, would he?"

"I doubt it. But it isn't for long."

Ouch. Mary Ellen had made the statement as if she were relieved of that fact. "Where are Abe and the boys?"

"In the far pasture. One of the cows is due any day, and they went to check on her."

Josie nodded, then Mary Ellen turned to go into the kitchen. Josie followed her.

"Mary Ellen, why did you ask me to stay here when I get the distinct impression you'd rather me not be here?" Josie folded her arms across her chest and waited for Mary Ellen to answer. She appeared in no hurry as she opened the refrigerator door and pulled out a stick of butter. Josie continued to wait.

Finally, Mary Ellen turned to face her. "I've asked myself that a hundred times." Josie's heart sank, but then Mary Ellen smiled before she walked to the stove. "I have a sense that you are meant to be here, Josie. Not just because you are Linda's birth mother either."

Josie sat down on the bench while Mary Ellen pulled two pots down from a rack near the stove. "What kind of sense?"

"The kind that comes from God." She turned her head around,

and her eyes flashed a gentle warning. "But I do not want Linda to be tempted by your ways." Then she turned back around and placed the pots atop the stove.

"That doesn't make sense, Mary Ellen." Josie scowled. "If you're so worried about that, then why did you invite me here?"

"Honestly?"

"Yes, honestly. I'd like to know." Josie paused. "You offered for Linda's sake, I suppose. Or just out of pity."

Mary Ellen turned around and twirled the wooden spoon in her hand as she spoke. "Because you are—ill. And because you don't know Jesus and His Father. I think that's tragic, and I thought perhaps you might learn from us. It's normally not our way to minister to others about the Lord, but I have a strong feeling that you are the exception."

"But how much could you teach me in only a day or two? Robert thinks he can catch a flight home from China any day now." Josie raised her shoulders and let out an exasperated breath. "I wish . . ."

Mary Ellen stood waiting.

Josie tapped her finger to her chin. "I wish I knew what was going on with me. I've felt different lately. Especially today, at the funeral. All those people together at one time, praying." She pulled her eyes from Mary Ellen's and focused on the brown mat in front of the sink. "I've even been praying." Then she shook her head. "I'm conflicted, I guess."

"There is much power in prayer, Josephine." Then Mary Ellen smiled. "A lot can be covered in a day or two."

Josie returned the smile. "I'm all ears."

If Mary Ellen could help her attain the hopefulness that she'd felt on brief occasions lately, Josie was willing to open her heart and her mind to the possibilities.

The days stretched into more than a week, but Robert was due home midmorning the next day. She missed Robert terribly, but until the end she'd treasure her time in this house, with this family. She spent lots of time during the day with Linda, by her side doing laundry, mending, or housecleaning. She'd only had two really bad headaches, and neither had lasted very long. The new medication Dr. Phillips prescribed for the seizures seemed to be working since she hadn't had one. Getting to know her daughter was all she wished for.

Late in the afternoons, Josie helped Mary Ellen with supper. Linda was glad that it gave her an opportunity to spend some extra time with Stephen. Each day she walked about a half mile to meet Stephen when he drove over the bridge in Ronks, and they would talk for about an hour before Stephen would bring her home.

In an ironic twist, Josie had never felt as alive as she had the past week, and something had changed between her and Mary Ellen as well. During the couple of hours that it took to prepare supper, Mary Ellen talked with Josie about the Bible and about the *Ordnung*, an unwritten code of conduct that most Amish know by heart. And they'd prayed. A lot. And with each prayer, Josie felt more hopeful about her circumstances. She'd begun to have dreams about heaven, and in her dreams it was the most beautiful place she could imagine.

As she felt possibilities springing forth around her, she fought a building resentment at Robert. Josie knew she was a grown woman perfectly capable of forming her own opinions, but she couldn't help but wonder how differently her life might have been if she'd married a man who had a strong faith like Mary Ellen did. But each time the thought presented itself, she worked to push it aside. Robert was the best man she'd ever known.

Josie was chopping tomatoes while she sat at the kitchen table that evening, sweat dripping down her face, and thinking how good it felt to not wear any makeup. It had seemed pointless after about the second day, as she only sweated it off, and no one else around here wore any.

Since Abe and the boys had gone into town and Linda was with Stephen, Josie wanted to share with Mary Ellen something that had been on her mind before she left in the morning.

"I want to thank you, Mary Ellen. For everything." Josie sliced the end off a tomato and began to chop it into tiny squares for the stew that night. "I know that my being here has been difficult for you from day one. But I just—just wanted to know her. That's all."

Mary Ellen stirred meat in a pot on top of the stove. She didn't turn around. "You're welcome."

"I guess I really didn't need to be here. I mean, I've had a couple of headaches, but no seizures, and overall I've felt pretty good."

Mary Ellen turned around. "*Ach*, I feel quite sure you needed to be here. For several reasons, no?" She smiled, then turned to stirring again.

"I guess you're right."

Josie continued chopping the tomatoes, but her mind was a whirlwind of activity. What if she hadn't stayed here, learned from Mary Ellen, opened herself up to a relationship with God? She'd even been fortunate enough to attend worship service with them all at Mary Ellen's sister's house. Rebecca and her husband,

Aaron, hosted the Sunday service at their home. It was a long three hours, sitting on the wooden benches, but Josie felt honored to have been invited. Even though she didn't understand most of the service spoken in High German, there was a sense of amazing fellowship. She still couldn't say that she wasn't afraid to die, but alongside her fears there was now hope, hope at an everlasting life.

"Do you mind if I keep seeing Linda in the next few months?" She piled the tomatoes on a plate to her left.

"Of course not." Mary Ellen was adding potatoes that Josie had peeled earlier to the stew, but she didn't turn around.

Josie stood up, picked up the plate, and took them to Mary Ellen. "Time for the tomatoes?" She held the plate over the pot.

Mary Ellen nodded but turned her face away from Josie. But not enough that Josie couldn't see the tears in her eyes.

"Mary Ellen? What is it?" Josie set the plate on the counter, latched onto Mary Ellen's shoulders, and gently turned her until Josie could see her face. Mary Ellen swiped at her eyes and shook her head.

"I'm fine."

"You're not fine. You're crying. What is it? What's wrong?"

Mary Ellen covered her face with her hands and sobbed. Then she looked up at Josie with tear-filled eyes. "Josephine . . ." She hung her head for a moment before she lifted her chin and locked eyes with Josie. "I've committed a sin against you, against God. I reckon I never wanted you here. I never wanted you to search for Linda, I never wanted her to know you, and I didn't want you to disrupt our lives."

None of this surprised Josie, but she wondered why Mary Ellen was telling her this now, when they seemed to have come so far. She waited for her to go on, hoping there would be a *but* coming.

"But I've grown to care deeply for you, and I would have never wished this on—on you, never, Josephine. Do you hear me? I never wanted something like this to happen, and . . ." Mary Ellen slumped over, crying hard.

"Mary Ellen." Josie spoke firmly, squeezed her arms gently, and nudged her to look up. "I know that. Do you hear me? I understand everything you are saying. I don't think you've experienced an emotion yet that wouldn't be human in this situation. You didn't make me sick, Mary Ellen. And I *did* disrupt your life. And I never expected to care for you like . . ." A lump in Josie's throat prevented her from going on. Instead, the women embraced, and Josie held on to Mary Ellen while her own tears spilled.

Mary Ellen eased away from Josie and gathered herself. "I know that God's will is to be done, but I will miss you, and it saddens me to think—to think . . ."

"I will miss you too." She dabbed at her eyes and smiled. "But if everything you are telling me is true, which I believe to be so, I'm going to a wonderful place, and we'll see each other again in heaven."

"*Ya, ya.*" Mary Ellen nodded as she sniffled.

A loud crash startled them both. They spun around to see a rooster slam through the screen in the door, ripping it in every direction as the winged animal hurtled toward them. Josie screamed.

Mary Ellen grabbed Josie's hand and pulled her to the other side of the kitchen just as the rooster rounded the corner and headed into the den.

"What do we do?" Josie yelled over the shrill squawking that echoed through the house.

Mary Ellen grabbed a broom in the corner. "Not sure! Something is wrong with that bird!" She ran into the den, and Josie followed behind. Then Mary Ellen screamed, and turned around, bumping right into Josie. "It's coming back!"

They ran back through the den, and Josie threw her hands over her head as the rooster began to flap his wings and lift off the ground, spewing horrible sounds. Josie didn't know much about roosters, but this didn't sound good at all. The bird skimmed the coffee table; books, Abe's glasses, and a lantern went crashing to the floor. Josie kept running until she got to the kitchen, but Mary Ellen stayed behind. Then it got very quiet.

"Mary Ellen, are you okay?" Josie peeked around the corner, and Mary Ellen had her shoulders scrunched up to her ears as she pointed to the couch.

Josie jerked her head to the left. That bird had perched itself on the back of the couch. Still and quiet. Josie didn't move. She looked back at Mary Ellen. "What do we do?"

That's all it took. The bird was in flight, and both women started screaming and trying to stay out of its path as it flew around the den, then into the kitchen, then back to the den. Josie even jumped over the coffee table to get out of the bird's way, toppling the wooden table over when her foot didn't quite clear it. Mary Ellen was trying to use the rocking chair to block the bird as it dove toward her, eventually toppling the chair over as well.

Mary Ellen began screaming something in Pennsylvania *Deitsch* when the bird slammed into the china cabinet up against the wall in between the kitchen and den. Then she yelled, "That's my wedding china!"

Josie was hovering on the couch with her hands over her head, but when she looked up and saw Mary Ellen holding the broom like a weapon and protecting her china, Josie burst into laughter, the type of laughter that causes you to snort and make all kinds of sounds you wouldn't necessarily want anyone to hear.

"You think this is funny?" Mary Ellen still had her hands gripped firmly around the broom, but her eyes were looking to the left, then to the right. "Where is that bird?"

Josie rolled onto her side on the couch, struggling to catch her breath because she was laughing so hard.

They both turned toward the kitchen when they heard the screen door slam. Linda's mouth dropped open. She looked back and forth between Josie and Mary Ellen. Then her hands moved over her mouth as she surveyed the area, which, Josie knew, looked like a war zone. When Linda looked at Josie lying on the couch, with tears streaming down her face, she turned to her mother.

Placing her hands on her hips, she said, "*Mamm*, put that broom down right now! What could you two possibly be fighting about? Look at this mess." She walked toward Josie, mumbling to herself in Pennsylvania *Deitsch*, before she addressed Josie directly. "Are you all right?"

Josie burst into laughter at Linda's assumption and, through watery eyes, noticed that Mary Ellen was bent over at the waist, laughing as hard as she was.

"Linda!" Mary Ellen yelled between gasps for air and laughter. "Do you really think I would hit Josie with a broom?"

Mary Ellen went to the couch and sat down beside Josie, who sat up next to her. Both women continued to laugh, but Linda didn't seem to see the humor.

"It smells like something is burning in the oven, and look at this mess!"

"Oops. Forgot to take the bread out." Mary Ellen started laughing again.

Linda walked toward them, laughing like school girls on the couch. She folded her hands across her chest. "Well, I reckon the two of you better get this mess cleaned up before *Daed* gets here and sees you carrying on this way. He'll think you've been hitting the wine, I reckon."

Josie heard the flapping of wings, and evidently Mary Ellen did too. "Cover your head," Mary Ellen yelled to her daughter as she scooted closer to Josie and held her hands above her head.

"What is that—" Linda looked toward the mudroom just in time to see that crazy bird come flying through. She screamed, then joined them both on the couch. All three were still huddled together when Abe walked through the door. He grabbed the rooster by the neck, then eyed the women on the couch, who were trying not to laugh but were unsuccessful.

He shook his head and walked out the door mumbling.

It took a few moments for Josie to gather herself. She took several deep breaths, then she looked to her left at—at—

Her head started to hurt in a way that it had never hurt before, and she slammed her hands to her temples. She could vaguely hear the women asking her if she was all right.

She panicked as her heart began to race, and her head was surely going to explode. *Please, dear God, help me. Oh, please help.*

I am here, My child.

Then everything went black.

21

JOSIE BLINKED HER EYES INTO FOCUS AND SQUINTED from the bright lights in the drafty room. She recognized the smell of the hospital right away.

"Hello, sleepyhead." Robert ran his hand through Josie's hair, then leaned down and kissed her on the lips. "How are you feeling?"

"I don't remember getting here. There was this bird, and . . ."

"You had a seizure last night, and Mary Ellen called an ambulance from their phone in the barn." Robert pulled a chair closer to the bed and sat down. "Mary Ellen stayed with you all night, until I got here this morning."

"She did?" Josie lifted her arm and eyed the IV. "I don't remember much." She reached for Robert's hand. "I'm so glad you're home. So very glad."

He leaned down and kissed her again. "Me too. And I'm not leaving you again. I don't care what kind of business presents itself." Robert hung his head. "I'm so sorry, babe."

Josie reached up and cupped his cheek with her hand. "It's all right, honey. I had an amazing time getting to know Linda. And Mary Ellen . . . well, who would have ever thought that we might become friends? She's a wonderful woman. And Robert, she taught me so much while I was there."

Robert smiled. "I imagine she did. I bet it was interesting to find out about their ways, live the life for a while."

"We prayed, she explained some of the *Ordnung*, their way of conduct, and we read the Bible. It was wonderful."

Robert stopped smiling, and his expression filled with concern. Then he seemed to be forcing a smile. "I'm glad you had a good time."

"I did." She paused, seeing the hurt in his eyes. "But I missed you terribly."

"The doctor said you can go home. They're sending home yet another new medication that hopefully will help with the seizures."

"Robert, I want you to get to know Linda."

"I'd like that."

"Maybe she can come stay with us some over the next few— few months."

"Josie, we can do anything you want to do. Anything." He ran a hand through her tangled hair again. "My precious Josie."

"She'll be eighteen in August. And I'll be praying that I make it to her birthday party."

Robert tried to hide the shadow that crossed his face, but Josie knew him too well for that.

"That bothers you, doesn't it?"

"What's that?"

"That I would mention praying."

Robert shrugged. "No."

She intertwined her fingers within his and stared into his eyes. "Do you know that people all over the country are praying for me? I know you don't believe, Robert, but I think that is just amazing."

Robert lifted her hand and kissed her fingers tenderly. "Josie, if you think it's amazing, then I think it's amazing."

"Get me out of here." She grinned. "Take me home and hold me all night long."

"Deal. We're just waiting for the nurse to come take out your IV. Then we can go."

Josie gazed into Robert's eyes, the love of her life. *Please help him to believe, God. Even if just a little.*

The door swung open, and the nurse walked in. "I understand someone is ready to go home?"

"Yes! Release me, please." Josie playfully lifted her hand with the IV up and down.

"You got it."

With Josie's IV out, Robert helped her dress and took her home.

Linda pushed herself along on the foot scooter, pumping her leg faster the closer she got to the bridge in Ronks. Stephen had told her he'd left a poem for her there, and sure enough, she saw a pink ribbon as soon as she entered the shade from the covered bridge. She fought to catch her breath and pulled the note from between the slats.

> *My heart belongs to the recipient of this letter; the one who makes my heart feel better.*
> *My emotions for you I cannot hide; as you are the warmth I feel inside.*
> *Please believe me as this is true; my entire world revolves around you.*
>
> > *I love you, Stephen*

She smiled at Stephen's gentle words. "I love you too," she whispered, and she wrote those same words on the note before stuffing it back in place. As much as she loved these exchanges on the bridge, her heart ached for Stephen to propose. She worried that Bishop Ebersol didn't think she was a suitable choice for a *fraa*, and perhaps Stephen would never get around to asking her to marry him. They'd been dating for over a year and were in love.

It was bothering her more and more, and even though she was only approaching her eighteenth birthday, she was sure she wanted to spend the rest of her life with Stephen. She sighed, then kicked the scooter forward, wishing she'd taken the time to hook the horse to the buggy. This July heat was almost unbearable. Lines of sweat rolled down her cheeks as she continued to Josie's house. She hadn't seen Josie in three days, and she knew that tomorrow Josie would get the results from the special test she'd had last week, the test to check the tumor inside her head.

"Hey, there," Robert said when Linda rolled onto the driveway. "Josie will be so glad to see you. She's had a great couple of days."

"*Ach, gut!*" Linda dragged her foot a bit, pulling the scooter to a stop. "What ya doing?"

Robert's hands were on his hips and he was staring at a leafy green plant in a big red container. "Wondering why this thing looks so sickly. I water it every day since it's so hot."

"Maybe it doesn't need water every day." Linda propped the scooter up on the stand, then leaned forward. "I reckon I've never seen a plant like that."

Robert chuckled. "Me either. It was actually here when we bought the place." He lifted his head and pointed toward the front door. "Go on in. Josie's making a shoofly pie."

"She learned that from me," Linda said.

"I'm quite sure I don't need to eat all the molasses in those things, but I sure enjoy her making them. You're probably just in time to have a warm slice." Linda turned to head toward the front door. "Save me a piece," Robert said.

"I will."

Over the past few weeks, she'd had time to get to know Robert. He was so good to Josie. He waited on her constantly, went out of his way to make her happy, and just the way he looked at her caused Linda's heart to fill with anticipation. *I want to live my life with Stephen like that.*

She entered the house, walked through the living room, and made her way to the kitchen. Josie was just pulling the pie out of the oven.

Linda walked to Josie's side as Josie placed the pie on a cooling rack. "Smells *gut.*"

"Linda!" She threw her arms around her. "I'm so glad you stopped by. You're just in time for pie."

"Robert said you've had a *gut* couple of days. I'm glad."

Josie eased out of the hug, then studied her pie. "A very special young lady showed me how to make the perfect shoofly pie, so let's have a piece." She paused. "And yes . . . it's been a great couple of days."

Linda nodded and went to the cabinet where she knew the plates were stored, and she pulled out two small ones. Josie sliced the pie, and they took a seat at the kitchen table. They both bowed their heads in silent prayer, and Linda added an extra special one for Josie. *Please God, leave her with me for a long time.*

"This air-conditioning feels so *gut.*" Linda took a bite of her pie, then grinned.

Josie chuckled. "I have to admit, I never appreciated air-conditioning so much until recently. Stay as long as you like."

"Tomorrow you find out about your test, no?" Linda tried to sound upbeat as she made the statement, but Josie's expression soured just the same.

"Yes. The results from my MRI. They'll be able to tell how fast the tumor is growing." Josie shrugged. "Whatever. I feel good today, so I'm going to enjoy it."

Linda watched Josie shoveling the rest of the pie into her mouth. "I guess you do feel better." She brought her hand up to stifle a giggle.

Josie chuckled. "Think I've put on a few pounds too."

Linda didn't want to focus on anything negative. For now, she was going to pretend that Josie would be around forever. "Guess what?"

"What?" Josie put her plate in the sink, then returned to the table.

"My birthday party is in two and half weeks. *Mamm* wanted me to tell you to come over at four o'clock that day, Saturday. She's going to make meatloaf. All my aunts and uncles and cousins will be there too. *Ach*, she's also making yellow cake with chocolate icing. My favorite."

Josie's face shriveled up until she looked like she might cry.

"What's wrong?" Linda reached across the table and touched her hand.

Josie sniffed. "I'm just incredibly grateful to be included. This year, I'll get to see you blow out your candles." Then she gasped. "You do blow out candles, right?"

Linda giggled. Englisch *folks, they can never keep things straight.* "Ya. We have birthday parties just like everyone else. Cake, candles, and homemade ice cream. We're making vanilla ice cream. Luke and Matt will take turns churning the ice cream during the afternoon, like I do when it's one of their birthdays."

"And singing?"

"*Ya*, singing too."

Josie smiled. "It will be a wonderful day."

Linda gazed into Josie's eyes, eyes still filled with happy tears. *Please God, don't let anything happen to her before my birthday.*

Stephen pulled the buggy to a stop in front of his house and wished he could see Linda's face one of the times she read his notes from the bridge. As he stepped down from the buggy, he heard wagon wheels churning the gravel on the driveway, and he turned to see his grandfather pulling up to the house.

Daadi pulled beside Stephen, but didn't get out of the buggy, so Stephen walked closer.

"Hello, *Daadi*. Are you here for supper?"

"No, I was just on my way home from Bird-In-Hand, and I saw you pulling in." He stroked his long gray beard. "How are things at the Huyard home? I understand the *Englisch* woman is back at her home, no?"

"*Ya*, she is."

"This pleases me, as I don't think it was appropriate for her to be their guest. Too complicated." He shook his head.

Stephen took a deep breath and smiled, too tired to argue with his grandfather.

"Does Linda plan to continue a relationship with this woman?"

"That *woman* is her birth mother. I reckon so." Stephen's heart started pounding in his chest the moment he made the wise comment, and he could tell by the look on *Daadi's* face that his statement was not well received.

His grandfather narrowed his eyes in Stephen's direction. "I was against Mary Ellen and Abe adopting Linda for reasons such as this. Linda is a fine *maedel*, but I worried something like this would happen, the girl's *mamm* showing up to claim her."

"She's not claiming her, just being friends with her."

Daadi's forehead wrinkled with concern. "We all have *Englisch* friends, Stephen, but this is not the same. Are you sure that Linda still plans to be baptized into the faith?"

"*Ya*. For sure she is."

Stephen knew his parents didn't have any concerns about Linda, but he worried his grandfather might persuade them.

"Even before this woman entered Linda's life, I heard many stories of Linda stretching her *rumschpringe* to the limit. Much time at the movies and malls with *Englisch* girlfriends. It wonders me if she will be able to stay on course with her studies of the *Ordnung*."

Stephen fought the anger building, but also realized he'd been guilty of having these same thoughts where Linda was concerned. But that was in the past.

"*Daadi*, Linda will not stray from her faith, even if she is friends with Josie. I'm sure of it." Stephen recalled briefly the scene with Linda wearing Josie's blue jeans, but quickly wiped it from his mind.

His grandfather tipped back the rim of his straw hat with his thumb. "I hope you're right."

I know I'm right.

If that was the case, why couldn't he bring himself to propose to Linda? He'd gotten up his nerve once, only to have her disappoint him.

"Besides, *Daadi* . . ." Stephen looked down and kicked the gravel with one foot. "Josie is sick."

"*Ya*, I know. God's peace be with her."

Stephen knew how much Josie's passing was going to affect Linda, and he was planning to be by her side.

"*Ya*, God's peace be with her," Stephen echoed.

The next morning in Dr. Phillips's office, Josie took a deep breath and crossed her legs while she and Robert waited for the doctor to bring in her MRI results. She'd thrown up earlier that morning but she attributed it to nerves. *I just want to make it to Linda's birthday in a couple of weeks. Please God.* And she felt hopeful, since she'd had a good few days. Surely she couldn't go down that fast, although she was well aware that the pressure on her brain stem could cause her to slip into a coma with little warning.

"What's taking so long?" Robert stood up and began to pace. "He's kept us waiting in here for thirty minutes."

Fear twisted around Josie's heart. Maybe things had worsened. She gazed at Robert, whose expression was filled with concern. "I'm sure he'll be here soon."

He walked up behind her and rubbed her shoulders. "Sorry, babe. I know this waiting is hard on you too." Robert leaned down from behind her and kissed her on the cheek.

"I guess I'm used to it."

Robert walked around Dr. Phillips's desk and eyed all the plaques on the wall. "He is one of the best in his field." He turned to face Josie. "And who knows, Josie. Who knows. Maybe it's taking so long because they are trying to decide whether or not surgery will be possible."

"Or maybe it's taking so long because they are deciding how to tell me that my time is shorter than they think." She knew she shouldn't have voiced her thoughts, and as Robert turned around, his eyes glazed with despair, she said, "Sorry."

Robert walked back to his chair and sat down. He stared straight ahead and didn't say anything, resting his head in his hand which he'd propped on the arm of the chair.

Please, God, be with Robert when I'm gone. He is going to be so lost. Please help him find his way to You.

They waited another ten minutes before Dr. Phillips entered the office, accompanied by two other doctors.

This must be bad.

Robert, always the optimist, didn't even wait for introductions. "Can you operate?"

"Hello, Josie . . . Robert." Dr. Phillips didn't answer Robert's question, but instead extended his hand to Robert, then Josie. "This is Dr. Bissmeyer and Dr. Simpson. I've invited them to join us."

Dr. Phillips eased back behind his desk and sat down. The two other doctors stayed standing by the door. After Dr. Phillips slid on his pair of dark-rimmed reading glasses, he pulled Josie's MRI films from a large envelope, then hung them over a lighted panel to his left for Josie and Robert to see.

As Dr. Phillips scratched his forehead, the other two doctors moved closer so they could also see the large X-rays.

"Sorry to keep you both waiting." Dr. Phillips leaned across his desk. "I wanted to confer with Dr. Bissmeyer and Dr. Simpson to make sure I wasn't missing something, but we're all in agreement about these results. You may want to do another test, but we're confident that these are accurate."

"Just tell us, Dr. Phillips," Robert said as he shook his head. "Has the situation changed? Is there any chance you can operate?"

Josie's heart was beating out of her chest, and her stomach churned with anxiety as she watched Dr. Phillips point to the middle of the film.

"See this?"

Josie and Robert leaned forward as the two doctors hovered above them. She focused on the spot above Dr. Phillips's fingertip.

"There won't be an operation, Josie." Dr. Phillips took a deep breath.

22

Linda opened the screen door and greeted her Uncle Samuel and Aunt Lillian, then David and the girls when they arrived for her birthday party. After giving each of them a hug on the front porch, she could see her Uncle Noah and his family pulling up the driveway in their car, followed by another buggy that looked like it was carrying Sarah Jane and Lizzie.

"I can't believe you're eighteen today," Lillian said. "All grown up."

Linda smiled. "*Ya*, eighteen today." She loved when the entire family was together. Aunt Rebecca and her family showed up next, followed by Uncle Ivan and Aunt Katie Ann.

"Snacks are in the kitchen, and there's also some chips on the coffee table." Linda's mother had been busy that morning, readying everything for the party, and as she scurried around the kitchen making sure everything was perfect, Linda wondered when Josie would get here. She'd only seen Josie twice in the past two weeks, and Josie had been unusually quiet. However, during their last visit, Josie had assured Linda she would be here. *Please God, I hope Josie is having a good day.*

"Matt, go help your brother with the ice cream," her father instructed as he walked into the kitchen. Then Abe gave Linda a big hug. "I reckon you'll always be *mei boppli*," he whispered in her ear.

"I know, *Daed*."

Only one thing kept the day from being perfect. Stephen had to work, but he'd promised to leave her something special at the bridge later.

Linda eyed the large cake in the center of the kitchen table—yellow cake with chocolate icing and eighteen candles ready for her to blow out. This would be a big day for her and Josie. *Where is she?*

Robert was coming with Josie, and it would be the family's first time to meet him. No doubt, everyone would like him. Linda had been fond of him from the very beginning, particularly the way he treated Josie. That made her thoughts roll back to the conversation she'd overheard between Aunt Katie Ann and Uncle Ivan, and she wondered if everything was all right.

She walked onto the porch and saw her brother working up a sweat. "You have to keep turning the handle, Matt." She thought about how good the homemade vanilla ice cream would taste with the cake later.

"*Ya*, I know." Matt pushed back his straw hat and wiped beads of sweat from his brow. "Maybe you could bring me a glass of tea, no?"

"Sure." Linda walked back into the house, and by the time she got back with Matt's tea, she saw Josie's SUV pulling into the driveway. She headed down the porch steps and waited for her to get out of the car.

"Sorry I'm late." Josie was holding the clock from the mantel. "I thought you might like to have this as a birthday present. Sorry I didn't get it wrapped. I couldn't find a box it would fit in."

Linda accepted the clock, cradled it on her hip, and then gave Josie a hug. "*Danki*, Josie." She stepped back after a moment and held the clock at arm's length to see it better. "I love this." Then she looked back at Josie. "Where's Robert?"

Josie sighed, wove her hands together in front of her, and looked down. "He couldn't come." When she raised her head, Linda could see the disappointment in her eyes. "But he said to wish you a very happy birthday." Josie smiled. "I'm here, though, and I've waited for this day for a very long time." She threw an arm around Linda's shoulder. "And I bet your mother has made all sorts of good food."

"*Ach, ya*, she has." They walked toward the house together, and Linda silently asked God to bless this day for Josie above all else.

Josie wound her way through Linda's family, who in many ways felt like the only family she had. Some of them she knew better than others, but Linda's home was a place where she felt comfortable. When the entire family got together, their fellowship seemed to spill over in abundance and touch anyone who was blessed enough to be present. More than anything, she wished Robert could be here to feel this. Maybe then he wouldn't be so confused and sad, when in reality, there was so much to be thankful for.

She recalled Dr. Phillips's conversation with her and Robert—and Robert's reaction. He'd broken into tears right there in the office.

Josie stood tall as everyone gathered in the kitchen to watch Linda blow out her candles. She refused to let his absence sadden this day that she'd waited so long for—for eighteen years—and today there would be no shadows across her heart. *This is a perfect day.*

Linda blew out her candles, and as celebrated in other homes outside of this peaceful community, everyone sang "Happy Birthday." Josie's words choked in her throat as her eyes filled with tears of joy. She felt a hand grab tightly to hers, and she looked to her left to see Mary Ellen singing at the top of her lungs. Mary Ellen squeezed her hand, then turned to her and smiled. Josie let the tears flow.

After the cake and ice cream, Josie watched Linda open her gifts. Her cousin David had made her a small wooden box to keep special trinkets in, and he'd etched her name on the front. Mary Ellen gave Linda a lovely black sweater that she'd knitted herself, and all her aunts had made her a special quilt for her bed. Then everyone gasped when Abe and the boys walked in with a cedar chest.

"We normally don't do this much for birthdays," Mary Ellen whispered to Josie as the boys placed the cedar chest in front of Linda, "but it's her eighteenth."

Linda cupped her mouth with her hands. "*Ach, Daed!* It's beautiful."

"We helped too," Luke said, breathing hard.

"*Danki*, Luke and Matthew, and *Mamm* too!" She gave each of them a hug. "*Danki*, all of you, for everything. What a wonderful birthday."

Josie knew she was about to steal the show, but she'd waited over two weeks to share her news with those she loved, and it had taken everything she had to hold back until now.

"I—I have some news," she said, barely in a whisper. She looked directly at Linda.

Linda's glowing expression left her beautiful face instantly. "Oh, no."

Josie walked closer to Linda, pushed back a strand of hair that had fallen across her cheek, and gazed into her daughter's eyes. Then she looked at Mary Ellen, and glanced around at all the others, before she turned back to Linda.

A tear rolled down her cheek and she clenched her jaw to stunt the sob in her throat.

She opened her mouth to try to speak, but everyone turned their attention toward the porch when they heard footsteps. Mary Ellen walked to the door in the kitchen and opened it. When Josie saw her husband walk into the den, she ran into his arms.

"Thank you for coming. Oh, Robert. Thank you." She embraced him tightly. "I need you right now," she whispered in his ear.

"Oh, Josie. I'm sorry for not being here. But the more I thought about it, I knew this is where I needed to be. Maybe—maybe I'll get some sort of understanding about all this."

Josie gently eased out of the hug and turned to face everyone. "I'd like you all to meet my husband, Robert."

She moved around the room to make introductions but noticed Linda impatiently tapping her bare foot on the wooden floor. "Josie, please. Tell us your news."

Robert reached for Josie's hand and held it tightly in his, and Josie gazed into Linda's eyes again. "Thank you for letting me share this special day with all of you. This is the happiest day of my life . . ." She turned to Robert, hoping to borrow some of his strength. He nodded for her to go on as tears poured down Josie's face. Linda was already moving toward her, dread on her face.

"What is it? Tell us, Josie."

Josie smiled, and as Linda reached her, she took her free hand and reached for Linda's. "The tumor is gone."

Linda's eyes narrowed. "What does this mean?"

"It means . . ." Josie drew in a breath and blew it out slowly. "I am going to be around for many more of your birthday celebrations." Josie glanced at Mary Ellen who had a hand clamped over her mouth and eyes filled with tears. "If that's okay with your mother and everyone else," Josie added as Mary Ellen moved toward her.

Linda's feet were rooted to the floor, her expression one of disbelief, but Mary Ellen cupped Josie's cheeks with her hands, and whispered, "You are a Daughter of the Promise. Miracles happen to those who believe."

"Yes," Josie whispered as she fell into Mary Ellen's arms. "Thank you. Thank you, Mary Ellen."

The room grew quiet, as if everyone was trying to absorb the magnitude of what was happening, but Josie heard sniffling among the women.

"The cancer is gone," Robert said, his voice cracking. He put a hand over his eyes, shielding his own emotions.

Josie left Mary Ellen's embrace and went to Robert. "It's all right," she whispered as she held him.

"I want to believe, Josie," he whispered, his words caught in his throat. "I really do."

Josie knew what it felt like when you began a spiritual cleansing, when you truly opened your heart to God, and she could see that happening now with Robert as he wept in front of all of them.

Josie recalled Dr. Phillip's explanation of her prognosis two weeks ago in his office.

"There won't be any operation, Josie," he'd said. "There is nothing to operate on."

Dr. Phillips had gone on to explain that doctors from all over the state had been brought in to look at Josie's MRI, and not one of them had a medical or scientific reason why the tumor would have just vanished.

"That's medically impossible," Robert had argued. "Redo the test or something, because you guys have messed up."

But Dr. Phillips, along with Drs. Bissmeyer and Simpson, just shook their heads. "No," Dr. Phillips said. "We did not mess up. The tumor is gone, and we are sure of it."

"But how—how in the world . . . I don't understand."

Josie hadn't spoken when she'd heard the results. Within a few minutes, Robert's and the doctors' words had faded away, and all she heard was, *Live well, My child.*

"Sometimes, there is no medical explanation as to why these things happen," Dr. Phillips had said. "It's a medical mystery."

But it was no mystery to Josie, and all the way home from the doctor's office, she'd cried and laughed, unable to stop doing either. "It's a miracle, Robert, and it's the power of prayer," she'd told him. "It's real, Robert. It's so real. My faith in my heart, the way I feel, it's the most incredible feeling in the world."

Robert had refused to open his mind to the possibility, even though she could tell that his heart kept slipping in that direction. Two weeks later, he remained confused—not just about the results, which of course he said he treasured, but about how he'd lived his life thus far if there was truly a God overseeing things. His befuddled thoughts dragged him further and further down, and only yesterday, he'd said he didn't think he could attend Linda's birthday party.

"What if—what if I've been wrong my entire life? Would I even be worthy to be in a room with all of them?"

Josie had tried to talk to him, to explain that it was never too late to reach out to God and His son, Jesus, but Robert just shook his head.

Now, as he stood before her, Josie knew that life as they knew it had changed. Perhaps a larger miracle than her own healing was her husband's change of heart.

When Linda moved toward her, Mary Ellen pulled back to make room for their daughter.

"God is *gut*," Linda said. "So very, very *gut*." And she wrapped her arms around Josie.

Lillian looked around her and knew that this was not the right time for her and Samuel to share their news, but Samuel disagreed.

"Now is as *gut* a time as any, I reckon."

"Samuel, this is Linda's day, and Josie's. I don't think we should share today. It wouldn't be right." Maybe if they didn't share today, it wouldn't come to pass, and they'd never have to tell anyone that it was ever a consideration. "Besides, what if we change our minds?"

"Lillian, everything is going to be fine," Samuel said, trying to assure her once again. The commotion in the kitchen had settled and folks had broken off into smaller groups. "I promise you." He paused with a sigh. "You know we need to do this."

David walked by them in the den, his eyes blazing in his father's direction.

"Your son is definitely not happy with this news." Lillian held the screen door open and motioned for Samuel to step onto the porch. She waited until the door shut behind him to ask, "Are you sure about this, Samuel?"

"Lillian, it makes the most sense." He lifted her chin and kissed her. "I love you. Please don't look so sad."

Just then, Linda rushed out of the screen door and ran down the porch steps.

"Hey! Where ya going?" Lillian called after her.

Linda edged her way around the volleyball game her cousins were playing. "I have to go do something. I'll be back soon, though!"

"Should we wait until she gets back?" Samuel pushed back the rim of his hat as he watched Linda kick the scooter into motion.

"No, Anna and Elizabeth are tired. I think we should go ahead and talk to everyone else so we can get them home." Lillian let out a deep sigh as she sat down in the rocker on the porch. Samuel sat down in the other chair, and a tense silence formed a gap between them. Samuel wasn't only her husband, but her best friend, so she resolved herself to support his decision and to be happy about it. "I love you."

He turned toward her. "I love you too, Lillian."

She smiled. "Then, let's do it."

Samuel nodded.

Linda was disappointed that she wouldn't be able to share her news about Josie with Stephen until the next day, when she saw him at worship service, but she couldn't wait to see what he might have left for her on the bridge. She pushed her scooter forward and felt a bottomless sense of peace and contentment.

Thank you, God. Thank you, God. Thank you, God.

She recalled a conversation she'd had with Jonas. It seemed like such a long time ago.

"Mamm *and* Daed *will always be* mei *parents," she'd told him. "That will never change."*

"*Of course not. And I reckon they'd lay themselves on the train track for you and both your brothers," Jonas had said. "But here's where it gets tricky." He squinted in her direction and then pointed a finger at her. "I reckon Josephine would lie down on a train track for ya, too, give her life willingly for you. That puts you in a unique position. All these people that love you. Do you have room in your heart for all of them?"*

Linda stared upward. "I miss you, Jonas. And I have enough love in my heart for all of them. I love Josie, and I thank you, God, for leaving her here for now." She scuffed her foot along the road even faster until the bridge was in sight.

Breathless upon arrival, she inched toward the special spot, then clenched her teeth. "Today's my birthday. And no note!" It had been a more than perfect day up until this moment. She hadn't expected a present, just one of his poems, maybe an extra long one. Something. She reminded herself how blessed she was, but anger and hurt still bubbled to the surface.

"You could have left me something!" She stomped her foot, knowing her behavior was childish. "A note, a poem. Something! If you really cared—"

"If I cared, I'd what?"

Linda spun around, her cheeks wet with sweat, but she could still feel the blush of embarrassment coming on.

"Stephen, where'd you come from?"

He squinted his eyes as he neared. "None of your business."

"Don't you talk that way to me, Stephen Ebersol." She stood taller and folded her hands across her chest. "Today is my birthday."

"Really? I had forgotten." A smile tipped the corner of his mouth on one side as it quivered.

"What you got behind your back?" She inched forward, but he stopped.

"Nothing for you."

"Then let me see."

"No."

Linda got within a couple of feet of him. "You have something behind your back."

Slowly, Stephen produced a bouquet of roses.

Linda gasped. "They're beautiful." She reached for them, only to have him pull them back.

"These are for a very special someone."

Linda raised her chin. "Really. And who might that be?"

Stephen's lip began to quiver in a way that Linda had never seen. "What's wrong with you?"

He dropped to one knee, pushed the flowers forward, and practically yelled, "Linda, will you marry me?"

Her heart sang as she accepted the flowers. "*Ya*, Stephen, I will marry you."

He stood up, wrapped his arms around her, and Linda basked in the feel of his embrace.

"I love you." He kissed her tenderly on the mouth.

"I love you too, Stephen." Then she pushed him away, and he blinked with bafflement.

"What'd you do that for?"

"I almost forgot!" Linda jumped up and down on her toes. "It's Josie! She's cured. She's well, Stephen! She's not going to die."

"But the tumor, what about—"

"Gone! It's a miracle." Her eyes clouded with tears. "Josie is not going to die. And I'm going to be Mrs. Stephen Ebersol. This is truly my most perfect day." Linda threw herself into his arms.

Thank you, God.

Linda was glad that all the family was still there when she and Stephen got back to the house. He'd parked his buggy out of sight a ways from the bridge, so they'd loaded up her scooter and headed to her house to spread the news. This wasn't the typical way to do things. Normally they would keep it rather hush-hush and then publish it a few weeks before the wedding, but Linda couldn't keep her joy to herself.

"Are you sure you don't want to wait?" Stephen secured the horse and buggy.

"No. I can't. This has been a perfect day, and I want to share this with my family today."

"All right, I reckon." He shrugged, but the spark in his eyes warmed her heart. They walked up to the house.

Everyone was gathered in the den. Linda heard a few mumblings, but the room grew quiet when they entered.

"We have some news!" She ran to her mother's side, still holding the flowers. Then she glanced at Josie and smiled. "Stephen asked me to marry him!"

"*Ach,* Linda!" Her mother hugged her as her father found his way to Stephen.

"Congratulations, Stephen. We'd be honored to have you in the family." *Daed* shook Stephen's hand, and then both Linda and Stephen made their way through the den, accepting congratulations from the family.

When she got to Josie, both of them started to cry. "I'll get to see you get married."

Linda threw her arms around Josie. "*Ya*, you will. We're so blessed."

"Yes. We are."

Linda withdrew from the hug and glanced around the room. Everyone was smiling, but Linda sensed an uneasiness. "Is everything all right?"

"*Ya*," several people answered at once.

Her cousin David stood up and folded his arms across his chest. "No, everything is not all right."

"David, that's enough!" Linda had never heard her Uncle Samuel speak with such authority, and she couldn't imagine why.

She felt a hand on her shoulder. "Honey, everything is fine." Lillian gave her a pat on the arm. "We were just telling everyone that we will be leaving for Colorado after the fall harvest."

Linda raised her brows. "How long will you be vacationing there?"

Lillian bit her lip, then turned to Mary Ellen.

"Linda, it's not a vacation. Samuel and his family will be moving there." Her mother glanced toward her right. "And your *Onkel* Ivan and Aunt Katie Ann are moving also."

"Why?" It had been a day filled with so many blessings. Why in the world would they move to Colorado?

"There is a place there called Canaan, a beautiful place there

that Jonas bought before he died," her mother said. "And Samuel
and Lillian have their reasons for wanting to move." She looked
cautiously at Ivan and Katie Ann and smiled. "As I'm sure your
Onkel Ivan and Katie Ann do, as well."

Aunt Katie Ann nodded, but Uncle Ivan just stared at the floor.
Again, Linda recalled the conversation she'd overheard between her
aunt and uncle.

"We won't be leaving until after the fall harvest," Samuel said.
"And today is a day of celebration. Stephen and Linda are getting
married!" He stood up. "I say we all go have another piece of birthday cake to celebrate."

Linda chose not to let this news dampen the blessings of the
day, so she followed everyone to the kitchen, her fiancé by her
side. She grabbed Josie's hand on the way, glad to see that Josie's
husband was better. Poor Robert had been quite a mess earlier.

She couldn't help but wonder why Samuel and his family, along
with Aunt Katie Ann and Uncle Ivan, would want to move to
Colorado, but God works in mysterious ways, and whatever His
plan was, Linda was sure His will would be done.

Life is good. God is good. What a perfect day.

Two months later, Josie pulled up at Linda's house to have lunch
with her and Mary Ellen. It had become their weekly thing, lunch
together on Wednesdays, just the three of them. Josie walked up
the cobblestone steps, glad she'd grabbed a light jacket at the last
minute. Cool October winds whipped across the yard, scattering
the fall foliage in whirlwinds around her. Rays of sunlight peeked
through blue-gray skies, and Josie could smell the comforting

aroma of Mary Ellen's cooking wafting through the screen door before she reached the front porch.

"Meatloaf today!" Linda swung the door wide for Josie and gave her a quick hug as she moved over the threshold.

Mary Ellen's meatloaf was no longer just Linda's favorite. Josie breathed in the familiar smell. "Ah, you're making my meatloaf." She edged over to Mary Ellen who was stirring potatoes atop the stove. Josie wrapped an arm around her shoulder.

"I've never seen two people get so excited about a simple meatloaf." Mary Ellen shook her head, placed the long wooden spoon on the counter, then turned to Josie and gave her a hug. "But I'll keep making it as long as you two keep requesting it."

Mary Ellen had given Josie the recipe weeks ago, but Josie just couldn't seem to get it to taste the same way Mary Ellen did—as moist and seasoned to absolute perfection.

Linda spread out sheets of paper across the kitchen table. "*Mamm* and I were going over the guest list for the wedding, and—"

"And I still can't believe we're planning a wedding this quickly." Mary Ellen chuckled, and Josie had never felt more blessed than to be included in all the plans. Both women leaned down to look at Linda's list.

"Josie, these are the people you and Robert said to add, Amanda from his office and a few others." Linda pointed about halfway down the list. "We're up to about two hundred now with Stephen's cousins from Ohio coming." Then Linda frowned. "I'm still sad that *Onkel* Samuel's family won't be here, or *Onkel* Ivan and Aunt Katie Ann."

Mary Ellen sighed. "I know, dear. But they are scheduled to move in mid-November, and it would just be too much for them to travel back here the first of December. I know they're all regretful about it. And you know we already tried to move the wedding up, but the first couple of weekends are already booked for weddings, weddings we'll be attending. You know how it is, everyone gets married in November and December, after the harvest. I'm sorry."

Linda tucked her chin. "They won't be here for Thanksgiving or Christmas either."

"Actually . . ." Josie drew in a deep breath, then blew it out slowly as Linda looked up at her. "I have a few people I'd like to add to that list, if it's all right with you."

Mary Ellen arched her brows. "*Ya*, it's fine with us. Anyone we know?"

"Um, no." Josie folded her arms across her chest and looked down for a moment, then looked up at the two of them and smiled. "It's my parents, and my brother and his family, if that's okay."

Linda's eyes widened. "But I thought you didn't really get along with your parents."

Mary Ellen smiled. "I think that's wonderful, Josephine. Just wonderful." Then she waited, as if knowing Josie had more to say.

"I've been talking to my mother a lot on the phone." Josie clasped her hands together in front of her. "I think I know now how special a relationship between mother and daughter can be, and I'd like to work toward that with my own mother."

Mary Ellen touched Josie's arm. "It's very special, the relationship you and Linda have formed." Then she smiled again.

Josie shook her head, then reached for Mary Ellen's hand. "No, Mary Ellen. I didn't mean *my* relationship with Linda. I meant *your* relationship with Linda. I am Linda's best friend. I hope to always be that, but what you and Linda have is everything that a mother and daughter should be."

Mary Ellen squeezed Josie's hand as her eyes filled with water.

Linda reached for Josie's free hand, then Mary Ellen clasped onto Linda's other one. The three of them stood in a circle, symbolic of the bond the women had formed.

"How blessed we are to all be Daughters of the Promise," Mary Ellen said.

"Yes." Then Josie closed her eyes and looked toward heaven. *Thank you.*

Reading Group Guide

1. When Linda finds out that she is adopted, do you think her anger at her parents is justifiable? Would the situation have been less awkward if Linda already knew she was adopted? Or would most of her fears and worries still have existed?

2. Is Josie being selfish by wanting to get to know her daughter, especially since she believes she only has a few months to live? What if Josie never went to Lancaster County—do you think Mary Ellen and Abe would have eventually told Linda about her adoption?

3. Have you ever known an adopted person who reconnected with their birth mother? Did it go well? Was a friendship or bond formed? How did each person react?

4. An unlikely friendship forms between Mary Ellen and Josie. Where do you see God's hand in this, and what did both Mary Ellen and Josie learn?

5. Josie's husband, Robert, is a non-believer, but a good man. What does Scripture tell us about good people who don't believe in God? What is happening to Robert by the end of the book?

6. Josie's healing was a miracle. Have you ever witnessed a miracle—medical or otherwise? Do you believe in miracles?

7. Think of all the lives that Jonas touched just by being himself. Who seemed to benefit the most from his wisdom?

8. Stephen worries that Linda might be tempted by life in the *Englisch* world. What are some examples depicted throughout the story? And why do you think Stephen was never interested in fully exploring his *rumschpringe*?

9. At Jonas's funeral, Katie Ann is upset because a woman named Lucy is there. Do you think this may have to do with Katie Ann and Ivan choosing to move to Colorado?

10. Jonas left letters for the people he loves. Have you ever known anyone who's done this? Why do you think Jonas did it?

11. What would make Samuel uproot his family and move to Colorado? Any speculations?

Acknowledgments

IT'S AN HONOR TO DEDICATE THIS BOOK TO MY FRIEND, Barbie, in Lancaster County. A huge thank you, Barbie, for continuing to read each manuscript prior to publication. I'm so grateful for the time you spend helping me keep the books authentic and for the friendship we share. May God's blessings shine on you always.

Thank you to my friends and family for continuing to support me and for understanding about the tight deadlines. Special thanks to my mother-in-law, Pat Mackey, for cooking for us twice a week.

And to my husband, Patrick . . . you're the best, baby. I couldn't travel this road without you by my side. I love you very much.

I'd like to thank Gary Leach, MD, for assisting me with the medical aspects in the book and for reading the manuscript prior to publication. Gary, I know this wouldn't normally be the type of book you would read, so it was extra special when you told me how much you enjoyed it. Many thanks, my friend, for taking the time to help me.

Karen and Tommy Brasher, Gayle Coble, and Bethany and Walter Guthmann—thank you all for hosting book signings each time a new book releases and for your continued support. You've all gone above and beyond, and I appreciate it so much.

Many thanks go to my editor, Natalie Hanemann. You're so special, Natalie. A bright light in my world! Thanks for all you do to make my books the best they can be and for being my friend. I'm so blessed to have you in my life.

Jenny Baumgartner, I love working with you. Your warmth and kindness shine through in every email you send me, and your editing expertise makes my books shine. I love hearing about your adventures with the twins. Thank you for everything. Peace and happiness to you and your beautiful family, always.

To my agent, Mary Sue Seymour—what a special friendship we share, and I hope we go shoe shopping again soon! Many blessings to you.

Renee Bissmeyer, my angel on Earth, thanks for reading each manuscript behind me and for being my life-long best friend. Our friendship is blessed by God, and I'd be lost without you, my kindred spirit.

My fabulous family at Thomas Nelson, you guys and gals are the best! Thank you so much for all you do.

To My Heavenly Father, you've blessed me way more than I deserve. Thank you for the stories You put in my head, tales that I hope will draw people closer to You.

Plain Proposal

To Eric and Cory

1

MIRIAM STEPPED BACK AND ADMIRED THE MATCHING quilts lying on the twin beds in her room. Gifts from her grandmother before she died. The pastel circles of yellow, powder blue, and pink were framed by a simple blue border in a traditional double wedding-ring pattern. They were finally making a debut—just in time for company.

"Your room looks nice." *Mamm* walked in carrying a wicker basket filled with towels to be folded. "Your *mammi* would be pleased that you saved her quilts for a special occasion." She glanced at the white vase full of pink roses on the nightstand and smiled. "*Ach,* fresh flowers too."

Her mother unloaded the towels onto Miriam's bed, and they each reached for one as *Mamm's* eyes traveled around the room.

When her mother nodded an approval, Miriam grinned. "When will she be here?"

Mamm placed a folded blue towel on top of Miriam's green one. "Not for a couple of hours. Your *daed* hired a driver, and they went to go pick her up at the airport."

Miriam couldn't wait to hear about her cousin's travels and life in the *Englisch* world. Shelby was eighteen too, and for Miriam, it would be like having a sister for the summer. A nice change from a house full of brothers. Even though Miriam was enjoying her *rumschpringe*, she'd done little more than travel to Lancaster to see a movie. Her *Englisch* cousin was coming all the way from Texas, a small town called Fayetteville.

"I'm excited about Shelby coming, *Mamm*. I can't wait to meet her." Miriam reached for the last towel to be folded as her mother let out a heavy sigh.

"I know you are, and we're glad to have Shelby come stay. But . . ." *Mamm* edged toward the nightstand, repositioned a box of tissue next to a lantern, then turned to Miriam. "We told you— times have been *hatt* for Shelby. Her parents got a divorce, and Shelby got in some kind of trouble."

Miriam couldn't imagine what divorce would be like. It was unheard of in their Old Order Amish district. "What kind of trouble?" Miriam sat down on her bed, crossed her ankles, and leaned back on her palms.

"Her mother said that Shelby was spending time with the wrong young people." *Mamm* sat down on the bed beside her, and Miriam watched her mother's forehead crinkle as her lips tightened into a frown. She knew her mother was concerned about having a young *Englisch* woman come for such a long visit.

"Was she shunned by her family?"

Mamm shook her head. "No. The *Englisch* don't shun the way—" Her mother cocked her head to one side, then met eyes with Miriam. "*Ya*. I guess, in a way, Shelby *is* being shunned. She is being sent away from her family and friends for not following the rules."

Miriam sat taller and folded her hands in her lap. "I'm going to try my best to make her feel welcome here."

"I know you will, Miriam." *Mamm* patted her leg, then cupped Miriam's cheek in her hand. "Please tell me that I don't need to worry about you being taken in by Shelby's worldly ways."

Miriam looked at her mother and said earnestly, "I won't, *Mamm*."

Her mother gently eased her hand from Miriam's face, then let out another heavy sigh. "I remember when your father's cousin left here. Abner was no more than your age at the time. He chose not to be baptized. We were shocked." *Mamm* leaned back on her hands like Miriam.

"Did he go to Indiana?" Miriam knew that her great grand-parents relocated here from Indiana. She'd been asked plenty of times what she was doing in Lancaster County with a name like Raber, an Indiana Amish name.

"No. Your *daed* said Abner went to Texas with three hundred dollars in his pocket and even took rides from strangers to get there. Evidently he had been corresponding with a man there about a job for months before he left. A job building Amish furni-ture." *Mamm* sat up and folded her arms across her chest.

"Have you seen Abner since he left?"

Mamm nodded. "Only twice, for each of his parents' funerals. It's a shame, too, because your *daed* and Abner were close when they were young."

"But you said he wasn't baptized into the community, so he wasn't shunned, right? He could have come to visit, no?"

"*Ya.*" *Mamm* stood up and smoothed the wrinkles from her black apron. "But Texas is a long way from here, and things between him and his folks weren't *gut*. They never did accept his choices." *Mamm* paused for a moment, then looked down at Miriam. "I remember that Abner met Janet not long after he arrived in Texas, and they were wed two years later. Then along came Shelby." Her mother shook her head. "After that, we heard less and less from your *daed's* cousin. But evidently his furniture was popular with the *Englisch* there, and he went on to own a big fancy store of his own. We got a letter every now and then, but . . ." *Mamm* picked up the stack of folded towels on the bed, then placed them in the laundry basket. "I met Janet, Shelby's mother, when they came here for Sarah Mae's funeral, which is when I met Shelby. But she was only four years old, so I doubt she remembers much."

Miriam tried to think of what she remembered from when she was four years old. Not much.

"I liked Janet a lot, and we exchanged letters for a while after they were here. But I hadn't heard from her in years until last month." *Mamm* bit her lip and was quiet for a few moments. "Anyway, as you know, Shelby doesn't have any brothers or sisters, and the only life she has known has included electricity and all the modern conveniences the *Englisch* have. Things will be different for her here." She picked up the basket, then smiled at Miriam. "But God is sending her here for a reason. I think the *maedel* needs time for healing."

"This is a *gut* place for that, I think." Miriam gave a final glance around her room. She'd dusted her oak rocking chair and chest of drawers and swept the hardwood floors after putting fresh linens on the bed. She'd even slipped a sprig of lavender in the top drawer of the chest, one of two drawers she had cleaned out for Shelby to use.

She was excited for her cousin to arrive, but her thoughts drifted to Pequea Creek where she knew her girlfriends were gathering. On

Saturday afternoons during the summer, the older girls in her district met at the creek to watch the young men show off their skills by swinging on a thick rope from the highest ledge and dropping into the cool water below.

Saul Fisher would be there. He was always there. And just the thought of him made Miriam's heart flip in her chest.

"My chores are done, *Mamm*. Can I take the spring buggy to the creek for a while?"

Her mother was heading out the door but turned briefly. "I guess so. But I'd like for you to be home before Shelby arrives."

Miriam nodded. Once her mother was gone, she opened the drawer to her nightstand, then pulled out the thin silver ankle bracelet she'd bought at the market in Bird-In-Hand. She knew Leah and Hannah would be wearing theirs too, and she liked the way the delicate chain looked dangling from her ankle. She sat down on the bed and fastened the tiny clasp. Her father frowned every time he saw the inexpensive purchase, but Miriam knew her parents wouldn't say anything since she was in her *rumschpringe*.

She stood up and walked to the open window. Through the screen, she could see the cloudless blue sky and the plush grass in the yard where her red begonias were in full bloom in the flower bed. Rays of sunshine warmed her cheeks, and she closed her eyes, feeling the June breeze and breathing in the aroma of freshly cut hay from her brothers' efforts the day before.

She looked down, wiggled her toes, and decided not to wear any shoes today, knowing that the cool blades between her toes would remind her of past summers, playing volleyball with her brothers in the yard or squirting each other with the water hose for relief from the heat. But today going barefoot was more about

Saul than her childhood memories. He'd said she had cute toes the last time they were at the creek, and since Saul Fisher wasn't big on conversation, Miriam hoped he might notice her ankle bracelet—maybe comment on it. Or her toes. It didn't matter. Any attention from Saul caused her insides to swirl with hope for the future. Saul didn't know it yet, but Miriam was going to marry him. She'd loved him from afar since they were children, and even though he was often withdrawn and had a reputation as a bit of a troublemaker, Miriam knew—*He is just waiting for the right woman to mold him into all he can be.*

Saul crept closer to the edge of the cliff until his toes hung over the smooth rock, a natural diving board that he had jumped from a hundred times. He tucked the thick rope between his legs and cupped his hands around the knot that met him at eye level.

Then he saw her. Miriam Raber. Sitting with her girlfriends on the bank. Her brilliant blue eyes twinkled in the distance as she watched him, and she was chewing the nail on her first finger—like she always did before he jumped. And his legs grew unsteady beneath him—like they always did when Miriam was watching him.

He pulled his eyes from her and gave his head a quick shake. He'd always felt confident about whatever he was doing, except when Miriam was around. She had a strange effect on him, always had—since they were kids. He recalled a time when he and Miriam were chosen as leads in the school Christmas pageant, playing Mary and Joseph. They were in the sixth grade, and Saul was still shocked at the amount of detail he remembered from that day. She'd worn a white sheet over her dress and belted it at the waist, and her long brown hair flowed freely past her shoulders instead of bound beneath her prayer covering. Mostly he remembered the way Miriam looked at him when she spoke her lines. And the way he went completely blank and forgot his.

"Jump, Saul!"

He straightened when he heard his buddy Leroy yelling from the bank. Then he took a deep breath and swung out over the water. As he let go of the rope, he didn't have more than a second before he plunged into the creek—but it was Miriam he saw the millisecond before his face submerged. He stayed down there longer than usual, enjoying the refreshing water and thinking about Miriam.

She was a good girl. The best. Every man of marrying age in Paradise had his eye on Miriam. Everyone except Saul. He'd known for as long as he could remember that one day he would leave Paradise. Leave *her*. So, despite their mutual attraction over the years, Saul had avoided her as best he could. But the older they got, the harder it was for him to keep his eyes from always drifting her way. And she seemed to have the same problem. She was always watching him.

He swam upward until his head popped above the water, and not surprisingly, his eyes found Miriam's right away, as she smiled and clapped from the water's edge. There were others around. But he only saw her.

"I don't know why you like him so much," Hannah said when she and Miriam sat back down on the bank, following Saul's jump. "He never pays you much mind." Hannah stretched her arms behind her and rested on her hands. "He never pays *any* of us much mind."

"He will someday." Miriam smiled. "He's just shy."

Hannah chuckled. "He's not shy, Miriam. He's a loner." Hannah leaned closer and whispered, "Some say that he isn't going to be baptized, that he will leave the community."

Miriam snapped her head to the side to face her friend. "Where did you hear that?"

Hannah lifted one shoulder, then dropped it slowly. "I don't remember. But he doesn't seem to—to fit in."

"I think he fits in just fine." Miriam smiled as she turned her attention back to Saul. She watched him climb out of the creek in a pair of blue swim trunks, then join his friends down the bank.

"He never attends singings, he doesn't gather with the other men after church service, and remember . . ." Hannah gasped. "Remember when he got in a fight on the school yard with that *Englisch* boy who passed by." She shook her head. "Not fit behavior, I say. Not at all."

Miriam swooned with recollection. "*Ya.* I remember. The boy called me a name as I walked across the school yard to get on my scooter."

"So because he stood up for you, he's your hero? That's not our way, Miriam." Hannah sat taller and folded her hands in her lap. "And that's not the only time he's been in trouble. There was that time with John Lapp when the bishop—"

"*Ya,* I know, Hannah." Miriam knew Hannah was referring to the time when Bishop Ebersol reprimanded Saul and John Lapp for fighting. Saul had refused to shave just after his sixteenth birthday, and John told Saul that only married men could grow a beard—*rumschpringe* or not—and that he'd better shave it off. Their harsh words led to a fistfight. Bishop Ebersol told Saul that the beard was not forbidden during *rumschpringe*, but the fighting was. Miriam couldn't understand why John made such a fuss about Saul having the facial hair, especially since the bishop wasn't very concerned. But John Lapp was married now, and he couldn't seem to grow a beard to save his life. Must have been a sensitive subject for him.

Miriam smiled. At least she'd had a small glimpse as to what her future husband would look like, his face covered with light-brown fuzz and sandy-red highlights.

"He's just a bit of a bad boy, Miriam." They both watched him laughing with his friends for a moment, then Hannah turned to her and grinned. "But he *is* a handsome bad boy."

"It's more than that." Miriam studied his back, the way he stood tall and straight like a towering spruce. His shoulders looked like they were a yard wide and molded bronze. She was glad when he put his shirt on. She took a deep breath. "He's just . . . *mysterious* in a kind sort of way."

Hannah narrowed her brows. "What does that mean?"

Miriam thought for a moment. How could she possibly put into words everything that she loved about Saul? His stunning good looks shouldn't matter, but his face kept her up at night, and the smooth way he spoke in a raspy voice, often barely above a whisper, caused her heart to flutter. He said very little, but Miriam was sure he was filled with goodness, even if his efforts might be misdirected from time to time.

She finally blew out a deep breath. "I don't know how to explain him. I just know that he's a *gut* person."

"How? Have you even been alone with him? You never even talk to him." Hannah's attitude was getting on Miriam's nerves.

"No. But I will."

"When?"

Miriam pulled herself up off the ground, brushed the wrinkles from her dark-blue dress, then put her hands on her hips and stared down at her friend. "I—I don't know for sure, but—but I will." She glanced toward Saul and the other men just in time to see Saul waving bye and leaving. He was nearing his spring buggy, and Miriam knew she would have to act fast. "I'm going to go talk to him right now."

Hannah stood up beside her. "Really?" She tipped her head to one side.

"*Ya.* I'm going to go talk to him right now."

"Well." Hannah folded her arms across her chest and grinned. "Go, then. You better hurry. He's leaving."

"I am." Miriam took a step, hesitated, then spun around to face Hannah. "I'm going."

Hannah smiled. "I see that."

"*Ach*, okay." She forced one foot in front of the other until she was close enough to call out his name, and she had no idea what she would say.

⁂

Saul recognized the voice and spun around a few feet from his buggy, wondering what Miriam could possibly want. They admired each other from afar. That's the way it had always been. He glanced down at her bare feet, then smiled as he remembered telling her she had cute toes not too long ago. He'd been walking by her at the creek, and she was alone, smiling up at him from her perch on top of a rock near the water's edge. He didn't know why he'd said it, except for the fact that it was true.

"Hi." She hesitated when she got closer, and Saul saw a tiny chain around her ankle.

"Nice ankle bracelet." It was easiest to look at her feet. If he took in the rest of her, he was afraid his mouth would betray him and say something *dumm*.

She kicked her beautiful bare foot forward. "This? *Danki*." She clutched the sides of her apron with both hands, then twisted the fabric. "Um, where are you going?"

Her face took on a rosy shade of pink, and Saul briefly wondered if his did too. "Home, I guess." He waited, and when she didn't say anything, he asked, "Why?"

She shrugged. "I don't know. It's a pretty day."

"Then let's go do something." His mouth had betrayed him after all. No good could come out of getting to know Miriam better. He already liked what he saw and knew. Why build on that just to leave her in the end? But he had no regrets when her whole face spread into a smile.

"Okay." She stepped closer, and Saul fought the urge to step back. Right now she was close enough to touch, and he wanted nothing more than to brush back a loose tendril of brown hair that had fallen from beneath her *kapp*. Then he locked eyes with her—those brilliant blue eyes.

"What do you wanna do?" He towered over her by at least a foot, and he rubbed his chin as he studied her. Her smooth skin glowed in the sunlight, the golden undertones evidence of the hard outdoor work everyone in their community did. Then, just like his mouth, his hand developed a mind of its own. Before his brain had time to realize what was happening, he reached up and pushed the wayward strand of hair off of her cheek. He didn't think he'd ever touched her before, and now he would lose sleep, wondering when he could do it again.

"*Danki.*" She avoided his eyes and lowered her chin as she spoke. When she looked back up at him, her eyes lit with excitement. "Let's go fishing at the old Zook farm. No one lives there, and the pond is full of fish."

Saul folded his arms across his chest. "You fish?"

"Of course. Don't you?"

He pulled his straw hat off and wiped sweat from his forehead. "*Ya.* I just didn't take you for the fishing type."

She giggled. "The fishing *type*? I can handle a fishing pole." The sound of her laughter made him want to hear it for the rest of his life. Then she grabbed at her chest with both hands. "Oh no!"

"What?"

"I can't go." She gazed into his eyes. "I'm sorry." And the way her face folded into a frown, she seemed to mean it. "I forgot that my cousin is coming this afternoon. She's staying with us for the summer."

Saul tried to hide his disappointment but knew it was for the best. "Do I know her?"

"No. She's *Englisch.* A cousin on my father's side." Her eyes brightened as she smiled. "She's coming all the way from Texas. She's our age." She paused. "I'm sure you'll meet her."

Saul nodded as he looped his thumbs beneath his suspenders, then glanced down to see his wet swim shorts had soaked through his black trousers. "I guess I'll see you around, then." He turned to leave, not sure what else to say to her. Spending time alone with her was a bad idea anyway.

"Saul?"

He unwrapped the reins from the tree where he had his horse tethered, not turning around. *"Ya?"* Then he felt a hand tap him on the back. Her simple touch rattled him so much that he dropped the reins. He quickly reached down and picked them up. "What is it?" As he stood, he couldn't look her in the face, so he stared at her toes again.

He watched her wiggle them, and he couldn't help but wonder if it was for his benefit. She looked up, and Saul finally locked eyes with her. When she smiled, Saul knew things were about to get complicated.

"Maybe we could go fishing tomorrow after church?" Her long eyelashes swept down across high cheekbones before she looked back at him.

This was a bad idea. But there wasn't one thing in the world that Saul could think of that he would rather do. So he nodded.

Tomorrow he would spend the afternoon with Miriam Raber. Alone. Something he had dreamed about for years but had put just as much energy into avoiding. His life, his plan, was set. And there was no place in any of it for Miriam.

But as she looked up at him with a smile that threatened to melt his resolve, he knew that he was going to do the unthinkable—date her for the summer. Then leave her in August. *God, forgive me.*

2

MIRIAM PUSHED HER HORSE HARD ON THE WAY HOME, grateful that the distance was short. She was late, and she feared Shelby would already be there. *Mamm* wouldn't be happy with her for not being home in time to welcome her cousin.

As the buggy neared her house, she reached up and cupped her cheek with her palm, surprised by the boldness of Saul's gentle touch, and decided being late was worth it. Tomorrow she would spend the afternoon alone with Saul, something she had wanted to do for as long as she could remember.

Mamm was sweeping the front porch when she parked the buggy, and she could see her three younger brothers out by the barn. Ben was carrying chicken feed inside, Elam had a shovel in his hand as he walked toward the barn, and little John was chasing an irritated rooster around the yard.

"You're lucky your cousin's flight was late, or she would have beaten you here." *Mamm* kept sweeping as she spoke, but finally looked up and gave Miriam a forgiving smile.

"I'm sorry, *Mamm*. But I'm here now." Miriam padded up the steps in her bare feet, feeling lighter than usual. "Can I help you with anything?"

Her mother pushed leaves from the porch with the broom,

although most of them blew back in her direction. "No, I think everything is ready for your cousin's arrival. Your *daed* called on the phone, and Ben happened to be in the barn and answered. *Daed* said that Shelby's flight was late, but they were leaving the airport about an hour ago." *Mamm* pushed a big leaf off the porch with her foot as she shook her head. "It wonders me where all this wind came from. It wasn't windy until I started to clear the leaves from the porch." She pushed back a strand of gray hair, then tucked it beneath her *kapp*.

Miriam thought of Saul.

"They should be here any minute." *Mamm* leaned the broom up against the house, then put her hands on her hips and inspected the area before she turned to Miriam. "I'm making cheddar meat loaf, a recipe your *Aenti* Lillian shared with me before they moved to Colorado."

Miriam thought about Aunt Lillian, Uncle Samuel, her cousins, and Aunt Katie Ann. They'd moved to Colorado in November to farmland that Lillian's *Daadi* Jonas had purchased before he died. "I miss them."

"*Ya.* I do too." *Mamm* sat down in one of the rocking chairs on the front porch, then crossed her legs. "But your *Aenti* Mary Ellen got a letter from Lillian just last week, and things are coming together for them there." *Mamm* gasped a bit. "Did I tell you that David is getting married? To a girl he met there named Emily."

David was a couple of years older than Miriam, and she missed him the most. "Will we travel to the wedding?" Miriam widened her eyes as she waited for her mother to answer. A trip to Colorado sounded exciting.

"We will see." Her mother smiled briefly, then her expression dropped. "I'm so glad that things are working out for Samuel, Lillian, and the *kinner*, but your *Aenti* Katie Ann is still having trouble adjusting to her new life there."

Miriam's heart hurt for Katie Ann. Her Uncle Ivan had left his dear wife shortly after moving to Colorado with the other members of their family. None of the family understood it, and her parents didn't talk about it much. And to make matters worse, Ivan had returned to Lancaster County and taken up with an *Englisch* woman they all knew. Her parents said they were not to speak to Ivan, and he was never invited to any family gatherings. That's how it was when you've been shunned.

"I don't know what's wrong with that *bruder* of mine." *Mamm* shook her head before she stood up and pointed to the end of the driveway. "There's a van pulling in. That must be them." She walked down the porch steps, raised a hand above her brow to block the sun, then called for Miriam's brothers to come up to the house.

Miriam strained to see the white van pull into the drive, then park beside the spring buggy. *Mamm* gathered Miriam's brothers around her in the yard, and they watched *Daed* slide a long door open and step out of the backseat. He turned and pulled out two large red suitcases and set them in the grass. As he slid his door closed, the passenger door popped open, and Miriam watched a brown boot land on the ground followed by a tall girl with flowing dark-brown hair.

Mamm leaned close to Miriam. "She's so *thin*."

Miriam studied the pretty girl who turned in their direction. She and Shelby probably weighed about the same, but her cousin stood at least five inches taller than Miriam's five-foot-five height.

She nodded at her mother's comment, then smiled as Shelby walked toward them.

Her cousin was dressed in blue jeans, and her brown boots looked like something her brothers might wear to work in the fields, except hers were pointed at the toe. Cowgirl boots. Miriam wondered if Shelby could ride a horse. They had two suitable mares in the barn.

Shelby's dark-blue shirt was buttoned almost to the neck. Miriam knew that *Mamm* would appreciate the conservative clothing. Many times they'd hosted *Englisch* guests for supper, and *Mamm* was appalled when the tourists showed up in short pants, or worse, backless tops or ones that showed their stomachs. But *Mamm* continued to host the suppers, in conjunction with bed-and-breakfasts in the area. It provided some extra income, but the truth was, Miriam knew her mother loved to cook for others. Visitors went on and on about how good her mother's cooking was.

"Welcome, Shelby." *Mamm* gave Shelby an awkward hug, then stepped back and pointed to Miriam. "This is our daughter, Miriam."

"Hi." Miriam didn't move. She was trying to decide if Shelby was happy to be here.

Her cousin said hello, but she wasn't smiling. She wasn't frowning either. Dark sunglasses hid her eyes, and her expression was confusing, rather blank.

Mamm introduced Shelby to the boys, then instructed Ben and Elam to carry her bags to Miriam's room as everyone else moved into the den.

"I will let you womenfolk talk. I think the cows are ready for milking." Miriam's father excused himself. Aaron Raber wasn't one for small talk, and Miriam suspected that he'd probably sat quietly in the backseat while the driver and Shelby talked on the way home from the airport.

Miriam watched her cousin eyeing her new surroundings. Shelby edged toward the couch when *Mamm* motioned her in that direction and told her to sit and rest, adding that she must be weary from her travels. As Shelby sat down on the tan sofa, Miriam saw her eyes darting around the room—to the two high-back rockers on the other side of the den, then to the hutch near the entryway. Miriam wondered what Shelby thought about their plain surroundings.

"I bet this is much different than what you are used to." *Mamm* sat down beside Shelby on the couch and twisted slightly to face her. Miriam sat down in one of the rockers, as did John.

"Not so much." Shelby showed the first hint of a smile. "It's nice."

Miriam breathed a small sigh of relief. Shelby had a soft, quiet voice, and when her brown eyes met with Miriam's, her smile broadened a bit.

John kicked his rocker into motion, his blond bob in need of a trim. "Do you have a cell phone?"

"Yes, I do." Shelby turned to *Mamm*. "Is that okay?"

"*Ya*, I think so." She paused. "If you wouldn't mind, we'd prefer if you use it outside. We have a phone in the barn. You're welcome to use that also."

Shelby nodded, then fumbled with the straps of the brown purse in her lap and bit her lip. Miriam wanted her to feel comfortable in their home.

"Do you want to see your room?" Miriam stood up from the rocker and smiled.

"Sure." Shelby rose, draped her purse over her shoulder, and waited for Miriam to motion toward the stairs.

"You girls get settled while I finish supper," *Mamm* said as she rose to her feet, then walked across the den toward the kitchen.

"We're the third door on the right at the end of the hallway." Miriam let Shelby walk in front of her, and her cousin's dark hair bounced against the middle of her back as she started up the stairs. Miriam's hair was just as long, although bound beneath her prayer covering. She thought about Saul again. *He'll see the length of my hair on our wedding night.*

Shelby stopped at the third door on the right. "This one?"

"*Ya.*" Miriam reached around her and pushed the door wide. "Your bed is that one." She pointed to the bed on the right side of the nightstand. "I put fresh linens on it just this morning."

Shelby sat down on the bed and ran her hand across the quilt. "Thank you."

"I also cleared two drawers for you and made room for you to hang your clothes on those hooks over there." Miriam pointed to a dozen hooks running along a two-by-four on the far wall.

Her cousin glanced in that direction, then hung her head before she looked back up at Miriam. "I'm sorry you have to share this small room with a stranger."

Miriam sat down on her own bed and faced her cousin, unable to ignore the sadness in Shelby's voice. "I don't mind at all. I've been looking forward to your visit." Miriam glanced around her room. She'd always thought it was a nice-sized room. "And you're my cousin, so not really a stranger." She smiled, and Shelby did so also, then quickly looked down.

When the silence grew uncomfortable, Miriam spoke again.

"Tomorrow is church, but maybe Monday I can take you to town after we do chores."

Shelby nodded, then stood up and walked toward the window. She leaned her nose close to the screen and peered outside for a moment, then spun around. "Would we go in a buggy? Do you drive one of those?" Her eyes lit up, and Miriam silently thanked God at the glimmer of happiness in her voice.

"*Ya.* I drive the buggy. I've been driving by myself since I was twelve, but mostly on the back roads. I was sixteen before I started taking my little brothers and going to town." She paused as she walked to where Shelby was standing by the window. "Have you ever been in a buggy?"

Shelby turned to face her. "No. I've never even been in an Amish town or been around an—an Amish person." She bit her lip again as her eyes grew round.

Miriam recalled her mother's earlier comments but assumed Shelby must not remember her visit here as a young child. She leaned closer to Shelby and whispered, "I promise we don't bite."

Finally, a full smile. "Good to know."

———

Shelby sat next to Miriam at the large wooden table in the kitchen. It felt like eating at a luxurious picnic table with a long backless bench on either side, and the breeze blowing through three different open windows in the kitchen only added to the picnic effect. At each end of the table was an armchair. Aaron was already seated in one, and Rebecca was standing at the counter pouring glasses of iced tea. The boys waited patiently on the bench across from Shelby and Miriam. Shelby surveyed the offerings already on the

table as her stomach growled. Aside from the meat loaf and potatoes, the rest was unfamiliar.

Rebecca placed the last two glasses of tea in front of Ben and
John, then took a seat at the opposite end of the table from her
husband.

"Shelby, we pray silently before and after a meal." Rebecca
smiled before she bowed her head along with the rest of the family.
Shelby followed suit, but she didn't have anything to say to God.
She lifted her head when she heard movement around her.

Miriam passed her a bowl first. "This is creamed celery."

Shelby spooned a generous helping onto her plate, trying to
remember the last time she'd sat down for a family meal like this.
She tried to recall when the problems had started between her parents. When had the two most important people in her life stopped
loving each other and started screaming at each other?

"Do you like to cook, Shelby?" Rebecca passed a tray with bread
toward Shelby, and Shelby nodded. She could remember spending
hours in the kitchen with her mother when she was young. Mom
would set her up on the counter, and together they would bake a
variety of cookies. Shelby's job was to lick the beaters clean and be
the tester for each warm batch that came from the oven.

She sat quietly, listening to the family talk about their day.
The oldest boy, Ben, told a story about running into someone
named Big Jake in a place called Bird-In-Hand. "He ain't ever
gonna sell that cow now that everyone knows it birthed a calf with
two heads." Ben laughed, then squinted as he leaned forward a bit.
"I heard he even took the animal to Ida King, and—"

"Ben!" Rebecca sat taller in her chair and scowled at her oldest
son. "We will not speak of such things at supper—or any time."

She turned to Shelby and spoke in a whisper. "Ida King practices powwowing."

Shelby laid a fork full of creamed celery on her plate. "What's that?"

Rebecca shook her head. "Her practices are not something the Lord would approve of."

"She's like a witch doctor," Miriam whispered to Shelby.

"Enough." Aaron didn't look up as he spoke, but everyone adhered to his wishes and ate silently for a moment, then Elam commented that he saw a raccoon trying to climb the fence to his mother's garden. Shelby had noticed the large garden on the side of the house when the van first pulled into the driveway.

"I put a bowl of freshly cut vegetables right outside the fence for that fellow, hoping he wouldn't get greedy," Rebecca said with a laugh.

The youngest boy—John—chuckled as he told a tale about chasing their rooster around the barn. Shelby saw the boy's father grimace, but he didn't say anything.

"And what about you, Miriam?" Rebecca pinched a piece of bread and held it in her hand as she waited for her daughter to answer. "How was your time at the creek?"

Shelby wondered what they did for fun here. She used to love to swim. She turned slightly toward her cousin and waited.

"It was fine," Miriam said.

"She only goes there to see Saul Fisher." Ben reached across his brother and pulled back a slice of bread. Shelby was sure this was the best bread she'd had in her life, warm and dripping with butter. She took another bite of her own slice as Ben went on. "But you're wasting your time. I've heard it told that he ain't gonna be baptized."

"You don't know that, Ben." Miriam's tone was sharp as she frowned at her brother.

Ben's glare challenged her as he leaned forward in his chair. "That's what folks are saying."

"No talk of rumors, Ben." Once again Aaron didn't look up from his plate, but the conversation ceased immediately, and Rebecca started to talk about a new schoolteacher named Sarah who would be taking over when school started up again in September. When she was done, she spoke directly to Shelby.

"Will you be attending college next year, Shelby?"

Shelby took a deep breath as she shifted her weight. That had certainly been the plan, until she learned that her parents used up her college fund fighting each other in their divorce. "No, ma'am. I'll be getting a job when I go home."

Aaron lifted his head for the first time and looked directly at her. "Hard work is good for the soul. Too much schooling can turn a person from what is important—the love of the land and a hard day's work."

"Aaron, now you know that the *Englisch* often send their children to college, and it's not our place to judge." Rebecca smiled at Shelby. "I'm sure you will find a *gut* job suited to you when you return, Shelby."

She doubted it. *What kind of job can I get without a college degree?* But she didn't much care what kind of job she found. She was having trouble caring about much of anything. Over the past few months, she'd made sure that she wouldn't feel much, and she was never going to forgive herself for the things she'd done. Things she knew God wouldn't approve of. She used to care what God thought, but she'd stopped when she realized . . . God had given up on her.

These strangers, with their odd clothes and strange lifestyle, seemed nice enough, but her parents were only further punishing her by sending her to this foreign place. *Haven't they hurt me enough?*

Miriam walked into her bedroom with her hair in a towel and dressed in her long white nightgown. Shelby was already tucked into bed with her head buried in a book.

"What are you reading?" Miriam pulled the towel from her wet hair, then reached for a brush inside the top drawer of her nightstand. She sat on the edge of her bed and fought the tangles.

"Your hair is so pretty." Shelby looked up from her book, but Miriam noticed that she also had a pen in her hand, which she began to tap against the book. "Why do you keep it up underneath those caps?"

Miriam continued to pull the brush through her hair as she spoke. "We believe a woman's head should be covered, and we try not to show the length of our hair to a man until after we're married." She stopped brushing for a moment as she recalled past trips to the beach when most Amish girls shed their caps and pulled their hair into ponytails. "Some boys have seen our hair at the beach, though."

"You're kidding, right?" Shelby stopped tapping her pen and sat taller in the bed, then propped the pillow up behind her. "I'm sorry, I didn't mean that to sound—"

"No, that's okay. I'm sure our ways must seem strange to you."

Shelby closed the pink book in her lap and put the pen on the nightstand. "I'm sure everyone else seems strange to you too. Us *'Englisch'* as I heard your mom say."

Miriam pushed her hair behind her ears and put the brush back in the top drawer, glad that a conversation was ensuing. "No. We have many *Englisch* friends, so we know how different things are outside of our community."

"How much school do you have left, or did you already graduate?"

"I'm done with school. We only attend school through the eighth grade." Miriam was surprised that Shelby didn't seem to know anything about them. Miriam thought Shelby might have done a little research before she got here, but she didn't fault her for that.

Shelby leaned farther back against the pillow. She was wearing a long blue nightgown, and again Miriam thought about how that would please her mother. Maybe someone had told Shelby that it would be appreciated if she dressed conservatively.

Her cousin began to kick her feet together beneath the covers. Miriam had noticed that Shelby was always fidgeting and couldn't seem to be still. Even during supper, Shelby kept moving in her seat, pushing her food around, and she wiped her mouth a lot with her napkin. *She must be nervous.*

"Will you leave here, since you're eighteen? Or do you plan to stay here forever?" Something about the way Shelby said *forever* made it sound like a bad thing.

"I would never leave here." Miriam settled into her own bed and also kicked the covers to the bottom. "I plan to be baptized in the fall, and . . ." *And marry Saul someday.* She smiled as she thought about her future. "And someday I'll get married and start a family of my own."

"Aren't you curious, you know . . . about everything outside of here?"

"No. I'm in my *rumschpringe.* That means that at sixteen, we get to experience the outside world, then choose if we want to stay here and be baptized as a member of the community, or leave." Miriam fluffed her pillow as she spoke. "So I think I've seen enough of the *Englisch* world the past couple of years. It's not for me."

Shelby twisted to face Miriam, then tapped a finger to her chin. "How many leave here?"

"Hardly any. I mean, a few do. But most of us stay." Miriam smiled slightly. "It's all we know, but what we know is *gut*, and I can't imagine living anywhere else."

"Who is Saul?"

Miriam sighed as she recalled the gentle way Saul brushed back a strand of her hair earlier that day, the feel of his touch. "A friend."

"You like him. I can tell." Shelby smiled a bit.

"*Ya*, I guess I do." She reached over and turned the flame on the gas lantern up since nightfall was upon them, then she eased down in the bed and propped herself up on one elbow. "What about you? Do you have a boyfriend in Texas?"

They both jumped when a gust of wind blew in through the screen and caused the green blind to bounce against the open window.

"I *did*. His name is Tommy." She shuffled in her bed. "He broke up with me when my parents were—were going through their divorce. I had thought . . . well, I thought we might get married someday."

"I'm sorry." Miriam had never had a real boyfriend. She'd been carted home by plenty of boys following Sunday singings since she'd turned sixteen, but her heart belonged to Saul. She knew she would wait for him.

"It's okay. I really don't care."

Somehow Miriam didn't think that to be true. "Was he your

boyfriend for a long time?" Miriam wanted to ask if they had kissed, but she didn't even know Shelby. That was something she might ask Leah or Hannah.

"About six months. Until things got bad with my family." She paused, then also propped herself up on one elbow and faced Miriam. They each strained to see each other over the nightstand in between them, so Miriam shifted upward a bit. Shelby did too. "Then he said I was sad all the time."

They were quiet for a while. "Are you still sad?" Miriam knew it was a dumb question. Of course she was sad. Her parents had recently divorced. "I mean, are you sad about *him*? Do you miss him?"

"No."

Again Miriam suspected otherwise.

"Did anyone tell you that breakfast is at four thirty?"

Shelby bolted upward, and Miriam could tell she was straining to see past the lantern in between them. "You're kidding, right?"

"No. We start our day early. The cows have to be milked, which *Daed* and the boys take care of. I usually go to the henhouse and collect eggs while *Mamm* gets breakfast started. Tomorrow is church service, so we will travel to the Dienner farm for that. We don't work on Sundays, but during the week, *Mamm* and I start the day by weeding the garden before the heat of the day is on us. Then we do our baking, and . . ." Miriam didn't want to overwhelm her cousin, so she trailed off with a sigh.

"I guess that's why everyone is already in bed, then." Shelby glanced at the battery-operated clock on the nightstand. "At eight thirty."

"*Ya.* Early to bed, early to rise." Miriam smiled, then turned the small fan on the nightstand toward Shelby. "Batteries. Sure saves us from the summer heat."

"It's not so bad."

Miriam chuckled. "Wait until August."

They were quiet again for a while, then Miriam reached over to extinguish the lantern. "Guess we'd best sleep. Morning will be here soon enough."

Shelby sat up in the bed. "Do you mind if we leave that on for just a little while longer? Will it bother you, keep you from sleeping?"

Miriam pulled back her hand. "No, I'll just face toward the window. Just turn the knob to the left when you're ready for sleep."

"Okay. Thanks. I like to write in my journal before I go to bed." Shelby reached for the pen on the nightstand.

"Do you do that every day?"

"Most days."

Miriam noticed the tiny lock dangling from the side of the small book, and she wondered if Shelby locked it when she was done writing in it. Would Shelby ever share the contents with her like she assumed sisters would?

"Good night, Shelby."

"Good night."

Miriam closed her eyes and said her nightly prayers. She wondered if Shelby prayed before sleep. Just in case she didn't . . . *Dear Lord, I sense sadness inside my cousin. Please wrap Your loving arms around her and guide her toward true peacefulness, the kind of peace and harmony that only comes from a true relationship with You. May her time here help to heal her heart.* Aamen.

Shelby stared at the page for a long while. Her cousin was snoring before Shelby wrote the first word. She sat thinking about her parents, images she wished she could erase from her mind. So much screaming. Especially when Shelby's mother found out that her father had cheated on her. Shelby recalled that night with more detail than the other fights she'd seen her parents have. Her mother called her father names that she'd never heard spoken in her house. And from that moment, things went from bad to worse. And no one seemed to care how it was affecting her. It was as if the ground dropped from beneath her and she just kept falling, with no one to save her. She'd always relied on her father to protect her, to keep her safe—but he was the one who had pushed her into this dark place she couldn't seem to escape. Her mother was too distraught to notice and focused much of her energy on how to get even with Shelby's father. Then Tommy chose to break her heart in the midst of everything. "You're sad all the time, Shelby," he'd said. "I just can't be around you like this anymore."

Shelby glanced around at her new accommodations for the next three months. She could run away, she supposed. But she didn't have much money, so she wouldn't get far. And she didn't want to take up with the kind of people that she had in Texas, other lost souls like herself who eased their pain with alcohol and drugs. But what did she want?

She put the pen to paper.

Dear Diary,

I've been shipped to Pennsylvania to live with my Amish cousins—people I don't even know, who dress funny, don't have electricity, and who get up at four thirty to start their day. They seem nice enough, but I don't want to be here. The only family I have ever known sent me here against my will. If my parents love me, why don't they want me with them? They only care about themselves. They have destroyed my life with their stupid decisions, and I'm the one who has to suffer along with them. If Tommy loved me, why did he break up with me? I know I've made some mistakes in my life, but I don't think I deserve this.

Or maybe I do. Maybe I'm being punished. I don't know. I just know that I feel bad all the time. I want to be loved, but my heart is so empty, and my faith in life, in God, is gone. I don't have anything to live for.

3

MIRIAM GENTLY NUDGED THE HUDDLED MASS UNDER the covers. "Shelby, breakfast is ready." It was already after five o'clock, but her cousin probably felt like she'd just gone to sleep.

"Already?" Shelby pulled the covers over her head. "It's not even daylight."

"It will be worth it when you see the feast *Mamm* and I have made for breakfast. *Mamm* always makes overnight blueberry French toast on Sunday, and we cook bacon and sausage."

Shelby poked her head from beneath the covers. "Blueberry French toast?" Then she sat up in bed and rubbed her eyes. "I love French toast."

"*Ya*, well . . . this is probably different from what you're used to, but it's a favorite around here." Miriam started to make her bed as she spoke. "*Mamm* makes the toast the night before in a casserole. It's got cream cheese, fresh blueberries, and all kinds of *gut* stuff. Then she refrigerates it so that on Sunday morning, she can just put it in the oven."

Shelby eased out of bed and also began straightening the covers on her bed. "Is there anything I should do while you are at church?"

Miriam stopped smoothing the quilt, stood straight up, and faced her. "You don't want to go to church with us?"

Shelby turned to face her. "Should I?"

"There are usually one or two *Englisch* folks there, friends or family of others in the community, so I don't think you would feel out of place." Miriam watched her cousin's expression sour. "Did—did you attend church in your hometown?"

"Not for . . . a while."

Miriam knew it was none of her business, so she didn't press. "We don't worship in churches. The gathering is always at someone's house, or if the house isn't big enough, we have the service in the barn. Today it's at the Dienners' home, and they have a large farmhouse, so it will be inside."

Shelby went back to making her bed and didn't say anything, so Miriam did the same. When she was done, she turned to Shelby. "The church service is in High German, so you might not understand any of it, but other *Englisch* folks say they enjoy the sense of fellowship."

Shelby grimaced. "I don't really have anything to wear." She opened the smaller of her suitcases on the floor by her bed and pulled out a brush. "And I'm not on good terms with God right now."

Miriam watched her run the brush through her hair and knew it was not her place to minister to Shelby, but her cousin seemed so unhappy, and being in a place of worship with so many others might help. "There's a wonderful offering of food following the church service." She smiled teasingly at Shelby. "And we play volleyball and other games outside this time of year."

Shelby slowed the brush through her long hair and seemed to be considering the idea.

"Better than staying here by yourself. You'll meet lots of folks." Miriam waited.

"I still don't have anything to wear."

"You can wear whatever you want. Did you bring a dress?"

Shelby twisted her mouth to one side. "Yes. But it's a short dress."

"How short?"

Her cousin unzipped the other suitcase on the floor by the bed. She pulled out a floral print dress with tiny straps, which was, indeed, short. "*Ya*, maybe too short." Miriam edged closer to where Shelby was squatting beside her suitcase. "What else do you have?"

Shelby held up two pairs of pants. "Which ones?"

Miriam studied the choices, then pointed to the pair of darker blue jeans. They were shorter than regular breeches, but not as faded as the longer pants Shelby was also considering. "What about those shorter pants, with maybe a nice blouse?"

Shelby held up a short-sleeved yellow pullover shirt. There was no fancy lace or low neckline. A little bright, but conservative.

"That will be just fine. I'll let you dress while I go help *Mamm* finish up breakfast."

Her cousin nodded, and Miriam closed the bedroom door behind her. When she returned to the kitchen, everyone was seated but her mother, who was placing a pitcher of orange juice on the table.

"Is she coming down for breakfast?" *Mamm* wiped her hands on her apron.

Miriam nodded as John propped his elbows on the table. "I bet she ain't used to gettin' up this early."

Mamm cut her eyes at him. "Elbows off the table, please."

They all turned when they heard footsteps coming through

the den. Miriam thought Shelby was so beautiful. She didn't wear makeup like most *Englisch* girls, although this morning there was a shine on her lips. Miriam didn't long for makeup, nor had she experimented with it during her *rumschpringe*, but she was wishing for some of the gloss that Shelby was wearing. Especially for when she saw Saul this afternoon. Her cousin's thick, long hair was pulled back into a ponytail. She slowed as she neared the kitchen, as if waiting to be invited to sit.

"I poured you some juice, Shelby." Miriam smiled, then pushed back on the bench to make room for her cousin.

"*Guder mariye*, Shelby." *Mamm* took her seat. "That's good morning in Pennsylvania *Deitsch*."

"Good morning to all of you." Shelby lowered her head when everyone else did for prayer. Miriam wondered what Shelby was saying to God, since she'd mentioned that she wasn't on good terms with Him.

Shelby enjoyed the buggy ride to the Amish farm where church service was being held. Miriam drove one buggy carrying Shelby, John, and Elam—a buggy with no top, which Miriam called a spring buggy. Aaron drove another buggy with a top on it, and he took Rebecca and Ben. Shelby was glad to be in the spring buggy, the wind in her face, on this early Sunday morning as the sun barely peeked above the horizon.

It was a short trip from her cousins' farm to the Dienner farm, but Miriam told several jokes on the way. They were the cleanest jokes Shelby had ever heard, but still funny, and she'd found herself laughing out loud—something she hadn't done in a long time.

She liked Miriam, and she appreciated the way Miriam seemed to be trying hard to make her feel comfortable. But Miriam didn't tell her that the church service was three hours long until she was parking the buggy. "You're kidding, right?" was all she said. Miriam just smiled.

Miriam kept close to Shelby's side, introducing her to everyone as they walked into the large home. Shelby was even related to some of them, but she couldn't keep everyone straight. They were all welcoming and thanked Shelby for coming to church with them, even though she'd already been told she wouldn't understand anything that was going on. And that was okay. She would just sit quietly and not have to feel guilty that she wasn't partaking in any sort of prayer. However, when she saw the backless benches set up in the large den, she thought about the three hours of sitting and wished she'd just stayed back at her cousins' farm.

"The men sit on one side, facing the women, who sit on the other side," Miriam whispered as they maneuvered through the crowd of about a hundred. "The bishop and deacons sit in the middle."

"Does it always last three hours?"

Miriam chuckled. "*Ya*, most of the time it does. Guess that's why we only have church every other Sunday."

Shelby followed Miriam, and they both sat down on a bench in the third row. Others were slowly filing into the room and taking a seat.

"Even though you won't understand the language, I think you will feel a sense of peace here." Miriam smiled.

Shelby didn't think so. Tiny distractions throughout her days provided her with brief reprieves from all that ailed her, but at the end of the day, when she laid her head down to sleep, life just seemed too much to bear. Her heart ached, and she missed the life she'd had before her parents' troubles. And if her parents loved her, they would have let her stay there to work through her problems. Especially her mother, whom she'd been living with before she was shipped away.

"You need a vacation, Shelby," her mother had said. "Far away from here. Away from those people you've been running around with and from the heartache associated with the divorce."

What her mother should have said was, "Shelby, I'm dating Richard Sutton and I don't have time to deal with your issues right now." That would have been a more honest reason to ship her only daughter to this foreign place. Her father had gotten on with his life, too, with the woman he'd left her mother for. Tina.

Shelby cringed. Yes, everyone was getting along with their lives just fine. She felt tears welling up in her eyes.

"Are you all right?" Miriam reached for Shelby's hand and squeezed. It was such a tender, endearing thing to do that a tear threatened to spill, but Shelby quickly blinked it back. She pulled her hand from Miriam's.

"Yes. I'm fine. I'm sorry." She hoped no one else saw. She was embarrassed enough.

Miriam smiled. "I'm so glad you're here, Shelby. So very glad. I know we're going to be like sisters."

Her cousin seemed so sincere, truly glad to have her here. *Why?* Shelby didn't have any brothers or sisters, and she wasn't sure that was a bad thing. That would only mean more people to hurt her. She didn't respond.

Two hours into the service, Shelby straightened her back and sighed. She felt no sense of fellowship, and she felt emptier than she did before. This was a mistake. Her life was a mistake. She had no sense of purpose, no guidance, and no faith. Why did her parents bother taking her to church all those years if things were going to end up like this? Clearly her parents hadn't been listening. People fell in love, they got married, and they stayed together forever—through the good and the bad.

"You will like this part," Miriam whispered. "When there are several *Englisch* folks, like there are today, Bishop Ebersol says a few verses in *Englisch*, so that the entire congregation will understand the blessings."

Shelby forced a smile, wishing she could close off her ears to whatever was forthcoming. She was wallowing in self-pity, mixed with a heavy dose of anger, but knowing this didn't deter the sadness that threatened to suffocate her. She couldn't bear it.

When Bishop Ebersol started to speak in *Englisch*, she closed her eyes and tried to will away his words, but they entered her mind just the same—and played havoc with her heart.

"There hath no temptation taken you but such as is common to man," the bishop said. "But God is faithful, who will not suffer you to be tempted above that ye are able; but will with the temptation also make a way to escape, that ye may be able to bear it."

Shelby didn't hear anything else the bishop said after the Scripture reading. The words echoed in her head. *"But will with the temptation also make a way to escape, that ye may be able to bear it."* She clamped her eyes closed and held her breath for a moment. *I can't bear it.*

Shelby could see her parents yelling, her mother pounding her fists against her father's chest as she sobbed. As she tried to clear the image, Tommy's face showed up in her mind's eye, and she could hear his voice saying he didn't want to be around her.

She released her breath but kept her eyes closed as she pictured her circle of friends back home—the parties, the drinking, the drugs. All things she knew were wrong, yet she'd allowed herself to partake.

Slowly she opened her eyes and looked around at these strange people dressed so differently from the rest of the world. Sweat dripped down her spine from the lack of air-conditioning, and her back ached from sitting on the backless bench. She shifted her weight but couldn't get comfortable. *What am I doing here?*

"Are you all right?" Miriam leaned toward her as she whispered.

"No. I—I actually think I need some air. Excuse me." Shelby stood up and quickly moved past her cousin, then walked as briskly as she could toward the nearest door. She could feel everyone's eyes on her, but she didn't care. *I don't want to be here. God let me down.*

Miriam turned to her mother and waited for instruction. She saw Shelby dab at her eyes on the way out the door, and she wondered if *Mamm* saw too.

Mamm glanced past Miriam toward the window, then said, "*Ya.* Go see to your cousin."

Miriam bowed her head in a brief, silent prayer, then took a quick peek in Saul's direction. He didn't catch her glance, so she got up and hurried to find Shelby. She crossed the Dienners' front yard and made her way to where Shelby was sitting, in one of two swings that hung from a large branch of an old oak tree. She slowed down as she approached and saw that Shelby was crying.

"What's the matter?" Miriam asked softly as she squatted down beside her cousin. "Is there anything I can do?"

Shelby shook her head but kept it hung low as she sniffled. "No. I'm all right. I'm sorry." She finally looked up. "I shouldn't be here."

Miriam bit her bottom lip. She didn't know what to say. *Help me to help her, Lord.* She stood up and eased her way into the other swing beside Shelby, then twisted the point of her black shoe into the worn area below her as she stared at the ground. "Do you want to go home, back to Texas?"

Shelby turned toward her and brushed away a tear. "I don't have a home anymore." She stood up and paced in front of the swings. "I don't have a home. I don't have a boyfriend. I don't have any friends. I made bad choices, and . . ." She paused, then took a deep breath and said, "And God let all this happen." She sat back down in the swing.

Miriam had never felt the call to minister to anyone until now. It wasn't their way. But she heard the voice in her head loud and clear. *It is of My will that Shelby is here.* She squeezed the rope supports on either side of her and prayed she would speak the right words. "Sometimes things happen, and it's hard to understand how it could be God's will." She glanced at Shelby, but her cousin had her head turned in the opposite direction. "But I know your faith will see you through this, and if you want to talk about—"

"Faith?" Shelby swung her head around to face Miriam. Her teary eyes were now blazing with anger. "I don't have any faith." Then she shook her head back and forth over and over again. "Never mind. I shouldn't be saying this to you. My problems are my problems, and I'll get through this somehow."

Miriam wanted to tell Shelby that faith and prayer were the only ways to get through it, but she stayed quiet.

"I'm sorry," Shelby said after a few moments. "You can go back in, Miriam. You don't have to stay out here with me. I'm okay."

Miriam straightened in the swing. "No. That's all right. There isn't that much left." She smiled. "I'll just stay here with you."

Shelby gazed for a long while at Miriam. "You're a good person, Miriam. I can tell."

"*Danki.*" Miriam twisted her mouth to one side. "But you don't even know me, so how can you tell that I'm a *gut* person?"

Shelby smiled slightly. "Most of the time, I'm a good judge of character." Her smile faded. "Although I wasn't such a good judge of character before I left home."

Miriam didn't want to pry, but she couldn't imagine what Shelby did that was so bad. She seemed like such a nice person.

"Miriam?"

"*Ya?*"

"Do you think God forgives our bad choices?"

Miriam thought for a moment. She wanted to tell Shelby that she needed to reach out to God, to have faith, but instead, she said, "*Ya.* I do."

"Hmm . . ." Shelby paused. "I don't know."

"I believe that . . ." Miriam didn't feel qualified to speak with Shelby about this. She wished Shelby could talk to Bishop Ebersol, even though she was *Englisch.*

"What? What do you believe?" Shelby twisted the swing so that her body faced Miriam's.

Miriam took a deep breath and hoped she was saying the right things. "I believe that we have to forgive ourselves first. Only then can God reach us. I believe . . ." She paused, glanced at Shelby. Her cousin was waiting for her to go on. "I believe it's hard to hear God when we are angry, or can't forgive ourself for something." Miriam smiled. "God forgives everything if we ask Him to."

Shelby faced forward again and stared straight ahead. "I don't know about that." After a few moments, she said, "Besides, I think maybe I'm being punished by Him."

By God? Miriam wanted to tell Shelby that wasn't how it worked, but she heard the screen door close, and she looked up to see people starting to emerge from the service. "Church is over early today." She stood up from the swing when she saw her mother heading their way.

"Shelby, are you all right?" *Mamm* asked when she got within a few feet of them.

Shelby stood up. "Yes, ma'am. I'm sorry. I just needed some fresh air."

Mamm smiled as she put a hand on Shelby's arm. "I'm sure you're still tired from your travels, and I bet you aren't used to getting up so early."

"No. But I'm fine. Really. I'm sorry I left the service early."

"It's no problem. As long as you're all right."

Shelby smiled, but Miriam knew she wasn't all right.

It was one o'clock when Miriam parked the buggy in front of their house. Shelby hadn't said anything on the way home, but she really didn't have a chance to. Little John was ribbing Elam about having a crush on thirteen-year-old Sarah King, and Elam spent most of the trip denying the accusation, though they all knew it was true. And Miriam spent the ride thinking about Saul and how she would meet him at the old Zook farm to go fishing soon. She'd only talked to Saul briefly after the service, and they'd confirmed plans. Miriam had also introduced him to Shelby. After they'd finished the meal, there was cleanup, so Miriam didn't see Saul again. She wondered if maybe he'd joined the men in the barn but suspected he'd left right after church, the way he usually did. Most of the younger folks had played volleyball that afternoon. Even Shelby joined in and played on Miriam's team. For a short while, Shelby seemed to be enjoying herself.

Miriam felt bad that she was going to have to leave Shelby this afternoon, but she'd waited so long to spend some time alone with Saul. Surely Shelby could occupy herself for a couple of hours.

Miriam tethered the horse while Shelby excused herself to hurry to the bathroom, and Elam and John took off toward the barn.

She was walking up to the house when her mother came down the porch steps and met her in the yard.

"I got the sense that Shelby is upset. Did she tell you what's wrong?" *Mamm* wiped her forehead as she spoke, her eyes showing concern.

"She's upset about her parents getting a divorce." Miriam didn't feel the need to tell her mother any more than that right now.

"Hmm . . . Well, you stay close to her. Her mother didn't tell me much about what happened there, but I want us to be her family right now, help her any way we can." *Mamm* turned and started back to the house.

Miriam wasn't surprised that *Mamm* had agreed to take Shelby in. Her mother was known to care for others in their community who were in a bad way or just needed a place to rest. And Shelby was family—a distant cousin perhaps, but still family.

Miriam cleared her thoughts and returned to the subject at hand. *"Mamm?"*

Her mother turned around. *"Ya?"*

Miriam caught up to her before she reached the porch. "Actually, I'm going to go meet Saul Fisher. We're going to go fishing at the old Zook farm. But I won't be gone for more than a couple of hours."

Her mother scowled, then softened her expression. "That's fine. You and Shelby have fun." *Mamm* turned again to head to the house.

What? She skipped across the yard to catch up with her mother again. "But, *Mamm* . . . I was going to go meet Saul by myself, and—"

Mamm turned around. "Why?"

"Why what?"

"Why do you need to meet Saul by yourself?"

Miriam took a deep breath, then let it out slowly as she shrugged. "I—we—it's like . . ."

Mamm put her hands on her hips and let out a sigh. "Miriam, your cousin just arrived yesterday, and I will not have you leaving her just yet."

So I have to babysit her? "But, *Mamm* . . ."

"No, Miriam. You take Shelby with you, or don't go at all." *Mamm* held up her first finger. "And no arguing." She turned to leave, and for the first time, Miriam considered how having Shelby here would alter her own choices.

It was a half hour later when Miriam told Shelby about the fishing trip. They were upstairs in Miriam's room because Shelby said she wanted to change blouses. Shelby emerged from the bathroom wearing a brown T-shirt with a slogan for Texas barbeque on it. Miriam agreed that Shelby's choice would be better for fishing than her pretty yellow blouse.

"Aren't you going to change clothes?" Shelby seemed in a better mood since Miriam had mentioned the fishing adventure, so Miriam tried to be happy that her cousin was going with her to meet Saul.

"I already did."

"But you're still in a dress. Aren't you allowed to wear anything else?"

"I changed from my nice Sunday dress to this older, worn one."

Miriam couldn't help but notice the way Shelby's jeans and T-shirt showed off her curves, and for the first time in her life, Miriam wished she had her own blue jeans and T-shirt to wear.

"I love to go fishing. I used to go all the time with my dad, but . . ." Shelby sighed. "Anyway, thank you for inviting me."

"Sure. We'll have a *gut* time." Miriam felt a tad guilty for not wanting Shelby to go, but she'd try to make up for it by making sure her cousin had fun.

Saul maneuvered his buggy down the dirt road that led to the abandoned Zook farm. Brown and green weeds flanked the path, and in the distance stood the white clapboard house, its paint chipped from neglect. Part of the white picket fence surrounding the front yard was down, and several cows meandered through the yard as if it was a pasture. It was a sad sight, and Saul recalled the times he'd played with the Zook kids in that yard. But when Amos, the youngest of the Zook children, got cancer six years ago, the family had relocated to a place where there was a fancy medical center that could take better care of him. The property had sold right away to a local *Englisch* man who didn't care anything about restoring the farmhouse. He'd purchased the land just to run cattle on, but at least he'd given permission for them to fish in the pond whenever they wanted. Saul rarely saw the owner of the property and figured he must just come to check on the cows from time to time. It was hard on the eyes to see the house in such disrepair. Saul wondered whatever happened to Amos Zook, if he had been cured of the cancer.

He did a double take when he edged closer and saw two buggies near the pond. Saul was pretty sure one of them was Miriam's. He strained to see, and his chest tightened when he saw Jesse Dienner standing next to Miriam. And who was the other woman? As he got closer, he recognized the other woman to be Miriam's cousin whom he'd met at church.

Saul tensed even more when he thought about the way Jesse had lingered around Miriam earlier in the day. It was the only reason he stayed around after the service and gathered with the men in the barn—where Jesse should have been. Twice he'd poked his head out and saw Jesse in the yard with Miriam while she picked up glasses from the tables outside. He knew plenty well that jealousy was a sin, but seeing the two of them laughing and talking had sent his heart to racing. Saul knew that once he left, it was just a matter of time before Miriam settled on one of the many interested fellows in their district. Probably Jesse. He was a fine man, and he would make a good husband for Miriam. But, right or wrong, Saul wanted one summer with Miriam. And he knew she wanted it too, even if she didn't know that he would be leaving her in late August or early September. He cringed for a moment about the betrayal, but then he got a glimpse of Miriam's smile and knew he couldn't stop himself.

He stepped out of the buggy. "I see we have lots of company." He forced a smile as he tethered his horse to a nearby tree.

Jesse smiled. "*Gut* thing I stopped by the Raber place to return a platter Miriam's *mudder* left this morning. Otherwise I wouldn't have known that Miriam and her cousin were meeting you here to go fishing." Jesse chuckled. "Guess you were going to keep these two pretty *maeds* all to yourself."

"He didn't know I was bringing Shelby," Miriam said in a shy voice.

Good. Now Jesse knows this was supposed to have been a date. At least they could pair up—Saul and Miriam and Jesse and Shelby.

"Well, I'm glad you did." Jesse smiled, and Saul thought again about how Miriam would probably end up with Jesse, but for today, maybe Miriam's *Englisch* cousin could keep him occupied. She was a pretty girl, even if she was a bit thin.

Saul figured most women thought Jesse was handsome. He was tall and broad like Saul, but his face was perfect. Perfect smile. Perfect teeth. And Jesse had never been in any kind of trouble.

Saul reached up and touched the scar that ran along his chin, then he ran his tongue along his not-so-straight front teeth. He disliked the fact that he felt inferior around Jesse just because of the man's looks. Besides, Saul knew he had gotten the scar on his chin in an honorable way, even if fistfights were not allowed. But he'd seen the man nab Mrs. Perkin's purse. The elderly *Englisch* woman attended quilting parties with his mother, and she was a nice lady who didn't deserve to have her bag taken.

The thief turned out to be almost more than Saul could handle. He'd gotten in one good punch before Saul stopped him. Then Bishop Ebersol had reprimanded Saul for his actions. Again.

"I went by my *haus* and picked up a couple of fishing poles." Jesse held up two cane poles.

"I brought three," Saul said as he reached into the back of his buggy. "I brought an extra one in case something happened to one of the other ones. So we have plenty."

Miriam smiled and batted her eyes at Saul, which caused him to once again go weak in the knees. "I brought my *own* pole," she said smugly. "It's my lucky fishing pole, and I catch fish every time I use it."

Saul couldn't take his eyes from hers for a moment. He recalled the way he'd pushed back a strand of her hair the day before. A vision he couldn't seem to shake, nor did he want to.

"Miriam, why don't you and me walk to the other side of the pond? We'll spread out a little." Jesse smiled his perfect smile, and Saul felt his temperature rise.

"Or . . . why don't we make this a competition, girls against the boys?" Shelby moved closer to Miriam. "Let's see who can catch the most fish."

"We don't usually compete against each other," Miriam said to her cousin. "Remember when we played volleyball after church? We didn't keep score."

Shelby looked toward the ground, her cheeks reddening, and Saul felt a little bad for her. "No one has to know," he said as he raised a brow playfully.

"Leave it to you, Saul." Jesse grinned, but Saul knew that his friend was hinting that he was always the one to break the rules. And maybe that was true. Another reason why he didn't belong here.

"But I'm in, if the girls are," Jesse added.

Miriam smiled. "I say let's do it." She latched onto her cousin's arm, and they started to walk to the other side of the pond.

Saul let out a heavy sigh. This was not at all how he planned to spend the afternoon.

4

An hour later Miriam and Shelby gazed across the pond at Saul and Jesse. Miriam shook her head.

"I don't understand. That's at least the tenth fish they've pulled in." Miriam twisted another worm on her hook, then dropped her pole in the water.

"Maybe I'm bad luck." Shelby set her pole on the ground, then sat down on a grassy patch next to it and twisted a strand of hair between her fingers.

Miriam glanced down at her and frowned. "Of course you're not."

"One thing is for sure, though." Shelby put her elbows on her crossed legs, then propped her chin in her hands. "They both have a thing for you."

"A thing?"

"Sure. Clearly this was supposed to be a date for you and Saul." Shelby paused. "And I really shouldn't have come." Miriam started to interrupt, but Shelby went on. "I saw the way both Saul and Jesse looked at you all morning." Miriam was glad to see Shelby smile. "Yep, you're a popular girl."

Miriam knew that Jesse liked her. She'd known that for years. But Saul had always held the key to her heart.

"So Saul is the one you're interested in?" Shelby picked up

her pole from where she was sitting, then tossed the line into the murky pond water.

Miriam sighed. *"Ya."* She dipped her pole up and down, hoping the action would attract a fish. "But Jesse is a *gut* man. He will be a fine husband for someone."

"Just not for *you?"* Shelby grinned.

"No. Not for me."

"Well, I think he's hot. Super good-looking."

Miriam glanced down at her cousin who was staring dreamy-eyed across the pond toward the men. While she was glad to see Shelby smiling and seemingly happy, her protective instinct kicked in. "He's going to be baptized in the fall, like I am. Then he'll be ready for marriage to someone in our community."

Shelby didn't say anything but continued to stare across the pond.

"Jesse is one of those who will never leave. Most of the boys here experience their *rumschpringe*—running-around period—to the full-est. They drink beer, drive cars, and lots of other things I probably don't know about. Not Jesse, though. He's not like that. He'll be baptized, marry, and eventually take over his father's blacksmith shop."

"So he can date anyone while he's running around, right?"

"I—I guess so." This was unsettling to Miriam. She didn't want to marry Jesse, but she didn't want to see him get hurt either. Shelby was beautiful, and Jesse might be tempted to get involved with her—a girl who wasn't Amish and someone who was leaving in three months. Plus, Shelby was having some problems with God, and Miriam knew Jesse had an unquestionable faith.

Shelby set her pole down, then leaned back on her hands. "It doesn't really matter anyway."

"Why do you say that?" Miriam heard the sadness in her cousin's voice again.

"You've probably noticed, I have some issues. Lots of issues. I wouldn't want to subject anyone to that."

Miriam was glad that Shelby didn't want anything romantic with Jesse, but she also wanted her cousin to feel whole and happy. "I think you will be fine, Shelby."

"How do you know that?"

"Because it's God's will for you to be here. He has a plan for you." Miriam would pray constantly that Shelby's faith would be restored, that she would feel close to God and trust His plan for her.

"I wish I could believe that. I feel like I'm being punished by being sent here." Right away Shelby looked up at Miriam. "I'm sorry. I didn't mean that the way it sounded."

"It's okay. I understand." Miriam couldn't imagine anyone not loving Lancaster County, its quiet people, simple ways, and love of the land and God. But Shelby was an outsider, and Miriam was sure she missed her home in Texas.

"I wish things were different for me." Shelby gazed out over the water with more unhappiness in her voice.

"They can be different. Things change according to God's plan, and we never know what time frame God is on."

"Oh, wow!" Shelby pulled back on her pole as her entire body fell backward onto the grass. "I've got one! And it's huge! Oh my!"

Miriam dropped her own pole when she saw Shelby struggling. She helped her cousin pull as they both scooted backward on their behinds, pulling the cane pole and line through the tall weeds.

"I've never worked so hard to pull a fish out of this pond!" Miriam screamed as they watched the enormous fish surface.

"Keep pulling!" They both kept hold of the pole and stood up. Miriam could see Saul and Jesse out of the corner of her eye running along the bank.

"We have to get it in before they get here and try to help us." Shelby was laughing, then Miriam started laughing, and together the girls pulled the fish onto the bank right before the men arrived, breathless—and speechless.

Shelby and Miriam looked on as Saul carefully picked up the large catfish. He held it by the mouth at arm's length and shook his head. "Can't believe a *girl* caught this." He chuckled as he tossed it back into the pond. Shelby was proud of her catch and wished she had a camera with her. She hadn't even bothered to bring hers from home, and Miriam told her that the Amish people didn't take pictures, something to do with their religion.

As the fish met with the water, it immediately disappeared. Shelby pulled the band that held her hair, then picked up the loose strands and twisted it back into a ponytail. "Yep, you boys were beat by a girl." She dropped her hands to her side. "I still say it's a shame not to have a picture."

Saul looked at Jesse. "I don't have a camera with me. Do you?"

Jesse shook his head, but Shelby was confused. She turned to Miriam. "I thought you said that no pictures were allowed."

"We're in our *rumschpringe*, running-around time," Miriam said. "So some people our age have cameras, cell phones, things like that."

"Oh." Shelby raised her brows. "Couldn't we have eaten it? I love fish."

"We throw most of them back." Jesse wiped his hands on his black pants, then looped his thumbs beneath his suspenders. His dark-green shirt brought out his eyes, and Shelby couldn't seem to look away from him. She reminded herself that Jesse liked Miriam, but her cousin had eyes for Saul. "Me and Saul threw ours back too. We'll let them all get bigger," Jesse added.

"Of course you threw yours back." Shelby giggled. "Because none of yours were even close to being as big as ours."

"The contest was to see who could catch the *most* fish," Jesse said, then chuckled. "And the men are the winners." He stood tall and smiled. "But you girls gave it your best try."

As the four of them stood at the bank's edge, Shelby glanced at Miriam, then at Saul. She'd ruined her cousin's date, so maybe she could make it up to Miriam, and also get to know Jesse Dienner a little better. Jesse carried his fishing pole and a bait bucket to his buggy, and Shelby followed him. As Jesse stowed the items in the back of the buggy, Shelby whispered, "Maybe you could take me home so they could spend some time alone together. I think I sorta barged in on their date."

Jesse grimaced instantly, and Shelby felt foolish to think that she could sway his feelings for Miriam. Miriam was very pretty and one of his own people. But Jesse was the first thing to pique Shelby's interest in a long time. She could knock out two things here, if Jesse would go along with her. Jesse glanced toward Saul and Miriam. They'd edged closer together and were talking. Jesse's scowl hardened, but then he took a deep breath and turned back to Shelby.

"Sure. I can take you home."

They walked back to where Miriam and Saul were standing,

and Jesse told them that he was going to give Shelby a ride home.
He didn't offer any additional information, and both Miriam and
Saul nodded. Shelby winked at Miriam as she walked away. Her
cousin winked back. Shelby hoped it went well for Miriam and
Saul, though she didn't understand why Miriam would choose
Saul over Jesse. Saul seemed quieter, and he wasn't nearly as good-
looking as Jesse. Jesse smiled a lot and was much more outgoing
too. But this worked out well for Shelby. She thought Jesse would
be a great catch, and Miriam did say that a small percent of the
Amish people did leave to go out into the real world. She hopped
into the passenger side of Jesse's buggy, anxious to learn more
about him on the way back to her cousin's farm.

Miriam helped Saul load the rest of the fishing equipment into the
back of his buggy. She had her own ride, so she wasn't sure whether
to say good-bye. After an awkward few minutes, Saul asked her if
she wanted to go sit on the porch swing. Miriam glanced at the
cows grazing in the yard, then up to the porch, which was barren
except for the old swing.

"Okay." She followed him through the overgrown yard as he
cleared the way and motioned with his arms to clear two cows in
their path. He stepped carefully up the creaky wooden steps, then
motioned to her with his hand.

"It's a mess but seems safe enough."

Miriam sat down on the small swing built for two. She eased as
far to one side as she could, but even then, Saul's leg brushed against
hers when he sat down, sending a rush of adrenaline through her
body, and she could feel her cheeks reddening.

"That was fun, fishing." She twisted the string on her prayer covering. "Shelby sure was excited to catch that big fish."

Miriam jumped when Saul shifted his weight slightly to face her, pushing his leg against hers. "How long is she here for?"

"For the summer, until August. Her parents got a divorce, and I think she got in some trouble back home." Miriam paused. "But she seems so nice, so I can't imagine what trouble she could have gotten into."

"Is it strange having an *Englisch* girl living with you?" Saul cocked his head to one side. "It's gotta be really different for her here."

Miriam shrugged. "She only arrived yesterday, but it doesn't seem so strange. It probably does to her, though."

Saul's body was still turned toward her, and when she turned her head to face him, there were only a few inches between their faces. His bobbed cut was longer than it should be, his light-brown hair boasting sandy-red highlights and brushing against his brows. Dark eyes stared into hers, and she watched him take a deep breath. *Is he as nervous as I am?*

Saul was lost in Miriam's blue eyes for the few moments that their eyes locked and held, but within seconds she turned away from him. And that was probably a good thing. Saul might have kissed her, and that would be moving too fast for Miriam. Why, after all these years, did she approach him? He could have just slipped away in a few months without hurting her. Saul knew that the right thing to do would be to avoid any more of these private times together, but he feared he didn't have the strength. Even though he'd often seen Miriam watching him, smiling at him, and whispering to her girlfriends when he was around, she always seemed out of reach for him. Miriam was a good girl, perfect for marrying and raising a family here in Lancaster County.

She turned to face him again and opened her mouth to say something. But she quickly snapped her lips together and looked away.

"What?" Her hand was on her leg, and without much thought, he stretched one of his fingers out and touched the top of her hand. "What are you thinking about?" He felt her hand tense beneath his touch.

"I—I don't know."

Saul eased his hand away from hers, and they were both quiet for a few moments.

"Miriam?"

She kept her eyes cast down and bit her lip for a moment. *"Ya?"*

He waited until she looked at him, then rubbed his chin. "Do you want to go on a date with me? I mean, a real date. Maybe to supper . . . and a movie?"

She bit her bottom lip, then grinned. "Sure. I've only been to a movie a couple of times."

"We're in our *rumschpringe.* Better see as many as you can," he said, even though he knew there would be plenty more opportunities in his future.

She faced him, the corner of her mouth curled upward. "I'd like to see a movie with you."

Saul pictured them in a dark movie theater and wondered if they would hold hands. Would he kiss her at the end of the night? "Do you want to go Friday night?"

She frowned. "I can't on Friday. *Mamm* hosts suppers for the tourists on Friday nights, and I'm expected to help."

"Okay," he said, trying not to sound as disappointed as he was. "Maybe some other time."

"When?" Her eyes widened as she faced him, and Saul didn't think he'd wanted to kiss anyone more than right now. He froze for a moment, then blinked his eyes a couple of times and forced himself to look away from her.

"*Mei daed* will expect me to work in the fields, then do chores on Saturday. But I could go Saturday night." He looked back at her. "Think your folks would let you go?"

Miriam dabbed at the sweat beading up on her forehead. Saul wondered how her parents would feel about him taking her to supper and a movie. But most of the teenagers in their district did things normally forbidden by the *Ordnung*, and parents just looked the other way while they were in their *rumschpringe*. This was the time to experience the outside world, but Saul suspected Miriam had never taken full advantage of her freedom.

"I'm sure it will be fine," she finally said, smiling.

Saul felt warm inside as he smiled back at her.

Shelby thanked Jesse for the ride home as he pulled to a stop in front of Miriam's farmhouse. Jesse had been polite enough, but when Shelby mentioned twice how much she enjoyed going fishing, he never suggested a return trip to the Zook farm. And he talked about Miriam a lot. Shelby didn't even think he realized it. Miriam's name just seemed to slide off his tongue in almost every conversation. Jesse was Amish anyway, so what was the point? But his stunning good looks had been a nice distraction today. For a while this afternoon, she hadn't thought about her parents or Tommy.

She waved to Jesse, then headed across the front yard.

"Where's Miriam?" There was an urgency in Rebecca's voice, and it caught Shelby a little off guard.

"She's still with Saul. I think they wanted to spend some time alone together. I think maybe today was supposed to be a date, but I ruined that for them." She smiled but quickly stopped when Rebecca's eyebrows drew into a deep frown.

"Did Miriam say when she would be home?"

"No, ma'am." Shelby regretted that she had apparently gotten Miriam in trouble. Maybe Amish girls weren't allowed to date. Maybe Shelby shouldn't have used that word. She'd talk to Miriam later when she got home. Besides, she had something to tell Miriam. Something Jesse told her that she didn't think Miriam was going to be happy about.

Rebecca lifted her chin and sighed. "Well, I'm sure she'll be along shortly. Why don't you go in and get yourself a glass of iced tea. Miriam knows to be home to help with supper, so she'll be here soon."

Shelby nodded and slid past Rebecca. She was hot and tired, and a glass of iced tea sounded wonderful.

Rebecca stood in the front yard and watched her husband washing his hands at the pump by the barn. When he was done, he slowly made his way toward her.

"Aaron, Miriam is with Saul Fisher." She clenched her hands at her sides. "And they are alone together."

Her husband took off his straw hat, then ran his sleeve across his forehead. He slowly put his hat back on as he let out a heavy sigh. "*Ach*, we've known this was coming. She's liked that boy for years."

"Aaron, how can you be so calm about this? Saul Fisher has been in more trouble than any other boy in this community." She folded her arms across her chest. "And you heard what Ben said at supper last night, that he heard Saul wasn't going to be baptized."

Her husband lowered his head, then lifted tired eyes to meet hers. "Now, Rebecca, those're just rumors."

Rebecca reached up and pulled a piece of fuzz from Aaron's black beard, speckled with gray. "I don't want her seeing that boy, Aaron." She knew it was wrong to judge another person, but Miriam was her only daughter.

"Rebecca." Aaron put one hand on his hip, then rubbed his forehead with the other. "She's in her *rumschpringe*. Let the *maedel* have some freedoms. We've raised Miriam well. She will make *gut* choices."

"I never said that Miriam shouldn't experience her *rumschpringe*." She sighed with irritation. "It just gives me worry that she might be thinking of dating Saul Fisher." She shook her head. "He's not right for her, Aaron."

"Who are we to decide that, Rebecca?" He sighed, and Rebecca knew her husband was ready to get into the house and have something cold to drink, but worry consumed her.

"We are her parents. That's *who* we are." Rebecca raised her chin and faced off with her husband.

Aaron kissed her on the cheek. "I'm goin' in the house, Rebecca. I'm hot and tired." He eased past her, and she spun around.

"Pray about this, Aaron! I will be."

He didn't turn around but waved an acknowledgment as he made his way up the porch steps.

Rebecca shook her head. Like her husband, she'd known for years that Miriam had a crush on Saul Fisher, but she'd always hoped that her daughter would have the good sense not to get involved with a boy like that. She recalled Miriam's hesitancy to take Shelby with her today, which certainly set off alarms. Now, after hearing what Shelby had to say about Miriam and Saul wanting to be alone, Rebecca felt her stomach clench with worry.

Miriam wished she could sit on the porch swing with Saul well into the evening, but she knew she was already going to be late getting home. *Mamm* wasn't going to be happy if she didn't arrive in time to help with supper.

Saul was a man of few words, but Miriam stayed persistent and eased him into a conversation, and during the past half hour, she'd learned a little bit more about him. All food related. It was a subject he was passionate about. He was allergic to shellfish, didn't care for whoopee pies, and once ate seven cheeseburgers on a dare from a friend. He also knew how to cook and told her that he could make a better shoofly pie than anyone in the district. She'd stifled a grin more than once as he spoke. *Saul Fisher can cook?*

Miriam remembered that Saul's mother and only sister had died in a buggy accident about five years ago. Since then, Saul had helped his *daed* raise his two younger brothers, and he'd probably learned to cook out of necessity. She couldn't believe how many different things he knew how to prepare, and she found herself sharing some of her secret recipes with him.

"Okay, Saul. I told you how to make cream of carrot soup.

Now . . ." Miriam nudged him with her shoulder. "I want to hear about this ultimate grilled cheese sandwich."

Saul chuckled. "No way."

"That's not fair, Saul Fisher. That cream of carrot soup was my great-*mammi's* recipe, and no one in the district knows how to make it but me and *Mamm.*"

"Not true. I've had cream of carrot soup before. *Mei mamm* used to make it before—" He took a deep breath. "Before the accident."

Miriam wasn't sure how much Saul wanted to talk about his mother, and they'd been having so much fun, so she just nodded.

"Fine." He shifted his weight in the swing, turning to face her even more, and grinned. "I'll tell you how to make the ultimate grilled cheese sandwich."

Miriam kept her eyes on his, but she was acutely aware of his knee pressed up against her leg. "*Gut.* Let's hear it."

Saul described preparation of the sandwich as if he was creating a work of art, talking with his hands as he spoke, but Miriam couldn't stay focused on anything but his mouth, his lips. It took everything in her power not to thrust forward and press her mouth to his. *How completely inappropriate!* She blinked a few times to refocus and caught the tail end of his explanation.

"You mix the cream cheese and mayo until creamy, and then you stir in the cheddar, mozzarella, garlic powder, and seasoned salt, and—" Saul stopped midsentence, and his dark-brown eyes locked with hers. "Do you think it's weird that I like to cook?"

Miriam was careful not to blurt out the first thing on her mind, since the truth was she thought it made him a thousand times more attractive. She didn't know any men who could cook, and she found this new information about Saul fascinating. "No,

I think it's wonderful that you cook!" She stared into his eyes and pictured the two of them in their own kitchen, cooking together and trying new recipes. It was a very non-Amish scenario, but Miriam had the vision just the same.

Saul's smile broadened. "Well, I like to eat, so I had to learn to cook. After *mei mamm* and Hannah died . . ." His smile faded as he momentarily pulled his eyes from her, then looked back up. "*Mei mammi* used to come cook for us. But then she got sick and wasn't able to come so much." He paused, then rubbed his chin as he spoke. "I just kinda taught myself."

This was the most she'd talked to Saul, and she wasn't ready for it to end. But her mother would start to stew if she didn't get home soon. "I guess I need to go," she said as she watched the sun begin to set.

"*Ya*. Me too." He smiled at her as they both stood from the swing. "Guess what everyone at my *haus* will be having for supper?" He rubbed his hand in a circular motion on his stomach.

Miriam giggled. "I'm guessing ultimate grilled cheese sandwiches."

Saul nodded, then they both headed down the creaky porch steps. "Watch that cow patty." He latched onto her arm and guided her around it, then let go and waved an arm at two cows in the yard. "Go on, now! You don't need to be in the front yard."

"This is so sad," Miriam said as they eased their way through the overgrowth in the yard. "This place was so pretty at one time."

"*Ya*. I know." Saul shook his head as he let Miriam go ahead of him through the rickety gate at the end of the sidewalk. He opened the door of Miriam's buggy, and she climbed in. Then Saul untied the reins and handed them to her.

"This was fun today." Miriam was sad to see it end, but she would have Saturday to look forward to.

"*Ya.*" Saul stuffed his hands in his pockets. "I guess I'll pick you up on Saturday. Seven o'clock?"

Miriam nodded but then said, "Why don't I meet you in town? On Saturday, I run errands in the afternoon, so I'll already be on Lincoln Highway. I could meet you at Yoder's Pantry. They stay open late." She paused, wondering how her parents were going to feel about her going on a date with Saul. "Can we make it eight o'clock?" She crinkled her nose, then grinned. "It's Saturday night."

"Sure."

She pulled back on the reins and clicked her tongue until her horse started to back up the spring buggy. She'd backed up a few feet when Saul walked briskly up to her.

"Miriam, wait!"

She stopped, raised her brows. "*Ya?*"

Saul cocked his head to one side and stroked his stubbly chin. "What made you come talk to me yesterday at the creek?" He captured her eyes and gazed at her, one side of his mouth hinting at a grin. "I mean, after all these years."

Miriam bit her lip and pulled her eyes from his. Then she looked back at him and held his gaze. "Don't you think it was time?"

His grin eased into a big smile. "*Ya.* I guess it was."

Miriam started backing the horse up again, and Saul walked to his own spring buggy. Then she stopped again. "Saul?"

He turned, took a few steps toward her. "*Ya?*"

Miriam brushed loose strands of hair away from her face, then found Saul's eyes. "Would you have come and talked to me?"

Saul lifted his eyes to hers. "No."

Miriam's heart thudded with disappointment, and she hung her head. A moment later Saul's hand was gently lifting her chin until her eyes met his again. "I'm not good enough for you, Miriam Raber." His finger brushed her cheek as he spoke in the raspy whisper that always sent her senses soaring.

She reached up, put her hand on his, then closed her eyes. "I think you are perfect for me, Saul Fisher."

Saul prayed all the way home. He knew what he was doing was as wrong as it could be, but nothing had ever felt more right to him. Being around Miriam, actually talking to her, getting to know her—it made his heart flip in his chest. But getting too close to her would only hurt them both in the end. And poor Miriam was going into this blind. Saul knew he would leave in August for the *Englisch* world, forgoing baptism and a future here in Paradise. When he visited Pittsburgh a few months ago, he never could have imagined how that trip would change his life. He'd answered the ad for an apprentice chef with little hope of landing his dream job. But soon after his trip and meeting with the owner of the restaurant, the letter came . . .

He'd saved enough money, and his brothers were old enough to fend for themselves. He'd taught them as much as he could. At fifteen and thirteen, Ruben and James both knew how to prepare some basic meals, tend to the fields, and handle the tools in the barn. Ruben was turning out to be a fine carpenter, and now that James was graduated from school, Saul knew he would find his calling too.

He tried to ease his guilt through prayer. It was bad enough that he would be leaving his father and brothers, but now he would be leaving Miriam too. Their feelings for each other would only grow if they dated through the summer, setting them both up for heartache. But he'd worked so hard to save his money, and *Daed* was on the mend. Surely everyone would be all right when he left.

Miriam would go on to find someone who deserved her. She'd been raised to be the perfect Amish *fraa*, and some lucky man would win her heart after Saul was gone. He promised himself that he would not break her heart. They would have fun, enjoy each other, but not get too close. But if that was true, then why couldn't he stop wishing he could just kiss her, hold her in his arms one time . . .

He pulled up his driveway. Ruben and James were sitting on the front porch, dangling their feet over the side. Ruben had his head in his hands, but James looked up when Saul pulled closer. His brother swiped at his eyes, and Saul knew immediately what was going on. This scene had played out a hundred times, but Saul thought they were past this. He walked across the yard and stood at the edge of the porch. Both his brothers locked eyes with him. Saul waited.

"It's worse than ever before," Ruben said as he stifled tears. "Go see for yourself."

5

MIRIAM'S MOTHER WAS MORE THAN A LITTLE MAD WHEN Miriam showed up too late to help with supper. *Mamm* had barely spoken to her, and Miriam was relieved when it was time to head upstairs for bed.

"I hope I didn't get you in trouble, Miriam. Are you not allowed to date?" Shelby fluffed the pillow behind her.

"*Ya*, I'm allowed to date." Miriam ran her brush the length of her hair. "I just think *Mamm* would prefer that I date Jesse." She rolled her eyes.

"Well, I gotta admit, I'm a little confused about that too. Jesse is so hot, and I could tell on our ride home how much he likes you. Your name came up in every conversation."

Miriam put the brush in the drawer, then got comfy in her bed. "Jesse is very nice, and *ya*, he's handsome. But Saul . . ." She smiled with recollections of their time alone sitting on the porch at the Zook farm. "He's just special."

Shelby sat up, hung her legs over the side of the bed, and faced Miriam. "He does seem nice, but . . ."

Miriam sat up, turned toward Shelby, and crossed her legs beneath her. "What is it?"

Her cousin looked down for a moment, then met eyes with Miriam. "Jesse said Saul is leaving here, that he's not going to be baptized." She paused. "And isn't that what your brother said too?"

Miriam was tired of these rumors. "I don't know why people are saying that. I'm sure it's not true." She leaned back on her palms. "Otherwise he wouldn't have asked me out on a date for this Saturday night."

"I take it this will be your first official date with him?" Shelby smiled.

"It will be my first official date with *anyone*."

Shelby bolted upright. "You're kidding me, right?"

Mirriam giggled. "You know, you say that a lot. But no, I'm not kidding. I've been waiting for Saul." She wrapped herself in a hug. "He's the one. I've always known that."

Shelby reached for her pink book and pen on the nightstand. "I just wouldn't want to see you get hurt." Her cousin leaned over the side of the bed and reached into her purse. Miriam watched her retrieve a key, then twist it in the tiny lock. She dropped the silver ring that held the key back into her purse.

Miriam lit the lantern. "I won't get hurt. Saul's not going anywhere. He belongs here." She smiled at Shelby as she leaned forward. "Here with *me*."

"Just be careful. Guys can be total jerks, and just when you think you've found the right one, they go and break your heart." Shelby opened the small book in her lap.

"Not Saul. He won't break my heart." Miriam hadn't always been right about everything, but this was one thing she was sure of. She saw the way he looked into her eyes today. "I'm going to go to sleep. You should too. Tomorrow is Monday, wash day. It always makes for a long day."

Shelby sighed. "I guess we get up again at four thirty tomorrow?"

"Every day." Miriam smiled as she rolled onto her side to avoid the soft glow of the lantern.

Shelby pressed the pen to the paper.

Dear Diary,

Today I went fishing with my cousin Miriam and two of her friends. It was the first time that I forgot about Mom and Dad and Tommy for a while. But now, as I try to calm my thoughts and get some sleep, images of the past are all over the place. I miss Tommy so much. And I'm so angry at Mom and Dad for the choices they made—choices that landed me here in Amish Country where I don't have any friends.

Shelby wiped sweat from her forehead, then turned the battery-operated fan more in her direction. She leaned closer to the breeze and thought about her friends back home.

I guess maybe they weren't true friends after all. I'm not sure I want or need any friends anymore. But I do like Miriam, even though I don't want to get too close to her. First of all, she's different. She's eighteen years old and she's just now going on her first date this Saturday night. Weird. Or maybe it's kind of sweet in a way. I don't know.

I met a guy. An Amish guy. His name is Jesse, and he is the hottest man I've seen in a long time. He seems to like Miriam a lot, but Miriam likes a guy named Saul. So, I don't know. We'll see what happens. But Jesse is easy on the eyes and seems so nice. Gotta watch it though—I don't want to get too close to him either.

Everyone I get close to hurts me. Even God.

Saul closed the door to his father's room after helping him into bed. *Daed* was snoring the minute his head landed on the pillow and before Saul even had a chance to pull his father's boots off. His father would wake up in the morning with all his clothes on and know what happened. But no one would mention it. That's the way it always was. Zeb Fisher was a kind, gentle man when he wasn't drinking. He loved the Lord, and he loved his sons. Maybe he'd loved their mother and Hannah more. Saul wasn't sure. But that's when the drinking started, after the accident, and it had gotten worse every year. Until three months ago. *Daed* just stopped drinking in the evening hours. *What made him start again?*

Ruben and James were cleaning up the mess when Saul walked into the den, the smell of red wine hovering in the air around them.

"What set him off this time?" Saul asked as he made his way to a spilled bottle of wine. He picked it up and recognized the brand to be none other than their own. For as long as Saul could remember, his father made his own wine from the muscadine grapes that grew along the back of their property. They grew wild and abundantly, and once Saul had taken a machete to the flourishing vines, hoping to banish them forever. But they came back even fuller the next year, along with *Daed's* appetite for the drink.

Saul glanced around the room at the toppled coffee table, overturned rocking chair, and slivers of glass surrounding the brick outlay of the fireplace. As he grew closer, he recognized the stems on the broken glasses at his feet. He squatted down and picked up one of his mother's favorite glasses that had remained housed in her china cabinet until tonight—glasses that she'd never used, a gift from an *Englisch* friend. *Mamm* said they were too fancy, but she kept them displayed so that her friend, Ida, would see them when she came to visit.

Ruben edged closer. "I don't know, Saul. Me and James were cleaning things up in the barn, and we heard *Daed* yelling and glass breaking. I went in, but when I saw the fire in his eyes again, I went back to the barn." Ruben hung his head. "I wasn't sure what to do. I told James I thought we should stay in the barn until *Daed* passed out." He looked back up at Saul. "I ain't ever seen him throwing things like that, and I just . . ."

Saul was glad his father had passed out on the couch, instead of just falling down on the floor. It was so much harder to get him off the floor. "You did the right thing. When he gets to that point, there's no reckoning with him, and he usually passes out not long after that."

Ruben picked up a piece of glass. "*Mamm* loved these glasses, even though she never would use them."

Saul picked up the two green blinds that were in the middle of the floor, window coverings ripped from the walls. He shook his head. "*Daed's* been doing so *gut*. I thought we were done with this."

James brushed by Saul and Ruben carrying a plate that he'd picked up from the other side of the room. Spaghetti and meatballs left over from the night before covered the whitewashed wall to the right of the fireplace. "I don't know how this plate didn't break," James said as he moved toward the kitchen.

"Well, we best get this cleaned up and try to make things look as back to normal as we can." Saul shook his head as he went to the mudroom to get a broom.

When he returned, he started sweeping up broken glass while Ruben scrubbed tomato sauce from the wall. He dreaded the next morning. They'd all eat breakfast together and no one would say anything. *Daed* would eat very little and head to the fields early, then he'd stay out later than usual, as if the extra hard work would in some way make up for what he'd done. He'd know what happened, even if he didn't remember all the details. Saul thanked God that his father had never laid a hand on any of them when he was in a drunken rage.

"It ain't ever gonna be normal," Ruben said as he carried a white rag soaked in red to the kitchen.

Saul sighed. He'd been counting on it being normal. Finally. So that he could leave in August knowing that his brothers wouldn't have to go through this in his absence. Ruben might be able to handle it, but James still cried after *Daed* had one of his fits like tonight.

Two hours later Saul set the lantern on his nightstand, then sat on the edge of his bed. He still needed to take a shower, but he'd told Ruben and James that they could bathe first. It was going to be late when they all finally got to sleep. He opened the drawer to his nightstand and pulled out the white envelope hidden beneath his Bible. He didn't need to read the letter since he knew it by heart. Instead, he opened the Bible and read for a few minutes but decided he needed some direct communion with God. He closed his eyes and bowed his head.

Dear Lord, please help me to help him.

Saul opened his eyes and questioned his plea. Was it selfish to want his father to be a well man so that he could leave and pursue his dreams?

He closed the Bible, set it on the bed next to him, then pulled the letter from the white envelope. As he moved the lantern closer to him, the words danced on the page in the dimly lit room.

Dear Saul,

I would like to extend a formal invitation for you to join me at my new restaurant in Pittsburgh. Our meeting confirmed your willingness to learn more about what it takes to be a chef, and you asked some fine questions. The dishes you prepared were delicious and distinct, and I enjoyed some of the other recipes you left with me too. Your pumpkin cinnamon rolls with caramel frosting were amazing, and the recipe you referred to as Heavenly Chicken was—indeed—heavenly. The ground ginger was a great touch. I look forward to tasting your traditional Amish recipes—shoofly pie, whoopee pies, and creamed celery.

I would like to offer you the position of apprentice chef if you are still interested in working with me. As we discussed while you were here, my bistro will open for business in September.

> *Warmest regards,*
> *Phil Ballentine,*
> *Owner and Head Chef,*
> *Ballentine's Bistro*

Miriam spent the week trying to get Shelby used to the family schedule, but her cousin still couldn't seem to get up and going in the morning. She'd thought that after almost a week, maybe Shelby would come help with breakfast, and today would be a busy day. Like Mondays, there was always more to do on Fridays because *Mamm* hosted supper for tourists. Their *Englisch* friend Barbie always suggested *Mamm's* suppers to the guests at her bed-and-breakfast, and tonight eight people were coming.

Miriam fought her irritation with Shelby as she marched up the stairs to tell her breakfast was ready. As expected, her cousin was still in bed with the covers over her head. Miriam didn't know how Shelby didn't burn up underneath those covers this time of year. She put one hand on her hip, shined the flashlight toward the bed, and prepared to speak loudly to her cousin and remind her that there was much to do today. But as she opened her mouth to speak, she noticed Shelby's pink book on the nightstand, her pen resting between the opened pages. She moved the flashlight toward it.

Every night Shelby would pull her book from the drawer, then pull the tiny key from her purse. It was always about that time when Miriam would roll over, face away from the lantern light, and fall asleep. Each night the book was tucked safely back in the top drawer. Locked. Miriam only knew this because she kept her hairbrush inside the drawer too, along with a spare *kapp* and a scarf for trips to the barn. There was only one drawer in the nightstand, so she couldn't help but notice.

From where she was standing, she could see blue ink scrawled across the pages, and there was not a doubt in her mind that Shelby kept the book locked for a reason. But Miriam could practically feel the Devil himself pushing her closer to the book as she tiptoed around Shelby's bed toward the nightstand. She held her breath for a moment, heard Shelby lightly snoring, then leaned her head down and pointed the flashlight toward the words on the page.

Dear Diary,

I'm so lonely. My cousins are doing their best to make me feel welcome, but I can tell that I just don't fit in here. Not surprising. Nothing is the same as back home, and I hate getting up at four thirty in the morning. I'm not missing Tommy as much. Now I'm just mad at him for hurting me. But I'm even madder at my parents. Neither one of them have called to check on me or anything. What kind of family is that? My cell phone has been dead for days because there is no electricity, another thing that I could never get used to. But there is a phone in the barn and Mom and Dad could have called. They've just written me out of their lives and moved on. Hope they're both happy.

Since I don't talk to God anymore, this journal is all I have. I wish I could talk to Miriam, but I don't think she'd understand any of this. We're just too different. Her parents are different. This whole family is different. In some ways, that's good, I guess. They are all nice to each other. There's no screaming or yelling.

I miss television. I wish I had a car here. I wish I had someone to love me.

Miriam didn't move or breathe when Shelby twisted beneath the covers in the bed. Then she eased her way back to the open doorway of the bedroom. She felt guilty for reading Shelby's private thoughts, but she immediately began to think of ways to help her cousin. *Doesn't she realize that God loves her?* Miriam knew that if Shelby didn't find her way back to God, it would be hard for her to come to peace with the other things bothering her. She tried to put herself in Shelby's shoes, although it was hard. *What if my parents didn't live together? What if I was cast out among the* Englisch *to live? What if my parents didn't check on me? What if Saul broke my heart?*

Maybe it was okay that Shelby didn't get up early to help make breakfast.

"Shelby." Miriam shined the light at the foot of her bed. "Time to get up and eat. Breakfast is ready."

Her cousin pulled the covers back but didn't open her eyes. "Okay. I'm coming."

Miriam glanced at the book on the nightstand, then turned and left the room. By the time she returned downstairs, everyone was seated at the table.

"Is everything okay?" *Mamm* spread her napkin on her lap. "Is Shelby coming?"

Ben let out a heavy sigh. "She's always late to breakfast."

"Hush, Ben," *Mamm* whispered as they all waited.

Miriam glanced at her father, his arms folded across his chest, then at each of her brothers who were eyeing the eggs, sausage, and biscuits. *Come on, Shelby.*

After a few moments, Miriam said in a whisper, "I think Shelby's sad, and I think she misses her family."

Mamm nodded. "I'm sure she does." She sat taller and gave her head a taut nod. "This morning everyone at this table is going to do our best to include Shelby in conversation and make her feel like part of this family. Understood?" *Mamm* glanced around the table.

"Elam can tell some of his *dumm* jokes." Ben chuckled.

"No joke telling at the breakfast table." Their father unfolded his arms and stretched. "Where is that *maedel*?"

"Sorry I'm late." Shelby scurried into the kitchen with sleepy eyes, her hair still tangled. She eased onto the bench next to Miriam.

"It's no problem, dear. Let's bow our heads."

Miriam was sure the prayer was the shortest on record. They always took a cue from their father. When he cleared his throat and lifted his head, so did everyone else. This morning *Daed* must have just said, "Thank You, Lord, let's eat."

Shelby dished out a small spoonful of eggs, one piece of sausage, and half a biscuit onto her plate. No wonder Shelby was so thin. She didn't eat enough. Miriam helped herself to a much larger helping of eggs, two pieces of sausage, and an entire biscuit.

Everyone was quiet for a few moments, but then Miriam was surprised when Shelby helped herself to more eggs. Barely a minute or two later, she spooned even more eggs onto her plate. Miriam realized that this was the first morning her mother had made what little John called "special eggs."

"These eggs are different, Rebecca." Shelby swallowed, then filled her fork again. "I love them."

"*Ya*, they're different all right," Elam said with a smile.

"Why, *danki*, Shelby." *Mamm* smiled, then shot a warning look to everyone at the table. "Let Shelby enjoy her eggs." She turned to Shelby. "This is the most I've seen you eat since you arrived."

Shelby nodded with a mouthful.

Ben put his hand over his mouth to stifle a giggle. Miriam knew why he was laughing, and she was fighting the urge to grin as well. Most *Englisch* folks didn't care for *Mamm's* secret ingredient in her "special eggs," but Shelby sure did.

Little John leaned forward across the table, his eyes wide with wonder as he spoke. "You're the first *Englisch* person I ever saw who liked head cheese."

Miriam held her breath as she watched Shelby stop chewing. "What?" Shelby asked with a mouthful.

"Mmm." John rubbed his small belly as he talked. "I seen *Mamm* make that cheese too. She takes them hogs' heads and scrapes 'em clean, then she pokes out their eyes and dumps 'em in a kettle—"

"John! I'm sure Shelby doesn't need to know how I make my special eggs." *Mamm* forced a smile, but the damage was done.

No one moved as they watched Shelby slap a hand across her mouth, which was filled with those special eggs.

Mamm let out a heavy sigh, then cut her eyes at Miriam's youngest brother. "See what you've done." Then she turned to Shelby and pointed at the trash can. "Go ahead, Shelby, dear. You won't be the first."

Shelby bolted from the chair, ran to the trash can under the sink, and spit *Mamm's* special eggs into the garbage. When she looked up at everyone, the expression on her face was totally blank.

Miriam couldn't help it; she burst out laughing, followed by her brothers. Then Shelby started laughing so hard that she bent over at the waist, and Miriam was sure her cousin was going to cry.

Her mother just shook her head and grinned. *Daed* shook his head too, but he smiled from ear to ear.

This was probably the last thing *Mamm* had on her mind to cheer Shelby up, but Shelby laughed longer and harder than any of them.

Which made her seem just like part of the family.

———

It was late morning when Rebecca sent Miriam and Shelby to the market to pick up a few things she needed to prepare supper that evening. Despite plans to go earlier in the week, this was Shelby's first time to visit the town of Bird-In-Hand, so she scanned her surroundings while Miriam parked the buggy.

"I'm sorry I haven't brought you sightseeing before now. This isn't where I would normally go shopping for groceries, but it's a fun place I thought you might like to see. The Bird-In-Hand Farmers Market is popular with the tourists." Miriam pulled back on the reins once she had the buggy parked next to another one in the parking lot. "We won't have much time today, but I promise soon we'll take a day so I can show you around."

Shelby stepped out of the buggy, then looked across the street from where they were parked. Bakeries and gift shops lined streets filled with bustling tourists. She walked around to where Miriam was tethering the horse and waited.

"Ready?" Miriam smiled, then took a few steps across the parking lot. Shelby followed, but she stopped abruptly when Miriam did. Her cousin raised her hands to her face, then sidestepped four women whose cameras flashed in their direction. Shelby felt unusually protective. Miriam had told her earlier in the week that they didn't take or pose for pictures. It was actually against their religion, for reasons Shelby didn't totally understand. Miriam also told her that most of the non-Amish people knew this, but that they took pictures anyway.

"Don't get *her* in the picture," said a woman with dark curls, toting several bags and pointing at Shelby. "She's not Amish."

Shelby glared at the women as she and Miriam passed by them and continued across the parking lot. She waited until they were out of earshot from the women, then turned to Miriam. "Doesn't that aggravate you?"

"Huh?" Miriam crinkled her nose.

Shelby had noticed throughout the week that Miriam's entire family had a limited vocabulary. "Doesn't that make you *mad*? People always snapping pictures and staring."

Miriam shrugged as they neared the entrance of the market. "No. We're used to it."

"Well, I think it's rude."

Miriam grinned. "I didn't say we liked it. We're just used to it." Miriam held the door open and let Shelby walk ahead of her. Then her cousin pulled out a handwritten list that Rebecca had given them. "It's a short list. Normally we go to Zimmermann's grocery store in the town of Intercourse. We'll go there next week to do our heavy shopping."

Shelby eased down the aisles with Miriam, where Amish and non-Amish vendors on both sides sold quilts, dolls, jewelry, baked items, canned vegetables, jams, jellies, and a hodgepodge of other things. Shelby could stay there all day looking and shopping, she thought. She pulled her purse up on her shoulder and remembered the small amount of money she had to last her for three months. Not enough to do any real shopping. She eyed a jewelry rack to her left, silver earrings and matching necklaces. Then she breathed in the aroma of freshly baked goods and decided that if she splurged, it would be on something to eat. Something safe—without head cheese in it. She grinned at the recollection. Her parents would have come unglued if she'd spit food into the trash and certainly not laughed about it. Shelby loved the laughter in Miriam's house.

Most of the people shopping were non-Amish, she noticed. She also took note of two men walking her way. Nice-looking guys about her age. For some reason Jesse popped into her head, but the vision vanished when one of the young men mumbled something in Pennsylvania *Deitsch* to Miriam as they walked by. Her cousin scowled but didn't say anything.

"Why were they speaking in Pennsylvania *Deitsch*? They weren't

Amish." Shelby turned around in time to see the men round the corner to the next aisle.

Miriam reached into a large wicker basket on a nearby counter and pulled out a large bag of homemade noodles, then blew a loose strand of hair that had fallen across her cheek. "No, they're not Amish. They're just *dumm*."

Shelby's jaw dropped momentarily. This was the first time she'd heard her cousin speak harshly of another. "What did they say?"

"*Schee beh*." Miriam shook her head, then started walking again. "It means nice legs, and non-Amish boys and some of the younger men say that to us. I don't know who first taught them to say that in Pennsylvania *Deitsch*, but it stuck." She shook her head. "We hear it all the time."

Miriam stopped abruptly, almost dropping the bag of noodles. "What's wrong?"

Her cousin spun around. "Hurry, let's go the other way."

Shelby looked over her shoulder. There was a man about her father's age holding hands with a pretty woman with blond hair, and there were also three women huddled together by one of the jewelry racks.

"Who are you avoiding?"

They both rounded the corner, and once they were halfway down the next aisle, Miriam stopped and took a deep breath. "That was my *Onkel* Ivan and his . . ." She scowled as she lifted her chin. "His *Englisch* girlfriend, Lucy Turner."

"Oh. The *bad* uncle." Shelby pressed her lips together. "Want me to go pull that woman's hair or something? Then I could kick your uncle in the shin."

Miriam's eyes grew wild and round. "We don't do things like that, Shelby!" She spoke in a harsh whisper.

She was so serious that Shelby couldn't help but laugh. "Miriam, I'm kidding."

Miriam grinned. "*Ya*, well . . . I wasn't sure." They slowly started walking again. "I've only seen *Onkel* Ivan once since he's been back. It was in a restaurant, but he didn't see me. I almost didn't recognize him. He looks different now." She faced Shelby with squinted eyes. "We're supposed to avoid him, and I didn't want it to be awkward."

"Where's your aunt?"

"*Aenti* Katie Ann is in Colorado with some other family members."

"Did that woman who was with your uncle break them up?"

Miriam sighed. "I think so."

Miriam paid for everything with the money her mother had given her, then looped the small bag over her wrist. They were almost out the door when she heard her name. She recognized the voice and slowly turned around.

Uncle Ivan eased ahead of Lucy and gazed down at Miriam with soft gray eyes, his lips parted slightly in a smile. His tan trousers were held up with a black belt instead of suspenders. His short-sleeved shirt was bright yellow, not dark brown, blue, or green, like she was used to seeing him wear. He seemed thinner and different in more ways than just his appearance. He seemed to stand taller, almost . . . proud. It was unsettling to see him this way, since pride was to be avoided, and it worsened as Lucy cozied up to his side and looped her arm through his.

She'd been praying for her uncle to see the wrong in his ways and return to the church. But based on this new look, she didn't feel hopeful.

Lucy's hair was so blond that it was almost white, and her wavy locks rested on her shoulders. She wore blue jeans that hugged her body in a way that made the pants look much too small, and her tight white blouse was cut low on her chest, so low that Miriam felt uncomfortable. Her pink lipstick matched the beaded belt around her waist.

"Wie bischt, mei maedel?" At the sound of his voice, memories filled Miriam's mind, but her heart beat with regret over Uncle Ivan's choices. Lucy scowled, as if maybe she didn't like him speaking their native dialect.

"I'm *gut, Onkel* Ivan." Miriam fought the tremble in her voice as she glanced at Lucy. "Hello, Lucy."

They'd all known the *Englisch* woman for years. Lucy's mouth turned up at one corner. "Hello, Miriam. Who is your friend?"

Miriam looked at Shelby, whose arms were folded across her chest, her chin lifted higher than usual. Her cousin spoke before Miriam had a chance to. "I'm Shelby," she said as she eyed Lucy with a critical squint. She looked back at Miriam. "We're late. Don't we need to go?"

"Uh, *ya.* We do."

Whatever pride Miriam thought she saw moments before seemed to fade from her uncle's expression. His eyelids drooped, and his shoulders slumped somewhat. He rubbed his shaven chin, and Miriam wondered if he was thinking about the times they'd spent together, regretting that he could no longer be a part of her life. *Onkel* Ivan was the first person to take her fishing when she was young, and they'd continued going as often as they could up until he left for Colorado. She'd missed those times together since he'd been back in Paradise. He locked eyes with her, and Miriam didn't look away. *Come back to us*, Onkel *Ivan*.

"Take care, *mei maedel*."

Miriam gave a quick nod, then turned away. She could hear Shelby's boots clicking behind her as they moved through the door and to the parking lot. Miriam didn't look back. She was sure Ivan and Lucy wouldn't be there anyway, but she didn't want Shelby to see her crying.

6

SHELBY HAD JUST FINISHED SETTING THE TABLE WHEN the first guests pulled into the driveway. Today she'd learned to make stromboli. One thing she had to admit, the food here was always great. Rebecca and Miriam were both good cooks, and Shelby thought she'd gained a pound or two over the past week. Though she enjoyed helping with supper, she still couldn't seem to get out of bed early enough to help with breakfast.

"So they each pay fifteen dollars for the meal?" Shelby carried a loaf of buttered bread to the table and placed it between a jar of rhubarb jam and a bowl of chow chow. She loved the sweet rhubarb jam, but she wasn't fond of the pickled vegetables they called chow chow.

"*Ya,*" Rebecca answered as she scurried past Miriam, toting a bowl of paprika potatoes.

Miriam placed the stromboli on the table next to a chicken casserole. There was also a bowl of creamed celery on the table, a plate of saucy meatballs, and something Miriam referred to as "shipwreck"—a casserole layered with potatoes, onion, ground beef, rice, celery, kidney beans, and tomatoes. It seemed an odd combination of offerings to Shelby, but her cousin had said that non-Amish folks expected to be served a variety of Amish dishes. And Rebecca had said these recipes were handed down from her mother. Even though Miriam told Shelby that pride was avoided in their community, Shelby could tell that Rebecca was proud of her cooking.

A spread of desserts beckoned from the counter: shoofly pie, whoopee pies, glazed apple cookies, and some molasses sugar cookies. Rebecca had been baking most of the day. Shelby wondered if it was worth it and quickly calculated fifteen times eight. She decided it probably was.

She heard footsteps coming up the porch steps.

"Don't forget. As soon as the meal is over, show them to the den." Rebecca gave instructions to Miriam as she pointed around the corner to the family room. Jams and jellies decorated with quilted doilies covered a long table against the far wall of the den. Shelby also noticed handwritten cookbooks, quilted pot holders, and individually wrapped whoopee pies.

"The *Englisch* love all that," Miriam said to Shelby before she turned to her mother. "I will, *Mamm*."

Rebecca crossed through the den and opened the door for the first of their guests. Shelby stayed in the kitchen with Miriam. She liked the way the kitchen was large enough for the long wooden table, unlike most homes she'd been in that had a separate dining room for such a large crowd. Their kitchen was the largest room in the house, much bigger than the family room, or den, as Rebecca called it. Shelby counted fifteen place settings. Each white china plate had a smaller white plate on top of it, a cloth napkin and silverware, and a glass already filled with ice water.

"Welcome to our home," Shelby heard Rebecca say as she ushered the first two dinner guests to the kitchen. "This is my daughter,

Miriam, and our cousin, Shelby." *Mamm* paused as she turned to the older couple. "And, girls . . . this is Frank and Yvonne."

"Nice to meet you," Shelby said in unison with Miriam.

Rebecca excused herself when there was another knock at the door, and she returned with the other six dinner guests—two couples who looked to be in their thirties, and two older women who appeared to be together. Rebecca made introductions, then asked everyone to have a seat.

Shelby wasn't sure what to do next, so she eased closer to Miriam and whispered, "What now?"

"*Daed* and the boys should be washing up outside at the water pump, then when they're seated, we'll sit down."

Shelby nodded as she checked out their company. One of the younger couples began to sit down. Both were well dressed, the woman in a peach-colored skirt and matching blouse that looked more appropriate for church, and the man in black slacks, a starched white shirt, and a black and white tie with tiny red dots. Her eyes drifted to the younger couple already seated. Both wore blue jeans and matching red T-shirts that said *Amish Dutch Country* on the back with a picture of a horse and buggy. The man had been introduced as Bruce, and his dark hair was pulled back in a ponytail that hung a few inches down his back. His arms were folded across his chest as he eyed the offerings in front of him. Frank and Yvonne took their seats, as did the two older women who'd arrived together.

Shelby stepped aside when Miriam brushed past her carrying another plate of buttered bread, and a few moments later Aaron and the three boys joined them.

"If we could please all bow our heads for silent prayer," Rebecca said after everyone was seated.

Shelby bowed her head, but she didn't close her eyes and instead glanced around the table. Bruce didn't bow his head or close his eyes, and when his eyes locked with Shelby's, a chill ran up her spine. She was relieved when his wife raised her head and began talking to him, pulling the man's dark, icy eyes away.

Rebecca identified the various dishes for their guests, then started passing bowls and platters to her left. "And please try some rhubarb jam on your bread if you'd like," she said, smiling.

"This looks delicious, Rebecca." Yvonne smiled as she passed the creamed celery to her husband.

Her sentiments were echoed throughout the group. All except for Bruce. There was something unsettling about him, and Shelby's eyes kept veering in his direction. Bruce's wife whispered to him several times, but she also commented to Rebecca about how good everything tasted.

"Why aren't you dressed like them?"

Shelby almost lost her grip on the bowl of potatoes at the sound of Bruce's gruff voice. "I'm not Amish. I'm their cousin, just visiting."

He narrowed bushy brows as one corner of his mouth twitched. His wife elbowed him to accept the plate of bread that she was holding, and he looked away. She was relieved when the two elderly women took over the conversation and began asking lots of questions about Amish life.

"I read somewhere that Amish children only attend school through the eighth grade. Is that true?" The gray-headed woman named Mary smiled as she posed the question to Rebecca.

Rebecca swallowed and took a moment before she answered. "*Ya.* It's true. We feel like that is enough education to prepare our young people for the type of work that we do."

Mary nodded, then spoke directly to Miriam. "Honey, are you in your *rumschpringe?*"

Even though the woman seemed pleased with her use of the Pennsylvania *Deitsch* dialect, Shelby recognized the fact that she mispronounced the word. But Miriam just smiled and said, "Yes, ma'am. I'm eighteen, and at sixteen, we are given the freedom to explore the *Englisch* world so that when we choose to stay here, it's not because we don't know what life outside of our community is like."

Bruce's throaty chuckle reeked of cynicism before he said, "Surely you all get out of here as soon as you can." He glanced around the room. "I mean, really. Who'd choose this life if they had a choice?"

His wife, a woman with shoulder-length blond hair, lowered her head, but Shelby saw her cheeks redden.

"I think I'd enjoy this life," the woman in the peach-colored outfit said. "It's so peaceful and without the distractions of our life—cell phones, tight schedules, and . . ." She paused and sat taller. "And the Amish have a strong faith in our Lord."

"Whatever," Bruce mumbled as he reached across his wife and scooped a large spoonful of chicken casserole from the dish. Rebecca shifted her weight in her chair and glanced at her husband. Shelby saw Aaron nod at her, as if they were having a secret conversation . . . one that perhaps they'd had before.

"Boys, finish up. You still have chores to finish." Aaron spoke with authority to Elam, Ben, and John, who all nodded and began to eat faster. A few minutes later all three boys excused themselves and headed outside.

"Uh, excuse me . . ." Bruce's wife glanced over Rebecca's shoulder toward the den. "Is the bathroom that way?"

Rebecca pushed herself away from the table. "*Ya.* Of course. Follow me."

"Nah, don't get up. I'll find it." The woman hurriedly stood up, lifted one leg over the bench, then the other, and was heading across the den before Rebecca could argue.

Mary cleared her throat. "You have a lovely home, Rebecca. Thank you for having us for supper." She smiled. "And this food is *wunderbaar gut.*" She nudged her friend, again proud of her use of the dialect.

"*Danki,*" Rebecca said as she glanced at Miriam, who lowered her eyes and grinned. Shelby would remember to ask both of them what was so amusing, even though Mary didn't seem to notice.

When the main meal was over, Shelby and Miriam helped Rebecca clear the table, then they placed the desserts in the middle. They supplied fresh plates for everyone and served hot coffee. Shelby noticed that Rhoda—Bruce's wife—wasn't back from the bathroom.

"Do you think your wife is all right?" Shelby avoided the man's eyes and glanced into the den.

"She's fine." He didn't look up but instead helped himself to a generous supply of each dessert offered.

It was at least another five minutes before Rhoda returned, and she slipped in beside her husband. "You got enough there on your plate, Bruce?"

"For fifteen dollars, I'm having everything they put out." He scowled at his wife.

"Everything is wonderful, Rebecca," Mary said as she daintily picked at a piece of shoofly pie.

"*Danki,*" Rebecca answered again, smiling. "I'd like to invite you all into the den to look at our homemade jams and jellies. We also have cookbooks that include the recipes for everything you have eaten here tonight. And there are some other things that might interest you." Rebecca motioned toward the table in the den.

"Don't even think about buying any of that junk," Bruce said to Rhoda, his forehead creasing as he spoke. Shelby watched Aaron take a slow, deep breath, but he didn't say anything. Miriam lowered her eyes but stood by her mother as everyone but Bruce and Rhoda walked into the den.

Aaron stayed at the table with Bruce and Rhoda while Bruce loaded up on another round of desserts. Everyone else was gathering up jams, jellies, cookbooks, and quilted pot holders in the other room.

"Thanks for dinner," Rhoda said a few minutes later as she and Bruce made their way across the den and toward the front door.

Rebecca quickly joined them, smiling. "Thank you for being a guest in our home."

"Yeah," Bruce said as he opened the door. "Come on, Rhoda."

Rhoda gave Rebecca a weak smile and followed her husband.

After Bruce and Rhoda were out the door, Shelby whispered to Miriam, "I'm glad they're gone."

Aaron followed the couple out the door, and it wasn't until tires met with the gravel road that Aaron came back in the house. He excused himself and thanked everyone for coming, then headed to the barn.

"I'm glad too," Miriam finally said.

Once everyone had paid for their goods, they thanked Rebecca and headed to their cars. Rebecca dropped onto the couch the minute everyone was gone. She put her head in her hands, and Miriam sat down beside her mother. "What's wrong, *Mamm*?"

Her mother didn't look up but pointed to the oak china cabinet on the far wall, next to the table of jams, jellies, and such. Miriam stood up and walked toward the cabinet, then hung her head for a moment. "It's okay, *Mamm*. We'll get another one."

"What?" Shelby walked to where Miriam was standing. "What's wrong?"

"*Mamm's* silver letter opener is gone."

"Someone stole it?" Shelby was sure who the culprit was. "Was it worth a lot?"

Rebecca pulled her hands away from her face, then joined Miriam and Shelby by the china cabinet. She let out a heavy sigh. "No. It was only silver-plated, but it was a gift from my grandmother years ago. It was inscribed to me, from her. It said, 'May all your letters be received with an abundance of love.'"

"Well, clearly that Rhoda woman took it when she went to the bathroom." Shelby shook her head, then looked up at Rebecca. "Is anything else missing?"

Rebecca glanced around the den. "No." She bit her bottom lip. "But the woman had to go down the hall to get to the bathroom, and she was gone a long time." She started down the hallway, Miriam and Shelby following. All the bedrooms were upstairs. The downstairs consisted of the large kitchen, a nice-sized den, a mudroom, and a hallway to the bathroom with a closed door on each side. Shelby knew that one room housed a pedal sewing machine and quilting supplies, but she'd never been in the other room.

"There's nothing missing in here," Rebecca said after she scanned the sewing room. Then she went to the door on the other side and pushed it open. "Oh no."

"What?" Shelby slid into the room with Miriam. "Rebecca, what is it?"

Rebecca walked to the middle of the room. There were racks and racks of jams, jellies, cookbooks, quilted pot holders, and other items marked with white price tags. "I left the cash box on the shelf." She walked to a cigar box and lifted the lid, then slowly closed it.

"How much did they take, *Mamm*?"

Rebecca turned around, tears in her eyes. "Your *daed* told me I needed to get the money to the bank last week after the Mud Sale, but I just didn't have time."

Miriam put a hand on her mother's shoulder. "How much, *Mamm*?"

Rebecca leaned her head back against her neck and closed her eyes. "A little over two thousand dollars."

"We need to call the police. I'll do it from the barn because my cell's dead." Shelby turned to leave the room.

"No, Shelby." Rebecca's voice shook, but the tone was firm. "We have no proof, and it's God's will. Perhaps whoever took the money needs it more than us."

"You're kidding me, right?" Shelby glanced at Miriam, recalling how her cousin said she overused the phrase, but in this case, she couldn't believe what she was hearing. "God's will? Are you saying that it's God's will for you to be robbed by people in your own home? People you served dinner to. You need to call the bed-and-breakfast where they are staying, let the owner know, then call the police."

Rebecca just shook her head, but she finally said, "I will call Barbie Beiler because she needs to know that someone in that group took things from our home. She needs to know that since those folks are guests at her place."

"*Mamm*, the only one who went this way was Rhoda. Where would she have put the letter opener? The cash she could put in her blue jean pockets, but not the letter opener." Miriam turned to Shelby. "The letter opener was long, maybe seven or eight inches long."

"In her sock," Shelby answered without hesitation, ashamed that she knew where the woman would conceal something she'd stolen. "She had on tennis shoes . . . and socks. She probably put it in her sock." Shelby's past flashed before her—a trip to the police station, a stolen necklace. She took a deep breath as she recalled how easy it was to steal the silver chain from the rack at the department store. Or so she'd thought. That's how it is when you're high—a false reality. Shelby was forced to watch the security tape later when she wasn't under any influence, and she'd cried hard, begging her parents for forgiveness. The department store went easy on her, but forgiveness never came from her parents.

Who was I back then? She wondered if she would be released from the guilt she felt about her shoplifting, especially now as she watched Rebecca close the door and dab at her eyes.

Shelby followed Miriam and Rebecca to the kitchen.

"I still think we need to call the police."

Rebecca walked to the table and began clearing the dessert plates. "No, Shelby. I will call Barbie from the phone in the barn, but not the police."

Shelby put her hands on her hips. "Rebecca, this just isn't right. We know who took that money, and this isn't God's will."

Maybe it was the way she said "God's will," but Rebecca's

expression turned sour quickly. "Everything that happens is God's will." She lifted her chin and sniffled. "I'd like no further talk of this."

Shelby glanced at Miriam, then sighed. "Okay." She walked to the sink and started placing the dishes in soapy water. "I'm sorry, Rebecca. I didn't mean to upset you."

Rebecca grabbed a towel and accepted a washed plate from Shelby. "You didn't upset me, Shelby. It upsets me that folks would come into our home and do this, but instead of calling the police, we handle things a bit different. We will pray for them every day and hope that they will find their way to God, and we'll ask God to forgive them for this."

Shelby momentarily wondered if anyone had prayed for her when she was making bad choices.

"I'm *not* praying for them." The words slipped out, and it was too late for Shelby to take them back. She glanced at Rebecca, then at Miriam. "I'm sorry. I just can't."

By Saturday afternoon Miriam couldn't stop thinking about her date with Saul.

"You never did tell me why you and your mother were grinning last night when that woman said *wunderbaar gut.*" Shelby ran the sweeper across the wooden floors in their bedroom.

"Because Amish folks don't really say that." She laughed. "Unless we're being funny, or making fun of the *Englisch* for saying it. The *Englisch* seem to think we say that all the time, but we don't."

Shelby just nodded, then she leaned the sweeper up against the wall. "Are you excited about your date?"

Miriam's insides warmed. "*Ya.* I am."

"What date?"

Miriam spun around at the sound of her mother's voice. "Uh . . . I meant to tell you . . . I have a date with Saul tonight. We're going to eat after I run my weekly errands in town." She held her breath when she saw the pained look on her mother's face, a squinting of her eyes as she pressed her lips together.

"Miriam, Shelby has just been here a week, and I don't think you should be off on a date when your cousin is—"

"It's okay, Rebecca." Shelby plopped down on her bed. "I'm fine. Really."

Miriam smiled at Shelby, then turned back to her mother. "See?" She raised her brows and waited.

Mamm shook her head. "Not tonight, Miriam. I need to wait another week or so before you make the weekly run to town, until I have—have more money." She held up a finger the way she was known to do when Miriam opened her mouth to argue. "And there might be a storm coming later. It's best you stay home tonight."

Miriam felt her heart sink to the pit of her stomach. "But, *Mamm* . . . I already told Saul that I would meet him in town. I don't have any way to tell him I can't be there."

"I'm sure the Fishers have a phone in their barn like everyone else." *Mamm* slapped her hands to her sides. "Please, *mei maedel*, don't argue with me. This is just not a *gut* night for you to be going out."

Miriam took a deep breath, then let it out slowly. She didn't say anything but nodded.

When she heard her mother's footsteps going down the stairs, she turned to Shelby. "That is not fair."

"Maybe your mom just can't accept that you are plenty old

enough to date." Shelby leaned back on her elbows. "I remember when I went on my first date when I was sixteen. I thought my dad was going to have a heart attack about it."

Miriam sat down on her own bed and faced Shelby. "She doesn't think Saul is right for me. I'm sure that's it." She leaned back on her palms. "She just doesn't know him very well. He's quiet around most people, and . . . he's been in a little trouble before. Nothing serious. But I think *Mamm* thinks he just isn't the right person for me." She sat up again. "But that is not her choice."

"Maybe your parents are worried that Saul will leave and that you will get your heart broken, or worse yet . . . that you'll leave with him."

Miriam shook her head. "Saul isn't leaving. Those are just gossipy rumors."

"I hope so, for your sake." Shelby rolled onto her side, then propped herself up on one elbow. "So are you going to go call Saul?"

Miriam thought for a few moments before she answered. *"Ya."*

"It's a shame you have to cancel, but maybe you can reschedule for another time."

"Ach, I'm not canceling." She grinned at Shelby. "I'm just going to tell him that I will meet him at nine thirty. After my parents are asleep." She tucked a loose strand of hair beneath her *kapp.* "This is *Saul Fisher.* I have been waiting for this night my entire life. I am not going to miss it."

7

SAUL LISTENED TO MIRIAM'S MESSAGE TWICE, JUST TO make sure he'd heard her correctly. He didn't understand why she wanted to meet so late at night, but that might be better anyway. He could make sure *Daed* was sound asleep by the time he left, and he wouldn't have to worry about there being trouble while he was gone. After his father's outburst a few days before, the rest of the week had gone fine. No drinking. And as Saul had suspected, his father never brought that night up. He merely went to the fields earlier on that day, and he stayed out working later . . . well past the supper hour. Saul wondered what time his father would come in tonight.

Saul had prayed extra hard every night that his father would stop drinking, and every night he would read his employment offer and ask God if he was doing the right thing by leaving his family and friends, particularly about leaving his brothers. He thought about the speedy response he'd sent to the owner of the bistro, and the way his hand had shook as he wrote the letter.

He pulled the lever on the water pump until the cool water splashed at his feet, then he ran his hands underneath. He caught a glimpse of his brothers as they walked toward the barn. James would collect eggs from the hens while Ruben brushed down the horses. Saul knew they were both going to be fine. They were strong and levelheaded. *They have to be fine.*

He strolled into the house, tired from a hard day's work in the fields but excited about his date with Miriam. Just the thought of holding her hand or putting his arm around her at the movies gave him a burst of energy he wouldn't normally have this time of day. When Saul walked into the den, his father was pulling off his work boots.

"It was a hot one today, no?" *Daed* dropped into his chair by the window, then fumbled for his glasses on the table next to him. Once he had the gold-rimmed glasses situated on his nose, he reached for *The Budget.*

Saul pulled off his own shoes, hung his hat on the rack, then let his suspenders drop to his sides. He sat down on the couch across from his father, one of the best men he'd ever known in his life. *Daed* was strong in his faith, and he went out of his way to help others. He just had this one problem. Saul leaned back against the couch, wishing he had the courage to tell his father about his plans in Pittsburgh. Since Saul hadn't been baptized yet and wouldn't face a shunning, maybe *Daed* would bless Saul's choices. He didn't realize he was staring until his father looked over the top of the newspaper at him.

"Something on your mind?" *Daed* pushed his reading glasses down on his nose.

If you only knew. Saul shook his head. "No, not really." His father seemed to be waiting for more. "I'll be going out later. I'm taking Miriam Raber for a late supper."

His father nodded as he pushed his glasses up and returned his eyes to the paper. "*Gut* folks, the Rabers." He lowered the newspaper. "Think she might be the one you'll settle with?"

Guilt tugged at Saul's heart as he shifted his weight. "I dunno." He leaned his head back against the couch and stared at the ceiling. He should never have set this date with Miriam.

But being with her was all he could think about.

Miriam closed the bedroom door behind her, then whipped the towel from her head. She leaned down and began to dry her hair in front of the small fan on the nightstand.

"What's that smell?" Shelby closed her pink book, locked it, then dropped the key in her purse like she always did, and Miriam wondered if she was writing about happier thoughts.

"It's vanilla lotion." Miriam held her arm up for Shelby to sniff. "I bought it at the market a few weeks ago."

"You smell like a candle." Shelby reached into her purse. "Here, try this. It's perfume, and you'll smell much better to Saul wearing this."

Miriam reached for the glass bottle. "Thank you, Shelby."

Shelby sat up and crossed her legs beneath her. "Miriam, sneaking out like this will only get you in trouble down the line, in one way or another." She shook her head. "Trust me. I know. Plus . . . don't you think your parents will hear you sneaking out? Those steps creak. . . . Then you'll have to hitch up the horse. They'll hear you leaving." She tapped a finger to her chin. "Do the Amish ground their kids? Because if so, I can already see you getting grounded for a long time."

"*Ya*, we get punished. But no worries. I have everything covered." Miriam knew her hair would never be completely dry by the time she needed to leave, so she wound it atop her head, then secured her prayer covering. She turned to Shelby. "Have you seen that huge fan in *Mamm* and *Daed's* room? It's run by the generator, and that thing is so loud that *Mamm* and *Daed* don't hear anything outside of their bedroom. They'll never hear the steps creak, and they won't hear me leaving."

"This has trouble written all over it, Miriam. I don't think you should go."

Miriam folded her arms across her chest. "Why? I'm not going to get caught. And I'm not exactly lying either."

Shelby twisted her mouth from side to side for a moment, then she sat up and dropped her legs over the side of the bed. She leaned closer. "Miriam, I kinda got in some trouble back home."

Miriam knew this, but she'd never known what kind of trouble. She eased her hands into her lap and folded them together. "What kind of trouble?"

Shelby took a deep breath, then blew it out slowly. "After my parents' divorce, and after Tommy broke up with me, I was sneaking out . . . and doing some things I shouldn't have done."

Miriam waited a moment to see if Shelby was going to share any details, but she didn't. "Saul is a wonderful person. My parents just don't know him, and they're judging him . . . My mother is, anyway. And *Mamm* knows that only God can judge."

Shelby let out a heavy sigh. "Maybe, Miriam. But I was running around with some people that my parents didn't like, and they ended up dragging me into a bunch of stuff that wasn't good for me."

"Have you heard from your parents?" Miriam wanted to change the subject.

Shelby frowned. "Your mom said my mom left a message on the

phone in the barn day before yesterday, saying that she couldn't get hold of me on my cell." Shelby rolled her eyes. "Duh. My cell phone has been dead, and Mom should know that." She raised one shoulder, then dropped it slowly as she spoke. "Whatever. Obviously, my mother wasn't in that big of a hurry to check on me."

Miriam didn't understand much about divorce, but she could tell that Shelby was bitter, and she hoped that her cousin would reach out to God for comfort. She wasn't sure what to say.

"I'm mad at my parents for getting a divorce, for ruining my life. But if they did anything right, it was pulling me away from the kids I was running around with before they shipped me here." Shelby turned away from Miriam and looked at the wall. "I wasn't exactly thrilled to come here." She turned to Miriam. "I'm sorry. It's just that everything is so different. I don't really know anyone. And I figured it would be like this. But . . . I do have to say . . . I was running around with a pretty rough crowd, and I was sneaking out all the time. Looking back, I should have made smarter choices, even if things were really bad at home."

"Saul is a *gut* man. The best. When *Mamm* and *Daed* get to know him, they'll see that."

"I hope you're right. But I'm going to get my two cents in, and I don't think you should be sneaking out at nine o'clock at night to go meet someone. It's not safe."

"Around here it is."

"How can you say that? Just yesterday a woman stole from your home." Shelby shook her head. "The world is not a safe place, Miriam. And your people aren't exempt just because they are Amish and live in the country." She paused. "And your mom said there might be a storm. Please don't go."

Miriam was touched by Shelby's concern. "I feel like we're sisters right now." She smiled. "But no worries. It's not like this is the first time I've snuck out of my house."

Shelby stiffened. "Huh?"

Miriam giggled. "I'm eighteen, Shelby. I've been in my *rumschpringe* for two years."

"But this is your first date?" Shelby's voice rose an octave as she spoke.

Miriam shrugged as she smiled. "That's just because I've been waiting for Saul. But I've snuck out to meet Leah and Hannah before."

"What in the world for?"

Miriam wasn't proud of her actions, but she wanted Shelby to stop worrying so much. "There was a country gospel band playing at a restaurant in Lancaster. That rarely happens, and we wanted to go. We all felt like our parents would forbid it because it was on a Thursday night and the music didn't start until ten o'clock." She shrugged again. "So we snuck out, met on Lincoln Highway, then walked to town and called a taxi cab."

"Did you get caught?"

"No." Miriam looked down for a moment. "I felt kinda bad about it, though."

"Trust me. You'll probably feel bad about this too, but I can see that you're determined to go." Shelby leaned over the side of the bed and reached into her purse. "Here." She pushed her cell phone and cord toward Miriam. "Plug it in somewhere when you get to the restaurant. Even thirty minutes will give you a little bit of a charge, and at least you'll have it on your way home, just in case you get into any trouble. I'm going to write in my journal some more for a while. I'll leave the window open so maybe I can hear the phone ringing in the barn if you need to call for something."

Miriam latched onto the phone, then took a deep breath. She had on her best green dress and black apron, and she smelled like orchids. Tonight was going to be the best night of her life.

It was nine o'clock when Shelby watched Miriam from the window. Her cousin seemed to be right. It appeared she was going to make a clean getaway. She waited until she saw Miriam maneuver the buggy onto the street before she climbed into bed. As she kicked back the quilt and tucked herself beneath the sheet, she felt an overwhelming urge. She leaned back against her pillow, then closed her eyes.

God, are You there?

She waited, not expecting an answer but not sure whether to go on.

I was wondering if maybe You could keep an eye on my cousin tonight. She's rather naive, and I don't want to see her get into any trouble. I think Saul is probably a good person, but sneaking around is never a good thing and can lead to other trouble. I should know.

Shelby opened her eyes and stared upward at the twinkling lights from the lantern, the smell of perfume still lingering in the air. She closed her eyes again.

I wish I knew why I'm being punished.

She paused.

Never mind. I know why. For the bad stuff I did. When will my penance be over? When will I feel happy again? Please, Lord. Please . . .

As she figured, no guidance came drifting into her mind, and her glimmer of hope was quickly replaced by anger. When she thought about the fellowship she used to feel when she went to church with her parents and the one-on-one connection with God she once had, her bitterness only escalated. Her parents had ruined her life in every way. Not only did they stop loving each other, but they'd stopped going to church. Shelby knew she was a grown woman, and she certainly could have gone to church on her own, but what was the point? God didn't care what happened to her, and all those years of praying and trying to live the right way hadn't served her well.

She recalled all the times she disobeyed her parents during the divorce, and she knew that drugs and alcohol hadn't served her well either, but God must still be punishing her for her bad choices. Otherwise He'd help her find some kind of peace in her heart. Especially at night, loneliness seemed to overtake her as recollections of better times haunted her. She reached for her journal, unlocked it, and then stared at the page. For the first time in a long while, she didn't have anything to write. She'd already voiced her thoughts . . . to God.

And He clearly wasn't hearing her.

Rebecca tossed and turned, just like she had the night before. She fought the anger building inside her about what happened yesterday. How could a guest in their home steal from them like that? She thought about the time and effort that had gone into making the quilts, and they were going to feel the loss of income for the next couple of months.

She rolled onto her side, tried to ignore Aaron's snoring, and then asked God to free her heart of anger . . . and worry. And as wrong as it was, she worried about Miriam's interest in Saul. She didn't know the boy well, but what she did know was that he'd been in trouble several times, even reprimanded by the bishop. But most troubling were the rumors that he might not get baptized and would leave the community. If that was true, where did that leave Miriam if she and Saul grew close? Miriam was eighteen, but in so many ways she was still a child, and Rebecca feared Miriam wouldn't be able to cope with a broken heart.

After another fifteen minutes of thrashing around because of her frustrating thoughts, she pushed back the sheet, reached for the lantern, then eased out of bed. Quietly she fumbled in the bedside drawer for a match. As she headed downstairs, the aroma of chocolate chip cookies still lingered in the air, and she smiled as she thought about John eating six of the warm treats earlier, straight from the oven. Her youngest boy had a sweet tooth for sure.

Rebecca poured herself a glass of milk, then peeled back the foil covering the cookies. She put the lantern on the counter and savored the moist cookie in her mouth, thinking that she could probably eat six cookies too, if she allowed herself. She rinsed it down with her milk, then slowly made her way back upstairs, hoping sleep would come soon and thankful she could sleep in a bit tomorrow since there was no church service.

Shelby would be glad she could sleep in. Poor girl just couldn't seem to get up in the morning. As she passed by the girls' room, she paused, then slowly turned the doorknob. Before she pushed the door wide, she lowered the flame on the lantern so as not to wake them. She smiled at Shelby, her head buried beneath the covers, wondering how she could sleep like that when it was so warm. Then she held the light a little higher toward the far bed, but Miriam was nowhere to be seen. Her heart thudded in her chest.

She stepped out of the bedroom and padded down the hallway to the bathroom. After shining the light into the small, empty room, she hurried back to the girls' bedroom. Gently she pulled the covers from Shelby's head and whispered, "Shelby, wake up, dear."

After a groan, Shelby cupped a hand above her eyes to block the light. "What is it, Rebecca?"

"Where's Miriam?"

Shelby bolted upright in the bed and cleared tangles from her face. "Huh?"

Rebecca's heart rate picked up. "Shelby, where is she?" She turned the flame up on the lantern. "Is she outside? Maybe on the porch? Did she go to the barn for some reason? Maybe she couldn't sleep." Rebecca walked to the window, but there wasn't a light coming from the barn. She spun around and edged closer to Shelby. "Did she tell you where she was going?"

Shelby rubbed sleep from her eyes, then blinked several times. "She isn't here right now."

Rebecca held the lantern higher and thrust her other hand on her hip. "I can see that. Where is she?"

"I'm not sure exactly."

"Shelby . . ." Rebecca took a deep breath, afraid her anger was going to boil over.

For nearly two hours, Miriam and Saul sat at Yoder's Pantry after they'd decided it was too late to go to a movie. It took awhile for Saul to seem comfortable, but once he started talking, Miriam hung on his every word. He loved to talk about cooking and recipes, especially about cooking for his family. Miriam could tell that it was Saul's way of loving and nurturing them, and it endeared him to her even more. Her Saul had an independent spirit, something she loved, and he was kindhearted.

As much fun as she was having with Saul, Shelby had been right about sneaking out. Guilt kept a steady hold on Miriam. She had to admit that regret about her choice was putting a damper on her time with Saul. She glanced at the clock again. Eleven thirty.

"This has been great," she said to Saul as he finished his second piece of pie, following the full meal they'd had earlier. "But I guess I need to go."

Saul chewed, then quickly swallowed. "*Ya*, this has been fun." He smiled, and momentarily Miriam forgot about everyone else but him. The dreamy way he'd been looking at her all night had caused her heart to flip several times. "And I have some new recipes to try out on *Daed* and the boys."

Miriam took a sip of her coffee, then stifled a yawn. But there was something else weighing on her mind, and even though she knew it was late, the question had been lurking on the tip of her tongue all night. "Saul, I've heard a couple of people say that you might not be baptized come the fall. That's not true, is it?"

Any hint of a dreamy look on Saul's face vanished instantly, and his eyes averted hers. "Where'd you hear that?"

Miriam shrugged, disappointed since that was not the outright denial she'd hoped for. "Just rumors, I guess."

Saul reached for his coffee, spilling a bit over the side before he took a sip. Then he reached for his hat on the seat beside him. "I guess we better get you home before your parents don't let you out of the *haus* again." Miriam could tell his smile was forced and something had changed. Saul stood up and waited for Miriam to do the same.

A few minutes later Saul opened the door of her buggy. "I'm going to follow you home. It's too late for you to be on the road."

Alarms went off in Miriam's head. If she got caught coming home, it would be even worse if Saul was following her. "No, no. You don't have to do that. The storm they predicted just moved around us. I'll be fine going home." Even though she'd forgotten to charge it, she pulled Shelby's cell phone from her apron. "See, I have a phone."

To her surprise, Saul reached for it, then flipped it open. "I thought about getting one of these, but . . ." He stopped mid-sentence as his forehead creased. "The battery is dead. The light doesn't even come on."

"*Ach, ya.* I was supposed to charge it inside somewhere." Miriam hung her head, knowing that she wasn't being completely truthful with anyone tonight.

He handed the phone back to her. "I'm following you home." His tone was firm and protective, and Miriam smiled at him. Her parents never got up during the night, and she'd just be quiet going into the house. They'd never see Saul. She refocused her thoughts on whether or not he would kiss her tonight. He closed the door, then promised to stay right behind her.

Ten minutes later, as she was pulling up her driveway with Saul right behind her, she gasped at the light on in the den downstairs. Maybe Shelby was up. Or one of her brothers, which wouldn't be good. Her brothers would tattle on her.

She slowed the buggy, jumped out as soon as it stopped, then ran to Saul's buggy. "*Danki* for supper. I have to go!" She turned to run toward the house, then he called her name. She turned around, her heart pounding in her chest. "I'm sorry. I have to go." She looked over her shoulder toward the house, then back at Saul.

"Do you want to do something again?"

Miriam wanted to stay in the moment and talk to him more, especially since Saul had clearly avoided her question about being baptized. But the longer she stayed outside talking to Saul, the worse things were going to be when she went inside. "I'll call you from our barn phone tomorrow at"—she thought for a moment, remembering that it was an off-Sunday for church service—"at ten in the morning."

"Okay."

Saul sounded confused, but Miriam ran toward the house, knowing she'd been caught. She waited until Saul rounded the corner before she reached for the screen door, glad that the wooden door was closed. Maybe her parents hadn't seen Saul. She pulled the screen door toward her and was just about to turn the knob on the main door when she heard the sound of car tires on their driveway. She pulled her hand back, turned around, and waited to see who it was. Her stomach knotted inside her at the thought of what faced her on the other side of the door, but she couldn't imagine who would be visiting them at midnight.

She waited. The car wasn't even parked before another car turned into their driveway. Miriam held her hand up to block the headlights from both vehicles. She turned around when she heard the front door open. Her mother stepped onto the front porch, supported by her father, and she was sobbing uncontrollably. They were followed by her brothers, who were also crying. Shelby appeared behind them, and Miriam wasn't sure, but it looked like Shelby had been crying too.

"*Mamm!* What is it?" Miriam clutched her mother's arm when it appeared she might fall. Her father lifted his wife into his arms and held her close as a tear ran down his face. "*Daed*, what's wrong? Someone tell me."

Her mother pulled herself from *Daed's* arms, then stumbled down the porch steps. She fell into her brother Noah's arms. *Mamm's* sister Mary Ellen stepped out of the other car and ran to her mother and Noah. Miriam watched the scene unfolding and began to cry herself. She didn't know what had happened, but it was bad, and it clearly didn't have anything to do with her sneaking out to meet Saul.

8

MIRIAM TRIED TO CALM HER BREATHING AND HER crying as they moved into the house. She couldn't believe it— her Uncle Ivan was dead. She'd just seen him at the market on Friday. Shelby kept her arm around Miriam as they moved into the house. Noah's wife, Carley, was doing her best to comfort Miriam's brothers, but all three boys couldn't stop crying.

It was bad enough that Uncle Ivan was in a car accident that killed him, but their loss felt even worse because he had been shunned recently, banned by his family for his recent choices. No one knew why her uncle was in a car so late at night.

Once Miriam was settled on the couch next to her aunts, Mary Ellen and Carley, Shelby offered to go make everyone some tea, but no one took her up on it. Shelby didn't even know Ivan, had only met him that one time, but yet she cried along with the rest of them.

"The policeman said he went quickly." Noah choked out the words as he ran a hand through his hair. "Never suffered. The other car hit the car Ivan was riding in head-on." Noah paused. "The driver of that car was also killed instantly, but the person who hit them survived. He's at Lancaster General in a coma."

"Oh no." *Mamm* wailed from the rocker across the room. Miriam's father leaned down beside the chair and clutched her hand, then *Mamm* said, "Poor Katie Ann . . . and their baby. Oh no, Aaron. As far as I know, Ivan still didn't know about the baby." *Mamm* dropped her head into her hands and sobbed.

They all knew Katie Ann was pregnant, but her aunt had chosen to keep her pregnancy a secret from Uncle Ivan, fearful he would return to Katie Ann out of obligation. Miriam's family had promised Katie Ann that they wouldn't mention anything to Ivan—at least for a while. Now he would never know, and Miriam wondered if they had done the right thing.

Mamm raised her head and continued, "Someone will have to call Katie Ann." *Mamm* dabbed at her eyes. "And we will need to call Samuel and Lillian."

Miriam tried to make sense of everything as she counted the other Stoltzfus siblings in her head. There was her mother, Samuel, Noah, and Mary Ellen. Everyone lived here in Lancaster County except for her Uncle Samuel, his wife, Lillian, and Ivan's wife, Katie Ann. Miriam missed her aunts and uncles, and she'd hoped to see them soon—but not like this.

"It's late, Rebecca." Her father squeezed *Mamm's* hand. "We'll call them at daylight."

Mamm nodded, and then Miriam's eyes met with her father's. His scowl caused Miriam to look away from him. She felt as low as a serpent slithering on the ground. She wanted to run across the room and comfort her mother, but her father's eyes kept her planted on the couch.

After about an hour, the group began to part ways, following more hugs and tears. Miriam couldn't stop thinking about her uncle, all the times she'd spent with him over the years, and how she'd been praying for him to come back to the church.

Once everyone was gone, Miriam cautiously eased toward her mother. "What would you like for me to do, *Mamm?*"

Her mother dabbed at her eyes, then glared at Miriam. "What would I like for you to do, Miriam?" She paused as her eyes narrowed with anger. "I would like for you not to sneak out of our home to go and meet a boy." She put both hands to her forehead and wept. "I can't talk about this right now." She turned to go up the stairs but turned around. "I don't want you seeing that boy."

"Let's go upstairs, Rebecca." Miriam's father coaxed her up the stairs, leaving the rest of them in the den. Shelby reached for John's hand and offered to take him back up to bed, but Miriam's eight-year-old brother wiped his eyes and said he didn't need her to. Ben and Elam eased past them, and Ben motioned for little John to follow them. Miriam stood in the middle of the den with Shelby, watching her family go upstairs. Then she cupped her face in her hands and cried. She felt Shelby's arms go around her, and she buried her face in her cousin's shoulder and wept.

———

Saul held the piece of plywood against the barn wall and nailed it firmly in place. It wasn't the best repair job, but it would keep things dry until he could fix it permanently. He released the breath he was holding, only to have his nostrils take in a full load of stench. Their mule, Gus, had kicked the siding in her stall yesterday after she got spooked by a skunk, which caused the skunk to spray everything in the stall. Saul pinched his nose and thought about how he was going to get the smell out of the barn—and off of Gus.

He glanced at the phone on *Daed's* workbench and figured it to be close to ten o'clock. Miriam would be calling soon, and thoughts about her had kept him up last night. *Daed* and James were working in the fields, and Ruben went to town for supplies they needed. Saul was glad to be alone with his thoughts this morning.

His father topped the list, and Saul fought to keep the worries from his heart. He knew that everything was the will of God, but he prayed constantly that God would see fit to cure his father of his drinking. It was like living with two different people—the man he admired and loved, and a strange being he didn't recognize when he drank. Once, in a drunken fit, his father had folded onto the floor like a small child and said that *Mamm's* and Hannah's deaths had left his soul without a spirit. It was a strange thing to say, but for some reason it stuck in Saul's mind. His father had never gotten over their deaths. *Daed* tried hard to stay focused for Saul and his brothers, but the alcohol seemed to just intensify his loss and turn him into a crazy man.

Saul fretted about Ruben and James. And his father. If he continued to see Miriam Raber, he'd only be adding her to his list of worries, and all this anxiety would drag a man down.

He picked up some tools that Ruben had left out on the workbench and began putting them in the proper storage bins. Then he glanced at the clock again.

Rebecca looked in the mirror hanging on a small chain in their bedroom. Even though they'd agreed to sleep late this morning, her eyes were puffy and red. She took a deep breath, then finished dressing. The thought of cooking breakfast made her feel sick to her stomach, but everyone had to eat.

"I shouldn't have been so hard on Miriam last night," she said to Aaron when he walked into their bedroom already dressed in a dark-blue shirt and black slacks. Rebecca had chosen a dark-brown dress and black apron to wear to the funeral home.

"Miriam shouldn't have snuck out to see the Fisher boy." Aaron pulled a pair of suspenders from the chest of drawers. "We will talk to Miriam about this after we've made Ivan's arrangements."

Rebecca sat down on the bed and pulled on a pair of black socks. "Ivan was Miriam's *onkel*, though, and I spoke cruelly to her even though I knew she was hurting." She reached for her black shoes and pulled them closer. With one shoe in her hand, she rose up and looked at Aaron. "It wasn't even Miriam's fault, I'm sure."

"What do you mean?"

"Miriam would never disobey us, and Shelby has a history of being disobedient." She leaned down and pulled her shoe on. "I'm sure Shelby convinced her to go against our wishes. Miriam would never do that."

"You don't know that, Rebecca." Aaron raked a hand through his dark hair. "It ain't fair to blame Miriam's choices on Shelby."

Rebecca stood up, but she didn't say anything.

"Shelby seems like a *gut* girl. She tried to help last night when we found out about Ivan, and she shed tears along with the rest of us, even though she didn't know him."

"I'm not sure she should be here, Aaron. I'm not sure she's a *gut* influence on Miriam . . . or the boys. Maybe we shouldn't have agreed to let her stay here for the summer."

Aaron put his hands on Rebecca's shoulders. "I think we have enough to worry about this morning without adding this to the list."

Rebecca leaned her forehead against her husband's chest. "You're right." A tear trickled down her cheek. "I can't believe Ivan's gone."

"I will call Samuel later if you want me to. It will be best if Samuel tells Katie Ann in person, I think. Katie Ann will take the news hard."

She nodded as she pulled back and lifted her eyes to her husband's. "Samuel will take the news of our *bruder's* death hard too."

"*Ya.* I know."

Rebecca dreaded going to the funeral home, but Mr. Roberts handled the Amish funerals in their area, and he would tell them how to proceed. He'd agreed to meet them there on a Sunday. "I guess I better go get breakfast started."

"Breakfast is already cooked and out on the table."

Rebecca put a hand on her chest. "What?"

"Miriam and Shelby were finishing up when I went downstairs earlier."

"They shouldn't have done that." Rebecca hung her head as another tear rolled down her cheek. "Those girls are bound to be tired, and there was no need for them to get up so early to finish before I even got downstairs."

Aaron offered her a comforting smile. "They're *gut* girls, Rebecca. Both of them." He kissed her on the forehead. "Now, come downstairs and eat a little. I know you're going to say you're not hungry, but it's gonna be a long day, and you're going to need your strength."

She nodded, then followed Aaron down the stairs toward the scent of frying bacon.

Ben, Elam, and John were already sitting at the table when Rebecca and Aaron walked into the room, and Miriam and Shelby were scurrying around the kitchen.

"*Danki,* girls, for making breakfast." Rebecca attempted a smile and knew she should apologize to Miriam for the way she'd spoken to her the night before, but Miriam *had* snuck out of the house . . . Fear of her only daughter taking up with Saul Fisher kept her silent.

"Here, Rebecca, sit down." Shelby pulled out Rebecca's chair for her, and although it was a sweet gesture, Rebecca knew that from now on, she wouldn't be able to let her guard down around the girl.

Miriam placed a cup of coffee in front of Rebecca. Her daughter's eyes were swollen and red also. She wanted to stand up, pull Miriam into her arms, and not only tell her that she was sorry for her harsh words the night before, but also vow to protect her from anything and anyone who threatened harm to her way of life. *"Danki,"* she said softly instead.

By the time eleven o'clock rolled around, Saul was sure that Miriam had changed her mind about wanting to spend time with him since she never called. Just as well. He had plenty to do around here and enough to worry about. But he couldn't deny that not hearing from her disappointed him. He squirted vinegar water on the inside of Gus's stall, hoping to rid the area of some of the smell.

"You still ain't got that skunk smell out of here?" Ruben walked into the barn carrying a plastic bag, his nose crinkling the closer he got to Saul. "Here's the plumbing parts you asked me to get in town, to fix the commode."

Saul took the bag and peeked inside. *"Danki."* He handed the bag back to Ruben. "I think you can handle fixing the toilet." He grinned. "Unless you wanna stay out here and try to get rid of the skunk smell."

Ruben snatched the bag from him. "I think I'll take care of the toilet. Have fun out here." His brother shuffled across the hay-covered floor and was almost out the door when he turned around. "Hey, did ya hear what happened last night? About the car accident?"

"No. What?"

"Ivan Stoltzfus was killed. He was ridin' in a car with another fella and was hit head-on by a truck last night around ten thirty."

Saul walked to his brother. "Are you sure?"

"*Ach, ya*, I'm sure." Ruben lifted his chin as he went on. "I heard some folks in town talkin' about it."

"That's Miriam's *onkel*," Saul hung his head and whispered, mostly to himself.

"Ain't he the one who was shunned and living with the *Englisch* woman?"

Saul looked up at Ruben. "*Ya*. He was living with Lucy Turner." He rubbed his chin as he grew concerned for Miriam and her family. "Did anyone say when the funeral is?"

"I don't think they know yet."

"All right." He waved his hand. "Get on to fixin' that toilet."

Saul was going to get cleaned up. Then he was going to go find Miriam and see if there was anything he could do for her or her family.

Shelby chose not to go to the funeral home. She felt out of place, and Rebecca had seemed relieved that she wasn't going. So much had happened in the short time she'd been here that Shelby was grateful to have some quiet time. She couldn't stop crying last night or this morning when she saw everyone else crying. So much sadness. But this morning she was reevaluating her life. Perhaps death did that—made you rethink things.

She was pondering as she sat in the swing on the front porch. When the phone started ringing in the barn, she darted down the steps, swung the door wide, and reached the phone right before the answering machine picked up. "Hello."

"You sound out of breath."

Shelby sighed. "Hi, Mom."

"Did Rebecca tell you I called the other day? I tried you on your cell phone, but it was dead."

"They don't have electricity, Mother." Shelby rolled her eyes.

"Shelby, I miss you, and I was just wondering if you were enjoying your time there. I know you aren't happy with your father and me for making this decision, but—"

"Don't refer to you and Dad like you're a couple making decisions together. You're not a couple. You're divorced."

Silence for a moment. "Shelby, when it comes to you, we are working together to make the best decisions. You were not making good choices on your own."

"I don't need you to remind me, Mom. I know this. But sending me out here to the boonies isn't going to help." Shelby knew she was lying. It *was* helping for her to be away from everyone and everything in her past, and slowly she was getting to know her cousins. "Oh, and someone died last night. Rebecca's brother."

"Oh no. That's terrible. I should send something. A basket or something."

"I'm sure that will help a lot." Shelby figured her mother could detect the heavy sarcasm, but just to be sure, she also grunted as she shook her head. "Seriously, Mom . . . they are all about family around here. I'm sure they will be just fine without one of your *baskets.*"

"It's the thought, Shelby, at a time like this."

She carried the cordless phone to the window in the barn when she heard the *clippety-clop* of hooves coming up the driveway. "I have to go, Mom. Someone is here, and I'm the only one home."

"Shelby, please call me back. I'm worried about you, and whether you believe it or not, your father and I love you, and even if we aren't together, we still—"

"I have to go, Mom. I'll call you later."

Shelby hung up, then left the barn. She walked toward the man tethering his horse, then saw it was Saul.

"Hi, Saul." She walked toward him and they met in the grass halfway between the barn and the house.

"How is everyone? Is Miriam okay?"

"They're all at the funeral home." Shelby shook her head and looked down for a moment. "It's terrible what happened." She thought about the man she'd met only briefly at the market. She'd been shocked to hear that Ivan's wife was pregnant, only making the situation even worse. She looked back up at Saul. "I'll tell them you came by, though."

Saul pushed back the rim of his hat. "I just wanted to tell them how sorry I am and see if there was anything me or my family can do."

Shelby twisted her mouth to one side, then crossed her arms across her chest. "I'm not sure you're on Rebecca and Aaron's happy list right now."

"What does that mean?" Saul frowned as he shifted his weight.

"No one's talking about it—in light of everything—but I don't think they're happy with Miriam for sneaking out of the house to see you. She'll probably get grounded or something when everything settles down."

"Sneaking out? What?"

Shelby squeezed her eyes closed for a moment, then opened them. "Oops. I assumed she told you."

Saul stood taller, shifting his weight from one foot to the other. "No, she didn't tell me." He paused, rubbing his chin. "And that ain't right. She shouldn't be sneaking around behind her parents' backs." He shook his head. "I wondered why they let her go out that late at night, but I just never asked her about it."

Shelby looked down and kicked the grass with her bare foot. She put her hands in the pockets of her blue jeans, then looked back up at him. "You know, she likes you a lot."

Saul looked toward the barn and didn't say anything for a moment. "I like her too," he said with a shrug.

Shelby leaned closer to him. "Don't be nonchalant, Saul."

"Huh?"

"She really likes you, but Jesse told me that you aren't going to be baptized here, and that you'll eventually leave this place. Is that true?"

Saul looped his thumbs beneath his suspenders, bit his lip, and looked toward the barn again. Shelby had her answer.

"Jesse needs to mind his own business." Saul finally faced Shelby. "I'll talk to Miriam."

"So it's true. You are leaving?"

"*Ya.*" Saul turned toward his horse. "She'll probably end up with Jesse anyway."

"She doesn't want Jesse." Shelby followed Saul as he walked toward his buggy. She knew she was overstepping her bounds, but she was feeling unusually protective of Miriam—probably because Shelby knew what it was like to be abandoned by the man you loved. "She wants *you*."

"I gotta go." Saul climbed into his buggy.

"I'm sure you do," Shelby mumbled as he pulled away. *Poor Miriam.*

Shelby waited until Saul was gone before she looked toward the sky. She closed her eyes to avoid the bright sun.

God, I thought that prayers for other people were answered before our own needs. I thought You'd help Miriam not to get hurt. Are You listening to me?

Shelby hung her head for a moment, then walked back to the house, dreading in her heart that she would have to tell Miriam that Saul was leaving here. But her cousin had a right to know before she got too involved with him.

Miriam sat quietly with her parents and brothers in a large room with empty caskets everywhere. Gold ones, blue ones, brown ones—all colors, and all very fancy. Her family was seated in the large room while Mr. Roberts went over the details of the funeral. As was custom, Uncle Ivan would be buried in a plain coffin with no ornament, then later laid to rest in a hand-dug grave in their community cemetery. The funeral home would take his body to her Aunt Mary Ellen's house tomorrow, where he would stay until the funeral two days later. Mary Ellen's home was the largest and would be best for receiving visitors. Uncle Noah wasn't Amish, so his wasn't an option. Miriam's Uncle Samuel, Aunt Lillian, cousin David, and

Aunt Katie Ann were scheduled to arrive from Colorado tomorrow and would be staying with Mary Ellen.

Everyone in the room looked toward the door when it eased open. Lucy Turner walked in, her ivory skin streaked with tears, and Miriam didn't think she'd ever seen her look so plain. Barely any makeup, and she was wearing gray sweat pants and a gray T-shirt.

"I'm—I'm sorry to interrupt. I just didn't know what to do, or where to go, and—and I just wanted to make sure that everything— I'm sorry. I'm so sorry. I shouldn't have come."

She turned to leave, but it was Miriam's mother who spoke up. "Lucy, you may stay."

Lucy faced the group, dabbed at her eyes, and took a couple of steps forward, finally settling into a chair that was set apart from the rest of the group. Mr. Roberts waited, then finished things up by asking if anyone had any questions. When no one did, he excused himself. "I'll let you have some time alone," he said quietly.

It seemed strange for Lucy to be among the family. They'd all been fairly certain that Lucy had lured Ivan away from Katie Ann, even though *Mamm* had said repeatedly that Ivan was a grown man making his own choices. Even though Miriam knew it was wrong in the eyes of God, she didn't care for Lucy Turner. But seeing Lucy so upset made Miriam realize that—right or wrong—Lucy obviously cared about Uncle Ivan a lot. She felt sorry for Lucy's loss too.

9

Miriam wasn't home for ten minutes before Shelby pulled her upstairs. "Saul was here earlier," she said.

"I forgot to call him!" Miriam slapped herself on the forehead and sat down on the bed. "I better go try now, or at least leave a message for him."

"Miriam . . ."

"Ya?"

Shelby bit her bottom lip for a moment. "Saul's not planning to be baptized here, Miriam. He's going to leave this place." Shelby waved her arm around the room.

Miriam was sad and exhausted. This was the last thing she needed at the moment. She let out a heavy sigh. "Shelby, what would make you say that?"

"He told me."

Miriam wrapped her arms around herself, more despair weighing on her. She didn't say anything.

"I'm sorry, Miriam." Shelby leaned her head down into her hands for a moment, then looked back up. "I just thought you'd want to know."

"I guess that's why he avoided the question when I asked him about it." She blinked a few times and told herself that she'd cried enough today.

"Because men are jerks. That's why. That's what they do. They get close to you, then leave you." Shelby nodded strongly as she pinched her lips together.

"I can't think about this right now." Miriam shook her head, and despite how sad she was about her uncle's passing, she knew that she would be thinking about Saul too. "But . . . why did he come by earlier?"

"He said he came to check on you and to see if he could do anything for your family."

Miriam smiled. "That was nice of him."

"Be careful, Miriam. Now that you know he's leaving, guard your heart."

"I have to go downstairs and help *Mamm*."

"I'll come too."

Miriam walked out the door and down the stairs, Shelby following close behind. Everything was going to be all right. It saddened her that Saul was going to leave the community, but almost instantly her mind began to scramble with what-ifs. She'd always pictured her and Saul in the community—married and raising a family together. But what if only *part* of that picture became a reality?

Saul had no doubt that Shelby told Miriam that he would be leaving the community, and he knew in his head that it was for the best. He'd had the best time with Miriam last night, and he longed to spend even more time with her. It was as if years of silent infatuation had risen to the surface and overtaken them both, and it felt wonderful. He'd always loved Miriam from afar. She was the kind of woman he hoped to marry someday, but her life was here. And Saul had known since he was fourteen that his wasn't. The world had too much to offer, and he got his first glimpse when his father took him to an auction, an *Englisch* auction in Lancaster. *Daed* needed a new plow and some other farm equipment, and his father spent all day surveying what he planned to bid on, then did so at the auction. While his father was preoccupied, Saul met Ted Stark, a sixteen-year-old *Englisch* boy—with a car. Saul wasn't old enough to be in his *rumschpringe* yet, but it didn't stop him from seeing the world beyond his district with Ted for the next several months. Saul's favorite part of his adventures—going to restaurants and critiquing the food. He'd worked part-time that summer, saved his money, and eaten at some mighty fine places. His favorite restaurant back then was one that used odd combinations of seasonings, and he could remember the taste long after he'd left.

One evening he'd worked up enough courage to speak to the chef, an *Englisch* fellow with no hair and a limp. After Saul questioned the man about a certain Italian dish, the chef—Claude—invited Saul to the back and actually showed him how to prepare the chestnut pasta with creamy porcini mushroom sauce. He decided that night that he would prepare fancy meals in a fancy restaurant if he was ever given the opportunity. Now, with a job offer in hand, it was time to act on his plans. *Best that Miriam knows now,* he supposed. And she'd surely not want to spend any more time with him.

Following family devotion, Saul noticed his father getting restless, pacing the room, and glancing out the window every few minutes.

"You waiting for someone?" Saul set down the Bible he was reading. Ruben and James were already upstairs, and Saul suspected Ruben was locked in his room reading a magazine *Daed* probably wouldn't approve of. Ruben liked cars, and he took every opportunity to buy an automobile magazine and sneak it upstairs.

His father shook his head and blew it out slowly. "No, just stretching my legs."

Saul picked up the Bible and started reading again when he saw his father wipe sweat from his forehead, then reach for his hat on the rack.

"I'm going to go take a walk, get some fresh air."

Saul's stomach churned. He'd covered every square inch of the house, barn, and property looking for wine or other forms of alcohol, and he'd never found any—but when *Daed* went for a walk, he always came back drunk or with a bottle in his hand. It was hidden somewhere. Saul just didn't know where. His heart started to beat out of his chest as he put the book down again and stood up. "I'll go with you. I could use some fresh air too."

As he could have predicted, his father shook his head. "No, you stay to your studies. I'd like to just clear my mind with a *gut* walk." *Daed* pulled the door open and wasn't even over the threshold when Saul called to him.

"*Ya?*" He smiled, and Saul didn't think there was a person on the planet whose eyes were kinder than his father's. Saul just stared at him for a few moments. "What is it, *sohn?*"

"*Daed.*" Saul slowly stood up as he bit his lip and walked toward his father. "Maybe tonight isn't really a *gut* night for a walk."

Daed lowered his head, a sad smile on his face when he looked up. "It's as good as any other night, Saul." And he left.

Tuesday morning Miriam gathered with the entire family at Mary
Ellen's home for the funeral. Her Uncle Samuel, Aunt Lillian, and
cousin David had flown in with Aunt Katie Ann, whose pregnant belly was easy to see. They'd arrived just last night from
Colorado. Miriam had never flown in a plane, and she hoped she
didn't ever have to. It was a last resort for travel and only in the
case of emergencies.

She glanced around and her heart ached even more at seeing her
Uncle Noah, Aunt Carley, and their daughter, Jenna; Aunt Mary
Ellen and Uncle Abe and their children; Lillian's mother, Sarah
Jane; close family friends Lizzie, Sadie, and Kade; their *Englisch*
friend Barbie Beiler; and so many more. She figured there were
close to two hundred people inside Mary Ellen's den, which was
set up just like church service, backless benches for the men facing
one way and more benches for the women facing toward the men.

Miriam was just taking her seat in between her mother and
Shelby when she saw Saul walk in with his two brothers but without Zeb Fisher. Miriam wondered why Zeb wasn't there and hoped
he wasn't ill. As she scanned the room, she saw Lucy Turner standing in the back, dressed in a knee-length black dress. When she
located Aunt Katie Ann sitting three seats in front of Miriam, she
wondered how it must feel for Katie Ann to know that Lucy was in
the back of the room. She looked at Saul again and thought about
what she would say to him later, when the time was appropriate.

Following the two-hour service, Miriam's heart was still heavy
with sadness but soothed by prayer. Amish folks went by buggy to
the cemetery, followed by a few cars. Bishop Ebersol spoke briefly

at the burial site about admonition for the living, then closed in prayer. As Miriam followed her family to their buggy, Saul walked up beside her.

"I'm sorry, Miriam."

"Danki." Miriam glanced around to see where her parents were. They were quite a ways in front of her with Shelby. "I'm sorry I didn't call. There was so much going on."

Saul brushed his hand against hers. "It's all right. I heard what happened, so I knew that's why you weren't able to call."

He started moving toward the buggies again, so Miriam did too, the two of them walking in silence for a few moments. They almost walked right into Miriam's mother and Shelby, who had turned around and seemed to be waiting on them.

Mamm raised her chin a bit as she sniffled. "Hello, Saul."

Saul removed his hat. "I'm sorry for your loss, Rebecca."

Miriam's mother nodded but quickly grabbed Miriam's hand. "Your *Aenti* Lillian is looking for you."

Saul nodded and didn't move as *Mamm* dragged her forward. She glanced over her shoulder and saw Saul's brothers walk up beside him, then they turned and walked the other way. She wondered if they would go to the meal at Mary Ellen's.

As soon as she arrived at her aunt and uncle's house, Miriam looked everywhere for Saul.

"I don't think he's here," Shelby said, standing in the yard and holding a glass of meadow tea. She took a sip of the drink. "I'm assuming you're looking for Saul?"

Miriam nodded, then Jesse walked up. "Miriam, I'm real sorry," he said as he removed his hat. "If there's anything me or my family can do, please let us know."

"*Danki*, Jesse."

Jesse turned to Shelby and gave a quick nod, then looked back at Miriam. "When you're feeling better, we should all go fishing at the Zook place again."

"Okay." Miriam wasn't much interested in going back to the Zook place unless Saul was going too.

"How about next Saturday? Do you think you'd be up to it then?" Jesse put his hat back on.

"I don't know if it will be too soon, or if I should—"

"I could stop by Saul's and see if he wants to go again too." Jesse smiled, and Miriam saw him glance at Shelby. Shelby said both Jesse and Saul liked her, but he seemed equally as focused on Shelby right now. Didn't Jesse realize that neither one of them was good for him? Miriam was in love with someone else, and Shelby wasn't Amish. But whatever his motives, his offer was too tempting.

"I guess by then we'd be able to go. We could meet you out there. Maybe lunchtime? Me and Shelby could bring a picnic lunch."

Jesse smiled. "Sounds *gut*. I'll let Saul know."

After he walked away, Miriam looked at Shelby and watched her cousin's left brow rise a fraction. "Wonder what he's up to," Shelby said, smirking.

Miriam was glad for a distraction from the sadness that surrounded them. "I'm not sure he's up to anything. He just wants to go fishing." She was mildly concerned that Jesse might be interested in Shelby, and she had to question exactly why that would bother her so much. *Has Jesse always been my backup plan in case things didn't work with Saul?* She quickly tossed the selfish thought aside. Then she thought for a moment about Saul leaving and what that might mean for her life.

"Look." Shelby nodded her head to their left. "Isn't that your Aunt Katie Ann talking to Lucy?"

Miriam tried to be discreet as she glanced toward the two women. "*Ya,*" she whispered. She saw her aunt swipe at her eyes, then touch her expanded stomach. Lucy hung her head as she spoke.

Miriam watched Katie Ann press her lips together, but her aunt eventually nodded. A few moments later the women parted ways.

"Katie Ann always wanted a baby. More than anyone I've ever known." Miriam sighed.

"I guess this is bittersweet, then."

"*Ya,* it is." She took a final look around for Saul, convinced that he and his brothers had gone home straight from the cemetery. At least she would see him next Saturday.

Miriam went to bed early Friday night, glad not to have any *Englisch* guests for supper for the second week in a row. *Mamm* had said earlier that even if she were not still mourning the death of her brother, she wouldn't have opted to host a supper tonight. Her mother couldn't seem to shake the fact that someone stole from her under her own roof. But Miriam knew her *mamm* had cried on and off most of the week following the funeral, saying that she would always regret that she didn't talk to Ivan before he died and, instead, had practiced the shunning to the fullest. Miriam recalled with regret how quickly she'd gotten away from her uncle while she and Shelby were in Bird-In-Hand. If she'd only known that it would be the last time she would see her uncle . . .

Surprisingly, Shelby was asleep before Miriam. She listened to her cousin snoring lightly, then reached for the lantern and darkened the room. Sleep wasn't going to come easy as her mind whirled with thoughts about Uncle Ivan. Then there was the fishing trip in the morning when she'd finally see Saul again.

Could Saul really the leave the community—and her? She kept asking herself what it was about Saul that made her so sure he was the one for her, even though they'd spent very little time together over the years. She was wise enough to know that mutual attraction was not enough. But something about Saul's personality had drawn her to him at an early age. He was edgy, adventuresome, but yet gentle and kind. He often bucked the traditional Amish ways, but always with the best of intentions. She thought again about how he defended her that day on the playground.

She rolled onto her side and stared out the window into a starlit night. She thought about everything outside of her small district, the only world she'd ever known. *Is it peaceful like it is here? Are folks good to each other?* Shelby had said it's a dangerous place.

She let her mind drift far away. She pictured her and Saul out in the *Englisch* world together. She thought about being able to listen to music all the time, something she really enjoyed and something forbidden in her community. She thought about wearing *Englisch* clothes and traveling to other parts of the world. Would they do those things? Mostly she thought about just being with Saul, loving him. No matter their location, she knew that the basis of marriage was unconditional love and a union blessed by God. Her thoughts were unresolved when she finally drifted off to sleep.

When she opened her eyes Saturday morning, Shelby was buried beneath the covers as usual, so she quietly climbed out of bed, got dressed, and headed downstairs. In the kitchen, her mother was scurrying around the kitchen. *Mamm's* eyes were swollen, so she knew her mother's heart was going to hurt for a long time about Uncle Ivan. As soon as breakfast was over, she went outside and found her father alone in the barn, carrying a stack of old newspapers. He smiled at her when she walked into the barn.

"I don't know why your *mamm* insists on keeping these old copies of *The Budget.*" He grinned as he shook his head. "She said it's like a scrapbook of everyone's birth announcements, obituaries, and news." He dropped the newspapers into a box in the corner. "I told her she didn't even know most of these folks from all over the United States, but you know how your *mamm* is. She doesn't really meet a stranger."

Miriam smiled as she moved closer to her father, and she pondered his statement. *Then why can't she accept Saul?*

Daed tipped back the rim of his hat. "What's on your mind, *dochder?*" He leaned against his workbench and looped his thumbs beneath his suspenders.

"Me and Shelby have a few chores to do this morning, then we were going to go fishing with Jesse and Saul . . . if that's okay." Miriam took a deep breath and waited.

Daed grinned. "So you came out here to ask me instead of asking your *mamm*, who's in the *haus?*"

Miriam hung her head as she kicked at the sandy floor of the barn with one foot.

"I guess it's all right, Miriam." *Daed* patted her on the shoulder as he moved past her toward the barn exit. "You *kinner* have fun."

Miriam lifted up on her toes. *"Danki, Daed!"* Then she ran to go find Shelby.

Rebecca marched to the barn to find Aaron.

"Hello, *mei lieb*," her husband said casually as he carried a pile of hay to the horse's stall. "What brings you out to the barn this fine morning?"

Her husband's smile quickly faded when Rebecca drew closer. Aaron dropped the hay.

"What's wrong?"

Rebecca thrust her hands on her hips. "What's wrong?" she huffed. "Do you really have to ask me that? Our *dochder* just told me that you gave permission for her and Shelby to go fishing with Saul and Jesse. Why did you do that?"

Aaron took off his hat, dabbed at his forehead with a hand-kerchief, then put his hat back on. "We already talked to Miriam about sneaking out of the house, and both girls have worked extra hard." He put his own hands on his hips and faced off with her. "It's just fishing, Rebecca, and if Miriam wants to see that boy, she's going to. Wouldn't you rather it be during the daylight hours, instead of sneaking around? She's in her *rumschpringe*, and it's her time to figure out—"

"Oh shush, Aaron!" Rebecca waved her hand in the air, despite the scowl stretching across her husband's face. "That boy is not *gut* for Miriam. You should have just said no." She stomped her foot.

"Rebecca." Aaron sighed. "You barely know him. And I thought you'd be glad that Shelby and Jesse are going too."

"We saw how that worked out last time. Shelby and Jesse went home early and left Miriam and Saul alone."

Aaron grinned. "I seem to recall a certain girl in her *rumschpringe* who snuck out on more than one occasion to see the boy she liked." He paused, lifting one brow playfully. "And look how that turned out."

"It's not the same, Aaron." She walked closer to him. "Do you really want our *dochder* involved with a boy who's been in trouble? And it's not just that. There is much talk about him wanting to leave the community. Doesn't that scare you?"

Aaron gently put his hands on Rebecca's shoulders. "I hope that all our *kinner* make the choice to stay here, Rebecca, but this is what their running-around time is for. And Miriam is a smart girl, dedicated to her faith and her life here. She isn't going to leave here."

Rebecca let him pull her into his arms, then she gently eased away. "Aaron, when we were courting . . . if you'd asked me to leave the community and go with you out into the *Englisch* world, I would have. I would have followed you anywhere. Young love is a dangerous thing."

Aaron smiled. "I didn't know that." He tipped the rim of his hat up a bit. "Not that I had any thoughts about leaving."

"I want you to talk to Saul. Find out what his intentions are."

"Rebecca, it's too soon for that. We don't even know if they are officially dating."

She blew out a breath of exasperation. "It's not too soon. It might already be too late!"

Shelby placed napkins in the picnic basket as she waited for Miriam to fill a thermos with tea. She had mixed emotions about the fishing trip. Even though there were four of them going, and she loved to fish, she still felt like the outsider—and not just because she wasn't Amish. Both men were vying for her cousin's attention, which did little for Shelby's fragile emotions. She was going to try to make the best of it anyway and enjoy the day outside fishing.

"Chicken salad sandwiches, potato chips, pickles, tea . . ." Miriam looked up at Shelby. "What am I forgetting?"

"Pie?"

Miriam snapped her fingers. *"Ya!"* She cut four slices of apple pie, wrapped them individually in plastic wrap, and placed them on top of the other items.

Shelby closed the lid and picked up the basket. They were almost to the door when they bumped into Rebecca coming in.

"We won't be late, *Mamm*," Miriam said meekly, avoiding her mother's eyes. Rebecca nodded, then scooted past them and into the den.

"Your mother is so unhappy," Shelby said as she placed the basket in the back of the spring buggy.

"I know. She's still real upset about *Onkel* Ivan." Miriam hung her head for a moment. "And she's still mad at me about sneaking out to see Saul, but I know it's more than that. She's afraid Saul will leave and that I'll go with him."

Shelby thought for a moment. "But you *know* Saul is leaving. I told you that."

Miriam grabbed the reins and backed up the horse. *"Ya.* I know."

"Are you going to say anything to him about it?"

"I don't know yet."

Shelby reached up and pulled her hair tighter within her ponytail holder, then adjusted her black sunglasses. "Well, I'd sure say something if I were you."

Miriam chewed her bottom lip for a moment. "Maybe he'll change his mind."

"And maybe he won't. Then what?"

Her cousin was quiet as she maneuvered the topless buggy onto the road. "I don't know."

Shelby couldn't imagine Miriam leaving this place. *It's all she knows.* Which is why this situation had nothing but heartbreak written all over it.

———

Saul pulled up to the Zook farm at the same time as Jesse. He didn't really like Jesse being here, but Jesse was the one who'd come to his house and invited him. Maybe he was truly interested in Shelby. Saul selfishly hoped so.

His stomach churned thinking about how long it would take for Miriam to say that she heard he was leaving the community. Things at home had gotten even more complicated over the past week anyway, and Saul wasn't sure how he could leave in good conscience.

"Are you and Miriam officially dating?" Jesse glanced at Saul as both men tethered the horses to the fence.

Saul shrugged. "We've only been out once, plus these fishing trips."

Jesse stood taller and faced Saul. "Miriam is a *gut* girl. I hope you won't hurt her. Rumor has it you're leaving here."

Saul tensed as he took a deep breath, but he knew Jesse really did care for Miriam, and Jesse was right to be concerned. "I'm not going to hurt her."

"If you leave here, you will hurt her." Jesse eyed Saul with curiosity, but Saul had no intention of confiding in him. If one word of his father's drinking got out, it would be all over the community. He prayed every day that his father would stop so that Saul could pursue his plans to go work at the bistro, but his *daed's* drinking was getting more frequent—and worse.

They both turned at the sound of Miriam's buggy on the gravel driveway. After she pulled up, Jesse quickly offered her a hand down. Saul walked to the other side to help Shelby, but she'd already jumped down by the time he got there and was reaching for a picnic basket in the back.

"We brought lunch," she said, holding the basket and grinning. "Although . . . I can't take credit."

Saul took the basket and waited while Jesse pulled Miriam's fishing pole from the back. They slowly made their way to the water's edge, and Miriam unfolded a red-and-white quilt to use as a big tablecloth. Once the food was spread out, everyone bowed their heads in prayer.

"Mmm. There's something different in this chicken salad." Saul wrapped his mouth around his sandwich and tried to figure out what Miriam's secret ingredient was. He swallowed, then smiled at her. "You gonna tell me?"

"Nope." She giggled. "But if you have a recipe you'd like to trade . . ."

Saul felt his face turning four shades of red.

"You cook, Saul?" Jesse grinned as he glanced at Shelby.

"He has to cook for his family, Jesse," Miriam said defensively, which warmed Saul's heart but also made him feel like a bit of a wimp.

"Sometimes," he added.

"Are we on for another competition?" Shelby asked as she helped Miriam gather up used paper plates and napkins.

"*Ya.* I'm in." Jesse stood up, then added, "But why don't we pair up differently? Probably ain't fair to have the girls against us, Saul."

Shelby laughed. "Why? Are you afraid we'll win again?"

"You didn't win." Jesse looped his thumbs underneath his suspenders. "Me and Saul caught more fish."

"But . . . we caught the biggest one!" Shelby stood with her shoulders back, grinning.

Saul took a deep breath. He could see where this was going. Despite Jesse's earlier comments, he was going to haul Miriam off to the other side of the pond.

"I say Shelby and me against you two." Jesse pointed to Miriam and Saul.

Saul tried not to show his surprise and looked at Miriam, who was smiling broadly. "Okay," he said. "Miriam?"

"*Ya.* I'm pretty sure me and Saul can catch more fish than the two of you!"

Saul was glad to see Jesse grab Shelby's hand, then pull her toward the other end of the pond. "May the best couple win!"

Miriam wanted nothing more than to be alone with Saul, but there was an uncomfortable feeling that emerged inside of her when she saw Jesse and Shelby skipping off happily together. She wanted to be with Saul, so it seemed strange that she would feel this way. If it hadn't been for Shelby telling her that Saul was leaving, Miriam knew she never would have thought about life outside of their district. Now she kept thinking of all the possibilities that would be available to her if she did leave. She'd always wanted to be a teacher here, but her mother had said that she was more suited for marriage and family. In the *Englisch* world, maybe she could have both? She'd always thought there was plenty of time to get to know Saul better, but time was no longer on her side. One thing she knew for sure . . . she couldn't imagine her life here without him in it.

But what if Saul has no plans to ask me to leave with him? Then Jesse might already be with . . . Shelby? No. That doesn't make sense either. Shelby is Englisch.

Her uneasiness calmed when she felt Saul's hand on her back. "Here, I got your pole ready." He offered her the pole with a wiggling worm dangling from the hook, then held his other palm toward her. "And *ya* . . . I know you could have done it yourself, but I was just helping."

"*Danki,*" she said as she accepted the pole. She liked that he recognized her independence but also acted as a gentleman every time he was around her.

As the afternoon sun beat down on them, Miriam wondered if maybe they shouldn't have planned this so late in the day. She reached up and wiped beads of sweat from her forehead. Next thing she knew, she felt a breeze on her face along with a shower of ice cold water. "Wow!" She closed her eyes and enjoyed the sensation.

"I found these at the market in Bird-In-Hand when I was there this past week. I got one for you, since I knew we were going fishing."

Miriam accepted the battery-operated fan that, with the push of a button, also sprayed cold water. She turned it and pushed the button until the icy droplets were sprinkling Saul's face. "I like this," she said as she pulled it back her way. "*Danki.*"

"I put some ice cubes in it before we came."

Miriam took her pole and her new fan and sat down on a stump near the edge of the water. Saul took a seat right next to her, causing her to jump. "This okay?" he asked.

She nodded, then tossed her line into the water.

"So what's in the chicken salad?" He grinned, and as Miriam turned to face him, their lips couldn't have been farther than six inches apart. She faced forward again.

"Uh, it's, uh—" She couldn't think.

"It almost tasted like lemon pepper?"

Miriam breathed a sigh of relief. "*Ya.* That's it." She didn't look at him but tried to stay focused on her line in the water. She picked up her fan, turned it on, and held down the button until cool water showered her face again.

"How 'bout a little of that this way?" Saul's leg brushed against hers as he shifted his weight to face her. Miriam pointed the fan toward his face. "Ah . . ."

She watched him close his eyes, enjoying the cool water. When he opened his eyes, he latched onto the fan, covering her hand, then turned it back toward her. After a few moments, he gently eased it down, then turned it off. Miriam tried not to look at him, but when his hand cupped her chin and he turned her toward him, she felt herself shaking. She'd never been kissed. And the moment was upon her. She'd always dreamed that Saul would be her first kiss. As his lips drew near hers, she watched him close his eyes, but her eyes seemed to have a mind of their own and remained wide open. With a jerk, she pulled away from him.

"Are you leaving here, Saul?"

Saul let out a heavy sigh, then scratched the back of his head. "I don't know."

"How can you not know? Shelby said you told her that you were leaving."

"That was my plan, but now I'm not sure."

Miriam's insides warmed. *It's because of me that he's not leaving.* She felt a smile cross her lips. "Oh," she said.

"I have something to ask you too." Saul backed up a bit but was still facing her. "Did you sneak out to meet me Saturday night . . . without telling your folks?"

Miriam avoided his accusing eyes as she twisted her mouth from side to side. *"Ya."*

Saul shook his head. "Please don't do that again, Miriam. Your parents won't want me being around you if they think I'm getting you to do stuff like that. We'll see each other when it's okay with your parents."

Miriam nodded, glad there was a mention about seeing each other again but not sure it would really be okay with her parents.

"Why would you leave here, Saul?" She eased away from him a little and faced him, still sitting on the stump.

His eyes averted hers, and he sighed. Then he looked up grinning. "Promise you won't laugh?"

"No." Then she giggled as she raised her palm to him. *"Ya.* I promise. I won't laugh."

He pulled his hat off and scratched his forehead. "I have a job offer to work in a fancy restaurant in Pittsburgh." Saul paused when Miriam's eyes widened. "I'd be the apprentice chef." He looked hard into Miriam's eyes. "I answered an ad in the newspaper, and then I went and cooked some of my recipes for the owner." Saul shrugged. "It's a great opportunity for me, and I really want to go, but . . ." He sighed again.

Miriam smiled, her heart warm, yet frightened at the same time. She knew she'd go anywhere with Saul, especially now that he was willing to forgo leaving because of her. "Don't worry, Saul."

Tense lines formed across his forehead. "There is much to worry about," he said as he put his hat back on.

Miriam wanted to ease his pain. Even though there would be strife and upset in the community, she wanted him to know how she felt.

"I'll go with you, Saul. So please don't change your mind because . . . because of me." She looked toward the ground, stifling a smile.

Saul jumped up from the stump they were sitting on and looked down at her, his face drawn into a scowl. "What?" He put his hands on his hips. "*What?* If I go, you can't go with me, Miriam."

10

SAUL CHASED AFTER MIRIAM AS SHE RAN TOWARD THE buggies. He felt like a louse, but he'd be even more of a louse if he asked Miriam to leave her family and all that she's ever known behind.

"Miriam, wait!" He finally caught up with her and grabbed her arm so she'd stop. Tears spilled from her eyes, and with little thought, except that he couldn't stand to see her cry, he cupped her cheeks in his hands and kissed the tears on her face. "Please, Miriam. Please don't cry," he whispered. When his lips finally met with hers, he kissed her softly, and when she kissed him back, something inside of Saul made him want to beg her to go with him if he left, but nothing could be more selfish. He eased away from her. "I'm sorry I made you cry." He brushed away her tears with his thumbs, then pulled her into his arms.

"I am such a *dummkopp*." Her body shook as she choked out the words, her face buried in his chest. "I should have known that you didn't feel the same way I do."

He gently pushed her away. "Is that what you think, Miriam? I've liked you since we were *kinner*." He kissed her again. "But I would never ask you to leave your family and your friends. Never."

She sniffled as she gazed into his eyes, and Saul wanted to drop to one knee right there in the old Zook front yard.

"I thought you had changed your mind about leaving our community because of *me*," she squeaked out as she started to cry again. "And I wanted you to know that I would go with you, if that were the case." She stepped back from him and stomped her foot. "I'm such a *dummkopp!*" she repeated even louder this time.

Saul pulled his eyes from hers as he rubbed his forehead. He couldn't tell her the real reason he might not be able to go, but her willingness to follow him certainly gave him cause for speculation—*Would she really go with me?* He could envision a life with Miriam. But just as quickly the image faded. *Ruben and James.* He couldn't leave his brothers, not with their father like this. "You're not a *dummkopp*, Miriam. Please don't say that."

"I want to go home, Saul." She swiped at her eyes, and Saul saw Jesse and Shelby heading their way. "I'm embarrassed, and I want to go home."

"Miriam, you don't understand."

"*Ya.* I do." She moved toward her buggy. Saul followed her.

"I can't ask you to leave here."

She faced him, her cheeks stained with tears, and she spoke softly. "No. It appears you can't."

Jesse walked up on them, Shelby trailing behind. "What's going on?" Jesse nudged Saul out of the way and put his hand on Miriam's arm. "Miriam, what is it?"

"It's nothing, Jesse." She sniffled again, and Saul didn't think he could feel any lower.

Shelby charged ahead, pushing Jesse out of the way. "Miriam, what's wrong?" She didn't wait for an answer but instead balled her hands into fists at her sides, moving closer to Saul. He backed up. "What did you do to her?"

"Shelby, he didn't do anything." Miriam grabbed her cousin's arm. "Come on, we need to get home."

Saul opened his mouth to say something, but everyone was glaring at him. "I'm sorry." It was all he knew to say.

Saul pulled into his driveway, and his stomach began to ache the way it always did. Who would he come home to? Which father would greet him?

However, when he saw Ruben and James happily playing basketball, his fears subsided.

He parked the buggy, then hollered, "Can one of you put Rascal in the barn? I'll go get supper started." He paused as he wrapped the reins around the post. "Everything okay?"

Both boys nodded, and Ruben started to make his way toward the horse and buggy. Saul walked inside. His father was sitting in his chair, reading the Bible. *"Wie bischt, Daed?"*

His father took off his reading glasses. *"Gut, gut.* I finished the last of the planting, and . . ." *Daed* smiled. "I took off early."

Saul let out a huge sigh of relief. This was the man he knew and loved, not the monster trapped in a way that Saul couldn't understand. *"Gut* for you, *Daed.* You work hard and deserve to take off early." Saul hung his hat on the rack by the door. "I'll go get supper started."

"Sohn, can we talk?"

Saul held his breath for a moment. "Sure."

His father motioned for Saul to sit down on the couch across from him. "I've been doing some thinking, and I've made arrangements to have a hundred acres deeded to you. That way when you find a *fraa*, you'll already have the land to build on. How does that sound? It's the acreage on the north side of the house. There's plenty of room for your own planting, and a house would be perfect up on the hill out there."

Daed smiled, and Saul knew that this was his father's way of apologizing for recent events. Saul could see his dream slipping further and further away, and he was still confused about Miriam and her willingness to leave the community to be with him. *Does she care about me that much?*

"*Danki, Daed,*" Saul finally said as he forced a smile.

"Tomorrow we'll walk the land, see what you think, and where might be the best place for you to build a home. I still think you could put a nice *haus* right on top of the hill." *Daed* stood up and walked to where Saul was standing. He put his hand on Saul's shoulder. "Today is a new day. A day blessed by our Lord." He paused as his eyes grew sad. "Perhaps we could think of it as a new beginning."

Saul was never affectionate with his father—or his brothers. It wasn't their way. But he couldn't help but put his arms around his father. "I love you, *Daed.*"

When his father squeezed him and whispered, "I love you too, *sohn,*" Saul knew everything was going to somehow be okay. Even if he never did become a chef in a restaurant.

Shelby was the last one in the tub this evening. After she finished in the bathroom, she passed by Rebecca and Aaron's room on the way to her room, and she heard her name. Instinctively she paused, even though she knew she shouldn't be eavesdropping.

"I don't care, Aaron. I still think that Miriam would have never snuck out if Shelby hadn't put her up to it."

"I told you before, Rebecca . . . you don't know if Shelby encouraged Miriam to do that. You ain't being fair about it."

Shelby brought her hand to her mouth, her feet rooted to the floor, and she listened.

"There is much worry in my heart concerning Miriam. Not only is she being influenced by an *Englisch* outsider, but we also have Saul Fisher to worry about. What if he leaves and tries to take our Miriam with him?"

Shelby kept her hand over her mouth as she blinked back tears. *An outsider?* She was just starting to feel more at home here than she had in Fayetteville. And today had been wonderful—Jesse had been wonderful. But hearing Rebecca speak about her this way pushed a tear down her cheek. She forced her feet to move and hurried down the hallway. When she opened the door, Miriam was sitting on the side of her bed, her eyes red and swollen. She knew her cousin needed to talk, but she just couldn't tonight.

She walked to her bed, crawled underneath the covers, then glanced at Miriam, whose eyes widened as if she couldn't believe Shelby was going to go to sleep. "I don't feel well, Miriam. I'm so sorry. Can we talk tomorrow? I know you're upset about Saul and sad about your uncle, but I feel like I need to go to sleep."

Miriam hung her head a bit but then looked at Shelby and sniffled. "Sure. We can talk tomorrow. I probably need to sleep too."

Sleep was the last thing on Shelby's mind. Her life was a wreck, and now the family she thought she'd found didn't want her either. No one wanted her. Not her parents. Not Tommy. And now . . .

not Rebecca. She covered her head with the sheet and buried her sobs in her pillow, hoping the sound of the fan would drown out her self-pity. Her cousin had enough worries, and Shelby couldn't even keep herself together enough to listen to the one person she'd come to trust and love. *Like a sister.*

God, if You're there, please, oh please, help me. I feel so lost and alone. I don't know who else to turn to.

Shelby realized right away that her plea sounded as though God was her last effort, her last hope. She could remember a time when she used to turn to God first. She took a deep breath.

Dear heavenly Father, lately I began to feel like I was part of a family again and that my life was on the mend. Now I'm confused and alone. Please, God, help me to find peace in my heart. Please . . . What is Your plan for me?

She buried her head into her pillow even farther, pulling the edges up over her ears, as if covering her ears would prevent her from hearing anything that she didn't want to hear. What did she expect to hear?

Please, God. Please . . .

She heard Miriam crawl underneath her covers and twist the knob on the lantern until the room went dark. All that could be heard was the steady spinning of the fan on the nightstand. She stifled her tears, pulled the sheet away from her head, then rolled onto her back. She stared at the ceiling, into darkness. *Please, God.*

She squeezed her eyes closed and mouthed the words over and over. *Please, God . . . Please, God . . .*

I am here for you, My child. I will never forsake you.

She held her breath, released it slowly, then felt a sense of calm . . . as if God had sent the Holy Spirit directly to her at that perfect moment, as only He could do. When she finally began to breathe, she slowly sat up in bed, hugged herself tightly, and began to sob.

"Shelby . . ."

She heard her cousin but didn't answer. The room seemed brighter somehow, and she wanted to bask in the knowledge that God was with her, that He would always be with her, even when she couldn't understand His plan for her.

"Dear Lord, I'm sorry. I'm sorry I doubted You." She cried harder until she felt Miriam's arms around her.

"I'm here, my sister. I'm here," Miriam said softly.

Shelby turned to Miriam, who was sitting on the edge of her bed. "God has not forsaken me."

"Of course He hasn't." Miriam rubbed her back as she spoke.

Shelby wept in Miriam's arms for a long time, knowing that the pains of her past were slowly being released into God's hands.

After a long while, Miriam turned the lantern up, then they sat like Indians and talked well into the night. Miriam told her everything that happened with Saul, and Shelby told Miriam about her parents' divorce, how her faith had slipped, and about the bad choices she'd made. It was painful to tell Miriam about the shoplifting and how she'd experimented with drinking and drugs, but her cousin never judged.

She didn't tell her what she overheard Rebecca saying. She knew Miriam well enough to know that she would go straight to her mother and tell the truth—that it was Miriam who insisted on sneaking out. And Shelby figured Miriam had enough troubles right now.

But her heart ached every time she heard Rebecca's voice, calling her the *"Englisch* outsider."

I want to belong somewhere.

But tonight, for the first time in a long while, she had faith that God would put her on the right path.

Rebecca's dreams continued to wake her up during the night and stayed with her throughout her days. She feared she would never get any sleep unless she had a heart-to-heart talk with Miriam. She could tell her daughter was reluctant to travel to town with her—just the two of them. Miriam had scoffed when Rebecca mentioned it, and then she'd shuffled across the yard toward the buggy like she was being punished.

"Why aren't we taking the spring buggy?" Miriam asked not long after they got on the road.

Rebecca enjoyed the topless buggy on a pretty day too, but today was a day for their covered buggy. "I need the room in the backseat for supplies, plus it's going to rain."

"It doesn't look like rain." Miriam's voice was bordering on snippy as she turned to face Rebecca.

Rebecca just smiled. "We'll see." She kept the buggy at a steady pace and waited until they had crossed Lincoln Highway before she brought up the subject that was causing her so much grief. She decided to ease into it slowly.

"I saw Zeb Fisher and the two younger boys at church Sunday, but I didn't see Saul."

Miriam kept her eyes straight ahead as she spoke. "Ruben said that he was feeling poorly that morning." She shrugged, then faced out her buggy window. "I haven't seen or talked to Saul in four days."

Relief flooded over Rebecca even though she hated to hear her daughter sound so sad. Maybe her worries were unfounded after all. She tried to think of a casual way to talk more about Saul, but before her thoughts could get organized, Miriam spoke again.

"I know you don't like him."

Rebecca waited for a car to cross in front of them, then flicked the reins until the horse picked up speed. She turned to face Miriam briefly, shocked at the way her daughter's eyes cut into her, but she took a deep breath, determined to keep things pleasant between them. "Please understand, Miriam . . . I don't really know Saul well enough to form an opinion of him, but the things I've heard . . ." Rebecca shook her head before turning to Miriam again. "All this talk about him leaving frightens me. If the two of you are close . . ."

"You don't need to be frightened." Miriam looked out her window to the right again. Rebecca couldn't see her expression, but she heard the sadness in her voice again. "He doesn't want me to go with him." Miriam dabbed at her eye, but Rebecca was having trouble getting past the fact that they had actually discussed such a thing. "Saul is probably leaving, but I won't be going with him." Miriam faced forward and raised her chin a bit. Rebecca watched as Miriam blinked back tears, but as much as her heart hurt for her daughter, relief was still her primary emotion.

Mamm sighed. "I'm sorry, Miriam."

"No, you're not."

Instinctively Rebecca opened her mouth to reprimand Miriam for her harsh tone, but she didn't. Instead, they rode quietly for a while. Finally, Rebecca spoke again.

"I'm sorry that you're hurting, Miriam. But the thought of you leaving here . . . I just can't . . ." Rebecca trailed off and shook her head, wondering when Miriam had gotten old enough for things to get so complicated between them.

Miriam twisted to face Rebecca, and while Rebecca kept her eyes on the road, she could feel her daughter's eyes blazing into her again. "*Mamm*, it's my choice. I choose whether or not to get baptized."

Rebecca took a deep breath and tried to choose her words carefully, keeping in mind that Miriam was hurting, but also knowing that she knew what was best for Miriam. "I know that, Miriam. But your father and I can't help but worry that you'll be drawn to a world you know little about."

"Worry is a sin," her daughter responded flatly, in the same tone that was getting harder for Rebecca to ignore. She took another deep breath.

"*Ya*, it is. But I'm human, Miriam." She paused. "Look at Shelby. She had troubles in her hometown, and now she's bringing you troubles."

Miriam scowled. "How is Shelby bringing me troubles?"

"You snuck out of the *haus*, Miriam. That is something you would never have done before. I'm sure that was Shelby's idea."

Miriam chuckled.

"You think this is funny?" Rebecca slowed the buggy as they neared the market. She braved a quick glance at Miriam, not finding humor in any of this.

"*Ya*. I do. Especially since Shelby is the one who tried to talk me out of it." They were quiet again for a few moments. "And I think Shelby only shares her experiences with me as a way to help me not to make bad choices."

Rebecca heard what Miriam was saying, but it was taking time for her words to sink in. *Have I been wrong about Shelby?*

"I hear her crying a lot at night, after she thinks I'm asleep."

Rebecca parked the buggy, then hung her head for a moment as she questioned what kind of mother figure she'd been for Shelby in the absence of her own mother. "Do you think she's homesick?"

"I don't think so. She just seems . . . lonely. I think she's been angry about a lot of things. Her parents, her ex-boyfriend, her old friends, and . . . at God."

Rebecca questioned her priorities for a moment as she stared at her only daughter. "You're a *gut* girl, Miriam. Maybe you can help her to find her way."

"God will do that."

Rebecca nodded, then they both stepped out of the buggy. She tethered the horse at the pole outside of the market, then stared up at the dark clouds forming to her west.

I was right.

About the rain.

Shelby thought about the conversation she'd overheard between Rebecca and Aaron. On her hands and knees, she scrubbed the bathtub even harder. Ben, Elam, and John were with Aaron, and Shelby wanted to surprise Rebecca when she got home. She planned to have the entire upstairs scrubbed clean, and then she'd do as much as she could downstairs. Nothing was ever really dirty here. Rebecca saw to that. But with six of them in the house, the bathtub always needed a good scrubbing.

She wasn't sure why Rebecca's approval was so important to her. She'd be gone in another six weeks—back to her home, or what was left of it. To her surprise, Paradise had started to feel like home. She loved cooking in the evenings with Rebecca and Miriam, and was even starting to make it downstairs in time to help with breakfast. Gardening wasn't her favorite thing, nor the lack of air-conditioning, but the freedom to not wear makeup or be judged by others—most of the time—made up for some of the inconveniences, such as not having a cell phone, computer, or television.

Aaron was a storyteller and often told tales in the evenings after devotion time, and everyone laughed. Despite the recent death in the family, there was still laughter in this house, something she couldn't remember hearing at home—at least not in a long, long time. No one screamed at each other here, and for the most part, everyone did as they were told, worked hard, and didn't complain. It was a simpler way of life that had started out as a punishment but had wrapped around her like a safe cocoon.

She wrung out the sponge, put it underneath the sink in the bathroom, then stopped and stilled herself when she thought she heard a knock at the door. Realizing she was right, she dried her hands on a towel, then headed down the stairs. When she opened the door, Jesse was standing on the porch holding a fishing pole.

"Jesse, hi." She pushed the screen open. "Come on in."

Jesse glanced around the yard, then looked over her shoulder. "Is Miriam here?"

Shelby's heart dropped. She should have known Jesse was here to see Miriam. "No. I'm sorry. She went to town with Rebecca. I'll tell her you stopped by to see her."

Jesse repositioned his weight. "I, uh—I didn't come to see Miriam. I came to see you."

Shelby smiled. "Oh. Well, come on in."

He looked over her shoulder again, then scanned the yard. "Is anyone home?"

"No. Aaron and the boys are out there." She pointed to her left toward the back fields. "And Rebecca and Miriam went to town." She pushed the door open wider.

"Maybe you could just come out on the porch," Jesse said as he scrunched his handsome face up and nodded to his side.

"Oh." Shelby joined him on the porch. "Are we not supposed to be alone in the house together?"

Jesse stood taller. "It wouldn't be proper."

Shelby loved Jesse's manners and the formality of his speech. "Okay." She sat down in one of the rocking chairs on the front porch and motioned for Jesse to do the same.

"I bought this for you." Jesse pushed the fishing pole toward her. "You can't keep using everyone's hand-me-downs. You need your own pole."

Shelby struggled not to burst into tears. It was the nicest thing anyone had done for her in a long time, and coming from Jesse, it warmed her insides even more.

"*Danki,*" she said in his dialect.

"*Ach,* you learnin' yourself the *Deitsch?*"

She laughed. "I'm picking up words and phrases here and there." She thought about hearing the young men at the market and their inappropriate comments in Pennsylvania *Deitsch.*

"Does Rebecca say *kumme esse? Mei mamm* always says that at supper time."

Shelby tapped her finger to her chin. "Hmm . . . no. I don't remember hearing Rebecca say that. What does it mean?"

"'Come eat.' Tonight, tell everyone *kumme esse,* and they'll think you're converting." He smiled, then stood up. "I best be gettin' on my way. I'm on lunch break from my job at the City Dump."

Shelby tried not to react, but her brows rose just the same.

Jesse grinned. "It's a furniture store in Ronks."

"Oh." Shelby brought her hand to her chest. "I thought you looked awfully clean to work at a dump." Then she squeezed her eyes closed and thought about how dumb that sounded.

"So when do you want to try out your new fishing pole? Saturday?" The beginning of a smile tipped the corner of his mouth, and Shelby felt like she was going to melt right there on the porch.

"Sure. Do you want Miriam to make us a lunch again? Maybe some chicken salad?"

Jesse looped his thumbs underneath his suspenders, and when he took a deep breath, it was hard for Shelby not to notice how well his broad shoulders filled out his blue shirt. "I—I was wondering if you wanted to go. I mean, just you. And me." His mouth twitched as he waited for her to answer.

Shelby's heart pounded against her chest so hard that when she finally did answer, it was more like a squeak. "Sure."

Jesse smiled. "*Gut.* Then can I come for you at noon?"

"Sure. Okay." She fought the swooning effect that overtook her. "Do you want me to bring lunch?"

"No. It is my invitation, so I'll ask *mei mamm* to make lunch for us."

Shelby put her hands on her hips and grinned. "You're scared of my cooking, huh? Believe me, I can whip up some sandwiches."

He laughed, then his expression stilled. "I ain't scared of your cooking, Shelby . . ." He paused. "But you do scare me." With a smile on his face, he winked, then turned and walked down the porch steps, waving when he got to his buggy.

She watched him maneuver the buggy down the driveway and onto the street. She couldn't wait to tell Miriam that she had a date. With Jesse Dienner.

11

MIRIAM WAITED WITH SHELBY ON THE FRONT PORCH
Saturday. It was almost noon, and Jesse was due to pick up Shelby
any minute. Miriam struggled to figure this out. For years she'd
known that Jesse was smitten with her, and it gave her a strange
sense of comfort. It was wrong, since she'd always wanted to be
with Saul, but the feelings were there anyway.

"I offered to make lunch." Shelby ran her hands along a crisp
white shirt that was tucked into a pair of dark blue jeans. "But
Jesse said he would have his mother pack us a lunch."

"Why did you wear a white shirt to go fishing?"

Shelby glanced down at her blouse. "I don't know. I like this
shirt." She cringed as she studied her choice further, as if seeing the bright white fabric for the first time. "I'm going to go
change." She jumped up from the rocker she was sitting in. "I
won't be long!"

Miriam slouched down into a rocker and tried to fight the self-
pity that lingered around her. No Saul. And now no Jesse. Why
was it that she'd never really noticed Jesse until he took an interest
in Shelby? He was handsome. And there would never be a worry
about Jesse leaving the community. Jesse would be a wonderful
husband and father.

What are you doing? Miriam shook her head to clear her wicked thoughts. She knew she didn't want Jesse, but rationally he would be the best person for her. Then everyone would be happy—everyone but Miriam. And—now—possibly Shelby.

She watched him pull into the driveway, so she straightened her curved spine. She reminded herself that there was a bigger issue at hand. What if Jesse really likes Shelby? Her cousin would be leaving, and Jesse could end up hurt. She briefly wondered if Jesse would consider leaving the community. What if he fell for Shelby? Would he so willingly follow her, like Miriam had been so ready to follow Saul—if he'd wanted her to?

"*Wie bischt*, Miriam?" Jesse strolled up wearing a light-blue shirt, black trousers, and a smile. Miriam was sure he'd never looked better in his life. She sighed.

"I'm *gut*. Shelby will be here in a minute."

Jesse smiled. "I bet it wonders you that I would be going out with an *Englisch* woman."

Miriam wondered briefly if Jesse was trying to make her jealous, but when the screen door slammed and Jesse's eyes darted to Shelby—it became obvious to Miriam where Jesse's interest lay. His eyes twinkled as a full smile spread across his face.

With no time to respond, Miriam said, "Well, you two kids have fun," then crossed her legs and plastered on a grin—just like her mother would. She wasn't sure why she said it, and both Shelby and Jesse gave her strange looks.

Once they were gone, Miriam slithered back down in the chair again, knowing her mother would reprimand her for such pitiful posture. But she didn't much care at the moment.

Little John strolled onto the porch holding a large piece of watermelon. He walked up to where she was sloped down in the chair.

"Want some?" Red juice dripped down his chin.

Miriam shook her head. "No. *Danki*, though."

Her youngest brother sat down on the porch and dangled his legs off the side. Miriam smiled when she saw watermelon juice on the tops of his bare feet. She could remember being eight years old, when there wasn't anything a piece of watermelon couldn't cure on a hot day. Brushing back a strand of hair that had fallen in front of her face, she decided that she could either sit here and feel sorry for herself or do something productive. She'd already weeded the garden and picked the tomatoes, strawberries, rhubarb, and cabbage that were ready. Housecleaning was done, and her parents allowed her Saturday afternoon to do anything she wanted. She wanted to go fishing. With Saul.

Scowling, she pulled herself up and headed into the house. When she walked into the den, she heard sniffling. Her mother quickly faced the window to the backyard, but Miriam saw her dab her eyes. Guilt flooded over her when she thought about how self-absorbed she'd been. Uncle Ivan had died just two weeks ago. Katie Ann and the rest of her family from Colorado had left two days after the funeral.

"*Mamm*, can I get you anything or do anything for you?"

Her mother slowly turned around, sniffled once. "No. *Danki*, Miriam. I'm all right." She walked to the couch, sat down, and picked up a book. Miriam sat down in the rocker across from her and kicked it into motion. She waited awhile, in case *Mamm* wanted to talk, but her mother kept her head buried in a book.

"*Mamm* . . . do you care if I take the spring buggy for a drive?"

"It's not hitched up, and your *daed*, Ben, and Elam are at your *Aenti* Mary Ellen's *haus* helping your *Onkel* Abe put up a new fence."

Miriam thought briefly about going to see if her cousin Linda wanted to go running around, but she really didn't feel like conversation. "I can hitch the buggy up."

Mamm looked up from the book. "I guess it would be all right."

Miriam stood up and shuffled across the wooden floor toward the front door.

"Miriam?"

"*Ya?*"

Mamm crossed one leg over the other and folded her hands atop the book in her lap. "Tell me about this—this outing with Shelby and Jesse."

"What do you want to know? They went fishing."

Mamm's forehead creased as she narrowed her eyes at Miriam. "You know what I mean. You don't think Jesse would be silly enough to date an *Englisch* girl, do you? I mean, Shelby will be leaving next month."

Miriam was dreading that day. She would miss Shelby. She wasn't sure that her cousin had completely opened up to her, but Shelby didn't write in that journal every night anymore, and Miriam thought that might be a good thing. She was hoping her cousin would seek the Lord for guidance and help with all that ailed her. Although . . . when she darted away with Jesse Dienner, she'd seemed just fine.

Finally, she shrugged. "I don't know, *Mamm*. I think they're just friends."

"Jesse will make a fine husband for a lucky *maedel* someday." She smiled all-knowingly at Miriam.

"I guess." She pulled the screen open. *But not for me.*

Saul regretted the way things ended the last time he saw Miriam, but he decided to leave well enough alone. Miriam was better off without him, and he didn't know how long he'd have the strength to tell her that she couldn't go with him when he left. He still couldn't believe what she'd said. It was like a dream—the thought of him and Miriam sharing a life together. But it was a dream that was out of reach. Leaving here was his dream, not hers. He could never let her do that.

He tried to stay focused on the positive, first and foremost his father, who hadn't had a drinking episode since he and Saul last talked. Soon Saul would need to tell him about his job offer. He needed to do it before *Daed* deeded over the property to him. But for the first time since he'd found out about his job, he felt a void in his life. Miriam never should have told him that she'd go with him. Now all he could do was think about the possibilities of a life with her.

He crawled into his buggy and headed toward the creek. He'd left Ruben and James an unfair amount of chores to do, but he'd make it up to them next weekend. Today he needed to be around friends, and he knew they would be gathered at Pequea Creek, like they always were on Saturday afternoons.

He'd barely turned onto Blackhorse Road when he saw Miriam drive by going the other direction. She waved but didn't even look his way. *Don't turn around. Keep going.* He gritted his teeth and managed to keep going for about a hundred yards before he grunted to himself and turned the buggy around. He picked up the pace until he was close to catching up with her. She eventually slowed to a stop, and he pulled up beside her.

"Are you following me?" She turned her head to face him, without even the hint of a smile on her face.

"*Ya.* I am. We need to talk, Miriam. Where are you off to?"

She raised her chin. "Nowhere. I'm just riding around. It's a nice day."

"Let's take your buggy back to your house, then you can ride with me to the creek. We can talk on the way." Saul waited a moment, then added, "Please."

She shifted in her seat and faced him from her buggy. "I don't know what we have to talk about, Saul. I misunderstood something, and now I feel . . . embarrassed."

Saul wanted to get out and go to her, but he didn't have anywhere to tie up his horse. "I don't think you really misunderstood. It's complicated, Miriam."

"It doesn't have to be," she said in the sweetest voice Saul had ever heard.

"Then, please, let's talk. I have some things I want to say to you." He knew she couldn't go with him. They'd barely started seeing each other. Then why did it seem like he'd been with Miriam his entire life? In some ways, he figured he had. His heart had belonged to her since they were young. In addition to his attraction to her, he also found that her goodness offset the trouble he often found himself in, and she made him want to be a better person.

His thoughts conflicted, he wasn't sure what he would say to her, but he couldn't stand to have her mad at him or not understand how he felt about her.

"Okay," she finally said.

She turned her horse around, and Saul followed her back to her house.

Rebecca hung little John's bedsheets out to dry. Her youngest still wet the bed every now and then, despite her many attempts to curb his late-night liquids and make sure he went to the bathroom before bedtime. She jumped when Aaron wrapped his arms around her from behind and nuzzled her neck.

"Aaron, what are you doing?" She pinned up the corner of the white sheet, squinting from the sun's glare. "I thought you were at Abe's putting up a fence?"

"That's what I have *sohns* for," he teased as he kissed her on the neck.

"You smell of work, so you must have been busy doing something." She clipped the last of the sheet on the line, then spun around to face her husband.

"We finished the fence, so the boys stayed to play volleyball, and I decided to come home and spend some alone time with *mei fraa*." He pulled her close. "I know Shelby is gone. Is Miriam here?" Frowning, he glanced around.

"No. She took the spring buggy and went for a drive. It's just us, Aaron." She pushed him away. "But I have chores to do."

Aaron grabbed her shoulders and drew her to him again. "I

think we best seize this moment, Rebecca." He looked up at the sky and squinted. "It's the middle of the day, and no one is at home." He smiled broadly.

"Shame on you, Aaron Raber. Such thoughts from a man your age in the middle of the afternoon."

Her husband of twenty years leaned in and kissed her with the same passion as when they were teenagers, and taking a nap didn't sound like such a bad idea. Next thing she knew, Aaron scooped her into his arms and started walking toward the house. "Why, Aaron . . ." She batted her eyes at him.

"Nap time, *mei leib.*"

"Don't drop me going up these porch steps."

Aaron didn't get up the first step when they heard the *clippety-clop* of hooves on the driveway. "Goodness! Put me down before someone sees!"

"It's Miriam." Aaron set her on the ground.

"She just left. I wonder what she's doing home so early." Rebecca held her hand to her forehead and strained to see. "Someone's behind her. I hope nothing's wrong." She moved across the yard until the second buggy came into view. "Oh no." She sighed. "It's Saul Fisher," she whispered to Aaron.

"*Ach,* Rebecca . . ." Aaron shook his head.

"Don't 'ach, Rebecca' me." She stood tall. "This won't be *gut.* I'm sure of it." She folded her arms across her chest and waited. Miriam tied the horse to the stump by the fence, then she waited for Saul to follow her into the yard.

"*Mamm, Daed,* I'm going to go with Saul to the creek, if that's all right." Miriam's eyes pleaded with hers, but Rebecca knew this was a terrible dilemma. She'd allowed her to go on a drive, and she could have just as easily met Saul at the creek, so how could she deny this request? Her mind worked doubly hard to think of a way.

"I don't know, Miriam. I mean—"

"Of course you can go, *mei dochder*. You go and have a *gut* time." Aaron stroked his beard, and Rebecca could have punched him.

Saul walked forward and nodded to Rebecca, then extended his hand to Aaron. "*Danki*, sir. I'll have her home well before the supper hour."

A smiled tipped the corner of Aaron's mouth as he glanced at Rebecca, then back at Saul. "That sounds mighty fine, Saul."

"*Danki, Daed.* I just have to go put the horse in the barn." Miriam turned to go back to the buggy.

"You *kinner* run along. I'll take care of that." Aaron waved his arm for them to go.

"*Danki*," Saul said as he and Miriam made their way to Saul's buggy.

Aaron waited until they had turned the corner before he attempted to scoop Rebecca back into his arms. Kicking, she fell out of his arms, almost all the way to the ground. "What are you doing?" she demanded.

"Taking up where we left off." He winked. "Nap time, remember?"

"I am no longer tired!"

She marched into the house and slammed the door.

———

"Did you see the look on your *mamm's* face?" Saul said as he got his horse into a steady trot. He shook his head. "I don't think she cares for you spending time with me."

Miriam was quite sure her mother didn't approve of her see-ing Saul. *"Mamm's* heard the rumors that you might be leaving the community."

Saul turned at the next gravel side road.

"This isn't the way to the creek."

"I know." He pulled the buggy to the side of the road, no houses visible, only a few cows grazing to their left. "We can talk here."

Miriam's heart started to pound. She wasn't sure she wanted to hear what he had to say. He twisted in his seat to face her, drew in a deep breath, and then let it out slowly.

"Like I told you, I got this job offer, and I wasn't going to get baptized this fall. I'd made up my mind about that, but I started to change my mind because—because of Ruben and James. I wasn't sure if I should leave them."

Miriam could feel her face turning pinker by the moment. "Saul, we really don't need to talk about this. I understand."

"No. I don't think you do." He reached for her hand, and visions of him kissing her flashed through her mind. He inter-twined their fingers, locking his eyes with hers. "I think I've always been *in lieb* with you, Miriam . . . since we were young *kinner.* That may sound crazy, but it's true."

Doesn't sound crazy to me. She held her breath as her heart danced.

"But, Miriam, every man in this community wants to be with you, and I never once considered that you might feel the way I always have."

Miriam held up one finger. "That's not true, Saul. We've watched each other and flirted for years. You had to have known I felt some-thing too."

"Ya, ya. I thought you liked me well enough, but I never felt

like I was *gut* enough for you, Miriam. And I can't give you what you want—a life here. I feel pulled to go do something else, and I want this job and the freedom to explore the world outside of our community. But since you told me you'd go with me, I can't stop picturing us together now." He pulled his eyes from her and sighed. "And I can't let you leave here."

Miriam was still reeling over the fact that he'd said he'd loved her for a long time. But now that the reality was set before her, it frightened her. She didn't know anything about the world outside of their district. In her fantasies, this was the time when she would tell him how much she loved him and vow to follow him anywhere. Instead, she sat speechless.

"Anyway, I didn't want you to think that I didn't care about you, or think about you going with me, because it's keeping me up at night now." Saul looked up and stared deeply into her eyes. "I love you, Miriam. I always have."

Miriam bit her lip as she blinked back tears. No matter their future, she couldn't let him not know how she felt too. "I love you too, Saul."

He let go of her hand, then pulled her into his arms. "It would be so unfair to ask you to come with me," he whispered.

Miriam felt like she couldn't breathe. *Why does he keep saying that?* Was he waiting for her to offer to go with him again? Being with Saul was all she'd dreamed about, but visions of her family kept popping into her mind. Could she really leave them and become part of a world that was foreign to her? Or could she stay here around all that was familiar—and not have Saul?

He eased away from her, cupped her cheek, then kissed her in a way that solidified her decision.

"I want to go with you, Saul. I'll go anywhere with you."

He smiled. "I can't *ask* you to do that, but I won't insist you stay. Are you sure? Is it really what you want, Miriam, to be with me as much as I want to be with you?"

Miriam felt herself trembling, unsure how much of it was from his kiss, the feel of his arms around her, or the fear of speaking the words she'd always dreamed about. She tried to calm her beating heart and prayed she was doing the right thing.

"*Ya.* I want to go with you."

12

MIRIAM SAT AT THE CREEK'S EDGE WITH LEAH AND Hannah and watched as Saul edged onto the diving rock and prepared to jump. She heard Saul's friends cheering him to jump, and his eyes met with hers right before he hit the water, like they'd done so many times before. But after their talk on the way to the creek, she knew things were different now. She felt a wave of excitement and confusion rush through her as she watched his head pop out of the water, searching until he found her.

"How are you doing, Miriam?" Leah asked. "We haven't seen you since your *onkel's* funeral."

"I'm fine." She hung her head for a moment but quickly looked back up.

"I like your cousin Shelby. I was sorry to meet her at such a sad time," Hannah said. "She seems sweet, though."

"She is," Miriam said, then for reasons she couldn't explain, she envisioned Shelby and Jesse alone together fishing at the Zook farm. *Am I doing the right thing by leaving with Saul?* It was all she'd ever wanted, to be with Saul. What would she do in the outside world? Would she work at a job outside the home? How often would she see her family? Would they join a church in the city?

Why haven't I thought of these things before?

"So tell us, Miriam . . . Last time we were here, you went to go talk to Saul. How did that go?" Leah nudged Hannah. "It must have gone *gut*, since he brought you here today."

Miriam smiled as she thought about the way Saul kissed her, and momentarily her worries drifted to the back of her mind where she hoped they would stay. "*Ya*, we're dating."

Hannah pressed her lips firmly together for a moment. "Be careful, Miriam. I don't think Saul is the settling-down type, and I still keep hearing that he might not be baptized in the fall. Some say he won't stay here."

"He's the settling-down type," Miriam said smugly.

Leah leaned across Hannah again. "I don't know." She giggled. "But he sure is handsome, and I sure do like watching him jump."

Miriam knew jealousy was a sin, but it reared its ugly head just the same. "He asked me to leave here with him."

"Who?" Hannah asked.

"Saul."

Hannah's mouth fell open, then she exchanged looks with Leah. When she turned back to Miriam, her forehead was creased with concern. "Of course you told him no, right?"

Miriam drew in a calming breath as she sat up taller. "I'm going with him. He has a job offer at a restaurant in Pittsburgh."

Leah was now practically in Hannah's lap as she leaned inward to hear Miriam.

"How did he propose? Tell us the details." Hannah nudged Leah out of her lap. "This happened so fast. I can't believe you'll be leaving here. What did your parents say?"

As the questions slammed into Miriam faster and harder, she

tried to gather her thoughts. And the first realization that hit her was—*He asked me to go with him, but he didn't ask me to marry him. What does that mean?*

Then she pondered some more. No, he didn't *ask* her to go with him. She volunteered. "I haven't told *Mamm* and *Daed* yet."

Hannah brought her hand to her mouth to stifle a gasp, and Leah's eyes got round as saucers.

"I'm going to tell them soon."

"Will you be married here before you go?"

"I—I don't know." Miriam stood up. "I have to go." She didn't look back as she hurried toward Saul's buggy, even though she heard Hannah call her name. Choking back tears, she squatted next to the buggy, out of view of everyone. She was breathing much too hard, and her hands were trembling.

"Miriam?" Saul squatted down beside her in the grass a few moments later. She didn't hear him walk up, and she felt ridiculous. He put his hand on her shoulder. "What's wrong?"

She forced herself to stand up. "I'm sorry to cut your time short with your friends, but I'm not feeling well."

"No problem." He helped her into the buggy, then went around to the other side. Within a few minutes he had them back on the road toward home. "Maybe you got too hot. Do you want me to stop at that little store when we get into town and get you something cold to drink?"

She shook her head. "No, I'll be okay."

They rode quietly for a while, and Miriam knew she wouldn't sleep tonight unless she asked Saul a few questions. "Do you think I'll have a job in Pittsburgh?"

"Do you want to work?"

She shrugged. "Maybe." They were quiet again, then she asked, "How often do you think we will see our families?"

"Pittsburgh isn't that far." He paused. "You're having second thoughts, aren't you?" Saul slowed the buggy to cross Lincoln Highway, then picked up speed when they turned onto Black Horse Road.

"Saul, I—I . . . Can you stop the buggy?"

Instantly Saul pulled back on the reins, then pulled off on the first gravel road he could. He turned to face her. "You haven't really thought this through, have you?" He searched her eyes. "I love you, Miriam. And I can picture our life together. But I would never, ever push you into leaving here. You have to be sure, Miriam."

"When would we go?"

"The end of August."

"That's only a month away." She heard the alarm in her voice. Saul reached up and touched her cheek.

"Sweet Miriam." He blinked a few times. "I think this is happening too fast for you." He pulled her into his arms and cupped the nape of her neck, and she rested her head against his chest. His heart was beating fast, and she wondered if he was having second thoughts. "I want you to be happy, whatever that is for you. I won't deny that I want you to make this journey with me, but you have to be sure." He lifted her face and kissed her gently on the lips. "I love you."

"How do you know that, Saul? We've barely spent any time together." It seemed odd to be asking him the question when she didn't have any doubts about how she felt about him. Only fears about this life-changing situation.

Saul was quiet for a few moments, then said, "Maybe I should be asking you the same thing." Before she could respond, he continued, "Do you remember the day at the creek when Lizzie Petersheim brought her sister, Annie?"

Miriam thought back. Little Annie had Down syndrome, but she'd died last year. "That was a few years ago, but *ya*, I remember. Why?"

"Everyone was occupied, even Lizzie, that day. Annie kept coughing, and she had all kinds of . . . *stuff* . . . dripping from her nose. I watched you that day. You cleaned Annie up, and you kept her by your side the rest of the time."

Miriam barely remembered that day. "Saul, anyone would have done that."

"Barbie Beiler fell and broke her leg. Remember that?"

"*Ya.*"

"You went over there every day and helped her run her bed-and-breakfast."

Miriam shook her head. "Saul, these are things anyone in our community would have done."

"But they didn't, Miriam. You did. And depending on how much time you've got, I can give you a dozen more reasons why I've grown to love you over the years." He shifted his eyes away from her. "You make me want to be a better person."

"Saul . . ." She reached up and touched his cheek until he turned to face her. "I think you're a wonderful person, and sometimes the way you help others is a bit different, perhaps more adventuresome than our ways . . . but I've watched you for years too. And your zestful spirit is one of the things that I love."

Saul leaned in and kissed her gently. "I want to spend the rest of my life getting to know everything about you. And I know this is happening fast, but I'm sure that I love you, and I'm sure that I want to be with you always. I know that we would have to throw a wedding together really fast, and—"

Miriam's eyes widened as she put some distance between them. "A wedding?"

"You didn't think we'd move to Pittsburgh together without being married, did you? But only if you're sure, Miriam."

"I'm sure!" She threw her arms around his neck, knowing that this was the piece of the puzzle she needed the most. Everything else would come together. Just knowing that Saul wanted to spend the rest of his life with her would ease the worry that was sure to come in the following weeks—she couldn't imagine how she would tell her parents.

Saul eased away from her, stepped out of the buggy, then walked around to her side. As he dropped to one knee, Miriam covered her mouth with her hand.

"I'm sorry I didn't do this properly." He reached for her hand. "Miriam Raber, I've loved you since I saw you in the first grade, and I love you more now than I thought possible. I'm a plain man making a plain proposal, but I will love you forever and always take care of you if you'll agree to marry me and become *mei fraa*."

Miriam jumped from the buggy and into his arms. "Oh, Saul! I will!"

Shelby couldn't believe how much time had passed. It was nearly four o'clock. She wouldn't be home in time to help with supper preparation, and she'd been trying so hard lately to impress

Rebecca. But she couldn't recall having as much fun as she'd had today in a long time.

She watched Jesse loading the fishing poles into the back of his topless buggy, and she wished this time with him could go on forever. They'd laughed, talked, and he'd shared Amish customs that she'd never heard of before. Her favorite was when he explained how a barn raising was done. When a young couple is starting out and needs a barn—or in the event of a fire—a new barn is erected in one day. Jesse told her that the entire community would arrive early in the morning to construct the barn. It was a family affair and a welcomed opportunity for fellowship in the community.

She reached into her purse sitting on the front seat of the buggy and glanced at her cell phone. She'd charged it earlier in the week in town, and she saw that she now had two missed calls from her mother and four from her father. *Suddenly they care about me?* She tossed it back into her purse.

"Missing your friends back home?" Jesse cradled her elbow and helped her into the buggy. He made her feel like a princess.

"No. I really don't."

He climbed into the buggy on the other side, flicked the reins, and backed the horse and buggy up. Shelby was hot, sweating like she couldn't recall sweating before, had no makeup on, no perfume, no jewelry, and she'd never felt better—or more appreciated for the person she was—than at this moment. Jesse had listened to her all afternoon, and she found herself telling him things she hadn't even told Miriam. Maybe it was an unintentional test to see if he would judge her for the mistakes she'd made. If so, Jesse had passed the test. He made her feel . . . worthy, like a person who deserved to be happy—and forgiven.

Thank You, Lord, for this beautiful day.

"So, Shelby. Tell me. What is the thing you like most about your visit here?"

Shelby leaned her head back, closed her eyes, and enjoyed the wind in her face while she thought about his question. "Family," she finally said as she turned to face him. "Not just Miriam's family, but the way the whole community is like one big family. Everyone helps each other, loves each other."

Jesse smiled. "And what do you like the least?"

Shelby laughed. "Would it be wrong of me to say the lack of air-conditioning?"

"I take every opportunity to go into town and walk the air-conditioned shops this time of year. We all do." He smiled, then whistled for his horse to pick up the pace. "I wonder what it would be like to leave here sometimes."

Shelby was shocked. From everything that Miriam had told her about Jesse, she didn't think Jesse would consider the idea. She blurted the first thing that popped into her head. "You don't want to leave here, Jesse."

"What makes you so sure? I think about it sometimes."

"Because—because there's a sense of peace here that's hard to find out there." She turned to look at him when she felt his eyes on her.

"That peace is in your heart, Shelby. You can have that any-where." He smiled. "You just happen to be finding it here. It sounds like you're working through things, healing from a bad time. But the peacefulness in your heart only comes from a true relationship with God. When you can let your cares go and trust that all things are of God's will, then there's no worry or fear, things that block the voice of God."

"Don't you worry about things?" Shelby often chewed her nails to the quick with worry, and she thought about how freeing it must be to just turn everything over to God. She was working on that.

"Of course. I'm Amish, but I'm still human. I struggle with it all the time. Right now my aunt is sick. I'm worried she'll die. It would be God's will for her to go to her heavenly home, but I still worry. I would miss her."

They rode along quietly for a while. Soon Jesse would be dropping her off at home.

Home. That's what her cousins' farm had become over the past couple of months. Only one thing bothered her about being here, and that was Rebecca, who still seemed guarded with her, as if her presence was a threat to their family somehow. If Rebecca only knew how much Shelby treasured what Rebecca's family had, she wouldn't be so fearful.

When Jesse pulled up the driveway, Shelby turned to him. "Thank you so much for today, Jesse. I had a wonderful time." She giggled. "Even though we didn't catch a single fish."

"I had a *gut* time too, Shelby. We will have to do it again."

When?

She waited until Jesse brought the buggy to a complete stop, then she picked up her purse and stepped out. She'd already asked him to hold on to her new fishing pole, hoping for another invite. "Thanks again." As she was walking away, he called her name.

"Yeah?" She turned to face him.

"I have my lunch hour at the City Dump from noon until one o'clock." He smiled. "Remember, that's the name of the place where I work."

Shelby nodded, guessing what he was about to ask her.

"Anytime you're in town, I'd be glad to buy you lunch. Maybe Miriam can bring you sometime."

"That would be great. I'll see you soon."

Jesse smiled. "I hope so."

Shelby wasn't sure she'd ever really felt butterflies in her stomach before today.

It was routine now for Miriam and Shelby to stay up late talking, later than they should considering that the day started at four o'clock in the morning. They were expected to help with breakfast no matter how late they'd stayed up the night before. But there was much to cover this evening. Miriam let Shelby go first, and her cousin told her about her day with Jesse. In light of Saul's proposal, any thoughts of Jesse as her "safe person" had vanished.

She was glad to see Shelby so happy, but she was worried for both her and for Jesse. Until, that is, Shelby told her what Jesse said.

"You mean he actually said he thinks about leaving sometimes?" Miriam was shocked.

Shelby's expression grew solemn. "Why would anyone want to leave here?"

Miriam laughed. "Usually the *Englisch* want to know why anyone would want to *stay* here."

Shelby ran her brush the length of her hair, and Miriam couldn't help but think about her wedding night when Saul would see her hair in its entirety. Then she cringed when she thought about having to tell her parents that she would be leaving the community with Saul, but she tried to stay focused on the life she knew they would have.

"I could live here."

Miriam sat perfectly still and stared at Shelby. "Really?" Then she folded her arms across her chest and stared at Shelby. "Shelby, you can't choose to live here just because you might be falling for Jesse. That's not right. That's not our way."

Shelby's eyes teared up, and Miriam regretted what she'd said. "I'm sorry."

"No, it's okay. I guess it must seem that way." Shelby hung her head. "I just like you—and your family. I like being here."

Miriam didn't say anything. Suddenly she wasn't sure that this was the best time to share her news with Shelby. But if not Shelby, then who? She was about to burst, needing to share with someone. That someone couldn't be her mother, which saddened her. She recalled a time when she used to tell her mother everything.

"Although . . ." Shelby stopped brushing her hair and frowned. "I think your mother is ready for me to go."

"Why would you say that?"

Shelby sighed as she stuffed her brush back into the drawer. "I overheard your mother saying that she thinks I'm a bad influence on you. More or less, that's what she said."

"Are you talking about me sneaking out to meet Saul? Because if so . . . I already cleared that up with *Mamm*."

"You did?" Shelby straightened. "Was she mad at you?"

"Not as mad as she's going to be."

"What do you mean?"

Miriam crossed her legs beneath her and folded her hands in her lap. "You can't tell anyone what I'm about to tell you. Not until I'm able to tell my parents."

Shelby's eyes widened. "I won't. I won't. What is it, Miriam?"

"I'm leaving here. With Saul. In one month."

13

REBECCA PULLED A RHUBARB PIE FROM THE OVEN and placed it on top of the stove to cool. She was alone in the house, so she sat down at the kitchen table and picked up a copy of *The Budget*. Before she started reading, she glanced around the room. It seemed almost sinful to just sit and do nothing. But Aaron and the boys were working outdoors, and Miriam and Shelby finished their chores in record time this morning, so Rebecca said they could take the buggy to town. Every day they charged through their chores so they could go to town at lunchtime. Those girls were up to something, but she wasn't sure what it was.

She opened the newspaper and began to scan the happenings in Amish and Mennonite communities in the United States. A warm breeze blew through the opened windows in the kitchen, and the smell of freshly baked rhubarb wafted through the air. As she began to relax and not feel guilty for allowing herself idle time, she heard a buggy coming up the driveway. She closed the newspaper and walked to the front door where she saw Marie King and her daughter, Leah, step down from their buggy.

"Marie, Leah. How nice to see you." She kept the door open while the women made their way up the porch steps. "I just pulled a rhubarb pie from the oven, and I was looking for an excuse to have a piece. Can I get you both some pie?"

"No. *Danki*, Rebecca." Marie didn't seem her usual bubbly self, and Leah kept her head hung low and avoided looking at Rebecca.

"Marie, is everything all right?" Rebecca motioned with her hand for both women to take a seat at the kitchen table. "Here, sit. No one is at home, and this is the perfect time to talk. Can I get either of you some *kaffi*?"

Marie shook her head, a solemn look on her face, and Leah still wouldn't look up.

"Rebecca . . ." Marie took a deep breath. "Leah told her father and me some—some upsetting news." She paused as a frown set into her features. "News that I don't think you are aware of, and I have much concern about it."

Rebecca's pulse picked up. "Marie, you're scaring me. What's wrong?"

"It's about Miriam." Marie reached across the table and put her hand on Rebecca's. "Leah tells us that Miriam is leaving the community, and maybe she's already told you, but—"

Rebecca pulled her hand away and brought it to her chest. "What?"

"Oh dear." Marie sighed. "I was afraid she hadn't told you, and maybe it's not our place, but it worries me so, this situation."

Rebecca stared hard at Leah as she tried to calm her beating heart. "Leah, what did Miriam tell you?" *Oh dear Lord, don't let it be true.*

Leah blinked back tears. "I shouldn't have said anything. I should have waited to tell *Mamm* until I was sure that Miriam told you."

"No, Leah. You did the right thing," Rebecca said as she fought her own tears. "What exactly did Miriam tell you?"

"She—she said that . . ." Leah turned to her mother. "Miriam is never going to forgive me for this."

"Leah, please," Rebecca prodded. "If I need to get Bishop Ebersol involved in whatever is going on, I need to know."

"She's going to marry Saul Fisher, and they are leaving the community." A tear rolled down Leah's cheek.

Rebecca stood from the table, turned, and faced the window, then covered her mouth with her hand. *This can't be happening.* She spun around and faced Marie and Leah. "Miriam told you this? When?"

"Saturday at the creek."

Marie stood up and walked to Rebecca. She put her hand on her shoulder. "I just thought you should know, that maybe there might be time to talk Miriam out of this."

Oh, I will talk her out of it. "*Danki,* Marie." She glanced at Leah. "And you did the right thing, Leah. We will surely have a talk with Miriam." She shook her head as she spoke. "Miriam has always been committed to live her life here." *I'm sure Saul has been pushing her to do this.*

Marie folded her arms across her chest. "They are evidently planning to get married and leave here the end of August."

"What?" Rebecca shrieked. "That's barely a month away."

Marie pulled Rebecca into a hug. "I know, dear. I'm so sorry. I can imagine how I would feel if it was Leah doing this. Please let me know if there's anything I can do."

"*Ya,* I will." Rebecca eased away from Marie. "Please don't tell anyone about this just yet. I want to have time to talk to Bishop Ebersol, and of course, I need to talk to Aaron. And Miriam."

"Hannah knows too," Leah said softly.

Rebecca drew in a deep breath. Hannah's mother, Eve, couldn't be quieted when it came to gossip. "All right. *Danki* for stopping by."

After they were gone, Rebecca sat back down at the kitchen table, covered her face with her hands, and cried.

Miriam dropped off Shelby at the City Dump at noon, then went to meet Saul at his place. When she pulled up in her buggy, Saul was leading two horses to the barn. She waved at his father and two brothers as she passed them on her right working in the fields.

"I brought turkey sandwiches." She stepped out of the buggy. "I would have brought enough for your *daed* and brothers too, but you said not to."

"Plenty of leftover meat loaf for them inside." He took the picnic basket from her. "I know it's hot, but do you care if we eat outside, by ourselves? I have some stuff to show you."

"Okay."

Saul led her to a picnic table nestled beneath a grove of oak trees. Miriam started laying out the food.

"You look so pretty," he said when she looked up and saw him staring at her.

"*Danki.* I'm happy."

"Me too." He glanced around to see if anyone was watching, then leaned over and kissed her. "Wait 'til you see what I have to show you. I went to the library yesterday, and the lady who works there helped me print some stuff."

Saul waited until after they ate to go into his house. When he came back, he was carrying a stack of papers. "These are places that we can rent, and they're close to my new job. I have enough saved for a year's rent."

Miriam looked through the pictures of small apartments not much bigger than their basement. She looked up at the man she was going to marry. "Saul, what will I do while you're at work?"

"I've thought about that, Miriam. What do you want to do? Do you want to try to go to school, or get a job, or stay at home and take care of our house?" He smiled. "And someday, our *kinner.*"

Miriam felt her cheeks reddening. "I think that I should probably get a job and work, don't you? We'll need to save our money so we can buy our own home someday. What do you think?"

The flow of Saul's smile warmed her. "I just want you to be happy. I'll make a *gut* life for you, Miriam." He paused, as if far away for a moment. "I can picture me as a chef in a fancy restaurant. And just think how *gut* we'll eat at home."

Miriam smiled as she thought about Saul cooking for her in their own home. She couldn't imagine her father or brothers ever cooking a meal. "Here comes your *daed,*" she said when she saw Zeb Fisher walking toward them. She stood up to greet him.

"Keep your seat, Miriam. Nice to see you." Zeb smiled as he walked past them and toward the house.

"Have you told your *daed* yet?"

Saul shifted his weight on the bench. "No. What about you? You tell your folks?" He shook his head. "Your parents are gonna be real upset. Do you want me to be with you when you tell them?"

"You'd do that?" Miriam's insides warmed as she sat back down across from him.

"Of course I would." He reached over and squeezed her hand. "I'll do anything for you."

Maybe it was the way he was looking at her, so solemn and serious, or maybe it was his soft, raspy, level tone of voice, but no matter what . . . she believed him. Saul was the kind of man she wanted to live the rest of her life with.

"I love you, Saul."

"I love you too, Miriam."

Miriam and Shelby talked and laughed all the way home. Miriam was still worried about what was happening between Shelby and Jesse, but it was good to see her cousin so happy. Turns out, Shelby used to be a big reader, and Jesse read a lot too. They'd read some of the same Christian books, and Shelby said they'd spent their entire lunch hour talking about books.

When Miriam pulled to a stop at home, she saw her parents sitting on the front porch in the rocking chairs, and they didn't look happy at all. *Mamm's* arms were folded across her chest, her legs were crossed, and she was kicking that rocker so hard it looked like it might lift off the ground at any moment. *Daed* was scowling in a way that made Miriam want to turn the buggy around and leave.

"Uh-oh," Shelby whispered. "Something's up."

They walked cautiously toward the porch. "Miriam, we need to speak with you," her father said in a voice that sounded frightfully unfamiliar.

"*Ya, Daed.*" Miriam didn't look at her parents as she padded up the steps to the porch. Shelby followed but passed by Miriam and went inside.

Daed stood up and started to pace. "Sit down, Miriam."

Miriam did as she was told. She glanced at her mother, and

Miriam could tell she'd been crying. She was pretty sure she knew what this was about. *I should have never told Hannah and Leah about me and Saul.* Miriam was hoping that her mother would take over the conversation, like she usually did. She wasn't sure that anything her mother could say would be nearly as scary as the way her father was looking at her, his mouth pinched together in a frown and his eyes squinted.

Daed took a few deep breaths, then stroked his beard several times before he glared at Miriam. "Do you have any idea how upsetting it was for your *mamm* today when Marie and Leah King came over to tell her about your plans? Did you not think that your parents should be the first to know that you are planning to marry Saul Fisher?" He walked closer and bent at the waist. "And that you are planning to leave the community? Do you not think us worthy of this news before it is spread around the community like sinful gossip? So tell me, Miriam, that this news is not true."

"I—I . . ." She sought help from her mother with her eyes, but *Mamm* just looked down at her feet and kicked the rocker even harder with her bare feet. "I love him, *Daed*. I love Saul." Her voice cracked as she spoke, but a tear rolled down her cheek when her father grunted. "I've always loved him," she added as she put her face to her hands.

"Look at me, *maedel*."

It wasn't a plea, it was a demand, and Miriam did as she was told. She met eyes with her father and waited.

"I've always known you liked Saul. But this rushed courtship so that you can move with him is disgraceful." Her father pulled his eyes from Miriam, and he stared out into the pasture. "Are you—are you in a family way?"

Miriam started to cry harder. "No, *Daed*. No. Never." She looked to her mother, but *Mamm* refused to look at her.

Her father turned around, then moved toward her. *Daed* had never laid a hand on her except as a young child who needed a spanking, but he was shaking so much that Miriam feared he might. But he squatted down beside her, and when he did, Miriam saw tears in his eyes.

"Then why, *mei maedel*, do you need to marry so quickly and leave us? Why not bring this boy around, let us get to know him better? And why do you both choose to leave your families?"

Miriam tried to breathe, to control her sobs. "Saul has a job in Pittsburgh working as a chef in a new restaurant. It starts in September."

Daed stood up and rubbed his eyes. "And he can support you doing this *job*?"

Miriam had thought of this too, despite the fact that Saul said he had some money saved. "I will work too, if I need to."

"A woman's place is in the home." *Mamm* finally spoke up. "Taking care of her husband, their *haus*, and their *kinner*. Working in the *Englisch* world in Pittsburgh is no place for you, Miriam."

Miriam knew that she needed to remind her parents that she was in her *rumschpringe*, and that according to the *Ordnung*, she had a right not to get baptized and to seek out a life among the *Englisch*. Fear kept her from doing just that. Everything her parents said only magnified her anxiety about going. She needed her family's support. She needed their blessing.

"I can still have a nice home and *kinner*," she said in a whisper between sobs.

"No." Her father crossed his arms across his chest. "You will not leave with Saul."

Miriam hung her head and cried. She needed Saul, but she needed her parents too.

Rebecca pulled back the covers and got into bed. She snuggled up against Aaron who had his head buried in a book. She'd prayed a lot since their conversation with Miriam, and the guidance she felt she was receiving from God surprised her. She felt called to share her feelings with Aaron.

"Aaron . . ."

"*Ya?*" He didn't take his eyes from his reading.

"We cannot keep her here against her will." She eased away from him, fluffed her pillow behind her, then crossed her ankles beneath the covers. "Besides, I thought you said you saw this coming, her seeing Saul."

Aaron closed the book. "*Ya,* I did. I've known for years those two were smitten with each other. One only has to watch them for a few minutes when they are in the same room to know that." Aaron looked at her for a moment, a hurt expression clouding his face. "But I never thought Saul would drag our only *dochder* away from the only place she's known." He paused, then scratched his head. "And to go be a cook. What kind of man goes to be a cook?"

Rebecca stifled a grin, although not one thing about this situation was funny.

"You told me to be firm, Rebecca. So I was."

She rubbed his arm. "*Ya,* you were." Rebecca's heart hurt for Miriam. But how could her daughter be in love? Surely she wasn't old enough. She sighed, recalling how she was the same age when she fell in love with Aaron. "But, *mei lieb,* we cannot stop her."

Aaron twisted to face her. "Why are you soft about this now? You don't want her to leave." He gave his head a taut nod. "We will stop her."

"She has free will, Aaron. We have to trust God to guide her."

"Is this the same woman who told me to make sure our *dochder* didn't leave the community?"

"I'm scared, Aaron. And I know you're scared too. Because usually where Miriam is concerned, you are a big ol' softie." She put her head on his shoulder. "But if she ends up leaving, we cannot shun her. It wouldn't be right."

"You sound like you've already given up. I will not give up."

"I'm not giving up either, Aaron. But . . ." She gazed into her husband's eyes. "Can you bear to see your only *dochder* with a broken heart?"

"If it means keeping her in the community, then *ya* . . . I can."

"*Ach*, Aaron. You don't mean that."

"If she chooses to leave with that boy, she will get no help from me. I'm not surprised that Saul Fisher is her choice for a spouse, but I always thought that boy would stay here." He shook his head. "How wrong I was."

Rebecca leaned up and kissed her husband. "We are both forgetting everything that we know and believe in, *mei lieb*. Everything is God's will. It's in His hands. We will have to trust that everything will work out."

Aaron sighed. "When you put it that way, I know you're right." He pulled Rebecca close. "But it scares me, the thought of our baby girl leaving."

Rebecca put her hand on her heart. "Me too." *And I plan to pay a visit to Saul Fisher as soon as possible.*

Shelby wasn't sure what to say to Miriam. Her cousin had been crying on and off all afternoon since her talk with her parents. No one said much at supper, and after helping clean up the kitchen, both Miriam and Shelby headed upstairs.

"I don't understand, though. I thought you got to choose if you wanted to stay or not." Shelby reached into her purse and pulled out her diary.

Miriam sniffled, then frowned. "You haven't written in that in a long time. Why are you writing in it?"

Shelby pulled the cap off of her pen. "I just feel like it. Maybe because I haven't written in it in a long time."

"I thought—I thought that you were happier now, and—and talking to God instead of that book."

Shelby briefly wondered if Miriam had looked at her diary. "It's not the same. Sometimes I just like to voice my thoughts to . . ." She paused, thought for a moment, then closed the diary, realizing that she *had* been voicing her thoughts—to God. "Maybe you're right." She dropped it back in her purse, then sighed. "So what are you going to do about you and Saul? Are you still going to go?"

"I love him. I'm going wherever he wants to go."

Shelby thought for a moment. "Is it really fair of him to ask you to leave here, though?"

"He didn't ask. He said he would never ask me. I offered."

"Hmm . . ." Shelby crossed her legs beneath her and faced Miriam on the other bed. "Will you be shunned by your family, like your Uncle Ivan was?"

Miriam sat taller as she dabbed at her eyes. "Well, I shouldn't be, that's for sure. I'm not baptized. Neither is Saul. We should both have the freedom to choose." She started to cry again. "*Mei daed* has never spoken to me like that."

"You'd be leaving in less than a month. It doesn't sound like your parents are going to help you get married, either." Shelby cringed when Miriam started to cry harder. "I'm sorry. I guess I shouldn't have said that."

"I'm scared. And I need my family's blessing. I don't know how I can leave without it. But I don't know how I can live without Saul in my life, either."

They were quiet for a few moments.

"Are you sure you can be happy away from here, Miriam? The *Englisch* world, as you call it, can be a scary place." She uncrossed her legs and dangled them over the side of the bed. "Hey, would Saul reconsider and stay here?"

"I'm not asking him to give up his dream."

"What about your dreams, Miriam?"

She smiled. "I just want to be with Saul. We will build dreams together."

Shelby thought about the time she'd been spending with Jesse and what good friends they were becoming. He wasn't like the guys back home. Jesse was polite, never pushy, and seemed interested in what she had to say. And more than once he'd said he wondered what it would be like to live away from here.

Was he just making conversation or would he really consider leaving this peaceful place? Shelby was starting to feel like her heart was back in a dangerous place. Maybe it would be best to stop spending so much time with Jesse—for both their sakes.

14

It took several more days before Rebecca found the right time to go see Saul. It was later in the evening but well before dark, and everyone was occupied after supper. Aaron and the boys were milking the cows and taking care of things in the barn. Miriam and Shelby were doing whatever they did up in that bedroom for hours each evening after their chores were done.

Rebecca couldn't help but worry about what sort of plans might be in the works. Was Miriam secretly planning a wedding, perhaps even somewhere far away? Rebecca's heart broke at the thought of not seeing Miriam get married, and she was equally as upset for Miriam, who moped around the house, barely speaking to anyone—except Shelby.

She thought about her first phone call with Shelby's mother. There was an urgency in the woman's voice, as if Shelby would never mend unless she was sent far away from friends who were causing her to make bad choices.

One thing that bothered her a lot was the lack of communication between Shelby and her parents. She'd asked Shelby about it, but the girl just shrugged and looked away, commenting that she had talked to each of her parents a few times.

Rebecca shook her head. She couldn't imagine Miriam being

away from her for one day, much less two months—with barely any conversation. Divorce must affect people in strange ways, Rebecca assumed, but to put oneself first over the well-being of one's children—well, it just seemed wrong.

She pulled into the Fisher driveway, surprised not to see anyone outside. This was Rebecca's family's favorite time of night. As soon as Aaron and the boys got through with the cows and secured things up for the night, they'd often sit on the porch and watch the sun set, or sometimes Aaron would even join the boys for a game of basketball. Miriam used to join in for those activities often as well, and Rebecca loved to sit and watch her family enjoying some fun after a hard day's work.

After parking the buggy, she tethered the horse to a pole by the fence. She hadn't taken two steps when Saul's two brothers came tearing across the yard from the barn. Breathless, the boys wound around her and stopped, almost blocking her way.

"Hello, Ruben. Hello, James." She waited while the boys caught their breath, and as she looked at them, she realized that she hadn't been here since Sarah and Hannah had died. Zeb and the boys didn't have any other family, and Rebecca had assumed that the bishop must not push Zeb to hold church service at his house. Rebecca silently reprimanded herself for not coming to check on Zeb and the boys over the years. Surely they would have enjoyed a home-cooked meal. Then she remembered Saul's job offer, and she doubted Zeb or the boys missed any meals. "I need to talk to Saul. Is he home?"

She hadn't planned out what she would say, but hopefully God would give her the right words to convince Saul not to take her baby girl away from the only life she'd ever known.

Rebecca looked on as Ruben and James both stuttered, looking back and forth at each other. "He's busy right now. Can we give him a message?" the older boy, Ruben, finally said.

"There is no message. I need to talk to him. Do you know when he'll be home?" Rebecca glanced to her right and saw three buggies. Surely the Fisher family didn't own more than three buggies. "Or is he home and just busy?"

"*Ya.* He's busy," James said. Rebecca knew him to be about thirteen now. Handsome boys, both of them. Saul was a nice-looking fellow too, so Rebecca could see Miriam's attraction, but hadn't she taught her daughter to look past just charm and looks?

"I would like to wait for him, please." Rebecca knew she was being rude, but this was an urgent matter that needed to be handled as soon as possible. She'd already waited too long to make this visit.

Both boys stood their ground, not moving. Rebecca folded her arms across her chest. "Perhaps I could wait on the porch for him. Can you please let him know that I am waiting to speak to him? It's important."

Ruben bit his bottom lip, glanced at James, then said, "Sure. Please have a seat on the porch, and I'll let Saul know you're here." He turned back to James. "Can you get Rebecca some tea?"

"No bother. I don't need any tea. *Danki*, though." She scooted past the boys, walked up the porch steps, then took a seat in the porch swing.

Ruben and James both went into the house, closing the screen and wooden door behind them. Rebecca could hear movement inside, but all the doors and windows were shut, which seemed ridiculous in this heat. She patted the sweat on her cheeks with her hands, then dabbed at her forehead. *Maybe they secretly have air-conditioning inside.*

Less than a minute later she heard a loud crash inside the house, followed by loud voices, though she couldn't understand what was being said. She rose from the swing, eased her way to the front door, then leaned her ear against it.

"I can't get him up. He's out cold!"

"What do we do? And by the way, Miriam's mother is on the porch."

Rebecca listened, unsure what to do. The voices grew softer for a few moments, then she heard James say, "Saul, maybe Miriam's mother can help us! We need some help! We need someone to tell us what to do!"

"No!"

Rebecca recognized Saul's voice as the one who'd denied his brother's request.

What in the world is going on in there? She took a deep breath, eased the screen away from the door, and grabbed the doorknob. In one quick motion, she turned the knob and pushed the door open. She stepped inside before anyone could say anything.

Bringing her hand to her mouth to stifle a gasp, she wished she could turn around and go back outside. She eyed the scene before her, and Saul was the first one to speak.

"Rebecca, please go home." Saul's eyes were wet with tears, and Rebecca started to do as he asked until she saw blood on Zeb Fisher's face. All three boys were squatting down around their father, and the rank smell of red wine filled the room. Rebecca moved toward them, squatted down between Saul and James, then spoke directly to Ruben as she leaned over Zeb.

"This isn't bad, boys. Ruben, go get me a wet rag, and see if you can find some ointment. We'll have your father fixed up in no time."

"Sarah, is that you?" Zeb could barely open his eyes as he spoke.

"No, Zeb. It's Rebecca Raber. You've got a nasty cut on your face, but we're going to doctor it for you. You'll be just fine."

"Hannah, *mei dochder?*" Zeb's lids flitted open for only a couple of seconds before they closed again.

Ruben returned with a wet rag and some ointment, and Rebecca dabbed at Zeb's chin. He could probably use a couple of stitches, but taking him to the hospital right now would cause scandal for this family.

Rebecca glanced around at the boys as sweat poured down everyone's faces. "Saul, why don't you open some windows?"

"But someone might come by or—"

Rebecca raised her brows. "Someone already did. *Me.* Now open those windows before everyone suffocates in here."

Saul did as she asked, and a breeze quickly filled the den. Once she'd tended to Zeb as best she could, she told the boys to just put him on the couch. "He'll wake up in the morning with a nasty headache, but he will be all right."

"We know," James said as he swiped at his eyes.

"Hush, James." Saul frowned at his brother as he reached underneath Zeb's shoulders. James and Ruben each grabbed a leg, and the boys lifted Zeb onto the couch.

Rebecca glanced around at the boys as she realized that they had done this more than once. *How many times?*

"Boys, has this happened before?" Rebecca directed the question to James, since he seemed the most willing to talk.

"All the time," James said as he shook his head.

Saul quickly grabbed both his brothers by the arm. "Go finish your chores. I'll take it from here."

Ruben and James moved toward the door. James turned around and faced Rebecca, his eyes somehow pleading with hers, and Rebecca's heart hurt for this family. The boys were barely out the door when Saul spoke.

"Please don't tell anyone, Rebecca. Please." Saul's eyes melded with hers in a way that left Rebecca speechless. "Please. I'm begging you."

"Saul . . ." she finally said. "Why don't we step into the kitchen?"

Saul pointed to his right. Rebecca walked ahead of him, and she was surprised how clean and fresh the kitchen was, especially for four men living alone. White countertops were shiny and clean, and nothing looked out of place. Rebecca sat down in one of six chairs around an oak table in the middle of the room.

"Do you want something to drink?" Saul didn't sit down.

Rebecca pulled the chair out next to her. "No, I'm fine. Sit down, Saul."

He sighed but did as she asked. "Are you going to tell anyone about this?"

Rebecca rubbed her forehead for a moment, then looked up at him. "Saul, if this goes on all the time, like James said, then you boys need—"

"It ain't that often." Saul leaned back in the chair and looped his thumbs beneath his suspenders. She noticed the blood on Saul's shirt and quickly glanced over him to see if he might be hurt. He didn't appear to be.

"Your father needs some help, Saul. You all do."

Saul pushed the chair from the table and stood up. His eyes blazed as he spoke to Rebecca. *"Mei daed* is the best man I've ever known. He is a loving man. He loves his family. He loves us!"

Rebecca stood up, slowly putting her hand on Saul's shoulder. "Of course he does, Saul."

Saul jerked away from her. "He would never do anything to hurt us." The boy blinked as fast as he could, but a tear still rolled down his cheek, and he quickly wiped it away.

"Saul . . ." She paused as their eyes locked. "How long has this been going on?"

He pulled his eyes from hers, folded his arms across his chest, and stared past Rebecca.

"Since your *mamm* and Hannah died?"

Saul bit his bottom lip and wouldn't look at her.

A knot was building in Rebecca's throat, but now was not the time to cry, even though her heart was breaking for Saul and his brothers. "Saul, you need some help."

"Why did you come here, Rebecca?" Saul leaned against the kitchen counter, his arms still folded across his chest. "Is it about me and Miriam?"

She cautiously took a step toward him. *"Ya,* but, Saul, I think right now we need to talk about what is happening here, and—"

"If you're worried about me taking Miriam away from here, don't worry about it anymore." He swiped at his eyes again. "I can't leave Ruben and James. They ain't old enough to take care of everything around here."

Rebecca was quiet for a moment. *You're only eighteen, dear child. You're not old enough either.*

"Is this why you are so anxious to leave our community, Saul?"

"No." He wouldn't look at her.

"I can understand. You've been raising your brothers, cooking, cleaning, taking care of your father, and—"

"*Mei daed's* drinking is not the reason why I want to leave. I'm not running away from everything."

Rebecca ignored Saul's sharp tone and softened her own. "Then why, Saul? Why do you want to take my baby girl and leave here?"

Saul uncrossed his arms, then rubbed his forehead for a moment. "I told you. I can't leave now anyway."

"Maybe in a few years when you are both older, you can rethink this, and—"

Saul shook his head, then locked eyes with Rebecca. "My job offer is only good for September." He paused, then stood taller. "I love Miriam. I would have made a *gut* home for her, taken care of her, and always made sure she was happy."

"Why cooking?" Rebecca eased herself back into a kitchen chair.

"What?"

Rebecca twisted her mouth to one side. "Why does cooking interest you so, and why do you think you need to leave here to go cook?"

Saul's blue eyes brightened for a moment as if he was about to tell her exciting news, then he looked away as his expression fell. "It ain't acceptable for a man to cook here. It's women's work."

Rebecca thought for a moment. "True. But I'm sure Miriam would let you do some of the cooking." Miriam marrying Saul might not be ideal, but if Rebecca could keep them both in the community—well, it seemed the lesser of the two evils.

Saul shuffled to a chair across from her, sat down, then leaned forward a bit. His eyes brightened again. "Do you know how many different recipes there are for rhubarb?"

Rebecca sighed, feeling they were getting off topic.

"There's rhubarb compote and all kinds of rhubarb sauces for fish, chicken, and beef." He shook his head. "It's not just for pies and jam." After he paused, he grinned. "And I have a great recipe for rhubarb soup with mint in it."

Rebecca opened her mouth to try to redirect the conversation, but Saul kept going. "And do you know how many different things you can make with eggs? Breakfast frittatas, crepes, quiches . . ." He shook his head. "It'll make you never want to scramble another egg for breakfast."

I enjoy scrambled eggs. Rebecca scowled a bit, realizing Saul knew more at his young age about cooking than she'd probably know in her lifetime.

"And the gadgets, electric gadgets that are available to help with the cooking . . . it's amazing." Saul let out a heavy sigh, then stood up from the table. "It was just a dream." He glanced around the corner into the den where his father was sleeping on the couch, and a big wave of reality brought them back to the subject at hand. Saul spun around and faced her. "Are you going to tell anyone about this?" He swallowed hard.

Rebecca stood up and took a deep breath. "Saul, don't you feel that you and your brothers could use some help, and that maybe—"

"No. Please." Saul took a step toward her. "I won't take Miriam away from here, but please don't tell."

Rebecca rubbed her forehead as she thought about how miserable Miriam had been. Was she really being fair to

Miriam—and Saul? She'd tried to rule out the possibility of true love between the two of them. *They're so young.* But just as soon as she saw fit to, she thought about her and Aaron. Their love was as real and true then as it was now. *Do Miriam and Saul have that kind of love?*

Miriam and Saul's whirlwind romance gave cause for speculation. Like her husband, Rebecca had known that Miriam admired Saul from afar. And yes, they'd grown up together. But true love was more than attraction, and Rebecca wondered if Miriam and Saul shared the kind of everlasting love blessed by God. Saul was standing at the counter, writing something on a piece of paper. He walked toward Rebecca and handed her the note.

Rebecca pulled the piece of paper closer, struggling to read it without her glasses. "A recipe for rhubarb mint soup." She scowled. "Saul, you can't bribe me with a recipe."

"It's not a bribe." Saul lifted one shoulder. "More of an offering of peace."

Rebecca tucked the recipe into her apron pocket. "I need to go." She left the kitchen and eased through the den, past Zeb on the couch, and toward the door. Saul followed. She'd won this round. Miriam wouldn't be leaving here. But as she glanced at Zeb on the couch, she didn't feel victorious at all.

"Good-bye, Saul."

* * *

It was two days later when Saul finally caught up with Miriam. He'd managed to get a message to Jesse, who gave it to Shelby for Miriam—for her to meet him at the covered bridge in Ronks on Thursday at six in the evening. Saul worried that Rebecca had told Miriam everything, and he wondered what she would be thinking—about him, his father, and their family. Miriam didn't seem one to judge, and it wasn't their way, but he was still fearful.

Today he would tell her that he planned to stay in the community. Marrying Miriam would be wonderful, but he couldn't help but feel that the dream he'd had for years was just out of reach, and that he'd never have this opportunity again. They'd both be baptized, and there'd be no need to rush a wedding. Plenty of time. Since he wouldn't be going anywhere.

He greeted Miriam with a kiss when he walked up to her. She was standing under the bridge, her buggy parked off the side of the road. "Do your folks know where you are?" He couldn't stand the thought of Miriam lying to her parents to sneak off and see him. It shouldn't be like that.

"I told them I was going for a ride."

"How is everything at home?"

"Tense. No one is saying much." She leaned closer to him. "But it doesn't matter, Saul. I love my family, but you are going to be my husband, and I'll go anywhere with you. Your dreams are my dreams."

Saul pulled her into a hug and held her tight for a few moments before he eased her away, feeling relieved that Rebecca hadn't shared anything. "Miriam, I've decided not to take the job in Pittsburgh."

She stepped back from him. "Why? Why not? Saul, please don't do this because of me. I've thought a lot about it, and I want to go out into the world. I want to experience things I've never been able to." She reached into the pocket of her black apron. "Look! I found this in a magazine. It's a person who helps you find houses—a realtor. And look at this." She pulled another piece of paper from her pocket. "This is a list of things to do in Pittsburgh." She smiled. "Look, there's museums and beautiful churches. All kinds of things for us to see and learn about." He watched her take a deep breath, then her face brightened even more. "And . . . I'm so excited about this! There is a job for a preschool teacher right near where you work. Oh, Saul. I've always wanted to work with children. And this is a class for what they call special needs children, *kinner* who need lots of extra love and care."

"That all sounds great, Miriam." Saul tried to share her enthusiasm, and there was nothing he wanted more than to take her with him to Pittsburgh, if she truly wanted to go. "I just don't think I can leave Ruben and James right now." Miriam actually hung her head, and it saddened him to see that she was genuinely disappointed. "I—I thought you'd be happy about this. Now we can stay in the community, raise a family here."

"But it's your dream. I want to be a part of your dreams, Saul. What made you decide you can't leave Ruben and James? Is your father ill? Does the farm need help? If so, maybe someone in the community can pitch in."

Saul avoided her eyes, knowing he was going to give her a partial version of the truth. "Maybe when they're older," he said, careful not to get locked into her gaze.

"But what about your job?" Her forehead creased as she spoke.

"I'm gonna write a letter to the owner of the restaurant and turn it down. There will be others." Although he knew there wouldn't.

"Saul, if we get baptized into the community, then we can't ever leave here without being shunned." She put her hand to her chest. "My family won't be happy if I leave here with you, but I won't be shunned."

Saul felt the life being zapped out of him. Too much was happening at once, and worry filled his heart. "I love you, Miriam. I want to marry you and be with you wherever we are."

She cut her eyes at him, then put her hands on her hips. "Saul, I love you too. And maybe I should feel happy about staying in our community, but . . ." She took a deep breath. "It's your *dream*."

"I'll build new dreams with you."

Miriam studied him for a few moments. Something was different about him, as if his spirit ran dry. His eyes drooped with sadness, and the smile that normally filled his face when he saw her seemed forced. "Did you talk with your *daed*? What did he say? Did he disapprove of you leaving? Is that why you don't want to leave? Because James and Ruben seem fine."

He shook his head, then leaned back against the inside of the bridge. "Miriam, you'll be happier here with your family. We'll have a *gut* life."

If that were true, then why did he look like he'd just settled for second best?

Saul shifted his weight, then pulled off his straw hat and wiped his brow. "I just changed my mind."

Miriam folded her arms across her chest. This didn't make sense. And she had a hunch who was behind this. Her parents. "Did *mei mamm* or *daed* talk to you?"

Saul scuffed one foot against the road and avoided her eyes. "Your *mamm* came for a visit, but—"

"I knew it!" Miriam stomped her foot. "I am eighteen years old and in my *rumschpringe*. She shouldn't be doing this. I have a right to make my own choices."

Saul gently grabbed both her shoulders and gazed into her eyes.

"Miriam, you wouldn't have made a choice to leave this place if it weren't for me. I know that."

"And you wouldn't have made a choice to stay if it weren't for—for my mother." She pulled away from him. "You are letting *mei mamm* take away your dreams, and that's not right." She shook her head. "I'm not letting her do that. We are going to get married, go to Pittsburgh, and you are going to be a great chef in that new restaurant."

Saul pulled her into a hug. "No, Miriam," he whispered. "I'm not going."

Such sadness in his voice. *This is not right.* Miriam wanted her mother to undo whatever she'd done to change Saul's mind.

15

FOR TWO DAYS, REBECCA HAD PONDERED WHAT, IF anything, she should do about Saul and his family. It didn't seem right for those three boys to be taking care of Zeb, then— understandably—hiding it from the community. They were too young to carry such burdens. Even Saul.

"Just stay out of it, Rebecca," Aaron said after Rebecca voiced her concerns. He raised his eyes above his Bible. "Be glad that Miriam will be staying here in the district. That's the most important thing."

"Keep your voice down. Miriam and Shelby are on the porch in the rockers." She spoke in a whisper, then tapped her finger to her chin as she thought about what her husband said. Keeping Miriam in the community should be Rebecca's only concern, but she couldn't ignore the little voice in her head pushing her to listen to her heart. And her heart hurt for everyone involved. She leaned her head back against the couch while Aaron sat across the room in the rocking chair reading. Closing her eyes, she prayed to do right by all concerned. The boys were upstairs. The house was so quiet. She didn't mean to eavesdrop, but she couldn't stop herself when she clearly heard her daughter's voice.

"Saul is so sad, Shelby. It's like his spirit has withered. I want to be with the Saul I'm in love with, the one with hopes and dreams.

He's adventuresome, and it's one of the things I love about him."

Rebecca opened her eyes and leaned one ear closer to the window, her heart heavy as she listened.

"Are you going to talk to your mom?"

"*Ya.* I am. I cannot believe that she would ruin Saul's life like this. And mine. Whatever she said to him, now he is refusing to go to Pittsburgh and follow his dreams. It's not right. In the *Ordnung,* it's clear that we get to experience the outside world and decide for ourselves if we want to leave."

Rebecca brought her hand to her mouth and held her breath, not wanting to miss what Miriam said, but with each word, her heart ached.

"Miriam, I probably sound like a broken record, but . . it's a rough world out there, and there are so many things that you don't know anything about. It's dangerous. There are bad people everywhere. I just don't understand why you would want to leave here. It's so safe, and everyone is so loving and kind. It's all about family, and I love that."

Rebecca heard Aaron grunt, and she looked at him.

"Guess you were wrong about Shelby, no?"

"Shh, Aaron." She narrowed her eyes at her husband, who could evidently hear the girls talking even though he was across the room. She listened as Miriam responded to Shelby's remarks.

"I could've been happy here, Shelby. But I can be happy in Pittsburgh too. I'm a Daughter of the Promise, and if I take those beliefs with me and live by them, it doesn't matter where I live."

Rebecca glanced at Aaron and whispered, "I don't want her to go, Aaron, but you must admit, we raised her right." Aaron scowled, but together they kept listening.

"What's a Daughter of the Promise?"

"It's a spiritual journey that a woman takes when she finds true meaning to the words *faith, hope,* and *love.* I have a strong faith, hope for my future, and I love God with all my heart." After a pause, Miriam added, "And Saul."

"I think you're lucky, Miriam. I would have loved to have grown up in a place like this, especially with your family. I love your family." She giggled. "Even your mom. I wish my mom cared about me even half as much as your mom cares about you."

Rebecca brushed away a tear.

"Let's go to bed, Rebecca. We've intruded on those girls enough." Aaron spoke in a whisper as he stood up and reached for her hand.

"I've been so wrong about Shelby."

"*Ya.* You have." Aaron put his arm around her as they moved toward the stairs, then he let her edge in front of him. She took a few steps, then turned around to face him.

"We got what we wanted today, Aaron. Saul isn't leaving, and Miriam isn't going anywhere with him." She looked down at her husband. "Why do I feel so bad?"

"I don't feel so *gut* either, *mei leib.* I don't like to see Miriam hurting. And my heart hurts for Zeb and those boys." He paused. "But I can't bear the thought of Miriam leaving."

Rebecca turned and started back up the stairs again, wondering if sleep would come tonight.

Miriam was nervous to face off with her parents, but by Friday, she'd made up her mind. *Mamm* still wasn't hosting suppers, and Miriam knew that it was partly because she was still mourning

Uncle Ivan's death, but also because of the money that was stolen during the last meal she hosted.

After supper Shelby coaxed Miriam's brothers outside, challenging them to a game of basketball, so that Miriam could speak privately with her parents. She wished she could talk only to her mother, tell her how wrong she'd been to convince Saul to stay here, but the decisions about her life affected her father too. Normally *Daed* was more easygoing than her mother, but when it came to her leaving, *Daed's* behavior went from calm to crazy. She wasn't looking forward to talking to either of them, but if there was any chance that they might see her side and convince Saul to accept his job offer, then it was worth a try.

"This is about Saul, no?" Her father eased into one of the rockers. *Mamm* sat in the other one while Miriam took a seat on the couch across from them.

"*Ya.*" Miriam folded her hands in her lap, then took a deep breath. She looked from one parent to the other. "*Mamm, Daed* . . . I love Saul. I've always loved him. I want to marry him. And his dream is to live in Pittsburgh and be a chef in a nice restaurant. Without that dream, he'll never be completely happy. He's carried that dream for a long time. I don't know what you said to him, *Mamm*, but now he's not going. Saul said he wants us to get baptized, married, and live our lives here. But I know that's not what he really wants. I don't think it's fair that—"

"Fair?" Her father scowled as he spoke. "It's not fair for Saul to take you away from here."

"*Daed*, he didn't talk me into this. And don't you think I'm scared and nervous?" Miriam felt the lump forming in her throat. She swallowed hard, then hung her head. "I need the blessing of my family."

"Miriam, what if you both get to Pittsburgh and you don't like it?" *Mamm* rubbed her eyes and shook her head. "Then what?"

"Then we come back. Or we do something else. We won't be shunned." Miriam wondered if there would be some type of private shunning if she left. "Will we? Because I don't think I could stand that." A tear rolled down her cheek. "I need you both. I need your blessing."

Mamm blinked back tears but didn't say anything. Her father abruptly stood up from his chair. "You will not have my blessing if you choose to leave here."

"*Daed!*" Miriam cried. "Please." She covered her face with her hands until she felt her mother's arm come around her. When she looked up, her father was gone.

"I will talk to your father, Miriam." *Mamm* patted her shoulder.

"The way you talked to Saul?" She pulled away from her mother. "The only reason you're saying you'll talk to *Daed* is because you know Saul isn't planning for us to leave now. You talked him out of going. He was ready for us to go start our lives. Now he isn't the same, *Mamm*. He is so sad. And both of us were so excited. *Ya*, I was nervous and scared, but still excited." She gazed into her mother's eyes. "You've raised me *gut, Mamm*. I'll carry my love for God wherever I go. I'm sorry you can't see that."

Tears flowed as she raced up the stairs.

"Why didn't you tell her the truth?" Aaron sat down on the edge of the bed, still in his work clothes. Rebecca sat down beside him and sighed. She leaned down and stepped out of her shoes.

"I think Saul should tell her."

"And in the meantime, you have to listen to her blame you?"

Aaron stood up, looked down at her, and put his hands on his hips. "I do not want that boy taking Miriam away from us."

"I know you don't. I don't either." Rebecca stood up. She pulled Aaron into a hug and kissed him on the cheek before she burrowed her head against his chest. "But we are going to have to let her make this decision."

He eased her away. "It sounds like the decision is made. Saul isn't going to leave his brothers with Zeb. So they will just get baptized, married, and live here in Paradise."

Rebecca rubbed her forehead. "And what about Saul's brothers, Ruben and James? They're only young teenagers. They shouldn't have to be handling this at their age. And what about Zeb? I think his drinking probably started after Sarah and Hannah were killed. But it doesn't give him the right to raise those boys that way. Zeb needs some help, Aaron."

"*Ach*, Rebecca." Aaron sat down on the bed again and put his head in his hands. "I wish we could just leave it alone, let the *kinner* get married and stay here."

She sat down on the bed and put her arm around her husband, then rested her head on his shoulder. "I know, Aaron. It would scare me to death for Miriam to venture out into the *Englisch* world." She paused, kissed him again on the cheek. "But it scares me even more that we might be trying to manipulate God's plans for them."

"We ain't doing that. Saul made the decision not to go so he could stay and tend to his *bruders* and *daed*."

Rebecca sighed. "I know." She paused. "It certainly says something about the type of person Saul is, no? He would give up his dreams for family. Isn't that the kind of person we want our daughter marrying, Aaron? Wherever they choose to live."

Her husband sighed. "I guess so. But still . . ."

"You know that a small percentage of our young people will venture out into the *Englisch* world."

Aaron slipped his suspenders off his shoulders and let them hang at his side. "I know. I just don't want Miriam in that percentage."

Rebecca couldn't agree more, but she also didn't want to be responsible for ruining her daughter's life, as Miriam had put it.

Shelby walked to the barn after everyone was in bed. She knew her mother would still be awake and probably worried since they hadn't spoken in a couple of weeks. Shelby's cell phone had been dead for a while. She put the lantern on the workbench, then lifted herself up to sit between it and the phone. As she picked up the cordless phone from the base, her stomach churned. She loved her parents, but she dreaded going home in a couple of weeks. She couldn't believe her stay here was almost over.

"Shelby! Thank goodness! Why haven't you called?"

"Why haven't *you* called?" Shelby's voice was flat as she spoke.

"I've tried several times. Your cell phone must be dead."

"Yes. But you have the number to their phone in the barn, the phone I'm calling you from."

"Well, we're talking now. Tell me what you've been doing."

"We stay busy, and like I told you before, we get up early, but I—"

"Honey, hold on a sec. I have another call."

Shelby sighed as her mother put her on hold. She waited.

"Okay. Sorry about that. It was Richard, telling me he's running late. We're going to Joe's Place tonight for dinner. I bet you miss the food at Joe's."

Shelby thought about the mouthwatering steaks she used to enjoy at her favorite restaurant back home. "I like the food here too. Rebecca is a great cook. Miriam is a good cook too. I help prepare the meals, so I'm learning to make a lot of different things."

"That's good. You'll have to try out some new recipes for me and Richard when you get home."

Shelby's heart leaped in her chest. "Mom? How often is Richard there?"

The line was silent for long enough that Shelby knew the answer.

"I was going to talk to you about that, Shelby. I know you don't know Richard all that well, but he's become so important to me, and we've been spending a lot of time together while you've been away. You'll love him as much as I do."

"Mom! Is he *living* there?"

"I know I always said I didn't believe in living together, but it's different because I'm older, Shelby, and I've already been married to your father."

"Lead by example, Mother." Shelby shook her head.

"Shelby, try to understand— Hang on, honey. Let me tell Richard I'll call him back."

Shelby stood still, the phone at her ear, for about ten seconds, then slammed it back into the carrier. She jerked around to grab the lantern but knocked it with her elbow. It rolled about two feet away and rested against a hay bale. Within seconds the hay swelled to a glowing orange ball, and Shelby froze.

Water. She ran out of the barn, turned on the faucet, and pulled a garden hose into the barn. By the time she got to the bale, the fire had spread to the workbench and the east wall. Chickens were cackling, the horses were reared up and kicking the stalls, and

Shelby's heart was pounding out of her chest. She was unsure whether to run for help or to keep spraying the stream of water on the fire.

Please, God. Help me. What do I do?

Instinctively she ran to the horse stalls and flipped the latches, and the animals ran free to safety. She opened the chicken coop, hoping the chickens would follow her as she ran out of the barn to get help. Aaron met her in the yard.

"Shelby! Are you all right? Are you hurt?"

She shook her head but couldn't speak. Ben, Elam, and John ran past her, followed by Miriam. But Aaron sent them back. "It's too late! Go back! Wet the yard in the front of the *haus* with the other hose—try to keep the fire from spreading to the house."

Why didn't I call 911? Shelby looked on as the rest of the family tried to control the spreading fire and made sure animals were a safe distance away. Even little John was coaxing the chickens toward the backyard. *What have I done?*

"Shelby! Are you all right?" Rebecca threw her arms around her. "Are you hurt?"

"I—I . . ." She couldn't talk.

Rebecca eased her away and cupped Shelby's cheeks in her hands, and even in the moonlight, Shelby could see the concern on Rebecca's face. "Nod if you're okay."

Shelby did.

"That's all that counts."

Rebecca kissed Shelby on the forehead, then went to help secure the animals. Shelby heard sirens, so she knew the fire wouldn't spread to the house. She stood alone in the middle of the yard and buried her face in her hands, sobbing.

16

MIRIAM WATCHED MEMBERS OF THE COMMUNITY CLEARING the rubble from the fire the next day. Even though the barn had been leveled, the animals survived and the fire never got near the house. Luckily, a neighbor down the road spotted the smoke from his place.

She smiled at Saul as he walked by her carrying a load of debris. Several areas still smoldered, and Saul's father and brothers were busy keeping the hot spots wet. Her own brothers were busy building temporary housing for the chickens and pigs, and her Uncle Noah, Uncle Abe, and friend Kade Saunders helped her father drag the larger pieces of burnt lumber to the far side of the house. Miriam counted more than sixty people helping out on this hot Saturday morning. The following Saturday most of those same people, plus some, would be back for the barn raising.

She blew a loose strand of hair from her face and accepted a tray of glasses of iced tea from Sadie Saunders before passing them out herself. It didn't matter that her mother was trying to ruin Saul's life; his entire family was still here helping. That was the way things were done, and Miriam briefly wondered how folks would be out in the *Englisch* world during a crisis. She still hadn't given up hope that she and Saul would be leaving for

Pittsburgh in a couple of weeks. She had to figure out a way to convince him to go.

"Do you know where Shelby is?"

Miriam turned at the sound of her mother's voice, sloshing tea from one of the glasses onto the tray. "She's upstairs."

Mamm frowned. "I'm worried about her. Poor thing was in shock last night and pale as a ghost before she went to bed. She didn't say much."

Miriam tried to put her own hurt and resentment toward her mother aside. "I thought I heard her crying during the night. And before she went to sleep, she just kept saying how sorry she was, over and over again."

Mamm shook her head. "It was an accident, and God saw fit to spare us any harm. I'll go check on her."

Rebecca knocked on the bedroom door, then pushed it open before Shelby had time to answer. "Shelby?" She stepped into the room, and her heart dropped. "What are you doing?" Rebecca eyed Shelby's packed suitcases. Her young cousin was sitting on the edge of the bed, her eyes swollen and red. Rebecca sat down beside her. "Shelby?"

Shelby sniffled as she kept her head hung. "I figured you would be ready for me to leave. I know I still have a couple of weeks, but after what happened—" She started to cry.

Rebecca put a hand on her shoulder. "Shelby. The fire in the barn was an accident. We are thanking the Lord that you are safe. That everyone is safe. Child, we hold no ill will toward you."

Shelby still didn't look at her. "I'm so sorry, Rebecca."

Rebecca twisted to face her. "Shelby, look at me." When Shelby finally did, Rebecca cupped her cheek in her hand. "Sweet Shelby, please don't leave yet."

A tear rolled down Shelby's cheek. "I would be leaving soon anyway. And I know you don't like me here, and—"

"That's not true." Rebecca lowered her hand and gazed into Shelby's eyes, realizing they'd never really had a heart-to-heart conversation. "I—I was worried when you arrived, Shelby. We're not used to having *Englisch* living in our home, and I admit . . ." Shame fell over Rebecca as she thought about the blame she'd mistakenly placed on Shelby in the past. "I was fearful." She lifted Shelby's chin, then smiled. "But you are part of this family. And I know that you have been a *gut* influence on our Miriam." Rebecca frowned. "Even if we've questioned her choices."

Shelby turned on the bed, bent one leg underneath her, then stared hard at Rebecca. "I think Saul loves Miriam very much. But I can understand why you wouldn't want her to leave here." Shelby looked away, stared at the wall for a moment as if remembering something, then said, "It's a scary place out there."

They were both quiet for a few moments. Rebecca finally stood up and folded her arms across her chest. "Young lady, you get busy unpacking those bags." Shelby looked up at her. "Because you haven't lived until you've experienced an Amish barn raising." She grinned. "Do you really want to miss that?"

Shelby's eyes teared up again. "You don't want to send me away? Seems like every time I did something bad, my parents were ready to ship me off. This wasn't the first time. When I was thirteen, I got sent to my aunt's to live because I failed two classes." Shelby paused, swiping at her eyes. "There were other times."

Rebecca sighed as she lowered her hands to her sides. "No, my dear. No one is shipping you anywhere, except perhaps outside to help serve tea to the neighbors helping us."

A grin tipped the corner of Shelby's mouth. "Yes, ma'am."

Rebecca folded her hands in front of her and stood taller. "Now, get these bags unpacked, and I'll see you downstairs." She winked at Shelby, then headed out the door.

Once downstairs Rebecca grabbed a pitcher of tea from the kitchen table and headed out the back door—just in time to see Bishop Ebersol pulling up. She'd prayed about this situation with Zeb and the boys, and now she knew that she must talk to the bishop. She took a deep breath and walked outside.

Saul stopped dead in his tracks with a handful of burnt wood when he saw Rebecca at the side of the house talking with Bishop Ebersol, and twice the bishop glanced toward Saul's father. There was no doubt in Saul's mind that Rebecca was telling the bishop about his *daed*. It would only be a matter of time before the entire community found out. How could she do this after Saul promised to stay here in the community? Clearly Rebecca's ultimate goal was to make sure that Saul didn't marry Miriam, here or anywhere else.

And I'm here helping your family while you go destroying mine?

He dropped the wood on the pile of debris and turned again toward the bishop, locking eyes with him briefly until he saw Miriam walk up beside him.

"I wonder what *Mamm* is talking to Bishop Ebersol about." Miriam handed Saul a glass of iced tea.

Saul accepted the tea, took a long drink, then shrugged. First, his dreams of going to Pittsburgh had been shattered, and now he couldn't help but worry that Miriam would change her mind about him once she found out about his father.

"Saul, no matter what, I still think we should go to Pittsburgh, like we planned."

"I told you. We can't. Because of Ruben and James." Saul didn't mean his words to sound so harsh, but it was hard to watch everything falling apart right before his eyes.

"I—I don't understand that. Your father will take care of Ruben and James, and—"

"I can't talk about this right now." Saul walked away, thinking it was only a matter of time before Miriam didn't want anything to do with him or his family. He couldn't look back.

Miriam stood completely still as she watched Saul walk away. Maybe he'd decided against marrying her after all. Maybe he couldn't deal with her meddlesome mother. She turned toward Bishop Ebersol and *Mamm* and watched them for a moment. Bishop Ebersol was stroking his long gray beard as her mother did most of the talking. She didn't see her father walk up beside her.

"I can't stand to see you leave here, *mei dochder*." *Daed* frowned as he spoke. "But I can't stand to see you unhappy either."

Miriam didn't say anything.

"You love that boy?"

She turned to face him. "With all my heart, *Daed*."

Her father shook his head and stared at the ground. "You don't know anything about the *Englisch* world, *dochder*."

Miriam kept her eyes on her mother and the bishop. "And apparently I'm not going to."

"What would be so terrible about you and Saul staying here, raising a family here?"

She turned to face her father. "Because Saul has a dream, *Daed*. A dream he's had for a long time. I would be the same person, *Daed*, whether I'm here or in Pittsburgh. I love God. I can love Him from anywhere." She lifted one shoulder, then dropped it. "But Saul is so unhappy right now, I don't even know if he still wants to marry me."

"If he loves you, he should want to marry you no matter where you live."

Miriam's mouth dropped for a moment. "You and *Mamm* should love me no matter where I live too."

Daed put one hand on his hip as he rubbed his forehead with the other, then he sighed. "Of course we will always love you, Miriam." He gazed at her with soft eyes and a gentle smile, and Miriam felt like a little girl all of a sudden.

"Then what is it, *Daed*? Why can't you stand the thought of me leaving with Saul?" She moved closer to him. "My faith will go with me wherever I go. Don't you believe that, *Daed*? You've raised me *gut*." She touched his arm. "Please, *Daed*. Have faith in me."

"I do."

Miriam kept her eyes locked with his and waited for him to go on.

"I would just—just miss you. So very much." He covered his eyes with one hand, and Miriam realized she'd never seen her father cry. Until now.

Miriam put her arms around him and cried with him for a moment.

I would miss all of you too.

Rebecca finished her conversation with Bishop Ebersol, then headed toward the house. Before going inside, she stopped and lowered her head to pray that she'd done the right thing. When she looked up, Aaron was standing right in front of her.

"This could all backfire on you, especially when Zeb finds out."

She lifted her head. "I have to believe I did the right thing, Aaron. I've prayed about this, and it's just not right—what's goin' on over there."

Her husband shook his head, then glanced around until he saw Zeb carrying a stack of wood, a smile on his face. "I know we don't know Zeb and the boys as well as we should, but it wonders me if it's right to interfere in a man's life like that, even if we're trying to do *gut* for everyone involved." He edged closer and stroked his beard. "He's here helping our family, and you're telling his family secrets."

"Secrets that can cause harm to his children." Rebecca's voice cracked as she began to second-guess what she'd just done.

"I hope it doesn't bring shame to Zeb's family. That's all I'm saying."

Rebecca bit her bottom lip for a moment, then eased closer to her husband. "You know that's not why I'm doing this."

"I know, Rebecca. But what you are doing is going to cost us something very precious."

Rebecca realized that there would be a cost for what she'd

done, but in her heart she believed it was the right thing for everyone. She could only hope and pray that she'd helped the Fishers, even if they never saw it that way. Just the same, her own actions frightened her, and she blinked back tears.

"Don't cry, Rebecca. Please don't cry." Aaron discreetly reached for her hand and squeezed. "We will pray extra hard about this." He paused when Shelby walked by them toward the barn. He waited until she was out of earshot before he asked Rebecca, "Where's she been?"

"She was upstairs packing. She thought we were going to send her home early because of what happened." Rebecca shook her head.

"She didn't mean to burn down the barn. It was an accident."

"That's what I told her." Rebecca watched Shelby join Miriam and take two glasses of tea from a tray, then pass them out to the fellows nearby. "I worry about her. I think divorce must cause all kinds of problems when there are *kinner* involved, no?"

"I don't know, Rebecca. Divorce or not—it seems odd to me that her folks don't call or check on her more often."

Rebecca couldn't agree more.

Shelby wound her way around the crowd, careful to avoid Jesse. She'd stopped going to lunch with him and hadn't made an effort to get in touch with him. She was leaving in two weeks, and they'd already become much too close. Saying good-bye was going to be hard enough.

She missed their lunches and talks about books, but she knew Miriam was right. If she were to get close to Jesse, it wouldn't be fair to either one of them, even if Jesse had hinted that he had a curiosity about the world outside of this safe community. He belonged here, and although she didn't want their friendship to come to a halt, she'd rekindled another relationship. Her time with the Lord brought her a sense of peace that she hadn't had in a long time. She credited Miriam and her family for reconnecting her with God, but Shelby knew that through prayer, He was changing her life.

She'd replaced writing in her diary with prayer, and instead of regret about her choices in the past, her parents' choices, and the life she'd led—now she was working on not carrying the burdens of the past, hers or her parents. Causing the barn fire could have been a setback and destroyed all that she'd been working toward—feelings and recognition that she hoped to take from here when she had to leave. But after talking with Rebecca, she found their forgiveness amazing. She wondered briefly how either of her parents would have reacted to such an accident. She recalled the time she accidentally broke her mother's favorite crystal vase. Not quite tall enough to smell the flowers at nine years old, she tipped the vase toward her and spilled the water. She knocked it off the table when she was wiping up the water. First there was yelling, then she was sent to her room for the afternoon. *But it was an accident.*

Lost in thought, she didn't see Jesse walk up beside her. "Got an extra one of those?"

Sweat ran the length of Jesse's face as he eyed the two glasses of iced tea Shelby was holding. "Sure." She eased one in his direction.

Jesse gulped the cold drink for several seconds, and Shelby started to walk away but stopped when she heard her name. She slowly turned around.

Jesse had one hand on his hip as his eyes narrowed. "Did I do something to upset you, Shelby?"

She avoided his intense green eyes as she nervously moistened her dry lips, then finally looked up at him, realizing how much she'd missed him. "No. Everything's fine."

He tipped back his straw hat and scratched his forehead for a few moments. "It sure don't seem fine. We were having lunch, talking . . . then you just didn't want to spend any more time with me." He paused, his lips pressed together for a moment. "I figure I must have done something."

She shook her head. "No, Jesse. You didn't do anything. It's just—I'll be leaving soon, and I just . . ." She bit her bottom lip, unsure how much to say.

Jesse eased closer to her, folding his arms across his chest. "Didn't want to break my heart?"

Shelby's eyes grew big as saucers, and she was sure her face was four shades of red. "What?"

"I like you, Shelby." His tight expression relaxed into a smile. "And I'm pretty sure you like me too."

She smiled tentatively, but her heart was racing. "Is that so?"

"*Ya.* And I figure you didn't want us to get too close, since you're leaving and all."

Just the thought of leaving caused her smile to fade. To agree with him would make it that much harder in two weeks. "I've just been busy, Jesse." She glanced around at everyone working, then hung her head. "And I feel terrible about what happened."

Jesse leaned down until Shelby was forced to lock eyes with him, eyes filled with tenderness. "Do you know how many barn fires we have each year from lanterns or propane heaters?" He waved his arm around the yard. "And you see how we handle it, no? And by the end of the day next Saturday, your cousins will have a brand-new barn." He chuckled, then whispered, "Theirs was old anyway."

She stifled a smile. "Thanks for saying that."

"So how about going for a ride with me Tuesday after work? I get off early that day." He winked at her. "We could go fishing at the Zook place."

Shelby took a deep breath, then lifted her chin a bit. "I can't, Jesse. I'm sorry." She handed him the full glass of tea she was holding and took his empty glass. "I have to go."

She didn't turn around as she headed back to the house. But she couldn't help but wonder if she was making a mistake. As she walked up the porch steps, she wondered if they would keep in touch or write letters.

Saul watched his father across the yard saying good-bye to Rebecca and Aaron. He heard Miriam's parents both thank *Daed* as they smiled. Saul cringed at the sight. From this moment forward, he would be watching out of the window, waiting for Bishop Ebersol to show up, and he would be praying it was on one of *Daed's* good nights. He had Rebecca Raber to thank for that.

He picked up his tool belt from where he'd left it earlier, then strapped it around his waist. He glanced up at his father a couple of times. The best man he'd ever known. And no matter his shortcomings, his father didn't deserve to be shamed by the community, as would surely happen when word of his drinking got out.

Saul had never seen his father drink a drop of alcohol until a few days after his mother and Hannah were buried. It seemed harmless enough at the time. Lots of folks in the district partook of wine, some even whiskey and beer. But for *Daed*, it slowly began to take him to a faraway place, somewhere free from the pain of *Mamm's* and Hannah's deaths. But it seemed like the more he drank, the more he began to change—into someone Saul didn't recognize anymore. But no matter what, Saul knew the man his father really was, the man buried beneath grief so thick he couldn't dig his way through it.

He headed toward his buggy as moments of his childhood flashed before his face. He recalled the time he'd begged his father for a sled one Christmas following a bad harvest. Money was tight, and the sled was on display at a fancy store in town. Saul didn't understand until he was much older why his father had taken on a job in the evenings. Saul and both his brothers each got brand-new fancy sleds that year, different than the kind they could have made themselves. These were faster and slicker, and Saul and his brothers had many a race down the hill behind the house that year.

More memories of his father breezed through his mind, and Saul fought not to question the Lord's will, why his mother and Hannah were taken away from them all. How different their lives might have been. He watched his father walking toward him, a smile stretched across his face.

"*Gut* people, Rebecca and Aaron. I regret that we haven't spent more time with them." His father's kind gray eyes brightened. "But I guess we will now that you and Miriam are getting married." He put his hand on Saul's shoulder. "She seems like a good choice for a *fraa, sohn.*" *Daed* pulled his arm back, then started unhitching the horse. "Your *bruders* said that they will get a ride home later." He walked around to the passenger side of the buggy, Saul's cue to drive. "Have you thought about the *haus* you will build on the property I'm deeding to you? Many bedrooms for many *kinner*, no?"

Saul stared at his father, blinked a few times, and forced the images of his father on the living room floor out of his mind. *How can this be the same man?* He managed a weak smile and nodded as he climbed into the driver's seat of the buggy. His father took a seat beside him, and Saul eased away, realizing he hadn't even said good-bye to Miriam. He knew she wasn't to blame for her parents' actions, but right now it seemed to be the Fishers against the Rabers. Rebecca Raber had seen fit to tell the bishop his family's secrets, even though he'd promised to stay here with Miriam and get married in the district.

It would serve Rebecca right if Saul swept Miriam away from here.

But what about Ruben and James?

Saul wondered if he was placing blame on the right person. He glanced at his father, then took a deep breath.

17

MIRIAM WALKED INTO THE KITCHEN ON WEDNESDAY, surprised that Shelby was up before her and already helping *Mamm*. It was the second time this week.

"Shelby scrambled some special eggs this morning," *Mamm* said, smiling. "They have onions, tomatoes, peppers, cheese, and . . ."

Mamm rattled off some more ingredients, but Miriam wasn't listening. She didn't feel like smiling this morning, and with each day that passed since Saturday, her mood had grown worse. Saul hadn't said good-bye after helping clean the fire debris, and she hadn't talked to him since. She wasn't sure who she blamed more—her mother for meddling, or Saul for letting her mother affect their relationship.

"I'm calling them *mei Englisch* special eggs." Shelby glanced at Miriam's mother, who chuckled.

"Even learning some *Dietsch* while you're here." *Mamm* placed a jar of rhubarb jam on the table.

"Mind if I call everyone to *kumme esse*?" Shelby said with a bright smile.

Mamm laughed again. "I think those hungry boys are already on their way, but I'm impressed, Shelby."

Miriam rolled her eyes as she pulled the orange juice from the refrigerator. *Must be nice that* Mamm *can be so cheerful.* She wanted to ask her mother what she'd talked to Bishop Ebersol about on Saturday, but most likely *Mamm* would say it was a private matter. Besides, her father and brothers were making their way into the kitchen.

Following prayer, they began to eat, and everyone loved Shelby's eggs. Miriam had to admit they were good. She savored the taste as she thought about how much Shelby had become a part of the family. Shelby and her mother had been interacting a lot more, especially since the barn fire, which Miriam didn't mind, especially right now, when Miriam had little to say to *Mamm.* Besides, it didn't sound like Shelby had nearly as good a mother as Miriam and her brothers.

Miriam reached for a piece of bacon and pondered her thought. Yes, she was angry with her mother, but she also knew her mother was a good person. And she loved her very much. She glanced around the table at her family. John stuffed his mouth with a biscuit, his hair unintentionally spiked on top as if he'd slept in the same position all night. His bright blue eyes shone with innocence, and Miriam felt like crying all of a sudden.

He's only eight years old. I'll miss seeing him grow up if I leave with Saul. Maybe pushing for this move with Saul, to fulfill his dreams, is a mistake.

What are my *dreams?*

Saul watched from the front yard as Miriam pulled into the driveway. He suspected she was angry with him for leaving Saturday without saying good-bye. He was angry at himself. Glancing at the sun, he figured it was nearing the supper hour, and he planned to make asparagus soup, a recipe of his mother's that he'd added some spices to, giving it a zestier flavor. He couldn't wait until he could cook for Miriam in their own home—even if it wouldn't be in Pittsburgh. He sighed as he thought about the times he'd fantasized about cooking at one of the fancy *Englisch* restaurants.

"I've missed you," he said as he approached her side of the spring buggy, and as her face lit with a smile, he didn't think he'd meant anything more in his life. He extended his hand to help her down. "I'm sorry I didn't say bye on Saturday."

"It's all right." She kept her hand in his as they stood facing each other. "You seemed upset that *mei mamm* was talking to Bishop Ebersol. I was wondering if she was talking about us."

"Maybe. Maybe about our wedding. We should choose a date, then publish it." He squeezed her hand.

Miriam's blue eyes sparkled. "*Mamm* made some rhubarb soup the other day, and she put mint in it. It was her third time to try to make the soup." Miriam crinkled her nose. "It was terrible—for the third time. She mumbled your name and gave it to the dog." She brought a hand to her mouth, stifling a grin. "Know anything about that?"

Saul laughed. "I gave her that recipe when she was here."

Miriam giggled, but then her smile faded. She looked down for a moment, then turned to him and asked, "What did she say to you that day, Saul?"

When he didn't answer, she said, "I can't wait to be your *fraa*, Saul, but are you sure you can be happy here? I still don't understand why you've given up going to Pittsburgh, and I think *mei mamm* had something to do with it."

Saul knew Rebecca wasn't to blame for his decision. She might have destroyed his family's reputation by talking to Bishop Ebersol, but Saul was making the best choices for his family. It just wasn't God's plan for him to leave here and pursue a life in the *Englisch* world. No matter how much he'd wanted it and prayed about it, there were just too many obstacles in his path. He remembered his mother saying once that if things are meant to be and part of God's plan, then they come easily and without forced effort. So instead of praying for a new life outside of his community, Saul had been praying that he would accept God's will for both him and Miriam, whatever that might be.

"No, Miriam. Your *mamm* didn't convince me to stay here. I just ain't ready to leave Ruben and James yet." He clutched her hand with both of his.

Miriam squared her shoulders and stood taller. "Maybe we shouldn't get baptized, then. Maybe we should wait and see if you decide to go to Pittsburgh later, in a few years."

"You would do that for me? Wait?"

"*Ya.* I would."

Saul heard her say she would wait for him, but her tone was reluctant, and he knew right then that he could never do that to her. He didn't feel worthy of all the sacrifices she was willing to make for him, especially since she didn't know the real reason why he couldn't go to Pittsburgh. Now was the time to be completely honest with her.

He touched her chin, quickly glanced around the yard, then kissed her lightly on the lips, grateful that his father and brothers were already inside. "I love you, Miriam. I don't want to wait to get married. We're going to get baptized in October, then marry in November. Nothing would make me a happier man." He smiled at her, then took a deep breath. "But there's something I want to tell you."

They both turned when they heard horse hooves clicking against the driveway.

"Bishop Ebersol," Saul said and hung his head. "This is what I wanted to talk to you about."

"About Bishop Ebersol? Why is he here?" The look of concern in her eyes made Saul's heart ache.

"*Ya.* He's probably here to talk to my father . . ."

"What? What are you talking about, Saul?" Miriam's hand was on his arm.

Bishop Ebersol pulled in beside Miriam's buggy before Saul had time to answer. He wasn't sure what to tell her anyway. Miriam dropped her hand to her side, and Saul's heart thudded in his chest as he watched the older man step down from his covered buggy, aided by a long black cane in one hand. Saul could feel his world getting ready to crash down around him.

Once everyone found out, his family would be avoided, shamed in the community. It wasn't their way to judge, but Saul knew there would be plenty who would practice their own private form of shunning. He locked eyes with Miriam and wondered how she would be affected by it. *Will you still want to marry me?*

"Hello, Saul. *Wie bischt?*" Bishop Ebersol extended his hand to Saul, then he turned to Miriam and nodded. "Hello, Miriam." He stroked his long gray beard that ran the length of his chest. "I need to see your father, Saul. Is he inside?"

Saul was sure Bishop Ebersol could see his heart beating beneath his dark-blue shirt. He took a deep breath. "*Ya.* He is inside with *mei bruders.*" Saul gestured toward the house, then turned to Miriam.

"I should go. *Mamm* will be waiting for me to help with supper."

Miriam backed up a step and offered a weak smile. "Bye, Saul. Good-bye, Bishop Ebersol."

"See you Saturday at the barn raising, Miriam." Saul gave her a quick wave of his hand, and Bishop Ebersol again nodded at her. They waited a few moments until Miriam was heading down the driveway, then the bishop said, "I know it is near the supper hour, but it's important that I speak with your father. I've not been well the past few days, or I would have come sooner."

Saul knew there was no way to avoid the crisis at hand, but he didn't want James and Ruben around when his father was humiliated. "I'll go let *Daed* know you're here, and I'll ask James and Ruben to help me in the barn so that you can talk."

"That will be *gut*."

Saul's steps were heavy as he walked into the house. *Daed* was reading but still in his work clothes, and James and Ruben were nowhere in sight.

"Where's James and Ruben?" Saul asked when he entered the den.

His father eased his reading glasses off and smiled. "We all worked hard today, so I told them to go ahead and bathe. I'll milk the cows later after supper. They deserve a break." His father chuckled. "I'd give you a break too, *mei sohn*, and cook us some supper, but I'm not much *gut* in the kitchen."

You're a gut *man. And now the bishop is here to humiliate you.*

"Bishop Ebersol is here to talk to you. Privately, I think."

Daed's eyes clouded as his expression soured. "I wonder why." Then he stood up. "The bishop is always welcome, of course."

"I'll go see if James and Ruben want to play basketball before I start supper, so you and the bishop can talk."

His father nodded. Saul darted up the stairs and summoned James and Ruben, who were always happy when Saul challenged them to play a game.

But a few minutes later, as Saul aimed the ball for his first shot, he watched his father opening the door for Bishop Ebersol. He threw, but the ball didn't go anywhere near the basket. *This is it.*

He saw Ruben toss the ball out of the corner of his eye, but he felt like his breath was being sucked out of him as he bent over and leaned his hands on his knees, wondering how this night would change all their lives.

A car coming up the driveway pulled his attention from the game. He waited and was surprised to see Noah Stoltzfus step out. Noah was Rebecca's brother who ran a clinic for both *Englisch* and Amish in the area. He'd been shunned years ago for leaving the Order to become a doctor, but his contributions to the community had earned him respect, and over time hardly anyone recognized the shunning. This was bad timing, though, and he couldn't imagine what Noah was doing here. He couldn't recall Noah visiting before.

"Hi, boys." Noah waved as he crossed the yard, hurrying across the grass and up the porch steps.

"Wait!" Saul called out to Noah as he ran toward him, dropping the basketball. "*Daed's* got company. Bishop Ebersol is here."

Noah spun around. "I know. I'm here to meet with them." He offered a brief smile, then quickly turned, pounded up the stairs, and was inside the house before Saul could say a word.

"Why's Noah here?" James asked as he ran to Saul's side.

Ruben joined them within seconds. "And why is the bishop here?"

They are all here to destroy our lives.

Friday morning Miriam, Shelby, and *Mamm* were busy preparing food to be served at the barn raising the next day. Miriam had been thinking about what had happened at Saul's. She didn't understand what Saul wanted to tell her or why Bishop Ebersol was at his house, but she suspected her mother knew something. She'd tried to catch her mother alone several times, but *Mamm* had been busy preparing for the barn raising. She'd also been teaching Shelby more Pennsylvania *Deitsch*. Her cousin seemed to enjoy learning new words and phrases, although Miriam wasn't sure why. Miriam had noticed the two of them growing even closer, and they hardly noticed Miriam was in the room that morning, which was fine by Miriam. She was glad to see her cousin happy.

Shelby's parents were due to arrive in a week, and Miriam was going to miss Shelby terribly, especially their late-night chats. It really was like having a sister.

Even with all of the windows and doors open in the house, the kitchen was still sweltering as they worked. Miriam could feel the sweat dripping down her back beneath her dress. *Mamm* wanted to get the cooking done early before it got too hot, but in August, it was hot all the time. She wiped her forehead with the back of her hand as she leaned down to pull a lemon sponge pie from the oven.

"Someone's here." Shelby walked to the opened door in the kitchen and peered through the screen. "In a car."

Mamm joined Shelby by the door. "I don't recognize that car."

Miriam put the pie on a cooling rack, then went to peer over Shelby's and *Mamm's* shoulders. "Uh-oh."

Shelby twisted her neck to face Miriam. "What?"

They watched the blond-haired woman balancing on heeled sandals as she made her way across the yard.

"What is Lucy Turner doing here?" *Mamm* asked in a whisper.

Lucy clicked up the stairs and stopped on the other side of the screen. "Hello, Rebecca. Can I talk to you for a moment?" She clasped her hands and held them against her sleeveless red blouse. "It's important."

"Of course." *Mamm* pushed the screen door open, and Miriam and Shelby backed up so Lucy could come into the kitchen. "Let's go into the den." *Mamm* motioned with her hand for Lucy to follow her. Miriam knew *Mamm* preferred folks to enter through the den, but with two doors on the porch, it was hard to direct people to the actual front door. Plus, Miriam was sure Lucy saw them staring at her through the screen door in the kitchen.

"I can see that you're in the middle of supper preparation, so I won't take up much of your time."

Miriam and Shelby didn't move. Miriam held her breath as she strained to hear what Lucy had to say.

Shelby leaned close. "I think the shoofly pie is probably ready," she whispered in Miriam's ear.

Miriam put her first finger to her mouth and kept it there until Shelby shrugged. She leaned her ear toward the entryway from the kitchen to the den, straining to hear Lucy.

"I need to know how I can reach Katie Ann. I know this must seem awkward, but it's important that I speak with her. So I was hoping that you could give me her address and phone number in Colorado."

Miriam blinked as she turned to Shelby and whispered, "Why would she want Katie Ann's address and phone number?"

"How should I know?"

Miriam put her finger back to her lip and leaned in again. It was her mother's voice she heard next.

"Lucy, I'm not sure what to do about this matter, but our Katie Ann is still grieving, I'm sure. It might be best not to call her right now."

"I understand, but what I have to tell Katie Ann, I would like to do in person. I'm planning to travel to Canaan to do so. I know from Ivan that's where they lived, but I think it would be less shocking for Katie Ann if she knew I was coming as opposed to my just showing up on her doorstep."

"I see."

It was quiet for a few moments, and Miriam wondered if her mother was going to hand over Katie Ann's phone number and address. She fumbled with the string on her prayer covering while she and Shelby waited, but when she heard footsteps moving in the opposite direction, Miriam knew that *Mamm* was ushering her to the door in the den that led to the front of the house.

Miriam heard their voices, but she could no longer make out what was being said. She heard Lucy's car on the driveway before her mother returned to the kitchen. Shelby was busy pulling the almost-burnt shoofly pie from the oven as Miriam asked, "Did you give her *Aenti* Katie Ann's address and phone number?"

Mamm drew her brows into a frown. "*Mei maedel*, were you eavesdropping?"

"It's hard not to hear when you're so close by." Miriam paused. "What do you think Lucy wants? Poor *Aenti* Katie Ann. I bet she doesn't think fondly of Lucy or want to talk to her." Miriam let out a small gasp. "I think it would be awful if Lucy just showed up on Katie Ann's doorstep, though, without Katie Ann being warned."

Mamm put her hands on her hips, pressed her lips together, then watched through the screen door as Lucy drove away in her car. "I did write down the phone number and address for her." *Mamm* turned slowly around and faced Miriam. "If Lucy is determined to go see Katie Ann, she will. It will be best if she calls her first to warn her." *Mamm* tapped her fingers on her crossed arms. "Maybe I'll call Katie Ann tomorrow to let her know that Lucy has her number and address and might pay her a visit. It sure wonders me why Lucy feels the need to travel all the way to Colorado to talk to Katie Ann, though."

They were all quiet for a minute, then Shelby changed the subject.

"I know I'm leaving here soon, but I sure hope I can come back for Miriam's wedding in November."

"You have to come back!" Miriam bounced on her toes as she wiped her hands on her black apron. She couldn't imagine getting married without Shelby nearby. Then she turned to her mother. "*Mamm*, you know, we need to start planning since that's only three months away. I'll need a new dress, and—"

"Plenty of time for all that," *Mamm* said abruptly, then walked across the den toward the mudroom. When she returned, she was toting a broom and dustpan. "Little John spilled his plate this morning, and I think I missed some of the crumbs." She began to sweep rapidly as if the conversation about Miriam's wedding was not up for discussion.

"*Mamm* . . ." Miriam edged closer to where her mother was sweeping. "Saul and I are going to be baptized in October. Don't you think we need to be planning my wedding?"

"Miriam, I'm busy right now. I told you that we have plenty of time."

Miriam recalled when her friend Anna Kauffman published her wedding announcement. They only had six months to plan the event, and everyone was panicking. Why was her mother acting so unconcerned? "I'm going to marry him, *Mamm*, even if you don't like it," Miriam grumbled.

"I'm sure you are," *Mamm* said as she scooped the tiny amount of crumbs into the dustpan.

Miriam folded her arms across her chest and knew the Lord would not be happy with her actions. Her tone with her mother was unacceptable, but her mother was refusing to accept Saul.

Miriam dried a few dishes, then paused as she closed her eyes and bowed her head, facing away from her mother and Shelby.

Dear Lord, please guide me and Saul onto the path You have planned for us—whether it's here or in Pittsburgh.

She opened one eye and glanced around the room at the only life she'd ever known, then closed her eyes again.

And please help Mamm to love Saul—or at least accept that I love him.

18

By two o'clock on Saturday, the barn was almost framed in, and a sense of fellowship had spread among the hundred or so folks present. But Saul felt lost as he mechanically worked alongside his father and wondered what he'd say to Miriam. He'd asked his father about the bishop and Noah's visit, but his father only said, "Always *gut* to have company." But there was a sadness in his father's eyes, so Saul knew there was more to it. He felt the need to stay close to his father, although watching Miriam throughout the day brought a longing to be near her as well.

Ruben and James knew something was going on, and they had asked Saul about their visitors several times. Saul told them he didn't know. It was the truth. But he felt a dark cloud looming over his family, and he kept waiting for the bottom to fall out.

"*Sohn*, I think we'll be done here soon." His father pounded a nail into a board high above them while Saul held it in place. "You and me need to talk privately when we get home."

His *daed* didn't look at him, but Saul couldn't take his eyes off his father, a complicated man with years of pain mapped across his face, his long dark beard speckled with gray and his tall frame thinner than in his younger years. "*Ya*, okay," he said softly.

Twice he'd seen Rebecca talking to the bishop again, and once he caught her in deep conversation with his father. What were they all plotting? Maybe they were planning to shun his father. Saul didn't know how he, Ruben, and James could keep the farm going by themselves. Despite *Daed's* shortcomings, his father could work circles around all three of them.

Rebecca walked by and gave him a hesitant smile. He glared at her, then hammered in another nail with strength he didn't know he possessed. He was beginning to think that Rebecca would do anything to keep him from marrying Miriam. His family would be shamed when the news leaked out, as it surely would, and even though Saul believed that Miriam loved him, could she hold up to the gossip that festered even among a community that preached against such a sin?

He took a deep breath and tried to calm his racing heart, wishing he didn't need to have that conversation with his father when he got home.

Rebecca knew that Bishop Ebersol had talked to Zeb, and she'd spoken to Zeb earlier in the afternoon, although it was one of the most awkward conversations she'd ever had. But she'd prayed hard about the situation, and she had to believe that God had guided her to busy herself in someone else's private life for the good of everyone involved, including her daughter.

She thought about Miriam, wondering how her daughter would take the events soon to unfold around her, and briefly worried that she should have talked to Miriam before she took matters into her own hands. There was no mistaking the way Saul had looked at her earlier, such anger in his eyes.

Lord, please continue to guide me. I pray I'm doing the right thing.

She waved as the last buggy left around four that afternoon with plans to finish out the inside of the barn the following Saturday. She felt Aaron's arm come around her waist.

"It's a fine barn, no?"

"*Ya.* Not as big as our other barn, but much sturdier." Rebecca crossed one arm on her chest and brought her other hand to her chin. "We needed a new barn."

"*Mei daadi* built that barn."

They both stood quietly in the yard as the August sun shone down on them from a cloudless sky. Rebecca dripped with sweat. Everyone had worked hard today, and there was nothing like seeing a new barn following a day of hard work and fellowship. But Rebecca couldn't fully enjoy their efforts. Saul and Miriam weighed heavily on her mind.

"Zeb said he is going to talk to Saul tonight." She turned to face Aaron. "Are we doing the right thing?"

"We?" Aaron smiled. "There is no 'we,' *mei fraa.* I told you I wasn't sure about any of this. You believe you are doing the right thing. I am praying you are."

"Do you think that we will lose our *dochder* once this unfolds?" She blinked back tears as she searched her husband's eyes.

"I don't know, Rebecca." He shook his head. "It fears me, keeps me up at night."

"Me too." She turned to face him, looked up into his hazel eyes. "But I believe I am doing the right thing, for everyone."

Aaron smiled, kissed her lightly on the lips. "I hope so."

Saul didn't think his stomach could churn any faster or harder. No one said much during supper, and with Ruben and James out milking the cows, Saul quickly finished cleaning up the kitchen dishes, then joined his father in the den. His father was sitting on the couch, leaning forward with his elbows on his knees and his hands folded under his chin. He looked up at Saul, then nodded for Saul to take a seat in the rocker across from him.

Daed was pale, and his hand was trembling. He'd seen his father's hands shake before, which happened when he hadn't had any alcohol for a while. Saul copied his father's posture and leaned forward, his elbows also on his knees. Outside, he heard crickets chirping and the cows mooing, and the evening sun shone through the window in the den. A normal night. But Saul knew things were far from normal.

His father stroked his beard and avoided making eye contact. "Saul, I have a drinking problem."

Saul didn't move or breathe. Even though he knew his father's drinking would be at the core of the conversation, he didn't expect his father to blurt it out. He waited for him to go on, keeping his eyes on his father's face.

Daed looked up, blinked a few times, and said, "I need to go away for a while, *sohn*." He fixed his eyes on Saul as if searching for a reaction. "Bishop Ebersol and me both agree that this is something I need to do. Noah Stoltzfus is helping us make the arrangements." His father leaned back against the couch and sighed. "I'm sorry for everything that I've put you and your *bruders* through."

Saul felt his eyes watering up, but he was determined not to cry. He stared hard into his *daed's* weathered face, the evidence of hard work, a nurturing father. "*Daed*, you've been a *gut* father." Saul blinked back tears as he sat up in his chair. "When *Mamm* and Hannah died,

I know it was hard, and"—Saul took a deep breath—"and you've always taken care of us."

His father stirred uneasily on the couch as he shook his head. "No, Saul. I have failed in the Lord's eyes, and I must right my ways." He choked out the words as if just talking caused pain in his throat. "I want to be a better father, and to do that, I need to go away for a while."

"No, *Daed*. Miriam and I are getting baptized in October, then married in November." Saul couldn't imagine his father not being at those two important events in his life. "You have to be here."

"I will be at your wedding, Saul."

Saul leaned forward again and laid his forehead in his hands for a moment, relieved that if his father left, he wouldn't be gone long. He looked back up after a few moments when his *daed* started to speak again.

"Bishop Ebersol and Noah are *gut* men. I have an illness, Saul. And that is what the bishop will tell our community if anyone asks, but we know that sometimes rumors and gossip can start, and I hope—"

"This is all Rebecca Raber's fault!" Saul bolted from the rocker and took two steps toward his father, feeling the heat in his face. "She told the bishop about your—your problem. She only did this because she doesn't want me to marry Miriam! And now you're going to be sent away! How am I going to run the farm with just Ruben and James? Miriam probably won't even want to marry me once this gets out, and—" Saul closed his mouth and took a deep breath when he saw the pain in his father's eyes. "I'm sorry, *Daed*." He backed into the rocker, sat down, and put his face in his hands, then looked back up. "I'm sorry."

"There will be talk, Saul. I'm sure of it. But you won't be here to hear of it, and your *bruders* are stronger than you think." *Daed* reached into his back pocket and pulled out an envelope that Saul recognized right away. "You will be working at your new job in Pittsburgh. With Miriam, after you're married, of course. If that's what you two want, that is."

Saul's heart leaped in his chest. "What?"

"Why didn't you tell me about this?" His father lifted the envelope, then put it in his lap and hung his head. "Never mind. I know why. You're a *gut* boy, Saul. You knew I wasn't able to properly tend to James and Ruben."

"I don't understand." Saul shook his head, trying to piece together what was going on.

"Saul . . ." *Daed* sighed. "I don't want you to leave our community, but in a strange way, I feel you deserve to pursue this dream. You've earned it. But I pray that you will take your faith with you as you and Miriam begin your life in Pittsburgh. It will not be easy for you to make this change. And marriage requires much work, even in the best of times."

Daed reached into an envelope that was on the couch beside him. "Here is the property that I promised you, the deed. Jake Petersheim has always wanted that tract. I'm guessin' he would buy it from you, and that will give you and Miriam some money to help you begin your life."

Saul stood up from the rocker again and paced for a moment. Then he faced his *daed*, unable to believe what his father was saying. "*Daed*, if you're leaving, that's even more reason why I can't leave." He shook his head, frustrated by all of this. "I can't leave Ruben and James. They aren't old enough. What are you thinking?"

His father stood up, approached him slowly, and put a hand on his shoulder. "I leave in two weeks for Chicago, to a place Noah suggested. You will leave for your new job that same week. James and Ruben will be staying with Rebecca and her family."

"What?"

"Rebecca spoke to Bishop Ebersol, and we can't be angry with her, Saul. She is not part of the problem but part of the solution. Bishop Ebersol said Rebecca cried when she told him of her visit to our *haus*." *Daed* hung his head and kept his eyes on the floor. "I feel shame for my behavior, but you and your *bruders* should not have to live like this." He looked up. "Rebecca said that her family will help with our farm while I am away, and Ruben and James will take their meals there and spend the nights there."

This was happening too fast for Saul. "But you said that you would be at my wedding. I don't understand how—" He shook his head.

"To leave our world, *sohn*, you won't be baptized, and you won't be married in the Amish faith . . . Are these things you are willing to give up to live your dream?"

Saul thought about marrying Miriam, leaving for Pittsburgh in the next couple of weeks, and living out his dream. And without hesitation he said, *"Ya, Daed."*

"I will pray that you take your faith with you wherever you go."

"And I will pray that you return soon." Saul embraced his father for the first time in years. "I love you, *Daed*."

"I love you too, Saul." His father squeezed tighter. "I hope you can forgive me for the life I've led over the past years."

"I forgave you a long time ago. You're the best father anyone could have."

He held his father, and they both cried, then agreed it was time that they go together to talk to Ruben and James.

———————

Rebecca took the pot from the stove and pounded across the kitchen floor. She kicked the screen open, marched down the steps, and tossed the rhubarb soup in the yard. The chickens sniffed briefly at the red mush, then turned up their beaks and toddled away.

"Even the birds won't eat that stuff." Aaron chuckled as he led one of the horses to the barn.

"It's not funny, Aaron."

"Why don't you just ask Saul how to make the soup? You must be doing something wrong."

"Because I have been cooking for over twice as long as that boy. I should be able to figure out how to make that recipe." Rebecca pushed back loose strands of hair blowing in her face. She was heading back to the kitchen when she heard a car pulling in, so she turned and put her hand above her forehead to block the sun. Aaron came across the yard and joined her. They waited until two heads came into view within the car.

"Is that . . . ?" Aaron strained to see. "It is. It's Abner and Janet."

"What? Shelby's mother isn't due here until next Friday." Rebecca twisted her neck to the right until she could see Miriam and Shelby on their knees in the garden. "Why are they here early?" She turned back toward the car and frowned, then spoke in a whisper to Aaron. "And I thought they were divorced. Why are they here together?"

Aaron shrugged.

As the car doors shut, Miriam and Shelby joined them in the front yard. Rebecca waited for Shelby to run into her parents' arms since she hadn't seen them in nearly three months, but Shelby walked tentatively toward them.

Abner threw his arms around his daughter, who looked like a limp doll before she slowly hugged her father. "Shelby, we've missed you."

Janet waved to Rebecca, Aaron, and Miriam, then moved toward Shelby. She waited until Abner released his daughter, then Janet hugged her. Shelby pulled out of the embrace right away.

"What are you doing here? You're not supposed to be here until Friday. That's almost a week away." Shelby stared back and forth between her parents, her expression tight with strain. "And what are you *both* doing here?"

Her parents didn't answer her, but both eased around and greeted Rebecca, Aaron, and Miriam. Ben, Elam, and John walked toward them from the chicken coops they were cleaning.

"What handsome boys," Janet said as Rebecca introduced her sons. "And, Miriam, what a lovely young woman you are. We haven't seen you since you were four years old."

"Mom, Dad . . ." Shelby approached her parents. "What are you doing here? Together? Plus, I'm not scheduled to go home until Friday. We just had the barn raising, and . . ." Shelby waved her hand toward the barn.

Janet reached for Shelby's hand. "Honey, we're both your parents, and we both missed you." She took a deep breath and seemed to force a smile. "Besides, your father and I are on friendly terms."

"Since when?" Shelby let go of her mother's hand.

"Sweetheart, we thought you'd be thrilled that we came early." Abner reached out to Shelby as he ignored her question, but she backed up.

"It's not time yet." Shelby stuffed her hands in the pockets of her blue jeans, then bit her lip. This wasn't the response Rebecca would have expected.

Janet pushed a shoulder-length strand of blond hair behind her ear, then pulled dark sunglasses down on her nose. "Honey, how long will it take you to pack? We tried to call, but of course your cell phone is dead, and we kept getting an answering machine for the number here."

"Why didn't you leave a message?" Shelby edged closer to Rebecca, and Rebecca could hear the desperation in her voice. "I'm not ready to go."

"Sweetheart, you've been here so long. We figured you'd had enough of . . ." Abner trailed off, then smiled. "I'm sure your hosts are ready to say good-bye to their houseguest."

"Not at all," Rebecca said, lifting her chin. "We'll miss Shelby very much." Rebecca's voice cracked as she spoke, and she realized how much she truly would miss Shelby.

"Maybe everyone can spend the night?" Miriam walked to Shelby and put an arm around her, and it touched Rebecca at how close the girls had become. She didn't know what kind of trouble Shelby had gotten into before her arrival here, but she had turned out to be a positive influence on Miriam.

"Of course you're all welcome to stay." Rebecca smiled at Janet.

Janet glanced at her watch. "We need to get back to the Harrisburg airport soon so Shelby can catch a flight home. Shelby's Aunt Charlotte, my sister, will be picking Shelby up at the airport when her flight gets in."

"What?" Shelby looked as confused as Rebecca felt.

Janet turned to Shelby. "Shelby, your father is catching another flight out of Harrisburg for a business trip, and I . . . well, I am leaving for another flight from Harrisburg to meet a—a friend." Janet pulled her eyes from Shelby's for a moment, then looked back up at her. "This was a way for your father and me to get to see you before we each leave, and you enjoy staying with Aunt Charlotte. Right?" Janet smiled. "Or Aunt Charlotte can drive you home, but I know you're not crazy about staying by yourself."

Rebecca stifled a gasp. "You're picking her up just to leave her again?" Right away she knew the remark was snide and uncalled for. It was not her business. But when she felt Shelby clutch her hand in hers, she didn't regret having said it. It was clear to Rebecca that Shelby's parents only came to pick her up because that's what fit into their schedules. *How can they do this?*

Shelby glared at her mother, then turned to Rebecca. "Please, Rebecca. Please let me stay here." Shelby wiped a tear from her cheek. "I'll never be any trouble, I'll be baptized here and live here forever, until I have a home of my own right here in this community. Please, Rebecca." Shelby threw herself into Rebecca's arms. Rebecca was unsure what to do or say.

"That is the most ridiculous thing I've ever heard!" Janet walked toward them, but Shelby did not pull from the embrace with Rebecca. "Are you saying you want to be Amish?"

Rebecca eased Shelby away and whispered, "*Ya,* Shelby. Is that what you're saying?"

Shelby wiped away a tear and faced Rebecca. "When I came here, Rebecca, I was a mess. But Miriam helped me to find my way back to God." She glanced at Miriam and Aaron, then looked back at Rebecca. "All of you did. And Miriam explained to me what a Daughter of the Promise is, someone who takes a spiritual journey where she finds out what faith, hope, and love really mean. I've done that, Rebecca. Please don't send me away."

Rebecca saw Janet throw her hands in the air before she started talking to Abner, but Rebecca grabbed each of Shelby's arms. "You dear, sweet girl. Finding your way to the Lord is a wonderful thing, no?" She smiled, and Shelby smiled back. "But you don't have to be Amish to be a Daughter of the Promise, Shelby. You can take your faith anywhere with you."

Shelby hung her head. "I understand. I'm sure you're ready for me to go."

Rebecca's heart was breaking. She wasn't sure what to do. *Help me to say and do the right thing, Lord.* "No, Shelby. I am not ready for you to go at all." She swallowed hard as she watched a smile tip the corner of Shelby's mouth.

"Honey, we should have contacted you before coming." Janet pushed her sunglasses up on her head. "I can see that you've become attached to Rebecca and all of them, but—"

"It's more than that, Mom." Shelby faced her mother, glancing at her father also. "I love it here. I love the fellowship, the honesty, the way families take care of each other. I love worshipping God in a way that I never have before. There's a peacefulness here that I've never felt before."

Rebecca felt the need to speak up, no matter how much she would love for Shelby to stay in the community. "Shelby . . ." She spoke softly. "You are welcome to stay here, but I want you to know that the peacefulness you speak of can also be found anywhere. The Lord is everywhere."

"Can I really stay?" Shelby turned to Aaron, who nodded with a smile on his face.

"Uh, this is ridiculous, Shelby." Janet thrust her hands on her hips. "You can't stay here."

"Why not, Mother? All you're going to do is send me home, then leave again. That's the way it has been my entire life. When I did something you didn't like, you sent me away." Shelby paused, blinking back tears.

"Shelby, that's not true, and—"

"Mom! Even when I didn't do anything bad, you and Daddy always had somewhere for me to go—summer camps or visits with relatives while you traveled. And it's no different now, even though you're divorced. You're just going in different directions."

"Shelby, we thought you enjoyed those things, and—"

"Mom, I'm happy here. I want to stay here. I can't be a hundred percent sure that I will become Amish, but I want to learn more about it and make that decision on my own."

"Absolutely not," Abner said strongly. "We need to go."

Shelby stood taller. "Dad, Mom . . . I love you both very much. But I'm not going."

Rebecca took a deep breath. "Aaron, Miriam, why don't we let Shelby talk with her parents."

Aaron and Miriam followed Rebecca into the house, and after Aaron went upstairs, Rebecca turned to Miriam. "I don't think I've ever been more proud of you than I was a few minutes ago. You've made a huge difference in Shelby's life."

Miriam smiled, but it wasn't the smile of times past, the smile that Rebecca so longed to see.

"Danki, Mamm."

Rebecca sat down on the couch and patted the spot beside her. She waited until Miriam sat down. "Now . . . we have less than a week to plan a wedding. It won't be an Amish wedding, most likely somewhere in town, but we will still need to have something memorable for you."

Miriam stared at her like she'd lost her marbles. "What are you talking about? Saul and I will be baptized in October, then married here in November."

Rebecca shook her head, then smiled. "No. I don't think so. There's been a change in plans."

19

MIRIAM TRIED TO WRAP HER MIND AROUND EVERYTHING. It was all happening so fast. Shelby was staying, and Miriam was leaving, moving to Pittsburgh with the love of her life. Miriam knew she should be the happiest girl on the planet. She was marrying Saul tomorrow at one o'clock. It would be a small private ceremony in a Christian church in town, the church that their friend Barbie Beiler attended. Barbie had helped make the arrangements. And the Fishers would get a new start. Her mother had explained the help Zeb would be receiving, which opened the door for Saul to have a chance at his dream.

Miriam sat down on her bed and glanced around the only bedroom she'd ever had. After a few moments, she put her face in her hands, and the tears came on full force. Once they started, she couldn't get them to stop. She couldn't believe that her mother had worked with the bishop and Saul's father to arrange all of this so that Miriam could go with Saul to Pittsburgh. It was the most unselfish thing a parent could do, and Miriam knew the cost for her parents. They'd never wanted any of their children to leave the community. But *Mamm* told Miriam that she knew the Lord would guide her steps no matter where she went, and that she wouldn't hold her back if she wanted to go with Saul to Pittsburgh.

She wanted to be with Saul, but leaving her community terrified her. It was exciting in the beginning, and Saul's face always lit up at the mention of it. But now she was going to be married—something exciting but frightening on its own—and moving to a new place, leaving the only home she'd known.

"What's the matter, *mei maedel*?"

Miriam lifted her head and quickly swiped at her eyes. "*Mamm.*" It was all she could say, then the tears started again. Her mother sat down beside her and pulled her into a hug. Miriam felt like she was five years old, and certainly not old enough to be getting married and venturing out on her own. "I'm scared, *Mamm.*"

Her mother held her, rocking back and forth the way she'd done when Miriam was a child. "I know, Miriam. A lot is happening for you all at once." *Mamm* eased her away. "But you don't have to do anything you don't want to do."

Sniffling, she said, "I know. And I want to be with Saul."

"These are decisions only you can make, *mei dochder.*"

Miriam reached for a tissue on her nightstand, then blew hard. "Saul said we can stay here and raise a family, that we don't have to go to Pittsburgh."

"And what did you say?"

"That I really want to go to Pittsburgh."

"Do you?"

Miriam thought long and hard about the new adventures they would be sharing together as husband and wife. "*Ya.* I do. I'm just scared."

"But it's also not too late to change your mind."

"I want to start a new life with Saul, and I'm excited about going to a new place." She stared into her mother's sympathetic eyes. "Will you come to visit us?"

Mamm smiled. "Pittsburgh is not that far." She paused, winked. "I think we can travel to the city to see our only *dochder*."

Miriam tried to smile, but another tear found its way down her cheek.

"Let me ask you something, Miriam." *Mamm* cupped Miriam's cheek. "Do you feel led to go on this new venture?"

"I'm so scared, *Mamm*. But not only do I love Saul with all my heart, I do feel led to go in this new direction. I really do think Saul would stay here if I really wanted him to, but I want to share his dream, and I feel like there is something there for me too." She took a deep breath. "I don't know what, though."

"Trust the Lord, Miriam. Follow your heart."

Miriam knew her next comment would be juvenile, but she couldn't marry Saul tomorrow and leave without asking. "I'm not being replaced, am I?"

Mamm smiled warmly. "You don't really believe that, do you?"

Miriam sighed. "No. I guess not. And I am glad that Shelby is staying. Do you think she'll join the church?"

"I don't know." Again she cupped Miriam's cheek. "But either way, *mei maedel*, you are not being replaced. A mother can love all kinds of folks, but there is no love like the love she feels for her *kinner*." She kissed Miriam on the cheek. "Take my love with you, Miriam, and know that I am always here for you."

"*Danki* for what you did, *Mamm*. Noah told Saul that his father could have died if he didn't get some help with his illness." She lowered her head, then looked up again. "And Saul and I wouldn't have been able to go to Pittsburgh if you hadn't offered to help with Ruben and James."

Mamm chuckled lightly. "We will have a houseful of new folks, and, Miriam, all of them put together will not replace you. But I walk in here and see you crying like this, and it makes me wonder if I did the right thing. Are you sure this is what you want? I don't want you to leave, Miriam, but I want you to follow your path, the one you feel led to follow."

"I'm sure. I'm just scared."

"I know. Me too." She kissed Miriam on the forehead. "Peace and blessings be with you always, my sweet Miriam."

Then *Mamm* swiped at her own tears and wrapped her arms around Miriam.

If there had been any doubts for Miriam, she couldn't remember them as she stared into Saul's eyes the next day in front of both their families. Shelby stood at Miriam's side as her bridesmaid, and both Ruben and James stood for Saul.

She and Saul were wearing *Englisch* clothes for the first time in their lives. Miriam had chosen a knee-length white dress from a dress shop in Paradise, and Saul was wearing a pair of tan slacks and a white button-up shirt. He'd never looked more handsome. Instead of Bishop Ebersol marrying them, it was a pastor from an unfamiliar church. It was nothing like the Amish wedding ceremony she'd dreamed of her entire life, but when Saul professed his love for her in front of everyone and with a tear in his eye, Miriam knew she was exactly where she was supposed to be. She couldn't seem to shake the feeling that her new life was opening up possibilities that she couldn't yet foresee, but for now, she just wanted to bask in the love of her new husband.

Both her parents cried, along with Shelby, during the short ceremony, but Miriam never hesitated, and she didn't have any more doubts. As she'd told Shelby months ago, you can take your faith anywhere in the world, and Miriam knew her faith in the Lord Jesus would go with her to her new home. Miriam couldn't believe that she was now Mrs. Saul Fisher.

Mamm insisted on making the traditional wedding dinner back at their house after the ceremony: turkey roast with all the fixings. Miriam was glad to have that tradition as a memory of her special day. This afternoon she and Saul would leave Paradise and head for Pittsburgh. Saul had rented them a small furnished apartment near his job.

"I love you so much, Miriam." Saul pulled her around the side of her house, out of sight, then kissed her in a way that made Miriam feel like his wife. She couldn't wait to start their life together.

"I love you too, Saul. With all my heart."

"I know you're scared, Miriam. But I'm going to make you happy for the rest of your life." He kissed her again, his lips lingering, and Miriam thought she would lift off the ground. Afterward he pulled her into a hug, and Miriam buried her head in his chest, closing her eyes.

"I'm not scared." And she wasn't.

Saul held Miriam tight, then they slowly made their way back to the front yard. Saul saw his father standing with Aaron and Rebecca, laughing and smiling, and it warmed Saul's heart. He felt confident that his father would get the help he needed and that Ruben and James would be tended to by Rebecca and Aaron. He hadn't had a chance to talk to Rebecca alone, so he needed to take the opportunity right away.

"Rebecca, can I talk to you for a minute?" Saul asked as he and Miriam approached the group. "Be back shortly," he said to Miriam with a wink. Rebecca followed him to an iron bench near the garden where they both sat down.

"I want to thank you for everything you're doing, Rebecca. It was hard for me in the beginning to understand . . ." He avoided her eyes for a moment, then looked back at her. "Anyway, *danki*."

Rebecca patted his leg. "I hope you will remember the *Deitsch* for when you bring my baby girl back to visit me." She smiled. "I wasn't sure that I did the right thing. But then something arrived in the mail yesterday." Rebecca reached inside the pocket of her apron and pulled out an envelope. "It was addressed to Ms. Raber, so I opened it, but it was clearly meant for Miriam. I haven't shown it to her yet." She pushed the envelope in Saul's direction. "But clearly our Miriam has dreams of her own."

Saul opened the envelope and pulled out a letter.

Dear Ms. Raber,

It would be a pleasure to have you work at the Watkins Christian School for Children with Special Needs. While we normally hire teachers and counselors with experience and/or a degree, we were so moved by the letter you sent us that we would like to offer you an entry-level position within our organization, and we would be happy to have you as a member of our team. We look forward to hearing from you.

Peace in the Lord's name,
Francis Parker, Director

"Wow." Saul stared at the letter, pleased that Miriam would be pursuing her dream too. "Can I be the one to tell her?"

"Of course. You're her husband." Rebecca smiled, then stood up. When Saul stood up, she hugged him, then kissed him on the cheek. "You're a *gut* man, Saul Fisher. I trust you to take care of my baby."

"I will."

Rebecca turned to walk away, but Saul called after her.

"*Ya?*"

Saul grinned, then folded his arms across his chest. "I have a little something for you, Rebecca."

"What's that?" She raised a brow.

Saul tipped his head to one side. "Miriam sure does want to make sure that you, Aaron, and the boys come to visit us. If I give you this, you have to promise to visit us in Pittsburgh."

Rebecca narrowed her eyes and lifted her chin. "All right, Saul. I'll play along. We'll come visit. Now what do you have for me?"

Saul reached into his pocket and then handed Rebecca a folded piece of paper. "Don't be mad," he whispered. Then he winked at her.

"What?" Rebecca unfolded the piece of paper, and Saul hurriedly walked off, cringing but laughing at the same time.

"I knew it! Saul Fisher, you get back here! I knew you didn't give me all the ingredients for that rhubarb mint soup. I knew it!"

Saul took off running—to go find his wife and share some news with her.

Shelby waved to Miriam and Saul as the car pulled away with them in it. They were going to spend their honeymoon night at Beiler's Bed-and-Breakfast in Paradise, then they were off to Pittsburgh in the morning. Shelby glanced at Rebecca, who was waving frantically following a long good-bye. Ben, Elam, and John were running behind the car waving, and Aaron had his hand over his mouth, as if trying to keep from showing his emotions. They watched the car turn the corner.

After a few minutes, everyone headed toward the house, but Shelby wanted to spend a few minutes by herself. Life had been a whirlwind of events the past week, but she'd never questioned her decision to stay with Rebecca and Aaron. Her parents had eventually realized that she was not going back with them. Shelby hoped they would both be happy, but she had a new life here, though she was going to try to communicate more with her parents, at Rebecca's urging more than anything.

She leaned against the fence, still wearing the plain green dress she'd worn for Miriam's wedding. It wasn't an Amish dress, but it also wasn't anything that Shelby would have chosen prior to arriving here. It was knee-length and conservative, and Shelby found herself to be more comfortable in the dress than something she might have chosen a few months ago.

Rebecca said that she would teach Shelby about the *Ordnung*, which she'd learned was the understood behavior by which the Amish were expected to live. Most of the rules the Amish knew by heart. Shelby wondered if she would be able to learn them all. Saul's father was leaving in a few days for Chicago, and Ruben and James would be moving in too. Shelby had asked Rebecca if she felt like she was running a house for wayward teens. Rebecca had merely laughed and said, "The more the merrier."

Saul had told Miriam that Ruben and James were glad that their father was going somewhere to help him get well, and Miriam's brothers, particularly Ben, had been going over to their house, spending time with them in an effort to make the move easier for them.

This was a new beginning for Shelby, in a place she'd grown to love, in a family that treated each other with kindness and respect. She leaned her head back, closed her eyes, and let the sun warm her cheeks. It was hot. Not as hot as Texas, but there was no doubt it was August.

She was excited about the prospect of becoming a true member of this wonderful community. Rebecca said they would be going to Sisters' Day next week where she would introduce Shelby to other young women her age. And Shelby had offered to take over the garden since Miriam was gone, since usually the women in the household took care of the garden and the yard while the men and boys took care of the fields and other outside chores.

Her newfound relationship with God provided her with a peacefulness she'd never had before, and when she'd tried to explain her feelings to Miriam, her cousin had said simply, "You're a Daughter of the Promise now."

Shelby smiled. "Thank You, Lord. Thank You for this new beginning. I pray for Your blessing and that I've made the right choice."

She slowly opened her eyes, breathed in the smell of freshly cut hay, then pulled her hair into a ponytail with the band she had on her wrist. Someday she hoped to have it pulled tight underneath a prayer covering. Movement on the driveway caught her attention. She anxiously watched the tall man coming toward her.

"Hello, stranger."

Shelby smiled. "Hello, Jesse."

"I hear you are going to be staying around." He tipped his hat back with his thumb, then shot her a slow, easy smile.

"I am."

Jesse's smile broadened. "I'm glad to hear that." Then he offered her his elbow. "How about going on a walk with me?"

Shelby looped her arm in his. "I'd like that."

She closed her eyes and smiled as she walked down the path she knew God had set before her.

Thank You.

Epilogue

MIRIAM SPRINTED AROUND THEIR SMALL APARTMENT, double-checking that everything was spotless. Saul had learned to cook all kinds of new dishes at his new job, but he'd chosen to make a simple pot roast for Miriam's family. As it turned out, her new husband wasn't as fond of baking, which was Miriam's specialty, so she'd prepared a pineapple cake for dinner.

She smoothed the wrinkles from her long blue jean skirt, something she'd bought on sale specifically for this occasion. And she'd chosen a conservative blue blouse to wear. Out of respect for her family, she decided against the blue-jean pants she'd become accustomed to. It had taken her some time to slowly convert her clothing in a way that blended in with the *Englisch,* but today she wanted to find a happy medium between her old life and her new one.

"Everything looks great," Saul said as he threw his arms around her waist when she whisked by him in the tiny den. "And so do you."

She fell into his arms, kissed him on the lips, then playfully pushed him away. "They'll be here soon. I want to make sure everything is perfect."

Miriam hadn't seen her family in three months. Pittsburgh was a four-hour drive from Paradise, and Miriam and Saul hadn't been able to make the trip to their hometown because of their job schedules. Miriam's family had to plan around working in the fields and their other commitments. Today they'd hired a driver to make the trip after their morning chores were done. Miriam wished she had extra bedrooms to offer her family, but right now she and Saul just had their one-bedroom apartment. Miriam was thrilled that they were coming, even if it would only be for a couple of hours. They were expecting her mother, father, brothers, and Shelby. The next visit would be from Saul's father and brothers. Zeb was back home and doing well after his treatment. Ruben and James had moved back in with him. Miriam felt like her life had been a continuation of one blessed event after the other.

Miriam couldn't still the butterflies in her stomach. She'd written to her family every detail of their lives in Pittsburgh— except for one.

"They're here," she squealed when the doorbell rang. Saul followed her to the door, and she threw herself into each of their arms. "I've missed you so much!" Then she stepped back and smiled at Shelby. "You look beautiful. I'm so sorry I missed your baptism."

"*Danki.*"

Shelby had written to ask Miriam if she could wear her clothes, and Miriam was honored to have her do so. In one of Miriam's dark-blue dresses and black aprons, Shelby looked like she'd been Amish all her life. Her hair was neatly tucked underneath one of Miriam's *kapps*. *Mamm* had written to say that Shelby was a good student, and that she'd picked up on the *Ordnung* quickly. Shelby had written to Miriam about a completely different subject matter. Seems she was spending lots of time with Jesse, and Miriam was glad to hear that.

The afternoon seemed to fly by as Miriam and Saul told her

family about their jobs, their plans for a bigger apartment soon, and the church they were attending a few blocks away. But Miriam could hardly contain herself any longer.

"We have some news to share." Miriam unconsciously touched her stomach, and her mother's hands flew to her mouth as her eyes rounded.

"Are you . . . ?" *Mamm* stood and walked toward her.

"*Ya.*" Miriam knew she would never completely give up her native dialect. "We are in a family way."

Miriam wasn't sure she'd ever seen her mother jump up and down until this moment. Her father blinked a few times, and Miriam thought he might shed a tear. It was a glorious moment, and Miriam realized that her relationship with family—and God—would be intact as long as she carried her faith with her the way she'd been taught her entire life.

Following congratulations, then dinner and dessert, *Mamm* said the driver would be back for them shortly.

"It all went too fast," Miriam said as she hugged her father, then Shelby and her brothers. She stayed in her mother's arms the longest. "I miss you, *Mamm.*"

"I miss you too, *mei maedel,*" she whispered, then eased Miriam away. "But if you think you will raise a *kinner* without *mammi* being a big part of his or her life, you are wrong. We will have to make arrangements to visit even more." *Mamm* kissed her on the cheek. "I have something for you." *Mamm* reached into her plain black purse that she'd carried for years. She handed Miriam a silver-plated letter opener that looked just like the one that had been stolen. Miriam turned it over and gasped when she saw the inscription— *May all your letters be received with an abundance of love.*

"*Mamm!* Your letter opener! Where did you get it?" Miriam handled it with care, knowing how much it meant to her mother.

Mamm reached into her purse again and dug around for a moment, then she handed Miriam a folded piece of paper. "This came in the mail." *Mamm's* eyes watered up as she spoke.

Miriam unfolded the letter and read silently.

Dear Mrs. Raber,

I have no good excuse for what I did, except that I was desperate to take my three-year-old daughter and get away from my husband, Bruce. He was an abusive man, and I'm sorry that he pushed me to do something so horrible. I picked up my daughter from my mother's house, then fled with her. I used the money I took from you to make a fresh start. I'm not sure why I took your letter opener, except that I was scared Bruce would try to harm me. I'm enclosing $10 and returning your letter opener. I saw the inscription on the back. I will pay you back every dime, no matter how long it takes. Please forgive me. I pray God forgives me.

Sincerely,

Rhoda Thompson

"Oh, *Mamm*," Miriam said softly as she handed the letter back to her mother. "Did you write her back?"

Mamm looked down for a moment, smiling, then her eyes met Miriam's. "*Ya.* I did."

Miriam started to ask her mother what the letter to Rhoda said, but she already knew in her heart that *Mamm* either sent her more money or told her not to worry about the debt. That was the way her mother was. She pulled her mother into another hug.

"Write me often, *mei* beautiful *maedel.*"

"I will, *Mamm*. I promise." Miriam thought about how events had unfolded, in a way she never would have thought possible for all of them. She said a silent prayer for Rhoda and her daughter.

They were almost out the door when her mother snapped her fingers. "*Ach*, Saul. I almost forgot something that I have for you." She handed Saul a piece of paper from her apron pocket. "Miriam tells me that you are unable to duplicate my famous stromboli." *Mamm* smiled, then raised her shoulders and dropped them slowly. "So here's the recipe for you."

Saul read through the recipe, looked up at *Mamm*, then grinned. "So . . . Rebecca . . . is everything in this recipe?" He folded his arms across his chest.

Mamm tapped her finger to her chin. "Hmm . . . I *think* I remembered everything." She winked at him on the way out the door.

Miriam just laughed as her husband took to reading the recipe again as the door shut. She glanced down at her bare feet, wiggled her toes, then focused on the same ankle bracelet she'd worn that day at the creek. *We've come a long way.*

"I'll figure this recipe out," he said, smiling.

Miriam pulled him into a hug, then kissed him. "I love you, Saul Fisher."

"I love you too, Miriam Fisher."

Miriam closed her eyes and thanked God for the peacefulness she'd carried with her from Lancaster County.

Reading Group Guide

1. Throughout the story, Miriam is sure she wants to be Saul's *fraa*, but when it finally comes time for her to marry him and leave, she cries on her mother's shoulder. What are some of the emotions Miriam feels as she enters this new phase in her life?

2. Rebecca has two strong reasons for not wanting Miriam to date Saul. What are they, and do you think Rebecca's concerns are valid? Or should she have trusted Miriam to make good decisions?

3. In the beginning of the story, Shelby is depressed, void of hope, and doesn't have much faith. What are some turning points for her? What and who inspire her to look within herself to seek God?

4. What are some of the things Shelby loves about life among the Amish? What does she have a hard time adjusting to? What about you—what could you not live without among an Old Order Amish district?

5. Saul is afraid for members of the community to find out about his father's drinking, fearing his family will be shamed.

Do you know of someone who kept a family secret that was perhaps not in the best interest of everyone involved? What was the outcome?

6. What would have happened if Rebecca hadn't stepped in to help Zeb? How could things have possibly played out differently?

7. At first, Aaron tells Rebecca that they must let Miriam make her own decisions, but his attitude changes when he finds out that Saul wants to leave the district and take Miriam with him. At what point does Aaron confess his true feelings about Miriam leaving?

8. More and more Amish families are giving up their phone shanties. Most of them have phones in the barn or even cell phones. What are your thoughts about the Amish embracing some forms of modern technology, but not others—such as electricity and automobiles?

9. Shelby uses her diary as a way to voice her private thoughts, but she stops writing in the journal after she begins to reconnect with God. Have you ever kept a journal, and if so, was it in addition to or in lieu of communion with God? Or neither one?

10. Forgiveness is a theme that runs throughout the book, and several characters must forgive either themselves or others. What are some examples of this?

11. By the end of the book, Shelby and Jesse have formed a friendship. Shelby is now a member of the Amish community, but

Jesse mentions earlier on that he has a curiosity about the outside world and what it would be like to leave the district. Do you think he was just saying that because he thought Shelby would be leaving their community, or do you think Jesse might leave? Or is it normal for him to be curious and casually ponder the idea?

12. Saul is driven to live in the outside world and be a chef in a fancy restaurant. Besides his love of food and cooking, how does this external desire reveal what is truly inside Saul? Is he a caregiver by nature? Does he enjoy pleasing others?

Acknowledgments

WITH EACH BOOK I WRITE, IT SEEMS THAT THERE ARE more and more people who deserve a big thank you. Please forgive me if I forgot anyone. I know there is no way I could share my stories without an abundance of love from family and friends, particularly my husband, Patrick. You're the best, baby!

To my wonderful sons—Eric and Cory—I dedicate this book to both of you, each so amazing in your own individual ways. Choose wisely in life, try to follow God's plan, and always know how very much I love you both.

To my family at Thomas Nelson, you guys and gals continue to bless me with your encouragement, hard work, and kindness. It's more than a job to all of you, and so often you go above and beyond even my highest expectations of what a top-rated publisher should do. I'm so blessed to have you on my team! (BIG hugs to my editor, Natalie Hanemann—love you!)

Barbie Beiler, are you getting tired of being mentioned in every single book . . . lol? Seriously, I couldn't do this without you. Peace and love to you always, my friend.

Big thanks to my Old Order Amish friends in Pennsylvania and Colorado for helping me to keep each book authentic—and for sharing your recipes with me. Peace and blessings to all of you.

To my mother, Pat Isley, for always being on hand to answer the smallest grammatical question on a regular basis. More importantly, for your encouragement, love, and constant support. I love you very much, Mother.

And everyone should be so fortunate to have a mother-in-law who cooks for them. To the best mother-in-law in the world—Pat Mackey—sending much love and thanks your way!

Janet Murphy, I've thought about the way things played out and how you came to work for me. This is a union truly blessed by God. Not only are you a fabulous assistant and publicity coordinator, but I'm also so fortunate to have you as my friend. I hope we make this entire journey together.

To my agent, Mary Sue Seymour—what a great year we've had! In addition to guiding my career, we've had some wonderful times together. I see more shoe shopping and trips to P.F. Chang's in our future!

Jenny Baumgartner, some authors dread their line edits, but with you, I know that you will make it as painless as possible, and your great suggestions always make the book so much better in the end. Love and blessings to you and your family. I can't wait to meet you in person someday, hopefully soon!

Not a day goes by that I don't recognize God's hand on my writing. It is only because of Him that I am able to pull together the screaming voices in my head and organize them into a story that I hope both entertains and draws people closer to Him. *Thank You.*

Coming Soon! *Plain Peace*—the next volume in Beth Wiseman's bestselling Daughters of Promise Series

All Anna wants to do is go on a date, but none of the Amish boys in her community have the courage to face her strict grandfather, the new bishop.

Available in Print and E-book
November 2013

Thomas Nelson
Since 1798

What would
cause the
Amish to move
to Colorado,
leaving family
and friends
behind?

The Land of Canaan Series

Available in Print and E-book

An Excerpt from
Seek Me with All Your Heart

--- *One* ---

EMILY STOOD BEHIND THE COUNTER OF HER FAMILY'S country store, watching as the tall man walked down each aisle, the top of his black felt hat visible above the gray metal shelving. First thing that morning, he'd strolled in and shot her a slow, easy smile, white teeth dazzling against bronzed skin. He moved slowly, sometimes glimpsing in her direction.

Emily twisted the strings on her apron with both hands and tried to slow down her breathing. Her heart pulsed against her chest as she glanced out the window toward her family's farmhouse in the distance. *Where is Jacob?* Her brother knew she didn't like to be left alone in the store, and he'd promised to be right back.

Their community was small, and all the members in the district knew each other, which was the only reason Emily agreed to work in the shop. But this Amish man was a stranger. And Amish or not, he was still a man.

Emily jumped when the man rounded the bread aisle toting a box of noodles in one hand and a can in the other. With the back of one hand, he tipped back his hat so that sapphire blue eyes blazed down on her. As he approached the counter, Emily clung to her apron strings and took a step backward.

"How come everything in this store is messed up?" Tiny lines creased his forehead as he held up a can of green beans with a large dent in one side. Then he held up the box of noodles. "And this looks like it's been stepped on. It's mashed on one side." He dropped them on the counter, then folded his arms across his chest and waited for her to answer.

He towered over her. Emily stared straight ahead, not looking him in the eye. The outline of his shoulders strained against a black jacket that was too small. Her bottom lip trembled as she turned her head to look out the window again. When she didn't see any sign of Jacob, she turned back to face the stranger, who looked to be about her age—maybe nineteen or twenty—which didn't make him any less threatening. His handsome looks could be a convenient cover up for what lay beneath. She knew he was not a married man since he didn't have a beard covering his square jaw, and his dark hair was in need of a trim.

He arched his brows, waiting for her to respond, looking anything but amused. Emily felt goose bumps on her arms, and chills began to run the length of her spine, even though Jacob had fired up the propane heaters long before the shop opened that morning.

"This is—is a salvage store." Her fingers ached as she twisted the strings of her apron tighter. "We sell freight and warehouse damaged groceries." She bit her lip, but didn't take her eyes from him.

"I can't even find half the things on my list." He shook his head as he stared at a white piece of paper. "What about milk and cheese?"

"No, I'm sorry. We mostly have dry goods."

He threw his hands in the air. Emily thought his behavior was improper for an Amish man, but raw fear kept her mouth closed and her feet rooted to the floor.

"Where am I supposed to get all this?" He turned the piece of paper around so she could see the list.

Emily unwrapped the strings of her apron and slowly leaned her head forward. She tucked a loose strand of brown hair underneath her *kapp*.

"What'd you do to your hand?"

Emily glanced at her hand, and a blush filled her cheeks when she saw the red indentions around her fingers. She quickly dropped her hand to her side and ignored his comment. "You will have to go to Monte Vista for most of those things. People usually come here to save money, just to get a few things they know we'll have for a lesser price."

"That's a far drive by buggy in this snow." He put both hands on the counter and hung his head for a few moments, then looked up as his mouth pulled into a sour grin. With an unsettling calmness, he leaned forward and said, "Just one more thing I can't stand about this place."

Emily took two steps backward, which caused her to bump into the wall behind her. "Then leave," she whispered as she cast her eyes down on her black shoes. She couldn't believe she'd voiced the thought, and when she looked back up at him, the stranger's eyes were glassed with anger.

"Please don't hurt me." She clenched her eyes closed.

ENJOY THESE AMISH NOVELLAS FOR EVERY SEASON

Brooke has only loved one man, her late
husband. Owen's rebuilding after a painful
divorce. Can a mysterious house bring them
together for a second chance at love?

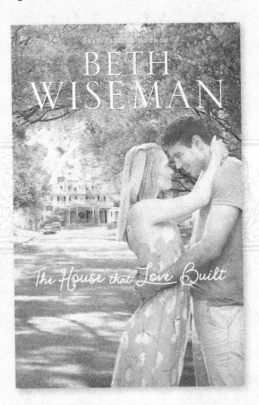

Darlene thought moving to a small town would bring their family closer together, but it just might tear them apart.

Need You Now

A NOVEL

BETH WISEMAN

Available in print and e-book

About the Author

BETH WISEMAN is hailed as a top voice in Amish fiction. She is a Carol Award winner and author of numerous bestsellers including the Daughters of the Promise and the Land of Canaan series. She and her family live in Texas.